ONE TRUE LOVES

~ A Novel ~

TAYLOR JENKINS REID

WASHINGTON SQUARE PRESS
New York Toronto London Sydney New Delhi

Washington Square Press
An Imprint of Simon & Schuster, Inc.
1230 Avenue of the Americas
New York, NY 10020

This book is a work of fiction. Any references to historical events, real people, or real places are used fictitiously. Other names, characters, places, and events are products of the author's imagination, and any resemblance to actual events or places or persons, living or dead, is entirely coincidental.

First Washington Square Press trade paperback edition June 2016

Manufactured in the United States of America

30 29 28

Library of Congress Cataloging-in-Publication Data

Names: Reid, Taylor Jenkins.
Title: One true loves : a novel / by Taylor Jenkins Reid.
Description: First Washington Square Press trade paperback edition. | New York: Washington Square Press, [2016]
Subjects: LCSH: Triangles (Interpersonal relations)—Fiction. | Man-woman relationships—Fiction. | Mate selection—Fiction. | GSAFD: Love stories.
Classification: LCC PS3618.E5478 O54 2016 | DDC 813/.6—dc23
LC record available at http://lccn.loc.gov/2015035902

ISBN 978-1-4767-7690-3
ISBN 978-1-4767-7691-0 (ebook)

Praise for *Maybe in Another Life*

A *People* Magazine Pick

Us Weekly Must Pick

Named a Best Book of the Summer by
Glamour, Good Housekeeping, USA TODAY,
Cosmopolitan, POPSUGAR, Working
Mother, Bustle, and Goodreads

"Entertaining and unpredictable; Reid makes a compelling argument for happiness in every life."

—*Kirkus Reviews* (starred review)

"Reid makes you think about love and destiny and then shows you the *what could have been*; I loved every word. A heartfelt, witty, and scintillating journey from one parallel universe to another, *Maybe in Another Life* takes the concept of fate and makes it tangible and engrossing; I couldn't put this book down!"

—Renee Carlino, *USA Today* bestselling author

"Readers looking for a romance with a twist won't be disappointed."

—*Library Journal*

Praise for *After I Do*

"Written in a breezy, humorous style familiar to fans of Jane Green and Elin Hilderbrand, *After I Do* focuses on Lauren's journey of self-discovery. The intriguing premise and well-drawn characters contribute to an emotionally uplifting and inspiring story."

—*Booklist*

"As uplifting as it is brutally honest—a must-read."

—*Kirkus Reviews*

"Taylor Jenkins Reid offers an entirely fresh and new perspective on what can happen after the 'happily ever after.' With characters who feel like friends and a narrative that hooked me from the first page, *After I Do* takes an elegant and incisively emotional look at the endings and beginnings of love. Put this book at the top of your must-read list."

—Jen Lancaster, *New York Times* bestselling author

"Taylor Jenkins Reid delivers a seductive twist on the timeless tale of a couple trying to rediscover love in a marriage brought low by the challenges of domestic togetherness. I fell in love with Ryan and Lauren from their passionate beginning, and I couldn't stop reading as they followed their unlikely road to redemption. Touching, perceptive, funny, and achingly honest, *After I Do* will keep you hooked to the end, rooting for husbands and wives and the strength of true love."

—Beatriz Williams, *New York Times* bestselling author

"Taylor Jenkins Reid writes with ruthless honesty, displaying an innate understanding of human emotion and creating characters and relationships so real I'm finding it impossible to let them go. *After I Do* is a raw, unflinching exploration of the realities of marriage, the delicate nature of love, and the enduring strength of family. Simultaneously funny and sad, heartbreaking and hopeful, Reid has crafted a story of love lost and found that is as timely as it is timeless."

—Katja Millay, author of *The Sea of Tranquility*

Praise for *Forever, Interrupted*

"Touching and powerful . . . Reid masterfully grabs hold of the heartstrings and doesn't let go. A stunning first novel."

—*Publishers Weekly* (starred review)

"Moving, gorgeous and, at times, heart-wrenching. Taylor Jenkins Reid writes with wit and true emotion that you can *feel*. Read it, savor it, share it."

—Sarah Jio, *New York Times* bestselling author of *The Violets of March*

"A moving novel about life and death."

—*Kirkus Reviews*

"You'll laugh, weep, and fly through each crazy-readable page."

—*Redbook*

"Sweet, heartfelt, and surprising, *Forever, Interrupted* is a story about a young woman struggling to find her way after losing her husband. These characters made me laugh as well as cry, and I ended up falling in love with them, too."

—Sarah Pekkanen, internationally bestselling author of *The Opposite of Me*

"Taylor Jenkins Reid has written a poignant and heartfelt exploration of love and commitment in the absence of shared time that asks 'what does it take to be the love of someone's life?' "

—Emma McLaughlin and Nicola Kraus, *New York Times* bestselling authors

"This beautifully rendered story explores the brilliance and rarity of finding true love, and how to find our way back through the painful aftermath of losing it. These characters will leap right off the page and into your heart."

—Amy Hatvany, author of *Somewhere Out There*

"*Forever, Interrupted* weaves a beautiful love story with a terrible tragedy. Told in alternating timelines, each chapter progresses sequentially from two different arcs: one of a blooming, forever love and another of overcoming a sudden, inexplicable loss. Each storyline moves effortlessly and seamlessly through the connected stages, while also emphasizing the strengthening of old friendships and the forging of new ones. Whether told in past or present voice, Reid's debut is a superb read from start to finish!"

—*Romantic Times*

Also by Taylor Jenkins Reid

Forever, Interrupted

After I Do

Maybe in Another Life

This is a book about Acton, Massachusetts.
So naturally, I would like to dedicate it to Andy Bauch
of Boxborough.
And to Rose, Warren, Sally, Bernie, Niko, and Zach
of Encino, California.

ONE TRUE LOVES

I am finishing up dinner with my family and my fiancé when my husband calls.

It is my father's sixty-fourth birthday. He is wearing his favorite sweater, a hunter green cashmere one that my older sister, Marie, and I picked out for him two years ago. I think that's why he loves it so much. Well, also because it's cashmere. I'm not kidding myself here.

My mother is sitting next to him in a gauzy white blouse and khakis, trying to hold in a smile. She knows that a tiny cake with a candle and a song are coming any minute. She has always been childlike in her zeal for surprises.

My parents have been married for thirty-five years. They have raised two children and run a successful bookstore together. They have two adorable grandchildren. One of their daughters is taking over the family business. They have a lot to be proud of. This is a happy birthday for my father.

Marie is sitting on the other side of my mother and it is times like these, when the two of them are right next to each other, facing the same direction, that I realize just how much they look alike. Chocolate brown hair, green eyes, petite frames.

I'm the one that got stuck with the big butt.

Luckily, I've come to appreciate it. There are, of course, many songs dedicated to the glory of a backside, and if my thirties have taught me anything so far, it's that I'm ready to try to be myself with no apologies.

My name is Emma Blair and I've got a booty.

I am thirty-one, five foot six, with a blond, grown-out pixie cut. My hazel eyes are upstaged by a constellation of freckles on the top of my right cheekbone. My father often jokes he can make out the Little Dipper.

Last week, my fiancé, Sam, gave me the ring he has spent over two months shopping for. It's a diamond solitaire on a rose gold band. While it is not my first engagement ring, it is the first time I've ever worn a diamond. When I look at myself, it's all I can see.

"Oh no," Dad says, spotting a trio of servers headed our way with a lit slice of cake. "You guys didn't . . ."

This is not false modesty. My father blushes when people sing to him.

My mother looks behind her to see what he sees. "Oh, Colin," she says. "Lighten up. It's your birthday . . ."

The servers make an abrupt left and head to another table. Apparently, my father is not the only person born today. My mother sees what has happened and tries to recover.

". . . Which is why I did not tell them to bring you a cake," she says.

"Give it up," my dad says. "You've blown your cover."

Thc servers finish at that table and a manager comes out with another slice of cake. Now they are all headed right for us.

"If you want to hide under the table," Sam says, "I'll tell them you're not here."

Sam is handsome in a friendly way—which I think might just be the best way to be handsome—with warm brown eyes that seem to look at everything with tenderness. And he's funny. Truly funny. After Sam and I started dating, I noticed my laugh lines were getting deeper. This is most likely because I am growing older, but I can't shake the feeling that it's because I am laughing more than I ever have. What else could you want in a person other than kindness and humor? I'm not sure anything else really matters to me.

The cake arrives, we all sing loudly, and my father turns beet red. Then the servers turn away and we are left with an oversized piece of chocolate cake with vanilla ice cream.

The waitstaff left five spoons but my father immediately grabs them all. "Not sure why they left so many spoons. I only need one," he says.

My mother goes to grab one from him.

"Not so fast, Ashley," he says. "I endured the humiliation. I should get to eat this cake alone."

"If that's how we are playing it . . ." Marie says. "For my birthday next month, please put me through this same rigmarole. Well worth it."

Marie drinks a sip of her Diet Coke and then checks her phone for the time. Her husband, Mike, is at home with my nieces, Sophie and Ava. Marie rarely leaves them for very long.

"I should get going," Marie says. "Sorry to leave, but . . ."

She doesn't have to explain. My mom and dad both stand up to give her a hug good-bye.

Once she's gone and my father has finally agreed to let us all eat the cake, my mom says, "It sounds silly but I miss that. I miss leaving someplace early because I was just so excited to get back to my little girls."

I know what's coming next.

I'm thirty-one and about to be married. I know exactly what is coming next.

"Have you guys given any thought to when you might start a family?"

I have to stop myself from rolling my eyes. "Mom—"

Sam is already laughing. He has that luxury. She's only his mother in an honorary capacity.

"I'm just bringing it up because they are doing more and more studies about the dangers of waiting too long to have a child," my mom adds.

There are always studies to prove I should hurry and studies to prove that I shouldn't and I've decided that I will have a baby when I'm goddamn good and ready, no matter what my mother reads on the *Huffington Post*.

Luckily, the look on my face has caused her to backpedal. "Never mind, never mind," she says, waving her hand in the air. "I sound like my own mother. Forget it. I'll stop doing that."

My dad laughs and puts his arm around her. "All right," he says. "I'm in a sugar coma and I'm sure Emma and Sam have better things to do than stay out with us. Let's get the bill."

Fifteen minutes later, the four of us are standing outside the restaurant, headed to our cars.

I'm wearing a navy blue sweater dress with long sleeves and thick tights. It is just enough to insulate me from the cool evening air. This is one of the last nights that I'll go anywhere without a wool coat.

It's the very end of October. Autumn has already settled in and overtaken New England. The leaves are yellow and red, on their way to brown and crunchy. Sam has been over to my parents' house once already to rake the yard clean. Come December, when the temperature free-falls, he and Mike will shovel their snow.

But for now the air still has a bit of warmth to it, so I savor it as best I can. When I lived in Los Angeles, I never savored warm nights. You don't savor things that last forever. It is one of the reasons I moved back to Massachusetts.

As I step toward the car, I hear the faint sound of a ringing cell phone. I trace it back to my purse just as I hear my father rope Sam into giving him a few guitar lessons. My father has an annoying habit of wanting to learn every instrument that Sam plays, mistaking the fact that Sam is a music teacher for Sam being *his* music teacher.

I dig through my purse looking for my phone, grabbing the only thing lit up and flashing. I don't recognize the number. The area code 808 doesn't ring a bell but it does pique my interest.

Lately, no one outside of 978, 857, 508, or 617—the various area codes of Boston and its suburbs—has reason to call me.

And it is 978 specifically that has always signified home no matter what area code I was currently inhabiting. I may have spent a year in Sydney (61 2) and months backpacking from Lisbon (351 21) to Naples (39 081). I may have honeymooned in Mumbai (91 22) and lived, blissfully, for years, in Santa Monica, California (310). But when I needed to come "home," "home" meant 978. And it is here I have stayed ever since.

The answer pops into my head.

808 is Hawaii.

"Hello?" I say as I answer the phone.

Sam has turned to look at me, and soon, my parents do, too.

"Emma?"

The voice I hear through the phone is one that I would recognize anywhere, anytime—a voice that spoke to me day in and day out for years and years. One I thought I'd never hear again, one I'm not ready to even believe I'm hearing now.

The man I loved since I was seventeen years old. The man who left me a widow when his helicopter went down somewhere over the Pacific and he was gone without a trace.

Jesse.

"Emma," Jesse says. "It's me. I'm alive. Can you hear me? I'm coming home."

~

I think that perhaps everyone has a moment that splits their life in two. When you look back on your own timeline, there's a sharp spike somewhere along the way, some event that changed you, changed your life, more than the others.

A moment that creates a "before" and an "after."

Maybe it's when you meet your love or you figure out your life's passion or you have your first child. Maybe it's something wonderful. Maybe it's something tragic.

But when it happens, it tints your memories, shifts your perspective on your own life, and it suddenly seems as if everything you've been through falls under the label of "pre" or "post."

I used to think that my moment was when Jesse died.

Everything about our love story seemed to have been leading up to that. And everything since has been in response.

But now I know that Jesse never died.

And I'm certain that *this* is my moment.

Everything that happened *before* today feels different now, and I have no idea what happens *after* this.

BEFORE

~

Emma and Jesse

Or, how to fall in love and fall to pieces

I have never been an early riser. But my hatred for the bright light of morning was most acute on Saturdays during high school at ten after eight a.m.

Like clockwork, my father would knock on my door and tell me, "The bus is leaving in thirty minutes," even though the "bus" was his Volvo and it wasn't headed to school. It was headed to our family store.

Blair Books was started by my father's uncle in the sixties, right in the very same location where it still stood—on the north side of Great Road in Acton, Massachusetts.

And somehow that meant that the minute I was old enough to legally hold a job, I had to ring up people's purchases some weekdays after school and every Saturday.

I was assigned Saturdays because Marie wanted Sundays. She had saved up her paychecks and gotten a beat-up navy blue Jeep Cherokee last summer.

The only time I'd been inside Marie's Jeep was the night she got it, when, high on life, she invited me to Kimball's Farm to get ice cream. We picked up a pint of chocolate for Mom and Dad and we let it melt as we sat on the hood of her car and ate our own sundaes, comfortable in the warm summer air.

We complained about the bookstore and the fact that Mom always put Parmesan cheese on potatoes. Marie confessed that she had smoked pot. I promised not to tell Mom and Dad.

Then she asked me if I'd ever been kissed and I turned and looked away from her, afraid the answer would show on my face.

"It's okay," she said. "Lots of people don't have their first kiss until high school." She was wearing army green shorts and a navy blue button-down, her two thin gold necklaces cascading down her collarbone, down into the crevice of her bra. She never buttoned her shirts up all the way. They were always a button lower than you'd expect.

"Yeah," I said. "I know." But I noticed that she didn't say, "*I* didn't have my first kiss until high school." Which, of course, was all I was really looking for. I wasn't worried that I wasn't like anyone else. I was worried that I wasn't like *her.*

"Things will get better now that you're going to be a freshman," Marie said as she threw away the rest of her mint chocolate chip. "Trust me."

In that moment, that night, I would have trusted anything she told me.

But that evening was the exception in my relationship with my sister, a rare moment of kinship between two people who merely coexisted.

By the time my freshman year started and I was in the same building as her every day, we had developed a pattern where we passed each other in the hallways of home at night and school during the day like enemies during a cease-fire.

So imagine my surprise when I woke up at eight ten one Saturday morning, in the spring of ninth grade, to find out that I did not have to go to my shift at Blair Books.

"Marie is taking you to get new jeans," my mom said.

"Today?" I asked her, sitting up, rubbing my eyes, wondering if this meant I could sleep a little more.

"Yeah, at the mall," my mom added. "Whatever pair you want, my treat. I put fifty bucks on the counter. But if you spend more than that, you're on your own."

I needed new jeans because I'd worn holes into all of my old ones. I was supposed to get a new pair every Christmas but I was so particular about what I wanted, so neurotic about what I thought they should look like, that my mother had given up. Twice now we had gone to the mall and left after an hour, my mother trying her best to hide her irritation.

It was a new experience for me. My mother always wanted to be around me, craving my company my entire childhood. But I had finally become so annoying about something that she was willing to pass me off to someone else. And on a Saturday, no less.

"Who's going to work the register?" I said. The minute it came out of my mouth, I regretted it. I was suddenly nervous that I'd poked a hole in a good thing. I should have simply said, "Okay," and backed away slowly, so as to not startle her.

"The new boy we hired, Sam," my mom said. "It's fine. He needs the hours."

Sam was a sophomore at school who walked into the store one day and said, "Can I fill out an application?" even though we weren't technically hiring and most teenagers wanted to work at the CD store down the street. My parents hired him on the spot.

He was pretty cute—tall and lanky with olive skin and dark brown eyes—and was always in a good mood, but I found myself incapable of liking him once Marie deemed him "adorable." I couldn't bring myself to like anything she liked.

Admittedly, this type of thinking was starting to limit my friend pool considerably and becoming unsustainable.

Marie liked everyone and everyone liked Marie.

She was the Golden Child, the one destined to be our parents' favorite. My friend Olive used to call her "the Booksellers' Daughter" behind her back because she even *seemed* like the sort of girl whose parents would own a bookstore, as if there was a very specific stereotype and Marie was tagging off each attribute like a badge of honor.

She read adult books and wrote poetry and had crushes on fictional characters instead of movie stars and she made Olive and I want to barf.

When Marie was my age, she took a creative writing elective and decided that she wanted to "become a writer." The quotation marks are necessary because the only thing she ever wrote was a nine-page murder mystery where the killer turned out to be the protagonist's little sister, Emily. I read it and even I could tell it was complete garbage, but she submitted it to the school paper and they loved it so much they ran it in installments over the course of nine weeks in the spring semester.

The fact that she managed to do all of that while still being one of the most popular girls in school made it that much worse. It just goes to show that if you're pretty enough, cool comes to you.

I, meanwhile, had covertly read the CliffsNotes in the library for almost every book assigned to us in English 1. I had a pile of novels in my room that my parents had given me as gifts and I had refused to even crack the spines.

I liked music videos, NBC's Thursday Must-See TV lineup, and every single woman who performed at Lilith Fair. When I was bored, I would go through my mom's old issues of *Travel + Leisure*, tearing out pictures and taping them to my wall. The space above my bed became a kaleidoscope of magazine covers of Keanu Reeves, liner notes from Tori Amos albums, and centerfolds of the Italian Riviera and the French countryside.

And no one, I repeat no one, would have confused me for a popular kid.

My parents joked that the nurse must have given them the wrong child at the hospital and I always laughed it off, but I had, more than once, looked at pictures of my parents as children and then stared at myself in the mirror, counting the similarities, reminding myself I belonged to them.

"Okay, great," I told my mom, more excited about not having to go to work than spending time with my sister. "When are we leaving?"

"I don't know," my mom said. "Talk to Marie. I'm off to the store. I'll see you for dinner. I love you, honey. Have a good day."

When she shut my door, I lay back down on the bed with vigor, ready to relish every single extra minute of sleep.

Sometime after eleven, Marie barged into my room and said, "C'mon, we're leaving."

We went to three stores and I tried on twelve pairs of jeans. Some were too baggy, some too tight, some came up too high on my waist.

I tried on the twelfth pair and came out of the dressing room to see Marie staring at me, bored senseless.

"They look fine; just get them," she said. She was wearing head-to-toe Abercrombie & Fitch. It was the turn of the millennium. All of New England was wearing head-to-toe Abercrombie & Fitch.

"They look weird in the butt," I said, staying perfectly still.

Marie stared at me, as if she expected something.

"Are you gonna turn around so I can see if they are weird in the butt, or what?" she finally said.

I turned around.

"They make you look like you're wearing a diaper," she told me.

"That's what I just said."

Marie rolled her eyes. "Hold on." She circled her finger in the air, indicating that I should go back into the dressing room. And so I did.

I had just pulled the last pair of jeans off when she threw a pair of faded straight-leg ones over the top of the door.

"Try these," she said. "Joelle wears them and she has a big butt like yours."

"Thanks a lot," I said, grabbing the jeans from the door.

"I'm just trying to help you," she said, and then I could see her feet walk away, as if the conversation was over simply because she wasn't interested in it anymore.

I unzipped the fly and stepped in. I had to shimmy them over my hips and suck in the tiniest bit to get them buttoned. I stood tall and looked at myself in the mirror, posing this way and that, turning my head to check out what I looked like from behind.

My butt was growing shapelier by the day and my boobs seemed to have stagnated. I had read enough of my mother's *Glamour* magazines to know that this was referred to as "pear shaped." My stomach was flat but my hips were growing. Olive was starting to gain weight in her boobs and her stomach and I wondered if I wouldn't prefer that sort of figure. Apple shaped.

But, if I was being honest with myself, what I really wanted was all that my mother had passed on to Marie. Medium butt, medium boobs, brown hair, green eyes, and thick lashes.

Instead, I got my father's coloring—hair neither fully blond nor fully brunette, eyes somewhere in between brown and green—with a body type all my own. Once, I asked my mother where I got my short, sturdy legs from and she said, "I don't know, actually," as if this wasn't the worst thing she'd ever said to me.

There was only one thing about my appearance that I truly loved. My freckles, that cluster of tiny dark spots under my right eye. My mom used to connect the dots with her finger as she put me to bed as a child.

I loved my freckles and hated my butt.

So as I stood there in the dressing room, all I wanted was a pair of jeans that made my butt look smaller. Which these seemed to do.

I stepped out of the dressing room to ask Marie's opinion. Unfortunately, she was nowhere to be found.

I stepped back into the dressing room, realizing I had no one to make this decision with but me.

I looked at myself one more time in the mirror.

Maybe I liked them?

I looked at the tag. Thirty-five bucks.

With tax, I'd still have money left over to get teriyaki chicken from the food court.

I changed out of them, headed to the register, and handed over my parents' money. I was rewarded with a bag containing one pair of jeans that I did not hate.

Marie was still missing.

I checked around the store. I walked down to the Body Shop to see if she was there buying lip balm or shower gel. Thirty minutes later, I found her buying earrings at Claire's.

"I've been looking all over for you," I said.

"Sorry, I was looking at jewelry." Marie took her change, delicately put it back into her wallet, and then grabbed the tiny white plastic bag that, no doubt, contained fake gold sure to stain her ears a greenish gray.

I followed Marie as she walked confidently out of the store and toward the entrance where we'd parked.

"Wait," I said, stopping in place. "I wanted to go to the food court."

Marie turned toward me. She looked at her watch. "Sorry, no can do. We're gonna be late."

"For what?"

"The swim meet," she said.

"What swim meet?" I asked her. "No one said anything about a swim meet."

Marie didn't answer me because she didn't have to. I was already following her back to the car, already willing to go where she told me to go, willing to do what she told me to do.

It wasn't until we got in the car that she deigned to fill me in. "Graham is the captain of the swim team this year," she said.

Ah, yes.

Graham Hughes. Captain of every team he's on. The front-runner for "best smile" in the yearbook. Exactly the sort of person Saint Marie of Acton would be dating.

"Great," I said. It seemed clear that my future entailed not just sitting and watching the fifty-meter freestyle, but also waiting in Marie's car afterward while she and Graham made out in his.

"Can we at least hit a drive-through on the way there?" I asked, already defeated.

"Yeah, fine," she said.

And then I mustered up as much confidence as I possibly could and said, "You're paying."

She turned and laughed at me. "You're fourteen. You can't buy your own lunch?"

She had the most amazing ability to make me feel stupid even at my most self-assured.

We stopped at a Burger King and I ate a Whopper Jr. in the front seat of her car, getting ketchup and mustard on my hands and having to wait until we parked to find a napkin.

Marie ditched me the minute we smelled the chlorine in the air. So I sat on the bleachers and did my best to entertain myself.

The indoor pool was full of barely clothed, physically fit boys my age. I wasn't sure where to look.

When Graham got up on the diving block and the whistle blew, I watched as he dove into the water with the ease of a bird flying through the air. From the minute he entered the water, it was clear he was going to win the race.

I saw Marie, over in the far corner, bouncing up and down, willing him to win, believing in him with all of her might. When Graham claimed his throne, I got up and walked around, past the other side of the bleachers and through the gym, in search of a vending machine.

When I came back—fifty cents poorer, a bag of Doritos richer—I saw Olive sitting toward the front of the crowd with her family.

One day last summer, just before school started, Olive and I were hanging out in her basement when she told me that she thought she might be gay.

She said she wasn't sure. She just didn't feel like she was totally straight. She liked boys. But she was starting to think she might like girls.

I was pretty sure I was the only one who knew. And I was

also pretty sure that her parents had begun to suspect. But that wasn't my business. My only job was to be a friend to her.

So I did the things friends do, like sit there and watch music videos for hours, waiting for Natalie Imbruglia's "Torn" video to come on so that Olive could stare at her. This was not an entirely selfless act since it was my favorite song and I dreamt of chopping off my hair to look just like Natalie Imbruglia's.

Also not entirely selfless was my willingness to rewatch *Titanic* every few weeks as Olive tried to figure out if she liked watching the sex scene between Jack and Rose because she was attracted to Leonardo DiCaprio or Kate Winslet.

"Hey!" she said as I entered her sight line that day at the pool.

"Hey," I said back. Olive was wearing a white camisole under an unbuttoned light blue oxford button-down. Her long jet-black hair hung straight and past her shoulders. With a name like Olive Berman, you might not realize she was half-Jewish, half-Korean, but she was proud of where her mother's family had come from in South Korea and equally proud of how awesome her bat mitzvah was.

"What are you doing here?" she asked me.

"Marie dragged me and then ditched me."

"Ah," Olive said, nodding. "Just like the Booksellers' Daughter. Is she here to see Graham?" Olive made a face when she said Graham's name and I appreciated that she also found Graham to be laughable.

"Yeah," I said. "But . . . wait, why are you here?"

Olive's brother swam until he graduated last year. Olive had tried but failed to make the girls' swim team.

"My cousin Eli swims for Sudbury."

Olive's mom turned away from the swim meet and looked

at me. "Hi, Emma. Come, have a seat." When I sat down next to Olive, Mrs. Berman turned her focus back to the pool.

Eli came in third and Mrs. Berman reflexively pumped her hands into frustrated fists and then shook her head. She turned and looked at Olive and me.

"I'm going to go give Eli a conciliatory hug and then, Olive, we can head home," she said.

I wanted to ask if I could join them on their way home. Olive lived only five minutes from me. My house was more or less between theirs and the highway exit. But I had trouble asking things of people. I felt more comfortable skirting around it.

"I should probably find Marie," I said. "See if we can head out."

"We can take you," Olive said. "Right, Mom?"

"Of course," Mrs. Berman said as she stood up and squeezed through the crowded bleachers. "Do you want to come say good-bye to Eli? Or should I meet you two at the car?"

"The car," Olive said. "Tell Eli I said hi, though."

Olive put her hand right into my Doritos bag and helped herself.

"Okay," she said once her mom was out of earshot. "Did you see the girl on the other side of the pool, talking to that guy in the red Speedo?"

"Huh?"

"The girl with the ponytail. Talking to somebody on Eli's team. I honestly think she might be the hottest girl in the world. Like ever. Like, that has ever existed in all of eternity."

I looked toward the pool, scanning for a girl with a ponytail. I came up empty. "Where is she?" I said.

"Okay, she's standing by the diving board now," Olive said as she pointed. "Right there. Next to Jesse Lerner."

"Who?" I said as I followed Olive's finger right to the diving board. And I did, in fact, see a pretty girl with a ponytail. But I did not care.

Because I also saw the tall, lean, muscular boy next to her.

His eyes were deep set, his face angular, his lips full. His short, light brown hair, half-matted, half-akimbo, the result of pulling the swimming cap up off his head. I could tell from his swimsuit that he went to our school.

"Do you see her?" Olive said.

"Yeah," I said. "Yeah, she's pretty. But the guy she's talking to . . . What did you say his name was?"

"Who?" Olive asked. "Jesse Lerner?"

"Yeah. Who is Jesse Lerner?"

"How do you not know who Jesse Lerner is?"

I turned and looked at Olive. "I don't know. I just don't. Who is he?"

"He lives down the street from the Hughes."

I turned back to Jesse, watching him pick up a pair of goggles off the ground. "Is he in our grade?"

"Yeah."

Olive kept speaking but I had already started to tune her out. Instead, I was watching Jesse as he headed back to the locker room with the rest of his team. Graham was right next to him, putting a hand on his shoulder for a brief moment before jumping ahead of him in the slow line that had formed. I couldn't take my eyes off of the way Jesse moved, the confidence with which he put one foot in front of the other. He was younger than any of the other swimmers—a freshman on the varsity team—and yet seemed right at home, standing in front of everyone in a tiny swimsuit.

"Emma," Olive said. "You're staring."

Just then, Jesse turned his head ever so slightly and his gaze landed squarely on me, for a brief, breathless second. Instinctively, I looked away.

"What did you say?" I asked Olive, trying to pretend I was engaged with her side of the conversation.

"I said you were staring at him."

"No, I wasn't," I said.

It was then that Mrs. Berman came back around to our side of the bleachers. "I thought you were meeting me at the car," she said.

"Sorry!" Olive said, jumping up onto her feet. "We're coming now."

"Sorry, Mrs. Berman," I said, and I followed them both behind the bleachers and out the door.

I paused, just before the exit, to see Jesse one last time. I saw a flash of his smile. It was wide and bright, toothy and sincere. His whole face lit up.

I wondered how good it would feel to have that smile directed at me, to be the cause of a smile like that—and suddenly, my new crush on Jesse Lerner grew into a massive, inflated balloon that was so strong it could have lifted the two of us up into the air if we'd grabbed on.

That week at school, I noticed Jesse in the hallway almost every day. Now that I knew who he was, he was everywhere.

"That's the Baader-Meinhof phenomenon," Olive said when I mentioned it at lunch. "My brother just told me about this. You don't notice something and then you learn the name for it and suddenly it's everywhere." Olive thought for a moment. "Whoa. I'm pretty sure I have the Baader-Meinhof phenomenon *about* the Baader-Meinhof phenomenon."

"Are you seeing Jesse everywhere, too?" I asked, entirely missing the point. Earlier that day, I'd walked right by him coming out of Spanish class. He was talking to Carolyn Bean by her locker. Carolyn Bean was the captain of the girls' soccer team. She wore her blond hair back in a bun, with a sporty headband every day. I'd never seen her without lip gloss. If that was the kind of girl Jesse liked, I stood no chance.

"I'm not seeing him any more than normal," Olive said. "But I always see him around all the time. He's in my algebra 1 class."

"Are you friends with him?" I asked.

"Not really," Olive said. "But he's a nice guy. You should just say hi to him."

"That's insane. I can't just say hi to him."

"Sure you can."

I shook my head and looked away. "You sound ridiculous."

"*You* sound ridiculous. He's a boy in our class. He's not Keanu Reeves."

I thought to myself, *If I could just talk to Jesse Lerner, I wouldn't care about Keanu Reeves.*

"I can't introduce myself, that's crazy," I said, and then I gathered my tray and headed toward the trash can. Olive followed.

"Fine," she said. "But he's a perfectly nice person."

"Don't say that!" I said. "That just makes it worse."

"You want me to say he's mean?"

"I don't know!" I said. "I don't know what I want you to say."

"You're being sort of annoying," Olive said, surprised.

"I know, okay?" I said. "Ugh, just . . . come on. I'll buy you a pack of cookies."

Back then, a seventy-five-cent bag of cookies was enough to make up for being irritating. So as we walked over to the counter, I dug my hand into my pocket and counted out what silver coins I had.

"I have one fifty exactly," I said just as I followed Olive to the back of the line. "So enough for both of us." I looked up to see Olive's eyes go wide.

"What?"

She directed me forward with the glance of her eyes.

Jesse Lerner was standing right in front of us. He was wearing dark jeans and a Smashing Pumpkins T-shirt with a pair of black Converse One Stars.

And he was holding Carolyn Bean's hand.

Olive looked at me, trying to gauge my reaction. But instead, I stared forward, doing a perfect impression of someone unfazed.

And then I watched as Carolyn Bean let go of Jesse's hand, reached into her pocket, took out a tube of lip balm, and applied it to her lips.

As if it wasn't bad enough she was holding his hand, she had the audacity to let go of it.

I hated her then. I hated her dumb, soccer-playing, headband-wearing, Dr-Pepper-flavored-lip-balm-applying guts.

If he ever wanted to hold my hand, I'd never, ever, ever let go.

"Let's get out of here," I said to Olive.

"Yeah," she said. "We can get something from the vending machine instead."

I walked off, depressed and lovesick, heading for the vending machine by the band room.

I bought two Snickers bars and handed one of them to Olive. I chomped into mine, as if it were the only thing that could fill the void in my heart.

"I'm over him," I said. "Totally dumb crush. But it's done. I'm over it. Seriously."

"Okay," Olive said, half laughing at me.

"No, really," I said. "Definitely over."

"Sure," Olive said, scrunching her eyebrows and pursing her lips.

And then I heard a voice coming from behind me.

"Emma?"

I turned to see Sam coming out of the band room.

"Oh, hey," I said.

"I didn't know that you had this lunch period."

I nodded. "Yep."

His hair was a bit disheveled and he was wearing a green shirt that said "Bom Dia!"

"So, I guess we've got our first shift together," he said. "Tomorrow at the store, I mean."

"Oh," I said. "Yeah." On Tuesday, Marie had borrowed my Fiona Apple CD without asking, prompting me to call her a "complete asshole" within hearing distance of my parents. My punishment was a Friday shift at the store. In my family, instead of getting grounded or having privileges revoked, you redeemed yourself by working more. Extra shifts at the store were my parents' way of both teaching lessons and extracting free labor. Assigning me Friday evening in particular meant I couldn't hang out with Olive and they could have a date night at the movies.

"Tomorrow?" Olive said. "I thought we were going to hang out at my house after school."

"Sorry," I said. "I forgot. I have to work."

The bell rang, indicating that it was time for me to start walking toward my world geography class.

"Ah," Olive said. "I have to go. I left my book in my locker."

Olive didn't wait for me, didn't even offer. Nothing stood between her and being on time for anything.

"I should get going, too," I said to Sam, who didn't seem to be in a rush to get anywhere. "We have a test in geo."

"Oh, well, I don't want to keep you," Sam said. "I just wanted to know if you wanted a ride. Tomorrow. To the store after school."

I looked at him, confused. I mean, I wasn't confused about what he was saying. I understood the simple physics of getting into a car that would take me from school to work. But it surprised me that he was offering, that he would even think to offer.

"I just got my license and I inherited my brother's Camry,"

he said. In high school, it seemed like everyone was inheriting Camrys or Corollas. "So I just thought . . ." He looked me in the eye and then looked away. "So you don't have to take the bus, is all."

He was being so thoughtful. And he barely knew me.

"Sure," I said, "that would be great."

"Meet you in the parking lot after school?" he asked.

"That sounds great. Thank you. That's really cool of you."

"No worries," he said. "See you tomorrow."

As I walked toward the double doors at the end of the hall, heading to class, it occurred to me that maybe it was time to just be friends with whomever I wanted to be friends with, to not try quite so hard to reject everything Marie liked.

Maybe it was time to just . . . be myself.

The next day I wore a red knit sweater and flat-front chinos to school, cognizant of my parents' request to never wear jeans at the store. And then, ten minutes after the last bell rang, I saw Sam leaning against the hood of his car in the school parking lot, waiting for me.

"Hey," I said as I got closer.

"Hey." He went around to my side of the car and opened the car door. No one had ever opened a car door for me before except my father, and even then, it was usually a joke.

"Oh," I said, taking my backpack off and putting it in the front seat. "Thank you."

Sam looked surprised for a moment, as if he wasn't sure what I was thanking him for. "For the door? You're welcome."

I sat down and sunk into the passenger's seat as Sam made his way to his side of the car. He smiled at me nervously when he got in and turned on the ignition. And then, suddenly, jazz music blasted through the speakers.

"Sorry," he said. "Sometimes I really have to psych myself up in the morning."

I laughed. "Totally cool."

He turned the music down but not off and I listened as it softly filled the air in the car. Sam put the car in reverse and twisted his body toward me, resting his arm on the back of my seat and then backing out of the spot.

His car was a mess. Papers at my feet, gum wrappers and guitar picks strewn across the dashboard. I glanced into the backseat and saw a guitar, a harmonica, and two black instrument cases.

I turned back to face the front. "Who is this?" I said, pointing to the stereo.

Sam was watching the steady stream of cars to his left, waiting for his chance to turn onto the road.

"Mingus," he said, not looking at me.

There was a small opening, a chance to enter the flow of traffic. Sam inched up and then swiftly turned, gracefully joining the steady stream of cars. He relinquished his attention, and turned back to me.

"Charles Mingus," he said, explaining. "Do you like jazz?"

"I don't really listen to it," I said. "So I don't know."

"All right, then," Sam said, turning up the volume. "We'll listen and then you'll know."

I nodded and smiled to show that I was game. The only problem was that I knew within three seconds that Charles Mingus was not for me and I didn't know how to politely ask him to turn it off. So I didn't.

My father was at the register when we came in through the doors. His face lit up when he saw me.

"Hi, sweetheart," he said, focused on me. And then he turned for a brief second. "Hey, Sam!"

"Hi, Dad," I said back. I didn't love the idea of my father calling me "sweetheart" in front of people from school. But groaning about it would only make it worse, so I let it go.

Sam headed straight for the back of the store. "I'm going to run to the bathroom and then, Mr. Blair, I'll be back to relieve you."

My dad gave him a thumbs-up and then turned to me. "Tell me all about your day," he said as I put my book bag down underneath the register. "Start at the beginning."

I looked around to see that the only customer in the store was an older man reading a military biography. He was pretending to peruse it but appeared to be downright engrossed. I half expected him to lick his fingertip to turn the page or dog-ear his favorite chapter.

"Aren't you supposed to be taking Mom on a date?" I asked.

"How old do you think I am?" he asked, looking at his watch. "It's not even four p.m. You think I'm taking your mother to an early bird special?"

"I don't know," I said, shrugging. "You two are the ones who made me work today so you could go see a movie together."

"We made you work today because you were being rude to your sister," he said. His tone was matter-of-fact, all blame removed from his voice. My parents didn't really hold grudges. Their punishments and disappointments were perfunctory. It was as if they were abiding by rules set out before them by someone else. *You did this and so we must do that. Let's all just do our part and get through this.*

This changed a few years later, when I called them in the middle of the night and asked them to pick me up from the police station. Suddenly, it wasn't a fun little test anymore. Suddenly, I had actually disappointed them. But back then, the stakes were low, and discipline was almost a game.

"I know that you and Marie are not the best of friends," my dad said, tidying up a stack of bookmarks that rested by the register. When the store opened, sometime in the sixties, my great-uncle who started it had commissioned these super cheesy bookmarks with a globe on them and an airplane circling it. They said "Travel the World by Reading a Book." My father loved them so much that he had refused to update them. He had the same exact ones printed time and time again.

Whenever I picked one of them up, I would be struck by how perfectly they symbolized exactly what I resented about that bookstore.

I was going to travel the world by *actually traveling it.*

"But one day, sooner than you think, the two of you are going to realize how much you need each other," my dad continued.

Adults love to tell teenagers that "one day" and "sooner or later" plenty of things are going to happen. They love to say that things happen "before you know it," and they really love to impart how fast time "flies by."

I would learn later that almost everything my parents told me in this regard turned out to be true. College really did "fly by." I did change my mind about Keanu Reeves "sooner or later." I was on the other side of thirty "before I knew it." And, just as my father said that afternoon, "one day" I was going to need my sister very, very much.

But back then, I shrugged it off the same way teens all over the country were shrugging off every other thing their parents said at that very moment.

"Marie and I are not going to be friends. Ever. And I wish you guys would let up about it."

My father listened, nodding his head slowly, and then looked away, focusing instead on tidying up another stack of bookmarks. Then he turned back to me. "I read you loud and clear," he said, which is what he always said when he decided that he didn't want to talk about something anymore.

Sam came out of the back and joined us up by the registers.

The customer reading the book came over to the counter with the book in his hand and asked us to keep it on hold for him. No doubt so he could come back and read the same copy tomorrow, as if he owned the thing. My father acted as if he was delighted to do it. My father was very charming to strangers.

Right after the man left, my mom came out of her office in the back of the store. Unfortunately, Dad didn't see her.

"I should tell your mother it's time to go," he said. I tried to stop him but he turned his head slightly and started yelling. "Ashley, Emma and Sam are here!"

"Jesus Christ, Colin," my mom said, putting a hand to her ear. "I'm right here."

"Oh, sorry." He made a scrunched face to show that he'd made a mistake and then he gently touched her ear. It was gestures like that, small acts of intimacy between them, that made me think my parents probably still had sex. I was both repulsed and somewhat assuaged by the thought.

Olive's parents always seemed on the edge of divorce. Marie's friend Debbie practically lived at our house for two months a few years earlier when her parents were ironing out their own separation. So I was smart enough to know I was lucky to have parents who still loved each other.

"All right, well, since you're both here, we will take off," my mom said, heading toward the back to grab her things.

"I thought you weren't leaving for your date until later," I said to my father.

"Yeah, but why would we hang around when our daughter is here to do the work?" he said. "If we hurry, we can get home in time to take a disco nap."

"What is a disco nap?" Sam asked.

"Don't, Sam; it's a trap," I said.

Sam laughed. I never really made people laugh. I wasn't funny the way Olive was funny. But, suddenly, around Sam I felt like maybe I could be.

"A disco nap, dear Samuel, is a nap that you take before you go out and party. You see, back in the seventies . . ."

I walked away, preemptively bored, and started reorganizing the table of best sellers by the window. Marie liked to sneak her favorite books on there, giving her best-loved authors a boost. My only interest was in keeping the piles straight. I did not like wayward corners.

I perked up only when I heard Sam respond to my father's story about winning a disco contest in Boston by laughing and saying, "I'm so sorry to say this, but that's not a very good story."

My head shot up and I looked right at Sam, impressed.

My dad laughed and shook his head. "When I was your age and an adult told a bad story, do you know what I did?"

"Memorized it so you could bore us with it?" I piped in.

Sam laughed again. My father, despite wanting to pretend to be hurt, gave a hearty chuckle. "Forget it. You two can stay here and work while I'm out having fun."

Sam and I shared a glance.

"Aha. Who's laughing now?" my dad said.

My mom came out with their belongings and within minutes, my parents were gone, out the door to their car, on their way to take disco naps. I was stunned, for a moment, that they had left the store to Sam and me. Two people under the age of seventeen in charge for the evening? I felt mature, suddenly. As if I could be trusted with truly adult responsibilities.

And then Margaret, the assistant manager, pulled in and I realized my parents had called her to supervise.

"I'll be in the back making the schedule for next week,"

Margaret said just as soon as she came in. "If you need anything, holler."

I looked over at Sam, who was standing by the register, leaning over the counter on his elbows.

I went into the biography section and started straightening that out, too. The store was dead quiet. It seemed almost silly to have two people out in front and one in the back. But I knew that I was here as a punishment and Sam was here because my parents wanted to give him hours.

I resolved to sit on the floor and flip through Fodor's travel books if nobody else came in.

"So what did you think of Charles Mingus?" Sam asked. I was surprised to see that he had left the area by the cash register and was just a few aisles down, restocking journals.

"Oh," I said. "Uh . . . Very cool."

Sam laughed. "You liar," he said. "You hated it."

I turned and looked at him, embarrassed to admit the truth. "Sorry," I said. "I did. I hated it."

Sam shook his head. "Totally fine. Now you know."

"Yeah, if someone asks me if I like jazz, I can say no."

"Well, you might still like jazz," Sam offered. "Just because you don't like Mingus doesn't mean . . ." He trailed off as he saw the look on my face. "You're already ready to write off all of jazz?"

"Maybe?" I said, embarrassed. "I don't think jazz is my thing."

He grabbed his chest as if I'd stabbed him in the heart.

"Oh, c'mon," I said. "I'm sure there are plenty of things I love that you'd hate."

"Try me," he said.

"*Romeo + Juliet,*" I said confidently. It had proven to be a definitive dividing line between boys and girls at school.

Sam was looking back at the journals in front of him. "The play?" he asked.

"The movie!" I corrected him.

He shook his head as if he didn't know what I was talking about.

"You've never seen *Romeo + Juliet* with Leonardo DiCaprio?" I was aware of the fact that there were other versions of *Romeo and Juliet*, but back then, there was no Romeo but Leo. No Juliet but Claire Danes.

"I don't really watch that many new movies," Sam said.

A mother and son came in and headed straight for the children's section in the back. "Do you have *The Velveteen Rabbit*?" the mom asked.

Sam nodded and walked with her, toward the stacks at the far end of the store.

I moved toward the cash register. When they came back, I was ready to ring them up, complete with a green plastic bag and a "Travel the World by Reading a Book" bookmark. When she was out the door, I turned to Sam. He was standing to the side, leaning on a table, with nothing to do.

"What do you like to do, then?" I asked. "If you're not into movies, I mean."

Sam thought about it. "Well, I have to study a lot," he said. "And other than that, between my job here and being in the marching band, orchestra, and jazz band . . . I don't have a lot of time."

I looked at him. I was thinking less and less about whether Marie thought he was cute, and more and more about the fact that I did.

"Can I ask you something?" I said as I turned away from the stacks in front of me and walked toward him.

"I think that's typically how conversations go, so sure," he said, smiling.

I laughed. "Why do you work here?"

"What do you mean?"

"I mean, if you're so busy, why do you spend so much time working at a bookstore?"

"Oh," Sam said, thinking about it. "Well, I have to buy my own car insurance and I want to get a cell phone, which my parents said was fine as long as I pay for it myself."

I understood that part. Almost everyone had an after-school job, except the kids who scored lifeguard jobs during the summer and somehow ended up making enough to last them the whole year.

"But why *here*? You could be working at the CD store down the road. Or, I mean, the music store on Main Street."

Sam thought about it. "I don't know. I thought about applying to those places, too. But I . . . I think I just wanted to work at a place that had nothing to do with music," he said.

"What do you mean?"

"I mean, I play six instruments. I have to be relentless about practicing. I play piano for at least an hour every day. So it's nice to just have, like, one thing that isn't about minor chords and tempos and . . ." He seemed lost in his own world for a moment but then he resurfaced. "I just sometimes need to do something totally different."

I couldn't imagine what it was like to be him, to have something you were so passionate about that you actually needed to make yourself take a break from it. I didn't have any particular passion. I just knew that it wasn't my family's passion. It wasn't books.

"What instruments?" I asked him.

"Hm?"

"What are the six that you play?"

"Oh," he said.

A trio of girls from school came in the door. I didn't know who they were by name, but I'd seen them in the halls. They were seniors, I was pretty sure. They laughed and joked with one another, paying no attention to Sam or me. The tallest one gravitated toward the new fiction while the other two hovered around the bargain section, picking up books and laughing about them.

"Piano," Sam said. "That was my first one. I started in second grade. And then, let's see . . ." He put out his thumb, to start counting, and then with each instrument another finger went up. "Guitar—electric and acoustic but I count that as one still—plus bass, too—electric and acoustic, which I also think counts as one even though they really are totally different."

"So five so far but you're saying that's really only three."

Sam laughed. "Right. And then drums, a bit. That's my weakest. I just sort of dabble but I'm getting better. And then trumpet and trombone. I just recently bought a harmonica, too, just to see how fast I can pick it up. It's going well so far."

"So seven," I said.

"Yeah, but I mean, the harmonica doesn't count either, not yet at least."

In that moment, I wished my parents had made me pick up an instrument when I was in second grade. It seemed like it was almost too late now. That's how easy it is to tell yourself it's too late for something. I started doing it at the age of fourteen.

"Is it like languages?" I asked him. "Olive grew up speaking English and Korean and she says it's easy for her to pick up other languages now."

Sam thought about it. "Yeah, totally. I grew up speaking Portuguese a bit as a kid. And in Spanish class I can intuit some of the words. Same thing with knowing how to play the guitar and then learning the bass. There's some overlap, definitely."

"Why did you speak Portuguese?" I asked him. "I mean, are your parents from Portugal?"

"My mom is second-generation Brazilian," he said. "But I was never fluent or anything. Just some words here and there."

The tall girl headed toward the register, so I put down the book in my hand and I met her up at the counter.

She was buying a Danielle Steel novel. When I rang it up, she said, "It's for my mom. For her birthday," as if I was judging her. But I wasn't. I never did. I was far too worried that everyone else was judging me.

"I bet she'll like it," I said. I gave her the total and she took out a credit card and handed it over.

Lindsay Bean.

Immediately, the resemblance was crystal clear. She looked like an older, lankier version of Carolyn. I bagged her book and handed it back to her. Sam, overlooking, pointed to the bookmarks, reminding me. "Oh, wait," I said. "You need a bookmark." I picked one up and slipped it into her bag.

"Thanks," Lindsay said. I wondered if she got along with Carolyn, what the Bean sisters were like. Maybe they loved each other, loved to be together, loved to hang out. Maybe, when Lindsay took Carolyn to the mall to get jeans, she didn't abandon her in the store.

I knew it was silly to assume that Carolyn's life was better than mine just because she had been holding Jesse Lerner's hand yesterday in line for a pack of cookies. But, also, I knew that simply because she *had* been holding Jesse's hand in line for a pack of cookies, her life *was* better than mine.

The sun was starting to set by then. Cars had turned on their headlights. Often, during the evening hours, the low beams of SUVs were just high enough to shine right into the storefront.

This very thing happened just as Lindsay and her friends were making their way outside. A champagne-colored oversized SUV pulled up and parked right in front of the store, its lights focused straight on me. When the driver turned the car off, I could see who it was.

Jesse Lerner was sitting in the front passenger's side of the car. A man, most likely his father, was driving.

The back door opened and out popped Carolyn Bean.

Jesse got out of his side and hugged Carolyn good-bye and then Carolyn got in her sister's car with her sister's two friends.

Then Jesse hopped back into his father's car, glancing into the store for a moment as he did it. I couldn't tell if he saw me. I doubted he was really *looking*, the way I had been.

But I couldn't take my eyes off of him. My gaze followed his silhouette even as Carolyn and Lindsay's car took off, even as Jesse's father turned the headlights back on and three-point-turned out of the parking lot.

When I spun back to what I was doing, I ached somehow. As if Jesse Lerner was meant to be mine and I was being forced to stare right into the heart of the injustice of it all.

My hand hit the stack of bookmarks, sending them into disarray. I gathered them and fixed them myself.

"So I was wondering," Sam said.

"Yeah?"

"If maybe you'd want to, like, go see a movie together sometime."

I turned and looked at him, surprised.

There was too much overwhelming me in that moment. Jesse with Carolyn, the headlights in my eyes, and the fact that someone was actually, possibly, *asking me out on a date.*

I should have said, "Sure." Or "Totally." But instead I said, "Oh. Uh . . ."

And then nothing else.

"No worries," Sam said, clearly desperate for this awkwardness to end. "I get it."

And just like that, I sent Sam Kemper straight into the friend zone.

Two and a half years later, Sam was graduating.

I had spent a good portion of my sophomore year trying to get Sam to ask me out again. I had made jokes about not having anything to do on a Saturday night and I had vaguely implied that we should hang out outside of the store, but he wasn't getting it and I was too much of a chicken to ask him outright. So I let it go.

And since then, Sam and I had become close friends.

So I went with my mom and dad to support him as he sat outside in the sweltering heat in a cap and gown.

Marie was not yet home for the summer from the University of New Hampshire. She was majoring in English, spending her extracurricular time submitting short stories to literary magazines. She had yet to place one but everyone was sure she'd get published somewhere soon. Graham had gone to UNH with her but she broke up with him two months in. Now she was dating someone named Mike whose parents owned a string of sporting goods stores. Marie would often joke that if they got married, they would merge the businesses. "Get it? And sell books and sports equipment at the same store," she'd explain.

As I told Olive, there was no end to the things Marie could say to make me purge my lunch. But no one else seemed to want to vomit around her, and thus, my parents were promoting her to assistant manager for the summer.

Margaret had just recently quit and Marie had lobbied for the job. I was surprised when my mom was reticent to let her do it. "She should be off enjoying herself in college," she said. "Before she comes back here and takes on all of this responsibility."

But my father was so excited about it that even I had softened to the idea. He made her an assistant manager name badge even though none of us wore name badges. And he told my mom that he couldn't be happier than to spend his summer with both of his daughters at the store.

The smile on his face and the gleam in his eye led me to promise myself to be nicer to Marie. But she hadn't even come home yet and I was already unsure it would take.

I was not looking forward to summer at the store. Sam had given his notice the month before and had worked his last day. Instead of staying in town, he was leaving in a few weeks to take an internship at a music therapy office in Boston. And then he was starting at Berklee College of Music in the fall.

It was his first choice and when he got in, I'd congratulated him with a hug. Then I quickly moved on to teasing him for staying so close to home. But I wasn't entirely joking. I truly couldn't understand why his first choice was to live in a part of the country he'd lived in all his life. I had set my sights on the University of Los Angeles. I got a pamphlet in the mail and I liked the idea of going to school in permanent sunshine.

As Sam's name was called out on the converted football field that afternoon, my parents were disagreeing about whether to restain our back patio. I had to nudge my father in the ribs with my elbow to get his attention.

"Guys," I said. "Sam's up."

"Samuel Marcos Kemper," the principal announced.

The three of us stood and cheered for him, joining his own parents, who were seated on the other side of the crowd.

When Sam sat down, I connected eyes with him for a moment and watched a smile creep across his face.

~

Four hours later, Olive and I were standing in the kitchen of Billy Yen's house, filling up our red Solo cups with generic-looking beer from an ice-cold steel keg.

Almost seventeen, I had made out with two guys and dated Robby Timmer for four weeks, during which time I let him get to a tame third base. It was safe to say I was looking to ditch my v-card as soon as the moment was right and I was hoping that moment was sooner rather than later.

Olive, for her part, had come out to her parents as bisexual and then confused them when she started dating Matt Jennings. Olive patiently explained to her parents that bisexual did not mean gay, it meant *bisexual*. And while they seemed to understand, they once again became confused when Olive and Matt broke up and Olive started dating a girl from her after-school job at CVS. They understood gay and they understood straight but they did not understand Olive.

"Did you see who's here?" Olive asked. She took a sip of the beer and made a grimace. "This tastes like water, basically," she said.

"Who?" I asked. I sipped from my cup and found that Olive was right—it did taste watery. But I liked watery beer. It tasted less like beer.

"J-E-S-S-E," Olive said.

"He's here?" I asked.

Olive nodded. "I saw him earlier, by the pool."

Olive and I were not aware, when we heard about the party, that there was a pool and people there would be running around in bikinis and swim shorts, throwing one another in and playing chicken. But even if we had been, we still would have come and we still wouldn't have worn our bathing suits.

I sipped my own drink and then decided to just throw it back in a series of chugs. Then I filled up my cup again.

"All right, well," I said. "Let's just walk around and see if we spot him."

Jesse and Carolyn broke up sometime over spring break earlier that year. It wasn't such a crazy thing to think that Jesse might notice me.

Except that it was. It was totally absurd.

He was now the captain of the swim team, leading our high school to three undefeated seasons. There was an article about him in the local newspaper, titled "Swim Prodigy Jesse Lerner Breaks 500 Meter Freestyle State Record." He was out of my league.

Olive and I took our cups with us out back, joining the chaos surrounding the yard and pool. There were girls on the redwood patio smoking clove cigarettes and laughing together, every single one of them wearing a spaghetti-strap tank and low-cut jeans. I was embarrassed to be wearing the very same thing.

I had on a black tank with flared jeans that came up two inches lower than my belly button. There was a gap between the tank and the jeans, my midriff showing. Olive was wearing flat-front camo-print chinos and a V-neck purple T-shirt, also exposing her lower abs. Now I look at pictures of us back then and I wonder what on earth possessed us to leave the house with our belly buttons hanging out.

"You look great, by the way," Olive said. "This might be your hottest phase yet."

"Thanks," I said. I figured she was referring to the way I'd been wearing my long, blond-brown hair low down my back, parted in the middle. But I also suspected it had something to do with the way that I was growing into my body. I felt more confident about my butt, less shy about my boobs. I stood taller and straighter. I had started wearing dark brown mascara and blush. I had become a slave to lip gloss like every other girl in school. I felt far from a beautiful swan but I no longer felt like an ugly duckling, either. I was somewhere in between, and I think my growing confidence had started showing.

Olive waved a hand in front of her face as the smoke from the cloves drifted over to us. "Why do girls think that just because the cigarette smells vaguely of nutmeg that I would want to smell it any more than a normal one?" She walked away, down toward the pool to put some distance between us and the smoke.

It was only once my feet hit the concrete surrounding the pool that I realized who was about to dive in.

There, in a wet red-and-white bathing suit clinging to his legs, toes lined up perfectly with the edge of the diving board, was . . . Sam.

His hair was wet and mashed down onto his head. His torso was entirely bare. There, underneath the faint chest hair and the sinewy pecks, was a six-pack.

Sam had a six-pack.

What?

Olive and I watched as he bounced slowly, preparing to take flight. And then he was in the air.

He landed with the familiar *thwack* of a belly flop.

Someone yelled, “Ohhhhh, duuude. That had to hurt.” And then Sam’s head popped up from the water, laughing. He shook the water from his ears and saw me.

He smiled and then started to swim to the edge as a second guy jumped in right after him.

I was suddenly nervous. If Sam came up to me, wet and half-naked, what did I want to happen?

“Another beer?” Olive asked me, holding her cup out to show me it was empty.

I nodded, assuming she would go get them.

But instead she said, “Be a doll,” and handed me her cup.

I laughed at her. “You are so annoying.”

She smiled. “I know.”

I walked up to the keg outside and pumped out enough for one cup before it sputtered out.

“Oh, man!” I heard from behind me.

I turned around.

Jesse Lerner was standing six inches from me in a T-shirt, jeans, and leather sandals. He was smiling in a way that seemed confident but vaguely shy, like he knew how handsome he was and it embarrassed him. “You drained the last of the keg,” he said.

It was the first time Jesse had ever said a complete sentence to me, the first time I’d heard a subject followed by a predicate come out of his mouth aimed for my ears.

The only thing that was weird about it was how *not* weird it was. In an instant, Jesse went from someone I saw from afar to someone I felt like I’d been talking to my entire life. I wasn’t intimidated, as I always imagined I’d be. I wasn’t even nervous. It was like spending years training for a race and finally getting to race it.

"You snooze, you lose," I said, teasing.

"Rules say if you take the last beer you have to chug it," he said.

And then, from the crowd, came the word that no teenager holding a Solo cup ever wants to hear.

"Cops!"

Jesse's head whipped around, looking to confirm that the threat was real, that it wasn't just a bad joke.

In the far corner of the yard, where the driveway ended, you could just make out the blue and red lights across the grass.

And then there was a *whoop*.

I looked around, trying to find Olive, but she'd already taken off into the back woods, catching my eye and pointing for me to do the same.

I dropped the cups on the ground, spilling my beer on my feet. And then I felt a hand on my wrist. Jesse was pulling me with him, off in the opposite direction of everyone else. We weren't going toward the woods in the back; we were headed for the bushes that separated the house from the one next to it.

Everyone was scrambling. What had previously been the controlled type of chaos that rages through a high school kegger became unruly disorder, teenagers running in every direction. It was the closest I'd come to seeing anarchy.

When Jesse and I got to the bushes, he guided me into them first. They were dense and thorny. I could feel the skin on my bare arms and ankles chafing against the tiny sharp blades in every direction.

But the bushes were big enough that Jesse could crawl in next to me and they were dark enough that I felt safe from the police officers. We were far enough away from everyone else that it started to feel quiet—if the background noise of a police siren and heavy running footsteps can ever really be described as quiet.

I could sense Jesse's body right next to me, could feel his arm as it grazed mine.

"Ow!" he said in a stage whisper.

"What?" I whispered back.

"I think I cut my lip on a thorn."

A harsh stream of light cascaded over the bushes we were hiding in and I found myself frozen still.

I could hear my own breath, feel my heart beating against the bone of my chest. I was terrified; there was no doubt about it. I was drunk by this point. Not plastered, by any means, but well past a buzz. There was real danger in getting caught: not only my parents' disappointment, but also the actual threat of being arrested.

That being said, it was impossible to deny the tingle of excitement running through me. It was a rush, to be stifling my own breath as I felt the shadow of a police officer grow closer and closer. It was thrilling to feel adrenaline run through me.

After some time, the coast started to clear. There were no more heavy footsteps, no more flashlights. We heard cars driving away, chattering stop. My ankles had started to itch considerably and I knew I'd been bitten by something or some*things.* It was, after all, May in Massachusetts—which meant that every bug in the air was out for blood.

I wasn't sure when to speak up, when to break the silence.

On the one hand, it seemed like it was safe to come out of the bushes. On the other hand, you never want to be wrong about that.

I heard Jesse whisper my name.

"Emma?" he said softly. "Are you okay?"

I didn't even know that he knew my name and there he was, saying it as if it were his to say.

"Yeah," I said. "Maybe a little scraped up but other than that, I'm good. You?"

"Yeah," he said. "I'm good, too."

He was quiet for a moment longer and then he said, "I think it's safe. Are you able to crawl out?"

The way he said it made me think that maybe he'd crawled into the bushes before, that maybe this wasn't the first time Jesse had been at a party he wasn't supposed to be at, doing things he wasn't supposed to be doing.

"Yeah," I said. "I got it."

A few awkward army-crawl-like steps forward and I was standing on the grass in front of Jesse Lerner.

His lip was cut and there was a scrape on the top of his forehead. My arms had a few tiny scratches down them. My ankle still itched. I lifted my foot up and saw a few small welts where my pants met the top of my shoes.

It was pitch-dark, the lights in the house all dimmed. Everything was deadly quiet. The only sound either of us could hear was the sound of our own breath and that of the crickets rubbing their wings together, chirping.

I wasn't sure what we were supposed to do now. How we were supposed to get home.

"C'mon," Jesse said, and then he took my hand again. Twice in one night, holding hands with Jesse Lerner. I had to remind myself not to take it too personally. "We will walk down the street until we find somebody else who escaped and bum a ride with them."

"Okay," I said, willing to follow his lead because I had no better idea. I just wanted to get home quickly so I could call

Olive and make sure she was okay and make sure she knew that I was.

And then, there was Sam. He'd been there, in the pool. Where had he gone?

Jesse and I set out down the dark suburban road, headed nowhere in particular, hoping it would lead us somewhere good.

"How come you weren't swimming?" I asked him once we were a few feet down the road.

Jesse looked at me. "What do you mean?"

"I mean, aren't you supposed to be the greatest swimmer of all time?"

Jesse laughed. "I don't know about that."

"You were written up in the *Beacon*."

"Yeah, but I'm not a fish. I do exist outside of the water," he teased.

I shrugged. "Question still stands, though," I said. "It was a pool party."

He was quiet for a moment. I thought maybe the conversation was over, maybe we weren't supposed to be talking, maybe he didn't want to talk to me. But once he finally started talking again, I realized that he had been caught up in his own head for a moment, deciding how much to say.

"Do you ever feel like everyone is always telling you who you are?" he asked me. "Like, people are acting as if they know better than you what you're good at or who you are supposed to be?"

"Yeah," I said. "I think so."

"Can I let you in on a very poorly kept secret?" he asked me.

"Yeah."

"My parents want me to train for the Olympic trials."

"Ah." He was right. That was a very poorly kept secret.

"Can I let you in on a better-kept secret?" he asked.

I nodded.

"I hate swimming."

He was staring forward, putting one foot in front of the other along the road.

"Do your parents know that?" I asked him.

He shook his head. "Nobody does," he said. "Well, I guess, except for you now."

At the time, I could not, for the life of me, understand why he told me this, why he trusted me with the truth about his life more than anyone else. I thought it meant that I was special, that maybe he had always felt about me the way I felt about him.

Now, looking back on it, I know it was just the opposite. I was a girl in the background of his life—that's what made me safe.

"I never really cared much for swimming anyway," I told him reassuringly. I said it because it was the truth. But there was a large secondary benefit in what I'd said.

Now I knew who he really was and I still liked him. And that made me different from anyone else.

"My parents run the bookstore," I said. "Blair Books."

"Yeah," he said. "I know. I mean, I put that together." He smiled at me and then looked away. We made our way around a corner and found ourselves on the main road.

"They want me to take over the store one day," I told him. "They are always giving me these five hundred–page novels as presents and telling me that one day I'll fall in love with reading just like they have and . . . I don't know."

"What?" Jesse asked.

"I hate reading books."

Jesse smiled, surprised and satisfied. He put his hand up, offering me a high five. He had confided in me because he thought I was a stranger, only to find that I was a comrade.

I laughed and leaned over, raising my palm to his. We slapped and then Jesse held on for a moment.

"Are you drunk?" he asked me.

"A little," I said. "Are you?"

"A little," he answered back.

He didn't let go of my hand and I thought maybe, just maybe, he was going to kiss me. And then I thought that was an insane thing to think. *That would never happen.*

Later on, when Jesse and I would tell each other everything, I asked him what he was thinking back then. I'd say, "That moment when you held on to my hand, right before the cops found us, were you going to kiss me?" He'd say he didn't know. He'd say that all he remembered was that he had just realized, for the first time, how pretty I was. "I just remember noticing the freckles under your eye. So, maybe. Maybe I was going to kiss you. I don't know."

And we will never know.

Because just as I built up enough confidence to look Jesse right in the eye in the wee hours of the morning, we were blinded by the stunning bright light of a police officer's flashlight, aimed directly into our eyes. We were drunk on the sidewalk, caught red-handed.

A litany of half-assed lies and two failed Breathalyzers later, Jesse and I sat handcuffed along the wall of the Acton Police Department waiting to be picked up.

"My parents are going to kill me," I said to him. "I don't think I've ever heard my dad as pissed as he was on the phone." In the bright light of the police station, the cut on Jesse's lip looked burgundy, the bug bites on my ankles almost terracotta.

I thought Jesse would react by telling me how much worse he had it, how much more unbearable his parents would undoubtedly be. But he didn't. Instead he said, "I'm sorry."

"No," I said, shaking my head. I never realized how often I used my hands to talk until they were constrained. "It's not your fault."

Jesse shrugged. "Maybe," he said. "But I'm still sorry."

"Well, then, I'm sorry, too."

He smiled. "Apology accepted."

There was a list of recent detainments on the table just to our left. I kept sneaking peeks at it to see if anyone else had been caught. I saw a few names of seniors I recognized but no Olive, no Sam. I felt confident I'd been the only one of us picked off.

"Are you worried about your parents?" I said.

Jesse thought about it and then shook his head. "My parents have a very specific set of rules and as long as I don't break any of those, I can pretty much do whatever I want."

"What are the rules?" I asked.

"Break state records and don't get anything below a B-minus."

"Seriously?" I said. "Those are the only rules you have to live by?"

"Do you know how hard it is to break state records *and* get a B-minus in all of your classes?" Jesse wasn't angry at me, but there was an edge to his voice.

I nodded.

"But the upside is they didn't seem too angry on the phone when I called them from the police station at one a.m. So I have that."

I laughed and then fiddled with my arms in the cuffs, trying to keep them from rubbing against the bone of my wrists.

"Why are they making us wear these?" I asked. "They didn't even arrest us. What do they think we are going to do? Run away?"

Jesse laughed. "Maybe. We could escape out of here. Go all Bonnie and Clyde." I wondered if he knew Bonnie and Clyde were lovers. I thought about telling him.

"So your parents aren't going to take it as well, huh?" Jesse asked.

I shook my head. "Oh, hell no. No, I'm going to be working shifts at the store from now until I'm ninety-two years old, basically."

"The bookstore?"

"Yeah; that's my parents' favorite mode of punishment. Also, they are under the illusion that my sister and I are going to one day take over the store, so . . ."

"Is that what you want to do?"

"Run a bookstore? Are you kidding me? Absolutely not."

"What do you want to do?"

"Get out of Acton," I said. "That's number one. I want to see the world. First stop, the Pacific Ocean, and then the sky's the limit."

"Oh yeah?" he said. "I've been thinking about applying to a few schools in California. I figured if I'm three thousand miles away, my parents can't force me to train doubles."

"I was thinking about doing that, too," I said. "California, I mean. I don't know if my parents will let me, but I want to go to the University of Los Angeles."

"To study what?"

"No idea. I just know that I want to join, like, every abroad program they have. See the world."

"That sounds awesome," Jesse said. "I want to do that. I want to see the world."

"I just don't know if my parents will go for it," I said.

"If you want to do something, you *have* to do it."

"What? That doesn't even make sense."

"Of course it does. If you want something as passionately as you clearly want this, that means you owe it to yourself to make it happen. That's what I'm doing. I want out so I'm getting out. I'm going far, far away. You should, too," he said.

"I don't think my parents would like that," I said.

"Your parents don't have to be you. You have to be you. My philosophy is that, you know, you did it their way for a long time. Soon, it's time for your way."

It was plain to see that Jesse wasn't really talking about my parents and me. But everything that he said resonated. It reverberated in my mind, growing louder instead of softer.

"I think you're right," I said.

"I know I'm right," he said, smiling.

"No, really. I'm going to apply to the University of Los Angeles."

"Good for you," he said.

"And you should, too," I told him. "Stop swimming if you hate it. Do something else. Something you love."

Jesse smiled. "You know, you're nothing like I imagined you'd be."

"What do you mean?" I asked him. It was hard for me to believe that Jesse had thought about me before, that he even knew I existed before tonight.

"I don't know; you're just . . . different."

"In a good way or a bad way?"

"Oh, definitely a good way," he said, nodding. "For sure."

"What did you think I was like before?" I asked, now desperate to know. How did I seem before that was bad? I needed to make sure I didn't seem like it again.

"It doesn't matter," he said.

"C'mon," I said. "Just say whatever it is."

"I don't want to, like, embarrass you or something," Jesse said.

"What? What are you talking about?"

Jesse looked at me. And then decided to just say it. "I don't know. I got the impression that maybe you might have had a crush on me."

I could feel myself move away from him. "What? No, I didn't."

He shrugged as if this was no skin off his back. "Okay, see? I was wrong."

"What made you think that?"

"Carolyn, my ex-girlfriend . . ." he said, starting to explain.

"I know who Carolyn is," I said.

"Well, she thought that you might."

"Why would she think that?"

"I don't know. Because she was always jealous when girls looked at me. And you must have looked at me once. And it made her think that."

"But, I mean, you believed her."

"Well, I mean, I hoped she was right."

"Why?"

"What do you mean, 'why'?"

"Why did you hope that she was right? Did you want me to have a crush on you?"

"Of course I did. Doesn't everyone want people to have crushes on them?"

"Did you want *me* in particular to have a crush on you?"

"Sure," Jesse said as if it were obvious.

"But why?"

"Well, it doesn't matter why, does it? Because you didn't. So it's irrelevant."

A conversational roadblock.

It was one I could only get past if I admitted the truth. I weighed the pros and cons, trying to decide if it was worth it.

"Fine—I had a crush on you once. Freshman year."

Jesse turned and smiled at me. "Oh yeah?"

"Yeah, but it's over."

"Why is it over?"

"I don't know; you were with Carolyn. I barely knew you."

"But I'm not with Carolyn and you know me now."

"What are you saying?"

"Why don't you have a thing for me now?"

"Why don't you have a thing for *me* now?" I asked.

And that's when Jesse said the thing that set my entire adult love life in motion. "I think I actually do have a thing for you. As of about an hour and a half ago."

I looked at him, stunned. Trying to find the words.

"Well, then I do, too," I finally said.

"See?" he said, smiling. "I thought so."

And then he leaned over when no one was looking and he kissed me.

That summer, I had to work triple the normal amount of shifts at the store as penance for my underage drinking. I had to listen to four separate lectures from my parents about how I had disappointed them, how they never thought I'd be the kind of daughter who got *detained*.

Marie took the assistant manager job, making her my boss

for a third of the hours I was awake. I learned that the only thing I disliked more than hanging out with her was taking orders from her.

Olive spent the summer on the Cape with her older brother, waiting tables and sunbathing.

Sam moved to Boston two weeks ahead of schedule and never said good-bye.

But I didn't mind any of that. Because that was the summer Jesse and I fell in love.

"Emma, would you just turn around?"

"What?" I said.

"Just turn around, for crying out loud!"

And so I did, to find Jesse standing behind me on a sandy beach in Malibu, California. He was holding a small ruby ring. It was nine years after he kissed me that first time in the Acton Police Station.

"Jesse . . ." I said.

"Will you marry me?"

I was speechless. But not because he was asking me to marry him. We were twenty-five. We'd been together our entire adult lives. We had both moved across the country in order to attend the University of Los Angeles. We'd spent our junior year abroad in Sydney, Australia, and backpacked across Europe for five months after we graduated.

And we had built a life for ourselves in LA, far away from Blair Books and five hundred–meter freestyles. Jesse had become a production assistant on nature documentaries, his jobs taking him as far as Africa and as close to home as the Mojave Desert.

I, in a turn of events that seemed to infuriate Marie, had become a travel writer. My sophomore year of school, I found out about a class called travel literature offered by the School of Journalism. I'd heard that it wasn't an easy class to get into.

In fact, the professor only took nine students per year. But if you got in, the class subsidized a trip to a different place every year. That year was Alaska.

I'd never seen Alaska. And I knew I couldn't afford to go on my own. But I had no interest in writing.

It was Jesse who finally pushed me to apply.

The application required a thousand-word piece on any city or town in the world. I wrote an essay about Acton. I played up its rich history, its school system, its local bookstore—basically, I tried to see my hometown through my father's eyes and put it down on paper. It seemed a small price to pay to go to Alaska.

My essay was fairly awful. But there were only sixteen applications that year, and apparently, seven other essays were worse.

I thought Alaska was nice. It was my first time leaving the continental United States and I had to be honest with myself and admit it hadn't been all it was cracked up to be. But imagine everyone's surprise when I found that I loved writing about Alaska even more than I liked being there.

I became a journalism major and I worked hard at improving my interviewing techniques and imagery, as per the advice of most of my professors.

I graduated college a writer.

That's the part that I knew killed Marie.

I was the writer of the family while she was in Acton, running the bookstore.

It had taken me a couple of years to get a job that sent me out on assignments, but by the age of twenty-five, I was an assistant editor at a travel blog, with a tiny salary but with the luxury of having visited five of the seven continents.

The downside was that Jesse and I had very little money.

On the cusp of twenty-six, neither of us had health insurance and we were still eating saltines and peanut butter for dinner some nights.

But the upside was so much sweeter: Jesse and I had seen the world—both together and separately.

Jesse and I had talked about getting married. It was obvious to everyone, ourselves included, that we would have a wedding one day. We knew it was what we would do when the time was right, the way you know that once you shampoo your hair, you condition it.

So I was not shocked that Jesse wanted to marry me.

What shocked me was that there was any ring at all.

"I know it's small," he said apologetically as I put it on. "And it's not a diamond."

"I love it," I told him.

"Do you recognize it?"

I gave it another glance, trying to discern what he meant.

It had a yellow-gold band with a round red stone in the middle. It was banged up and scratched, clearly secondhand. I loved it. I loved everything about it. But I didn't recognize it.

"No?" I said.

"Are you sure?" he said, teasing me. "If you think about it for a second, I think you might."

I stared again. But the ring on my finger was much less interesting to me than the man who had given it to me.

Jesse had grown up to be even more handsome than he had been cute. His shoulders had grown wider, his back more sturdy. No longer training, he had gained weight in his torso, but it was weight that fit him fine. His cheekbones stood out in almost any light. And his smile had matured in a way that made me think he'd be handsome late into life.

I was madly in love with him and had been for as long as I could remember. We had a deep and meaningful history together. It was Jesse who had held my hand when my parents were furious to find out I'd never sent in my application to the University of Massachusetts, and in doing so, had forced their hand to send me to California. It was Jesse who supported me when they asked me to move home after we graduated, Jesse who dried my tears when my father was heartbroken that I would not come home to help run the store. And it was also Jesse who helped me remain confident that, eventually, my parents and I would see eye-to-eye again one day.

The boy that I first saw that day at the swimming pool had turned into an honorable and kind man. He opened doors for me. He bought me Diet Coke and Ben & Jerry's Chunky Monkey when I had a bad day. He took photos of all the places he'd been, all the places he and I had been together, and decorated our home with them.

And now, as we firmly settled into adulthood and the resentments of his childhood faded away, Jesse had started swimming long distance again. Not often, not regularly, but sometimes. He said he still couldn't stand the chlorine smell of the pool, but he was starting to fall in love with the salt of the ocean. I was so enamored with him for that.

"I'm sorry," I said. "I don't think I've ever seen this ring before."

Jesse laughed. "Barcelona," he said. "The night of—"

I gasped.

He smiled, knowing that he didn't need to finish the sentence.

"No . . ." I said.

He nodded.

We had just gotten into Barcelona on the Eurail from Madrid. There was a woman selling jewelry on the street. The two of us were exhausted and headed straight for our hostel. But the woman was hounding us to please take a look.

So we did.

I saw a ruby ring.

And I'd said to Jesse, "See? I don't need anything fancy like a diamond. Just a ring like this is beautiful."

And here it was, a ruby ring.

"You got me a ruby ring!" I said.

Jesse shook his head. "Not just *a* ruby ring . . ."

"This isn't *the* ruby ring," I said.

Jesse laughed. "Yes, it is! This is what I've been trying to tell you. This is *that* ring."

I looked at it, stunned. I pulled my hand away from my face, getting a better view. "Wait, are you serious? How did you do that?"

I had visions of Jesse making international phone calls and paying exorbitant shipping fees, but the truth was much simpler.

"I snuck back and bought it when you went looking for a bathroom that night," he said.

My eyes went wide. "You've had this ring for five years?"

Jesse shrugged. "I knew I was going to marry you. What was the point of waiting to buy you some diamond when I knew exactly what you wanted?"

"Oh, my God," I said. I was blushing. "I can't believe it. It fits perfectly. What are . . . what are the odds of that?"

"Well," Jesse said shyly, "actually pretty high."

I looked at him, wondering what he meant.

"I took it to a jeweler to have it resized based on another one of your rings."

I could tell he was worried this made it less romantic. But to me, it was only more so.

"Wow," I said. "Just . . . wow."

"You didn't answer my question," he said. "Will you marry me?"

It seemed like an absurd thing to ask; the answer was so obvious. It was like asking if someone liked French fries or whether rain was wet.

Standing there on the beach, with the sand underneath our feet, the Pacific Ocean in front of us, and our home just a few miles away, I wondered how I got so lucky to be given everything I ever wanted.

"Yes," I said as I wrapped my arms around his neck. "Absolutely. Of course. Definitely. Yes."

We were married Memorial Day weekend at Jesse's family's cabin in Maine.

We had talked about a destination wedding in Prague but it wasn't realistic. When we resigned ourselves to marrying in the United States, Jesse wanted to do it in Los Angeles.

But for some reason I didn't want to do it anywhere but back in New England. The impulse surprised me. I had spent so much time exploring everywhere else, had put so much emphasis on getting away.

But once I had put enough distance between myself and where I grew up, I started to see its beauty. I started to see it the way outsiders do—maybe because I had become an outsider.

So I told Jesse I thought we should get married back home, during the spring, and though he did take a bit of convincing, he agreed.

And then it became obvious that the easiest place to do it was up by Jesse's parents' cabin.

Naturally, my parents were thrilled. In some ways, I think the night I was caught by the cops and the day I called my parents and told them we were going to get married in New England shared a lot in common.

Both times, I had done something my parents thought was wildly out of character for me, and it surprised them so much that it instantly changed things between us.

Back in high school, it had made them distrust me. I suspect it had been the trouble with the police that did it more than the drinking. And the fact that I started dating the very boy with whom I'd been detained only served to compound the problem. To them, I had gone from a precious little girl to a hooligan overnight.

And with the wedding, I went from their independent, globe-trotting daughter to a bird flying home to the nest.

My mom handled a lot of the finer details, coordinating with Jesse's parents, reserving the spot by the lighthouse on the water just a mile away, and choosing the wedding cake when Jesse and I couldn't make it back for the taste test. My dad helped negotiate with the inn down the street, where we'd have our reception. Marie, married to Mike just nine months before us, lent us the place settings and table linens from their wedding.

Olive flew to Los Angeles from her home in Chicago to host my bachelorette party and my bridal shower. She got rip-roaring drunk at the former and wore a shift dress and an oversized hat to the latter. She was the first to arrive the weekend of the wedding—always proving that Olive didn't do anything half-assed.

Our friendship had been a long-distance one since we went off to college. But I never met another woman who meant to me what she did. No one else could make me laugh like she could. So my oldest friend remained my best friend, despite however many miles kept us apart, and it was for that reason that I made her my maid of honor.

There was a brief moment when my mother and father seemed unsure whether to acknowledge that Marie and I had not chosen each other for that esteemed role. But we were bridesmaids for each other and this seemed to mollify them.

As for Jesse's side of the bridal party, those spots went to his two older brothers.

Jesse's parents didn't ever really care for me very much and I always knew that it was because they blamed me for the fact that he stopped swimming. Jesse had confronted them, had told them the full truth: that he hated training, that he was never going to pursue it on his own. But all they saw was the convenient chronology: I showed up and suddenly Jesse didn't want what they believed he'd always wanted.

But once Jesse and I became engaged—and once Francine and Joe found out we were willing to have the wedding at their cabin—they opened up a bit more. Maybe they just saw the writing on the wall—Jesse was going to marry me whether they liked me or not. But I like to think that they simply started seeing me clearly. I think they found there was a lot to like about me once they started looking. And that Jesse had grown into an impressive man regardless of whether or not he followed their dream.

Aside from a few minor breakdowns over my dress and whether we should practice for our first dance, Jesse and I had a relatively painless wedding-planning experience.

As for the actual day, the truth is I don't remember it.

I just remember glimpses.

I remember my mother pulling the dress up around me.

I remember pulling the train of it high enough as I walked to avoid getting the edges dirty.

I remember the flowers smelling more pungent than they had in the store.

I remember looking at Jesse as I walked down the open aisle—looking at the black sheen on his tux, the perfect wave of his hair—and having a sense of overwhelming peace.

I remember standing with him as we had our picture taken during the cocktail hour between the ceremony and the reception. I remember he whispered into my ear, "I want to be alone with you," just as a flash went off on the photographer's camera.

I remember saying, "I know, but there's still so much . . . wedding left."

I remember taking his hand and escaping out of sight when the photographer went to change the battery in his camera.

We rushed back to the cabin when no one was looking. It was there, alone with Jesse, that I could focus again. I could breathe easy. I felt grounded. I felt like myself for the first time all day.

"I can't believe we just snuck out of our own wedding," I said.

"Well . . ." Jesse put his arms around me. "It's our wedding. We're allowed to."

"I'm not sure that's how it works," I said.

Jesse had already started unzipping my dress. It would barely budge. So he pushed the slim skirt of it up around my thighs.

We had not made it past the kitchen. Instead, I hopped up on the kitchen counter. As Jesse pushed up against me, as I pressed my body against his, it felt different from all the other times we'd done it.

It meant more.

A half hour later, just as I was coming out of the bathroom fixing my hair, Marie knocked on the door.

Everyone wanted to know where we were.

It was time to be announced.

"I guess we have to go, then," Jesse said to me, smiling with the knowledge of what we'd been doing as we kept them waiting.

"I guess so," I said in the same spirit.

"Yeah," Marie said, none-too-amused. "I guess so."

She walked ahead of us as we made the short walk over to the inn.

"Looks like we've angered the Booksellers' Daughter," Jesse whispered.

"I think you're right," I said.

"I have something really important to tell you," he said. "Are you ready? It's really important. It's breaking news."

"Tell me."

"I'll love you forever."

"I already knew that," I said. "And I'll love you forever, too."

"Yeah?"

"Yeah," I said. "I'll love you until we're so old we can barely walk on our own and we have to get walkers and put those cut-up yellow tennis balls on them. I'll love you past that, actually. I'll love you until the end of time."

"You sure?" he said, smiling at me, pulling me toward him. Marie was just up ahead, grabbing the door to the reception hall. I could hear the din of large-scale small talk. I imagined a room full of my friends and family introducing themselves to one another. I imagined Olive already having made friends with half of my father's extended family.

When this was over, Jesse and I were leaving on a ten-day trip to India, courtesy of his parents. No living out of backpacks or sleeping in hostels. No deadlines or film shoots while we were there. Just two people in love with each other, in love with the world.

"Are you kidding?" I asked. "You are my one true love. I don't even think I'm capable of loving anyone else."

The double doors opened and Jesse and I walked through,

into the reception hall, just as I heard the DJ announce, "Introducing . . . Jesse and Emma Lerner!"

Hearing my new name felt jarring to me, for a moment. It sounded like someone else. I assumed I would get over it in time, that it would grow on me, likening this moment to the first few days of a haircut.

Besides, the name didn't matter. None of that mattered when I had the man of my dreams.

It was the happiest day of my life.

Emma and Jesse. Forever.

Three hundred and sixty-four days later, he was gone.

The last time I saw Jesse he was wearing navy blue chinos, Vans, and a heather gray T-shirt. It was his favorite. He'd done the laundry the day before just so he could wear it.

It was the day before our anniversary. I had managed to snag a freelance assignment writing up a piece on a new hotel in the Santa Ynez Valley in Southern California. Despite the fact that a work trip isn't exactly the most romantic way to spend an anniversary, Jesse was going to join me on the trip. We would celebrate one year of marriage touring the hotel, taking notes on the food, and then squeezing in a visit to a vineyard or two.

But Jesse was asked to join an old boss of his on a quick four-day shoot in the Aleutian Islands.

And unlike me, he had not yet been to Alaska.

"I want to see glaciers," Jesse said. "You've seen them but I haven't yet."

I thought about how it felt to stare at something so white it looked blue, so large that you felt small, so peaceful you forgot just what an environmental threat they posed. I understood why he wanted to go. But I also knew that if I were in his position, I'd turn down the opportunity.

Some of it was travel fatigue. He and I had spent almost ten years grabbing on to every opportunity to get on a plane or a train. I was working at a travel blog and writing freelance on the side, doing my best to get placed in loftier and loftier publications.

I was a professional at navigating security checkpoints and baggage claims. I had enough frequent-flyer miles to go absolutely anywhere I dreamed of.

And I'm not saying that travel wasn't incredible, that our life wasn't incredible. Because it was.

I had been to the Great Wall of China. I'd hiked a waterfall in Costa Rica. I'd tasted pizza in Naples, strudel in Vienna, bangers and mash in London. I'd seen the *Mona Lisa*. I'd been inside the Taj Mahal.

I had some of my most incredible experiences abroad.

But I'd also had a lot of them right in my own home. Inventing cheap at-home dinners with Jesse, walking down the street late at night to split a pint of ice cream, waking up early on Saturday mornings to the sun shining through the sliding glass door.

I had predicated my life on the idea that I wanted to see everywhere extraordinary, but I'd come to realize that extraordinary is everywhere.

And I was starting to yearn for a chance to settle in somewhere and maybe, perhaps, not need to rush to get on a plane to go somewhere else.

I had just found out that Marie was pregnant with her first child. She and Mike were buying a house a short commute from Acton. It seemed all but finalized that she would take over the store. The Booksellers' Daughter realizing her full potential.

But here is what surprised me: I had the smallest inkling that her life didn't sound quite so bad.

She wasn't always packing or unpacking. She was never jetlagged. She never had to buy a phone charger she already had because she'd forgotten the original thousands of miles away.

I had mentioned all of this to Jesse.

"Do you ever just want to go home?" I said.

"We are home," he'd said to me.

"No, *home* home. To Acton home."

Jesse looked at me suspiciously and said, "You must be an impostor. Because the real Emma would never say that."

I laughed and let it go.

But I wasn't *actually* letting it go. Case in point: If Jesse and I were going to have children, were we still going to be hopping on a quick flight to Peru? And maybe more important: Was I ready to raise children in Los Angeles?

The very moment these questions occurred to me, I started to realize that my life plans had never really extended past my twenties. I had never asked myself if I *always* wanted to be traveling, if I *always* wanted to live so far from my parents.

I began to suspect that this jet-setting Jesse and I had been living had always felt temporary to me, like something I knew I needed to do and then one day would be over.

I think that I wanted to settle down one day.

And the only thing that shocked me more than realizing it was realizing I had never realized it before.

Of course, it did not help matters that I was pretty sure Jesse hadn't been thinking any of this. I was pretty sure Jesse wasn't thinking this at all.

We had created a life of spontaneous adventure. Of seeing all the things people say one day they will see.

I couldn't very well change the entire modus operandi of our lives.

So even though I wanted him to skip Alaska and go to Southern California with me, I told him to go.

And he was right. I'd already seen a glacier. But he hadn't.

So—instead of preparing to celebrate our one-year wedding anniversary—I was driving Jesse to LAX so that he could hop on a flight to Anchorage.

"We'll celebrate our anniversary when I get home," he said. "I'm gonna go all out. Candles, wine, flowers. I'll even serenade you. And I'll call you tomorrow."

He was meeting the rest of the crew in Anchorage and then getting on a private plane, landing in Akun Island. Most of the time after that, he'd be filming aerial shots from a helicopter.

"Don't stress out about it," I said. "If you can't call, I totally get it."

"Thank you," he said as he gathered his bags and looked at me. "I love you more than anyone has ever loved anyone in the history of the world. Do you know that? Do you know that Antony didn't love Cleopatra as much as I love you? Do you know that Romeo didn't love Juliet as much as I love you?"

I laughed. "I love you, too," I said. "More than Liz Taylor loved Richard Burton."

Jesse came around the side of the car and stood at my window.

"Wow," he said, smiling. "That's a lot."

"All right. Get out of here, would you? I have errands to run."

Jesse laughed and kissed me good-bye. And then I watched him walk in front of our car through the automatic doors, into the belly of Los Angeles International Airport.

Just then, my favorite song came on the radio. I turned up the volume, sang at the top of my lungs, and pulled the car away from the curb.

As I navigated the streets back home, Jesse texted me.

I love you. I'll miss you.

He must have sent it just before he went through airport security, maybe right after. But I didn't see it until an hour or so later.

I texted him back.

I'll miss you every second of every day. Xoxo

I knew that he might not see it for a while, that I might not hear from him for a few days.

I pictured him riding in a small plane, landing on the island, hopping into a helicopter, and soon seeing a glacier so big it left him breathless.

I woke up the morning of our anniversary, sick to my stomach. I rushed to the bathroom and vomited.

I had no idea why. To this day, I don't know if I ate something bad or if, on some level, I could just sense the looming tragedy in my bones, the way that some dogs can tell a hurricane is coming.

Jesse didn't call to wish me a happy anniversary.

The commercial flight made it to Anchorage.

The Cessna made it to Akun Island.

But the first time they took the helicopter out, it never came back.

The best anyone could conclude was it went down somewhere over the North Pacific.

The four people on board were lost.

My husband, my one true love . . .

Gone.

Francine and Joe flew into LA and moved into my apartment. My own parents came and rented a hotel a few minutes' walk away but spent every waking minute with me.

Francine kept saying that she didn't understand why this wasn't a national news story, why there wasn't a nationwide search party.

Joe kept telling her that helicopters crash all the time. He said it as if it were good news, as if that meant there was a plan in place for moments like these.

"They will find him," he would say to her over and over. "If anyone can swim to safety, it's our son."

I held it together for as long as I could. I held Francine as she sobbed in my arms. I told her, just as Joe did, that it was only a matter of time until we got a call saying he was safe.

My mom made casseroles and I would cut them up and put them on plates for Francine and Joe and say things like, "We need to eat." But I never did.

I cried when no one was around and I found it hard to look in the mirror, but I kept telling everyone that we would find Jesse soon.

And then they found a propeller of the helicopter on the shore of Adak Island. With Jesse's backpack. And the body of the pilot.

The call we had been waiting for came.

But it went nothing like we expected.

Jesse had not yet been found.

He was believed to be dead.

After I hung up the phone, Francine broke down. Joe was frozen still. My parents stared at me, stunned.

I said, "That's crazy. Jesse didn't die. He wouldn't do that."

~

Francine developed such strong panic attacks that Joe flew her home and checked her into a hospital.

My mom and dad stayed on an air mattress at the foot of my bed, watching my every move. I told them I had a handle on it. I thought, for certain, that I did.

I spent three days walking around in a daze, waiting for the telephone to ring, waiting for someone *else* to call and say the first call had been wrong.

That second call never came. Instead, my phone was tied up with people checking in to see if I was OK.

And then, one day, Marie called and said she'd left Mike in charge of the store. She was flying in to be here for me.

I was far too numb to decide whether I wanted her around.

The day Marie arrived, I woke up late in the afternoon to find that my mom had gone to the store and my dad had left to pick Marie up from the airport. My first time alone in what felt like forever.

It was a clear day. I decided I didn't want to be in my house anymore. But I didn't want to leave it, either. I got dressed and asked the neighbors if I could borrow their ladder so that I could clean the gutters.

I had no intention of cleaning anything. I just wanted to stand, high up on the earth, unencumbered by the safety of walls, floors, and ceilings. I wanted to stand high enough that if I fell, it'd kill me. This is not the same thing as wanting to die.

I climbed up to the roof and stood there, with glassy bloodshot eyes. I stared straight ahead, looking at treetops and into the windows of high-rises. It didn't make me feel any better than being in the house. But it didn't make me feel any worse, either. So I stayed there. Just standing and looking. Looking at anything that didn't make me want to crawl into a ball and fade away.

And then I saw, in the sliver of a view between two buildings, so far in the distance you almost couldn't make it out . . .

The ocean.

I thought, *Maybe Jesse is out there in the water. Maybe he's swimming. Maybe he's building a raft to get home.*

The hope that I clung to in that moment didn't feel good or freeing. It felt cruel. As if the world were giving me just enough rope to hang myself.

I got down off the roof and searched through Jesse's things. I ransacked his closet, dresser, and desk before I found them.

Binoculars.

I got back up on the roof and I stood right where I could see the sliver of sea. I waited.

I was not enjoying the view. I was not relishing the peace and quiet. I was not reveling in my solitude.

I was looking for Jesse.

I saw waves cresting onto the shore. I saw a boat. I saw people under umbrellas, lying on towels, as if there wasn't important work to be done.

I heard my dad and sister enter the house and start looking around for me. I heard, "Emma?" coming from them in every room of the house. I recognized the worry as it grew in their voices, as each time they said my name they were met with more silence. Soon, my mom came home and her voice joined the chorus.

But I couldn't respond. I had to stand there and watch for Jesse. It was my duty, as his wife. I had to be the first to spot him when he made landfall.

When I noticed someone coming up to the roof, I assumed it was my dad and I thought, *Good, he can look, too.*

But it was Marie.

She stood there, looking at me, as I held the binoculars up to my face and stared at the ocean.

"Hi," she said.

"Hi."

"What are you doing?" she said as she started walking toward me.

"I'm going to find him."

I felt Marie put her arm around my shoulder. "You can't . . . that won't . . . work," she said.

"I have to be looking for him. I can't give up on him."

"Em, give me the binoculars."

I wanted to ignore her, but I needed to explain my logic. "Jesse could come back. We have to be watching."

"He isn't coming back."

"You don't know that."

"Yes. Yes, I do."

"You just can't stand that I'm no longer in your shadow," I said to her. "Because it means you aren't the center of the world anymore. Jesse is coming back, Marie. And I am going to sit here and wait until he does. Because I know my husband. I know how incredible he is. And I'm not going to allow you to make me feel like he's anything less just because you like it better when I feel small."

Marie reared her head back, as though I'd struck her.

"I have to stay here and watch for him. It's my job. As his wife."

When I saw the look on my sister's face in that moment, a mixture of compassion and fear, I realized that she thought I was crazy.

For a moment, I wondered, *Oh, my God. Am I crazy?*

"Emma, I'm so sorry," she said as she put her arms around me and held me the way a mother holds a child, as if we were of the same body. I was not used to that type of sister, the type of sister that is also a friend. I was used to having *just* a sister, the way some of your teachers are just teachers and some of your coworkers are just coworkers. "Jesse is dead," she told me. "He's not out there somewhere trying to come home. He's gone. Forever. I'm so sorry. I'm so, so sorry."

For a moment, I wondered, *What if she's right?*

"He's not dead," I said, my voice wavering and rocky. "He's out there."

"He's not out there," she said. "He's dead."

For a moment, I wondered, *Is that possible?*

And then the truth washed over me like a flood.

~

I sobbed so hard for so long that every day I would wake up with my eyes swollen shut. I didn't get dressed for three weeks.

I cried for him, and for what I'd lost, and for every day left of my life that I had left to live without him.

My mom had to force me to bathe. She stood in the shower with me, holding my naked body up to the water, carrying my entire weight in her arms because I wouldn't stand up on my own.

The world seemed so dark and bleak and meaningless. Life seemed so pointless, so cruel.

I thought of how Jesse took care of me and how he held me. I thought of how he felt when he ran his hands down my back, how his breath smelled sweet and human.

I lost hope and love and all of my kindness.

I told my mom that I wanted to die.

I said it even though I knew it would hurt her to hear it. I had to say it because of how much it hurt to feel it.

She winced and closed her eyes and then she said, "I know. But you can't. You have to live. You have to find a way to live."

Six weeks after I left Jesse at the airport, I came out of my bedroom, walked into the kitchen where my parents were talking, and I said, with a calmness and clarity of purpose that I had been lacking for weeks, "I want to go back to Acton. I don't want to stay here anymore."

My father nodded and my mom said, "Whatever you need."

I do not remember who packed up my things, who sold my car and my furniture. I do not remember getting on the plane. All I know is that, a week later, I landed at Logan Airport.

Home.

Emma and Sam

Or, how to put yourself back together

When you lose someone you love, it's hard to imagine that you'll ever feel better. That, one day, you'll manage to be in a good mood simply because the weather is nice or the barista at the coffee shop on the corner remembered your order.

But it does happen.

If you're patient and you work at it.

It starts just by breathing in the Massachusetts air again. Your soul recharges ever so slightly when you see brick walkways and brownstones in Boston, when you pull into your parents' driveway and move back into your old bedroom.

Your emotional fortitude grows stronger as you sleep in your childhood bed and eat your mother's pancakes for breakfast and hide from most of the world.

You spend all of your time watching the Travel Channel and you get so bored of it that you pick up a novel from the stack of books in your bedroom, the books that your parents have given you over the years that you refused to crack open until now.

You read all the way through to the end of one, only to find out that the husband dies. You hurl the book across the room, breaking the bedside lamp. When your mom comes home that night, you tell her what happened. You ask her for books to read where no one dies.

Two days later, you find both of your parents in the living

room with a pile of novels on the coffee table. They are skimming through them one by one, making sure every character lives to the end. That night, you have a new stack of books to read and you open up the first one, confident it won't break you down.

It is the first time in a long time that you have felt safe.

Marie finds out that she is having identical twin girls. You want to buy her a pair of matching onesies but you don't want to leave the house. You order them online to have them sent to her. When the site asks you for a gift message, you know that you should congratulate her and use a lot of exclamation points but you don't have it in you. You can't summon up enthusiasm, can't even bring yourself to type it. Instead, you type, "For my little baby nieces."

Your mom comes home with a new bedside lamp for you, made just for reading. It shoots up from the base and then hangs over your head, hovering just above the pages. You read three books from the stack that week, by the light through the window during the day and the lamplight hovering above you at night.

Your nieces are born. They are named Sophie and Ava. You hold them. They are beautiful. You wonder how it's possible Marie got everything she ever wanted and you . . . ended up here. You know this is called self-pity. You don't care.

Olive flies in from Chicago to see you. Everyone assumes she will stay at her parents' place but you feel immense relief when she says she'd rather make up a bed on the floor of your room. She doesn't ask how you are because she knows there's no answer. Instead, she tells you that she's thinking of giving up caffeine and makes you help her Facebook-stalk the man she just began seeing. You feel less alone when she's there, which is a welcome reprieve from the crushing loneliness you feel almost all the time. When she packs up to go back to Chicago, you joke about going with her, fitting in the overhead compartment. Olive says, "You probably can't see it just yet, but this place is good for you."

One day, the memories that haunt every section of your town and your house, the memories of where you and Jesse met and fell in love as teenagers, feel contained and manageable. So you venture outside.

You head to your family's bookstore.

You realize you aren't ready for a full day out of the house when you break down next to the Shel Silverstein collection Marie put up in the back corner.

You don't even know why you're breaking down. Nothing about Shel Silverstein reminds you of Jesse. Except that Shel Silverstein wrote about what it meant to be alive and you feel like you aren't alive anymore. Because Jesse isn't. You feel like you stopped living when he went missing. You feel like the rest of your days are killing time until it's time to die.

You know the only thing you can do is get in the passenger's seat of your dad's car and allow him to drive you back home and put you to bed.

But then you feel yourself growing stronger in that bed, as if you're squeezing the tears out of yourself, wringing yourself dry of pain. You imagine yourself bleeding grief, as if the water from your eyes is the pain itself. You imagine it leaving your body and being soaked up by the mattress.

You wake up one morning feeling dry and completely empty, so empty that if someone knocked on you, you'd sound hollow.

Hollow and empty are terrible ways to feel when you're used to being full of joy. But it's not so bad when you're used to feeling full of pain.

Hollow feels okay.

Empty feels like a beginning.

Which is nice, because for so long you have felt like you were at the end.

You ask your parents for a new bed. You feel childish doing it. But you don't have any money because you have not pitched a story in a very long time and you quit working at the blog.

Your parents don't understand why you're asking and you can't quite explain it to them. You just say, "This one is tainted." But what you mean is that you feel like it absorbed your suffering. You know it sounds crazy but you believe your pain is in the mattress and you don't want to absorb it back into your own body.

You know it's not that simple. But it feels like it is.

Two weeks later, you have a new mattress and box spring. You watch your dad tie the old ones to a friend's truck. You watch him drive down the street headed for the dump.

You feel better. Freer.

You realize this is called superstition.

You're OK with that.

You know that you will never truly be free of the grief. You know that it is something you must learn to live with, something you manage.

You start to understand that grief is chronic. That it's more about remission and relapse than it is about a cure. What that means to you is that you can't simply wait for it to be over. You have to move through it, like swimming in an undertow.

Toward the end of Marie's maternity leave, your parents come down with food poisoning. There is no one to open the store. You offer to do it. They tell you that you don't have to.

They say they can ask one of the sales clerks. You tell them you've got it under control.

When they say thank you, you realize that you have missed being relied upon. You remember the pride of being useful.

You wake up early and you take a shower and you get in the car. When you put the key in the door of the bookstore, you realize that Jesse is gone but maybe your life is still here. Maybe you can do something with it.

Three days before Marie is supposed to return to the store, she tells your parents that she doesn't want to come back to work. She has tears in her eyes. She says she's sorry that she's disappointing them but she just wants to stay at home with her babies. She says she can't imagine spending her days away from them. Your parents are caught off guard. They quickly become supportive.

That night, you overhear them talking about it. You hear your mother console your father, you hear her tell him that the store doesn't have to go to you or Marie. She says it's going to be fine.

The next day, they start looking for a new store manager.

You know what you need to do.

You sit them down at the kitchen table that night and you ask for the job. When they ask if you're sure that's what you want to do, you say you are but the truth is somewhere in the gray area between yes and no.

Surprised but pleased, your parents agree, saying nothing would make them prouder.

Now, you have a job.

And then, slowly, day by day, minute by minute, at such a snail's pace that you can barely register that anything is happening at all, you find a life's purpose again.

It is right there, in Blair Books, the very place you've spent your life running from. It is in the children's reading nook and the messy stockroom. It is in the curated display table at the front of the store and the bargain bin in the back. You look at the bookmarks. The ones that say "Travel the World by Reading a Book."

You have already seen the world.

Marie and Mike bring the girls over for dinner one Sunday, and right before dessert, Mike mentions that they have an appointment with a hearing specialist on Tuesday. That night, you overhear your parents saying that it's about time. You realize that you spend so little time with your nieces, so little time with your sister, that you didn't realize the twins have stopped responding to the sound of their names or to loud noises.

You resolve to call Marie after the appointment. You are going to be an attentive sister. You are going to be a good aunt.

Marie answers the phone in tears but you are able to piece together what has happened.

Your nieces are going deaf.

It has something to do with a gene called connexin 26.

You go over to Marie's house that night and bring her what you used to love on a bad day. You bring her Diet Coke and Ben & Jerry's. You find a flavor with coconut and chocolate because you know her favorite candy bar is an Almond Joy. She puts the ice cream in the freezer and leaves the Diet Coke on the counter. But she hugs you so hard you think it might leave a mark. You hold her and let her sob.

You move out of your parents' house into a studio apartment in Cambridge. You say you're moving out because you want to live in a brownstone but the truth is you're moving out because Olive agrees that it's time for you to start to meet people. Any people. New people.

Five months into your job as the manager, you sit your parents down and pitch them on selling e-books and e-readers. You outline how to do it. When they tell you that you're great at your job, you start crying and you miss Jesse. Happy moments are the worst, that's when the ache is strongest. But you wipe your eyes, get back to work, and when you put your head on the pillow that night, you consider it a good day.

An old college friend of your father's comes into the store looking for him but he's not in. The man sees that you are the manager and asks your name. You say your name is Emma Lerner and the man frowns. He says he knows Colin always wanted one of his girls to take over the store. You say that you *are* one of his girls. The man apologizes for his mistake.

Marie and Mike buy a house down the street from your parents. Mike will have to commute far to the sporting goods stores but Marie thinks it's important to be near your parents.

After she's settled in, you call her and ask her if she'd like to take a sign language class with you in Boston. You tell her you're excited to learn how to talk with your hands. She agrees and it is the only time she takes to do something out of the house, without her children. After a few weeks, you realize that you are your sister's entire social life.

One day after class, Marie asks if you'd like to stay out and get lunch. You take her to a Mongolian barbecue place and you run into Jesse's older brother Chris. You say hello and you catch up and you are surprised to find that you do not cry.

As you and Marie are walking back to the T, she asks if you're okay. As you're explaining how you feel, it hits you like a ton of bricks. For years now people have said to you, "May his memory be a blessing." You realize, finally, that's exactly what it is.

You are happier to have known him than you are sad to have lost him.

You wonder if grief is less chronic than you think. If remission can last for years.

You go to the hairdresser one day and she asks you if you've ever considered highlights. You tell her to go for it. When you walk out of the salon, you feel like a million bucks. You start scheduling future appointments.

Your parents partially retire and give you the store. You are so proud, so happy, so eager to take it over that you decide to change your name back. You are a Blair. You haven't ever been more proud to be a Blair. The day your new license comes you cry and look up to the sky, as if Jesse is there, and you say, "This doesn't mean I don't love you. This just means I love where I come from."

When Marie finds out the store is being handed over to you, she gets upset. She accuses you of taking it from her. You tell her you're just picking up the ball that she dropped. The two of you erupt. She's yelling and you're yelling. In anger, she screams, "Oh, please. We all know you're the favorite. Perfect Miss Emma who does everything exactly as Mom and Dad want."

You start laughing. Because it's so absurd.

But then you realize it's true.

You have become the person your parents always wanted you to be and you've done it almost entirely by accident.

You didn't think you wanted to work with books or live in Massachusetts or be close to your sister. But it turns out you do. That's what makes you happy.

And then you say to yourself, *Wait, no, that's not right. I can't be happy.*

Because you don't have him. He's gone. You can't be happy, can you?

And then you stop and truly ask yourself, *Am I happy?*

And you realize that you just might be.

You apologize to Marie. She apologizes to you. You spell out, "I was being an idiot," in sign language. Marie laughs.

Later, you ask her if it's a betrayal to Jesse to feel good, to like your life now. She just says, "Not at all. That's all he'd want for you. That's exactly what he'd want."

You think she might be right.

You take off your wedding ring and you put it in an envelope of your love letters and pictures. You will never let it go but you do not need to wear it.

You go back to your hairdresser and ask her if she thinks you'd look good with a pixie cut. She says you'd look great. You trust her. You go home, newly shorn, and you aren't quite sure what to make of yourself.

But then Marie sees it and tells you that you look like a movie star, and when you look at yourself in the mirror again, you sort of see what she means.

Six months later, you decide to take up the piano.

And just by walking into a music store, you set a whole second life in motion.

I could have started by trying to take piano lessons. But I decided to just leap into it. I wanted something to do with my hands at home. It was either piano or cooking and, well, cooking seemed messy.

So I found a secondhand-instruments shop in Watertown and drove over on a Sunday afternoon.

The doors chimed as I walked through them and they caught on themselves as they closed behind me. The store had a leathery scent to it. It was filled with rows of guitars. I found a magazine stand and rifled through it for a minute, unsure of what I was actually looking for.

I suddenly felt uncomfortable and completely out of my element. I didn't know what questions to ask or of whom to ask them.

Standing there surrounded by a sax, trumpets, and a series of instruments I couldn't even name, I realized I was out of my league. I was tempted to give up, to turn around and go home. I took a step away from the magazines and bumped right into two bronze drums. They made a clang as I accidentally knocked them into each other. I straightened them out and looked around to see if anyone saw me.

There was a salesman a few feet over. He looked up at me and smiled.

I timidly smiled back and then turned to the magazines again.

"Hey," the salesman said. He was now standing right next to me. "Are you a timpanist?"

I looked up at him and I saw the recognition in his eyes at the very same time it clicked in mine.

"Sam?" I said.

"Emma Blair . . ." he said, taken aback.

"Oh, my God," I said. "Sam Kemper. I don't even . . . I haven't seen you in . . ."

"Ten years or more, maybe," he said. "Wow. You . . . you look great."

"Thanks," I said. "You do, too."

"How are your parents?"

"Good," I said. "Really good."

It was quiet for a moment as I stared at him, surprised at how much he'd changed. I was trying to remember if his eyes had always been that stunning. They were a warm brown that seemed so kind and patient, as if they saw everything with compassion. Or maybe I was simply projecting what I remembered of him onto his face.

But there was no doubt that he'd grown up to be an attractive man. His face had angled out a bit, had grown some character.

I realized I was staring.

"Do you play the timpani now?" Sam said.

I looked at him as if he were speaking French. "What?" I said.

He pointed to the bronze drums behind me. "I saw you by the timpani; I thought maybe you had started to play."

"Oh," I said. "No, no. You know me. I don't play anything. I mean, except for when they made us learn 'Mary Had a Little Lamb' on the recorder, but I hardly think that counts."

Sam laughed. "It's not exactly the timpani, but I think it counts."

"We all can't play a bajillion instruments or however many it was that you play," I said. "Six, was it?"

Sam smiled shyly. "I've picked up a few since then, actually. Most of them amateur-level, though."

"And here I just have the recorder. Oh!" I said, suddenly remembering. "I also played the finger cymbals in the fourth-grade holiday concert! So there's two."

He laughed. "You're an expert, then! I should be asking you questions."

I played along with him, pretending to be a humble genius. "Well, finger cymbals are pretty basic. You mostly just want a pair of cymbals that will fit on your fingers and then you hit them together to make a clanging noise." I hit my own pointer fingers together enthusiastically to show him. "Finger cymbaling is really about confidence."

He laughed again. He always made me feel like I was the funniest person in the room.

"And from there, the sky's the limit," I said. "I know a girl who started out on the finger cymbals; now she plays the actual cymbals."

I grew slightly embarrassed, as if because he'd laughed, I'd taken that as license to perform a stand-up comedy routine. But he laughed again. A hearty laugh. And my anxiety faded away.

"Actually, all of that is a lie. I mean, I did play the finger cymbals but . . . I'm considering learning the piano. Hence, why I'm standing in the middle of this shop looking really confused."

"Ah," he said, nodding his head. "Well, if you want my opinion . . ."

"I do," I said. "Yours is exactly the opinion I want."

He smiled. "Then I think you should get one of the Yamaha PSRs in the back by the drum machines. They're only sixty-one keys and they aren't weighted, but if you're just starting out or you're not really sure you're going to make it a lifelong passion, I think it's silly to spend four hundred bucks on a keyboard. But that's just me."

"No, that's great advice. Would you mind showing me one of the ones that you're talking about?"

"Oh," he said as if he was surprised that I was actually listening to him. "Sure. I think they have one back here."

He turned around and headed toward the back of the store. I followed him. "Do you still play a lot of piano?" I asked him.

He nodded as he looked back at me slightly. "For fun, yeah," he said as he stopped at a short black keyboard on a stand. "This one would probably be great for you."

I hit a few of the keys. They were silent except for the dull *thunk* of the key physically hitting the board.

"I don't think it's plugged in . . ." he said.

"Right. That makes sense." I was legitimately embarrassed that I'd tried to play an unplugged keyboard, perhaps the most embarrassed I'd been since a few months prior when a customer told me my fly was down. "How much is it?"

"Oh, uh . . ." He bent down to look at the price tag. It was about half as much as I'd assumed I'd have to spend.

I decided to seize the day and go for it.

"OK, I'll take it."

He laughed. "Are you serious?"

"Yeah," I said. "You have to start somewhere, right?"

"I guess that's true," he said.

Quiet settled over us.

"Wow," I said. "I can't believe I ran into you."

"I know!" he said. "What are the odds of that?"

"Well, if we both live in the same city, I guess fairly high."

Sam laughed. "I just assumed you were out in California somewhere."

I nodded, unsure just how much Sam knew. "Yeah, well, you know."

Sam nodded somberly. "Yeah," he said, a dryness in his voice. "I hear you."

And now I knew that he knew it all. And my impulse was to get as far away from him as possible as quickly as I could. "Well, my parents will be so happy to hear you're doing well," I said. "Thanks for your help, Sam. It was great to see you."

I put my hand out and watched as Sam was surprised by my ending the conversation.

"Oh, yeah, sure," he said.

And then I excused myself and headed to the register.

"Did anyone help you with your purchase today?" the woman behind the counter said to me as she handed my credit card back.

"Hm?" I asked her. I took it and placed it back into its spot in my wallet.

"Did any salespeople help you decide on your purchase today?" she asked.

"Oh," I said. "Sam helped me out. He was great."

"Sam?"

"Yeah."

"There's no one that works here named Sam."

For a minute, I thought maybe I was in a ghost story.

"Sam Kemper," I said. "He just advised me on this keyboard."

The woman shook her head, unsure what I was talking about.

I turned around, shifted my gaze from left to right, then stood on my tippy toes to get a better view. But I couldn't see him anywhere. I was starting to feel like maybe I was crazy. "Like six feet tall, wearing a black shirt, a little bit of stubble . . ." The cashier looked at me like she might know who I was talking about. I pushed forward. "Really nice eyes?"

"Oh, yeah, I know who you're talking about."

"Great."

"That guy doesn't work here," she said.

"What do you mean he doesn't work here?"

"He's a customer. He comes in a lot, though."

I closed my eyes and sighed. I'd been talking to him as if he were a salesman the whole time. "My mistake," I said. "I'm an idiot."

She started laughing. "No worries." She handed me my receipt. "Do you need help bringing it out to your car?"

"Um . . ." I looked at it and decided I could do it on my own. "I think I'm good. Thanks."

I picked up the keyboard and headed for the door, looking for Sam as I went. I made it all the way to the front of the store before I saw him. He was coming down the stairs.

"Sam!" I said.

"Emma!" He said it in my exact same inflection.

"You're still here," I said. "I thought maybe you'd left."

"I was upstairs. I'm here looking at baby grands."

Admittedly, it took me a second to realize that baby grand wasn't some sort of candy bar.

"Oh, wow, you're buying a baby grand piano," I said, setting the keyboard down for a moment. "Further proof that you don't actually work here."

He smiled.

"I'm so sorry I assumed that you were a salesperson. I think I just figured because you worked at our store and . . . Anyway, I just made an ass out of myself when I went up to the register and tried to give you commission on my purchase."

Sam laughed. "You know, I suspected at the end there that you might have thought I worked here, but I wasn't sure how to clear it up without . . ."

"Making me feel dumb?"

He laughed. "Kinda."

"Well, I officially feel dumb."

"No, don't," he said. "It was my pleasure to help you. Really. It's so nice to see you again." The sincerity with which he looked at me was disarming. And I wasn't sure whether I liked that or not. I was thinking maybe I did.

"I owe you a thank-you," I said. "You were a great help."

"Do you need lessons?" Sam said. "If you wanted I could . . . teach you. I'd be happy to do it. Show you a few things, just to get you started maybe."

I looked at him, unsure how to respond.

"Or if not that, maybe I could just take you out for a drink sometime," he said.

The realization of what was happening washed over me like a wave. Not one of those small waves that runs over your feet and gets the bottom of your jeans wet as you walk along the sand, either. The kind of wave that happens when you're coming out of the water, with your back to the ocean, and it just appears out of nowhere and pummels you.

"Oh, my God," I said, stunned. "You're asking me out?"

I saw Sam's shoulders slump and I caught the disappointment pass across his face before he covered it up.

"I was trying to be casual and subtle about it. Maybe one of those dates neither of us are sure is a date," he said, and then he shook his head. "It's over ten years later and I'm just as bad at it now as I was the first time, huh?"

I felt myself blushing and my blushing made Sam start to blush.

"Sorry," he said. "I'm just getting out of a really long relationship, so I'm out of practice. You might not believe it but I used to be very good at talking to women back in college. As my dad always says, be direct but—"

Sam looked at me like he'd just revealed a terrible secret. He put his hand on his face and pinched the bridge of his nose. "Did I just admit that I ask my father for dating advice?" he said, without changing his expression.

I laughed. A quiet laugh. A "Yes, you did, but it's totally fine" laugh.

That's when I remembered how much I always liked him.

I *liked* him.

Sam was *cute*. And *sweet*. And he thought I was *funny*.

"It's fine," I said. "Look. I thought you were a salesperson. You ask your dad how to hit on women. We're like the Tweedledee and Tweedledum of social interaction."

He laughed. He looked so relieved.

I wanted to see him again. That was the truth. I wanted to spend more time with him. I wanted to be around him.

"How about this?" I said. "You can teach me 'Chopsticks' and I'll buy you a beer."

"Well, if it's just 'Chopsticks' you're after, I have a great idea."

I looked at him, willing to hear him out.

He took my keyboard and I followed him as he led me up the stairs. The rickety, tight staircase led to a room full of huge instruments. A few upright pianos, a harp, a cello. Sam led me toward a sleek black baby grand. He put my keyboard down and then sat at the piano, tapping the spot next to him on the bench. I joined him.

He looked over at me and put his hands delicately on the keys. Then leaned into it and started playing "Chopsticks."

I watched as his hands flew across the keys, the way they seemed to instinctually know what to do. He had nice hands, strong but gentle. Short, clean nails; long, lean fingers. I know women sometimes say they like men to have calluses and knobby knuckles, that they like a man whose toughness shows on his palms. But looking at Sam's hands, I decided that way of thinking was all wrong. I liked the way his hands were agile and almost elegant. I found myself looking up his wrists to his arms and shoulders.

Watching Sam play the piano, remembering how skilled he was, how talented he was, how dexterous—I found myself wondering what else he could do with his hands.

You think you know who you are, you think you have your identity down pat, signed and sealed in a box that you call "me," and then you realize you're attracted to musicians—that "dexterous" is sexy to you—and you have to rethink everything you know about yourself.

He stopped playing. "All right, now you go."

"Me?" I said. "Do that? I don't even know where to start."

He pressed down on a white key in front of me. I, dutifully, put my pointer finger on it.

"Try this finger," he said as he pulled my middle finger onto the key.

I nodded.

"Now, hit that key like this."

He hit another key in a rhythm, six times.

So I did the same with my key.

"And now hit this one," he said as he pointed to another.

I followed each of his instructions, just as he told me. I was supposed to be looking at the keys, but half the time I was looking at him. He caught me once or twice, and I turned my head back to my fingers and the keys beneath them.

I played slowly and unmelodically. My fingers hesitated and then moved too quickly, sort of panicked and squirrelly. But I could recognize a faint pattern in my own movements.

His body brushed up against mine as we sat on that bench. He kept touching my hands with his.

"All right," he said. "Think you can do that fast now? I'll play the other part as you do it."

"Sure," I said. "Yeah, I got it."

I rested my finger on the first key. He put his hand, gently, on the one just below it. "On three," he said. "One . . . two . . . three."

I hit mine.

He hit his.

And there it was.

Duh Duh Duh Duh Duh Duh *Duh Duh Duh Duh Duh Duh* Duh Duh Duh Duh *Duh Duh Duh* . . .

"Chopsticks."

We only played for a few seconds before I had hit all the notes I knew. Feeling shy, I pulled my hands back into my lap.

A part of me hoped he'd continue to play. But he didn't. He stopped his hand in place and rested it gently on the keys. He looked at me.

"So now that you know 'Chopsticks,'" he said, "let's go get a beer."

I laughed. "You're smoother than you think," I said.

"My dad says it's best to be persistent," he said, joking. He looked confident. Hopeful.

I thought about it for a minute.

I thought about how nice it would be to order a gimlet and sit and talk to someone who was both a handsome man and an old friend.

But as Sam looked at me, waiting for my response, I suddenly felt a very sharp sense of fear. True fear.

This wouldn't be dinner with an old friend.

This would be a date.

I couldn't just throw myself into something like that.

I looked at Sam's smile. It was fading as I made him wait for a response.

"It's a rain check," I said. "Is that OK?"

"Yeah," he said, shaking his head. "Totally. Of course."

"I really want to," I said, reassuring.

"No, I get it."

"I just have a thing."

"No worries."

"I'll give you my number," I said, wanting him to know that I did want to see him again, that I *was* interested. "And maybe we can go out next weekend."

Sam smiled and handed me his phone.

I called myself, so his number showed up on my phone, too. I handed his phone back.

"I should get going," I said. "But we'll talk soon?"

"Yeah," he said. "Sounds good."

"It was really nice to see you," I said.

"You, too, Emma. Seriously."

He reached out his hand and I grabbed it. We shook but then let our hands hang there for a moment. The effect was somewhere between shaking and holding.

As I drove back to my apartment that afternoon, with a keyboard in the back and Sam's number in my phone, I found myself wondering whether I could be with someone like Sam, whether Sam could mean something to me.

I had always had a tender spot for him, always cared for him. And maybe it was time that I went out on a date with a nice guy. A nice guy who had always been good to me, who I might have even said yes to back in high school if things had been different.

Good things don't wait until you're ready. Sometimes they come right before, when you're almost there.

And I figured when that happens, you can let them pass by like a bus not meant for you. Or you can *get* ready.

So I got ready.

I thought about it all night. I tossed and turned. And then, the next morning, on my way into the store, I texted Sam.

Drinks on Friday around 7:30? Somewhere in Cambridge? You pick.

It was before nine. I didn't expect him to answer.

But my phone dinged right away.

McKeon's on Avery Street?

And there it was.

I had a date.

With Sam Kemper.

I had never been so excited and so sick to my stomach at the same time.

What was I going to do if I started to have feelings for someone?

Maybe it wouldn't be Sam. Maybe it would be years in the future. But realizing you want love in your life means you have to be willing to let love *in.*

And that meant I needed to let Jesse *go.*

I could think of no other way to do it, no other way of processing it, than putting it into words. So, after work that night, I sat down on my couch, grabbed a piece of paper and a pen, and I wrote a letter.

Dear Jesse,

You've been gone for more than two years but there hasn't been a day that has gone by when I haven't thought of you.

Sometimes I remember the way you smelled salty after you'd gone for a swim in the ocean. Or I wonder whether you'd have liked the movie I just saw. Other times, I just think about your smile. I think about how your eyes would crinkle and I'd always fall a little bit more in love with you.

I think about how you would touch me. How I would touch you. I think about that a lot.

The memory of you hurt so much at first. The more I thought about your smile, your smell, the more it hurt. But I liked punishing myself. I liked the pain because the pain was you.

I don't know if there is a right and wrong way to grieve. I just know that losing you has gutted me in a way I honestly didn't think was possible. I've felt pain I didn't think was human.

At times, it has made me lose my mind. (Let's just say that I went a little crazy up on our roof.)

At times, it has nearly broken me.

And I'm happy to say that now is a time when your memory brings me so much joy that just thinking of you brings a smile to my face.

I'm also happy to say that I'm stronger than I ever knew.

I have found meaning in life that I never would have guessed.

And now I'm surprising myself once again by realizing that I am ready to move forward.

I once thought grief was chronic, that all you could do was appreciate the good days and take them along with the bad. And then I started to think that maybe the good days aren't just days; maybe the good days can be good weeks, good months, good years.

Now I wonder if grief isn't something like a shell.

You wear it for a long time and then one day you realize you've outgrown it.

So you put it down.

It doesn't mean that I want to let go of the memories of you or the love I have for you. But it does mean that I want to let go of the sadness.

I won't ever forget you, Jesse. I don't want to and I don't think I'm capable of it.

But I do think I can put the pain down. I think I can leave it on the ground and walk away, only coming back to visit every once in a while, no longer carrying it with me.

Not only do I think I can do that, but I think I need to.

I will carry you in my heart always, but I cannot carry your loss on my back anymore. If I do, I'll never find any new joy for myself. I will crumble under the weight of your memory.

I have to look forward, into a future where you cannot be. Instead of back, to a past filled with what we had.

I have to let you go and I have to ask you to let me go.

I truly believe that if I work hard, I can have the sort of life for myself that you always wanted for me. A happy life. A satisfied life. Where I am loved and I love in return.

I need your permission to find room to love someone else.

I'm so sorry that we never got the future we talked about. Our life together would have been grand.

But I'm going out into the world with an open heart now. And I'm going to go wherever life takes me.

I hope you know how beautiful and freeing it was to love you when you were here.

You were the love of my life.

Maybe it's selfish to want more; maybe it's greedy to want another love like that.

But I can't help it.

I do.

So I said yes to a date with Sam Kemper. I like to think you would like him for me, that you'd approve. But I also want you to know, in case it doesn't go without saying, that no one could ever replace you. It's just that I want more love in my life, Jesse.

And I'm asking for your blessing to go find it.

Love,
Emma

I read it over and over and over. And then I folded it, put it in an envelope, wrote his name on it, and tucked it away.

I got in bed and I fell asleep.

I slept soundly and woke as the sunlight started beaming in from my window. I felt rested and renewed, as if the earth and I were in perfect agreement about when the sun should rise.

When I showed up at the bar, Sam was wearing a dark denim button-down shirt and flat-front gray chinos. He looked like he might have put pomade in his hair, and when I leaned in to hug him hello, I noticed that he was wearing cologne.

I'd known it was a date. I'd wanted it to be a date.

But the cologne, the smell of wood and citrus, made it all crystal clear.

Sam liked me.

And I liked him.

And maybe it was that simple.

I knew it wasn't. But maybe it could be.

"You look great," Sam said.

When I got ready that evening, I'd put on a tight black skirt and a long-sleeved black-and-white-striped T-shirt that clung to the better parts of me. I took more care applying my mascara than I had in years. When it clumped, I used a safety pin to straighten my lashes, the way I'd seen my mom do when I was a child.

And then I put on pale pink ballet flats and headed toward the door.

I caught a glimpse of myself in the mirror just as I was leaving the house.

Something wasn't right. This wouldn't do. I turned around

and exchanged my flats for black heels. Suddenly, my legs looked longer than they had any right to be.

Feeling confident, I went back into the bathroom and outlined the edges of my lips in a perfect crimson line, filling it in with a lipstick that was called Russian Red. I'd only worn it once a few months ago when I took Marie out for a fancy dinner in Back Bay. But I'd liked it then. And I liked it now.

When I made my way back to the front door and once again caught a glimpse of myself in the mirror, I felt borderline indestructible.

I looked good.

I knew I looked good.

This was my good look.

"Thank you," I said to Sam there at the bar. I pressed my lips together and I sat down on the stool next to his. "You're no slouch yourself."

The bartender, a tall, formidable woman with long, dark hair, came over and asked me what I wanted to drink. I quickly perused their signature cocktails list and nothing struck a chord. It all just looked like various ways to mix fruit juice and vodka.

"Gimlet?" I said.

She nodded and turned away, starting to mix.

"What are you having?" I asked him. He was sitting in front of a pale draft beer. "I hope you haven't paid for that yet. It's supposed to be on me."

Sam looked over at me and smiled a sorrowful smile. "They made me pay when they handed over the beer," he said. "But that just means you'll have to buy my second."

"Fair enough."

The bartender put my drink in front of me and I handed her my credit card. She disappeared.

"I mean, you say that, but for my second beer, I plan on ordering the most expensive one on the menu."

We were both sitting facing forward, looking at each other with glances and side eyes.

"That's OK," I said. "It's the least I can do since you took the time to teach me this."

I started playing "Chopsticks" on the bar with my right hand as if the keys were underneath it. Sam angled his body toward me to watch.

"Very good!" he said when I was done.

"A plus?" I asked.

He thought about it while sipping his beer. "A-minus," he said as he put his beer down. "You just missed it by a hair."

"What?" I said. "Where did I go wrong?"

"You missed a note."

"No, I didn't!" I said.

"Yes, you did. You did this," he said, hitting the bar with the same fingers I'd hit it with just a few moments ago. "And it's this." He hit the bar again. It looked exactly like the first one.

"That's the same thing."

Sam laughed and shook his head. "Nope. It's not."

"Do it again."

"Which one?"

"Do what I did and then do what the real thing is."

He started to repeat mine.

"No, no," I said. "Slower. So I can spot the difference."

He started over and slowed it down.

He did mine.

And then he did his.

And there it was. Right toward the end. I'd skipped a key.

I smiled, knowing I was wrong. "Aw, man!" I said. "I did mess it up."

"That's OK. You're still very good for a beginner."

I gave him a skeptical look.

"I mean," he said, his whole body shifting away from the bar and toward me. "You play the bar beautifully."

I rolled my eyes at him.

"I'm serious, actually. If you got into it, I bet you could be really good."

"You probably say that to all the girls," I said, waving my hand at him, dismissing the compliment. I gracefully picked up my gimlet and slowly brought the filled-to-the-brim glass to my lips. It was sweet and clean. Just the littlest bit dizzying.

"Just my students," he said.

I looked at him, confused.

"Now seems like a good time to tell you I'm a music teacher," he said.

I smiled at him. "Ah, that's awesome. What a perfect job for you."

"Thanks," he said. "And what about you? Are you some big travel writer now? My mom said she saw your name in *Travel + Leisure*."

I laughed. "Oh yeah," I said. "I was. I did that for a while. But, uh . . . no, now I'm actually running the store."

"No way," Sam said, disbelieving.

"Shocking, I know," I said. "But it's true."

"Wow," he said. "Colin Blair's greatest wish. There's a Blair running Blair Books."

I laugh. "I guess dreams do come true," I said. "For my dad at least."

"But not for you?" Sam said.

"Not the dream I originally dreamt, as you know," I said. "But I'm starting to think you don't always know what your dreams are. Some of us have to run smack into one before we see it."

"Ah," Sam said. "Cheers to that." He tilted his glass toward me and I clinked mine against his. "May I change the subject ever so briefly?" he said.

"Be my guest," I said.

"You seem to get even more beautiful with time," he said.

"Oh, stop it," I said, pushing his shoulder away with my hand.

I was flirting. Me. Flirting.

It feels so good to flirt. No one ever talks about that. But in that moment, I felt like flirting was the very thing that made the world go around.

The excitement of wondering what the other person will say next. The thrill of knowing someone is looking at you, liking what they see. The rush of looking at someone and liking what you see in them. Flirting is probably just as much about falling in love with yourself as it is with someone else.

It's about seeing yourself through someone's eyes and realizing there is plenty to like about yourself, plenty of reasons someone might hang on your every word.

"So you're a music teacher," I told him. "Where do you teach?"

"Actually, not far from Blair Books. I'm just over in Concord," he said.

"Are you serious?" I said. "You've been that close by and you never stopped in to say hello?"

Sam looked at me and said, very sincerely, "If I had known you'd be there, I assure you, I'd have rushed over."

I could not stop the smile from spreading across my face. I grabbed my gimlet and took a sip. Sam's beer was almost finished.

"Why don't I get you another?" I said.

He nodded and I waved the bartender over.

"Your most expensive beer on the menu," I said to her gallantly. Sam laughed.

"That's a pretty rich stout, are you sure you want that?" the bartender asked.

I looked at Sam. He put his hands in the air as if to say, "You're in charge."

"That'll be fine," I said to her.

She left and I turned back to him. We were both quiet for a minute, unsure what to say next.

"What's your favorite song to play?" I asked him. It was a stupid question. I knew it when I asked it.

"On the piano?"

"Sure."

"What do you want to hear?" he asked.

I laughed. "I didn't mean now. There's no piano now."

"What are you talking about? We played 'Chopsticks' right here on this bar."

I laughed at him, game to play, but suddenly having a hard time remembering what songs are played on a piano. "How about 'Piano Man'?"

Sam made a face. "A little on the nose, don't you think?"

"It's all I could think of!"

"All right, all right," he said. "It's actually a good choice anyway because it has a nice bit of show-off flair at the beginning."

He straightened his posture and rolled up his sleeves, as if he were playing an actual instrument. He moved a napkin out of the way and then picked up my drink. "If you could please get this out of my way, miss," he said.

"Certainly, sir," I said.

He interlaced his fingers and stretched them out away from his chest.

"Are you ready?" he asked me.

"I was born ready."

He nodded his head dramatically and began to run his hands over the bar, as if there were a full piano right there in front of him. I watched as his fingers glided over the nonexistent keys. He was so confident as he pretended to play that I almost believed it.

"Excuse me," he said as he was playing, "but I believe the harmonica would have come in by now."

"What? I can't play the harmonica."

"Sure you can."

"I don't know the first thing."

"You must know how musicians hold harmonicas. I assume you've seen at least one blues band in your life."

"I mean, sure."

He kept his head down, looking at the bar, playing. People were starting to look at us. He didn't care. Neither did I.

"Let's hear it."

I surprised myself and I did it. I put my hands up to my mouth as if there were a harmonica between them and I ran my mouth over the space it would have occupied.

"Slower," Sam said. "You're not Neil Young."

I laughed and stopped for a minute. "I don't even know what I'm doing!"

"You're doing great! Don't stop."

So I played along.

"All right, wait for a minute; there's no harmonica in this part."

I put my fake harmonica down as he kept playing. I could tell he was going through the full song, each note. I watched how effortless it was for him, how his fingers seemed to move with the expectation they'd make a beautiful sound. And yet they were making no sound at all.

"Now!" he said. "Get that harmonica going. This is your moment."

"It is? I didn't know!" I said, desperately pulling my hands up to my face and really committing to it.

And then Sam slowed and I could tell the song was ending. I took my hands down and I watched him as he hit the last few notes. And then he was done. And he looked at me.

"Next request?" he asked.

"Have dinner with me?" I asked him.

It just popped out of my mouth. I wanted to talk more, to spend more time with him, to hear more about him. I wanted more. "We can eat here or anywhere nearby if you're in the mood for something in particular."

"Emma . . ." he said seriously.

"Yeah?"

"Can we get burritos?"

~

Dos Tacos was brightly lit with orange and yellow undertones instead of the flattering blue light of the bar. But he still looked handsome. And I still felt beautiful.

Even when I bit into my gigantic carne asada deluxe burrito.

"If I could only eat Mexican food for the rest of my life, that would be fine with me," Sam said. "Completely fine."

I wanted to tell him that food in Mexico tasted nothing like this. I wanted to tell him about the three weeks Jesse and I spent in Mexico City, where we found this tiny little restaurant that served amazing chiles rellenos.

But I didn't want to talk about the past.

"I wouldn't mind at all," I said. "Not one bit." I reached over and took a chip out of the basket in front of us at the same time that Sam did.

We collided, ever so briefly, and I liked the feel of his hand on mine. *This is what it's like to be on a date,* I thought. *This is what it's like to be normal.*

"But if we're talking about desserts," Sam said, "I don't know if I'd choose Mexican for the rest of my life. French maybe, éclairs and custards. Italian could be interesting, tiramisu and gelato."

"I don't know," I said. "Indian desserts are pretty incredible. They are all really creamy and nutty. Like rice puddings and pistachio ice cream type stuff. I might have to go with that."

"Wow, that sounds great."

I nodded. "But maybe nothing beats tres leches. Which is Mexican, I suppose. Although, almost every Latin American country you go to claims it's theirs. It's like baklava. I swear, I've spoken to at least twenty people who all claimed they know for a fact their people invented baklava."

"That's funny, because my family invented tres leches right here in the United States."

I laughed. "And I personally invented baklava."

Sam laughed and I looked around to see that everyone appeared to have cleared out and the staff behind the counter had started cleaning up.

"Oh no," I said. "I think they're closing." I pulled my phone out of my purse to check the time. It was 10:02.

"Are you saying the night is over?" Sam asked as he finished the chips sitting in between us. The way he said it, the way he smiled at me and held my gaze, told me that he didn't think the night was over, that he knew I didn't, either.

"I'd say we should go to a bar and get a drink," I said. "But we already did that."

Sam nodded. "We sort of did things in reverse, didn't we? Maybe we should go get lunch now."

"Or meet for coffee." I gathered all the trash onto my tray. "Either way, we should get out of here. I don't want to be like that guy who would always come read books ten minutes before closing. Remember that guy?"

"Remember him?" Sam said, standing up. "I still resent him."

I laughed. "Exactly."

Sam and I threw everything away, thanked the man behind the counter, and walked out onto the sidewalk. It was one of those Boston nights that almost make the winters worth it. The air was warm but fresh. The moon was full. The tall, age-old buildings that often looked dirty in the day glowed at night.

"I have a crazy idea," Sam said.

"Tell me."

"What if we went for a walk?"

My first thought was that it sounded wonderful and my second was that I wouldn't last more than ten minutes in my heels.

"Too quaint?" he asked. "Like it's the nineteen fifties and I'm asking you to split a milk shake?"

I laughed. "No!" I said. "I love the idea. I just know that my feet will start to hurt."

Up ahead, I saw one of the ubiquitous crimson red signs that litter the city—CVS.

Seven minutes later, I had my high heels in my purse and a pair of five-dollar flip-flops on my feet. Sam had a king-sized Snickers.

"Where to?" I asked him, ready to take on the city.

"I didn't really have a plan," Sam said. "But, uh . . ." He looked up and down the street. "This way?" He pointed away from the cluster of buildings.

"Great," I said. "Let's do it."

And off we went. Slowly at first, just putting one foot in front of the other, talking as we did.

The city was humming. Groups of girls out together, college kids walking around, tipsy drinkers smoking cigarettes out on the sidewalk, men and women holding hands on their way out or way home.

Sam told me about teaching eighth-grade orchestra and jazz band, about how he had recently started picking up extra money as a studio musician a few times a month.

I told him how the store was doing, how my parents were doing. I updated him on Marie, told him about Sophie and Ava, even showed him a few signs I'd learned recently. I told him about a few days before when I recognized Ava signing, "Milk, please."

Sam listened as if I was the most fascinating woman in the universe and I realized how long it had been since someone listened to me like that.

We both made fun of ourselves for living in the city and working in the same suburban area where we grew up, a reversal of the common commute.

We stepped over gum and we made way for other pedestrians and we bent down to pet dogs. We walked past Harvard dorms and Harvard Yard. Twice we walked past a T stop and I wondered if we both wouldn't gravitate toward it, using it as a way to say good-bye. But my feet didn't head in that direction and neither did Sam's. We just kept walking, slowly and peacefully, deeper into the night.

We eventually found ourselves walking along the Charles. My feet started to hurt and I asked Sam if we could sit on one of the benches along the river.

"Oh, I thought you'd never ask. I think I started forming a blister around Porter Square."

We sat down on a bench and I picked up my phone to check the time. It was one in the morning. I wasn't tired. And I didn't feel like going home.

There was so much we had already talked about. We had talked about work and music and families and books. We had talked about anything and everything—other than Jesse.

But once we sat down on that bench, it somehow became impossible to ignore.

"So I suppose you know I'm a widow," I said.

Sam looked at me and nodded. "I had heard," he said. "But I wasn't sure if I should bring it up." He reached over and grabbed my hand, gently and with tenderness. "Emma, I'm so sorry."

"Thank you," I said.

"I hope this feels okay to you," he said. "Us being out here. Together."

I nodded. "Surreal, maybe," I said. "But, yeah, it feels okay."

"I can't even imagine how hard it has been for you," he said. "How long has it been?"

"A little over two years," I said.

"Is that a long time or a short time?"

That's when I knew that Sam was sincerely listening, that he was interested in learning exactly who I was in that moment. I realized that Sam understood me, maybe had always understood me, in a way that very few people did. And that meant that he knew that two years was both forever and just a moment ago.

"It depends on the day," I said. "But right now, it feels like a long time. How about you? Who broke your heart?"

Sam sighed, as if preparing himself to rehash it all. "I was with someone for years," he said. He wasn't looking at me. He was looking out onto the water.

"What happened?" I asked.

"What always happens, I guess."

"Werewolf got her?" I asked him.

He laughed and looked at me. "Yeah, brutal. Took her right out of my arms."

I smiled and continued to listen.

"We just outgrew each other," he said finally. "It sounds so banal. But it hurt like nothing before."

I didn't know anything about growing apart. I only knew being *ripped* apart. But I imagined it felt like a tree root slowly growing so big and strong that it breaks through the sidewalk. "I'm sorry," I said. "It sounds awful."

"I just wasn't the same person at thirty that I was at twenty," he said. "And neither was she."

"I don't think anybody is," I said.

"I feel a bit jaded by it now, to be honest," he said. "Like, will I be the same person at forty? Or . . ."

"Will we outgrow this, too?" I said, completing his thought.

And then Sam said something that has stayed with me ever since.

"I think it's a good sign, though," he said, "that I was crazy about you at sixteen and I'm still crazy about you now."

I smiled at him. "It certainly seems promising," I said.

Sam shortened the distance between us and put his arm around me. My shoulder crept into the pit of his arm and he reached across the length of my back. He squeezed me just the littlest bit.

It didn't seem easy, the idea of loving someone again.

But it did seem possible.

So I sat there with him, watching the river, and allowing myself to feel hope again, to feel joy again, to feel how nice it was to be in a man's arms on a bench by the river.

I don't know how long we stayed like that.

I just know that it was four a.m. when I finally made it home.

At my front door, in the early hours of the morning, fifteen years after we met, Sam Kemper finally kissed me.

It was sweet and fresh and gentle. He smelled like morning dew, like a wonderful beginning.

"When can I see you again?" he asked as he looked at me.

I looked right back at him, no artifice between us. "I'm here," I said. "Call me."

Four and a half months into our relationship, I told Sam I loved him. He'd said it a few weeks before and told me that I didn't need to say it back, not then anyway. He said he'd been head over heels for me all through high school, carrying a torch for me since the first time he met me at the store. He told me that part of the reason he left Acton without saying good-bye the summer before college was that he knew that I had fallen in love with Jesse, that he didn't have a shot.

"What I'm saying is that loving you—even if I'm not sure you love me—it's familiar territory," he said. "I've picked it right back up like riding a bike. And I can do it for a little while longer, if that's what you need."

I was immensely grateful because it was exactly what I needed.

It wasn't that I didn't love him. I did. I knew I loved him even before he said it. But I couldn't utter the words. I wasn't prepared to acknowledge the shift that had already happened. I wasn't ready to let go of the word "wife" and grab on to the word "girlfriend."

But that night, four and a half months in, as we both lay in my bed, naked and touching, entangled in blankets and sheets, I realized that even if I wasn't ready for the truth, that didn't make it untrue.

"I love you," I said into the darkness, knowing the sound had nowhere to go but into his ears.

He grabbed my hand and squeezed it. "I thought you might," he said. I could tell he was smiling just by his tone.

"I'm sorry I couldn't say it until now."

"It's OK," he said. "I get it."

Sam always seemed to have a grasp on what was truly important. He never seemed bogged down by petty things. He prioritized the heart of the situation over the details. He paid attention to actions more than words.

I didn't like sleeping in my own bed anymore without him. I always held his hand at the movies. I waited all day to see him again just so I could kiss the soft spot by his eye, where his wrinkles were settling in.

He knew I was head over heels in love with him. So he was OK if it took me a while to say it. And that just made me love him more.

"I just . . . it's sometimes hard not to associate moving forward with forgetting the past," I said.

"If it helps . . ." Sam said as he moved closer to me. My eyes were adjusting to the darkness and I could see the glow of his skin. "I don't expect you to stop loving him just because you love me."

I probably should have smiled or kissed him. I should have told him how much I appreciated his magnanimous spirit and his selflessness. But instead, I started crying so hard I shook the bed.

He held me, kissing the top of my head, and then he said, "Is it OK if I tell you a few more things I've been thinking?"

I nodded.

"I think you and I have something that could last for a very long time, Emma. Maybe I even knew that back in high school, maybe that's why I was as infatuated with you as I was. But I feel—I have always felt—more myself with you than anyone I've ever met. And for the first time, I'm starting to see what it would mean to grow *with* someone, as opposed to merely growing beside someone, the way I did with Aisha. I'm not worried about our future, the way I thought I'd be when I fell in love again. I'm OK just being with you and seeing where it goes. I just want you to know that if what we have lasts, and one day we talk about getting married or having kids, I want you to know I'll never try to replace Jesse. I'll never ask you to stop loving him. You can love your past with him. My love for you now isn't threatened by that. I just . . . I want you to know that I'll never ask you to choose. I'll never ask you to tell me I'm your one true love. I know, for someone like you, that isn't fair. And I'll never ask it."

I was quiet for a minute as I processed what he'd said. He put his arm underneath me and held me tight. He smelled my hair. He kissed my ear. "I've just been thinking about that for a while and I wanted to tell you."

I stopped crying and I took a very deep breath in.

The room smelled of sweat and sleep. The bed beneath us felt soft and safe. I had found a man who understood who I was and accepted me entirely, who was strong enough to make peace with the tender spot in my heart for the love I used to have.

"I love you," I said to him, again. The second time, it came out of my mouth with less effort.

"I love you, too," he said. "I love everything about who you are. Always have."

I moved onto my side to face him with my hands underneath my head. He turned to meet me. We looked at each other and smiled.

"It makes me so happy to have you in my life," I said. "I don't know what I did to deserve you."

Sam smiled. "Think of all the people in the world," he said, tucking my longest hair behind my ear. "And I was lucky enough to find you twice."

"Think of all the women trying to buy a piano," I said. "And I'm the one you hit on."

Sam laughed.

"Turn around, would you?" he said. He said this when he wanted to spoon me, when he wanted to fit my body into the cradle of his. I did so happily.

"Good night, sweetheart," he said. I could smell the mint and sweetness of his breath.

"Good night," I told him, and then I said, "I don't know how I got so lucky."

I kept it at that. I didn't say the rest of the sentence that popped into my head.

I don't know how I got so lucky to have both of you. My two true loves.

Sam got us tickets to the symphony. We had been together for over a year. The two of us had just moved in to an apartment in Cambridge and adopted a pair of cats. My parents, ecstatic to have Sam back in their lives, had jokingly started to call him "son."

That night as I was walking out of Symphony Hall in an emerald green dress, Sam in a handsome dark suit, I probably should have been reflecting on the music we'd heard or asking Sam what he thought of some of the performers.

But instead, all I could think about was how hungry I was.

"You look lost in thought," Sam said as we walked through the streets of Boston, headed for the Green Line.

"I'm ravenous," I said to him. "I realize we ate dinner but I just had that tiny salad and now I feel like I could eat a full meal."

Sam laughed. "Should we stop somewhere?" he asked.

"Please," I said. "Somewhere with french fries."

Soon enough, I was eating a hamburger with the wrapper still half on as Sam and I walked down the street in black-tie attire. Sam was holding the rest of the bag in one hand—I'd already eaten the carton of french fries—and drinking a chocolate milk shake with the other.

"How are your feet feeling?" Sam asked me.

"OK," I answered. "Why?"

"What if we walked around for a bit before getting on the T?" he asked. "You look gorgeous and the weather is nice and . . . I don't know. I want to prolong the moment."

I smiled. I figured I had a few minutes of walking before my heels started to rub up against the broad bones of my feet.

"I'm in," I said, and then I took another bite of my burger. When I swallowed, it occurred to me that there was a flaw in his argument. "How are you going to try to say that this is a beautiful moment between us when I'm eating a Whopper?"

Sam laughed. "I think I just love you that much," he said. "That even standing next to you as you cram Burger King into your mouth is special to me." He took a sip of his milk shake after he said it. I watched as his cheeks sucked in to pull the ice cream up the straw while he stood on the sidewalk looking dapper in his dark suit. I knew exactly what he meant. I felt exactly what he felt.

"You look cute trying to inhale that milk shake," I told him.

"See?" he said. "That's how I know you're in love with me. You've also gone crazy."

We continued to walk along the sidewalk as I took another bite of my burger.

"I really mean it," Sam said. "I'm madly in love with you. I hope that you know how much."

I smiled at him. "I suspect I do," I said teasingly.

"I don't know if this is exactly the right time but . . . I want to make sure you know that I want to spend the rest of my life with you. I don't know if I've properly conveyed it but I am committed to this, to us. I'm in, you know? For life. I want you forever. My only concern is that I don't want to pressure you."

"I don't feel pressure," I said. I was still processing what he was saying, still beginning to understand how monumental this moment we were having truly was.

"Are you sure?" he said. "Because I have to be honest. I'm ready to cash in. I'd commit to you for the rest of our lives without a single doubt in my mind. I have never been happier than I have been during this year with you. And—the way I see it—you're it for me. You're everything."

I looked at him, listening to him. I didn't respond because I was wrapped up in how wonderful it felt to be me just then, how nice it felt to be loved the way he loved me.

Sam shifted his gaze and drank from his milk shake. And then he looked at me and said, "I guess what I'm saying is I'm ready. So now I'll just wait until you're ready, if you're ever ready. If you ever want to."

"If I ever want to . . ." I wanted to make sure I understood exactly what he was saying.

"Marry me," he said, taking another sip of his milk shake.

"Wait, are you . . ." I wanted to ask him if he was proposing but something about the word seemed so formal, so daring.

"I'm not proposing," Sam said. "But what I'm saying is that I'm not 'not proposing' because I don't want to. I want to. I just want to wait until you're ready for me to propose."

"I don't think I understood half of that sentence," I said, smiling at him.

"It wasn't the best one I've ever said," he said, laughing.

"Can you just say what you're saying clearly and succinctly?" I asked.

Sam smiled and nodded. "Emma Blair, if you ever decide that you want to marry me, please tell me. Because I would like to marry you."

I dropped the hamburger onto the street. I didn't mean to;

it just fell out of my hand, as if my brain had said to my fingers, "Stop whatever you're doing, and pay attention to what's happening." And then I took both of my free hands and wrapped them around Sam's face and kissed him with everything I felt in my heart.

When I pulled away, I didn't let him speak. I said, "Let's do it."

"What?" Sam said.

"I want to marry you."

"Wait," Sam said. "Are you sure?" I could tell that he couldn't believe what he was hearing and it made me love him even more.

"I'm absolutely positive," I said. "I want to marry you. Of course I do. I love you. So much."

"Oh, wow," Sam said, smiling so wide his eyes crinkled. "Are we . . . are we getting engaged?"

I laughed, blissful. "I think we are," I said.

Sam took stock of the moment. "No, no, no," he said, shaking his head. "This won't do. It has to be better than this. We can't get engaged while I'm holding a milk shake."

He dropped his milk shake in the trash can. I picked my hamburger off the ground and threw it away.

"OK," Sam said. "We're gonna do this right."

He got down on one knee.

"Oh, God," I said, overwhelmed and stunned. "Sam! What are you doing?"

"I just don't have a ring yet," he said. "But I know everything else. Come here." He reached for my hand and held it in his.

"Emma," he said, teary. "I want to spend the rest of my life with you. I always have. You and I . . . we fit like the gears of a machine, like interlocking pieces that join together effortlessly, turning in tandem, perfectly in sync.

"I believe in us, sweetheart. I believe that I am good for you and that I am a better man because of you. And I want to spend the rest of my life by your side. So, Emma Blair, here it is: Will you marry me?"

The first thought that popped into my head was, *This is too soon.* But then the second thought was, *I think I deserve to be happy.*

"Yes," I said quietly. I was surprised just how hard it was to project my voice in that moment, how much my astonishment had muted me. But he heard me. He knew my answer. He stood up and kissed me as if it were the first time.

I felt a welling in my eyes that I knew I stood no chance of holding back. I started bawling.

"Are you okay?" Sam asked me.

I nodded emphatically. "I'm wonderful," I said. "I'm . . ."

I wasn't sure what word I was looking for, what adjective I could possibly use to describe the chaotic elation that was running through my heart.

"I love you," I said, realizing that it was as close as I could ever get.

"I love you, too."

I was tempted to say, "I'm so grateful for you," and "I can't believe you're real," but instead I pulled him close to me and held him as tight as I possibly could.

He dried my tears as we hailed a cab. He held my hand as we rode back to our apartment. He brushed the hair out of my face as we walked in.

He helped me unzip my dress. We made love on our bed, parallel to the headboard, as if there wasn't any time to lie right. We lost ourselves in each other, the last vestige of a wall between us had been knocked down.

Afterward, Sam opened a bottle of champagne. He got his phone and held it in his hand as we called everyone on speakerphone to tell them the good news.

When we were done, we walked into the living room and played "Heart and Soul" together, half-naked, drunk, and swooning.

As I sat next to him on the piano bench, I said, "What if I'd never walked into the music store . . ."

Sam smiled gently and looked at me as he played the keys on the piano ever so softly. And then he said, "But you did."

I decided that was my answer to questions of fate. I could go around asking myself what if *x* hadn't happened, and the answer would always be, "But it did."

What if Jesse hadn't gotten on that helicopter?

But he did.

I decided to no longer wonder what would have happened if things had worked out differently. And instead, I would focus on what was in front of me. I would focus on reality instead of asking myself questions about fictions.

I kissed Sam's temple. "Take me to bed!" I said.

Sam laughed and took his hands off the piano. "OK, but most of the time when women say that, they mean it sexually."

I laughed. "I mean it sleep-ually," I said.

And then I let out a yelp as Sam stood up and lifted me into his arms.

"Sleep-ually it is," he said as he laid me down on my side of our bed and tucked me in. I fell asleep in the crook of his arm just as he said, "I'm going to find you the perfect diamond ring. I promise."

I was joyful that night.

I felt as if I was moving forward.

I thought that if Jesse could see me from wherever he was, he'd be smiling.

What I was not thinking was, *Jesse is alive. He'll be home in two months. Look what I've done.*

AFTER

~

Both

Or, how to put everything you love at risk

I am lying awake in bed next to Sam, staring at the ceiling. Our gray cat, Mozart, is lying on my feet. Homer, his brother, is black and white and never leaves his spot underneath the piano in the living room except to eat.

It's almost nine a.m. on Wednesday, one of my days off and the day Sam doesn't have to be at school until eleven. On these late mornings, I have illusions about the two of us going out for breakfast, but Sam always refuses to open his eyes until the very last second. This school year so far we have gone to breakfast on a Wednesday exactly zero times. Right now, Sam is sound asleep beside me.

It's been seven weeks since I found out that Jesse was alive. Our initial conversation was kept brief, and due to concerns of Jesse's well-being, contact has been limited. I have been getting most of my updates via e-mail from his mother, Francine.

All I know is that he's been at risk for refeeding syndrome and complications from hypoglycemia.

The doctors did not clear him to be released until yesterday.

That means that he is coming home tomorrow.

When I told Sam about this last night, he said, "OK. How are you feeling?"

I told him the God's honest truth. "I have no idea."

I am very confused right now. In fact, I'm so confused that I'm confused about how confused I am.

What Sam and I have . . . it's love. Pure and simple and true.

But I'm no longer feeling pure, nothing is simple, and I'm no longer sure what's true.

"What's on your mind?" Sam asks me.

I look over at him. I didn't realize he had woken up yet.

"Oh," I say, turning back to the ceiling. "Nothing. Really. Nothing and everything."

"Jesse?" he asks.

"I guess, yeah."

Sam swallows and stays silent and then he turns away from me, getting up and going into the bathroom. I can hear the faucet start and then the water splash as he brushes his teeth. I hear the familiar squeak and rumble of the shower.

My phone rings and I reach onto my bedside table to see who it is. I do not recognize the number. I should put it through to voice mail but I don't. Lately, I can't stand to miss a single call.

"Hello?"

"Is this Emma Lerner?" It is the voice of a young woman.

"It's Emma Blair," I say. "But yes, speaking."

"Mrs. . . ." The woman stops herself. "Ms. Blair, my name is Elizabeth Ivan. I'm calling from the *Beacon*."

I close my eyes, cursing myself for answering.

"Yes?"

"We are doing a piece on the rescue of Jesse Lerner of Acton."

"Yes."

"And we wanted to give you an opportunity to comment."

I can feel myself shaking my head, as if she could pick up on any of my nonverbal clues. "I'm sorry. I don't think I'd like to publicly comment."

"Are you sure? The Lerners are contributing."

"Yeah," I say. "I hear you. I just don't think I'm comfortable, but thank you very much for the opportunity."

"Are you—"

"Thank you, Ms. Ivan. Have a great day."

I hang up the phone before she can speak again. I double-check twice that my phone is off and I throw myself back down onto my pillows, covering my face with my hands, wondering if I will ever feel only one emotion again in my life.

Because lately it's happiness *and* fear, joy *and* sorrow, guilt *and* validation.

It is not simply happiness. Simply fear. Simply joy. Simply sorrow.

The deafening silence in the room means that my ears can only focus on the sound of the water spraying from the shower in the bathroom.

I think of the steam building up.

I think of how warm it must be.

I think of the way the hot water must feel soothing and comfortable. I think of Sam. The way he looks when he's wet. I think of the hot water running down his shoulders. The shoulders that carried my obscenely large desk up four flights of stairs when we moved in together. The shoulders that brought up two boxes of books at a time as he teased me that I should stop hoarding books, knowing full well that would never happen.

Sam is my life. My new, beautiful, wonderful, magical life.

I get up out of bed and I open the bathroom door. It's just

as steamy in here as I imagined. The mirror is too fogged up to see myself as I take off my shirt and slide out of my underwear. But I know what I'd see if I could: I'd see a short, blond, pear-shaped thirtysomething woman with a pixie cut and a smattering of freckles under her right eye.

I slide the curtain open just barely and I step into the shower. Sam opens his eyes. I can tell he is relieved to see me. He puts his arms around me and holds me tight. The warmth of his skin warms me up exactly as I knew it would.

His chin is nestled into my shoulder.

"I know everything is really complicated right now," he says to me. "I'll do whatever you want. I just . . . I need to know what you're thinking."

"I love you," I say into his shoulders as the hot water hits my face and pastes my hair to my forehead. "I love you so much."

"I know," he says, and then he pulls himself away from me and turns toward the water.

He washes the shampoo out of his hair.

With his back to me, I grab the bar of soap and lather it up in my hands. I rub it across his shoulders and down his back. I reach forward and soap up his chest. As the water washes it away, I put my cheek on his back. I put my arms around him. I'd glue myself to him if I could. For the past three nights, I've had dreams of wrapping the two of us together in one rope. I've dreamed of tying it tight so neither of us can escape. I've dreamed of knots so taut they can't be undone. Rope so thick it can't be cut.

Sam puts his arms forward onto the shower wall to steady himself. And then he says, "Just . . . just do me a favor."

"Anything."

"Don't stay with me if you want to be with him," he says. "Don't do that to me."

My dreams, the rope and the knots, I know exactly what they mean.

You don't tie yourself to something unless you're scared you might float away.

The beginning of December is one of my least favorite times of year in Massachusetts. It always feels like the calm before the storm.

The air is often thin and frigid, as if it could shatter like glass. But, today at least, it's warm enough that the light precipitation is just a drizzle of rain and not the beginning of flurries. Although this is a somewhat unwelcome reminder that our first snow is looming.

I am wearing black jeans, a slouchy cream sweater, tall brown boots, and a black peacoat. I never wondered what I'd be wearing when I saw Jesse again because I never thought it would happen.

And yet here is the answer to the question I never knew to ask myself: jeans and a sweater.

There's no dress code for this sort of thing, for seeing the love of your life who has been missing since your first anniversary.

One of the loves of your life.

One of.

Sam left early this morning and didn't wake me up to say good-bye. I opened my eyes only when I heard him shutting our front door on his way out. I watched him from the bedroom window. I saw him walk to his car and get in. His face looked stoic but his posture betrayed him. Shoulders slumped, head bowed, he looked like a man at the end of his rope.

He pulled away before I could call out to him, and when I dialed his number, he didn't answer.

Meanwhile, Jesse lands at three. Which means I have the whole morning and most of the afternoon to get through as if this isn't the most unbelievable day of my life.

Just before nine, I pull into the parking lot behind Blair Books and make my way inside, turning on all the lights and bringing it to life—the way I do almost every morning.

My parents are officially retiring next year. But at this point, they have retired all but in name. I run the store. I am in charge. The clerks report to my assistant manager, Tina, who reports to me.

My dad still oversees the bookkeeping. My mom comes in on Saturday afternoons and works the floor—she wants to know what people are reading and she likes to keep in touch with the same customers she's grown to care for over the past twenty years.

Everything else is me.

Blair Books is the one thing in my life right now that I am unequivocally proud of.

I may be a bit overwhelmed and sometimes feel like I'm in over my head, but I am good at running this store.

Sales are staying solid in light of the changes in the industry. Not many people can say that. Just being able to keep the lights on at a time when even big-box chain stores have closed is, obviously, the most important thing. But the truth is that's only a fraction of where my pride lies. I am, more than anything, incredibly excited about how we are engaging readers.

We have author events at least twice a month. We have signed copies of best-selling books. We have eleven different reading groups and a writers workshop that each meet here once a month. We have a thriving online business. We have exceptional customer service. We have free doughnuts once a week.

I am especially proud of the free doughnuts.

When I'm done tidying up the store this morning, I head to my office and sit down at my desk to check my e-mail. I see a message from my mother at the top of my in-box.

The subject line says *Did You See This?* The body of the e-mail is a link to the article in the *Beacon* about Jesse. It must have gone live this morning. Underneath the link, my mother wrote, *Call me anytime today if you need to talk. I'm thinking of you.*

I'm not sure that I want to read the article but I can't stop myself from clicking.

Missing Local Man Surfaces on Pacific Island

BY ELIZABETH IVAN

Jesse Lerner, 31, from Acton, has been found after having gone missing three and a half years ago.

Lerner had been involved in a fatal helicopter crash that killed the other three passengers on board. The team was on their way to film in the Aleutian Islands when the helicopter experienced a critical engine failure. Lerner, then 28, was presumed dead. Seven weeks ago, he was discovered at sea by a ship heading to Midway Atoll.

Midway is a former naval air facility and is currently

managed by the United States Fish and Wildlife Service. Though it is far out into the Pacific, a third of the way between Honolulu and Japan, there are anywhere from thirty to sixty FWS members stationed there at any given time.

Lerner is believed to have spent the majority of his time stranded on an islet within a thousand kilometers of Midway. There has been no official word on how he made his way to safety.

Hospitalized shortly after rescue, Lerner has recently been cleared for travel and will arrive back in Massachusetts sometime this week, most likely by way of Hanscom Field. His parents, Joseph Lerner and Francine Lerner of Acton, eagerly await his arrival. "We cannot tell you the depth of the pain of losing a child. And we cannot begin to describe the relief in finding out he's coming home," said the Lerners in a joint statement.

Over a decade ago, Lerner made headlines when he beat the high school state record for the five hundred-meter freestyle. A year before he went missing, Lerner married local woman Emma Blair. When contacted, Blair had no comment.

I finish reading the article and I read it again. And then again. And then again. I snap out of it only when Tina calls my name.

"Good mornin', Emma," she says to me as she comes in through the back just before ten. With her thick Boston accent, my name sounds more like "Emmer" than "Emma."

She pronounces "library" as "libry," calls water fountains "bubblahs," and leaves work on time so she's not late for "suppah."

Boston accents are warm and cozy and wonderful to me.

When I hear people make fun of them on TV, I always wonder if they've ever been here. So many people in Massachusetts don't even speak with a Boston accent, and the ones who do would never *pahk they-ah cah in Hahvahd Yahd.*

There's nowhere to park in Harvard Yard.

"Good morning, Tina," I say.

Tina is the sort of employee you search high and low for. She's an empty-nested stay-at-home mom who loves books more than anyone I've ever met. She is sweet to everyone, but firm with people who are unkind. She misses her kids, who are all in college, and works here to busy her mind. I don't think she or her husband needs the money she makes. It's not that I've asked, it's just that she uses at least a quarter of her paycheck every week to buy books with her discount.

When I start to get overwhelmed by all that there is to do running this store, it is Tina who I count on.

The other thing that I like about her is that she has absolutely no interest in being my friend. We work together. I am her boss. We are kind to each other and occasionally share a laugh in the stockroom. That's the beginning and the end of it.

When I first started managing people, I had a hard time setting boundaries and expectations. I wanted everyone to like me. I wanted the people here to feel like they were part of a family—because that is what this store has always been to me. Family. But business doesn't work like that. And I don't need my employees to like me. I need them to respect me and do their jobs well.

I've learned that lesson the hard way a few times, but at least I can say I've learned it. Now, I have a group of employees who might sometimes go home and complain about me but take pride in their jobs and run a great bookstore.

Today I am especially grateful that my employees are not my friends. I know that Tina reads the *Beacon*. I'm sure she read the article. But I know she will not ask me a single thing.

When the Acton Ladies Reading Society comes in at eleven to start their book group, I begin to get anxious.

Jesse's plane lands in four hours.

Jesse, my Jesse, will be home today.

I dropped him off at LAX three years and seven months ago and I will be at the airfield this afternoon when he lands.

I am not good at my job for the hours between noon and two. I am scatterbrained, unfocused, and impatient.

I ring up a woman for $16.87 and when she hands me a twenty-dollar bill, I give her $16.87 back.

A man calls asking if we have any copies of *Extremely Loud & Incredibly Close* and I tell him, "Yes, we carry all of Jonathan Lethem's books."

When I see Mark, the only one of my employees whom I would say classifies as a book snob, come to relieve me, I am the very definition of relieved.

It's time to go.

I can go.

I can get out of here.

As I gather my things and take a look at myself in the bathroom mirror, I regret, for a moment, that I'm not better friends with Tina. It would be nice to look at someone and say, "OK, how do I look?" And have them say, "You look great. It's all gonna be fine."

I consider calling Marie when I get to my car. She might be the perfect person to give me whatever sort of pep talk a person needs before they go meet their long-lost husband. But when I pick up my phone, I'm sidetracked by a text from Sam.

I love you.

It's the sort of thing we text to each other every day, but seeing it now, it is both life-affirming and heartbreaking.

I stare out the windshield, stunned at what is happening to my quiet and stable life.

I have a husband and a fiancé.

I turn the ignition, start my car, and head out of the parking lot.

After years without him, the man I lost is coming home.

I pull into the airfield to see that the parking lot is empty. I check the time. I'm eighteen minutes early.

I fidget in the car, unsure how to contain all of the nervous energy in my body. And then my phone erupts with the sound of my ringtone and I see Olive's face on my screen.

I answer.

"How are you doing?" she asks, even before saying hello.

"I don't know," I say.

"Is he home yet?"

"He will be soon. He's supposed to land in fifteen minutes."

"Jesus," she says.

"Tell me about it."

"What can I do?"

This is Olive's go-to mode of function. *What can I do?* It's a wonderful quality in a friend. It means that she is always the one that is clearing the plates when she's staying at your house. She is always the one sending thoughtful gifts and checking in on you at opportune moments. But in a situation like this, she's not in her element.

Because there is nothing for her to do.

There is nothing to be done.

All of this just . . . *is.*

"Can I at least send you flowers?" she says.

I smile. "I don't think flowers are going to help me deal with the fact that I have a husband and a fiancé at the same time," I tell her.

"What you're describing is completely absurd," she says. "Flowers help with everything."

I laugh. "Thank you," I say, "for managing to be funny right now."

"And thank you for thinking that joking about intense things is appropriate," Olive says. "Tracey does not agree."

Tracey is Olive's girlfriend. I have to say that their pairing makes absolutely no sense to me. Tracey is serious and erudite and corrects other people's grammar. She's regal, thin, and gorgeous. Whereas the best part of Olive, to me, has always been that she says whatever pops into her brain, eats whatever is in front of her, and will try anything you propose.

Sam easily explains it away by saying that opposites attract, but I'm still digging for some piece that I'm missing. Sam must say to me, "Do we really have to keep talking about Olive and Tracey?" at least once a month.

"Do you think he is OK?" Olive says. "I mean, I know he's alive and they say he's healthy enough, but do you think he's going to show up and have gone mad? I mean, wouldn't you? Three years alone? He was probably living off of coconuts and talking to volleyballs."

"This isn't helping," I tell her. "This is the opposite of helping."

"Sorry. I'll shut up."

"No," I say. "Don't shut up. Just stop talking about how my husband is probably mentally unstable. Talk about something else. I have time to kill until everyone gets here and I'm afraid if I have to kill it alone, I'll be the one that's mentally unstable."

Olive laughs. "Like I said, you keep a good sense of humor in a crisis."

"I wasn't joking," I tell her.

And then we both start laughing because that's the funniest thing of all, isn't it? How serious this is, how unfunny it is.

Just as I'm laughing my hardest, I see a white SUV pull into the parking lot and I know, even before seeing the driver, that it is Jesse's parents.

"Ah," I say to her. "I have to go. Francine and Joe are here."

"Oh, my God," Olive says. "This all sounds so uncomfortable."

"A bit, yeah," I say as I turn off the car.

"I mean, when was the last time you talked to them?"

"I basically haven't since he disappeared," I tell her. The three of us kept up the pretense of family for a few months, calling one another on holidays and birthdays. But that faded quickly. To be honest, I think it was too painful for all of us. For the past few years, we've lived in the same town and not seen each other except for the occasional run-in at the grocery store.

"All right, wish me luck dealing with this. I gotta go."

Olive has a very bad habit that I never noticed until we moved away from each other and had to conduct our entire relationship over the phone. When you say you have to go, she says OK and then talks for another half hour.

"OK," she says. "Good luck. I'm here for you. Is Sam okay? How's he doing?"

"Sam is . . ." I don't know how to finish the sentence and I don't have time to. "I don't know. I really have to go," I say. "Thank you for calling. I don't know how I would do this without you."

"I'm here anytime, you know that," Olive says. "If there is anything I can do, please let me know."

"I will," I say. "I promise. All right, I'll talk to you soon."

"Talk to you soon. Are you and Sam definitely going through with the wedding? I mean, at this point everything is up in the air, right?"

"Olive!" I say, losing my patience.

"Sorry," she says, realizing what she's doing. "I'm being such an Olive right now."

I laugh. "You kind of are," I say.

"OK, I'm going. I love you. I'm here for you. I won't even ask how Sophie and Ava are because I know you don't have time."

"Great. Thank you. I love you. Good-bye."

"Bye."

When she hangs up the phone, I realize how alone I am. For a moment, I thought the problem was just that I needed to get Olive off the phone. Now, I remember what the real challenge is.

I get out of my car. Francine waves as she sees me.

I wave back and start walking over to them.

Francine is wearing a fitted burgundy dress with a navy peacoat. Her wavy dark brown hair just grazes her shoulders.

She hugs me, firmly and passionately, as if she's missed me all these years. I pull away from her just as Joe puts his arms around me. He looks like he's dressed for church. Gray slacks, light blue button-down, navy blue blazer. I notice that he has started losing his hair. His face has low valleys in places that used to be plains.

"Hi, sweetheart," he says to me.

"Emma," Francine says, putting a scarf around her neck. "It's like a breath of fresh air to see you."

"Thanks," I say back to her. "You, too." I don't know what to call her. When I was a teenager, I called her "Mrs. Lerner." When I was married to her son, I called her "Franny."

"Look at your hair!" she says, moving her hand toward my short hair but not actually touching it. "It's so different."

I am stronger than when I knew them. I stand straighter. I am more patient. I hold fewer grudges. I am more thankful for what I have, less resentful for what I don't. I am less restless. I read a lot more books. I play the piano. I'm engaged.

But, of course, she can't see all that.

The only change she can see is my short, blond hair.

"It's very gamine."

"Thanks," I say back as if I am confident this is a compliment but, by the way Francine says it, I'm not.

"How are you?" she says.

"Um," I say. "Good. You?"

"Us, too," she says. "Us, too. The Lord works in mysterious ways but I am stunned, humbled really, at what a gift today is."

Jesse wasn't raised with any religious instruction and in high school I once heard Francine say she didn't "care what you think God wants" to a proselytizing Mormon who rang their doorbell. Now I'm wondering if that's changed. If losing Jesse made her a born-again Christian and if getting him back serves as all the proof she needs that she's on the right track.

Joe looks at me briefly and then looks away. I can't tell what he's thinking. But he appears to be much more conflicted about everything. Francine seems to think that life is going to be perfect again, just as soon as Jesse gets off that plane. But I think Joe understands that everything is going to be a lot more complex.

"All right," Francine says. "Shall we head in there? I can't believe he lands soon. Look at this, the three of us on our way to see our boy."

She pulls out her phone and checks it.

"Looks like Chris, Tricia, and the boys will be here with Danny and Marlene in a minute."

I knew Chris and Tricia had kids not because anyone told me but because I saw Tricia in T.J. Maxx last year, many months pregnant with a toddler at her side.

I don't actually know who Marlene is. I can only assume she's Danny's girlfriend, fiancée, or wife.

The simple fact is that I know almost nothing about the Lerners anymore and they know almost nothing about me. I don't even know if they know about Sam.

Joe and I follow Francine as she walks confidently in the direction of the terminal.

"It is hard to predict how he'll be feeling," Francine says as we walk. "From what I've heard and the advice that I've been given by professionals, our job right now is to make him feel safe."

"Of course," I say.

Right before we get to the door, Francine turns and looks at me. "In that vein, we have chosen not to tell him you've moved on."

So they do know. Of course they do.

"OK," I say, unsure how else to respond other than to acknowledge that I've heard her.

The wind picks up and I find myself wishing I had brought a warmer coat. The air here is sharper than I expected. I button up tighter and I watch as Joe does the same.

"You can tell him if you want," Francine says. "I just don't know if he can handle finding out you are already engaged to someone else."

It is the "already" that bothers me. The "already" nested firmly in the sentence, as if it's right at home between "you are" and "engaged."

I resolve to stay quiet. I tell myself the best response is stoicism. But then, before I realize I've done it, I've let the feelings in my chest become words out of my mouth.

"You don't need to make me feel guilty," I tell her. "I feel plenty guilty all on my own."

Even though I know she hears me, she pretends she's heard nothing. It doesn't matter; even if she did acknowledge it, I know there's no way she could possibly understand what I mean.

I feel awful for giving up on Jesse. For thinking he was dead. For moving on. For falling in love with someone else. I'm actually furious at myself for that.

But I'm also really angry at myself for not being loyal to Sam, for not remaining steadfast and true in my devotion, like I have promised him I would be. I am mad at myself for being unsure, for not being the sort of woman who can tell him he's the only one, for not giving him the kind of love he deserves.

I'm mad at myself for a lot of things.

So much so that I barely have time to consider what anyone else thinks of me.

"OK," Joe says abruptly. "Let's go. Jesse's going to land any minute."

I watch through the plate-glass window in front of me as a plane flies low in the sky and lands on the runway.

My heart starts beating so hard in my chest that I am afraid I am having a heart attack.

A man on the ground wheels out a staircase. A door opens. A pilot walks out.

And then there is Jesse.

Worse for wear and yet, somehow, never more beautiful to me than right now.

Pictures never did his smile justice. I remember that now.

He's also thin and frail, as if his body is made only of muscle and bone. His once-gentle face is sleek, hard edges where soft cheeks used to be. His hair is longer, shaggier. His skin is mottled light brown and pink, looking very much like a three-year sunburn.

But his mannerisms are the same. His smile is the same. His eyes, the same.

I stare at him as he gets off the plane. I stare at him as he hugs Francine and Joe. I stare at him as he comes closer to me, as he looks me in the eye with purpose. I notice that the pinkie on his right hand stops at the first knuckle. He lost a finger somewhere along the way.

"Hi," he says.

Just hearing that one word makes me feel as though I have gone back in time, to a part of my life when things made sense, when the world was fair.

"Hi."

"You are a sight for sore eyes."

I smile. I bury my face in my hands. He grabs me, holding me. I can feel my pulse beat erratically, as if it isn't sure whether to speed up or slow down.

I wonder if this is all real.

But when I open my eyes again, he's still there. He's right here in front of me, surrounding me.

I grieved him as if he were dead. But here he is.

It's almost terrifying, how much it defies logic and reason. What else do we know about the world that isn't true?

"You're home," I say.

"I'm here."

You know how every once in a while you look back on your life and you wonder how so much time has passed? You wonder how each moment bled into the next and created the days, months, and years that now all feel like seconds?

That's how I feel.

Right now.

In this moment.

It feels like our entire past together spans eons and the time I've spent without him is an insignificant little flash.

I have loved Jesse since the day I saw him at that swim meet.

And I'm having a hard time remembering how I lived without him, how I could bear to look at a world that I thought he wasn't in, and why I thought I could ever love anyone the way I love him.

Because it has been him.

My whole life.

It has always, always been him.

How have I spent all of my time forgetting who I am and who I love?

The last couple of hours have been a daze. I've stood by, saying barely anything, as the whole family embraced Jesse's return home. I watched as Francine cried her eyes out and prayed to God at the sight of him, as Chris and Tricia introduced him to their son, Trevor, and their baby girl, Ginnie. As Danny introduced him to his new wife, Marlene.

My phone has rung a number of times but I have yet to bring myself to even look at the caller ID. I can't handle real life right now. I can barely handle what's happening right in front of me.

And I can't even begin to reconcile what is happening right in front of me to my real life.

There is so much for Jesse to process. You can tell there is a great deal that his family wants to say, so much they want to do. I find myself wanting to tell him every thought I've had while he's been gone, wanting to describe every moment I've spent without him, every feeling I have right now. I want to plug my heart into his and upload the past three and a half years right into his soul.

I can only imagine that everyone else here wants to do that same thing.

It must be so overwhelming to be him, to be the person everyone is staring at, the person everyone wants to see with their very own eyes and hold in their own hands.

As I watch Jesse interact with his family, I feel suddenly like I don't belong here.

Jesse is holding his niece, Ginnie, for the first time, trying to remain calm. But I know him. I know what the downturn of the corners of his eyes means. I know why he pulls his ears back, why his neck looks rigid and stiff.

He's uncomfortable. He's confused. This is all so much for him. Too much.

I catch his eye. He smiles.

And I realize it's everyone else who doesn't belong here. There may be twenty people in this room but there are only two people in the whole world to Jesse and me and they are Jesse and me.

When his family has calmed down, they all start discussing how they will make their way back to Francine and Joe's house. I watch Jesse pull apart from the pack and then I feel his arm on me, pulling me aside.

"Is your car here?" he says.

"Yeah. Just right outside."

I can't believe I'm talking to him. He's right in front of me. Talking to me. Jesse Lerner. My Jesse Lerner. Is alive and talking to me. Nothing has ever been so *impossible* and yet *happening*.

"All right, great. Let's get out of here soon, then."

"OK," I say, stone-faced.

"Are you OK?" he asks me. "You look like you've seen a ghost." The moment he hears it come out of his mouth, he closes his eyes. When he opens them back up, he says, "I'm sorry. You are seeing a ghost. Aren't you?"

I look at him and I am hit with a wave of exhaustion.

Do you know how tiring it is to see a dead man in front of

you? To have to remind your brain every half second that your eyes aren't lying?

I'm overwhelmed by the stunning incredibility of the truth. That I can, right this very second, reach out and touch him. That I can ask him any of the questions I've spent years of my life wishing I'd asked him. That I can tell him I love him.

The desire to tell him, and the belief that he would never hear me, has gutted me year after year after year.

And now I can tell him. I can just open my mouth and say it and he will hear it and he will know.

"I love you," I say. I say it because I mean it right now, but I also say it for every single time I couldn't say it then.

He looks at me and he smiles a deep and peaceful smile. "I love you, too."

It all hurts so bad and feels so good that I'd swear my heart is bleeding.

There is such immense relief of an ache so deep that I fall to pieces, as if I hadn't realized until now how much effort it was taking to seem normal, to stand up straight.

My legs can't hold me. My lungs can't sustain me. My eyes stare ahead but don't see a thing.

Jesse catches me before I fall to the ground. Everyone is looking but I barely care.

Jesse supports my weight and leads me around the corner, into the bathroom. When the door shuts, he puts his arms around me, tightly, holding me so close that there's no air between us. For years there were immeasurable miles separating us and now, not even oxygen.

"I know," he says, "I know."

He is the only person who can understand my pain, my astonishment, my joy.

"I'm going to tell my family we need some time, OK?"

I nod vehemently into his chest. He kisses the top of my head. "I'll be right back. Stay here."

I stand against the bathroom wall and watch him walk out the door.

I look at myself in the mirror. My eyes are glassy and bloodshot. The skin around them is blotched red. The diamond ring on my finger catches the dingy yellow light.

I could have taken it off before I came here. I could have slipped it off my finger and left it in my car. But I didn't. I didn't because I didn't want to lie.

But right now, I cannot for the life of me understand why I thought wearing it was better than tossing it in my jewelry box and replacing it with my little ruby ring.

Both of them are only half the truth.

I close my eyes. And I remember the man I woke up next to this morning.

Jesse is back.

"OK," he says. "Let's go."

He grabs my hand and leads me out through a back door. He walks toward the parking lot. His family is still inside. The wind blows through our hair as we run toward the bank of cars.

"Which one is yours?" he asks. I point to my sedan at the corner of the lot. We get into the car. I turn on the ignition, put the car in reverse, and then I put the car right back into neutral.

"I need a minute," I say.

Sometimes I think this is a dream that I'm going to wake up from and I don't know whether that would be good or bad.

"I get it," Jesse says. "Take all the time you need."

I look at him, trying to fully process what is happening. I find myself staring at the space where the rest of his pinkie used to be.

It will take us days, maybe weeks, months, or years, to truly understand what each other has gone through, to understand who we are to each other now.

Somehow that makes me feel calmer. There's no rush for us to make sense of all of this. It will take as long as it takes.

"All right," I say. "I'm good."

I pull out of the spot and toward the road. When I get to the main drive, I take a right.

"Where are we going?" he says.

"I don't know," I tell him.

"I want to talk to you. I want to talk to you forever."

I look at him, briefly taking my eyes off the road.

I don't know where I'm driving; I just drive. And then I turn on the heat and I feel it blaze out of the vents and onto my hands and feet. I can feel the smothering warmth on my cheeks.

We hit a red light and I come to a stop.

I look over at him and he's looking out the window, deep in thought. No doubt this is even more bewildering for him than it is for me. He must have his own set of questions, his own conflicted feelings. Maybe he loved someone out there in the world while he was gone. Maybe he did unspeakable things to survive, to get back here. Maybe he stopped loving me somewhere along the way, gave up on me.

I have always thought of Jesse as my other half, as a person that I know as well as I know myself, but the truth is he's a stranger to me now.

Where has he been and what has he seen?

The light turns green and the sky is getting darker by the minute. The weather forecast said it might hail tonight.

Tonight.

I'm supposed to go home to Sam tonight.

When the winding back roads we are traveling get windier, I realize I'm not headed anywhere in particular. I pull over onto a well-worn patch on the side of the road. I put the car in neutral and pull up the hand brake, but I keep the heat on. I unbuckle my seat belt and I turn to look at him.

"Tell me everything," I say. He's hard for me to look at, even though he's all I want to see.

Wherever he was, whatever he was doing, has weathered him. His skin has a leatheriness that it didn't have when he left. His face has wrinkled in the overused spots. I wonder if the lines around his eyes are from squinting off in the distance, looking for someone to save him. I wonder if his pinkie isn't the only wound, if there are more beneath his clothes. I know there must be a great deal beneath the surface.

"What do you want to know?" he asks me.

"Where were you? What happened?"

Jesse blows air out of his mouth, a telltale sign that these are all questions he doesn't really want to answer.

"How about just the short version?" I say.

"How about we talk about something else? Absolutely anything else?"

"Please?" I say to him. "I need to know."

Jesse looks out the window and then back to me. "I'll tell you now, and then will you promise that you won't ask about it again? Nothing more?"

I smile and offer him a handshake. "You've got yourself a deal."

Jesse takes my hand, holds it. He feels warm to the touch. I have to stop myself from touching more of him. And then Jesse opens his mouth and says, "Here it goes."

When the helicopter went down, he knew he was the only survivor. He declines to tell me how he knew that; he doesn't want to talk about the crash. All he'll say is that there was an inflatable raft with emergency supplies, including drinking water and rations, that saved his life and got him through the weeks it took to find land.

Land is a generous description for where he ended up. It was a rock formation in the middle of the sea. Five hundred paces from one end to the other. It was not really even an islet, let alone an island, but it had a gradual enough slope on one side to give it a small shore. Jesse knew he'd traveled far from Alaska because the water was mild and the sun was relentless. Initially, he planned to stay there only long enough to rest, to feel earth under his feet. But soon, he realized that the raft had been punctured along the rocks. It was almost entirely deflated. He was stuck.

He was almost out of water and running low on food bars. He used the old water containers to collect rainwater. He searched the rocks for any signs of plants or animals but found only sand and stone. So he figured out how to fish.

There were some missteps along the way. He ate a few fish that made him vomit. He drank the water faster than it replenished. But he also found oysters and mussels growing on the shoreline and during a particularly relentless rainstorm managed to store over a week's worth of water—getting him ahead of the game. During the scorching sun of midday, he hung the deflated raft between two rocks and slept in the shade. Soon, he figured out a fairly reliable routine.

Jesse was eating raw fish, barnacles, and food bars, drinking rainwater, and hiding from the sun. He felt stable. He felt like he could make that work for as long as he needed to until we found him.

But then, after a few weeks, he realized we were never going to find him.

He says he had a breakdown and then, after, an epiphany.

That's when Jesse started training.

He knew that he couldn't spend the rest of his life living alone on a small patch of rocks in the Pacific. He knew his only way out was the very thing he had been raised to do.

He trained to swim a race.

He counted his strokes and each day swam out farther than he had the day before.

He started out slow, frailer and more fatigued than he'd ever been.

But after a few months, he was able to make it far out into the ocean. He felt confident that one day he'd be strong enough to swim the open water as long as he had to.

It took him almost two years to work up the stamina and the guts to do it. He had setbacks both minor (a jellyfish sting) and major (he saw a shark circling the rocks on and off for a few weeks). And when he finally set out for good, it wasn't because he believed that he could make it.

It was because he knew he'd die if he didn't.

He had run out of food bars long ago and the oysters had dried up. Half of the raft had been torn and lost to the wind. He feared that he was not growing stronger but weaker.

There was a rainstorm that brought him days' worth of water. He drank as much as he could and managed to strap a few bottles on his back using pieces of the raft.

And then he got in the water.

Ready to find help or die trying.

He does not know exactly how long he was out in the open sea and he lost count of the strokes. He says he knows it was less than two days when he saw a ship.

"And that's when I knew it was all over," he says. "That I would be OK. That I was coming home to you."

He never mentions his finger. In the whole story, in his telling me everything, he never mentioned that he lost half of his finger. And I don't know what to do because I agreed not to ask anything more. I start to open my mouth, to ask what I know I'm not supposed to. But he cuts me off and I get the message. We're done talking about that now.

"I thought of you every day," he says. "I have missed you for all these years."

I start to say it back and then realize I'm not sure if it's true. I thought of him always—until one day I thought of him less. And then I thought of him often but . . . that's not really the same thing.

"You were always in my heart," I finally say. Because I know that's true. That's absolutely true.

No matter how much history Jesse and I have shared, no matter how much we may feel like we understand the other, I'm not sure I can ever understand the pain of living alone in the middle of the ocean. I don't know if I can ever truly appreciate the courage it takes to swim the open water.

And while I'm in no way comparing the two, I don't think Jesse can understand what it feels like to believe the love of your life is dead. And then to be sitting across from him in your car off the side of the road.

"Now you go," he says.

"Now I go?"

"Tell me everything," he says. The minute he says it, I know that he knows I'm engaged. He knows everything. Between the acute awareness of his voice and the sense of "here it comes" that lives in his focused eyes and tight lips, I can tell he figured it out on his own.

Or he noticed my diamond ring.

"I'm engaged," I say.

Then, suddenly, Jesse starts laughing. He looks relieved.

"What? Why are you laughing? Why is this funny?"

"Because," he says, smiling, "I thought you were already married."

I feel a smile erupt across my face even though I can't tell you where, exactly, it comes from.

And then I start laughing and playfully hit him. "It's practically the same thing!" I say to him.

"Oh, no, it's not," he says. "No, it absolutely is not."

"I'm planning to marry someone else."

"But you haven't yet."

"So?" I say.

It's so easy to talk to him. It was always easy to talk to him. Or maybe it's just that I've always been good at it.

"I'm saying that I have spent the last three and a half years of my life hoping with everything I have in me to see you again. And if you think that you being engaged to someone else is going to stop me from putting our life back together, you've lost your goddamn mind."

I look at him, and at first the smile is still spread wide across my face, but soon, reality starts to set in and the smile fades. I put my head in my hands.

I am going to hurt everyone.

The car becomes so quiet all I can hear is the roll of the cars whizzing past us on the road.

"It's more complicated than you realize," I say finally.

"Emma, look, I get it. You had to move on. I know everybody did. I know that you thought I was . . ."

"Dead. I thought you were dead."

"I know!" he says, moving toward me, grabbing my hands. "I can't imagine how hard that must have been for you. I don't want to imagine it. All these years, I knew you were alive, I knew I had you to go back to. And I know you didn't have that. I'm so sorry, Emma."

I look up at him and I can see there are tears in his eyes to match the ones forming in mine.

"I'm so sorry. You have no idea how sorry. I should never have done it. I should never have left you. Nothing on this earth, no experience I could ever have, would be worth losing you or hurting you the way that I did. I used to lay awake at night and worry about you. I would spend hours and hours, days, really, worried about how much you must be hurting. Worried about how you and my mother and my whole family must be aching. And it nearly killed me. To know that the people I loved, that you, you, Emma, were grieving for me. I am so sorry that I put you through that.

"But I'm home now. And what drove me to get home, what kept me going, was you. Was coming home to you. Was coming back to the life that we had planned. I want that life back. And I'm not going to let the decisions that you made when you thought I was gone affect how I feel about you now. I love you, Emma. I've always loved you. I never stopped loving you. I'm incapable of it. I'm incapable of loving anyone but you. So I absolve you of anything that happened while I was gone and it's now our time. Our time to put everything back together the way it was."

It's now so hot in the car that I feel like I have a fever. I turn down the heat and I try to wrestle out of my jacket. It's hard, in the small space of the driver's seat, to wiggle left and right just enough to get my arms out. Jesse, wordlessly, takes hold of one of the sleeves and pulls for me, helping me finally free myself.

I look at him, and if I push away the shock and the confusion and the bittersweetness, what I'm left with is extreme comfort. Opening my eyes and seeing his face staring back is more like home than anything I can remember. Right here in this car is the best part of my teenage years, the best part of my twenties. The best part of me. The whole beginning of my life is this man.

The years he's been gone have done nothing to erase the warmth and comfort we have from the years we spent in each other's lives.

"You were the love of my life," I say.

"I *am* the love of your life," Jesse says. "Nothing's changed."

"Everything has changed!"

"Not between us, it hasn't," he says. "You're still the girl with the freckles under her eye. And I'm still the guy that kissed you in the police station."

"What about Sam?"

It is the first time I see sadness and anger flash over Jesse's face. "Don't say his name," he says, moving away from me. The sharpness of his tone disarms me. "Let's talk about something else. For now."

"What else could we possibly talk about?"

Jesse looks out the window for a moment. I can see his jaw

tense, his eyes fixate on a point. And then he relaxes and turns back to me. He smiles. "Seen any good movies?"

Despite myself, I'm laughing and soon he is, too. That's how it's always been with us. I smile because he's smiling. He laughs because I am laughing.

"This is really hard," I say when I catch my breath. "Everything about this is so . . ."

"It doesn't have to be," he says. "I love you. And you love me. You're my wife."

"I don't even think that's true. When you were declared dead, it . . . I mean, I don't even know if we're still married."

"I don't care about a piece of paper," he says. "You're the woman I've spent my entire life loving. I know that you had to move on. I don't blame you. But I'm home now. I'm here *now.* Everything can be the way it's supposed to be. The way it should be."

I shake my head and wipe my eyes with the back of my hand. "I don't know," I say to Jesse. "I don't know."

"*I* know."

Jesse leans forward and wipes away the tears that have fallen down my neck.

"You're Emma," he says as if that's the key to all of this, as if the problem is that I don't know who I am. "And I'm Jesse."

I look at him, half smiling. I try to feel better the way he wants me to. I try to believe that things are as simple as he is telling me they are. I can almost believe him. Almost.

"Jesse—"

"It's going to be OK, OK?" he says. "It's all going to be fine."

"It is?"

"Of course it is."

I love him. I love this man. No one knows me the way he knows me, no one loves me the way he loves me.

There is other love out there for me. But it's different. It isn't this. It isn't this exact love. It's better and it's worse. But I guess that's sort of the point of love between two people—you can't re-create it. Every time you love, everyone you love, the love is different. You're different in it.

Right now, I want nothing but to revel in *this* love.

This love with Jesse.

I throw myself into his arms and he holds me tight. Our mouths are now close together, our lips just a few inches from touching. Jesse moves the littlest bit closer.

But he doesn't kiss me.

Something about that strikes me as the most gentlemanly thing he has ever done.

"Here is what we are going to do," he says. "How about you drop me off at my parents'? It's getting late and my family is probably wondering where I am. I can't . . . I can't keep them wondering where I am . . ."

"OK," I say.

"And then you head home. To wherever you live," he says. "Where do you live?"

"In Cambridge," I tell him.

"OK, so you go home to Cambridge," he says.

"OK."

"Where do you work? Are you at a magazine or freelance?" Jesse asks expectantly.

I'm almost hesitant to disappoint him. "I'm at the bookstore."

"What are you talking about?" he says.

"Blair Books."

"You work at Blair Books?"

"I moved back here after you . . ." I drift off and go another route. "I started working there. And now I really like it. Now it's mine."

"It's yours?"

"Yeah, I run it. My parents are in and out, sort of. Mostly retired."

Jesse looks at me as if he can't compute it. And then he changes his face entirely. "Wow," he says. "I did not expect that."

"I know," I say. "But it's good. It's a good thing."

"All right," he says. "Then I'd imagine you'll be at the bookstore tomorrow?"

"I usually get in around nine. Open at ten."

"Can I see you for breakfast?"

"Breakfast?"

"You can't expect me to wait until lunch to see you . . ." he says. "Breakfast is already too long."

I think about it. I think about Sam. With guilt weighing me down, I start to speak.

Before I can respond, Jesse adds, "C'mon, Emma. You can have breakfast with me."

I nod. "Yeah, OK, yeah," I say. "Seven thirty?"

"Great," he says. "It's a date."

It is just after eight when I pull into the parking lot of my apartment. I tighten my coat as I step out. The wind is starting to pick up, the temperature dropped as the sun went down, and I can feel the rough breeze and the cold air on my shoulders and neck. I rush into my building.

I walk into the elevator. I press the button for the fifth floor. I watch the elevator close and as it does, I close my eyes.

When he asks me what happened today, what do I say?

How do I tell the truth when I don't know what it is?

I'm so lost in my own thoughts that I jump when the elevator dings and the doors open.

Standing in the hallway, right at our front door, is Sam.

Beautiful, kind, fractured, heartbroken Sam.

"You're back!" he says to me. "I thought I saw your car pull up in front just now when I was taking out the trash but I wasn't sure. I . . . I called you earlier, a few times actually, but I never heard from you, so I wasn't sure when you were coming home."

He wasn't sure *if* I was coming home.

His eyes are glassy. He's been crying. He seems to think that if he's peppy enough I won't notice.

"I'm sorry." I put my arms around him and feel him lean into me. His relief is palpable. "I lost track of time."

We head back into our apartment. The moment the door is

open, I can smell tomato soup. Sam makes the most incredible tomato soup. It is spicy, light, and sweet.

I come around the corner into the kitchen and I can see that he has ingredients out to make grilled cheese, including vegan cheddar because I'm convinced I'm growing lactose intolerant.

"Oh, my God," I say to him. "You're making tomato soup and grilled cheese for dinner?"

"Yeah," he says, trying to act cool, putting in considerable effort to make his voice sound carefree. "I thought it might be nice since it's so cold today."

He moves toward the cutting board and starts assembling sandwiches as I put my bag on the table and sit down at the counter. I watch him, carefully grating cheese, softly buttering the bread, as I unzip my boots and put them by the door. Sam's hands are shaking ever so slightly. His face looks pained, as if it's working overtime just to remain even.

It aches to look at him, to know that he's trying so hard to be OK right now, that he's trying to be understanding and patient and secure, when he's anything but. He is standing there, putting a frying pan down over a medium flame, trying to pretend that the fact that I saw my (former?) husband today isn't tearing him up inside.

I can't put him through this any longer.

"We can talk about it," I say to him.

He looks up at me.

Mozart walks into the kitchen and then turns around, as if he knows he doesn't want to be here for this. I watch as he joins Homer under the piano.

I grab Sam's hand. "We can talk about anything that is on your mind; you can ask me anything you want. This is your life, too."

Sam looks away from me and then nods.

He turns off the flame.

"Go ahead. Whatever you want to know. Just ask me. It's OK. We're gonna be honest and we're gonna be OK." I don't actually know what I mean by that, about us being OK.

He turns to me. "How was he?" Sam asks.

"Oh," I say, surprised that Sam's first question is about Jesse's well-being.

"He's OK. He's good. He seems . . . like he's adjusting." I don't mention that he seems almost bizarrely unflappable, that he is singularly focused on restoring our marriage.

"How are you?"

"I'm OK, too," I say. "I'm a little stunned by everything. It's very weird to see him. I'm not sure what to make of it." I'm choosing vague words because I'm afraid to narrow anything down. I'm afraid to commit to any particular feeling more than another. I honestly don't know what words I'd choose even if I was committed to specifics.

Sam nods, listening. And then he breathes in and asks what he really wants to know. It's clear the first two questions were warm-ups and this is game time. "Did you kiss him?"

It's funny, isn't it? So often men see betrayal in what you've done instead of how you feel.

"No," I say, shaking my head.

Sam is instantly relieved but I feel worse. I'm getting by on a technicality. Jesse didn't even try to kiss me, so I don't know if I would have let him, or if I would have kissed him back. But I still get credit as if I'd resisted. I don't feel great about that.

"I'd understand if you did kiss him," Sam says. "I know that . . . I guess what I'm saying is . . ."

I wait for him to finish his sentence but he doesn't finish it.

He just gives up, as if it's too overwhelming to try to choose words for his thoughts.

I know how he feels.

He turns the burner on again and goes back to making sandwiches.

"You're in an impossible situation," I tell him. I want him to know that I understand what he's going through. But I could never really understand it, could I? I have no idea what it's like to be him right now.

"You are, too," he says.

We're both playing the same game with each other. We want to understand, we want to make the other person feel understood, but the truth is we're on opposite sides of the street right now, looking over at each other and imagining what life must be like.

I watch him as his eyes narrow and his shoulders broaden from the tension in his body. I watch as he puts butter on a piece of bread.

Maybe I understand him more than I think.

Sam is making his fiancée a grilled cheese sandwich while worrying that she might leave him.

He's scared he's about to lose the person he loves. There's not a fear on this earth more common than that.

"Let's make these together," I say, stepping toward the pan and taking the spatula out of his hand.

I'm great at flipping things with a spatula.

I'm not great at choosing what to add to a lackluster soup and I have no idea what cheese to pair with anything. But show me a half-baked omelet and I will flip it with the ease of a born chef.

"You keep buttering; I'll flip," I tell him.

He smiles and it's honestly just as striking as watching the sun shine through the clouds.

"All right," he says. He puts more energy into swiping butter across the sliced bread. It's so yellow, the butter.

Before I met Sam, I kept sticks of cheap butter in the refrigerator and when I needed it for toast, I chopped it off in tiny chucks and futilely tried to spread the cold mess over the hot toast like a woman in a faded dramatization of an infomercial.

When Sam and I moved in together, he had this small little porcelain container that he put on the counter and when I opened it up, it looked like an upside-down cup of butter sitting in a puddle of water.

"What the hell is this?" I'd asked him as I was plugging in the toaster. Sam was putting glasses away in the cupboards, and when I said it, he laughed at me.

"It's a French butter dish," he said as he got off the step stool he'd been using and flattened the box the glasses had been in. "You keep the butter in the top part, put cold water in the bottom, and it keeps it chilled but spreadable." He said it as if everyone knew this, as if I was the crazy one.

"I have been all over France," I said to him, "and I have never seen one of these. Why is this butter so yellow? Is this some sort of fancy organic butter?"

"It's just butter," he said as he grabbed another box and started unloading its contents into the silverware drawer.

"This is not just butter!" I held the top cup part out to show him, as if he'd lost his mind. "Butter butter is pale yellow. This butter is yellow yellow."

"All I just heard was, 'Butter butter yellow butter yellow yellow.' "

I laughed.

"I think we're both saying the same thing," he said. "Butter is yellow."

"Admit there is something up with this butter," I said, pretending to interrogate him. "Admit it right now."

"It's not Land O'Lakes, if that's what you're asking."

I laughed at him. "Land O'Lakes! What are we, Bill and Melinda Gates? I buy store-brand butter. The name on my butter is exactly equal to the name of the store I bought it from."

Sam sighed, realizing he'd been caught. He confessed. "It's all-natural, organic, hormone-free, grass-fed butter."

"Wow," I said, acting as if this was a great shock. "You think you know a person . . ."

He took the butter from me and proudly put it on the counter, as if to say that it was officially a member of our home. "It *might* cost almost twice as much as regular butter. But once you try it, you will never be able to eat normal butter again. And *this* will become your normal butter."

After we had fully unpacked the kitchen, Sam opened the bread and took out two slices. He put them in the newly plugged-in toaster. When they were done, I watched how easy it was for him to spread butter on the slices. And then my eyes rolled back into my head when I took a bite.

"Wow," I said.

"See?" Sam had said. "I'm right about some stuff. Next, I'm going to convince you we should get a pet."

It was one of many moments in my life since Jesse left that I wasn't thinking about Jesse. I was very much in love with Sam. I loved the piano and I loved that butter. A few months later, we adopted our cats. Sam was changing my life for the better and I was curious to see what else he would teach me. I was reveling in how bright our future felt together.

Now, watching him place evenly buttered bread onto the pan in front of me, I desperately want to simply love him—unequivocally and without reservation—the way I did back then, the way I felt until I found out Jesse was coming home.

We were so happy together when there was nothing to muddy the waters, when the part of myself that loved Jesse was happily and naturally repressed, kept neatly contained in a box in my heart.

Sam moves the slices of bread around the sizzling pan and I propose something impossible.

"Do you think, maybe just for tonight, that we could put a pin in all of this? That we could pretend I had a normal day at the bookstore and you had a normal day teaching and everything could be the way it was before?"

I'm expecting Sam to tell me that life doesn't work like that, that what I'm proposing is naive or selfish or misguided. But he doesn't.

He just smiles and then he nods. It's a small nod. It's not an emphatic nod or a relieved nod. His nod isn't saying anything along the lines of "I thought you'd never ask," or even "Sure, that sounds good," but rather, "I can see why you'd want to try that. And I'll go along with it." Then he gathers himself and—in an instant—seems to be ready to pretend with me.

"All right, Emma Blair, get ready to flip," he says as he puts the top slices on the sandwiches.

"Ready and willing," I tell him. I have the spatula in position.

"Go!" he says.

And with two flicks of the wrist, I have flipped our dinner.

Sam turns the heat up on the soup to get it ready.

He grabs two bowls and two plates.

He grabs himself a beer from the fridge and offers me one. I take him up on it. The cool crispness of it sounds good, and for some reason, I have it in my head that having a beer helps to make this seem like just another night.

Soon, the two of us are sitting down to eat. Our dining room table has benches instead of chairs and that allows Sam to sit as close to me as physically possible, our thighs and arms touching.

"Thank you for making dinner," I say. I kiss him on the cheek, right by his ear. He has a freckle in that spot and I once told him I considered it a target. It is what I aim for. Normally when I kiss him there, he reciprocates by kissing me underneath my eye. Freckles for freckle. But this time he doesn't.

"Thank you for flipping," he says. "Nobody flips like you."

The sandwich is gooey in the center and crunchy on the outside. The soup is sweet with just a little bit of spice.

"I honestly don't know which I love more, this or your fried chicken," I say.

"You're being ridiculous. No tomato soup has ever been as good as any fried chicken."

"I don't know!" I tell him, dunking my sandwich. "This stuff is really outstanding. So cozy and comforting. And this grilled cheese is toasted to—"

Sam drops his spoon into his soup. It splashes onto the table. He drops his hands and looks at me.

"How am I supposed to pretend everything is OK right now?" Sam says. "I'd love to pretend things were different. I would love for things to *be* different but . . . they aren't."

I grab his hand.

"I can't talk about soup and cheese and . . ." He closes his eyes. "You're the love of my life, Emma. I've never loved anyone the way I love you."

"I know," I tell him.

"And it's OK if, you know, I'm not that for you. I mean, it's not. It's not at all OK. But I know that I have to be OK if that's what ends up being the truth. Does that make sense?"

I nod and start to speak but he keeps going.

"I just . . . I feel . . ." He closes his eyes again and then covers his face with his hands, the way people do when they are exhausted.

"Just say it," I tell him. "Whatever it is. Just let it out. Tell me."

"I feel naked. Like I'm raw. Or like I'm . . ." The way he's trying to find the words to describe how he feels makes him look like he wants to jump out of his skin. He's jittery and chaotic in his movements. And then he stops. "I feel like my entire body is an open wound and I'm standing next to someone that may or may not pour salt all over me."

I look at him, look into his eyes, and I know that whatever pain he's admitting to is a drop in the bucket compared to how he feels.

I'm not sure that emotional love can be separated from physical love. Or maybe I'm just a very tactile person. Either way, it's not enough for me to say, "I love you." The words feel so small compared to everything that's in me. I have to show him. I have to make sure that it's felt as much as heard.

I lean into him. I kiss him. I pull him close to me. I press my body against his and I let him run his hands up and down my back. I push the bench back slightly, to make room for me to fit, straddling his lap. And I rock, back and forth, ever so gently, as I hold him and whisper into his ear, "I need you."

Sam kisses me aggressively, like he's desperate for me.

We don't make it to the bed or to the couch. We clumsily move only as far as the kitchen floor. Our heads bang against the hardwood, our elbows bump against the low cupboards. My pants come off. His shirt comes off. My bra rests underneath the fridge, next to Sam's socks.

As Sam and I moan and gasp, we keep our eyes closed tightly except for the fleeting moments when we are looking directly into each other's eyes. And it is in these moments that I know he understands what I am trying to tell him.

Which is the whole point, our only reason for doing what we are doing.

We don't really care about pleasure. We are aching to be felt by the other, aching to feel each other. We move to tell each other what's in our souls, to say what words can't. We are touching each other in an attempt to listen.

Toward the end, I find myself pressing my heart into his, as if the problem is that we are two separate people, as if I could fuse us together and when I did, the pain would be gone.

When it's over, Sam collapses on top of me.

I hold him close, my arms and legs wrapped around him. He moves and I hold him tighter, my limbs asking him to stay.

I don't know how long we lie like that.

I swear I'm almost asleep when Sam knocks me back into reality by pulling himself off me and rolling onto the floor between me and the dishwasher.

I roll over onto his shoulder and put my head down, hoping that this reprieve from reality isn't over.

But I can tell that it is.

He puts his clothes back on.

"He's your husband," he says. His voice is quiet and stoic, as if it's all hitting him right now. I find that this happens a lot with shocking things; it seems to hit you all at once even though you could have sworn it hit you all at once an hour ago. "He is your *husband*, Emma."

"He *was*," I say, even though I'm not sure that's exactly true.

"It's semantics, really, isn't it?"

I grab my shirt and throw it over myself, but I don't respond. I don't have anything comforting to say. It *is* semantics. I think I'm heading into a time in my life where words and labels will lose their meaning. It will only be the intent behind them that will matter.

"I'm so miserable. I feel torn apart," he says. "But it's not about me, right? He's the one that spent three years lost at sea or wherever he was. And you're the one that lived as a widow. And I'm just the asshole."

"You're not an asshole."

"Yes, I am," Sam says. "I'm the asshole who's standing in the way of you two being reunited."

I am, again, at a loss for words. Because if you replace the word "asshole" with "man"—"I'm the *man* who's standing in the way of you two being reunited"—then, yeah. He's right.

If I hadn't run into Sam that day at the music store, if I hadn't fallen in love with him, this would have been the greatest time in my life.

Instead of the most confusing.

For a moment, I let myself think of what my life would be like right now if all of that had never happened, if I'd never allowed myself to move on.

I could have done it. I could have shut myself off to life and to love. I could have pinned Jesse's name to my heart and lived every day in honor of him, in remembrance of him. In some ways, that would have been a lot easier.

Instead of writing that letter telling him that I needed to let him go and find a new life, I could have spent my days waiting for him to return from a place I thought he could never come back from. I could have dreamt of the impossible.

And my dream would be coming true right now.

But I gave up on that dream and went out and found a new one.

And in doing so, I'm ruining all of us.

You can't be loyal to two people.

You can't yearn for two dreams.

So, in a lot of ways, Sam is right.

He is the wild card.

In this terrible-wonderful nightmare-dream come true.

"It's like I'm eighteen all over again," he says. "I love you and I have you and now I'm terrified I'm going to lose you to Jesse for the second time."

"Sam," I say. "You don't—"

"I know this isn't your fault," Sam says, interrupting me. His mouth turns down and his chin shakes. I hate watching him try not to cry. "You loved him and then you lost him and you loved me and now he's back and you didn't do anything wrong but . . . I'm so mad at you."

I look at him. I try not to cry.

"I'm so angry. Just at everything. At you and at him and at myself. The way I told you . . ." he says, shaking his head. He looks away. He tries to calm down. "I told you that I didn't need you to stop loving him. I told you that you could love us both. That I would never try to replace him. And I really thought that I meant what I said. But now, I mean, it's like the minute I find out he's back, everything's changed. I'm so mad at myself for saying those things back then because . . ." He stops talking. He rests his back against the dishwasher, his arms over his knees. "Because I think I was kidding myself," he says, looking at his hands as he picks at his nails.

"I think it was just this thing that I said because I knew it was theoretical. It wasn't real. I wanted to give you the comfort of knowing that I wasn't trying to replace him because I knew that I *was* replacing him. He wasn't a threat because he was gone and he was never coming back. And he was never going to be able to take you away from me. He couldn't give you what I could. So I said all of that stuff about how I didn't expect you to stop loving him and how we could both fit into your life. But I only meant it in theory. Because ever since I heard he was back, I haven't been happy for you. Or even really that happy for him. I've been heartsick. For me."

He looks at me, finally, when he says this. And between the look on his face and the way his voice breaks when the words escape from his mouth, I know that he hates himself for feeling the way he does.

"Shhh," I say to him, trying to calm him down, trying to hold him and comfort him. "I love you."

I wish I didn't say it so often. I wish that my love for Sam wasn't so casual and pervasive—so that I could save that phrase for moments like this. But that's not very realistic, is it? When you love someone, it seeps out of everything you do, it bleeds into everything you say, it becomes so ever-present, that eventually it becomes ordinary to hear, no matter how extraordinary it is to feel.

"I know you do," he says. "But I'm not the only one you love. And you can only have one. And it might not be me."

"Don't say that," I tell him. "I don't want to leave you. I couldn't do that. It's not fair to you. It's not right. With everything that we've been through and how much you've done for me, how you've stood by me, and how you've been there for me, I couldn't . . ." I stop talking when I see that Sam is already shaking his head at me as if I don't get it. "What?" I ask him.

"I don't want your pity and I don't want your loyalty. I want you to be with me because you want to be with me."

"I do want to be with you."

"You know what I mean."

My gaze falls off of his eyes, down to his hands, and I watch him fiddle with the beds of his nails—his own version of wringing his hands.

"I think we should call off the wedding," he says.

"Sam . . ."

"I've thought about it a lot for the past few days and I thought, for sure, you were going to pull the trigger. But you haven't. So I'm doing it."

"Sam, c'mon."

He looks up at me, with just a little hint of anger. "Are you ready to commit to me?" Sam says. "Can you honestly say that no matter what happens from this moment on, we are ready to spend our lives together?"

I can't bear to see the look in his eyes when I shake my head. So I look away as I do it. Like every coward in the history of the world.

"I have to let you go," Sam says. "If we have any chance of surviving this and one day having a healthy, loving marriage."

I look up at him when I realize what's happening.

He's leaving me. At least for now. Sam is leaving me.

"I have to let you go and I have to hope that you come back to me."

"But how can—"

"I love you," he says. "I love you so much. I love waking up with you on Sunday mornings when we don't have any plans. And I love coming home to you at night, seeing you reading a book, bundled up in a sweater and huge socks even though you have the heat up to eighty-eight degrees. I want that for the rest of my life. I want you to be my wife. That's what I want."

I want to tell him that I want that, too. Ever since I met him I've wanted that, too. But now everything is different, everything has changed. And I'm not sure what I want at all.

"But I don't want you to share those things with me because you have to, because you feel it's right to honor a promise we made months ago. I want us to share all of that together because it's what makes you happy, because you wake up every day glad that you're with me, because you have the freedom to choose the life you want, and you choose our life together. That's what I want. If I don't give you the chance to leave right now, then I don't know," he says, shrugging. "I just don't think I'll ever feel comfortable again."

"What are we saying here?" I ask him. "What exactly are you suggesting?"

"I'm saying that I'm calling off the wedding. For now, at least. And I think one of us should stay somewhere else."

"Sam . . ."

"Then you'll be free. To see if you love him the way you love me, to see what's left between you. You should be free to do that. And you can't do that if I'm with you or if I'm pleading for you to stay. Which I don't trust myself not to do. If I'm with you, I will try to get you to choose me. I know that I will. And I don't want to do that. So . . . go. Figure out what you want. I'm telling you it's OK."

My instinct is to grab on to him tightly, to never let go, to put my hand over his mouth in order to stop him from saying all of this.

But I know that even if I can stop the words from coming out of his mouth, that won't make them any less true.

So I grab Sam by the neck and pull his head close to mine. I am, not for the first time, deeply grateful to be loved by him, to be loved the way he loves.

"I don't deserve you," I say. Our foreheads are pushed so close together neither of us can see the other. I am looking down at his knees. "How can you be so selfless? So *good*?"

Sam shakes his head slowly, without peeling away from me. "It's not selfless," he says. "I don't want to be with a woman who wants to be with someone else."

Sam cracks his knuckles, and when I hear the sound of it, I notice that my own hands feel tight and cramped. I open and close them, trying to stretch out my fingers.

"I want to be with someone who lives for me. I want to be with someone who considers me the love of her life. I deserve that."

I get it. I get it now. Sam is pulling his heart out of his chest and handing it to me, saying, "If you're going to break it, break it now."

I want to tell him that I'll never break his heart, that there is nothing to worry about.

But that's not true, is it?

I pull away from him.

"I should be the one to go," I say. I say it just as I can't believe I'm saying it. "It's not fair to make you leave. I can stay with my parents for a while."

This is where everything starts to shift. This is where it feels like the room is getting darker and the world is getting scarier, even though nothing outside of our hearts has changed.

Sam considers and then nods, agreeing with me.

And just like that, we have transitioned from two people considering something to two people having made a decision.

"I guess I'll pack up some stuff," I say.

"OK," he says.

I don't move for a moment, still stunned that it's happening. But then I realize that staying still doesn't actually pause time, it's still passing, life is still happening. You have to keep moving.

I stand up and head to my closet to gather my clothes. I make it to our bedroom before I start crying.

I should be thinking of outfits to pack, things to wear to work. I should be calling my parents to tell them I'm going to be sleeping at their house. But instead, I just start throwing things into a duffel bag, with little attention paid to whether the clothes match or what I might need.

The only thing I take on purpose is the envelope I have of keepsakes from Jesse. I don't want Sam to look through them. I don't want him hurting himself by reading love letters I once wrote to the boy I chose all those years ago.

I walk back into the kitchen, saying good-bye to Mozart and Homer on the way.

Sam is in the exact same position I left him.

He stands up to say good-bye to me.

I can't help but kiss him. I'm relieved that he lets me.

As we stand there, still close to each other, Sam finally allows himself to lose his composure. When he cries, his eyes bloom and the tears fall down his cheeks so slowly that I can catch every one before they reach his chin.

It breaks my heart to be loved like this, to be loved so purely that I'm capable of breaking a heart.

It is not something I take lightly. In fact, I think it might be the most important thing in the world.

"What am I gonna do?" I ask him.

I mean, what am I going to do *right now*? And, what am I going to do *without him*? And, what am I going to do *with my life*? And, *how* am I going to do this?

"You'll do whatever you want," he says, brushing the side of his knuckle under his eye and taking a step back from me. "That's what it means to be free."

By the time I pull into my parents' driveway, it's almost two a.m. Their front light is on, as if they've been waiting for me, but I know that they leave it on every night. My father thinks it wards off burglars.

I don't want to wake them up. So I'm planning on tiptoeing into the house and saying hello in the morning.

I turn the car off and grab my things. I realize as I step out onto the driveway that I didn't bring any shoes other than the boots on my feet. I guess I'll be wearing these indefinitely. I remind myself that "indefinitely" doesn't mean forever.

I slowly shut the car door, not so much closing it as tucking it gently into place. I sneak around to the rear of the house, onto the back deck. My parents never lock the back door and I know that it doesn't squeak like the front door does.

There is a small click as I turn the knob and a swish as I move the door out of my way. Then I'm in.

Home.

Free.

I walk over to the breakfast table and grab a pen and a piece of paper. I leave my parents a note telling them that I am here. When I'm done, I take off my boots so they don't clang against the hard kitchen floor. I leave them by the back door.

I tiptoe across the kitchen and dining room, down the hall.

I stand outside my bedroom door and slowly, gently turn the knob.

I don't dare turn on the light in my bedroom. I've made it this far and I'm not going to throw it all away now.

I sit down on the bottom edge of the bed and take off my pants and shirt. I feel around in my bag for something to wear as pajamas. I grab a shirt and a pair of shorts and put them on.

I pad over to the bathroom that my room has always shared with Marie's. I feel around for the faucet and turn the water on to a trickle. As I brush my teeth, I start to question whether I should have just woken up my parents by calling or ringing the front door. But by the time I'm running water over my face, I realize that I didn't want to wake them because I don't want to talk about any of this. Sneaking in was my only option. If your daughter shows up at two in the morning the night that her long-lost husband comes home, you're going to want to *talk about it*.

I walk back to my bedroom, ready to fall asleep. But as soon as I go to turn the blankets down, I hit my head against the overhanging lamp on the nightstand.

"Ow!" I say instinctually, and then I roll my eyes at myself. I know that goddamn lamp is there. I worry for a moment that I've blown my cover, but it remains quiet in the house.

I rub my head and slip into the covers, avoiding the lamp the way I now remember you have to.

I look out the window and I can see a few windows of Marie's house down the street. All of the lights in her house are off and I imagine that she, Mike, Sophie, and Ava are sound asleep.

I'm shaken out of it by blinding light and the sight of my father in his underwear with a baseball bat.

"Oh, my God!" I scream, scrambling to the farther corners of the bed, as far away from him as possible.

"Oh," my dad says, slowly putting down the bat. "It's just you."

"Of course it's just me!" I say to him. "What were you going to do with that?"

"I was going to beat the ever-living crap out of the thief who had broken into my home! That's what I was going to do!"

My mother comes rushing in in plaid pajama bottoms and a T-shirt that says, "Read a Mother F&#king Book." There is no way that that shirt is not a gift from my father that my mother refuses to wear out of the house.

"Emma, what are you doing here?" she says. "You scared us half to death."

"I left a note on the kitchen table!"

"Oh," my dad says, falsely assuaged, and looking at my mother. "Never mind, Ash; looks like this is our fault."

I give him a sarcastic look that I swear I haven't given since I was seventeen.

"Emma, our apologies. The next time we fear we are being attacked in the night, we will first check the kitchen table for a note."

I'm about to apologize, realizing the full extent of the absurdity of breaking into my parents' house and then blaming them for their surprise. But my mom steps in first.

"Honey, are you OK? Why aren't you with Sam?" I swear, and maybe I'm just being sensitive, but I swear there's a small pause in between "with" and "Sam" because she is unsure whom I'm supposed to be with.

I breathe in, allowing all of the formerly tensed muscles in my shoulders and back to relax. "We might not be getting married. I think I have a date with Jesse tomorrow. I don't know. I honestly . . . I don't know."

My dad puts the bat down. My mom pushes past him to sit down on the bed next to me. I move toward her, resting my head on her shoulder. She rubs my back. Why does it feel better when your parents hold you? I'm thirty-one years old.

"I should put on pants, shouldn't I?" my father asks.

My mother and I look up, as one unit, and nod to him.

He's gone in a flash.

"Tell me everything about how today went," she says. "All the parts you need to get off your chest."

As I do, my father comes back into the room, in sweats, and sits on the other side of me. He grabs my hand.

They listen.

At the end of it, when I've said everything that's left in me, when I get out every piece I have, my mom says, "If you want my two cents, you have the unique ability to love with your whole heart even after it's been broken. That's a good thing. Don't feel guilty about that."

"You're a fighter," my dad says. "You get back up after you've been knocked down. That is my favorite part about you."

I laugh and say, in a jovial tone, "Not that I run the bookstore?"

I'm joking but *I'm not joking.*

"Not even close. There are so many things to love about you that, honestly, that's not even in the top ten."

I put my head on his shoulder and rest there for a moment. I watch my mom's eyes droop. I hear my dad's breathing slow down.

"OK, go back to bed," I tell them. "I'll be OK. Thank you. Sorry again about scaring you."

They each give me a hug and then go.

I lie on my old mattress and I try to fall asleep, but I was a fool to ever think that sleep would come.

Just before six a.m., I see a light come on in Marie's house.

I take off my engagement ring and put it in my purse. And then I throw on some pants, grab my boots, and walk right out the front door.

Marie is with Ava in the bathroom with the door open. Ava is sitting on the toilet and Marie is coaxing her to relax. The twins are potty trained, but as of a few weeks ago, Ava has started backsliding. She will only go if Marie is with her. I have decided to hang back and stand by the door, as is my right as an aunt.

"You can go ahead and take a seat," Marie says to me as she sits down on the slate gray tile of the bathroom floor. "We're gonna be here a while."

The girls' cochlear implants mean that they have learned to talk only a few months behind other children. And Marie and Mike both use sign language to communicate with them, too. My nieces, whom we were all so worried about, may just end up speaking two languages. And that is in large part because Marie is a phenomenal, attentive, unstoppable motherly force.

At this point, she knows more about American Sign Language, the Deaf community, hearing aids, cochlear implants, and the inner working of the ear than possibly anything else, including all of the things she used to love, things like literature, poetry, and figuring out what authors use what pseudonyms.

But she's also exhausted. It's six thirty in the morning and she's both talking and signing to her daughter to please "go pee in the potty for Mommy."

The bags under her eyes look like the pocket on a kangaroo.

When Ava is finally done, Marie brings her to Mike, who is lying in bed with Sophie. As I'm standing in the hallway, I get a glimpse of Mike under the covers, half asleep, holding Sophie's hand. For a moment, I get a flash of what sort of man I'd want to be the father of my own children and I'm embarrassed to say that the figure is only vague and blurry.

Marie comes back out of the bedroom and we head toward the kitchen.

"Tea?" she says as I sit down at her island.

I'm not much of a tea drinker, but it's cold in here and something warm sounds nice. I'd ask for coffee, but I know that Marie doesn't keep coffee in the house. "Sure, that sounds great," I say.

Marie smiles and nods. She starts the kettle. Marie's kitchen island is bigger than my dining room table. Our dining room table. Mine and Sam's.

I am, instantaneously, overcome with certainty.

I don't want to leave Sam. I don't want to lose the life I've built. Not again. I love Sam. I love him. I don't want to leave him. I want to sit down together at the piano and play "Chopsticks."

That's what I want to do.

Then I remember that way Jesse looked when he got off that plane. All of my certainty disappears.

"Ugh," I say, slouching my body forward, resting my head in the nest I've made with my arms. "Marie, what am I going to do?"

She doesn't stop pulling various teas out of the cupboard. She pulls them all out and puts them in front of me.

"I don't know," she says. "I can't imagine being in your shoes. I feel like maybe both options are equally right *and* wrong.

That's probably not the answer you were looking for. But I just don't know."

"I don't know, either."

"Does it help to ask what your gut tells you?" she says. "Like, if you close your eyes, what do you see? Your life with Sam? Or your life with Jesse?"

I indulge her game, hoping that something as simple as closing my eyes might tell me what I want to do. But it doesn't. Of course it doesn't. I open my eyes to see Marie watching me. "That didn't work."

The kettle starts to whistle and Marie turns toward the stove to grab it. "You know, all you can do is just put one foot in front of the other," she says. "This is exactly the sort of thing people are talking about when they say you have to take things one step at a time." She pours hot water into the white mug she's set out for me. I look up at her.

"Earl Grey?" she asks.

"English Breakfast?" I ask in return and then I start laughing and say, "I'm just messing with you. I have no idea what tea names mean."

She laughs and picks up an English Breakfast packet, tearing off the top and pulling out a tea bag. "Here, now you'll know what English Breakfast tastes like for next time." She puts it in my mug and hands it to me. "Splenda?" she offers.

I shake my head. I stopped drinking artificial sweeteners six months ago and I feel entirely the same but I'm still convinced it's for a good cause. "I'm off the sauce," I say.

Marie rolls her eyes and puts two packets in her tea.

I laugh and look down toward my cup. I watch as the tea begins to bleed out of the bag into the water. I watch as it swirls, slowly. I can already smell the earthiness of it. I put my hands on the hot mug, letting it warm them up. I start absent-mindedly fiddling with the string.

"Do you think you can love two people at the same time?" I ask her. "That's what I keep wondering. I feel like I love them both. Differently and equally. Is that possible? Am I kidding myself?"

She dips her tea bag in and out of the water. "I'm honestly not sure," she says. "But the problem isn't who you love or if you love both, I don't think. I think the problem is that you aren't sure who you are. You're a different person now than you were before you lost Jesse. It changed you, fundamentally."

Marie thinks, staring down at the counter, and then tentatively starts talking again. "I don't think you're trying to figure out if you love Sam more or Jesse more. I think you're trying to figure out if you want to be the person you are with Jesse or you want to be the person you are with Sam."

It's like someone cracked me in half and found the rotten cancer in the deepest, most hidden part of my body. I don't say anything back. I don't look up. I watch as a tear falls from my face and lands right in my mug. And even though I was the one who cried it out, and I saw it fall, I have no idea what it means.

I look up.

"I think you're probably right," I say.

Marie nods and then looks directly at me. "I'm sorry," she says. "It's important to me that you know that. That you know I regret what I did."

"Regret what? What are you talking about?"

"For that day on the roof. The day that I found you looking out . . ." It feels like yesterday and one hundred years ago all at once: the binoculars, the roof, the grave anxiety of believing I could save him just by watching the shore. "I'm sorry for convincing you Jesse was dead," Marie says. "You knew he wasn't . . ."

Marie isn't much of a crier. She isn't one to show how she feels on her face. It's her voice that tells me just how deep her remorse is, the way some of the syllables bubble up and burst.

"I was the wrong person to be up there that day. I hadn't supported you, at all, really, in any of the years prior. And suddenly, I was the one telling you the worst had happened? I just . . . I thought he was gone. And I thought that I was doing you a kindness by making you face reality." She shakes her head as if disappointed in her old self. "But instead, what I did was take away your hope. Hope that you had every reason to hold on to. And I . . . I'm just very sorry. I'm deeply sorry. You have no idea how much I regret taking that away from you."

"No," I say. "That's not what happened. Not at all. I was crazy up on that roof. I'd gone absolutely crazy, Marie. It was irrational to think that he was alive, let alone that I could save him, that I could spot him up there, looking at that tiny piece of the shore. That was madness.

"Anyone thinking clearly would have made the assumption that he was dead. I needed to understand that the rational conclusion was that he was gone. You helped me understand that. You kept me sane."

For the first time, I find myself wondering if facing the truth and being sane aren't the same thing, if they are just two things that tend to go together. I'm starting to understand that they might be correlational rather than synonyms.

And then I realize that if I don't blame Marie for thinking he was dead—if I don't see her belief that he died as a sign she gave up on him—then I shouldn't be blaming myself for doing the same thing.

"Please don't give it another thought," I say to her. "What you did on the roof that day . . . you saved me."

Marie looks down at her tea and then nods. "Thank you for saying that."

"Thank you for what you did. And I'm glad it was you. I don't know if you and I would be as close . . . I mean, I think we would have just gone on . . ."

"I know what you mean," Marie said. "I know."

After all of our shared experiences and our parents' cajoling, it has been our hardships that have softened us to each other. Losing my husband and the challenges of raising Marie's twins are the things that have brought us together.

"I'm just glad that things between us are the way they are now," Marie says. "I'm very, very glad."

"Me, too," I say.

Instinctively, I grab Marie's hand and hold it for a moment and then we break away.

It is hard to be so honest, so vulnerable, so exposed. But I find that it always leads you someplace freer. I feel the smallest shift between my sister and me, something almost imperceptible but nevertheless real. We are closer now than we were just three minutes ago.

"I've been thinking about writing again," Marie says, changing the subject.

"Oh yeah?" I ask. "Writing what?"

She shrugs. "That's the part I'm not sure about. I just need to do something, you know? Anything that is not revolving around my kids. I need to get back to me, a little bit. Anyway, it might be a dumb idea because I say that I want to start writing again but I can't find anything I want to write *about*. I'm not inspired. I'm just . . . well, bored."

"You'll find something," I say. "And when you do, it will be great. Just don't make it a murder mystery where you pin the murders on a character that is clearly supposed to be me, like you did back then," I say, teasing.

She laughs, shaking her head at me. "No one ever believed me that it wasn't supposed to be you," she says.

"You named her Emily."

"It's a common name," Marie says, pretending to defend herself. "But, yeah, OK. I'm mature enough now to admit that might not have come from a totally innocent place."

"Thank you," I say magnanimously.

"I was just so annoyed that you were always copying me."

"What?" I say. "I was never copying you. I was basically the opposite of you."

Marie shakes her head. "Sorry, but no. Remember when I got really into TLC? And suddenly, you started telling everyone you loved 'Waterfalls'? Or when I had a crush on Keanu Reeves? And then suddenly, you had his picture up over your bed?"

"Oh, my God," I say, realizing she's totally right.

"And then, of course, you went and started dating the captain of the swim team. Just like me."

"Whoa," I say. "That honestly never occurred to me. But you're totally right. You and Graham. And then me and Jesse."

Marie smiles, half laughing at me. "See?"

"I must have really wanted to be like you," I say. "Because I thought Graham was so lame. And then I went and *also dated the captain of the swim team*."

Marie lifts her tea to her mouth, smiling. "So, I think we can agree that on some level, you've always wanted to be me."

I laugh. "You know what? If being you means having just the one man in your life, I'll take it."

"Boohoo," she says. "Two men love you."

"Oh, shut up," I say as I find a dish towel and throw it at her.

Our laughter is interrupted by Mike coming down the stairs with Sophie behind him and Ava on his hip.

"Breakfast!" he says to the girls, and I see Marie reanimate, opening up the refrigerator, ready for the day.

I know when to excuse myself.

"I'm around if you need anything today," Marie says as I gather my things. "Seriously. Just call. Or stop by. I'm here for you."

"OK," I say. "Thank you."

She gives me a hug and then picks up Sophie into her arms. I head out the door.

On the way back to my parents', my phone dings. I'm not sure who I thought would be contacting me but I definitely wasn't expecting a text message from Francine.

So excited to see you again that I didn't sleep all night. This is Jesse, btw. Not my mom. Pretty weird if my mom couldn't wait to see you.

When I'm done reading it, I notice that my feet walk faster toward the door to my parents' house.

I rush my warm shower. I rush the shampoo through my hair, rush the soap over my body.

I rush putting on clothes and getting out the door.

I rush all of it, every second. There is a kick in my step and a smile on my face.

I am happy. In this brief moment of time. I am happy.

When I pull my car into the parking lot of Julie's Place a little before seven thirty, Jesse is standing right in front. He's even earlier than I am.

He looks just like he used to, even if he does look totally different.

I open my car door, step out into the cold, and I realize just why this morning feels a little bit better than the others recently.

It's finally OK to love him.

It's OK to love Jesse.

I have been given the freedom to do that.

Sam did that for me.

What else did you miss?" I ask Jesse as the waitress brings us our breakfasts. He's been listing everything he missed about home.

I was number one.

The sweet-and-sour chicken at the tacky Chinese restaurant in the middle of town was number two.

"I mean, there are so many people and places, but right now, honestly, all I can think about is the food."

I laugh. "So tell me, then; tell me all the food."

"All right," he says, looking down at his plate. He has barely touched his meal and I can't blame him. I can't focus on actually eating right now, either. My stomach is in knots, flooded with butterflies, twisting and turning to try to keep up with the flutter in my heart.

"Oh, God. There are just too many to name. How can I choose? I mean, there's the pizza at Sorrentos, the Snickers sundae from Friendly's, the sandwiches at Savory Lane . . ."

"Savory Lane closed," I tell him. "Actually, Friendly's did, too."

He looks at me, focused on my eyes, trying to figure out if I'm messing with him. When he sees that I'm serious, a flash of sorrow wipes across his face. He quickly replaces it with a smile, but I wonder if maybe it's all the evidence he needs that the world went on without him, that we couldn't even keep Savory Lane going as a courtesy.

"Friendly's is now a Johnny Rockets," I tell him. "It's good, though. Plus, you know, once Kimball's opens in the spring, you're not going to be thinking about a Snickers sundae. You're gonna be thinking about two scoops of black raspberry ice cream in a waffle cone."

Jesse smiles and then looks away from me, shifting his body toward the counter and away from our table, repositioning his legs. "What about Erickson's? Is that still open? Or have they forsaken me, too?"

The way he says it, the word "forsaken," and the fact that he doesn't look at me, it all adds up to make me think Jesse's angrier than he's letting on. That he does resent me for moving on. He says he understands, but maybe he doesn't really understand at all.

"They are still open, yeah," I say, nodding, trying to please him. "Most stuff is still open. Most stuff is still the same."

"Most stuff," he says, and then he changes his tone. "And Blair Books? Is Blair Books the same? I mean, clearly there's new management."

"Yeah," I say, smiling, proud of myself. "Although I've kept it mostly the same. And my parents are still involved a bit. It's not like I've gone rogue. I do things pretty much the way they did them."

"Do you even put out those little 'Travel the World by Reading a Book' bookmarks?"

"Yes!" I say. "Of course I do."

"What? No way!"

"Yeah, totally."

I have pushed the food around my plate. He's pushed his around his. Neither one of us has taken so much as a bite. When the waitress comes over, she frowns.

"Looks like you aren't very hungry," she says as she pours more water in my glass.

"It's delicious," I say. "But we're just . . ."

"We have a lot of catching up to do," Jesse says. "Can we get it to go?"

"Sure thing, sweetheart," she says, taking both of our plates with her.

When she leaves, we have no food to play with and nothing to look at but each other.

"You used to hate those bookmarks," Jesse says.

"I know," I say. I find myself embarrassed about how much I've changed. I am tempted to lie, to rewind, to remember exactly who I was before he left and try to be that version of myself again.

The Emma he knew wanted a different life. She wanted adventure. She ached with wanderlust. She used to think you couldn't find joy in simple things, that they had to be big and bold and wild. That you couldn't feel amazed at how good it feels to wake up in a nice bed, that you could only feel amazed by petting elephants and visiting the Louvre.

But I don't know if I was totally that person when he left.

And I'm definitely not that person now.

The future is so hard to predict. If I had a time machine, would it even make a difference to try to go back there and explain to my young self what was ahead?

"I guess I did say that," I tell him. "But I like them now."

"You never cease to surprise," Jesse says, smiling. Maybe it's OK with him if I'm not exactly the way I was when he left.

The waitress comes back with our meals in boxes and the check. Jesse hands her cash before I can grab my wallet.

"Thank you," I say. "That was very nice of you."

"It's my pleasure."

I check my phone and see that it's eight fifty. The time has flown by so quickly.

"I have to head to work," I tell him. "I'm running late as is."

"No . . ." he says. "C'mon. Stay with me."

"I can't," I say, smiling at him. "I have a store to open."

Jesse walks me to my car and pulls a set of keys out of his pocket, unlocking, from afar, a gray sedan a few spaces down.

"Wait a minute," I say to Jesse, as something is occurring to me. "You don't have a license. You can't be driving."

Jesse laughs. "I had a license before I left," he says. "I'm approved to drive a car."

"Yeah," I say, opening my door. "But didn't it expire?"

Jesse smiles mischievously and it slays me. "Expired, schmexpired. It's harmless."

"You just always have to push things, don't you?" I say, teasing him. "Why do you think that is?"

"I don't know," he says, shrugging. "But you can admit you find it charming."

I laugh. "Who said I find it charming?"

"Will you get in the car with me?" he says.

"In your car?"

"Or yours," he says.

"I have to go to work."

"I know. I'm not asking you to go anywhere with me. I just want to be in the car with you. It's cold outside."

I should tell him good-bye. I'm already running later than I want to be.

"OK," I say. I click both doors open and watch as Jesse sits in my passenger seat. I sit in the driver's seat next to him. When

I shut my car door, the outside world mutes, as if we can keep it at bay.

I watch as his eye line settles on my now-bare ring finger. He smiles. We both know what the empty space on my left hand means. But I get the impression there is a strange code of silence between us, indicative of the two things we don't talk about. We won't talk about what happened to my finger, just like we don't talk about what happened to his.

"I missed you, Emma. I missed us. I missed your stupid eyes and your awful lips and that super-annoying thing you do when you look at me like I'm the only person that's ever mattered in the history of the world. I missed your very un-adorable freckles."

I laugh and I can feel myself blushing. "I missed you, too."

"You did?" he says, as if this is news, as if he wasn't sure.

"Wait, are you kidding?"

"I don't know," he says. His voice is teasing. "It's hard to know what happened while I was gone."

"I was more heartbroken than I've ever been or I think I will ever be again."

He looks at me, and then out the windshield, and then out the window on the other side of him.

"We have so much to talk about and I don't even know where to start," he says.

"I know, but even if we did know where to start, I can't now. I have to go to work. I should have been there fifteen minutes ago." Tina won't be in until the afternoon. If I'm not there, the store doesn't open.

"Emma," he says, looking at me like I'm a fool. "You're not going to be at work on time, that's clear. So what's a few more minutes? What's an hour more?"

I look at him and find myself considering it. And then I feel his lips on mine. They are just as bold and surprising as they were almost fifteen years ago, kissing me for the first time.

I close my eyes and reach for him. I kiss him again. And again and again and again. I am soothed and invigorated all at once. Never before has something felt so exciting and yet so familiar.

I lose myself in him, in the way he feels, the way he smells, the way he moves.

Can you ever put things back the way they were? Can you chalk the intervening years up as a mistake and pick up as if you never left each other?

I feel Jesse's hand slide down my arm and then I hear myself accidentally hit the horn with my elbow.

I snap out of it. I pull myself away from him and look forward, out the windshield. Two of the servers at Julie's Place, including the woman who waited on us, are staring at us through the window. When they see that I see them, they start to turn away.

I look down at my phone. It's almost a quarter of ten. The store is supposed to be open in less than twenty minutes.

"I have to go!" I say, shocked that I could be running this late.

"OK, OK," Jesse says, but he doesn't move.

"Get out of my car," I say, laughing.

"OK," he says, putting his hand on the door handle. "There's just one thing I wanted to talk to you about."

"Jesse! I have to go!"

"Come to Maine with me," he says as he gets out of the car.

"What?"

"Come to my family's cabin in Maine with me for a few days. We can leave tonight. Just the two of us."

"I have a store to run."

"Your parents can manage it. For a little while. It's their store."

"It's my store," I say.

"Emma, we need time. And not stolen moments before you go to work. Real time. Please."

I look at him, considering.

He knows I'm considering it. Which is why he already starts smiling. "Is that a yes?" he says.

I know my parents will step in and I'm late and I don't have time for this.

"OK, a couple of days."

"Three," he says. "Three days."

"OK," I tell him. "Three."

"We'll leave tonight?"

"Sure. Now I have to go!"

Jesse smiles at me and then shuts the door behind him so I can finally leave. He waves at me through the window. I find myself grinning as I drive away from him, leaving him there in the parking lot.

I make my way to the road and wait for a clear opening to take a left. I watch as Jesse gestures for me to roll down my window from the other side of the lot. I roll my eyes but I do it.

He cups his hands over his mouth and yells, "I'm sorry I made you late! I love you!"

I have no choice but to scream, "I love you, too!"

I bang a left onto the main road and fly through town. I get to the parking lot of Blair Books at ten eleven and I can already see there is a customer waiting at the door.

I jump out of the car, open the back door, and run through the store turning on all the lights.

I gather myself and calmly walk to the front door and unlock it.

"Hi," I say to the woman waiting.

"Your store says that you're open from ten to seven. It's ten fifteen."

"My apologies," I say.

But when the woman heads right to the bestseller section and is no longer in my line of sight, I can't stop a smile from erupting, pulling my cheeks as wide as my ears.

Jesse.

My dad comes into the store around eleven. He is here to grab some books that he ordered for my mom, but I pull him aside to discuss the idea of my leaving for Maine.

"What do you mean you're going to Maine with Jesse?"

"Uh . . ." I say, unsure which part my dad is confused about. "I think I mean that I am going to Maine with Jesse?"

"Are you sure this is a good idea?"

"Why wouldn't it be?"

That is such a stupid thing to say. There are about twenty thousand reasons why it might not be.

"Emma, I just . . ." He stops there and doesn't finish his sentence. I see him rethink his entire train of thought. "I read you loud and clear. Of course Mom and I can cover. We'd love to, actually. I'm bored stiff at home now that I have finished watching all five seasons of *Friday Night Lights*."

"Great!" I say. "Thank you."

"Certainly," he says. "My pleasure. Will we see you tonight, then? To get your things?"

"Yeah," I say, nodding. "I'll come by to get some clothes and stuff."

"OK, great," he says.

And then he heads out. "Mom's making BLTs for lunch and you know I can't miss that."

"I know," I say.

My mom makes him BLTs multiple times a week and he loves them so much you'd think he would learn to make them himself. He's tried, a number of times. I've tried for him and Marie's tried for him. He swears it tastes different when she makes them. Something about the bacon being hot and the lettuce being sweet. I honestly have no idea. All I know is that my parents have always made love seem easy and sometimes I wish they'd prepared me for how truly complicated it can be.

Later on in the afternoon, as I'm picking up a very late lunch, I get a text message from Sam.

You forgot your allergy meds and phone charger. I left them on your desk.

The first thing I think when I see the message isn't how sweet he is or that I'm glad to be able to charge my phone. My first thought is that there's a chance he's still at the store. So I rush to my car, sandwich in hand, hoping that I can get back to the parking lot before he leaves.

I hit absolutely no red lights and I turn right into the parking lot just as Sam is in his car with his blinker ready to turn left. I wave him down.

I don't know what I'm doing, what good I think will come of this. I just know that there is nothing like thinking that you might lose your fiancé to make you realize how much you ache to see your fiancé. That remains true even if you think it's you who might be leaving, you who might be messing it all up.

Sam backs up and rolls down his window. I park my car and walk over to him.

"Hi," I say.

"Hi."

He is wearing his black wool coat with a white oxford button-down and a navy chambray tie. I bought him that tie.

He liked the tiny anchors printed on it and I said I wanted to treat him to something he'd get excited to wear at work.

"Thank you for my meds," I say. "And the charger. That was really nice of you."

Sam nods. "Yeah, well . . ."

I wait for him to finish and then realize that he's not going to.

"How are you?" I ask.

"Been better," he responds. He looks sad but also distant. It feels as if the two of us can't reach each other. I find myself moving physically closer to him, trying to connect. "I will be fine. It's just weird sleeping in our bed alone," he says. "I miss you."

"I miss you, too," I say, and then—I don't know what possesses me—before I know it, I have bent down and kissed him. He kisses me back but then pulls away. I wonder if it's because he can tell I've kissed someone else.

"Sorry," I say. "Force of habit."

"It's OK," he says.

"How were the cats this morning?" I ask. I love talking to Sam about our cats. I love inventing silly names for them and making up stories about what they do when we're not around.

"Homer slept in the bathtub," Sam says.

Before I had a cat, before I loved those two little furballs, I would have thought someone saying, "Homer slept in the bathtub," was boring enough to put me to sleep. But now it's as fascinating as if you'd told me he'd landed on Mars.

"He wasn't under the piano?"

Sam shakes his head. "Nope, he won't leave the bathroom. When I tried to take a shower this morning, I had to pick him up and lock him out of the room."

I should be back in that house. I should be with Sam and

Mozart and Homer. I don't know why Homer's in the bathtub or what it means. But I know it wouldn't happen if I was there.

Good Lord.

There is so much guilt lying around here, just waiting for me to pick it up and carry it with me. There is so much I can torture myself about.

Maybe I deserve to.

But I resolve, right now, to leave it waiting. I'm not taking it on. Even if I should. It does no one any good, least of all me, to have it clawing at my back.

"I love you," I tell him. It just slips out. I don't know what I mean by it. I just know that it's true.

"I know," he says. "I have never once doubted that."

We are quiet for a moment and I fear that he might leave. "Will you play 'Piano Man'?" I ask him.

"What?" he says.

"Will you play 'Piano Man'? On the steering wheel? And I can do the harmonica?"

I always ask him to do it when I want to fall a little bit more in love with him. I like remembering the first time he did it. I love watching how skilled he truly is. Now, it's become so familiar that I can hear the notes when he plays it, even though he's always playing in silence.

But instead of pushing up his sleeves and positioning his fingers like he has always done in the past, he shakes his head. "I'm not gonna do that."

"You always do it."

"I'm not going to perform for you," he says. "I hope you change your mind and realize that you love me and that we should be together for the rest of our lives, but . . . I'm not going to audition for the part."

It's one thing to break a heart. It's an entirely different thing to break someone's pride.

And I think I have done both to him.

"You're right," I say. "I'm sorry."

"Listen, you've been through something I can't even imagine. I know it's shaken you to your core. I love you enough to wait for a little while until you figure it out."

I grab his hand and squeeze it—as though if I could just squeeze enough, hold it the right way, the gratitude I feel in my heart might run through my arms, out my hands, and straight into his soul. But it doesn't work that way. I know it doesn't.

"Thank you," I say. "I don't know how to thank you. But thank you."

Sam takes his hand away. "But you can't have both of us," he continues. "I can't pretend things are OK until they're actually OK. OK?"

"OK," I say, nodding my head.

He smiles. "That was a lot of 'OKs' at one time, huh?"

I laugh.

"I'm gonna go," Sam says, putting his car in drive. "Otherwise, I'll be late for rehearsal. And then, you know, I suppose I'll just go home, eat some dinner, and watch ESPN Classic. A rousing good time."

"Sounds like quite a night," I say.

"I'm sure you've got big plans, too," he says, and then I watch as his face freezes. It's clear he wasn't thinking when he spoke. He doesn't want to know what I'm doing tonight. But now that he's said it, I can't get out of this without in some way acknowledging whether I do have plans. "I just meant . . . uh, you know what? Just don't say anything."

"Yeah, OK," I say. "Not saying anything."

But not saying anything is saying something, isn't it? Because if there truly was nothing for him to worry about, I would have just said, "No, Sam, seriously, don't worry."

I didn't say that. And we both know it.

Sam looks at me. And I can tell that he has reached his limit. He cannot do this anymore. "Bye, Emma," he says, starting to turn the wheel. He stops himself and starts talking again. "You know what? I'm going to keep the ball in my court."

"What do you mean?" I ask.

"I'll call you when I'm ready. But . . . don't call me. I know it probably makes the most sense for you to tell me what you've chosen after you've chosen but . . . I'd rather you tell me once I'm ready to hear it."

"I can't call you at all?"

Sam shakes his head somberly. "I'm asking you not to."

This is the smallest amount of control he can claim over his own fate. I know that I have to give it to him.

"Whatever you want," I say. "Anything."

"Well, that's what I want," he says, nodding, and then he puts his foot on the gas and drives away.

Gone.

I realize just how cold I am, how frigid it is outside, and I race back into the store. I remember that I left my sandwich on the front seat of my car and I don't even bother to go get it. I'm not hungry.

I didn't eat breakfast, either. It appears my appetite had been the first thing to go.

Tina is ringing up a pair of books for two older ladies when I walk in. "Hey, Emma," she says. "Do you remember when we are getting more copies of the new Ann Patchett?"

"It should be next Tuesday," I say as if today is any normal day, as if I can think straight. "Ladies, if you give your contact info to Tina, she or I will call you when the copies are in."

I smile and then briskly walk into the back of the store. I sit down at my desk. I put my head in my hands and I breathe.

My mind races from Sam to Jesse and back.

I keep saying that I feel like I don't know what I'm doing. But the truth is, I know exactly what I'm doing.

It's one thing to play coy with them, I suppose. But what I have to do is stop playing coy with myself.

I am going to choose one of them.

I just don't know which one it is.

Love and Maine

Or, how to turn back time

The store closed about forty-five minutes ago. The register has been tallied. The sales floor is clean. Tina went home. I'm done. I can get in the car and go. But I'm just standing in the dark stockroom. Thinking about Sam.

My phone rings and I pick it up to see that it's Jesse. Just like that, Sam flies out of my head, replaced by the man he replaced.

"Hey," Jesse says when I answer. "I thought I'd meet you at the store."

"Oh," I say, surprised. I just assumed I'd meet him at my parents' house once I'd grabbed my things.

"Is that cool?"

"Sure," I say, shrugging. "Yeah. That's good. I'm still here."

"Well, that's good," he says. "Because I'm outside the front door."

I start to laugh as I head toward the front.

"Are you serious?" I say, but he doesn't need to answer because as I step onto the sales floor from the stockroom, I see him through the glass doors.

He is silhouetted by the streetlights in the parking lot. His body, in a heavy jacket and relaxed pants, fills the glass.

I unlock the door and let him in.

He grabs me, not just with his arms, but with his whole

body, as if he needs all of me, as if he can't bear another minute apart.

And then he kisses me.

If loving them both makes me a bad person, I think I'm just a bad person then.

"So . . . Maine?" I say, smiling.

"Maine," Jesse says, nodding once in agreement.

"All right," I say. "Let me just grab my purse. Actually, we can both go out this way. My car's in the back."

"It's OK, I'll drive us."

I give him a skeptical look. Jesse waves me off. "C'mon. Grab your stuff. I'll meet you in the car."

I go back and get my purse, then lock up the store and get into his car. All despite the fact that he shouldn't be driving.

Sometimes I worry Jesse could lead me into hell and I'd follow along, naively saying things like, "Is it getting hot to you?" and believing him when he told me it was fine.

"We have to stop at my parents'," I say when we're on the road. "I need to get some clothes."

"Of course," Jesse says. "Next stop, the Blairs'."

When we pull into their driveway, I can tell just by what lights are on that everyone is over at Marie and Mike's.

Jesse and I head into my parents' house to grab my things, and I warn him we'll have to say good-bye to everyone over at Marie's.

"That's fine," he says as I unlock the front door. "How far away is Marie's?"

"No, that's Marie's," I say, pointing to her house.

Jesse laughs. "Wow," he says. I watch as he looks at the distance between Marie's house and my parents'. "The Booksellers' Daughter strikes again."

It has been so long since someone called her that. It's become moot, for a lot of reasons.

Jesse turns and looks at me. "But I guess you're more of a Booksellers' Daughter than we thought, huh?"

I smile, unsure if he means this kindly or not. "A bit more, maybe," I say.

Once we're in the house, I bound up the stairs heading to my old room, but when I turn around behind me, I notice Jesse is still in the entryway, staring.

"You OK?" I ask.

He snaps out of it, shaking his head. "Yeah, totally. Sorry. I'll wait here while you get your stuff."

I get my bag and gather the things I've left on the bathroom sink.

When I come back down, Jesse is again lost in thought. "It's weird to see that some things look exactly the same way they did before."

"I bet," I say as I make my way to his side.

"It's like some things went on without me and other things paused the moment I left," he says as we head out the front door. "I mean, I know that's not true. But all your family got was a new TV. Everything else looks exactly the same. Even that weird cat painting. It's in the exact same place."

Sam and I picked out Mozart because he looks exactly like the gray cat in the painting above one of my parents' love seats.

I never would have even considered getting a cat without Sam. But now I'm a cat person. A few weeks ago, Sam sent me a picture of a cat sitting on a peanut butter and jelly sandwich and I laughed for, like, fifteen minutes.

I put my things in Jesse's car and then the two of us start walking over to Marie's.

"You sure you're ready to see my family again?" I ask him.

"Of course," he says with a smile on his face. "They're my family, too."

I knock on Marie's door and I hear commotion.

And then Mike answers the door.

"Emma," he says, giving me a hug and then moving out of the way for us to come in. "Two times in one day. What a treat. Jesse, nice to see you again," he says, and puts his hand out. Jesse shakes it. "Pleasure's mine," Jesse says.

Jesse and Mike hung out at family gatherings, but there was never a reason to confide in each other anything more than "How've you been?" They weren't close because Marie and I weren't close. When I think back on it now, it seems best likened to boxing coaches, with Marie and I as the fighters, our husbands pouring water into our mouths and psyching us up to go back in there.

We walk into the dining room to see Marie and my parents. Sophie and Ava have gone to sleep. The moment everyone sees Jesse, they stand up to greet him.

My dad shakes Jesse's hand heartily and then pulls him in for a hug. "Son, you don't know how good it feels to set my eyes on you."

Jesse nods, clearly a bit overwhelmed.

My mom hugs him and then pulls away, holding him out at the end of her arms and squeezing him on the shoulders, and then she shakes her head. "Never been so happy to see a person."

Marie gives him a sincere and kind hug, catching Jesse off guard.

I watch as Jesse smiles and tries to politely extricate himself from the situation. He is uncomfortable and desperately trying to hide it.

"We just wanted to stop in and say good-bye. We should probably be on our way," I say.

"Where are you going?" Marie asks. I assumed my dad would fill everyone in, but apparently not. I'm surprised just how slow gossip travels in my family.

"Jesse and I are headed up to Maine for a few days," I say. I say it as if it's perfectly natural. As if I don't have a fiancé. Actually, maybe I don't have a fiancé. I really don't know what I have anymore.

"Oh, OK," Marie says, her tone matching my own. "Well, I hope you two have a nice time." She holds my gaze for just a little too long, looks at me just a little too intently. The message is clear. She wants details soon. No doubt because she cares about me but also, I'm going to guess, because this is starting to get juicy.

"Thanks," I say, and the way I look at her out of the side of my eye makes it clear I will make sure she is the first to know anything there is to know.

And then Sophie and Ava come bounding down the stairs together, holding hands. Sophie is in a set of sea green thermal pajamas, desperate to see what all the fuss is about. Ava is in mismatched yellow and orange, being dragged along.

They get about three stairs from the bottom when they stop. Ava plops down. Sophie has one hand shielding her eyes from the light and she's squinting ever so slightly.

"Hey," Marie says gently. "You two know you're not supposed to be up." I look at Jesse as he watches Marie sign every word she's saying.

My father stands up. "I'll put them back to bed," he says. "I'd like to spend some time with my grandbabies."

Jesse watches as my dad signs the words "bed" and "children." My dad then scoops up Ava and takes Sophie's hand and disappears up the stairs.

"All right," I say. "We will see you all later."

Jesse waves good-bye to everyone as I take his other hand and lead him out. But when our feet hit the street, Jesse appears lost in his own thoughts.

"Everything OK?" I ask.

Jesse snaps out of it. "What?" he says. "Yeah. Totally."

"What's on your mind?"

I assume he's going to ask about the sign language or their cochlear implants. But he doesn't. He doesn't even mention the fact that they are hearing impaired. Instead he says, "I don't know . . . it's just that . . . wow."

"What?"

"Those are my nieces."

My appetite came back just before we hit the Massachusetts border. Jesse and I drove through a fast-food place and now we're pulled over on the side of the road.

I'm eating a hamburger and french fries.

Jesse ordered a bacon cheeseburger and a Coke but he hasn't had much of either.

"I think we've actually stopped here before," Jesse says.

"At this exact one?" I ask him.

Jesse nods. "After the senior prom."

I laugh. The prom feels like a lifetime ago. We told our parents we were staying over at friends' houses but escaped early and drove up to the very cabin we're leaving for now. Olive and I had gone to Victoria's Secret the week before. She was trying to find a bra to fit under her dress but I ventured toward the more adult lingerie and bought a black strappy G-string, saving it for prom night. It was the first time I had really *tried* to be sexy. Jesse didn't even notice it that night. All he cared about was that we were alone, no one to hear us or stop us.

"Sometimes when I think about what I wore to prom, I wonder why you and Olive didn't try to stop me. Remember I had those temporary butterfly tattoos all over my body?"

He laughs. "Honestly, I thought that was hot as hell. Remember, I was eighteen."

"I don't think you're remembering just how trashy I looked."

"I remember it like it was yesterday," he says. "You were the hottest girl there."

I shake my head and finish my hamburger, balling up the wrapper and throwing it into the bag.

"Hold on," I say. "I think I have a picture. I need you to truly remember what I'm talking about. I need you to admit that I looked incredibly cheesy."

Jesse laughs while I turn around and grab the duffel bag I put in the backseat. I pull it onto my lap and shuffle through it, grabbing the envelope I took from my apartment and searching for the picture I'm talking about. I can't find it at first, even though I know it's there.

I toss the bag back into the backseat and dump the contents of the envelope onto my lap.

"Whoa," Jesse says. "What is all of this?"

"Just stuff of yours, ours," I say. "That I kept."

Jesse looks touched. "Wow," he says.

"I never forgot about you," I say. "I could never forget about you."

He looks at me briefly and then down at my lap, to the photos and papers I've saved.

He doesn't acknowledge what I've said. Instead, he grabs a picture from the pile. "Is this from New Year's Eve in Amsterdam?" he asks me.

I nod my head.

That night, we kissed other people at midnight because we were in a fight. At 12:07 a.m., we made up in the bathroom of a dingy bar in De Wallen and made out sitting on top of the sink. The photo is a selfie from the wee hours of the morning, when he and I were sitting out on a bench by the river.

Jesse picks up a candid photo of us on top of a mountain in Costa Rica and a picture of him on a beach in Sydney. You can tell I am the one taking the picture. You can tell, just from the smile on his face, how much he loves me.

"God, look at us," he says.

"I know," I say.

"Do you remember when this photo was taken?" Jesse says, showing me the one of him on the beach.

"Of course I do," I say.

"That was the day we decided we were never going to make a backup plan, so that we had to pursue our dreams," he says. "Remember? We were going to take jobs that allowed us to see the world."

"I remember."

I riffle through a few more pictures until I find another envelope inside. It's addressed to him in my handwriting. It is the letter I wrote him before I went out on my date with Sam. I push it aside, allowing it to make its way, without being noticed, back into the larger envelope it came from.

And then I find the photo I'm looking for. Our prom. Me with my butterflies.

"All right," I say. "Look at this picture and tell me the truth."

We are standing in front of a large glass window, overlooking Boston. You can see city lights in the background. Jesse is in a cheap tux with a wayward boutonniere that I pinned on him in my front yard as all of our parents watched. I'm right beside him, turned slightly to the side but looking at the camera. I am standing in a bright red dress, with way too many clips in my hair and a series of already-faded and splotchy fake butterfly tattoos down my back.

A victim of early-2000s fashion.

Jesse immediately starts laughing.

"Oh, my God," he says. "You look like you have some sort of skin condition."

I start laughing. "Nope, just fake butterflies."

"I remember thinking that those butterflies were the sexiest thing I'd ever seen."

"Oh, I remember thinking I was the coolest girl at the prom," I say. "Just goes to show things aren't always the way we remember them."

Jesse looks up at me, trying to see if I meant anything by that. I decide to ignore how much it resonates.

"But you," I say. "You nailed it. Handsome then. Handsome now."

Jesse smiles and then turns back toward the steering wheel, getting ready to get on the road.

I gather the rest of the contents of the envelope and try to put them all back. But, of course, some fall to the floor and others get caught on the edge, unwilling to be crammed in.

I pick up what's fallen, including my ruby ring, put it all back in the envelope, and then throw it in the backseat. Only then do I see that I've left something on the center console between us.

It's an almost four-year-old article from the *Beacon*.

"Local Man Jesse Lerner Missing."

Next to the headline is an old photo of him standing in his parents' yard, waving, his right hand perfectly intact.

I was still in LA when the article was published, but a copy of it made its way to me shortly after I got back to Massachusetts. I almost threw it away. But I couldn't. I couldn't bring myself to get rid of anything with his picture on it, anything that bore his name. I had so little of him left.

I grab it and fold it back in two, the way it has lived in the envelope for years.

Jesse watches my hands as I do it.

I know that he saw it.

I put it in the backseat, with the envelope. When I turn back around, I open my mouth to tell Jesse about it, to acknowledge it, but he looks away and starts the car.

He doesn't want to talk about it.

Do you ever get over loss? Or do you just find a box within yourself, big enough to hold it? Do you just stuff it in there, push it down, and snap the lid on it? Do you just work, every day, to keep the box shut?

I thought that maybe if I shoved the pain in there hard enough and I kept the box shut tight enough that the pain would evaporate on its own, that I'd open the box one day to find it was empty and all of the pain I thought I'd been carrying with me was gone.

But I'm sitting in this car right now and I'm starting to think that the box has been full for the past three and a half years. I'm pretty sure that the lid is about to come off and I'm scared to see what's inside.

After all, Jesse has a box, too.

And his is packed tighter than mine.

Jesse's family cabin.

I never thought I'd see this place again.

But here I am.

It's about two in the morning. The roads to get here were so quiet, you'd think it was a ghost town.

The cabin, an oddly shaped house that resembles more of an oversized chalet, is warm and inviting—wood siding, big windows, a wraparound deck. It has the slightly mismatched sense that it used to be a tiny home but has weathered a number of additions.

There's not a single lit lamp on the property, so Jesse leaves the high beams on in order for us to get our stuff.

I grab my bag. Jesse grabs a few things from the trunk. We head toward the front door.

"You chilly?" he says as he fiddles with the key. "I'll get a fire going after we get in."

"That sounds great," I say.

The key turns and clicks, but the door sticks. Jesse has to lean into it to push through.

When it finally gives, the first thing that grabs me is the familiar woodlike musk.

Jesse walks through and turns on all the lights and the heat before I've even had a chance to put my things down.

"Settle in, I'm going to go turn off the lights in the car."

I nod and rub my hands together, trying to warm them. I look around at the stone fireplace and the cabin furniture, the afghan blankets that cover most of the chairs. The bar is stocked with half-empty bottles of liquor. The wood plank stairs are so old you can tell they creak just by looking at them.

There's not a single thing about this place that surprises me, not a single thing that feels out of place in comparison with my memory, except that I am a different person than I was the last time I was here.

I think I understand a little of how Jesse must feel coming back. I can see now what he meant back at my parents' house, how it is equally weird how much things don't change as how much they do.

Jesse comes in and shuts the door.

"This place should heat up in a few minutes, I think," he says. "Although it goes without saying that I haven't been here in years."

"The last time we were here was—"

"Our wedding," Jesse says, finishing my sentence.

I smile, remembering. Jesse smiles, too. After the reception, we spent the night at the inn so, in fact, the last time we were here was when we had sex—he in his tux, me in my wedding dress—on the kitchen counter that is currently just off to my left. I remember how romantic it seemed. Now, I find myself sort of cringing that we had sex on the counter. That's where people prepare food! What were we thinking?

"So how about this fire?" I say.

"On it!" he says as he walks over to the fireplace. It's dusty and bare, with a stack of old wood next to it.

I watch him as he moves. I watch as he selects the pieces of wood. I watch him stack them. I watch him strike a match.

"Are you tired?" he asks me. "Do you want to go to bed?"

"No," I say, shaking my head. "I'm oddly awake. You?"

He waves me off. "I'm not exactly on Eastern Standard Time."

"Right," I say.

Jesse steps to the bar. "Wine, then?"

"Gin?" I say.

"Oh, wow," he says. "All right."

He pours me a glass of Hendrick's. He pours another one for himself. I sit down and grab the afghan that's hanging on the back of the couch.

Jesse ducks underneath the bar and grabs a tray of ice from the freezer. He has to hit it against the counter in order for any of the ice to pop out.

"It might have been months, maybe years, since someone made a cocktail in this place," Jesse says. "This ice isn't exactly grade-A material."

I laugh. "It's fine, honestly."

He brings me my glass and puts his down. He moves toward the fire and stabs at it with the poker. It starts to build into a gentle roar. I straighten my posture and grab my glass. I gesture for Jesse to get his.

"To you," I say.

"To us."

I smile and we toast. I shoot back a quarter of the glass. Jesse tries to do the same and winces. "Sorry," he says, shaking his head. "It's actually been quite a long time since I had liquor."

"Don't worry," I say, throwing the rest of the contents of the glass into my mouth. "I'll get you caught up."

Soon, the fire is warming up the whole room. Our sometimes stilted conversation grows more uproarious and loquacious as the alcohol hits our system. In no time, the two of us are reminiscing about how bad the cake tasted at our wedding and I've had three glasses of Hendrick's.

Jesse is sitting at one end of the couch with his feet on the coffee table. I'm sitting on the other end with my feet underneath me. My shoes are off; my sweater is on the floor.

"So tell me," he says. "What stamps have you acquired on your passport?"

I am sorry to disappoint him. "Uh, none actually. None since you left."

Jesse is clearly surprised. "Not even to Southern Italy?" he asks. "You were up for that piece about Puglia."

"I know," I say. "I just . . . you know, life sent me in another direction."

We are quiet for a minute and then Jesse sits forward, his torso leaning toward me.

"I'm sorry I took that job," he says. "I'm sorry I left you. What was I thinking? Leaving the day before our anniversary?"

"It's OK," I say back. I want to add, "I'm sorry I got engaged to someone else," but I can't bring myself to say it. The apology would only draw attention to the most vulnerable and insecure parts of me, like a teenager wearing a bikini to a pool party.

"Do you have any idea what it's like to wish for someone every day and then finally see yourself sitting next to them?" he asks me.

"Lately, it feels like that's all I know," I tell him. "I still have trouble believing that all of this is real. That you're here."

"I know. Me, too," Jesse says. He grabs my hand and holds it in his and then he says, "You cut your hair."

I find my hand moving to the back of my head, along the nape of my neck where my hairline ends. I do it as if I'm too shy to have hair so bold. Something about the way I move irritates me. It's as if I'm not entirely myself, as if I'm performing a role. "Yeah," I say. I can hear there is an edge to my voice. I soften it. "A few years ago."

"And it's blonder," he says. "Your hair wasn't really blond before."

"I know," I say. "But I like it."

"I almost didn't recognize you," he says. "At the airport."

"I recognized you the moment you stepped out of that plane."

"You are so different," he says, moving closer. "But you're also everything I dreamt of for all of those years. And you're right in front of me." He puts his hand to my face and looks into my eyes. He leans in to me and presses his lips against mine. My brain gives way to my heart as I sink into him.

He pulls away. "I think we should sleep together," he says. He looks me in the eye and doesn't shy away.

I know that if I say yes, there is no turning back.

It will change things between Sam and me forever.

But I also know that what we're talking about is inevitable. I will sleep with him, whether it's this second or tomorrow or in two weeks. It will happen.

I want to know what Jesse feels like now—a desire that is only heightened by the memories I have of what he felt like then.

I know the consequences. I know what this might cost me.

I'm going to do it anyway.

"I think so, too," I say.

Jesse smiles and then laughs. "Then what the hell are we doing down here?" he says. He stands up and puts his hand out for me, like a gentleman.

I laugh and take it. But the moment I'm on my feet, Jesse has lifted me right back off of them, swooping me up into his arms.

"When was the last time you did it in a twin-size bed?" he asks. It is a joke. And I know better than to answer. But I'm starting to wonder if it's not such a good sign how often I'm cherry-picking the truth.

Jesse rushes us out of the living room to the stairs.

"Oh, my God!" I cry out, stunned at how easily he can move about the house with me in his arms. "You're gonna drop me!"

He doesn't listen. Instead, he bounds up the stairs, taking them two at a time. He pushes open the door to the room that was once considered his. Jesse throws me onto the bed and lands on top of me.

Nothing I've ever done has felt as much like home as this, being underneath him, feeling his lips on mine, his hands running down my body.

He unbuttons my shirt and opens it wide.

My body has changed since he left, the somewhat natural process of time. But I don't feel shy or embarrassed. I feel invigorated. As if I want to be as naked as possible, as quickly as possible—as if I want to show him all of me.

I watch as he takes his own shirt off, as he puts his arms over his head and pulls. I am surprised to see that he's even skinnier than I imagined and that there is a tangle of faded puce scars running down the left half of his torso. They look like lightning bolts tied up in knots. He wears so much of his pain and hardships on his body.

"All those years that I missed you," he says as he runs his nose gently down my collarbone, "I missed your face and your voice and your laugh."

My body is hot, my face is flush. His hands feel so much better than I remember. His body fits into the corners of mine effortlessly, like our limbs were formed around each other, ebbing and flowing in relation to the other.

He tears the button of my jeans open with a flick of his wrist. "But more than anything I missed the feel of you," he says as he pulls my jeans off of me, struggling at first to get them around my hips and then flinging them across the room. He wordlessly takes off his own. He lies back down and presses his whole body onto mine.

"I missed the way your hands feel on my back," he says. "And the way your legs feel around me."

I move slightly, inviting him.

And then I am lost.

I am no longer anyone but the Emma that loves Jesse Lerner, the Emma I've been for so much of my life.

And when we are moving together, breathing together, aching together, I hear him whisper, "Emma."

And I whisper back, "Jesse."

~

We are lying in bed.

We are naked.

We are tangled in sheets, covered in sweat.

We lie in each other's arms and I am reminded of all of the other times we lay next to each other, catching our breath side by side, limbs intertwined. We learned how to do this together, explored ourselves with each other. We loved and desired each other when we were bad at it, and we grew good at it together, in tandem.

Now, we are great at it. The best we have ever been. Even though we are done, I roll over to Jesse and we begin once more.

He reciprocates easily, pressing into me and moaning.

His breath has gone sour. His hair smells dirty. It is my favorite form of him.

"Again," he says. It is neither a question nor a command. Rather a simple fact, observed. We will do this again. We have to be closer again. Here we are again.

And this time, the passion is no longer akin to a house burning down, but instead feels like a steady burning flame, hot and warm.

Neither of us is in a rush. Neither of us could rush even if we wanted to.

We are slow and we are purposeful.

More than anything, I relish the feel of his skin against mine, the feeling of our chests touching ever so briefly before pulling away again.

Right now, in this moment, I am stunned that I am even capable of having sex with anyone else. That the world wouldn't—didn't—stop me. Before I lost him, sex always seemed like something we invented together. Now that he's back, now that he's again here with me, I wonder how I ever went crazy enough to think it could be this good with anyone else.

What I am feeling, what we are doing, is sending signals all throughout my body, like a shot of caffeine, the rush of sugar, the burn of liquor. I can feel my brain rewiring.

This is what I want.

This is what I've always wanted.

I will always want this.

We fall asleep sometime around six in the morning, just as the sun is waking up the rest of the world.

I wake up to the creak of the front door closing and the thud of two shoes hitting the interior floor. I open my hungover eyes to find that there is no one in bed beside me.

I slowly roll out of the sheets, find my underwear, and slip it on along with Jesse's shirt from yesterday. I head down the stairs as I start to smell coffee.

"There she is," Jesse says from the kitchen. He walks closer and grabs me, lifting me up. I wrap my legs around him. I kiss him. He tastes like mint and it reminds me just how awful my morning breath is. I look at the clock on the microwave. It's almost two p.m. Afternoon breath, I guess.

I haven't slept this late since we were in college. I wasn't hammered last night, but ever since the age of twenty-nine or so, my body can't shrug off a drink like it used to.

I pull away from Jesse and he puts me down.

"I should probably brush my teeth," I say.

"You noticed that, too, huh?" Jesse says, teasing me.

"Hey!"

I lightly hit him on the torso and find myself wondering if I've hit the scar that runs down his body, wondering if it's sensitive, if I've hurt him. I want to know what those scars are. I want to know if his teeth are OK after years without dental care or whether he's suffering from vitamin deficiencies. And then, of course, there's his finger.

I also know that I can't ask. I promised not to ask.

But he has to talk about it eventually. If not with me, then with someone else. I know that he is pretending to be OK, but no one would be OK after what he's been through. He can't pretend forever.

"I'm kidding," he says soothingly. "I have waited years to smell your morning breath. Everything about you, morning breath, stray hairs . . . I love it all."

When he disappeared, I kept his hairbrush for months. I didn't want to throw away something that had any of him on it.

"I love you, Emma," he says. "I want to be with you for the rest of my life."

"I love you, too," I say.

Jesse smiles. Toast pops out of the toaster with a swish and a ding.

"All right," Jesse says. "Coffee, orange juice, toast and jam, and I got us microwaveable bacon. I will be honest, this stuns me. Microwaveable bacon. Am I crazy or did they not have that a few years ago?"

I laugh as I move into the kitchen. "I think it's relatively new, yeah."

"I thought so. OK, sit down at the counter and I'll make you a plate."

"Wow," I say, impressed.

I sit down as I watch Jesse move around the small kitchen as if his life depends on it. He pours two glasses of orange juice. He pulls the toast out of the toaster. He gets the strawberry jam and searches for a knife. And then he opens the bacon and puts it on a plate and into the microwave.

"Are you ready for this? Apparently, this is going to be perfectly crisp bacon in a matter of seconds."

"I'm ready," I say. "Dazzle me."

Jesse laughs and then grabs two mugs for coffee. He pours the coffee and hands it to me. I take a sip just as the microwave beeps.

Jesse moves around the kitchen and then he's right next to me, putting two full plates of food on the counter, complete with perfectly crisp bacon.

He sits down and puts his hand on my bare leg. There was once a time when I wasn't sure where I ended and Jesse began. When we were so intertwined, so very much one being in two bodies, that my nerve endings barely lit up when he touched me.

Now is not that time.

Instead, my skin warms underneath his touch. His hand absently moves just slightly higher up my thigh and it gets hotter, brighter. And then he takes it back to eat his toast.

"Breakfast for lunch," I say. "Very charming."

"What can I say? I'm a charming guy. I also, while I was out, got you a twelve-pack of Diet Coke because I know Emma Lerner, and Emma Lerner needs a steady supply of Diet Coke in the house."

My name is not Emma Lerner and I don't drink Diet Coke anymore and I'm not sure how to respond to any of it, so I don't.

"What else did you get?" I ask him.

"Actually, not much else," he says. "I figured we could go into town for dinner."

"Oh, awesome," I say. "That sounds great."

"I'm thinking me, you, a bottle of wine, maybe lobster." I look at him, surprised. "We are in Maine," he adds, explaining himself.

"I didn't know that you ate shellfish," I say. But the minute I say it, I realize how stupid that is to say.

"Don't worry about it," he says. "Lobster will be good."

"Well, then, great. Maine lobsters and wine it is. And what's on the docket for this afternoon?"

"Anything you want," Jesse says, finishing the last of the toast and giving me the rest of his bacon. I greedily chomp it down. I want even more than what's on my plate.

"Anything?" I say.

"Anything."

It's been such a long time since I had a day where I could do anything. "What about a walk to the lighthouse?" I say.

Jesse nods. "That's a great idea. I mean, it's really cold outside, but assuming we can stand it . . ."

I laugh. "We'll bundle up," I tell him. "It will be great."

"I'm in," he says. "Let's go."

I grab his hand and pull him upstairs. I put on thick pants and a sweater. I grab my coat and a scarf. Jesse already has on jeans and a shirt but I insist he wear something warmer. I look through the closets for an old sweatshirt. I find a sweater in the back of the closet in the master bedroom. It's cream and hunter green with a reindeer on it. It obviously once belonged to his dad.

"Here," I say as I hand it to him.

He takes it from me and looks at it. He brings it up to his nose. "I am not kidding when I say this smells like mothballs and death."

I laugh. "Just put it on! Otherwise, you'll just have a jacket and a T-shirt."

He begrudgingly lifts it up over his head and pulls it down around his chest. When it's fitted on him, he claps his hands together. "To the lighthouse!"

We head out onto the front porch, wrapped tightly in our coats, scarves, and boots. It is even colder than I was expecting. The air is whipping against my ears. I can feel it sharply in the vulnerable spots between my scarf and my neck. It is one of the only things I miss about having long hair. In the summer, you feel nice and cool. But in moments like this, you're exposed.

"Onward?" Jesse asks.

"Onward," I say.

Jesse and I talk about his family. We talk about college, about high school, about our months in Europe, our honeymoon in India. I feel like my old self with him, the carefree version of me that died when I thought he did. But it would be a lie to say that I am so entranced with our conversation that I forget the cold. The cold is impossible to forget.

We can see it as our breath hits the air. We can feel it in our bones. Our lips feel cracked, our cheeks blistered, our shoulders are hunched around our necks.

We huddle close to warm each other. We hold hands inside the warmth of Jesse's coat pocket. We find a spot in the sun and we stand in it, letting the subtle heat save us.

"Come here," Jesse says, even though I am already right next to him. He takes me closer, pulling me into his chest. He rubs my back and shoulders, runs his hands up and down my arms, trying to warm me up.

It occurs to me that my memory of him was a poor substitute for the real thing.

They say that when you remember something, you are

really remembering the last time you remembered it. Each time you recollect a memory, you change it, ever so slightly, shading it with new information, new feelings. Over the past years without him, my memories of Jesse have become a copy of a copy of a copy. Without meaning to, I have highlighted the parts of him that stood out to me, and the rest have faded away.

In the copy of a copy, what stood out to me about him was how much I loved him. What faded into the background was how much he loved me.

But I remember it now, how it feels to be the recipient of this much love, this type of dedication.

I wonder what stood out to him when he remembered me. I wonder what faded to gray.

"All right," Jesse says. "We can't stand right here in the sun forever. I say we start running to the lighthouse, to warm up."

"OK," I say. "You got it."

"On the count of three."

"One . . . two . . ."

"Three!"

He takes off like a cheetah. I pump my legs as fast as I can to keep up.

As I run, the wind grows worse on my face but soon I start to heat up in my chest, in my arms, in my legs.

Jesse turns his head back and checks in on me as we're running. And then we come around the bend.

Even though it's still a bit in the distance, the lighthouse and the ocean are in plain view. The stark white of the tower against the dark blue-gray of the water is just as beautiful today as it was when we were married here. Back when I still believed that love was simple, that marriage was forever, that the world was safe to live in.

Can we start again, from this very spot?

"I'll race you to the fence," I say, even though I know that I have no shot of winning.

Jesse gets to the fence and turns around, claiming his victory. I slow down, giving up once I've lost. I walk toward him.

As I gulp the cold air into my lungs, it cuts like a knife. I take it slower; I calm my body down. There is a faint line of sweat on my skin, but it cools down and disappears in an instant.

"You won," I say as I stand next to Jesse and put my head on his shoulder. He puts his arm around me.

We stand next to the lighthouse, catching our breath, looking out onto the rocky ocean. That's the thing about Maine. The water splashes onto rocks more than sand, onto the side of cliffs more than beaches.

I can't imagine living for years on rocks and sand, using an inflatable raft as shade from the sun. There is no way that Jesse can be adjusting as simply as he's presenting.

I want to believe him. I want, so badly, to believe that he is *this* OK. I mean, I have to let him do this all at his own pace, don't I?

It's just so nice to think that things can be as beautiful as they once were.

"That was the happiest day of my life," Jesse says. "Here with everyone, marrying you."

"Mine, too," I say.

Jesse looks at me and smiles. "You look so cold you might shatter."

"I'm pretty freezing," I say. "Should we head back?"

Jesse nods. "In sixty seconds."

"OK," I say. "Sixty seconds. Fifty-nine . . . fifty-eight . . ."

But then I stop counting. I just enjoy the view and the company, a sight I never thought I'd see again with a man I thought I'd lost.

Candles on the table. Pinot Gris in our glasses. Warm bread that I've managed to crumb all over the cream-colored tablecloth.

And one small, very expensive lobster on the table. Because December is not exactly the high season.

"What are we doing?" Jesse says to me. He's sitting across the table, wearing a long-sleeve black shirt and gray chinos. I'm in a red sweater and black jeans. Neither one of us brought nice enough clothes to dine here. The maître d' was clearly hesitant to even seat us.

"I don't know," I say. "It seemed like a nice idea, but I just think . . ."

Jesse stands up and puts his napkin on the table. "C'mon," he says.

"Now?" I'm standing up.

I watch as Jesse pulls out a few bills from his pocket, counts out a reasonable figure, and puts it on the table, nestled under his glass. He doesn't have credit cards or a bank account or any sort of identification. I bet Francine gave him cash and told him she'd take care of getting him everything he needed.

"Yeah," Jesse says. "Now. Life is too short to be sitting in some restaurant drinking wine we don't care for, eating a lobster we don't like."

That is absolutely true.

We run to the car and I hop in the passenger seat, quickly shutting the door behind me. I rub my hands together. I stomp my feet. None of it warms me up.

"The wind is nuts out there!" Jesse says as he starts the car. I have offered to drive every time I've been in the car with him and he keeps turning me down.

"I'm still hungry," I say to him.

"And the night is young."

"Should we head down to the Italian place and grab some subs or a salad to go?"

Jesse nods and heads out of the parking lot. "Sounds good."

The roads are dark and winding and you can tell by the way the trees sway that the wind isn't letting up. Jesse slowly pulls into the makeshift parking lot of the restaurant. He parks and turns off the ignition, leaving the heat on.

"You stay here," he says. "I'll be back soon." He's out the door before I have time to respond.

In the quiet dark of the car, I have a moment to myself.

I use it to check my phone.

Work e-mails. Coupons. Texts from Marie and Olive asking how I'm doing. I open up a few of the work e-mails and find myself overwhelmed by one from Tina.

Dear Colin, Ashley, and Emma,

It is with a heavy heart that I have to render my resignation. My husband and I have decided to sell our home and buy a condo outside of Central Square.

Unfortunately, this means I will be leaving Blair Books. Of course, I can stay on board for the standard two weeks.

Thank you so much for the opportunity to work at your wonderful store. It has meant a lot to me.

Sincerely,
Tina

There were assistant managers before Tina and I always knew there would be assistant managers after her. But I'm having a hard time imagining it all running smoothly when she leaves. My parents are also taking a step back in the coming months and that means that everything really will rest on me—and only me—in the future. On any other day, I think I'd probably have some perspective on this, but for right now, all I can do is ignore it. I archive the e-mail and am taken to the next message in my in-box. I quickly realize it is from my wedding venue.

Dear Ms. Blair,

Our records indicate that you have inquired about the cancellation fee for your event scheduled for October nineteenth of next year. As discussed in your initial consultation, we reserve the right to hold the entire deposit.

However, as we also discussed at the time, that weekend is a popular one. Seeing as how a number of couples have expressed interest in your date, our owner has agreed to release half of your deposit if you cancel before the end of the month.

I hope this answers your question.

Sincerely,
Dawn

I didn't contact Dawn. Which means there's only one explanation.

Sam's really prepared to leave me.

I'm truly on the verge of losing him.

This isn't how my life is meant to go. This isn't what my inbox is meant to look like.

I am supposed to have love notes. I am supposed to have cat pictures and e-mails about caterers and invitations.

Not messages from the Carriage House telling me that my fiancé is a few clicks away from canceling our wedding, that I could lose him, lose a wonderful man, because of my own confusion, my own conflicted heart.

What am I doing here in Maine?

Have I lost my goddamn mind?

I am suddenly overwhelmed by the desire to get in the driver's seat and drive home to Sam right now. But if I did, if I went back to him right now, could I honestly say that I wouldn't think about Jesse anymore?

If I go home to Sam, it needs to be with the confidence that I will never leave him. I owe him that much. I mean, I owe him everything. But taking him seriously and not toying with him is the absolute least I can do. And I'm aware that even then it might not be enough.

By loving the two of them, I am no longer sure about either. And by being unsure, I might just lose them both.

Romantic love is a beautiful thing under the right circumstances. But those circumstances are so specific and rare, aren't they?

It's rare that you love the person who loves you, that you love *only* the person who loves *only* you. Otherwise, somebody's heartbroken.

But I guess that's why true love is so alluring in the first place. It's hard to find and hold on to, like all beautiful things. Like gold, saffron, or an aurora borealis.

"The guys inside said it's going to snow tonight," Jesse says as he gets back in the car. He has a pizza in his hand. "I got us a pepperoni and pineapple pizza, your favorite." He puts the pizza in my lap.

I feel myself feigning a surprised smile. I can't eat cheese. "Great!" I say.

And then we're off, heading back to the cabin over the same snowy streets. Jesse takes the turns confidently now, like a man who knows his way around.

But the roads are winding and they curve unpredictably. I find myself grabbing on to the handle above my head not once but twice.

"Maybe slow down?" I offer after the second time.

I glance at the speedometer. He's going fifty in a thirty-five-mile zone.

"It's fine," he says. "I've got it." And then he looks at me briefly and smiles. "Live a little."

I find myself relaxing even though we're going just as fast. In fact, I become so at ease within the car that I am actually surprised when I hear the whoop of a cop car stopping us.

Jesse pulls over, slowly but immediately.

My heart starts racing.

He's driving with no license at all.

None.

"Jesse . . ." I say, my voice somewhere between a panicked whisper and a breathy scream.

"It's going to be fine," he says. He's so confident about everything. He always has been. He's always the one who believes everything is going to be fine.

But he's wrong, isn't he? Everything isn't always fine. Terrible things happen in this world. Awful things. You have to do your best to prevent them.

A middle-aged man in a police uniform comes up to Jesse's window and bends over. "Evening, sir," he says.

He has a no-nonsense haircut and a stoic stance. He's got a short frame, a clean-shaven face, and hard edges. His hair, even his eyebrows, are starting to gray.

"Good evening, Officer," Jesse says. "How can I help you?"

"You need to take these turns a bit more cautiously in this weather, son," the man says.

"Yes, sir."

"License and registration."

This is my nightmare. This is a nightmare I am having.

Jesse barely shows a moment's hesitation. He leans forward into the glove box and grabs a few papers. He hands them over to the officer.

"We're in the beginning of a storm. You can't be driving like it's the middle of June," the cop says as he takes the documents from Jesse and looks them over.

"Understood."

"And your license?" The officer looks down, staring at Jesse directly. I look away. I can't stand this.

"I don't have it," Jesse says.

"Excuse me?"

"I don't have it, sir," Jesse says. This time I can hear in his voice that he is struggling to maintain his composure.

"What do you mean you don't have it?"

I just sort of snap. My arms start moving on their own. I grab the envelope I left in the car when we drove up here.

"Officer, he's just come back from being lost at sea."

The officer looks at me, stunned. Not because he believes me, but because he can't seem to believe someone would try a lie this elaborate.

"She's . . ." Jesse tries to explain, but what's he going to say? I'm telling the truth.

"I can prove it to you," I say as I look through the envelope and pull out the article from years ago about Jesse being missing. His picture is right there, in the middle of the clipping. I hand it over to the cop.

I'm not sure why he humors me enough to take it, but he does. And then he looks at the picture, and then at Jesse. And I can see that while he's still not convinced, he's not entirely sure I'm lying, either.

"Sir," Jesse starts, but the cop stops him.

"Let me read this."

And so we wait.

The cop looks it over. His eyes go from left to right. He looks at the picture and then once again at Jesse.

"Say I believe this . . ." the cop says.

"He got back a couple of days ago," I say. "He's still waiting on a license, credit cards, really any sort of ID."

"So he shouldn't be driving."

"No," I say. I can't deny that. "He shouldn't. But after being lost for almost four years, all he wants is to be able to drive a car for a few minutes."

The cop closes his eyes for a moment and when he opens them back up, he's made his decision.

"Son, get out of the driver's seat and let this young woman drive."

"Yes, sir," Jesse says, but neither of us move.

"Now," the officer says.

Jesse immediately opens up the door and stands as I get out of the car on my side and switch places with him. I walk past the officer and I can tell he's not exactly entertained by all of this. I get in the driver's seat and the officer closes the door for me.

"It's cold as hell out here and I don't feel like standing on the side of the road trying to figure out if you two are pulling something over on me. I'm deciding to err on the side of . . . gullibility."

He bends down farther to look right at Jesse. "If I catch you driving a car without a license in this town again, I will have you arrested. Is that clear?"

"Absolutely," Jesse says.

"All right," the cop says, and then he turns back. "Actually, I'd like to see your license, miss."

"Oh, of course," I say, turning toward my purse. It's at Jesse's feet. Jesse leans forward and grabs my wallet from it, pulling my license out.

"I don't have all night," the cop says.

I take it from Jesse and hand it over to the cop. He looks at it and then at me. He hands it back.

"Let's stick to the speed limit, Ms. Blair," he says.

"Certainly," I say.

And then he's gone.

I roll up the window and the car is once again dark and starting to warm. I hand my license back to Jesse.

I watch the cop pull onto the road and drive away. I put on my blinker.

I look over at Jesse.

He's staring at my driver's license.

"You changed your name back?"

"What?"

He shows me my own ID. He points to my name. My younger face smiling back at me.

"You changed your name," he says again. This time it's more of a statement than a question.

"Yeah," I say. "I did."

He's quiet for a moment.

"Are you OK?" I ask.

He puts the license back in my wallet and gets hold of himself. "Yeah," he says. "Totally. You thought I was dead, right? You thought I was gone forever."

"Right."

I don't mention that I'm not sure I was ever really comfortable changing my name to Emma Lerner in the first place, that I am and have always been Emma Blair.

"OK," he says. "I get it. It's weird to see, but I get it."

"OK," I say. "Cool."

I pull onto the road and I drive us back to the cabin. It's silent inside of the car.

We both know why the other one isn't talking.

I'm mad at him for getting pulled over.

He's mad at me for changing my name.

It isn't until I pull up in front of the cabin, and the tires crunch over the gravel, that either of us speaks up.

"What do you say we call it even?" Jesse says with a smirk on his face.

I laugh and reach for him. "I'd love to," I say. "Even-steven." I kiss him firmly on the lips.

Jesse grabs the pizza and the two of us run out of the car, heading straight to the cabin.

We shut the door behind us, keeping out the cold and the wind and the cops and the fancy restaurants where we don't like the wine.

It's warm in here. Safe.

"You know, you saved my ass out there," Jesse says.

"Yes!" I say. "I did! You'd be halfway to jail by now if it wasn't for me."

He kisses me against the door. I sink into him.

"Emma Blair, my hero," he says, a slightly sarcastic edge in his voice.

I'm still a little mad at him and now I know he's still mad at me, too.

But he pushes into me and I open myself up to him.

He runs his hands along my stomach, underneath my shirt. I gently bite his ear.

"You know where I think we should do this?" he says as he kisses me.

"No, where?"

He smiles, pointing to the kitchen counter.

I smile and shake my head.

"Remember?" he says.

"Of course I remember."

He pulls me over there and stands up against it, the way he did that day. "I couldn't get your dress off, so I had to push the bottom of it up around your . . ."

"Stop," I say, but not emphatically. I say it the way you say, "Don't be silly" or "Give me a break."

"Stop what?"

"I'm not going to have sex with you on the kitchen counter."

"Why not?" he asks.

"Because it's gross."

"It's not gross."

"It is gross. We ate there this afternoon."

"So we won't eat there again."

That's all it takes. A very simple, very misconceived idea—and I'm doing what just thirty seconds ago I said I wouldn't.

We are loud and we are fast, as if there's a time limit, as if there's a race to the finish. When we are done, Jesse pulls away from me and I hop down. I see a line of sweat on the counter.

What is the matter with me?

What am I doing?

Run-ins with the police aren't as thrilling at thirty-one as they were at seventeen. It's one of those things that was charming *once*. Ditto having sex in the kitchen and speeding. I mean, c'mon, I'm talking cops out of tickets and doing it next to a box of microwaveable bacon? This isn't me. I'm not this person.

"We forgot to eat the pizza," Jesse says as he gets up and walks to pick it up off the table by the door. He puts it on the dining table. I get dressed, eager now to be covered. Jesse opens the box.

I stare right at the pepperoni and pineapple pizza. If I eat it as is, my stomach is going to hurt. But if I pull the cheese off, I'll just be eating gummy tomato bread.

"You know what?" I say. "You go for it. I'm not feeling pizza at the moment."

"No?"

"I don't really eat cheese anymore. It doesn't sit well with me."

"Oh," he says.

It occurs to me that there are a few more things he should know, things I should be clear about.

"I changed my name back to Emma Blair because Blair Books is my store. I love it. And I've built a life around it. I am a Blair."

"OK," he says. A noncommittal word, said noncommittally.

"And I know I used to be the sort of person who always wanted to bounce around from place to place but . . . I'm happy being settled in Massachusetts. I want to run the store until I retire—maybe even hand it over to my own children one day."

Jesse looks at me but doesn't say anything. The two of us look at each other. An impasse.

"Let's go to bed," Jesse says. "Let's not worry about pizza and last names and the bookstore. I want to just lie down next to you, hold you."

"Sure," I say. "Yeah."

Jesse leaves the pizza behind as he leads me up the stairs to the bed. He lies down and holds the blanket open for me. I back into him, my thighs and butt nestled into the curve of his legs. He puts his chin in the crook of my neck, his lips by my ear. The wind is howling now. I can see, through the top of the window, that it is starting to snow.

"Everything is going to be OK," he says to me before I fall asleep.

But I'm not sure I believe him anymore.

I wake well after the sun has come up. The snow has stopped falling. The wind has retreated. For a moment after I open my eyes, everything seems peaceful and quiet.

"Not sure if you can tell from the view out the window but I think we're snowed in," Jesse says. He is standing in the doorway of the bedroom in a T-shirt and sweatpants. He is smiling. "You look adorable," he adds. "I guess those are the big highlights of the morning. We're snowed in, you're as cute as ever."

I smile. "How snowed in is snowed in?"

"We're as snowed in as you are adorable."

"Oh, God," I say, slowly sitting up and gathering myself. "We'll be stuck here for years, then."

Jesse moves toward the bed and gets in next to me. "Worse fates."

I lean into him and quickly realize that both of us could stand to bathe.

"I think I might hop in the shower," I say.

"Great idea. My parents told me they put in a walk-in sauna in the master. Last one there has to make breakfast." And off we go.

The water is warm but the air is damp and humid. The steam fogs the glass doors. There are more showerheads than I care to count, two coming from the ceiling and a number of jets coming from the walls of the shower. It is hot and muggy in here. My hair is flattened and smoothed back across my head. I can feel Jesse just behind me, lathering soap in his hand.

"I wanted to ask you . . ." Jesse says. "Why did you leave LA?"

"What do you mean?" I ask.

"I mean, I just assumed you'd still be out there. Why did you come back?"

"I like it here," I say.

"You liked it there, though," he says. "We both did. It was our home."

He's right. I loved my life in California, where it never snowed and the sun was always shining.

Now, my favorite day of the year is when daylight savings begins. It's usually when the air starts to thaw and the only precipitation you can be threatened with is a little rain. You're tired in the morning because you've lost an hour of sleep. But by seven o'clock at night, the sun is still out. And it's warmer than it was yesterday at that time. It feels like the world is opening up, like the worst is over, and flowers are coming.

They don't have that in Los Angeles. The flowers never leave.

"I just knew I needed to come home to my family."

"When did you move back?"

"Hm?"

"How long after . . . how long was it before you moved back to Acton?"

"I guess soon," I say, turning away from him and into the water. "Maybe two months."

"Two months?" Jesse says, stunned.

"Yeah."

"Wow," he says. "I just . . . all these years I always pictured you there. I never . . . I never really pictured you here."

"Oh," I say, finding myself unsure how to respond or what to say next. "Do you see the shampoo anywhere?" I say finally. But I'm not paying attention to the answer. My mind is already lost in the life that Jesse never pictured.

Me and Blair Books and my cats and Sam.

I close my eyes and breathe in.

It's a good life, the one he never imagined for me.

It's a great life.

I miss it.

Sam knows I can't eat cheese. And he knows that I never want to change my last name from Blair again. He knows how important the store is to me. He likes to read. He likes to talk about books and he has interesting thoughts about them. He never drives without a license. He never attracts police officers. He drives safely in bad weather. Sam knows me, the real me. And he has loved me exactly as I am, always, especially as the person I am today.

"Em?" Jesse says. "Did you want the shampoo?"

"Oh," I say, snapping out of it. "Yeah, thanks."

Jesse hands me the bottle and I squeeze it into my palm. I lather it through my hair.

And suddenly, it takes everything I have not to dissolve into a puddle of tears and go down the drain with the soapy water.

I miss Sam.

And I'm scared I've pushed him away forever.

Jesse notices. I try to hide it. I smile even though the smile doesn't live anywhere beyond my lips. Jesse stands behind me, putting his arms around me, his chest against my back. He nestles his chin into my shoulder and he says, "How are you?"

There is nothing like a well-timed "How are you?" to reduce you to weeping.

I have no words. I just close my eyes and give myself permission to cry. I let Jesse hold me. I lean into him, collapse onto him. Neither of us says anything. The air grows so hot and oppressive that eventually breathing takes more effort than it should. Jesse turns off the steam, turns down the temperature of the faucets, and lets the lukewarm water run over us.

"It's Sam, right? That's his name?"

I had split my world into two, but by simply uttering Sam's name, Jesse has just sewn the halves back together.

"Yeah," I say, nodding. "Sam Kemper." I want to pull away from Jesse right now. I want him to go stand on the other side of the shower. I want to use the water and the soap to clean my body and I want to go home.

But I don't do any of that. Instead, I freeze in place—in some way hoping that by standing still I can stop the world from spinning for just a moment, that I can put off what I know is eventually going to happen.

I watch as Jesse places the name.

"Sam Kemper?" he asks. "From high school?"

I nod.

"The guy that used to work at your parents' store?"

There's no reason for Jesse to dislike Sam other than the fact that I love Sam. But I watch as Jesse's face grows to show contempt. I should never have said Sam's full name. It was better when Sam was an abstract. I've done a stupid thing by giving him a face to match. I might as well have stabbed Jesse in the ribs. He bristles and then gets hold of himself. "You love him?" Jesse asks.

I nod but what I want to do is tell him about what Marie said, that she told me this isn't about who I love but rather who I am. I want to tell him that I've been asking myself that question over and over and it's starting to seem glaringly obvious that I am different from the person Jesse loves.

I am not her. Not anymore. No matter how easy it is for me to pretend that I am.

But instead of saying any of that, I just say, "Sam is a good man."

And Jesse leaves it there.

He turns off the water and I'm instantly cold. He hands me a towel and the moment I wrap it around myself, I realize how naked I feel.

We dry ourselves off, not speaking.

I'm suddenly so hungry that I feel ill. I throw some clothes on and head downstairs. I start brewing coffee and put bread in the toaster. Jesse comes down shortly after, in fresh clothes.

The mood has shifted. You can feel it in the air between us. Everything we've been pretending isn't true is about to come tumbling out of us, in shouts and tears.

"I started making coffee," I say. I try to make my voice sound light and carefree but it's not working. I know it's not working. I know that my inner turmoil isn't so inner, that trying to cover it up is like brushing a thin coat of white paint over a red wall. It's seeping out. It's clear as day what I'm trying to hide.

"I'm starting to think you don't want to be here," Jesse says.

I look up at him. "It's complicated," I say.

Jesse nods, not in agreement with me but as if he's heard this all before. "You know what? I gotta tell ya. I don't think it's that complicated."

"Of course it is," I say, sitting down on the sofa.

"Not really," Jesse says, following suit, sitting down opposite me. His voice is growing less patient by the second. "You and

I are married. We have been together, have loved each other, forever. We belong together."

"Jesse—"

"No!" he says. "Why do I feel like I have to convince you to be with me? This isn't . . . You should never have done what you did. How could you agree to marry this guy?"

"You don't—"

"You're *my* wife, Emma. We stood in front of a hundred people right down the road at that goddamn lighthouse and promised to love each other for the rest of our lives. I lost you once and I did everything I could to get back to you. Now I'm here, I'm back, and I'm in danger of losing you all over again? This is supposed to be the happy part. Now that we're here together. This is all supposed to be the easy stuff."

"It's not that simple."

"It should be! That's what I'm saying. It should be that fucking simple!"

I am both stunned at the anger directed at me and surprised it took this long for it to surface.

"Yeah, well, it's not, OK? Life doesn't always work out the way you think it will. I learned that when you left on a plane three years ago and disappeared."

"Because I survived a crash over the Pacific Ocean! I watched everyone else on that helicopter die. I lived on a tiny scrap of a goddamn rock, alone, trying to figure out a way to get back to you. Meanwhile, what did you do? Forget about me by August? Submit for a name change by Christmas?"

"Jesse, you know that's not true."

"You want to talk about the truth? The truth is you gave up on me."

"You were gone!" My voice goes from zero to sixty in three

seconds and I can feel that my emotions are bursting out of me like a horse kept too long behind a gate. "We thought you were dead!"

"I honestly thought," Jesse says, "that you and I loved each other in a way that we could never, ever forget about each other."

"I never forgot you! Never. I have always loved you. I still love you."

"You got engaged to someone else!"

"When I thought that you were dead! If I had known you were alive, I would have waited every day for you."

"Well, now you know I'm alive. And instead of coming back to me, you're sitting on the fence. You're here with *me,* crying about *him* in the shower."

"I love you, Jesse, and even when I thought you were gone, I loved you. But I couldn't spend my life loving a man who was no longer here. And I didn't think that's what you'd want for me, either."

"You don't know what I'd want," he says.

"No!" I say. "I don't. I barely know you anymore. And you barely know me. And I feel like you want to keep pretending that we do."

"I know you!" he says. "Don't tell me I don't know you. You are the only person in my entire life that I have truly, truly known. That I know loved me. That I have understood and accepted for exactly who they are. I know everything there is to know about you."

I shake my head. "No, Jesse, you know everything about the person I was up until the day you left. But you don't know me now. Nor do you seem to have any interest in seeing me for who I am today, or for sharing with me who you are today."

"What are you talking about?"

"I'm different, Jesse. I was in my twenties when you left. I'm thirty-one now. I don't care about Los Angeles and writing travel pieces anymore. I care about my family. I care about my bookstore. I'm not the same as I was when you left. The loss of you changed me. I changed."

"I mean, fine. You changed because I was gone, I get that. You got scared, you were grieving, so you came back to Acton because it felt safe and you took over your parents' store because it was easy. But you don't have to do any of that anymore. I'm back. We can go home to California. We can finally go to Puglia. I bet you can even sell some pieces to a few magazines next year. You don't have to have this life anymore."

But I'm already shaking my head and trying to tell him no before he's even finished. "You are not understanding me," I say. "Maybe at first I came home to retreat from the world, and sure, initially, I took the job at the store because it was available. But I love my life now, Jesse. I choose to live in Massachusetts. I choose to run my store. I want this for myself."

I look at Jesse's face as he searches mine. I try a different tactic, a different way of explaining to him.

"When I'm in a sad mood, do you know what I do to cheer myself up?"

"You eat french fries and have a Diet Coke," Jesse says, just as I say, "I practice the piano."

The difference in our answers startles him. His body deflates slightly, pulling away from me. I can see, as it quickly wipes across his face, that it's hard for him to reconcile my answer with who he believes that I am.

I imagine, for a moment, that the next words out of his mouth might be, "You play the piano?"

And I'd say yes and I'd explain how I got started and that I only know a few songs and that I'm not that good, but that it relaxes me when I'm feeling stressed. I'd tell him how Homer is normally asleep under it when I want to play, so I have to pick him up and put him on the bench beside me, but that it's so nice to sit there next to my cat and play "Für Elise." Especially when I pretend "Für Elise" is about his fur.

It would mean so much if Jesse wanted to fall in love with who I am today. If he opened up and let me fall in love with the truth about who he is now.

But none of that happens.

Jesse just says, "So you play piano. What does that prove?"

And when he says it, I know that the gap between us is even larger than I thought.

"That we are different people now. We grew apart. Jesse, I don't know anything about what your life has been like for the past three and a half years and you won't talk about it. But you are different. You can't go through what you went through and not be different."

"I don't need to talk about what happened to me to prove to you that I still love you, that I'm still the person you've always loved."

"That's not what I'm saying. I'm saying that I think you're trying to pretend that we can just pick up where we left off. I was, too. But that's not possible. Life doesn't work that way. What I've been through in my life affects the person that I am today. And that's true for you, too. Whatever you went through out there. You can't keep it bottled inside."

"I've told you I don't want to talk about it."

"Why not?" I say to him. "How are we supposed to be honest with each other about our future if you won't even tell me the most basic elements of your past? You say that you know that everything can be exactly how it was, but before you left we never had huge parts of our lives that we just *didn't talk about*. We didn't have any history that we didn't share. And now we do. I have Sam and, c'mon, Jesse, you have scars on your body. Your finger is—"

Jesse slams his fist into the pillow cushions underneath us. It would be a violent action if it hadn't landed in such a soft place, and I wonder if that was by design or by accident. "What do you want to know, Emma? For crying out loud. What do you want to know? That the doctors found two types of skin cancer? That when they found me, you could see the bone of my wrists and my ribs through my chest? That I had to have four root canals and it feels like half my mouth is fake now? Is that what you want to know? You want to know that I was stung by a Portuguese man-of-war as I swam looking for safety? You want to know I couldn't get it off of me? That it just kept fucking stinging me? That the pain was so bad I thought I was dying? That the doctors say I'll have this scar for years, maybe forever? Or maybe you just want me to admit how awful it was living out on that rock. You want me to tell you how many days I spent looking out at the sea, just waiting. Telling myself I just had to make it until tomorrow, because you'd come for me. You or my parents or my brothers. But none of you came. None of you found me. No one did."

"We didn't know. We didn't know how to find you."

"I know that," he says. "I'm not mad at anyone for that. What I'm mad about is that you forgot about me! That you moved on and replaced me! That I'm back and I still don't have you."

"I didn't replace you."

"You got rid of my name at the end of yours and you told

another man you'd marry him. What else could that possibly be? What other word would you use?"

"I didn't replace you," I say again, this time weakly. "I love you."

"If that's true, then this is simple. Be with me. Help me put us back together."

I can feel Jesse's eyes on me even as I look away. I turn to look out the window, to the blanket of snow covering the backyard. It is white and clean. It looks as soft as a cloud.

When I was a kid, I loved the snow. Then when I moved to California, I used to tell people I'd never leave the sun, that I never wanted to see snow again. But now, I can't imagine a green Christmas and I know that if I left, I would miss that feeling of coming in from the cold.

I have changed over time. That's what people do.

People aren't stagnant. We evolve in reaction to our pleasures and our pains.

Jesse is a different man than he was before.

I am a different woman.

And what has confused me ever since I found out he was alive is now crystal clear: We are two people who are madly in love with our old selves. And that is not the same as being in love.

You can't capture love in a bottle. You can't hold on to it with both hands and force it to stay with you.

What has happened to us is no one's fault—neither of us did anything wrong—but when Jesse left, life took us in opposite directions and turned us into different people. We grew apart because we *were* apart.

And maybe that means that even though we can finally be together . . .

We shouldn't be.

The thought cracks open my chest.

I am perfectly still but feel as if I'm caught in a riptide, barely able to see how I can get my head out and above the water.

I don't think I was ever afraid that loving both of them made me a bad person.

I was afraid that loving Sam made me a bad person.

I was afraid that I would pick Sam. That my heart would love Sam. That my soul would need Sam.

You're not supposed to forsake the man who journeyed home to you.

You're supposed to be Penelope. You're supposed to knit the shroud day in and day out and stay up every night unraveling it to keep the suitors at bay.

You're not supposed to have a life of your own, needs of your own. You're not supposed to love again.

But I did.

That's exactly what I did.

Jesse moves closer to me, gently puts his hands on my arms. "If you love me, Emma, then be with me."

It's a scary thought, isn't it? That every single person on this planet could lose their one true love and live to love again? It means the one you love could love again if they lost you.

But it also means I know Jesse will be OK, he will be happy one day, without me.

"I don't think I can be with you," I say. "I don't think . . . I don't think we're right for each other. Anymore."

Jesse's arms slump down around him. His posture sinks. His eyes collapse shut.

It's one of those moments in life when you can't believe that the truth is true, that the world shook out like this.

I don't end up with Jesse.

After all of this, all we've been through, we aren't going to grow old together.

"I'm sorry," I say.

"I have to go."

"Where are you going to go? We're snowed in."

He grabs his jacket and puts on his shoes. "I'll just go to the car. I don't care. I just need to be alone right now."

He opens the front door and slams it behind him. I go to the door and open it again to see his back as he walks toward the car, trudging through the snow. He knows I'm behind him but stops me before I can even say a word by lifting his arm up and giving me the universal sign for "Don't." So I don't.

I close the door. I lean against it. I slink down to the floor and I cry.

Jesse and I were once ripped apart. And now we've grown apart.

The same hearts, broken twice.

Over an hour has passed and Jesse has not yet come back. I stand up and peek through the front window to see if he's still in the car.

He's sitting in the driver's seat with his head down. I look around the front of the house. The warm sun has started to melt some of the snow. The roads in the distance look, if not cleared, at least a bit traveled. We could leave here right now if we wanted to. We'd just have a little shoveling to do. But my guess is Jesse is in no rush to be trapped in a car with me.

My eye drifts back to the car and I see him moving in the driver's seat. He's looking through my envelope. He's looking at pictures and reading notes, maybe even the *Beacon* article about his disappearance.

I shouldn't watch him. I should give him the privacy that he walked out there for. But I can't look away.

I see a white envelope in his hands.

And I know exactly what it is.

The letter I wrote him to say good-bye.

He fiddles with the envelope, flipping it back and forth, deciding whether he's going to open it. My heart beats like a drum in my chest.

I put my hand on the doorknob, ready to run out there and stop him, but . . . I don't. Instead, I look back out the window.

I watch as he puts a finger under the flap and tears it open.

I turn away from the window, as if he spotted me. I know that he didn't. I just know that I'm scared.

He's going to read that letter and everything is going to get worse. It will be all the proof he needs that I forgot him, that I gave up on us, that I gave up on him.

I turn back to the window and watch him read it. He stares at the page for a long time. And then he puts it down and looks out the side window. Then he picks it up again and starts reading it a second time.

After a while, he puts his hand on the car door and opens it. I run from the window and sit on the sofa, pretending I've been here the whole time.

I never should have written that goddamn letter.

The front door opens, and there he is. Staring at me. He has the letter in his hand. He's perfectly still, stunningly quiet.

I wrote the letter so that I could let go of him. There's no hiding that. So if that's the evidence he's looking for that I've been a terrible wife, an awful person, a disloyal soul, well, then . . . I guess he got what he was looking for.

But Jesse's reaction surprises me.

"What is this about going crazy on the roof?" he says calmly.

"What?" I ask.

He hands me the letter as if I've never read it. I stand up and take it from him. I open it even though I already know what it says.

The handwriting looks hurried. You can see, at the end, that there are splotches of ink where water must have hit it. Tears, obviously. I can't stop myself from rereading it, seeing it through new eyes.

Dear Jesse,

You've been gone for more than two years but there hasn't been a day that has gone by when I haven't thought of you.

Sometimes I remember the way you smelled salty after you'd gone for a swim in the ocean. Or I wonder whether you'd have liked the movie I just saw. Other times, I just think about your smile. I think about how your eyes would crinkle and I'd always fall a little bit more in love with you.

I think about how you would touch me. How I would touch you. I think about that a lot.

The memory of you hurt so much at first. The more I thought about your smile, your smell, the more it hurt. But I liked punishing myself. I liked the pain because the pain was you.

I don't know if there is a right and wrong way to grieve. I just know that losing you has gutted me in a way I honestly didn't think was possible. I've felt pain I didn't think was human.

At times, it has made me lose my mind. (Let's just say that I went a little crazy up on our roof.)

At times, it has nearly broken me.

And I'm happy to say that now is a time when your memory brings me so much joy that just thinking of you brings a smile to my face.

I'm also happy to say that I'm stronger than I ever knew.

I have found meaning in life that I never would have guessed.

And now I'm surprising myself once again by realizing that I am ready to move forward.

I once thought grief was chronic, that all you could do was appreciate the good days and take them along with the bad. And then I started to think that maybe the good days aren't just days; maybe the good days can be good weeks, good months, good years.

Now I wonder if grief isn't something like a shell.

You wear it for a long time and then one day you realize you've outgrown it.

So you put it down.

It doesn't mean that I want to let go of the memories of you or the love I have for you. But it does mean that I want to let go of the sadness.

I won't ever forget you, Jesse. I don't want to and I don't think I'm capable of it.

But I do think I can put the pain down. I think I can leave it on the ground and walk away, only coming back to visit every once in a while, no longer carrying it with me.

Not only do I think I can do that, but I think I need to.

I will carry you in my heart always, but I cannot carry your loss on my back anymore. If I do, I'll never find any new joy for myself. I will crumble under the weight of your memory.

I have to look forward, into a future where you cannot be. Instead of back, to a past filled with what we had.

I have to let you go and I have to ask you to let me go.

I truly believe that if I work hard, I can have the sort of life for myself that you always wanted for me. A happy life. A satisfied life. Where I am loved and I love in return.

I need your permission to find room to love someone else.

I'm so sorry that we never got the future we talked about. Our life together would have been grand.

But I'm going out into the world with an open heart now. And I'm going to go wherever life takes me.

I hope you know how beautiful and freeing it was to love you when you were here.

You were the love of my life.

Maybe it's selfish to want more, maybe it's greedy to want another love like that.

But I can't help it.

I do.

So I said yes to a date with Sam Kemper. I like to think you would like him for me, that you'd approve. But I also want you to know, in case it doesn't go without saying, that no one could ever replace you. It's just that I want more love in my life, Jesse.

And I'm asking for your blessing to go find it.

Love,
Emma

I know I'm adding new splotches, new tears, to the page. But I can't seem to stop them from coming. When I finally look at Jesse, his eyes are watery. He puts his arm around me and pulls me in tight. The pain between us feels sharp enough to cut, heavy enough to sink us.

"What did you do on the roof?" he says again, this time softer, kinder.

I catch my breath and then I tell him.

"Everyone said you were dead," I start. "And I was convinced they were all wrong and that you were trying to come home to me. I just knew it. So one day, when I couldn't take it anymore, I went up to the roof and saw this small sliver of ocean and I just . . . I became convinced that you were going to swim to shore. I got your binoculars and I . . . I stood there, watching the small little piece of shoreline, waiting for you to surface."

Jesse is looking right at me, listening to my every word.

"Marie found me and told me you weren't going to swim back to me. That you weren't going to just appear on the beach like that. That you were dead. She said that I had to face it and start dealing with it. And so I did. But it was the hardest thing I've ever done. I wasn't sure I'd make it through the day. Sometimes I was living hour by hour. I've never been more confused or felt less like myself."

Jesse pulls me in tighter, holding me. "Do you realize that we were both looking out at the same ocean looking for each other?" he says.

I close my eyes and think of him waiting for me. I remember what it felt like to wait for him.

"I had this idea in the car that I would look through that envelope and find all of the stuff in there, the memories and the pictures, and that I would show you how happy we were together. I thought I'd be able to make you see that you were wrong. That we are the same people we were when we loved each other. That we are meant to be together forever. But you know what I realized?"

"What?" I say.

"I hate your hair."

I pull back from him and he laughs. "I know that's not very nice to say but it's true. I was looking at those pictures of you back then with your gorgeous long hair, and I always loved how it wasn't really blond, but it wasn't really brown. I mean, I loved your hair. And now I'm back and you've chopped it off and it's blond and, you know, maybe I'm supposed to like it, but I was sitting in the car thinking, 'She'll grow her hair out again.' And then I thought, 'Well, wait, she likes her hair like that.' "

"Yes, I do!" I say, stung.

"That's exactly my point. This is you now. Short blond hair. My Emma had long, light brown hair. And that's not you anymore. I can't just look at you and ignore your hair. I have to look at you as who you are. Right now. Today."

"And you don't like my hair," I say.

Jesse looks at me. "I'm sure it's beautiful," he says. "But, right now, all I can see is that it's not like it used to be."

I find myself leaning back into him, putting my head back onto his chest. "The Emma I knew wanted to live in California, and she wanted to be as far away from her parents' bookstore as possible. And she wasn't going to sit still until she'd seen as much of the world as she could. She loved tiny hotel shampoo bottles and the smell of the airport. She didn't know how to play a single note on a piano. And she loved me and only me," he says. "But I guess that's not you anymore."

I shake my head without looking at him.

"And I have to stop pretending that it is. Especially because . . . I'm not the same, either. I know it seems like I don't know that, but I do. I know I've changed. I'm know I'm . . ." I'm surprised to see that Jesse has begun to cry. I hold him tighter, listening, wishing I could take the pain away, spare him any more hardship on top of what he's already faced. I want so badly to protect him from the world, to ensure nothing ever hurts him again. But I can't, of course. No one can do that for anybody.

"I'm messed up, Emma," he continues. "I'm not OK, I don't think. I keep acting as if I feel OK here, but . . . I don't. I don't feel like I belong anywhere. Not here, not there. I'm . . . struggling to keep it together almost every moment of the day. One minute I feel overwhelmed by how much food is around and then the next minute I can't bring myself to eat any of it. The night I landed I woke up around three and went down to the kitchen and ate so much I made myself sick. The doctors say that I still need to be mindful of what I eat and how much, but I just want to eat nothing or everything. There's no in-between. It's not just food, either. When we were in the shower earlier, I was thinking, 'We should get a bucket and save some of this water. Store it.'"

He's finally ready to say how he really feels and it's all spilling out of him like a turned-over gallon of milk.

"I can't even stand to look at my hand. I can't stand to see that my finger is still gone. I know it sounds so stupid, but I think I thought that if I could just get home, then things could go back to the way they were. I'd get you back, and I'd feel normal again, and my pinkie would, I don't know, magically reappear or something."

He looks at me and he breathes in and then breathes out, all with great effort.

"Do you want to sit?" I ask him, pulling him toward the sofa. I sit him down and I take a seat beside him. I put my hand on his back. "It's OK," I say. "You can talk about it. You can tell me anything."

"I just . . . I hate even thinking about it," he says. "It was . . . awful. All of it. Losing my finger was maybe one of the most painful things I've ever been through. I have been working so hard to block it out."

I am quiet in the hopes that he will keep talking, that he will continue to be honest with me and with himself, that he will share what he's been through, what plagues him.

"I sliced it almost clean through," he says finally. "Trying to open an oyster with a rock. I thought it might heal on its own but it wouldn't. I lived with it growing more and more infected until I finally just had to . . ."

I can see that he can't bring himself to speak the words.

But he doesn't have to.

I know what he can't say.

He had to cut off his own finger.

Somewhere in the years he's been gone, he was forced to save his hand the only way he could.

"I'm so sorry," I say to him.

I can't imagine what else happened, how many days he went without food, how near he came to grave dehydration, the searing pain of being stung over and over as he was trying to swim to rescue. But I am starting to think that he will tackle that pain when he is ready, talking and admitting more as he grows stronger. It will be a long process. It may even be years until he can unpack it all. And even then, he'll never be able to erase it completely.

The same way I'll never be able to erase the ache of grieving him.

These are the things that have made us who we are.

I step away from Jesse for a moment and head into the kitchen. I look through the cabinets and find an old box of Earl Grey.

"How about some tea?" I offer.

He looks up at me and nods. It is so gentle as to be almost imperceptible.

I put two mugs of water in the microwave. I grab the tea bags.

"Keep talking," I say. "I'm listening."

His voice picks up again and I realize that he must have, whether it was conscious or subconscious, been waiting for permission.

"I think I've been trying to *undo* the last however many years," he says. "I've been trying to put everything back the way it was before I left so it can be as if it never happened. But that doesn't work. I mean, obviously it doesn't. I know that."

I stop the microwave before it beeps, pulling the mugs out and putting the tea bags in. The smell of the tea reminds me of Marie. I sit back down next to Jesse, putting his steaming cup in front of him. He takes it into his hand but he doesn't drink it yet.

"I'm not the same person that I was back then," he says. "You know it and I know it, but I just keep thinking that with a little effort, I can change that. But I can't. I can't, can I?"

He puts the mug down and starts gesticulating with his hands. "I don't want to spend the rest of my life in Acton," he says. "I've spent too long trapped somewhere I didn't want to be. I want to go back to California. I respect that Blair Books means as much to you as it does, but I don't get it. We worked so hard to move away from New England, to get away from the life that our parents were pushing us toward. We sacrificed so much so that we could travel, not so that we could stay in one place. I don't understand why you came back here, why you chose to spend your life here, doing exactly what your parents always told you you should do.

"I'm really, really angry, deep down in my heart. And I wish that I didn't feel that way and I hate myself for feeling it. But I'm furious that you could fall in love with someone else. I know you say that it doesn't mean you forgot me, but, you know, at least right now, it sure sounds like it to me. And I'm not saying that we couldn't get past that, if everything else about us made sense, but . . . I don't know.

"I'm mad at you and I'm mad at Friendly's for turning into a Johnny whatever you called it. I'm mad at almost everything that changed without me. I know I need to work on that. I know it's just one of the strings of issues that I'm facing. I know I said that now was supposed to be the easy part but I don't know why I thought that. Coming home is hard. This was always going to be hard. I'm sorry I didn't see that until now.

"Of course I've changed. And of course you've changed. There is no way we could be the same after losing each other; we meant too much to each other for that to happen. So, I guess what I'm saying is that I'm miserable and I'm angry, but I guess I do get it. What you said in that letter makes some sense to me. You had to let go of me if you were ever going to have a chance at a normal life. I know you loved me then. I know it wasn't easy. And, obviously, I know this is hard for you, too. I'd be lying if I said that I didn't see what you see."

He puts his arms around me, pulling me close to him, and then he says what has taken us days to understand.

"We loved each other and we lost each other. And now, even though we still love each other, the pieces don't fit like they used to."

I could make myself fit for him.

He could make himself fit for me.

But that's not true love.

"This is it for us," Jesse says. "We're over now."

I look in his eyes. "Yeah. I think we are."

After everything we've been through, I never predicted it ending like this.

Jesse and I stay still, holding each other, not yet ready to fully let go. His hands are still a little bit frozen. I take them in my own. I hold them, sharing the heat of my body.

He pulls one hand away to brush a hair off of my face.

I think, maybe, *this* is what true love means.

Maybe true love is warming someone up from the cold, or tenderly brushing a hair away, because you care about them with every bone in your body even though you know what's between you won't last.

"I don't know where we go from here," I say.

Jesse puts his chin on my head, breathing in. And then he pulls away slightly to look at me. "You still don't have to be back until late tomorrow, right?"

"Yeah," I say.

"So we can stay," he says. "For another day. We can take our time."

"What do you mean?"

"I'm saying that I know what's ahead of us, but . . . I'm not ready yet. I'm just not ready. And I don't see why we can't spend a little bit more time with each other, a little bit more time being happy together. I've waited so long to be here with you; it seems silly to squander it just because it won't last."

I smile, charmed. I consider what he's saying and realize that it feels exactly right to me, like being handed a glass of water just as you realize you're thirsty. "That sounds good," I say. "Let's just have a nice time together, not worry about the future."

"Thank you."

"OK, so until tomorrow, you and I will leave the real world on the other side of that door, knowing that we will face it soon. But . . . for now, we can let things be the way they were, once."

"And then tomorrow we go home," Jesse says.

"Yeah," I say. "And we start to learn how to live without each other again."

"You'll marry Sam," Jesse says.

I nod. "And you'll probably move to California."

"But for now . . . for one more day . . ."

"We'll be Emma and Jesse."

"The way we were."

I laugh. "Yeah, the way we were."

Jesse builds a fire and then joins me on the sofa. He puts his arm around me and pulls me into the crook of his shoulder. I rest my head on him.

It feels good to be in his arms, to be satisfied with this moment, to not wonder what the future holds. I relish the way he feels next to me, cherish the joy of having him near. I know I won't always have it.

It starts snowing again, small flurries landing on the already white ground. I get up from Jesse's arms and walk over to the sliding glass doors to watch it fall.

Everything is quiet and soft. The snow is white and clean, not yet crushed under the weight of boots.

"Hear me out," I say, turning back to Jesse.

"Uh-oh," he says.

"Snow angels."

"Snow angels?"

"Snow angels."

As soon as we step out into the snow, I realize the flaw in my plan. We will sully the unsullied snow by walking in it. We will crush the uncrushed just by being here.

"Are you sure this is what you want to do?" Jesse asks me. "Imagine how good it will feel to watch a movie inside by the fire."

"No, c'mon, this is better."

"I'm not sure about that," Jesse says, and from the tone of his voice, I now understand why people sometimes describe the air as "bitter cold." The cold is not bitter. They are bitter about the cold.

I run ahead, hoping he'll catch up to me. I try to remember what it felt like to once be a teenager with him. I trip and let myself fall. I drop face-first into the snow. I turn around. I see Jesse running to catch up with me.

"Come on, slowpoke," I say as I stretch my arms out and widen my legs. I windshield-wiper them back and forth, until I hit the icy snow that has crystalized onto the grass beneath it.

Jesse catches up and plops himself down next to me. He extends his limbs and starts pushing the snow out of the way. I get up and watch him.

"Nice work," I say. "Excellent form."

Jesse stands and turns to look at his creation. Then he looks at mine.

"You can say it," I tell him. "Yours is better."

"Don't beat yourself up," he says. "Some people just have a natural raw talent for snow art. And I'm one of them."

I roll my eyes and then step lightly in the center of his angel where the footprints won't show. I lean forward and draw a halo where his head once was.

"There," I say. "*Now* it's art."

But I have made a rookie mistake, out here in the snow. I have turned my back to him. And when I stand up, he pelts me with a snowball.

I shake my head and then very slowly and deliberately make a snowball myself.

"You don't want to do that," he says, just a hint of fear in his voice.

"You started it."

"Still. What you're planning on doing would be a mistake," he says.

"Oh yeah? What are you gonna do?" I ask, slowly sauntering up to him, savoring the very trivial power I currently wield.

"I will . . ." he starts to say, but then he swiftly leans toward me and knocks the snowball out of my hand. It hits my leg on the way down.

"You just hit me with my own snowball!" I say.

I gather up another one and throw it at him. It hits him square in the neck. I have declared war.

Jesse gets in a snowball to my arm and one to the top of my head. I get one that hits him straight in the chest. I run away when I see a huge one forming in his hand.

I run and I run and then I trip on the snow and fall down. I brace myself, waiting for a snowball to hit me. But when I open my eyes, I see that Jesse is standing right above me.

"Truce?" he asks.

I nod and he throws the last snowball far out in the distance.

"How about that warm fire and those blankets?" he asks me.

This time I don't hesitate. "I'm in."

When we're thawed, Jesse heads to the stack of books and movies that have been sitting in this cabin for years. There are supermarket paperbacks so well-worn that they have white line creases on the spine. There are DVDs from the early 2000s and even a few VHS tapes.

We pick out an old movie and try to turn on the TV. It doesn't respond.

"Is it just me or does it appear that the television is dead?" Jesse says.

I look behind to see if it's plugged in. It is. But when I hit a few buttons, nothing happens.

"It's broken," he says. "I bet it's been broken for years and no one thought to turn it on."

"A book, then," I say, walking over to the stack of paperbacks. "I've come to realize it's a wonderful way to pass the time." I glance through the spines of the books on the shelf and spot a thin detective novel that I've never heard of among the John Grishams and James Pattersons. I pull it out. "Why don't we read this?"

"Together?"

"I'll read to you, you read to me," I say. Jesse isn't entirely sold.

The sun starts to set and even though we aren't in danger of being cold in here, Jesse adds logs to the fire. He finds an old bottle of red wine underneath the bar and I grab two jelly jars from the cabinets.

We drink the bottle as we sit by the fire.

We talk about the times we made each other blissfully happy, and we laugh about the times we made each other blisteringly mad. We talk about our love story like two people reflecting on a movie they just saw, which is to say, we talk about it with the fresh knowledge of how it all ends. All of the memories are ever so slightly different now, tinged with bittersweetness.

"You were always the voice of reason," Jesse says. "Always the one stopping us from going just one step further than we should."

"Yeah, but you always gave me the courage to do what I wanted to do," I say. "I'm not sure I would have had the guts to do half the things I did if I didn't have you believing in me, egging me on."

We talk about our wedding—the ceremony by the lighthouse, our brief dalliance here, our reception down the street. I tell Jesse that my memories of that day aren't darkened by what happened later. That it still brings me nothing but joy to think about. That I'm thankful for it, no matter where we have ended up.

Jesse says he's not sure he agrees with me. He says it feels sad to him, that it represents a painful naivete about the future, that he feels sorry for the Jesse of that day, the Jesse who doesn't know what is ahead of him. It feels like a reminder of what he could have had if he hadn't ever gotten on that helicopter. But then he says that he hopes, one day, to see it the way I do.

"If I ever come around to your way of thinking," Jesse says, "I promise I'll find you and tell you."

"I would like that," I say. "I'll always want to know how you are."

"Well, then it's a good thing you'll always be easy to find," he says.

"Yeah," I say. "I'm not going anywhere."

The fire slows and Jesse moves toward it, rearranging the logs, blowing on it. He turns back to me, the calm fire now starting to roar again.

"You think you would have ever gone to school in LA if it wasn't for me?" he says.

"Maybe," I say. "Maybe not. I know that I wouldn't have been as happy there without you. And I wouldn't have even applied to that travel-writing class without you. And I definitely wouldn't have spent a year in Sydney or all those months in Europe if you weren't with me. I think there were a lot of things I never would have done—good, bad, beautiful, tragic, however you want to describe them. I think there were a lot of things I wouldn't have had the nerve to do if it wasn't for you."

"Sometimes I wonder if I would have just let my parents push me toward pro training if I hadn't met you," he says. "You were the first person who didn't care how good of a swimmer I was. The first person who just liked me for me. That . . . that was life changing. Truly."

He turns and looks at me intently. "You're a lot of the reason why I am who I am," he says.

"Oh, Jesse," I say, so much tenderness and affection that my heart is soaked, "there is no me without you."

Jesse kisses me then.

A kiss is just a kiss, I guess. But I've never been kissed like this before. It is sad and loving and wistful and scared and peaceful.

When we finally pull away from each other, I realize I'm tipsy and Jesse might just be drunk. The bottle is gone and as I go to put down my glass, I accidentally tip it over. That unmistakable cling and thud of a wine bottle hitting the floor is not followed by the familiar crash that sometimes accompanies it. Grateful, I pick up the intact bottle and our glasses.

I think it's time to switch to the soft stuff.

I get us some glasses of water and remind him about the book.

"You really want to read a book together?" he says.

"It's that or Taboo."

Jesse acquiesces, grabbing blankets and pillows from the couch. We lie down on the floor, close to the fire. I open up the book I pulled aside earlier.

"The Reluctant Adventures of Cole Crane," I begin.

I read to children's groups on Sunday mornings sometimes. I've started getting more confident, making up voices for the characters and trying to make the narration come alive. But I don't do any of that now. I'm just me. Reading a book. To someone I love.

Unfortunately, it's a very bad book. Laughably bad. The women are called dames. The men drink whiskey and make bad puns. I barely get through five pages before handing it over to Jesse. "You have to read this. I can't do it," I say.

"No," he says, "c'mon. I waited years just to hear your voice."

And so I read some more. By the time my eyes feel dry from the fire, I'm reluctantly invested in what happens to the Crooked Yellow Caper and I find myself wanting Cole Crane to just kiss Daphne Monroe already.

Jesse agrees to read the second half while I lie in his lap with my eyes closed.

His voice is soothing and calm. I listen as it ebbs and flows, as his words fall up and down.

When he's been reading for over an hour, I sit up and take the book out of his hand. I put it on the floor.

I know what I'm about to do. I know that it is the last time that I will ever do it. I know that I want it to mean something. For years I never had a chance to say good-bye. Now that I have it, I know this is the way I want to do it.

So I kiss him the way you kiss people when it is the start of something. And it starts something.

I pull my shirt over my head. I unbutton the fly of Jesse's jeans. I lay my body flush against his. It is the last time I will feel his warmth, the last time I will look down to see him below me, with his hands on my waist. It is the last time I will tell him I love him by the way I sink my hips and touch his chest.

He never looks anywhere but at me. I watch as his gaze moves down my body, watching me, taking it all in, trying to pin it to memory.

I feel seen. Truly seen. Cherished and savored.

Don't ever let anyone tell you the most romantic part of love is the beginning. The most romantic part is when you know it has to end.

I don't know that I've ever been as present in a moment as I am this very second, as I make love to a man I once believed was my soul mate, who I now know is meant for some*one* else and some*thing* else, is meant to build his life some*where* else.

His eyes have never looked more captivating. His body underneath me has never felt safer. I trace my hands over the scars on his body; I intertwine my left hand with his right one. I want him to know he's beautiful to me.

When it's over, I am too tired and stunned to mourn. I crawl back into the crook of his arm and I hand him the book again.

"Read?" I say. "Just a little while longer."

All of this. Just a little while longer.

"Yeah," Jesse says. "Anything you want."

I fall asleep in his arms, listening to him read the end of the book, happy to learn that Cole grabs Daphne by the shoulders and says, finally, "My God, woman, don't you know it's you? That it's always been you?"

Falling out of love with someone you still *like* feels exactly like lying in a warm bed and hearing the alarm clock.

No matter how good you feel right now, you know it's time to go.

Errr Errr Errr Errr Errr.

The sun is shining brightly in my face. And Jesse's watch is beeping.

The cover of *The Reluctant Adventures of Cole Crane* is bent back, underneath his leg.

The fire is out.

"Time to get up," I say.

Jesse, still trying to adjust to wakefulness, nods his head and rubs his face.

We both head into the kitchen and grab some food. I drink a full glass of water. Jesse drinks cold coffee from the pot. He looks out the kitchen window as he drinks and then he turns back to me.

"It's snowing again," he says.

"Hard?" I ask. I look around to the front window to see that there's a fresh blanket of snow on the driveway.

"We should get on the road soon," he says. "I think it looks pretty clear right now, but we don't want to wait too much longer."

"OK, good idea. I'm going to get in the shower."

Jesse nods but doesn't say anything else. He doesn't follow me up the stairs to join me. He doesn't make a joke about me being naked. Instead, he moves toward the fireplace and starts to clean up.

It is then, as I start walking up the stairs alone, that I feel the full weight of the new truth.

Jesse is home. Jesse is alive.

But Jesse is no longer mine.

Within forty-five minutes, Jesse and I have gathered our things and are ready to go. The dishes are done, the remaining groceries are packed up, the mess we made has been cleaned. Even *The Reluctant Adventures of Cole Crane* is back on the shelf, as if it had never been read. If I didn't know better, I'd swear we were never here.

Jesse grabs the keys and opens the front door for me. It is with a heavy heart that I pass through it.

I don't offer to drive because I know he won't let me. He's going to do things his way and I'm going to let him. So I get into the passenger seat and Jesse puts the car in reverse.

I take one last look as we pull away from the cabin.

There are two tracks of footprints leading from the front door.

They start out close together and veer off in different directions as our feet head for opposite sides of the car.

I know those footprints will be gone soon. I know they might not make it to tonight if it keeps snowing like this. But it feels good to be able to look at something and understand it.

The footprints start off together and they grow apart.

I get it.

It's fine.

It's the truth.

Two True Loves

Or, how to make peace with the truth about love

Jesse and I are almost to New Hampshire by the time we start actually having a conversation. We've just been listening to the radio, stuck in our own heads for the past hour and a half.

I have thought mainly of Sam.

About the stubble that always grows on his face, about the fact that he's clearly going to go gray early, about how I am eager to go back to spending my evenings with him at the piano.

I hope that when I tell him he's the one I want, he believes me.

It's been rough going but I have finally figured out who I am and what I want. In fact, never has my identity felt so crystal clear.

I am Emma Blair.

Bookstore owner. Sister. Daughter. Aunt. Amateur pianist. Cat lover. New Englander. Woman who wants to marry Sam Kemper.

That doesn't mean that it's without pain and sadness. There is still loss.

I know, I know deep in my gut that the moment when I get out of this car, when Jesse drops me off and says good-bye, I will feel as if I am breaking.

I feel the same way I did when I was nine and my mom took me to get my ears pierced for my birthday.

My party was that night. I had a blue dress that I had picked out myself. My mom and I picked out fake sapphire stud earrings to match. I felt very grown-up.

The woman put the gun to my right ear and told me it might hurt. I told her I was ready.

The pierce shot through me like a shock. I wasn't sure which was worse: the pressure of the squeeze, the pain of the puncture, or the sting of the air on a fresh wound.

I shuddered and closed my eyes. I kept them closed. My mom and the lady with the piercing gun asked me if I was OK and I said, "Can you do the other one now? Please."

And that ache—that sense that I knew exactly what to expect and I knew that it would be awful—feels exactly like the ache inside me now.

I know exactly how much it hurts to lose Jesse. And I'm in this car, waiting to be pierced.

"When my parents have adjusted a bit," Jesse says as we approach the state border, "and I feel like they will be OK if I leave, I'm just going right back to Santa Monica."

"Oh, Santa Monica? Not interested in trying out San Diego or Orange County?"

Jesse shakes his head. "I think Santa Monica is my place. I mean, I thought you and I would spend the rest of our lives there. I wasn't sure what to make of the fact that you were back here. But you know what? I think it will be really good to go back on my own." He says it as if it's just occurring to him that by letting me go, he has freed himself of some things.

"If you do go, will you let us all know how you are?"

"I have no intention of ever leaving anyone wondering where I am again."

I smile and squeeze his hand for a brief moment. I look out the window and watch as we pass bare brown trees and green highway signs.

"And you," Jesse says after a while. "You're gonna marry Sam and live here forever, huh?"

"If he'll have me," I say.

"Why do you say that? Why wouldn't he have you?"

I fiddle with the heat controls on my side of the car, aiming the air right on me. "Because I've put him through hell," I say. "Because I haven't been the easiest woman to be engaged to lately."

"That's not your fault," Jesse says. "That's not . . . that's not the whole story."

"I know," I say. "But I also know that I've hurt him. And the last time I spoke to him he said not to call him. That he would call me when he was ready to talk."

"*Has* he called you?"

I check my phone again, just to be sure. But of course he hasn't called. "No."

"He'll take you back," Jesse says. He's so sure of it that it makes me realize just how unsure I really am.

I risked my relationship with Sam to see if there was something left with Jesse. I knew what I was doing when I did it. I'm not pretending I didn't.

But now I know what I want. I want Sam. And I'm afraid that I may have lost him because I didn't know it earlier.

"Well, if he doesn't take you back . . ." Jesse says, just as he realizes that he needs to be three lanes over. He doesn't finish his sentence right way. He's focused on the road. I wonder, for a moment, if he's going to say that if Sam doesn't marry me, he'll take me back.

I am surprised at how unnatural and inaccurate that would be.

Because I haven't been choosing between Sam or Jesse. It was never one or the other. Even though at times, I thought it was exactly that.

It was about whether Jesse and I still had something, or whether we didn't.

I know, like I know that stealing is wrong and my mom is lying when she says she likes my dad's mint juleps, that what has happened between Jesse and me is because of Jesse and me. And not because of anyone waiting in the wings.

We are over because we aren't right for each other anymore.

If Sam doesn't want me to come home after all of this, Jesse will call me to make sure I'm OK and send postcards from sunny places. And we'll both know that I could join him. And we'll both know that I'm not going to. And we'll be OK with that.

Because we had this.

We had three days in Maine.

Where we reunited and broke our own hearts.

And walked away in two pieces.

"Sorry," Jesse says now that he's been able to make it through the interchange and can focus on talking again. "What was I saying? Oh, right. If Sam doesn't take you back, I will personally kick his ass."

I laugh at the idea of Jesse kicking Sam's ass. It seems so absurd. Jesse could probably kick Sam's ass in about three seconds. It would be like one of those boxing matches where the one guy gets in a punch right off the bat and the poor sucker never knew what hit him.

Sam, my Sam, my adorable, sweetheart Sam, is a lover, not a fighter. I love that about him.

"I'm serious," Jesse says. "This is an insane situation. If he can't see that, I will personally see to it that he is in physical pain."

"Oh!" I say, joking with him. "No, don't do that! I love him."

I don't mean it as a profound announcement, despite how profoundly I feel it. But no matter *how* I say it, it's sort of an uncomfortable thing to say, given the circumstances.

I watch Jesse swallow hard and then speak. "I'm happy for you," Jesse says. "I am."

"Thank you," I say, relieved at his magnanimity. I don't think he's being honest, right now. But he's trying really hard. I have so much respect for him for that.

"And that's going to conclude our discussion of him," Jesse says. "Because otherwise, I'm going to be ill."

"Fair enough," I say, nodding my head. "Happy to change the subject."

"We'll be home not too long from now," he says. "We're almost in Tewksbury."

"Should we play I Spy or something?"

Jesse laughs. "Yeah, all right," he says. "I spy with my little eye . . . something . . . blue."

Maybe relationships are supposed to end with tears or screams. Maybe they are supposed to conclude with two people saying everything they never said or ripping into each other in a way that can't be undone.

I don't know.

I've only really ended one relationship in my life.

It is this one.

And this one ends with a good-natured game of I Spy.

We spot things and we guess them and we make each other laugh.

And when Jesse pulls the car into the front parking lot of Blair Books, I know I only have a moment before the piercing gun comes to my ear.

"I love you," I say. "I've always loved you. I'll always love you."

"I know," he says. "I feel the same way. Go grab the life you made for yourself."

I kiss him good-bye like you kiss your friends on New Year's. I don't have it in me to kiss him any other way.

I gather my things and I put my hand on the car door, not yet ready to pull the handle.

"You were a wonderful person to love," I say. "It felt so good to love you, to be loved by you."

"Well, it was the easiest thing I ever did," he says.

I smile at him and then breathe in, preparing myself for the piercing pain of leaving.

"Will you promise me that you will take care of yourself?" I say. "That you'll call me if you need anything. That you'll . . ." I don't know exactly how to phrase what I mean. He has been through so much and I want him to promise me, promise all of us who care about him, that he will work through it.

Jesse nods and waves me off. "I know what you mean. And I promise."

"OK," I say, smiling tenderly. I open the door. I put my feet onto the pavement. I get out of the car and close it behind me.

Jesse waves at me and then puts his car in reverse. I watch him as he does a three-point turn out of the lot. It hurts just as much as I thought it would. The pressure, the ache, the sting.

I wave as he makes a left onto the main road.

And then he's gone.

I close my eyes for a moment, processing what has just happened. *It's over. Jesse is alive and home and our marriage is over.* But then when I open my eyes again, I realize where I am.

My bookstore.

I turn around and walk toward the door.

I'm walking toward books and my family and that one day in spring when the sun feels like it will shine for you forever and the flowers will bloom for months. I am walking toward vegan cheddar grilled cheese and cat GIFs and "Piano Man."

I am walking toward Sam.

I am walking home.

And just like the day I got my ears pierced, once the pain has come and gone, I've grown up.

My mother and father are both in the store. Before I'm even close enough to say hi to them, I hear children crying in the far corner.

"Are the girls here?" I ask the moment I hug my parents hello.

"With Marie in the children's section," my mom says.

"How are you? How did everything go?" my dad asks.

I start to answer but there's so much to explain and I'm not up for getting into the details just yet. "I missed Sam," I say. Actually, that might just cover all of it. Succinct and painless.

They look at each other and smile, as if they are part of a two-man club that knew this is what I'd do all along.

I hate the idea of being predictable, especially predictable to my parents. But, more than anything, I'm relieved that I seem to have made the right set of decisions. Because, after all, they are my parents. And when you get to be old enough, it's finally OK to admit that they often do know best.

I can hear Marie trying to calm down Sophie and Ava. I come around the side of the register to get a better view. The two girls are crying, red faced. They are both holding opposite sides of their heads. I look back to my parents.

"Ava ran into Sophie and they hit each other in the head," my mom says.

My father puts his finger to his ear, as if the sound of their screaming is going to burst his eardrum. "It's been great for business."

As the girls' sobbing dies down, reduced to the far more quiet but equally theatrical gulping for breath and frowning, Marie spots me and comes walking over.

I turn to my parents. "By the way, we have to talk about Tina," I say.

Neither of my parents look me in the eye directly. "We can talk about it another time," my dad says. "When things aren't so . . . dramatic."

My mother averts her gaze, instantly focusing on straightening things underneath the register. My dad pretends as if he's deeply engaged in the store calendar sitting on the counter. I have been their daughter for too long to fall for this kind of crap. They are hiding something.

"What's going on?" I ask. "What are you two not saying?"

"Oh, honey, it's nothing," my mom says, and I almost believe her. But then I see the look on my dad's face, a mixture of "Is she buying this?" and "Oh, God, we should just tell her."

"We just have some, you know, ideas for the management of the store," my dad says finally. "But we should talk about it later."

When Marie makes her way to me and looks like she's afraid to tell me she borrowed my favorite sweater, I know she's in on it, too.

"C'mon, everybody, I'm dealing with too much stuff right now to have the patience for whatever this is."

"It's nothing," Marie says. I frown at her to let her know I don't believe it for a second. She folds like a cheap suit. "Fine. I want the job."

"What job?" I ask.

"The assistant manager position."

"Here?"

"Yeah, I want it. Mom and Dad think it's a great idea, but obviously it's up to you."

"You want to work here?" I say, still disbelieving. "With me?"

"Yes."

"At this store?" I say.

"See? I knew it wasn't the right time to talk about this."

"No," I say, shaking my head. "I'm just surprised."

"I know," she says. "But this could be my something. Like we talked about. Something outside of the house that has nothing to do with potty training or hearing and deafness. I think this idea is better than writing, actually. I'm excited about it and it's something with adults, you know? A reason to put on a nice pair of pants. Emma, I need a reason to put on pants."

"OK . . ." I say.

"I can't take on a full-time job but an assistant manager position could be really good. Especially because Mom and Dad could help fill in for me with the kids or here if need be. I guess what I'm saying is . . . Please hire me."

"But you used to be the manager. I'd be your boss," I say.

Marie puts both of her hands up, in mock surrender. "It's your show. I know that I gave up the position and you've done a great job at it. I'm not trying to usurp anything. If, later on down the line, I decide that I want to take on more or be a more vocal participant in the store, that's my problem and I'll deal with it. I can always take on a manager job at one of Mike's stores if it comes to that. But right now, what I really want is to spend my time here, with you."

Marie has said her piece and now it's up to me to respond.

I can feel my sister's, my father's, and my mother's eyes on me. Sophie and Ava, now calm, are pulling on Marie's leg.

"So?" Marie says.

I start laughing. It's all so absurd. All three of them start to worry, unsure what, exactly, I find so funny. So I get hold of myself in an effort to not keep them in suspense any longer.

It scares me, the idea of having Marie working under me. It makes me sort of uncomfortable and I'm slightly worried that it will undermine the good relationship we've started to build. But I also think that it could turn out to be great. I'd have someone to share this store with, someone who understands how important it is, who has a passion for not just books but this store's history. And working together, spending more time with each other, could bring us even closer.

So I think this is a risk I'm willing to take.

I'm ready to bet on Marie and me.

"OK," I say. "You're hired."

The smile that erupts across my father's face is so wide and sincere that the teenage version of me would have threatened to barf. But I'm not a teenager anymore and it won't kill me to give my father everything he's ever dreamed of. "All right, Dad," I say. "Your girls are running your store."

For the first time in my entire life, I wonder if perhaps Marie and I might actually prove to be greater together than the sum of our parts.

Emma and Marie.

Our moment of celebration is interrupted by a man who tells my dad he is looking for a book for his wife. I overhear as my dad asks what it's called. The man says, "I don't know and I'm not sure who wrote it. I don't remember what it's about, but I do remember that the cover was blue."

I watch my parents give each other a knowing glance and then both of them try to help him.

As they walk away, Marie looks at me. "So what happened in Maine? Are you going home to Sam?"

"I don't know, exactly."

"What do you mean?" she asks.

"I know that I want to be with Sam, but he told me not to call him even if I've made a decision. He said that he would let me know when he was ready to talk. Not the other way around."

Marie waves it off. "He just meant that if you were going to turn him down. He doesn't mean that if you have good news you shouldn't tell him."

"I don't know. I think he's really upset."

"Of course he's upset. But that's all the more reason to find him and talk to him."

"I want to respect his wishes," I say.

"Emma, listen to me. Go find him right now and tell him that you want to be with him."

"You mean like go to his office at school?" I say.

"Yes!" Marie says. "Absolutely do that. I mean, don't propose to him in front of band kids or whatever. But yes! Find him now."

"Yeah," I say, starting to build up the confidence. "Yeah, I think you're right."

My parents come over and ring up the man. He must not have found what he came in for. He is, instead, purchasing a copy of *Little Women*. No doubt my parents gave up trying to figure out what book he was talking about a few minutes into it and just decided to sell him on Louisa May Alcott.

They want to sell everyone a copy of *Little Women*. Because it's a great book, sure. But also because they are proud that it was written just a few miles away. They probably also tried to sell him any Henry David Thoreau or Ralph Waldo Emerson we have in stock.

I haven't been pushing the transcendentalists like they do. Copies stay on the shelf longer than they did when my parents were running things.

They have never given me a hard time about it. My father has never asked why there are copies of *Civil Disobedience* that have managed to earn dust on them.

My parents have given me an incredible gift: they gave me this store, and they set up a future for me, but they never told me theirs was the only way to do it.

We sell more journals and candles now. We sell tote bags with literary quotes on them. We sell more Young Adult than we have in years. And we sell less of the classics and less hardcovers. That all might be because of how the business is changing. But I also think it's because of me. Because I do things differently, for better and for worse.

Now, things might change again with Marie coming back. We might grow even stronger.

The man leaves and I prepare to head out to my car and try to win back the love of my life.

"OK," I say. "I'm out of here. Wish me luck."

I get to the door before I turn around. I decide that something I've left unsaid needs to be explicit.

"Thank you," I say to my parents. "For trusting me with this store and for waiting for me to fall in love with it on my own, in my own way. Thank you for guiding me toward a life that makes me happy."

For a minute, my mom looks like she might cry, but she doesn't.

"Of course, honey," she says as my dad gives me a wink. That's parents for you.

You say thank you for gifts they've given that have shaped your entire world and their answer is, "Of course."

As I'm out the door, I turn to Marie and say, "Welcome back."

As I get into my car in the back lot, I find my days-old sandwich sitting in the front seat. It has already given my car a sour, acrid odor. I grab it and throw it away in the Dumpster and then open up both of my car doors for a minute, trying to air it out.

That's when I see a car pulling in.

I don't need to look through the windshield to know who it is.

But of course I do anyway.

Sam.

My heart starts beating rapidly. I can feel rhythmic bass throbbing in my chest.

I run toward his car just as he steps out of it.

He's in slacks and a button-down with his tie untied and hanging loosely around his neck. His coat is unbuttoned.

It's the middle of the day and he should be at school.

Instead, he's standing in the lot of my store with his eyes bloodshot.

I look at him and I see a broken heart.

"I have to talk to you," he says, his breath visible in the cold.

"I have to talk to you, too," I say.

"No," Sam says, putting his hand up. "I'm going first."

I can feel my heart start to break in my chest. *Is it over?* I am devastated that my being unsure has led to the man I love being unsure about me. I feel the urgent need to stall, to draw out this moment, to spend as much time as possible with him before he leaves me for good—if that's what he's going to do.

"Can we get in the car?" I say. "Turn on the heat?"

Sam nods and opens up his car door. I run around to the passenger side, rubbing my hands together for warmth. Sam turns on the ignition and we wait for the heat to warm up. Soon, my hands start to thaw.

"Listen," Sam says. "I've spent the past four days thinking."

It feels like a lifetime has passed but it's only been four days.

"I can't do this," he says as he turns his whole body toward me. "I can't live like this. I can't . . . This isn't working for me."

"OK," I say. I can feel my chest start to ache as if my body can't stand to hear this.

"You have to come home," he says.

I look up at him. "What?"

"Fifteen years ago, I watched you go off with Jesse and I told myself that you had made your decision and there was nothing that I could do about it. And here we are, all this time later, and I'm doing the same thing. That's not . . . I can't do it again. I'm fighting for you.

"I left work after fifth period today because I was considering teaching the jazz band how to play 'Total Eclipse of the Heart.' I'm heartbroken without you. I have spent this time alone moping around like a bird with a broken wing just hoping that you'd come back to me. But it's not enough to hope. I'm an adult now. I'm not a teenager like I was back then, the first time. I'm a man now. And it's not enough for me to hope for you. I have to fight for you. So here I am. That's what I'm doing. I'm putting up a fight."

Sam takes my hand and implores me. "I am right for you, Emma. What we have is . . . it's true love. I love you. I want to spend the rest of my life with you. You're my soul mate. I can make you happy," he says. "I can give you the life you want. So marry me, Emma. Marry *me*."

"Oh, my God," I say, relief washing over me. "We are so ridiculous."

"What are you talking about?" Sam asks. "What do you mean?"

"You're fighting for me?" I say.

"Yeah."

"I was about to come find you at your job to fight for you."

Sam is disarmed and stunned. He is quiet. And then he starts to tear up and says, "Really?"

"I love you, sweetheart," I say to him. "I want to be with you for the rest of my life. I'm so sorry that I had unfinished business. But it is finished now. It's over. And I know that you are the man I want to spend every day of my life with. I want our life. I want to marry you. I'm sorry I was lost. But I'm so sure now. I want you."

"And Jesse?" Sam asks.

"I love Jesse. I'll always love him. But he was right for me then. You are right for me now. And always."

Sam breathes in, letting my words flow into his ears and settle in his brain.

"Do you mean all of this?" he asks me. "It's not just something you're saying to be dramatic and wonderful?"

I shake my head. "No, I'm not trying to be dramatic and wonderful."

"I mean, you've succeeded in it, for sure."

"But I mean it. All of it. Assuming that you can forgive me

for being uncertain, for needing to leave, for needing more time with him, to find out what I think I already knew."

"I can forgive that," Sam says. "Of course I can."

It's important to me that he knows what I've done, that I face it. "We went to Maine together, alone," I say.

I don't say anything more because I don't have to.

Sam shakes his head. "I don't want to hear about it. I don't want to know. It's over. It's in the past. All that matters is from here on out."

I nod my head, desperate to assure him. "I don't want anyone or anything except you from here on out, forever."

He takes it all in, closing his eyes.

"You'll be my wife?" he says, smiling wide. I don't know if I've ever felt more loved than in this moment, when the idea that I might marry a man brings that much joy to his face.

"Yes," I say. "God, yes."

Sam leans over to my side of the car and kisses me, beaming. The tears in my eyes are finally happy tears. My heart is no longer pounding but swelling.

No more conflicted feelings. No more uncertainty.

"I love you," I say. "I don't think I ever knew just how much until now." It's a good sign, I think, that our love has proven to grow, rather than wane, when faced with a challenge. I think it bodes well for our future, for all of the things ahead of us: marriage, children.

"Oh, God, I was so scared I'd lost you," Sam says. "I was capsizing over here. Worried I'd lose the greatest thing that has ever happened to me."

"You didn't lose me," I say. "I'm here. I'm right here."

I kiss him.

The two of us are sitting awkwardly half over the console

with cricked necks and the stick shift digging into my knee. I just want to be as close to him as possible. Sam kisses my temple and I can smell our laundry detergent on his shirt.

"Take me home?" I ask.

Sam smiles. It is the sort of smile that any minute might turn to tears. "Absolutely."

I move away from him, putting myself firmly in the passenger seat as he puts the car in reverse and backs out.

My phone and my wallet are in my car, as well as my weekend bag with all of my things. But I don't stop him. I don't ask him to wait just a minute while I grab them. Because I don't need them. Not right now. I don't need anything that I don't have right this minute.

Sam holds my left hand with his right. He does so the entire way home except for a twenty-second period when I lean forward and dig through his glove compartment for his favorite Charles Mingus CD that he keeps buried in the dash. I still can't stand jazz and he still loves it. In both important and unimportant ways, Sam and I are the same to each other that we were back then. When the music begins, Sam looks at me, impressed.

"You hate Mingus," he says.

"I love you, though, so . . ."

This seems like a good enough explanation for him and so he grabs my hand again. There is no tension, no pressure. We are at peace simply being next to each other. A deep calm comes over me as I watch the snowplowed streets of Acton turn to those of Concord, as the evergreens that hug the highway leading us through Lexington and Belmont turn to brick sidewalks and brownstones in Cambridge. The world feels like a mirror, in that what I see in front of me is finally in perfect synchronicity with what I am made of.

I feel like myself on these streets, with this man.

We park and head up to our apartment. I am tucked into the crook of his arm, using his body as a shield against the cold.

Sam turns the key and when the door shuts behind us, it feels like we've locked the whole world out. When he kisses me, his lips are still chilled and I feel them warm up with my touch.

"Hi," he says, smiling. It is the kind of "hi" that means everything except hello.

"Hi," I say back.

The smell of our apartment, a scent I'm not sure I've ever noticed before, is spicy and fresh, like cinnamon toothpaste. I spot both of the cats under the piano. They are OK. *Everything* is OK.

Sam pushes himself against me as I rest against the back of our front door. He puts his hand to my cheek, his fingers slip into my hair as his thumb grazes under my eye.

"I was afraid I'd lost these freckles of yours forever," he says as he looks right at me. His gaze feels comforting, safe. I find myself moving my head toward his hand, pressing against it.

"You didn't," I say. "I'm here. And I will do anything for you. Anything. For the rest of our lives."

"I don't need anything from you," Sam says. "Just you. I just want you."

My arms reach up around his shoulders and I pull him close to me. The weight of his body against mine is both stirring and soothing. I can smell the drugstore pomade in his hair. I can feel the short stubble of his cheeks. "You're it for me," I say. "Forever. Me and you."

I was wrong before, when I said there's nothing more romantic than the end of a relationship.

It is this.

There is nothing more romantic than this. Holding the very person that you thought you lost, and knowing you'll never lose them again.

I don't think that true love means your only love.

I think true love means loving truly.

Loving purely. Loving wholly.

Maybe, if you're the kind of person who's willing to give all of yourself, the kind of person who is willing to love with all of your heart even though you've experienced just how much it can hurt . . . maybe you get lots of true loves, then. Maybe that's the gift you get for being brave.

I am a woman who dares to love again.

I finally love that about myself.

It's messy to love after heartbreak. It's painful and it forces you to be honest with yourself about who you are. You have to work harder to find the words for your feelings, because they don't fit into any prefabricated boxes.

But it's worth it.

Because look what you get:

Great loves.

Meaningful loves.

True loves.

I wear a pale lavender dress at my second wedding. It is sleek and ornate. It feels like the wedding dress of a woman who has lived a full life before getting married. A dress that signals a strong, well-rounded person making a beautiful decision. Marie is my maid of honor. Ava is our flower girl; Sophie is our ring bearer. Olive gives a speech that leaves half the room in tears. Sam and I honeymoon in Montreal.

And then eight months and nine days after Sam and I say our vows in front of all of our friends and family, I am talking to Olive on the phone as I close up Blair Books on a balmy summer night.

Marie left early to pick up the girls from our parents'. We are all meeting up for dinner at Marie and Mike's house. Mike is grilling steaks and Sam promised Sophia and Ava he'd make them grilled cheese.

Olive is talking about the first birthday party that she is throwing for her baby, Piper, when I hear the familiar beep of call-waiting.

"You know what?" I say. "Someone's on the other line. I gotta go."

"OK," she says. "Oh, I wanted to ask you what you think about sea animals as a theme for—"

"Olive!" I say. "I gotta go."

"OK, but just . . . do you like sea animals as a theme or not?"

"I think it depends on what animals but I have to go."

"I mean, like, whales and dolphins, maybe some fish," Olive explains as I groan. "Fine!" she says. "We can FaceTime tomorrow."

I hang up and look at my phone to see who is calling me.

I don't recognize the number. But I recognize the area code.

310.

Santa Monica, California.

"Hello?"

"Emma?" The voice is instantly familiar. One I could never forget.

"Jesse?"

"Hi."

"Hi!"

"How are you?" he asks me casually, as if we talk all the time. I have gotten postcards from California a few times, even one from Lisbon. They are short and sweet, simple updates on how he is, where he's headed. I always know he's OK. But we don't text that often. And we never talk on the phone.

"I'm good," I say. "Really good. How about you?"

"I'm doing well, yeah," he says. "Miss you guys in Acton, obviously."

"Obviously," I say.

"But I'm good. I'm . . . I'm really happy here."

I don't know what else to say to him. I can't quite tell why he's calling. My silence stalls us. And so he just comes out with it.

"I met someone," he says.

Maybe it shouldn't surprise me—that he met someone, that he wants to tell me. But both things do.

"You did? That's wonderful."

"Yeah, she's . . . she's really incredible. Just very unique. She's a professional surfer. Isn't that crazy? I never thought I'd fall in love with a surfer girl."

I laugh. "I don't know," I say, locking up the shop, walking out to my car. It's still bright out even though the evening is fully under way. I will miss this come October. I make a point to appreciate it now. "It kind of makes perfect sense to me that you'd fall in love with a surfer girl. I mean, it doesn't get much more California than that."

"Yeah, maybe you're right." Jesse laughs.

"What's her name?"

"Britt," Jesse says.

"Jesse and Britt," I say. "That has a nice ring to it."

"I think so. I think we're good together."

"Oh, Jesse, that's so wonderful. I'm really so glad to hear it."

"I wanted to tell you . . ." he says, and then he drifts off.

"Yeah."

"I get it now. I get what you were saying. About how falling in love with Sam didn't mean that you forgot me. That it doesn't change how you once felt. It doesn't make the people you loved before any less important.

"I didn't get it back then. I thought . . . I thought choosing him meant you didn't love me. I thought because we didn't work out, it meant we were a failure or a mistake. But I understand it now. Because I love her. I love her so much I can't see straight. But it doesn't change how I felt about you or how thankful I am to have loved you once. It's just . . ."

"I'm the past. And she's the present."

"Yeah," he says, relieved that I've put it into words for him, that he doesn't have to try to find them himself. "That's exactly it."

I think you forsake the people you loved before, just a little bit, when you fall in love again. But it doesn't erase anything. It doesn't change what you had. You don't even leave it so far behind that you can't instantly remember, that you can't pick it up like a book you read a long time ago and remember how it felt then.

"I guess what I'm saying is I've come around to your way of thinking. I am immensely thankful I was married to you once. I am so grateful for our wedding day. Just because something isn't meant to last a lifetime doesn't mean it wasn't meant to be. We were meant to have been."

I am sitting in the front seat of my car with the phone to my ear, unable to do anything but listen to him.

"You and I aren't going to spend our lives together," Jesse says. "But I finally understand that that doesn't take away any of the beauty of the fact that we were right for each other once."

"True love doesn't always last," I say. "It doesn't always have to be for a lifetime."

"Right. And that doesn't mean it's not true love," Jesse says.

It was real.

And now it's over.

And that's OK.

"I am who I am because I loved you once," he says.

"I am who I am because I loved you once, too," I say.

And then we say good-bye.

ACKNOWLEDGMENTS

My grandmother Linda Morris lived her entire life in Acton. She passed away a few weeks before I sat down to start this book. It was my trip home that October for her memorial, with the beautiful leaves and crisp air, that made me realize just how deeply I love the place I am from. And just how much I wanted to write about it in tribute to my grandmother. The people in my life whom I have cherished the longest are people from Acton and its surrounding towns. So this is my way of saying not just *thank you* but also *I love you*.

This book—and every book I've written—would not be possible without three particular women: my editors, Greer Hendricks and Sarah Cantin, and my agent, Carly Watters.

Greer, thank you for seeing all the things I can't see and for having the faith to know I will find a way to fix them. Both of those qualities were in dire need this go-around and I could not be more grateful that you were on my team. Sarah, thank you for being such a great champion. I know that my work is in great hands at Atria and that is because of how good you are at what you do. Carly, thank you for always getting just as excited about my work as I do and for knowing what I'm going to ask before I ask it. Four books in, I still feel so lucky to have you as the face of this operation.

Crystal Patriarche and the BookSparks team, you are unbelievable publicity all-stars. Tory, thank you for handling every crazy question I have with patience and grace. Brad Mendelsohn, thank you for not only being an awesome manager who thinks ten steps ahead, but also finally putting together your daughters' trampoline.

Thank you to everyone at Atria, especially Judith Curr, for making Atria such an exceptional imprint to be a part of. I feel incredibly fortunate that my book travels from one talented hand to another on its way to publication.

To all the bloggers who have supported me time after time, this book exists because you've rallied readers. You make my job fun and your passion for great stories and characters is infectious. Thanks for always reminding me why I love what I do and for helping me reach a diverse and incredible readership. I owe you one (million).

To all the friends and family I've thanked before, I thank you again. To Andy Bauch and my in-laws, the Reids and the Hanes, I have dedicated this book to you because as much as I love Acton, I also love Los Angeles, and it is in no small part because of all of you. Thank you for always supporting me and for making this huge city feel like home.

To mi madre y mi hermano, Mindy and Jake, I love you guys. Mom, thanks for moving us to Acton so I had an exceptional education, an incredible support system, and, eventually, a place to write about. Jake, thanks for moving to LA so I have someone who I can talk to when I miss the Makaha and the Honey Stung Drummies from Roche Bros.

And last but not least, Alex Jenkins Reid. Thank you for reading all of my work as if it were your own—for being thoughtful enough to see what there is to love about it and honest enough to tell me when it sucks. And—on those occasions when it does, in fact, suck—thank you for going to get me an iced tea and a cupcake. Thank you for waiting until I'm ready to try again and then rolling up your sleeves with me and saying, "We'll figure this out." You're always right. We always do.

ONE TRUE LOVES

A Q&A with

TAYLOR JENKINS REID

When you set out to write *One True Loves,* did you know whether Emma would end up with Jesse or Sam? Did you find yourself rooting for one or the other as you wrote?

That is *the* question! I spent a lot of time, before I even sat down to write the first word of the book, trying to decide what I believed the truth of the situation would be. I asked myself (and a lot of my friends) what they thought they would do. I decided that there was one answer that simply felt more honest than the other answer. And I went with it. So when I started writing the first draft, I knew the ending.

As for whether I was rooting for either, I swear that I remained entirely neutral—and that I'm still neutral—about who I *wanted* to win out in the end. I only felt that one was more likely and I told the story I felt was the most real. But I love both Jesse and Sam madly and I worked hard in the hopes that readers would, too.

How have you developed as a writer over the course of crafting your four novels? Are there differences in how you approached writing *One True Loves* compared with your debut, *Forever, Interrupted*?

I'm embarrassed to say I don't have a concrete answer for this! I think my readers might be a better judge of that than I. I'm inclined to turn the question around and ask, of those who have read all of my work thus far, how do they see [my writing] changing?

One of the most obvious evolutions for me to recognize is that once I've talked about something in one book, I find myself working double time to avoid talking about it in another. So with *One True Loves*, I put in a great deal of effort to create challenges that my characters in other books haven't faced before. The more you write, the more you have to go out of your way not to emulate your past work—and that has led me to some really fun places I might not go [toward] as naturally.

What does "true love" mean to you? What about this concept did you want to explore in *One True Loves*?

My main goal was to put forth the idea that just because a relationship ends, it doesn't mean that it has failed. I don't think that true love means lasting love. If you remove that requirement and you start looking at the people you have loved in the past, you start to ask yourself: Did I love that person with all my heart? Did they change me for the better? Was I good to them? Am I glad it happened? And if that's the case, I think we should call that relationship a success.

What inspired you to set part of *One True Loves* in your hometown?

As I say in the acknowledgments, my grandmother passed away right before I was to start writing this story and it absolutely devastated me. My brother and I were raised by our mother with a lot of help from my grandmother, Linda. I dedicated my first book to her. She was so encouraging and believed in me with everything she had. I am a stronger and kinder person because of her influence on me. She lived her entire life in Acton, Massachusetts. I was lucky enough to spend what to me are my most formative years, from twelve to eighteen, living there. And I always took it somewhat for granted.

When my grandmother passed away in the fall of 2014, I went home to attend her memorial. I usually only go home during Christmas, or perhaps the summer. This was the first time I'd been home in the fall in probably a decade. When I got to town and saw how beautiful the changing leaves were, and how kind the people of Acton were in supporting my family during a very hard time, I realized I had not given enough credit to the wonderful town I am from.

Some of my very best friends—people that feel like my family—are people I met in Acton. And I have such fond memories of growing up there. So I decided to set the book in Acton as a way to honor both how much I appreciate the town and how much my grandmother loved it.

You based the bookstore Blair Books on Willow Books in Acton, MA. Do you have any memories of Willow Books you'd like to share?

My most fond—and very New England—story about Willow Books is from when I was about fourteen. My best friend, Erin, and I went to see *The Vagina Monologues* when it came to Boston. We were both completely riveted by it. We loved it. This was revolutionary stuff back then. So after we saw it, we decided we wanted to get the book, but it wasn't easy to find. We went into Willow Books and they kindly agreed to order copies for us.

A week later, I got a message on my family's home answering machine from this older woman who said, "I'm calling from Willow Books. The uh . . . the book that you . . . the monologues . . ." And then she just gave up and said, "The book you ordered is here." The poor woman couldn't bring herself to say the word "vagina." But she got me the book. And I read it cover to cover. That was probably my first unequivocally feminist moment, that book. No other store had it for me. But Willow did.

What is your favorite aspect of the writing process? What aspect is the most challenging for you? What are some things you do to overcome that challenge?

Oh, boy. When I'm writing a first draft, I'll tell you my favorite part is editing. When I'm editing, I'll say my favorite part is when it's done. When it's done, and I'm promoting it, I'll tell you that I want to get back to *writing.* I'm always convincing myself that the grass is greener on the other side of the street. I think, truthfully, the only part that is always as fun as I think it will be is coming up with ideas. The very beginning, when it's all potential, is very intoxicating.

And I find, somehow, even when I'm cursing whatever stage I'm in, the cumulative effect of all the stages still manages to be joy. Sort of [like] how they say, "The days are long but the years are short." Writing is frustrating, but being a writer is near bliss.

How were you able to imagine Jesse's mindset and experience after the helicopter crash? Did you do any research on crash survivors or near-death experiences?

I did some research about real people who have survived being lost at sea. There is a wide range of stories to pull from and no two stories are alike, which, at first, was very frustrating because there was nothing I could really pin down. But then I realized it was freeing because it gave me permission to be entirely unique.

The biggest research came from deciding where he could land, what he could live on, what challenges he would face. When I decided he would be in the Pacific, I had to narrow down what areas made the most sense, what vegetation was there, what the currents were like. And then comes the human element: What happens to the human body without protein? Without social interaction? What happens when you've cut yourself or been stung? What happens to your teeth when you can't brush them?

I wanted the reader to focus on Emma's tragedy, so I used only as much information about Jesse's as necessary to move the story forward. We've seen desert island stories. We've seen tales of men's adventures trying to get home. I wanted this to be about the woman left behind.

What do you think is the most important step in creating three-dimensional characters?

People don't make sense. They lie without even realizing they are lying. They are selfish while believing they are selfless, etc. I think the biggest thing I focus on is making sure that my characters are recognizable and knowable but not convenient or streamlined. Real people are messy. They are interesting because of the mess. I try to recreate that on the page.

In the book, Emma takes a circuitous route to becoming an avid reader and bookshop owner. What inspired you to have your protagonist have such a strong—and at times conflicted—relationship with a bookstore? Have you always wanted to be an author? What initially drew you to writing?

Yes, Emma definitely has an untraditional love story with books. And I did that because I think so often in the reading community, we focus on people who have loved reading their entire lives. But [in my case], I was not an avid reader until after college. And even then, I don't think I realized just how much I loved reading books until I realized I liked *writing* them. I feel vaguely embarrassed about that sometimes. Because I was the kid who didn't do her summer reading so that she could watch TV. I wanted to show a different story about how someone falls in love with reading.

It took me until I was about twenty-five to realize I wanted to be a writer and until [I was]about twenty-eight to admit it to people out loud. I floated around from job to job, attracted to various different elements of the work I was doing. And it wasn't until it occurred to me to try to write fiction that I realized being an author was exactly the thing I had been searching for. When I added up all of the elements of the other jobs I'd been doing, it hit me that writing fiction was my dream job.

It came as such a relief, honestly. To finally have that

direction. I knew it was a long shot but I also finally had a target to aim for.

You've also written for television and for film. How is this type of writing different from crafting a novel? How has your work as a novelist influenced your work as a screenwriter?

Writing for books, film, and TV are somehow all completely different and all essentially the same. In every medium, your goal is to connect with an audience, to bring them into a story, to thrill them, to make them feel. So the underlying skills are identical. How do I make this world seem real? How do I make this character someone people feel passionately about?

But of course there are different formulas for each one and different strengths to each. Part of what is the most fun about working in all three is coming up with an idea and then deciding how it will work best. Is this a book that could also be a TV show? Is it a book that would make a great film? Is it an idea that is really best only as a movie?

I've never painted or sculpted a day in my life but I'd imagine it's similar to having a vision of a woman in your head and trying to decide if she should be made out of paint, marble, or clay. Again, we're talking about the conception phase of a story—where you get to start making decisions about what it will be *someday.* And that is—and will forever be—the very thing that drives me.

Praise for *Forever, Interrupted*

"Touching and powerful . . . Reid masterfully grabs hold of the heartstrings and doesn't let go. A stunning first novel."

—*Publishers Weekly* (starred review)

"You'll laugh, weep, and fly through each crazy-readable page."

—*Redbook*

"A moving novel about life and death."

—*Kirkus Reviews*

"A poignant and heartfelt exploration of love and commitment in the absence of shared time that asks, what does it take to be the love of someone's life?"

—Emma McLaughlin and Nicola Kraus,
#1 *New York Times* bestselling authors

"Moving, gorgeous, and at times heart-wrenching."

—Sarah Jio, *New York Times* bestselling author

"Sweet, heartfelt, and surprising. These characters made me laugh as well as cry, and I ended up falling in love with them, too."

—Sarah Pekkanen, internationally bestselling
author of *The Opposite of Me*

"This beautifully rendered story explores the brilliance and rarity of finding true love, and how we find our way back through the painful aftermath of losing it. These characters will leap right off the page and into your heart."

—Amy Hatvany, author of *Safe with Me*

Praise for *After I Do*

"As uplifting as it is brutally honest—a must-read."

—*Kirkus Reviews*

"Written in a breezy, humorous style familiar to fans of Jane Green and Elin Hilderbrand, *After I Do* focuses on Lauren's journey of self-discovery. The intriguing premise and well-drawn characters contribute to an emotionally uplifting and inspiring story."

—*Booklist*

"Taylor Jenkins Reid offers an entirely fresh and new perspective on what can happen after the 'happily ever after.' With characters who feel like friends and a narrative that hooked me from the first page, *After I Do* takes an elegant and incisively emotional look at the endings and beginnings of love. Put this book at the top of your must-read list!"

—Jen Lancaster,
New York Times bestselling author

"Taylor Jenkins Reid delivers a seductive twist on the timeless tale of a couple trying to rediscover love in a marriage brought low by the challenges of domestic togetherness. I fell in love with Ryan and Lauren from their passionate beginning, and I couldn't stop reading as they followed their unlikely road to redemption. Touching, perceptive, funny, and achingly honest, *After I Do* will keep you hooked to the end, rooting for husbands and wives and the strength of true love."

—Beatriz Williams,
New York Times bestselling author

"Taylor Jenkins Reid writes with ruthless honesty, displaying an innate understanding of human emotion and creating characters and relationships so real I'm finding it impossible to let them go. *After I Do* is a raw, unflinching exploration of the realities of marriage, the delicate nature of love, and the enduring strength of family. Simultaneously funny and sad, heartbreaking and hopeful, Reid has crafted a story of love lost and found that is as timely as it is timeless."

—Katja Millay,
author of *The Sea of Tranquility*

MAYBE IN ANOTHER LIFE

Also by Taylor Jenkins Reid

Forever, Interrupted
After I Do
One True Loves
The Seven Husbands of Evelyn Hugo

MAYBE IN ANOTHER LIFE

~ *A Novel* ~

TAYLOR JENKINS REID

WASHINGTON SQUARE PRESS
New York Toronto London Sydney New Delhi

Washington Square Press
An Imprint of Simon & Schuster, Inc.
1230 Avenue of the Americas
New York, NY 10020

This book is a work of fiction. Any references to historical events, real people, or real places are used fictitiously. Other names, characters, places, and events are products of the author's imagination, and any resemblance to actual events or places or persons, living or dead, is entirely coincidental.

First Washington Square Press trade paperback edition July 2015

Manufactured in the United States of America

30 29 28

Library of Congress Cataloging-in-Publication Data

Reid, Taylor Jenkins.
Maybe in another life : a novel / Taylor Jenkins Reid. —First Washington Square Press trade paperback edition.
pages ; cm
1. Chick lit. I. Title.
PS3618.E5478M39 2015
813'.6—dc23

2014039873

ISBN 978-1-4767-7688-0
ISBN 978-1-4767-7689-7 (ebook)

To Erin, Julia, Sara, Tamara,
and all of the other women I feel destined to have met.
May we know each other in many universes.

MAYBE IN ANOTHER LIFE

It's a good thing I booked an aisle seat, because I'm the last one on the plane. I knew I'd be late for my flight. I'm late for almost everything. That's why I booked an aisle seat in the first place. I hate making people get up so that I can squeeze by. This is also why I never go to the bathroom during movies, even though I always have to go to the bathroom during movies.

I walk down the tight aisle, holding my carry-on close to my body, trying not to bump anyone. I hit a man's elbow and apologize even though he doesn't seem to notice. When I barely graze a woman's arm, she shoots daggers at me as if I stabbed her. I open my mouth to say I'm sorry and then think better of it.

I spot my seat easily; it is the only open one.

The air is stale. The music is Muzak. The conversations around me are punctuated by the clicks of the overhead compartments being slammed shut.

I get to my seat and sit down, smiling at the woman next to me. She's older and round, with short salt-and-pepper hair. I shove my bag in front of me and buckle my seat belt. My tray table's up. My electronics are off. My seat is in the upright position. When you're late a lot, you learn how to make up for lost time.

I look out the window. The baggage handlers are bundled

up in extra layers and neon jackets. I'm happy to be headed to a warmer climate. I pick up the in-flight magazine.

Soon I hear the roar of the engine and feel the wheels beneath us start to roll. The woman next to me grips the armrests as we ascend. She looks petrified.

I'm not scared of flying. I'm scared of sharks, hurricanes, and false imprisonment. I'm scared that I will never do anything of value with my life. But I'm not scared of flying.

Her knuckles are white with tension.

I tuck the magazine back into the pouch. "Not much of a flier?" I ask her. When I'm anxious, talking helps. If talking helps her, it's the least I can do.

The woman turns and looks at me as we glide into the air. " 'Fraid not," she says, smiling ruefully. "I don't leave New York very often. This is my first time flying to Los Angeles."

"Well, if it makes you feel any better, I fly a fair amount, and I can tell you, with any flight, it's really only takeoff and landing that are hard. We've got about three more minutes of this part and then about five minutes at the end that can be tough. The rest of it . . . you might as well be on a bus. So just eight bad minutes total, and then you're in California."

We're at an incline. It's steep enough that an errant bottle of water rolls down the aisle.

"Eight minutes is all?" she asks.

I nod. "That's it," I tell her. "You're from New York?"

She nods. "How about you?"

I shrug. "I was living in New York. Now I'm moving back to L.A."

The plane drops abruptly and then rights itself as we make our way past the clouds. She breathes in deeply. I have to admit, even I feel a little queasy.

"But I was only in New York for about nine months," I say. The longer I talk, the less attention she has to focus on the turbulence. "I've been moving around a bit lately. I went to school in Boston. Then I moved to D.C., then Portland, Oregon. Then Seattle. Then Austin, Texas. Then New York. The city where dreams come true. Although, you know, not for me. But I did grow up in Los Angeles. So you could say I'm going back to where I came from, but I don't know that I'd call it home."

"Where's your family?" she asks. Her voice is tight. She's looking forward.

"My family moved to London when I was sixteen. My younger sister, Sarah, got accepted to the Royal Ballet School, and they couldn't pass that up. I stayed and finished school in L.A."

"You lived on your own?" It's working. The distraction.

"I lived with my best friend's family until I finished high school. And then I left for college."

The plane levels out. The captain tells us our altitude. She takes her hands off the armrest and breathes.

"See?" I say to her. "Just like a bus."

"Thank you," she says.

"Anytime."

She looks out the window. I pick up the magazine again. She turns back to me. "Why do you move around so much?" she says. "Isn't that difficult?" She immediately corrects herself. "Listen to me, the minute I stop hyperventilating, I'm acting like your mother."

I laugh with her. "No, no, it's fine," I say. I don't move from place to place on purpose. It's not a conscious choice to be a nomad. Although I can see that each move is my own decision, predicated on nothing but my ever-growing sense that I don't belong where I am, fueled by the hope that maybe there is, in fact, a place I do belong, a place just off in the future. "I guess . . . I don't know," I say. It's hard to put into words, especially to someone I barely know. But then I open my mouth, and out it comes. "No place has felt like home."

She looks at me and smiles. "I'm sorry," she says. "That has to be hard."

I shrug, because it's an impulse. It's always my impulse to ignore the bad, to run toward the good.

But I'm also not feeling great about my own impulses at the moment. I'm not sure they are getting me where I want to go.

I stop shrugging.

And then, because I won't see her again after this flight, I take it one step further. I tell her something I've only recently told myself. "Sometimes I worry I'll never find a place to call home."

She puts her hand on mine, ever so briefly. "You will," she says. "You're young still. You have plenty of time."

I wonder if she can tell that I'm twenty-nine and considers that young, or if she thinks I'm younger than I am.

"Thanks," I say. I take my headphones out of my bag and put them on.

"At the end of the flight, during the five tricky minutes when we land, maybe we can talk about my lack of career choices," I say, laughing. "That will definitely distract you."

She smiles broadly and lets out a laugh. "I'd consider it a personal favor."

When I come out of the gate, Gabby is holding up a sign that says "Hannah Marie Martin," as if I wouldn't recognize her, as if I wouldn't know she was my ride.

I run toward her, and as I get closer, I can see that she has drawn a picture of me next to my name. It is a crude sketch but not altogether terrible. The Hannah of her drawing has big eyes and long lashes, a tiny nose, and a line for a mouth. On the top of my head is hair drawn dramatically in a high bun. The only thing of note drawn on my stick-figure body is an oversized pair of boobs.

It's not necessarily how I see myself, but I admit, if you reduced me to a caricature, I'd be big boobs and a high bun. Sort of like how Mickey Mouse is round ears and gloved hands or how Michael Jackson is white socks and black loafers.

I'd much rather be depicted with my dark brown hair and my light green eyes, but I understand that you can't really do much with color when you're drawing with a Bic pen.

Even though I haven't visited Gabby in person since her wedding day two years ago, I have seen her every Sunday morning of the recent past. We video-chat no matter what we have to do that day or how hungover one of us is feeling. It is, in some ways, the most reliable thing in my life.

Gabby is tiny and twiglike. Her hair is kept cropped close in a bob, and there's no extra fat on her, not an inch to spare. When

I hug her, I remember how odd it is to hug someone so much smaller than I am, how different the two of us seem at first glance. I am tall, curvy, and white. She is short, thin, and Black.

She doesn't have any makeup on, and yet she is one of the prettiest women here. I don't tell her that, because I know what she'd say. She'd say that's irrelevant. She'd say we shouldn't be complimenting each other on our looks or competing with each other over who is prettier. She's got a point, so I keep it to myself.

I have known Gabby since we were both fourteen years old. We sat next to each other in earth science class the first day of high school. The friendship was fast and everlasting. We were Gabby and Hannah, Hannah and Gabby, one name rarely mentioned without the other in tow.

I moved in with her and her parents, Carl and Tina, when my family left for London. Carl and Tina treated me as if I were their own. They coached me through applying for schools, made sure I did my homework, and kept me on a curfew. Carl routinely tried to persuade me to become a doctor, like him and his father. By then, he knew that Gabby wouldn't follow on his path. She already knew she wanted to work in public service. I think Carl figured I was his last shot. But Tina instead encouraged me to find my own way. Unfortunately, I'm still not sure what that way is. But back then, I just assumed it would all fall into place, that the big things in life would take care of themselves.

After we went off to college, Gabby in Chicago, myself in Boston, we still talked all the time but started to find new lives for ourselves. Freshman year, she became friends with another Black student at her school named Vanessa. Gabby would tell me about their trips to the nearby mall and the parties they went to. I'd have been lying if I said I wasn't nervous back then, in some small way, that Vanessa would become closer to Gabby than I ever could, that Vanessa could share something with Gabby that I was not a part of.

I asked Gabby about it over the phone once. I was lying in my dorm room on my twin XL bed, the phone sweaty and hot on my ear from our already-hours-long conversation.

"Do you feel like Vanessa understands you better than I do?" I asked her. The minute the question came out of my mouth, I was embarrassed. It had seemed reasonable in my head but sounded irrational coming out of my mouth. If words were things, I would have rushed to pluck them out of the air and put them back in my mouth.

Gabby laughed at me. "Some things, sure. But overall, no. Do you think white people understand you more than I do just because they're white?"

"No," I said. "Of course not."

"So be quiet," Gabby said.

And I did. If there is one thing I love about Gabby, it is that she has always known when I should be quiet. She is, in fact, the only person who often proves to know me better than I know myself.

"Let me guess," she says now, as she takes my carry-on bag out of my hand, a gentlemanly gesture. "We're going to need to rent one of those baggage carts to get all of your stuff."

I laugh. "In my defense, I am moving across the country," I say.

I long ago stopped buying furniture or large items. I tend to sublet furnished apartments. You learn after one or two moves that buying an IKEA bed, putting it together, and then breaking it down and selling it for fifty bucks six months later is a waste of time and money. But I do still have *things*, some of which have survived multiple cross-country trips. It would feel callous to let go of them now.

"I'm going to guess there's at least four bottles of Orange Ginger body lotion in here," Gabby says as she grabs one of my bags off the carousel.

I shake my head. "Only the one. I'm running low."

I started using body lotion somewhere around the time she and I met. We would go to the mall together and smell all the lotions in all the different stores. But every time, I kept buying the same one. Orange Ginger. At one point, I had seven bottles of the stuff stocked up.

We grab the rest of my bags from the carousel and pack them one after another onto the cart, the two of us pushing with all our might across the lanes of airport traffic and into the parking structure. We load them into her tiny car and then settle into our seats.

We make small talk as she makes her way out of the garage and navigates the streets leading us to the freeway. She asks about my flight and how it felt to leave New York. She apologizes that her guest room is small. I tell her not to be ridiculous, and I thank her again for letting me stay.

The repetition of history is not lost on me. It's more than a decade later, and I am once again staying in Gabby's guest room. It's been more than ten years, and yet I am still floating from place to place, relying on the kindness of Gabby and her family. This time, it's Gabby and her husband, Mark, instead of Gabby and her parents. But if anything, that just highlights the difference between the two of us, how much Gabby has changed since then and how much I have not. Gabby's the VP of Development at a nonprofit that works with at-risk teenagers. I'm a waitress. And not a particularly good one.

Once Gabby is flying down the freeway, once driving no longer takes her attention, or maybe once she is going so fast she knows I can't jump out of the car, she asks what she has been dying to ask since I hugged her hello. "So what happened? Did you tell him you were leaving?"

I sigh loudly and look out the window. "He knows not to contact me," I say. "He knows I don't want to see him ever again. So I suppose it doesn't really matter where he thinks I am."

Gabby looks straight ahead at the road, but I see her nod, pleased with me.

I need her approval right now. Her opinion of me is currently a better litmus test than my own. It's been a little rough going lately. And while I know Gabby will always love me, I also know that as of late, I have tested her unconditional support.

Mostly because I started sleeping with a married man.

I didn't know he was married at first. And for some reason, I thought that meant it was OK. He never admitted he was married. He never wore a wedding ring. He didn't even have a paler shade of skin around his ring finger, the way magazines tell you married men will. He was a liar. A good one, at that. And even though I suspected the truth, I thought that if he never said it, if he never admitted it to my face, then I wasn't accountable for the fact that it was true.

I suspected something was up when he once didn't answer my calls for six days and then finally called me back acting as if nothing was out of the ordinary. I suspected there was another woman when he refused to let me use his phone. I suspected that *I* was, in fact, the other woman when we ran into a coworker of his at a restaurant in SoHo, and rather than introduce me to the man, Michael told me I had something in my teeth and that I should go to the bathroom to get it out. I did go to the bathroom. And I found nothing there. But if I'm being honest, I also found it hard to look at myself in the mirror for more than a few seconds before going back out there and pretending I didn't know what he was trying to do.

And Gabby, of course, knew all of this. I was admitting it to her at the same rate I was admitting it to myself.

"I think he's married," I finally said to her a month or so ago. I was sitting in bed, still in my pajamas, talking to her on my laptop, and fixing my bun.

I watched as Gabby's pixelated face frowned. "I told you he was married," she said, her patience wearing thin. "I told you this three weeks ago. I told you that you need to stop this. Because it's wrong. And because that is some woman's husband. And because you shouldn't allow a man to treat you like a mistress. I told you all of this."

"I know, but I really didn't think he was married. He would have told me if he was. You know? So I didn't think he was. And I'm not going to ask him, because that's so insulting, isn't it?" That was my rationale. I didn't want to insult him.

"You need to cut this crap out, Hannah. I'm serious. You are a wonderful person who has a lot to offer the world. But this is wrong. And you know it."

I listened to her. And then I let all of her advice fly right through my head and out into the wind. As if it was meant for someone else and wasn't mine to hold on to.

"No," I said, shaking my head. "I don't think you're right about this. Michael and I met at a bar in Bushwick on a Wednesday night. I never go to Bushwick. And I rarely go out on a Wednesday night. And neither does he! What are the odds of that? That two people would come together like that?"

"You're joking, right?"

"Why would I be joking? I'm talking about fate here. Honestly. Let's say he is married . . ."

"He is."

"We don't know that. But let's say that he is."

"He is."

"Let's *say* that he is. That doesn't mean that we weren't fated to meet. For all we know, I'm just playing out the natural course of destiny here. Maybe he's married and that's OK because it's how things were meant to be."

I could tell Gabby was disappointed in me. I could see it in her eyebrows and the turn of her lips.

"Look, I don't even know that he's married," I said. But I did. I did know it. And because I knew it, I had to run as far away from it as I could. So I said, "You know, Gabby, even if he is married, that doesn't mean I'm not better for him than this other person. All's fair in love and war."

Two weeks later, his wife found out about me and called me screaming.

He'd done this before.

She'd found two others.

And did I know they had two children?

I did not know that.

It's very easy to rationalize what you're doing when you don't know the faces and the names of the people you might hurt. It's very easy to choose yourself over someone else when it's an abstract.

And I think that's why I kept everything abstract.

I had been playing the "Well, But" game. The "We Don't Know That for Sure" game. The "Even So" game. I had been viewing the truth through my own little lens, one that was narrow and rose-colored.

And then, suddenly, it was as if the lens fell from my face, and I could suddenly see, in staggering black-and-white, what I had been doing.

Does it matter that once I faced the truth I behaved honorably? Does it matter that once I heard his wife's voice, once I knew the names of his children, I never spoke to him again?

Does it matter that I can see, clear as day, my own culpability and that I feel deep remorse? That a small part of me hates myself for relying on willful ignorance to justify what I suspected was wrong?

Gabby thinks it does. She thinks it redeems me. I'm not so sure.

Once Michael was out of my life, I realized I didn't have much else going for me in New York. The winter was harsh and cold and only seemed to emphasize further how alone I was in a city of millions. I called my parents and my sister, Sarah, a lot that first week after breaking up with Michael, not to talk about my problems but to hear friendly voices. I often got their voice mails. They always called me back. They always do. But I could never seem to accurately guess when they might be available. And very often, with the time difference, we had only a small sliver of time to catch one another.

Last week, everything just started to pile up. The girl whose apartment I was subletting gave me two weeks' notice that she needed the apartment back. My boss at work hit on me and implied that better shifts went to women who showed cleavage. I got stuck on the G train for an hour and forty-five minutes when a train broke down at Greenpoint Avenue. Michael kept calling me and leaving voice mails asking to explain himself, telling me that he wanted to leave his wife for me, and I was embarrassed to admit that it made me feel better even as it made me feel absolutely terrible.

So I called Gabby. And I cried. I admitted that things were harder in New York than I had ever let on. I admitted that this wasn't working, that my life was not shaping up the way I'd wanted it to. I told her I needed to change.

And she said, "Come home."

It took me a minute before I realized she meant that I should move back to Los Angeles. That's how long it's been since I thought of my hometown as home.

"To L.A.?" I asked.

"Yeah," she said. "Come home."

"You know, Ethan is there," I said. "He moved back a few years ago, I think."

"So you'll see him," Gabby said. "It wouldn't be the worst thing that happened to you. Getting back together with a good guy."

"It *is* warmer there," I said, looking out my tiny window at the dirty snow on the street below me.

"It was seventy-two the other day," she said.

"But changing cities doesn't solve the larger problem," I said, for maybe the first time in my life. "I mean, *I* need to change."

"I know," she said. "Come home. Change here."

It was the first time in a long time that something made sense.

Now Gabby grabs my hand for a moment and squeezes it, keeping her eye on the road. "I'm proud of you that you're taking control of your life," she says. "Just by getting on the plane this morning, you're getting your life together."

"You think so?" I ask.

She nods. "I think Los Angeles will be good for you. Don't you? Returning to your roots. It's a crime we've lived so far apart for so many years. You're correcting an injustice."

I laugh. I'm trying to see this move as a victory instead of a defeat.

Finally, we pull onto Gabby's street, and she parks her car at the curb.

We are in front of a complex on a steep, hilly street. Gabby and Mark bought a townhouse last year. I look at the addresses on the row of houses and search for the number four, to see which one is theirs. I may not have been here before, but I've been sending cards, baked goods, and various gifts to Gabby for months. I know her address by heart. Just as I catch the number on the door in the glow of the streetlight, I see Mark come out and walk toward us.

Mark is a tall, conventionally handsome man. Very physically strong, very traditionally male. I've always had a penchant for guys with pretty eyes and five o'clock shadows, and I thought Gabby did, too. But she ended up with Mark, the poster boy for clean-cut and stable. He's the kind of guy who goes to the gym for health reasons. I have never done that.

I open my car door and grab one of my bags. Gabby grabs another. Mark meets us at the car. "Hannah!" he says as he gives me a big hug. "It is so nice to see you." He takes the rest of the bags out of the car, and we head into the house. I look around their living room. It's a lot of neutrals and wood finishes. Safe but gorgeous.

"Your room is upstairs," she says, and the three of us walk up the tight staircase to the second floor. There is a master bedroom and a bedroom across the hall.

Gabby and Mark lead me into the guest room, and we put all the bags down.

It's a small room but big enough for just me. There's a double bed with a billowy white comforter, a desk, and a dresser.

It's late, and I am sure both Gabby and Mark are tired, so I do my best to be quick.

"You guys go ahead to bed. I can get myself settled," I say.

"You sure?" Gabby asks.

I insist.

Mark gives me a hug and heads to their bedroom. Gabby tells him she'll be there in a moment.

"I'm really happy you're here," she says to me. "In all of your city hopping, I always hoped you'd come back. At least for a little while. I like having you close by."

"Well, you got me," I tell her, smiling. "Perhaps even closer than you were thinking."

"Don't be silly," she says. "Live in my guest room until we're both ninety years old, as far as I'm concerned." She gives me a hug and heads to her room. "If you wake up before we do, feel free to start the coffee."

After I hear the bedroom door shut, I grab my toiletry bag and head into the bathroom.

The light in here is bright and unforgiving; some might even go so far as to describe it as harsh. There's a magnifying mirror by the sink. I grab it and pull it toward my face. I can tell I need to get my eyebrows waxed, but overall, there isn't too much to complain about. As I start to push the mirror back into place, the view grazes the outside of my left eye.

I pull on my skin, somewhat in denial of what I'm seeing. I let it bounce back into shape. I stare and inspect.

I have the beginnings of crow's-feet.

I have no apartment and no job. I have no steady relationship or even a city to call home. I have no idea what I want to be doing with my life, no idea what my purpose is, and no real sign of a life goal. And yet time has found me. The years I've spent dilly-dallying around at different jobs in different cities show on my face.

I have wrinkles.

I let go of the mirror. I brush my teeth. I wash my face. I resolve to buy night cream and start wearing sunscreen. And then I turn down the covers and get into bed.

My life may be a little bit of a disaster. I may not make the best decisions sometimes. But I am not going to lie here and stare at the ceiling, worrying the night away.

Instead, I go to sleep soundly, believing I will do better tomorrow. Things will be better tomorrow. I'll figure this all out tomorrow.

Tomorrow is, for me, a brand-new day.

I wake up to a bright, sunny room and a ringing phone.

"Ethan!" I whisper into the phone. "It's nine o'clock on a Saturday morning!"

"Yeah," he says, his gritty voice made grittier by the phone. "But you're still on East Coast time. It's noon for you. You should be up."

I continue to whisper. "OK, but Gabby and Mark are still sleeping."

"When do I get to see you?" he says.

~

I met Ethan in my sophomore year of high school at Homecoming.

I was still living at home with my parents. Gabby was offered a babysitting job that night and decided to take it instead of going to the dance. I ended up going by myself, not because I wanted to go but because my dad teased me that I never went anywhere without her. I went to prove him wrong.

I stood at the wall for most of the night, killing time until I could leave. I was so bored that I thought about calling Gabby and persuading her to join me once her babysitting gig was over. But Jesse Flint was slow-dancing with Jessica Campos all night in the middle of the dance floor. And Gabby loved Jesse Flint, had been pining away for him since high school began. I couldn't do that to her.

As the night wore on and couples started making out in the dimly lit gym, I looked over at the only other person standing against the wall. He was tall and thin, with rumpled hair and a wrinkled shirt. His tie was loose. He looked right back at me. And then he walked over to where I was standing and introduced himself.

"Ethan Hanover," he said, putting out his hand.

"Hannah Martin," I said, putting out my own to grab his.

He was a junior at another school. He told me he was just there as a favor to his neighbor, Katie Franklin, who didn't have a date. I knew Katie fairly well. I knew she was a lesbian who wasn't ready to tell her parents. The whole school knew that she and Teresa Hawkins were more than just friends. So I figured I wasn't hurting anyone by flirting with the boy she brought for cover.

But pretty soon I found myself forgetting anyone else was even at the dance in the first place. When Katie did finally come get him and suggest it was time to go, I felt as if something was being taken from me. I was tempted to reach out and grab him, to claim him for myself.

Ethan had a party at his parents' house the next weekend and invited me. Gabby and I didn't normally go to big parties, but I made her come. He perked up the minute I walked in the door. He grabbed my hand and introduced me to his friends. I lost track of Gabby somewhere by the Tostitos.

Soon Ethan and I had ventured upstairs. We were sitting on the top step of the staircase, hip to hip, talking about our favorite bands. He kissed me there, in the dark, the wild party happening just underneath our feet.

"I only threw a party so I could call you and invite you," he said to me. "Is that stupid?"

I shook my head and kissed him again.

When Gabby came and found me an hour or so later, my lips felt swollen, and I knew I had a hickey.

We lost our virginity to each other a year and a half later. We were in his bedroom when his parents were out of town. He told me he loved me as I lay underneath him, and he kept asking if it was OK.

Some people talk about their first time as a hilarious or pathetic experience. I can't relate. Mine was with someone I loved, someone who also had no idea what we were doing. The first time I had sex, I made love. I've always had a soft spot in my heart for Ethan for that very reason.

And then everything fell apart. He got into UC Berkeley. Sarah got into the Royal Ballet School, and my parents packed up and moved to London. I moved in with the Hudsons. And then, one balmy August morning a week before the beginning of my senior year of high school, Ethan got into his parents' car and left for Northern California.

We made it until the end of October before we broke up. At the time, we assured each other that it was just because the timing was wrong and the distance was hard. We told each other we'd get back together that summer. We told each other it didn't change anything; we were still soul mates.

But it was no different from the same old song and dance at every college every fall.

I started considering schools in Boston and New York, since

living on the East Coast would make it easier to get to London. When Ethan came home for Christmas, I was dating a guy named Chris Rodriguez. When Ethan came home for the summer, he was dating a girl named Alicia Foster.

When I got into Boston University, that was the final nail.

Soon there was more than three thousand miles between us and no plan to shorten the distance.

Ethan and I have occasionally kept in touch, a phone call here or there, a dance or two at mutual friends' weddings. But there has always been an unspoken tension. There is always this sense that we haven't followed through on our plan.

He still, all these years later, shines brighter to me than other people. Even after I got over him, I was never able to extinguish the fire completely, as if it's a pilot light that will remain small and controlled but very much alive.

"You've been in this city for twelve hours, according to my calculations," Ethan says. "And I'll be damned if I'm going to let you be here for twelve more without seeing me."

I laugh. "Well, we'll be cutting it close, I think," I say to him. "Gabby says there is some bar in Hollywood that we should go to tonight. She invited a whole bunch of friends from high school, so I can see everybody again. She's calling it a housewarming. Which makes no sense. I don't know."

Ethan laughs. "Text me the time and place, and I will be there."

"Awesome. Sounds great."

I start to say good-bye, but his voice chimes in again. "Hey, Hannah," he says.

"Yeah?"

"I'm glad you decided to come home."

I laugh. "Well, I was running out of cities."

"I don't know," he says. "I like to think you've just come to your senses."

I am pulling things out of my suitcase and flinging them around the guest room. "I swear I will clean this up," I say to Gabby and Mark. They are dressed and standing by the door. They have been ready to go for at least ten minutes.

"It's not a fashion show," Gabby says.

"It's my first night back in Los Angeles," I remind her. "I want to look good."

I had on a black shirt and black jeans, with long earrings and, of course, a high bun. But then I thought, you know, this isn't New York anymore. This is L.A. It was sixty degrees out this afternoon.

"I just want to find a tank top," I say. I start filtering through the clothes I have already thrown across the room. I find a teal shell tank and throw it on. I slip on my black heels. I look in the mirror and fix my bun. "I promise I will clean this all up when we get back."

I can see Mark laughing at me. He knows I sometimes don't do exactly what I say I'll do. No doubt, when Gabby asked him if I could stay here, she prepared him by saying, "She will probably throw her stuff all over the place." Also, I have no doubt he said that was OK. So I don't feel too bad.

But I don't think that is why Mark is laughing, actually. He says, "For someone so disorganized, you look very pulled together."

Gabby smiles at him and then at me. "You do. You look, like, glowy." She grabs the doorknob and then says, "But looks aren't the measure of a woman." She can't stop herself. This political correctness is just a part of who she is. I love her for that.

"Thank you both," I say as I follow them to their car.

When we get to the bar, it's fairly quiet. Gabby and Mark sit down, and I go up to get our drinks. I order beers for Mark and me and a glass of chardonnay for Gabby. The bill comes to twenty-four dollars, and I hand over my credit card. I don't know how much money I have in my account, because I'm afraid to look. But I know I have enough to live for a few weeks and get an apartment. I don't want to be a person who nickels-and-dimes, especially when Mark and Gabby have been sweet enough to give me a place to stay, so I just put it out of my head.

I bring the two beers to the table and turn back to get Gabby's wine. By the time I sit down, another woman has joined us. I remember meeting her at Gabby and Mark's wedding a couple of years ago. Her name is Katherine, I believe. She ran the New York City Marathon a few years ago. I remember faces and names really well. It's easy for me to remember details about people I have only met once. But I learned a long time ago not to reveal this. It freaks people out.

Katherine extends her hand. "Katherine," she says.

I shake her hand and say my name.

"Nice to meet you," she says. "Welcome back to Los Angeles!"

"Thanks," I say. "Actually, I think we've met before."

"We have?"

"Yeah, at Gabby and Mark's wedding. Yeah, yeah," I say, as if it's coming back to me. "You were telling me about how you ran a marathon somewhere, right? Boston or New York?"

She smiles. "New York! Yes! Great memory."

And now Katherine likes me. If I'd come right out with it, if I'd said, "Oh, we've met before. You were wearing a yellow dress at their wedding, and you said that running the New York Marathon was the hardest but most rewarding thing you've ever done," Katherine would think I was creepy. I have learned this the hard way.

Soon some of my old friends from high school start trickling in, the girls Gabby and I hung out with: Brynn, Caitlin, Erica. I scream and shout at the top of my lungs when I see each of them. It is so nice to see familiar faces, to be somewhere and know that the people who knew you at fifteen still like you. Brynn looks older, Caitlin looks thinner, Erica looks just the same.

Some of Mark's friends from work show up with their spouses, and soon we are crowding around a table too small for us.

People start buying other people drinks. Rounds are on this person or that person. I nurse my beer and a few Diet Cokes. I drank a lot in New York. I drank a lot with Michael. Change starts now.

I'm up at the bar again when I see Ethan walk in the door.

He's even taller than I remember, wearing an untucked blue cotton button-down and dark jeans. His hair is short and tousled, his stubble a few days old. He was cute in high school. He's handsome now. He will only get more handsome as he ages, I suspect.

I wonder if he has crow's-feet like I do.

I watch as he scouts around, searching for me in the crowd. I pay for the drinks in my hand and walk toward him. Just when I worry he'll never see me, I finally catch his eye. He lights up and smiles wide.

He moves toward me quickly, the gap between us almost instantly reduced to zero. He throws his arms around me and squeezes me tight. I briefly put the drinks down on the edge of the bar so I don't spill them.

"Hi," he says.

"You're here!" I say.

"*You're* here!" he says.

I hug him again.

"It's really great to see you," he tells me. "Beautiful as ever."

"Thank you kindly," I say.

Gabby makes her way toward us.

"Gabby Hudson," he says, leaning in to give her a hug.

"Ethan!" she says. "Good to see you."

"I'm going to grab a drink, and I'll meet you in a minute," he says to us.

I nod at him, and Gabby and I turn back toward our table.

She raises her eyebrows at me.

I roll my eyes at her.

An entire conversation without a word spoken.

Soon the music is so loud and the bar is so crowded that conversation becomes difficult.

I'm trying to hear what Caitlin is saying when Ethan gets to the table. He stands next to me, resting with his arm up against mine without a hint of self-consciousness. He sips his beer and turns to Katherine, the two of them trying to hear each other over the music. I glance over for a moment to find him looking intently at her, gesturing as if he's making a joke. I watch as she throws her head back and laughs.

She's prettier than I realized. She seemed plain before. But I can see now that's she's quite striking. Her long blond hair is blown out straight. Her sapphire-blue dress flatters her, hanging off her body effortlessly. It doesn't even look as if she needs to wear a bra.

I can't go anywhere without a bra.

Gabby pulls at my hand and drags me onto the dance floor. Caitlin joins us and then Erica and Brynn do, too. We dance to a few songs before I see Ethan and Katherine come over to join us. Mark hangs back with the others, nursing his beer.

"He doesn't dance?" I ask Gabby.

Gabby rolls her eyes. I laugh as Katherine, twirling, catches my eye. Ethan is spinning her.

I wonder if he'll take her home. I am surprised at how much this idea bothers me, just how unsubtle my feelings are.

He laughs as the song ends. They break apart, and he high-fives her. It seems like a friendly gesture, as opposed to a romantic one.

Looking at him now, recalling what it used to be like between us, how I liked myself around him, how I felt good about the world and my place in it with him by my side, how I ached when he left for college, I remember what it feels like to truly love someone. For the right reasons. In the right way.

Gabby taps my shoulder, bringing me back to reality. I turn to look at her. She is trying to tell me something. I can't hear her.

"Some air!" she yells, pointing to the patio. She waves herself off like a fan. I laugh and follow her out.

The moment we step outside, it's an entirely different world. The air has cooled, and the music is muted, contained by the building.

"How are you feeling?" Gabby asks me.

"Me?" I say. "Fine, why?"

"No reason," she says.

"So Mark doesn't dance, huh?" I ask, changing the subject. "You love dancing! He doesn't take you dancing?"

She shakes her head, scrunching her eyebrows. "Definitely not. He's not that kind of guy. It's fine. I mean, nobody's perfect but you and me," she jokes.

The door opens, and Ethan walks through. "What are you guys talking about out here?" he asks.

"Mark doesn't like dancing," I tell him.

"I'm actually going to go see if I can get him to cut a rug once and for all," Gabby says. She smiles at me as she leaves.

It's just Ethan and me alone out here now.

"You look a little bit cold," he says as he sits down on the empty bench. "I'd offer you my shirt, but I'm not wearing anything underneath."

"Might break the dress code," I say. "I thought since I'm in L.A., I should wear a tank top, but . . ."

"But it's February," he says. "And this is Los Angeles, not the equator."

"It's crazy how new this city feels to me, even though I lived here for so long," I tell him as I sit down next to him.

"Yeah, but you were eighteen when you left. You're almost thirty now."

"I prefer the term *twenty-nine*," I say.

He laughs. "It's nice to have you back," he says. "We haven't lived in the same city for . . . I guess almost thirteen years."

"Wow," I say. "Now I feel even older than when you called me almost thirty."

He laughs again. "How are you?" he asks me. "Are you well? Are you good?"

"I'm OK," I say. "I have some things to work out."

"You want to talk about them?"

"Maybe," I say, smiling. "At some point?"

He nods. "I'd love to listen. At some point."

"What's going on with you and Katherine over there?" I ask. My voice is breezy. I'm trying to sound as if this is casual, and I'm pulling it off.

Ethan shakes his head. "No, no," he says. "Nothing. She just started talking to me, and I was happy to entertain her." He smiles at me. "She's not who I came to see."

We look at each other, neither one of us breaking the gaze. His eyes are on me, focused on my eyes, as if I am the only other person in the world. And I wonder if he looks at every woman that way.

And then he leans over and kisses me on the cheek.

The way it feels, his lips on my skin, makes me realize I have spent years looking for that feeling and never finding it. I have settled for casual flings, halfhearted love affairs, and a married man, searching for that moment when your heart jumps in your chest.

And I wonder if I should really kiss him, if I should turn my head ever so slightly and put my lips on his.

Gabby and Mark come through the door.

"Hey," Gabby says, before staring at us. "Oh, sorry."

"No," I say. "Hey."

Ethan laughs. "You're Mark, right?" he says, getting up and shaking his hand. "Ethan. We didn't formally meet earlier."

"Yeah. Hey. Nice to meet you."

"Sorry," Gabby says. "We have to head out."

"I just found out I have an early-morning thing," Mark says.

"On a Sunday?" I ask him.

"Yeah, it's this thing at work I have to do."

I look at my watch. It's after midnight.

"Oh, OK," I say as I start to rise.

"Actually, I could take you home," Ethan says. "Back to Gabby's place later. If you want to stay for a while. Whatever you want."

I catch a coy smile come across Gabby's face for a split second.

I laugh to myself. It's so obvious, isn't it?

By coming back to L.A., I'm not just trying to build a better life with the support of my best friend. I've also reopened the question of whether Ethan and I have unfinished business between us.

We've spent years apart. We've gone on to live two very different lives. And we're right back here. Flirting off to the side at the party, while everyone else is dancing.

Will we or won't we? and *If I let him take me home, will it mean more to me than it means to him?*

I look at Ethan, and then I look at Gabby.

Life is long and full of an infinite number of decisions. I have to think that the small ones don't matter, that I'll end up where I need to end up no matter what I do.

My fate will find me.

So I decide to . . .

So I decide to go home with Gabby.

I don't want to rush into anything.

I turn and give Ethan a good-bye hug. I can hear, through the door, that the DJ just started playing Madonna's "Express Yourself," and for a moment, I sort of regret my decision. I love this song. Sarah and I used to sing it in the car together all the time. My mom never let us sing the part about satin sheets. But we just loved the song. We'd listen to it over and over.

I consider taking my good-bye back, as if the universe is telling me to stay and dance.

But I don't.

"I should go home," I say to Ethan. "It's late, and I want to get on West Coast time, you know?"

"I totally understand," he says. "I had a great time tonight."

"Me, too! I'll call you?"

Ethan nods as he moves to give Gabby a hug good-bye. He shakes Mark's hand. He turns to me and whispers into my ear, "You're sure I can't convince you to stay out?"

I shake my head and smile at him. "Sorry," I say.

He smiles and sighs ever so subtly, with a look that says he's accepted defeat.

We walk back into the bar and say good-bye to everyone—Erica, Caitlin, Brynn, Katherine, and the rest of the people I've met tonight.

"I thought for sure you were going home with Ethan," Gabby says as we are heading back to the car.

I shake my head at her. "You think you know me so well."

She gives me a doubting look.

"OK, you know me perfectly. But I just feel like if things with Ethan and me are going to happen, they will happen on their own time, you know? No need to rush anything."

"So you do want something to happen?"

"I don't know!" I say. "Maybe? Eventually? It seems like I should be with an honest, stable, nice guy like him. He seems like a move in the right direction, men-wise."

When we get to the car, Mark opens the doors for us and tells Gabby he's just going to take Wilshire Boulevard home. "That seems easiest, right? Less traffic?"

"Yeah," Gabby says, and then she turns around and asks me if I've ever heard of the Urban Light installation at the Los Angeles County Museum of Art.

"No," I say. "I don't think so."

"I think you'll really like it," she says. "They installed it a few years ago. We're gonna end up driving by it, so I'll point it out. This is all part of my campaign to make you fall in love with L.A. again, by the way."

"I'm excited to see it," I say.

"People always say that Los Angeles has no culture," Gabby says. "So, you know, I'm going to prove them wrong in the hopes that you'll stay."

"You do remember that I lived here for almost twenty years," I tell her.

"I meant to ask you." She turns toward me as Mark looks ahead, driving. "How are your parents and Sarah?"

"Mom and Dad are good," I say. "Sarah's at the London Ballet Company now and living with her boyfriend, George. I haven't met him, but my parents like him, so that's good. My dad's doing well at work, so I think my mom is considering only working part-time."

They don't send me money in any traditional sense. But for years, they have given me such a large amount of money every Christmas that I almost feel like I'm getting a Christmas bonus. I don't know how much money my family actually has, but it certainly seems like a lot.

"Your family doesn't come to the U.S. anymore?" Mark asks.

"No," I say. "I always go over to see them."

"Any excuse to go to London, right?" Mark says.

"Right," I say, although that's not really true. They've never offered to come back to the U.S. And since they are the ones buying the ticket, I don't have a lot of say in the matter.

I turn toward the car window and watch the streets go by. They are streets I didn't frequent as a teenager. We're in a part of town I don't know that well.

"Did you have fun tonight?" Gabby asks me.

"Yeah, I did," I tell her, my gaze still on the sidewalks and storefronts we're passing. "You have a lot of great friends out here, and it was awesome to see the girls from high school. Did Caitlin lose like thirty pounds?"

"Weight Watchers, I think," Gabby says. "She's doing really well. She was doing well before, though, too. Women don't need to be thin to be valuable."

I can see Mark smile into the rearview mirror, and I smile back at him. It is a small intimacy between us, our mutual eye-rolling at Gabby's political correctness. I start to laugh, but I hold it in. Gabby's not wrong. Women don't have to be thin to be valuable. Caitlin was the same person before she lost the weight as she is now. It's just funny that Gabby always feels the need to spell it out all the time. She can't take it for granted.

Gabby's phone dings, and she picks it up. I watch as she reads the text message and immediately hides her phone. She's terrible at keeping things from me.

"What is it?" I ask.

"What is what?"

"On your phone."

"Nothing."

"Gabby, c'mon," I say.

"It's not important. It means nothing."

"Hand it over."

She reluctantly puts the phone in my hand. It's a text message from Katherine.

Going home with Ethan. Is this a terrible idea?

My heart sinks in my chest. I look away and hand the phone back to Gabby without a word.

She turns back to look at me. "Hey," she says softly.

"I'm not upset," I say back, but my voice is thin and high-pitched. Upset is exactly how I sound.

"C'mon," she says.

I laugh. "It's fine. He can do what he wants." I'm glad I didn't stay out late with him, looking to see if there was something between us. "I specifically did not stay out with him tonight because I didn't want it to be a one-night thing. If it was anything. So there you go. Spares me the embarrassment."

Gabby frowns at me.

I laugh defensively, as if the harder I laugh, the harder I can push her pity off me and out the window. "He's a great guy. I'm not saying he's not, but, you know, if that's how it gonna be with him, I don't need that."

I look out the window again and then immediately back at Gabby.

"I like Katherine, actually," I say. "She seems great."

"If I may," Mark interjects. "I don't know much about the history between the two of you, but just because he's sleeping with someone else doesn't necessarily mean . . ."

"I know," I say. "But still. It makes it clear to me that he and I are best left in the past. I mean, we dated forever ago. It's fine."

"Do you want to change the subject?" Gabby asks me.

"Yes," I say. "Please."

"Well, should we go to breakfast tomorrow while Mark goes into work?"

"Yeah," I say, turning away from her and looking out the window. "Let's talk about food."

"Where should I take her?" Gabby asks Mark, and the two of them start rattling off names of restaurants I've never heard of.

Mark asks me if I like sweet or savory breakfasts.

"You mean, do I like pancakes or eggs?"

"Yeah," he says.

"She likes cinnamon rolls," Gabby answers at the exact same time I say, "I like places with cinnamon rolls."

When I was a kid, my dad used to take me to this doughnut shop called Primo's Donuts. They had big, warm cinnamon rolls. We'd go get one every Sunday morning. As I got older, we got busier. Eventually, a lot of my parents' time was spent shuttling Sarah to and from various rehearsals and recitals, so it became harder to find time to go. But when we did, I always ordered a cinnamon roll. I just love them so much.

When I moved in with Gabby's family, Tina used to buy the cans of raw cinnamon rolls and bake them for me on the weekends. The bottoms were always burned, and she had a light hand with the prepackaged icing, but I didn't care. Even a bad cinnamon roll is still a good cinnamon roll.

"With a lot of icing," I tell Mark. "I don't care if it's a day's worth of calories. Gabby, if you're up for it, I can try to find Primo's, and we can go there tomorrow."

"Done," she says. "OK, we're almost at the museum. Up on the right here. You can sort of see the lights now, just right there."

I look forward, past her head, and I think I see what she's talking about. We breeze through the green light, hitting a red in front of LACMA, and now I see it perfectly.

Streetlight after streetlight, rows of them, tightly lined up and lit. These are not the streetlights that you see today, the kind that shoot toward the sky and then curve over above the street. These are vintage. They look as if Gene Kelly might have swung on them while singing in the rain.

I look at the installation, staring with purpose out the window. I suppose there is something very simple and beautiful about it. City lights against a backdrop of a pitch-black night does have a sense of magic to it. And maybe there's a metaphor here, something about brightness in the middle of . . . Oh, hell. I'm lying. The truth is, I don't get it.

"Actually," Gabby says, "why don't we get out? Is that cool, Mark? Can we park and take a quick picture by the lights? Hannah's first real night back in L.A.?"

Mark nods, and when the light turns green, he pulls up to the curb. We get out of the car and head to the center of the lights.

We take turns taking pictures of each other, round robin–style. Gabby and I stand between two rows of lights, and Mark takes pictures of us with our arms around each other. We wear oversized grins. We kiss each other on the cheek. We stand on either side of a lamppost and mug for the camera. And then I offer to take a picture of Mark and Gabby together.

I switch places with Mark, getting out my own phone to take the photo. Gabby and Mark tuck themselves together, holding each other tight, posing underneath the lamps. I back up just a little, trying to frame the picture as I want.

"Hold on," I say. "I want to get all of it." I can't get far enough away from them to get the top of the lights in the shot, so I walk to the edge of the sidewalk. It's still not far enough away, so I push the walk button and wait for a signal so I can stand on the street.

"Just one sec!" I call out to them.

"This better be good!" Gabby yells.

The light turns red. The orange hand changes to a white-lit pedestrian, and I step down into the crosswalk.

I turn around. I frame my shot: Mark and Gabby in the middle of a sea of lights. I hit the shutter. I check the photo. I start to take another for good measure.

By the time I hear the screeching of tires, it's too late to run.

I am thrown across the street. The world spins. And then everything is shockingly still.

I look at the lights. I look at Gabby and Mark. The two of them rush toward me, mouths agape, arms outstretched. I think they are screaming, but I cannot hear them.

I don't feel anything. Can't feel anything.

I think they are calling to me. I see Gabby reach for me. I see Mark dial his phone.

I smell metal.

I'm bleeding. I don't know where.

My head feels heavy. My chest feels weighed down, as if the entire world is resting on it.

Gabby is very scared.

"I'm all right," I tell her. "Don't worry. I feel fine."

She just looks at me.

"Everything is going to be OK," I tell her. "Do you believe me?"

And then her face blurs, and the world mutes, and the lights go out.

So I decide to stay out with Ethan.

I'm eager to spend time with a good man for a change.

I turn and say good-bye to Gabby and Mark. That very second, "Express Yourself" comes on in the bar, and I know I've made the right decision. I absolutely love this song. Sarah and I used to make our parents listen to it over and over in the car, singing at the top of our lungs. I've got to stay and dance to this.

"You don't mind, right?" I say as I hug Gabby. "I just want to stay out a bit longer. See where the night takes me."

"Oh, please, go for it!" she says as I hug Mark good-bye. I can see a sly smile on her face, visible only to me. I roll my eyes at her, but a small grin sneaks out at the last minute. Then Gabby and Mark head for the door.

"So," Ethan says as he turns to me, "the night is ours for the taking." The way he says it, with a little bit of scandal in his voice, makes me feel as if we're teenagers again.

"Dance with me?" I say.

Ethan smiles and opens the door to the bar. He holds it for me to walk through. "Let's do this," he says.

We only get a minute or so before the song ends and another starts playing. This new one has a Spanish feel to it, a Latin beat. I feel my hips start to move without my permission. They sway for a moment, back and forth, just testing the waters. Soon I just let go and allow my body to move the way it wants to. Ethan slips his arm around the lowest part of my back. His leg just barely grazes the inside of mine. He moves back and forth and then pulls me quickly against him. He spins me. We forget about everyone else around us, and we stay like this, song after song, moving in tandem. Our faces stay close together but never touch. Every once in a while, I catch him looking at me, and I find myself blushing ever so slightly.

By the end of the night, when the dancing is over and the bar is thinning out, I look around and realize that everyone else in the group has gone home.

Ethan grabs my hand and leads me outside. As our feet hit the sidewalk, away from the din of the bar, I feel the effects of a night spent in a small place with loud music. The outside world feels muted compared with the bar. My eyes feel a bit dry. The balls of my feet are killing me.

Ethan's leading me down the street as the rest of the bar funnels out.

"Where's your car?" I ask him.

"I walked. I live only a few blocks from here. This way," he says. "I have an idea."

I stumble to try to keep up with him. He's going too fast, and my feet are killing me. "Wait, wait, wait," I say.

I bend over and take my shoes off. The sidewalk is grimy. I can see wads of gum so old they are now black spots in the concrete. Up ahead, a tree has rooted itself so firmly into the ground that it has broken up the sidewalk, creating jagged edges and crevices. But my feet hurt too much. I pick up my shoes and follow Ethan.

Ethan looks down at my feet and stops in place. "What are you doing?"

"My feet hurt. I can't walk in these. It's fine," I say. "Let's go."

"Do you want me to carry you?"

I start laughing.

"What's so funny?" he asks. "I could carry you."

"I'm good," I say. "This isn't the first time I've walked barefoot through a city."

He laughs and starts walking again. "As I was saying . . . I have a great idea."

"And what is that?"

"You've been dancing," he says as he pulls me forward.

"Obviously."

"And you've been drinking."

"A bit."

"And you've been sweating up a storm."

"Uh . . . I guess so?"

"But there is one thing you haven't been doing."

"OK?"

"Eating."

The second he says it, I am suddenly ravenous. "Oh, my God, where do we eat?" I say.

He quickens his pace toward the major intersection up ahead. I start to smell something. Something smoky. I run with him, my feet hitting the gritty concrete with every step, until we make our way to the crowd forming on the sidewalk.

I look at Ethan. He tells me what I'm smelling. "Bacon. Wrapped. Hot dogs."

He cuts through the crowd and walks up to the food cart. He orders two for us. The cart looks like a glorified ice cream wagon that you might see someone pushing at the park. But the woman running it is keeping up with the orders of all the tipsy people out on the street.

Ethan comes back with our hot dogs nestled in buns. He puts one under my nose. "Smell that."

I do.

"Have you ever smelled anything that good this late at night in any other city you've been to?"

Right now, this second, I honestly can't think of a time. "Nope," I say.

We walk around the block and find ourselves on a residential street. The sounds of the crowd and the smoke of the cart are gone. I can hear crickets. *While standing in the middle of a city.* I forgot that about Los Angeles. I forgot how it's urban and suburban all at once.

The street is lined with palm trees so tall you have to throw your neck back to see their full scope. They continue on up and down this block, up and down the blocks to the north and south. Ethan walks to one of the trees and the surrounding grass. He sits down on the thin curb that separates them from the street. He puts his feet on the road, his back up against the tree. I do the same next to him.

The bottoms of my feet are black at this point. I can only imagine how dirty I will make Gabby's shower tomorrow morning.

"Dog me," I say, holding my hand out, waiting for Ethan to give me the one he has decided is mine.

He does.

"Thank you," I say. "For buying me dinner. Or breakfast. Not sure which this is."

He nods, having already taken a bite. After he swallows, he says, "Ah, I made a rookie mistake. I should have gotten us water, too."

The world is starting to come into focus a bit more now

that we have left the bar. I can hear better. I can see better. And maybe most important, I can taste this delicious hot dog in all of its bacon-wrapped glory.

"I know it's become a cliché now," I say. "But bacon really does make everything else taste better."

"Oh, I know," he says. "I don't want to sound pretentious, but I really feel like I knew that before everyone else. I have loved bacon for years."

I laugh. "You were into bacon when it was just a breakfast food."

He laughs and adopts an affected tone. "Now it's changed. It's so commercial."

"Yeah," I say. "You probably put bacon on a doughnut back in oh-three."

"All kidding aside," Ethan says, "I really do think I figured out candied bacon first."

I start laughing at him between bites.

"I'm not joking! When I was a kid, I would always put maple syrup on my bacon. Maple syrup plus bacon equals . . . candied bacon. You're welcome, America."

I laugh at him and put my hand on his back. "I'm sorry to break it to you," I say, "but everyone's been doing that for years."

He looks right at me. "But no one told me about it. I came up with it on my own," he says. "It's my own idea."

"Where do you think people got the inspiration for maple bacon doughnuts or brown sugar bacon? All around the country for years and years, people have been putting maple syrup on their bacon and loving it."

He smiles at me. "You have just ruined the only thing I've ever considered a personal achievement."

I laugh. "Oh, come on. You're talking to a woman with no

career, no home, barely any money, and no potential," I say. "Let's not bring up personal achievements."

Ethan turns to me. His hot dog is long gone. "You don't really think that," he says.

Normally, I would make a joke. But jokes take so much effort. I wave my head from side to side, as if deciding. "I don't know," I say. "I sort of really think that."

Ethan shakes his head, but I keep talking. "I mean, this is just not where I thought my life was going, at all. And I look at someone like Gabby or someone like you, and I mean, I sort of feel like I'm behind. It's not a big deal," I say, finally realizing that I'm complaining. "Just something for me to work on. I mean, I guess I am just hoping to find a city and stick with it one of these days."

"I always thought you should be back here," Ethan says, looking at me directly.

I smile, but when Ethan doesn't break his gaze, I get nervous. I slap my hands on my thighs lightly. "Well," I say, "should we get going?"

Ethan stares forward for a moment, his eyes focused on the ground underneath his feet. Then he sort of comes to, snaps out of it. "Yeah," he says. "We should head back." He stands up as I do, and for a moment, our bodies are closer together than either of us anticipated. I can feel the warmth of his skin.

I start to back away, and he lightly grabs my hand to stop me. He looks me in the eye. I look away first.

"Something I've been wanting to ask you for a while," he says.

"OK," I say.

"Why did we break up?"

I look at him and feel my head cock to the side ever so slightly. I'm genuinely surprised by the question. I laugh gently.

"Well," I say, "I think that's what eighteen-year-olds do. They break up."

The tension doesn't dissipate.

"I know," he says. "But did we have a good reason?"

I look at him and smile. "Did we have a good *reason*?" I say, repeating his question. "I don't know. Teenagers don't really have to have good reasons."

He laughs and starts walking back in the direction we came from. I walk with him.

"You broke my heart," he says, smiling at me. "You know that, right?"

"Excuse me? Oh, no, no, no," I say. "I was the heartbroken one. I was the one who got dumped when her boyfriend went to college."

He shakes his head at me, smiling despite himself. "What a load of crap," he says. "*You* broke up with *me*."

I smile and shake my head at him. "I think we're dealing in revisionist history here," I tell him. "*I* wanted to stay together."

"Ridiculous!" he says. His hands are buried deep in his pockets, his shoulders hunched forward. He is walking slowly. "Absolutely ridiculous. A woman breaks your heart, comes back to town a decade later, and pins it on you."

"OK, OK," I say. "We can agree to disagree."

He looks at me and shakes his head. "Nope!" he says, laughing. "I don't accept."

"Oh, you're being silly," I say.

"I am not," he says. "I have proof."

"Proof?"

"Cold, hard evidence."

I stop in place and cross my arms. "This should be good. What's your proof?"

He stops with me, comes closer toward me. "Exhibit A: Chris Rodriguez." My senior-year boyfriend.

"Oh, please," I say. "What does Chris Rodriguez prove?"

"You moved on first. I came home from Berkeley for Christmas ready to knock on your door and sweep you off your feet," he says. "And the minute I get into town, I hear you're dating Chris Rodriguez."

I laugh and roll my eyes just a little bit. "Chris didn't mean anything. I wasn't even with him by the time you came home from school for the summer. I thought, you know, maybe you'd come home for those three months and . . ."

He moves his eyebrows up and down at me, the visual version of *hubba hubba*.

I laugh, slightly embarrassed. "Well, it didn't matter anyway, right? Because you were with Alicia by then."

"Only because I thought you were with Chris," he says. "That's the only reason I dated her."

"That's terrible!" I say.

"Well, I didn't know that at the time!" he says. "I thought I loved her. You know, I was nineteen years old at that point. I had the self-awareness of a doorknob."

"So maybe you did love her," I say. "Maybe it was you who moved on from me."

He shakes his head. "Nah," he says. "She broke up with me when we got back to school that year. Said she needed someone who could tell her she was the only one."

"And you couldn't do that?"

He looks at me pointedly. "Nope."

It's quiet again for a moment. Neither of us having much to say or, maybe more accurately, neither of us knowing *what* to say.

"So we broke each other's heart," I say at last. I start walking forward again.

He joins me and smiles. "Agree to disagree," he says.

We continue walking down the street, stopping at a red light, waiting for a cross signal.

"I never had sex with Chris," I tell him as we walk farther and farther into the residential section.

"No?" Ethan says.

"No," I say, shaking my head.

"Any reason why not?" Ethan asks.

I sway my head from side to side, trying to find the words to explain what I felt back then. "I . . . I couldn't stand the thought of sharing that with someone other than you," I finally say. "Didn't seem right to do it with just anybody."

I was twenty-one by the time I had sex with someone else. It was Dave, my college boyfriend. The reason I slept with him wasn't that I thought he might mean something to me the way Ethan did. I did it because *not* doing it was getting weird. If I'm being honest, somewhere along the way, I lost that feeling that the person had to be special, that it was something sacred. "I bet you didn't turn down Alicia's advances," I say, teasing him. For a moment, I think I see him blush.

He guides me toward an ivy-covered building on a dark, quiet street. He opens the lobby door and lets me in first.

"You have me there," he says. "I'm embarrassed to admit that there have been times in my life when rejection from the woman I love has served only to encourage me sleeping with others. It's not my best trait. But it does numb the pain."

"I'm sure it does," I say.

He guides me to his apartment on the second floor.

"Doesn't mean anything, though," he says. "Sleeping with

Alicia didn't mean that I didn't love you. That I wouldn't have dropped everything to be with you. If I thought . . . well, you know what I'm getting at."

I look at him. "Yeah, I do."

He opens the door and gestures for me to walk in. I look at him and walk in front of him into his place. It's a studio apartment but big, making it cozy without seeming cramped. It's neat but not necessarily clean, which is to say that everything is in its place, but there are dust bunnies in the corners, a water ring on the dark wood coffee table. He has painted the walls a deep but unobtrusive blue. A flat-screen TV is mounted on the wall opposite the couch, and shelves overloaded with books cover every available space. His bed linens are a dark, forgiving gray. Did I know, back then, that this was the kind of adult he'd grow up to be? I don't know.

"It was very hard to get over you," he says.

"Oh, yeah?" I say. There is a lump in my throat, but I try to cover it up by being flirtatious and light. "What was so hard to get over?"

He throws his keys onto a side table. "Three things," he says.

I smile, letting him know I'm ready to listen. "These should be good!"

"I'm serious. Are you ready to hear them? Because I'm not messing around."

"I'm ready," I say.

Ethan puts up his thumb to start the count. "One," he says. "You always had your hair up, just like it is now, in that high bun thing. And very occasionally, you would take it down." He pauses and then starts again. "I just loved that moment. That moment between up and down, when it fell across your neck and around your face."

I find myself fiddling with the bun on the top of my head. I have to stop myself from adjusting it. "OK," I say.

"Two," he says. "You always tasted like cinnamon and sugar."

I laugh. If I wasn't sure before, I am now positive that he is being sincere. "From the cinnamon rolls."

He nods. "From the cinnamon rolls."

"And what's the third?" I ask. I almost don't want to know, as if it's the third thing he says that will undoubtably and irrevocably usher forth all those teenage feelings, a flood of blushing cheeks and quickening heartbeats. It is the teenage feelings that are the most intoxicating, the ones that have the power to render you helpless.

"You smelled like tangerines," he says.

I give him a look. "Orange Ginger."

"Yeah," he says. "You always smelled like Orange Ginger." He comes ever so close to my neck. "Still do."

He is close enough that I can smell him, too, the mixture of laundry detergent and sweat.

I can feel the skin of my cheeks start to burn, my pulse start to speed up.

"You smell good, too," I say. I don't move away.

"Thank you," he says.

"In high school, you smelled like Tide."

"I think that's what my mom used," he says.

"When you left, I smelled your old T-shirts," I say. "I used to sleep in them."

He listens to me. He takes my words, my feelings, and he spits them back out into facts. "You loved me," he says.

"Yeah," I say. "I did. I loved you so much it sometimes burned in my chest."

He leans forward ever so slightly. "I want to kiss you," he says.

I breathe in. "OK," I say.

"But I don't want to do this if . . . I don't want this to be a one-time thing."

"I don't know what it is," I say. "But it's not a one-time thing."

He smiles and leans in.

It's gentle at first, the touch of lip to lip, but I lean into it, and when I do, it overtakes us.

We back up to the closed front door behind us, my shoulders just grazing the door frame.

His lips move just like they used to, and his body feels just like it used to, and as much as two people can rewind the clock, as much as they can erase time, we do.

By the time we're in his bed, it feels as if we never left each other. It feels as if we never broke up, my parents never moved, I never started dating Chris Rodriguez, and Ethan never met Alicia Foster. It feels as if I never felt the chill of Boston in my hands or the wind of D.C. in my hair. As if I never felt the rain of Portland and Seattle on my shoulders or the heat of Austin on my skin. It's as if New York City, and all of its disappointments, never entered my heart.

It feels as if I finally made a good decision for once.

THREE DAYS LATER

I open my eyes.

My head feels heavy. The world feels hazy. My eyes adjust slowly.

I'm in a hospital bed. My legs are stretched out in front of me, a blanket covering them. My arms are by my sides. There is a blond woman in front of me with a stoic but kind look on her face. She's about forty. I can't be sure, but I don't think I've ever seen her in my life.

She is wearing a white coat and holding a folder.

"Hannah?" she says. "Nod if you can hear me, Hannah. Don't try to talk just yet. Just nod."

I nod. It hurts, just that little nod. I can feel it down my back. I can feel a dull ache all over my body, and it seems to be increasing exponentially.

"Hannah, my name is Dr. Winters. You're at Angeles Presbyterian. You've been in a car accident."

I nod again. I'm not sure if I'm supposed to. But I do.

"We can get into the details later, but I want to go over the big news now, OK?"

I nod. I don't know what else to do.

"First, on a scale of one to ten, how much pain are you in? Ten being so excruciating you don't think you can bear it for another second. One being you feel perfectly fine."

I start to try to talk, but she stops me.

"Show me on your fingers. Don't hold them up. Don't move your arms. Just show me with your hands at your sides."

I look down at my hands, and then I pull back the four fingers on my left hand.

"Six?" she says. "OK."

She writes something down in the folder and starts fiddling with one of the machines behind me.

"We're going to get you down to one." She smiles. It's a reassuring smile. She seems to think everything is going to be OK. "Soon you'll have an easier time moving your arms and torso, and speaking won't be too hard once you've been up for a little while. You have suffered blood loss and broken bones. That's an oversimplification, but it will work for now. You're going to be OK. Walking, at first, is going to be hard. You will need to practice a bit before it comes naturally to you again, but it will, one day, come naturally to you again. That's what I want you to take away from this conversation."

I nod. It hurts less this time. Whatever she did, it hurts less this time.

"Now, you've been unconscious for three days. Some of that time was because of the blow to the head you sustained during the accident, but the rest is because we put you under for surgery."

She's quiet for a moment, and I see her look off to the side. She turns back to me.

"It's perfectly normal if you don't remember the accident. It may take some time to come back. Do you remember the accident?"

I start to answer her.

"Just nod or shake your head for now," she says.

I shake my head slightly.

"That's fine. That is completely normal. Nothing to be concerned about."

I nod to let her know I understand.

"Now, as I said, we can go over the details of your injury and your surgery when you are feeling a bit stronger. But there is one last thing that I want to make sure you know as soon as possible."

I stare at her. Waiting to hear what she has to say.

"You were pregnant," she says. "At the time of the accident."

She picks up my chart and consults a piece of paper.

Wait, what did she just say?

"It looks like you were about ten weeks along. Did you know? Nod or shake your head if you feel up for it."

I can feel my heart start to beat faster. I shake my head.

She nods in understanding. "OK," she says. "That's more common than you think. If you're not trying to get pregnant and you don't always have regular periods, it's possible not to figure it out at this stage of the pregnancy."

I continue to stare, unsure what, exactly, is happening right now, stunned silent.

"The fetus did not make it through," she says. "Which, unfortunately, is also common."

She waits for me to respond, but I have no response. My mind is blank. All I can feel is my eyes blinking rapidly.

"I am sorry," she says. "I imagine this is a lot for you to digest at once. We have a number of resources here at the hospital to help you deal with everything that has happened. The good news, and I really do hope you are able to see the good news, is that you are going to be physically back to normal soon."

She looks at me. I avert my eyes. And then I nod. It occurs to me that my hair is down around my face. I must have lost my hair tie. It feels sort of uncomfortable like this, down. I want it back up in a bun.

Did she just say I lost a baby?

I lost a baby?

"Here is what we are going to do," the doctor says. "You have a lot of people here who have missed you these past few days. A lot of people who have been excited for this moment, the moment when you wake up."

I close my eyes slowly.

A baby.

"But I find that some patients need some time alone right after they have woken up. They aren't ready to see Mom and Dad and their sister and friends."

"My mom and dad?" I start to say, but my voice comes out as an unintelligible whisper. It's scratchy and airy.

"You've had a tube in your throat for some time. Talking is going to be difficult but will come back the more you do it. Just take it slowly. One or two words at a time at first, OK? Nod and shake your head when you can."

I nod. But I can't resist. "They're here?" I say. It hurts to say it. It hurts on the edges of my throat.

"Yep. Mom, Dad, your sister, Gabby, right? Or . . . Sarah? Sorry. Your sister is Sarah, friend is Gabby?"

I smile and nod.

"So this is the question. Do you need some time on your own? Or are you ready for family? Lift your right arm for time alone. Left for family."

It hurts, but my left hand shoots up, higher than I thought it would go.

I open my eyes.

My head feels heavy. The world feels hazy. My eyes adjust slowly.

And then I smile wide, because right in front of me, staring back at me, is Ethan Hanover.

I stretch slowly and push my head further into the pillow. His bed is so soft. It's the kind of bed you never want to leave. I suppose, for the past few days, I really haven't.

"Hi," he says gently. "Good morning."

"Good morning," I say back. I am groggy. My voice is scratchy. I clear my throat. "Hi," I say. That's better.

"You haven't had a cinnamon roll since you've been here," he says. "That's at least three entire cinnamon-roll-less days." He is shirtless and under the covers. His hair is scattered and unkempt. His five o'clock shadow is way past five o'clock. I can smell his breath as it travels the short distance from his pillow to mine. It leaves something to be desired.

"Your breath stinks," I say, teasing him. I have no doubt that mine smells much the same. After I say it, I put my hand over my mouth. I talk through the spaces between my fingers. "Maybe we should brush our teeth," I say.

He tries to pull my hand away, and I won't let him. Instead, I dive under the covers. I am wearing one of his T-shirts and the underwear that I picked up from my suitcase at Gabby's yesterday. Other than the trip to her place to grab some stuff, Ethan and I haven't left his apartment since we got here Saturday night.

He dives under the covers to find me and grabs my hands, holding them away from my own face.

"I'm going to kiss you," he says.

"Nope," I say. "No, my breath is too terrible. Free me from your superhuman grip, and let me brush my teeth."

"Why are you making such a big deal out of this?" he says, laughing, not letting go of me. "You stink. I stink. Let's stink together."

I pop my head out of the covers to inhale fresh air, and then I go back under.

"Fine," I say, and I breathe onto his face.

"Ugh," he says. "Absolutely revolting."

"What if my breath smelled this bad every morning? Would you still want to be with me?" I say, teasing him.

"Yep!" he says, and then he kisses me deeply. "You're not very good at this game."

That's the joke we came up with Sunday night. What would it take to derail this thing between us? What could ruin this great thing we have going?

So far, we've established that if I became an Elvis impersonator and insisted that he come to all of my shows, he'd still want to be with me. If I decided to get a pet snake and name it Bartholomew, he'd still want to be with me. Perpetual halitosis, it looks like, isn't a deterrent, either.

"What if everything I put in the washing machine shrinks?" This one isn't hypothetical. This one is very real.

"Doesn't matter," he says as he moves off me and gets out of bed. "I do my own laundry."

I lie back down, my head on the pillow. "What if I mispronounce the word *coupon* all the time?"

"Clearly, that's fine, because you just mispronounced it." He picks his jeans up off the floor and pulls them on.

"No, I didn't!" I say. " 'Cue-pawn.' "

"It's 'coo-pawn.' " He slips on his shirt.

"Oh, my God!" I say, sitting upright and outraged. "Please tell me you are joking. Please tell me you don't say 'coo-pawn.' "

"I can't tell you that," he says. "Because it would be a lie."

"So this is it, then. This is the thing that stands in our way."

He throws my pants at me. "Sorry, but no. You'll just have to get over it. If it makes you feel better, we will never use coupons for the rest of our lives, OK?"

I stand up and put my pants on. I leave his shirt on but grab my bra from the floor and slip it on underneath. It's such a bizarre and uncoordinated thing to do, to put on a bra while you still have a shirt on, that about halfway through, I wonder why I didn't just take the shirt off to begin with.

"OK," I say. "If you promise we will never talk about coupons, then fine, we can be together."

"Thank you," he says, grabbing his wallet. "Get your shoes on." I pull my hair down briefly so that I can redo my bun. He stares at me for a moment as it falls. He smiles when I put it back up. "Where are we going?" I ask him. "Why are we leaving the bed?"

"I told you," he says as he puts on his shoes. "You haven't had a cinnamon roll in three days."

I start laughing.

"Hop to it, champ," he says. He is now fully dressed and ready to go. "I don't have all day."

I put on my shoes. "Yes, you do."

He shrugs. I grab my purse and head out the front door so quickly he has to catch up. By the time we get down to the garage, he's narrowly in front of me and opens my door.

"You're quite the gentleman these days," I say as he gets into the front seat and turns on the car. "I don't remember all of this chivalry when we were in high school."

He shrugs again. "I was a teenager," he says. "I hope I've grown since then. Shall we?"

"To the cinnamon rolls!" I say. "Preferably ones with extra icing."

He smiles and pulls out of the driveway. "Your wish is my command."

My dad is sitting to my right, holding my hand. My mom is at the foot of the bed, staring at my legs. Sarah is standing by the morphine drip.

Gabby came in with them an hour ago. She's the only one who looked me in the eye at first. After giving me a hug and telling me she loved me, she said she'd leave us all alone to talk. She promised she'd be back soon. She left so that my family would have some privacy, but I also think she needed some time to pull herself together. I could see as she turned to leave that she was wiping her eyes and sniffling.

I think I am hard to look at.

I can tell that my mom, my dad, and Sarah have been crying on and off today. Their eyes are glassy. They look tired and pale.

I haven't seen them since Christmas the year before last, and it is jarring to see them in front of me now. They are in the United States. Los Angeles. The four of us, the Martin family, haven't been together in Los Angeles since I was a junior in high school. Our yearly family reunions have since taken place in their London apartment, a space that Sarah very casually and unironically refers to as a "flat."

But now they are here in my world, in my country, in a city that once was ours.

"The doctor said you're going to be able to walk again pretty soon," Sarah says as she fiddles with the arm of the bed. "Which

I guess is good news? I don't know." She stops and looks down at the floor. "I don't know what to say."

I smile at her.

She's wearing black jeans and a cream luxe sweater. Her long blond hair is blown dry and straightened. She and I have the same hair color naturally, a deep brown. But I see why she went blond. She looks good blond. I tried it once, but Jesus, did you know you have to go to the salon to get your roots done like every six weeks? Who has that kind of time and money?

Sarah's twenty-six now. I suppose she might look a bit more like me, have some curves to her, if she wasn't dancing all day. Instead, she's muscular and yet somehow willowy. Her posture is so rigid that if you didn't know her better, you might suspect she was a robot.

She's the type to do things by the book, the proper way. She likes fancy clothes and fine dining and high art.

For Christmas a few years ago, she got me a Burberry purse. I said thank you and tried really hard not to scuff it up, not to ruin it. But I lost it by March. I felt bad, but I also sort of felt like, *Well, what was she thinking giving* me *a Burberry purse?*

"We brought you magazines," she says now. "The good British ones. I figured if I was in a hospital bed, I'd want the good stuff."

"I'm . . . we're just so glad you're OK," my mom says. She's about to start crying again. "You gave us quite a scare," she adds. My mom's hair is naturally a dirty blond. Her coloring is lighter than the rest of us.

My dad has jet-black hair, so thick and shiny that I used to say his picture should be on boxes of Just For Men. It wasn't until I was in college that it occurred to me he was probably *using* Just For Men. He's been squeezing my hand since he sat down. He now squeezes it harder for a moment, to second my mom's statement.

I nod and smile. It's weird. I feel awkward. I don't have anything to say to them, and even though I couldn't really say anything anyway, it seems odd for us all to be sitting here, not speaking to one another.

They are my family, and I love them. But I wouldn't say we are particularly close. And sometimes, seeing the three of them together, with their similar non-American affectations and their British magazines, I feel like the odd man out.

"I'm sleepy," I say.

The sound of my voice causes them all to snap to attention.

"Oh, OK," my mom says. "We will let you sleep."

My dad gets up and kisses my temple.

"Right? We should leave? And let you sleep? We shouldn't stay, right? While you're sleeping?" my mom says as Sarah and my dad start laughing at her.

"Maureen, she's OK. She can sleep on her own, and we will be in the waiting room whenever she needs us." My dad winks at me.

I nod.

"I'll just leave these here," Sarah says, pulling a stack of magazines out of her bag. She drops them onto the tray by my bed. "Just, you know, if you wake up and you want to look at pictures of Kate Middleton. I mean, that's what I'd do all day if I could."

I smile at her.

And they leave.

And I am finally alone.

I was pregnant.

And now I'm not.

I lost a baby I didn't know existed. I lost a baby I was not planning for and did not want.

How do you mourn something like that? How do you mourn something you never knew you had? Something you never wanted but something real, something important.

My mind rolls back to thinking about *when* I got pregnant. Rolls back to the times I took a pill later than I meant to or the time one accidentally rolled underneath the bed and I couldn't find it. I think about when I told Michael we should use a condom as backup for a few days and Michael said he didn't care. And for some reason, I thought that was OK. I wonder which exact time it was. Which time we made a mistake that made a baby.

For the first time since waking up, I start crying.

I close my eyes and let the emotion wash over me. I listen to what my heart and mind are trying to tell me.

I am relieved and devastated. I am scared. I am angry. I am not sure if any of this is going to be OK.

The tears fall down my face with such force that I cannot possibly catch them all. They make their way to my hospital gown. My nose starts to run. I don't have the physical capacity to wipe it on my sleeve.

My head hurts from the pressure. I roll toward my pillow and bury my face in the sheets. I can feel them getting wet.

I hear the door open, and I don't bother to look and see who it is. I know who it is.

She sighs and gets into bed next to me. I don't turn to see her face. I don't need to hear her voice. Gabby.

I let it erupt. The fear and the anger and the confusion. The grief and the relief and the disgust.

Someone hit me with their car. Someone ran me over. They broke my bones, and they severed my arteries, and they killed the baby I didn't love yet.

Gabby is the only person on the planet I trust to hear my pain.

I howl into the pillow. She holds me tighter.

"Let it out," she says. "Let it out."

I breathe so hard that I exhaust myself. I am dizzy with oxygen and anguish.

And then I turn my head toward her. I can see she's been crying, too.

It makes me feel better somehow. As if she will bear some of the pain for me, as if she can take some of it off my hands.

"Breathe," she says. She looks me in the eyes and she breathes in slowly and then breathes out slowly. "Breathe," she says again. "Like me. Come on."

I don't understand why she's saying this to me until I realize that I am not breathing at all. The air is trapped in my chest. I'm holding it in my lungs. And once I realize that's what I'm doing, I let it go. It spills out of me, as if the dam has broken.

Air comes back in as a gasp. An audible, painful gasp.

And I feel, for maybe the first time since I woke up, alive. I am alive.

I am alive today.

"I was pregnant," I say, starting to cry again. "Ten weeks." It is the first real thing I've said since I woke up, and I can feel now how much it was tearing up my insides, like a bullet ricocheting in my gut.

Talking isn't as hard as I thought it would be. I think I can talk just fine. But I don't need to say anything else.

I don't need to tell Gabby that I didn't know. I don't need to tell Gabby that I wouldn't have been ready for the baby I don't have.

She already knows. Gabby always knows. And maybe more to the point, she knows there is nothing to say.

So she holds me and listens as I cry. And every couple of minutes, she reminds me to breathe.

And I do. Because I am alive. I may be broken and scared. But I am alive.

Ethan and I are circling the block around the café he wants to go to. Despite the fact that it is Tuesday morning and you'd think most people would be working, the street is packed with cars.

"When are you going back to work, by the way?" I ask him. He's called in sick twice now.

"I'll go back tomorrow," he says. "I have some vacation days saved up, so it's not a problem."

I don't want him to go back to work tomorrow, even though, you know, clearly, he should. But . . . I've been enjoying this reprieve from the real world. I quite like hiding out in his apartment, living in a cocoon of warm bodies and takeout.

"What if I eat so many cinnamon rolls that I turn into a cinnamon roll? Then?"

"Then what?" he says. He's only half listening to me. He's focused on trying to find a place to park.

"Then would this be over? Would that be a deal breaker?"

He laughs at me. "Try all you want, Hannah," he says. "But there are no deal breakers here."

I turn and look out the window. "Oh, I'll find your weak spot, Mr. Hanover. I will find it if it's the last thing I do."

He laughs as we slow to a red light. He looks at me. "I know what it means to miss you," he says. The light turns green, and he speeds down the boulevard. "So you'll have to find a pretty insurmountable problem if I'm going to let you go again."

I smile at him, even though I'm not sure he can see me. I've been doing a lot of that lately, smiling.

We finally find a spot relatively close to the café.

"This is why people leave this city, you know," I say as he squeezes into the spot.

He turns the key and pulls it out of the ignition. He gets out of the car. "You don't have to tell me that," he says. "I hate this city every time I circle a block like a vulture."

"Well, I'm just saying, in New York, there's the subway. And in Austin, you can park anywhere you want. The Metro in D.C. is so clean that you could eat off the floor."

"Nowhere is perfect. But, you know, don't go racking up reasons to leave already."

"I'm not," I say. I'm slightly defensive. I don't want to be the person no one thinks is going to stick around.

"OK," he says. "Good."

He turns and opens the door to the café, letting me in first. We get in line, and it so happens that the line snakes around the bakery case. I see the cinnamon rolls on the top shelf. They are half the size of my head. Covered in icing.

"Wow," I say.

"I know," he says. "I've wanted to take you here ever since I first found this place."

"How long ago was that?" I ask, teasing him.

He smiles. For a moment, I wonder if he's embarrassed. "A long time. Don't feel like you need to trick me into admitting I've been hung up on you for years. I'm confident enough to say it outright." I smile at him as he laughs and steps forward. "A cinnamon roll, please," he says to the cashier.

"Wait, aren't you having one?"

"They are huge!" Ethan says. "I thought we'd split one."

I give him a look.

He laughs. "Excuse me," he says to the cashier. "Make that two cinnamon rolls. My apologies."

I try to pay, but Ethan won't let me.

We grab some waters, sit down by the window, and wait for a server to warm up the rolls. I fiddle with the napkin dispenser.

"If I hadn't stayed out with you on Saturday, would you have tried to sleep with Katherine?" I ask him. It's been in the back of my mind since that night. I'm trying to be better at actually asking the questions I have instead of avoiding them.

He starts sipping his water. I can tell he is put off by the question. "What are you talking about?"

"You were flirting with her. And it bothered me. And I just want to make sure this is . . . that this is just me and you, and we aren't . . . that there is no one else."

"As far as I'm concerned, there's not another woman on the planet. I'm into you. I'm only into you."

"But if I hadn't stayed out . . ."

Ethan puts his water down and looks me right in the eye. "Listen, I went to that bar hoping to get you alone, hoping to talk to you, to gauge how you felt. I tried on ten different shirts to find the right one. I bought gum and kept it in my back pocket in case I had bad breath. I stood in front of the mirror and tried to get my hair to look like I didn't do my hair. For you. You are the only one. I danced with Katherine because I was nervous talking to you. And because I want to be honest with you, I'll admit that I don't know what I would have done if you had turned me down on Saturday, but no matter what I would have done, it would have been because I thought you weren't interested. If you're interested, I'm interested. And only in you."

"I'm interested," I say. "I'm very interested."

He smiles.

The cinnamon rolls arrive at the table. The smell of the spice and the sugar is . . . relaxing. I feel as if I am at home.

"Maybe all of this time," I say to Ethan, "I've been looking for home and not realizing that home is where the cinnamon roll is."

Ethan laughs. "I mean, if you're going to go all over the country looking for where you belong, I could have told you years ago you belong in front of a cinnamon roll."

I grab a knife and fork and make my incision, right into the deep heart of the swirl. I put the fork to my mouth. "This better be good," I say before I finally taste it.

It is absolutely delicious. Wonderfully, indulgently, blissfully delicious. I put down my utensils and look up at the ceiling, savoring the moment.

He laughs at me.

"Would it surprise you if I finished this entire roll myself?" I ask.

"Not since you insisted on having your own," he says. He takes a bite of his. I watch as he chews it casually, as if it's a ham sandwich or something. He'll indulge my sweet tooth, but he doesn't share it.

"How about if I finish yours, too?" I ask.

"Yes, I would actually go so far as to say that would shock me."

"Challenge accepted," I say, except that none of the syllables comes out clearly. There is too much dough in my mouth. I accidentally spit cinnamon on him.

Ethan moves his hand to his cheek to wipe it away. On a scale of one to ten, I'm about a six for embarrassment. I think my cheeks turn red. I swallow.

"Sorry," I say. "Not very ladylike."

"Kinda gross," he says, teasing me.

I shake my head. "How about that? If I make a habit of spitting cinnamon roll chunks on you, is that a deal breaker?"

Ethan looks down at the table and shakes his head. "Just get over it, OK? You and me. It's happening. Stop trying to find cracks in it." He puts down his knife and fork. "Maybe there are no cracks in this. Can you handle that?"

"Yeah," I say, "I can handle that."

I can, right? I can handle that.

I've noticed that in TV shows, visiting hours are only certain set times. "Sorry, sir, visiting hours are over" and that sort of thing. Maybe this is true in the rest of the hospital, but here on whatever floor I'm on, no one seems to care. My parents and Sarah were here until nine. They only left because I insisted they go back to their hotel. My nurse, Deanna, was in and out of here all day and never said anything to them about leaving.

Gabby showed up about two hours ago. She insisted on setting up camp on the poor excuse for a sofa in here. I told her that she didn't have to stay the night with me, that I'd be OK on my own, but she refused. She said she'd already told Mark she was sleeping here. Then she handed me the bouquet he sent with her. She put it on the counter and gave me the card. And then she made a bed for herself and talked to me as she closed her eyes.

She fell asleep about a half hour ago. She's been snoring for at least twenty minutes. I, myself, would love to fall asleep, but I'm too wired, too restless. I haven't moved or stood up since I was standing in front of LACMA four days ago. I want to get up and move around. I want to move my legs.

But I can't. I can barely lift my arms above my head. I turn on a small light by my bed and open up one of Sarah's magazines. I flip through the pages. Bright photos of women in absurd outfits in weird places. One of the photo shoots looks as if it took place in Siberia with women wearing polka-dot bikinis. Apparently, polka dots are in. At least in Europe.

I throw the magazine to the side and turn the TV back on, the volume low. No surprise to find that *Law & Order* is on. I have yet to find a time when it isn't.

I hear the show's familiar *buh-bump* just as a male nurse walks into my room.

He's tall and strong. Dark hair, dark eyes, clean-shaven. His scrubs are deep blue, his skin a deep tan. He has on a white T-shirt underneath.

It only now occurs to me that Deanna probably isn't working twenty-four hours a day. This guy must be the night nurse.

"Oh," he says, whispering. "I didn't realize you had company."

I notice that he has a large tattoo on his left forearm. It appears to be some sort of formal script, large cursive letters, but I can't make out exactly what it says. "She won't wake up," I whisper back.

He looks at Gabby and winces. "Geez," he says softly. "She sounds like a bulldozer."

I smile at him. He's right.

"I won't be too long," he says. He moves toward my machines. I've been hooked up to these things all day, to the point where they are starting to feel like a part of me.

He starts checking things off his list just as Deanna did earlier today. I can hear the sound of the pen on the clipboard. *Check. Check. Check. Scribble.* He puts my chart back into the pocket. I wonder if it says in that file that I lost a baby. I push the thought out of my head.

"Would you mind?" he asks me, gesturing to the stethoscope in his hand.

"Oh," I say. "Sure. Whatever you gotta do."

He pushes the neck of my gown down and slips his hand between my skin and the cloth, resting the stethoscope over my heart. He asks me to breathe normally.

Deanna did this earlier, and I didn't even notice. But now, with him, it feels intimate, almost inappropriate. But of course, it's not. Obviously, it's not. Still, I find myself slightly embarrassed. He's handsome, and he's my age, and his hand is on my bare chest. I am now acutely aware of the fact that I am not wearing a bra. I turn my head so I'm not looking at him. He smells like men's body wash, something that would be called Alpine Rush or Clean Arctic.

He pulls the stethoscope off me when he's satisfied with his findings. He scribbles something on the chart. I find myself desperate to change the mood. A mood he's probably not even aware of.

"How long have you worked here?" I ask, whispering so as not to wake up Gabby. I like that I have to whisper. At a whisper, you can't tell my voice is shot.

"Oh, I've been here since I moved to L.A. about two years ago," he whispers as he stares at my chart. "Originally from Texas."

"Whereabouts?" I ask.

"Lockhart," he says. "You wouldn't have heard of it. Small town just outside of Austin."

"I lived in Austin," I say. "For a little while."

He looks up at me and smiles. "Oh, yeah? When did you move here?"

It's hard to answer succinctly, and I don't have the voice to give him the whole story, so I simplify it. "I grew up here, but I moved back last week."

He tries to hide it, but I can see his eyes go wide. "Last week?"

I nod. "Last Friday night," I say.

He shakes his head. "Wow."

"Seems sort of unfair, doesn't it?"

He shakes his head and looks back down at the chart. He clicks his pen. "Nope, you can't think about that," he says, looking back up at me. "From experience, I can tell you that if you go around trying to figure out what's fair in life or whether you deserve something or not, that's a rabbit hole that is hard to climb out of."

I smile at him. "You might be right," I say, and then I close my eyes. Conversation takes more energy than I thought.

"Anything I can get you?" he whispers before he leaves.

I shake my head slightly. "Er, actually . . . maybe a hair tie?" I point to my head. My hair is down around my shoulders. I am lying on it. I hate lying on my hair.

"That's an easy one," he says. He pulls one out of his shirt pocket. I look at him, surprised.

"I find them all over the hospital. Someday maybe I'll tell you about the elaborate reminder system I use them for." He comes close and puts one in my hand. I only get a slightly better look at his tattoo. I still can't make it out.

"Thanks," I say. I lean forward, trying to get a good angle, trying to gather all of my hair. But it's hard. My entire body aches. Moving my arms high enough seems impossible.

"Hold on," he whispers. "Let me."

"Well," I say, "I don't want a ponytail."

"OK . . ." he says. "I don't have to braid it, do I? That seems complicated."

"Just a bun. High up." I point toward the crown of my head.

I don't care if the bun looks good. I just want it out from under my head and neck. I want it contained and out of the way.

"All right, lean forward if you can." He starts to gather my hair. "I think this is the beginning of a complete disaster."

I laugh and push my body forward. I wince.

"Let's get you a bit higher dosage on the pain meds. Does that sound OK?" he says. "You shouldn't be in that much pain."

I nod. "OK, but I think they've turned it as high as it will go."

"Oh, I don't know about that. We might be able to go higher." He drops my hair momentarily and moves toward my IV. I can't see what he's doing; he's behind me. And then he's in front of me again, picking up my hair. "I mean, you might start saying weird things and having hallucinations," he jokes, "but better that you're not in pain."

I smile at him.

"All right, so I'm just gathering all of this hair and putting it on the top of your head and then wrapping a rubber band around it?"

"Yeah."

He leans into me, our faces close together. I can smell the coffee on his breath. I feel slight tugging and pressure. He's got some of my hair caught, pulling tightly against my scalp.

"Looser? Maybe?" I say.

"Looser? OK." His arms are in my face, but the tattoo is facing the other direction. I bet it's a woman's name. He seems like the kind of guy who met a woman on some exotic island and married her and they have four beautiful children and live in a house with a gourmet kitchen. She probably makes beautiful dinners that incorporate all the food groups, and I bet they have fruit trees in their backyard. Not just oranges, either. Lemons, limes, avocados. I think the medication is up too high.

"OK," he says. "Voilá, I guess." He backs away from me ever so subtly to check his work.

By the look on his face, I can tell that my bun looks ridiculous. But it *feels* right. It feels like a high bun. I feel like myself for the first time today. Which . . . feels great. I feel great. Also, I'm definitely high.

"Do I look silly?" I ask.

"It's probably not my best work," he says. "You pull it off, though."

"Thanks."

"You're welcome," he says. "Well, if you need any other hairstyles, just press that button. I'm here for the next eight hours."

"Will do," I say. "I'm Hannah."

"I know," he says, smiling. "I'm Henry."

When he turns and leaves, I finally get a good glimpse of his tattoo. *Isabelle.*

Man, all the good ones are taken by Isabelles.

I lay my head down, relishing the free space behind my neck.

Henry's head pops back in.

"What's your favorite flavor of pudding?" he asks me.

"Probably chocolate," I say. "Or tapioca? And vanilla is good."

"So all of them? You like all flavors of pudding?" he says, teasing me.

I laugh. "Chocolate," I say. "Chocolate is good."

"I take my break at two a.m.," he tells me. He looks at his watch. "If you're still up, which I hope for your sake you aren't, but if you are still up, maybe I'll bring you some chocolate pudding."

I smile and nod. "That'd be nice," I whisper.

It's quiet on the floor, and it's dark. Gabby is snoring so

loudly I think for sure that I will not be able to fall asleep, that I will be wide awake when Henry comes back.

I turn on the TV. I flip through the channels.

And then I wake up in the morning to the sound of Gabby's voice. "Where did this chocolate pudding come from?"

I lie on Ethan's couch and stare up at the ceiling. He went to work today. I spent the morning cleaning up his apartment. Not *his* messes, mind you. But my own. My clothes were strewn across all of his furniture. His kitchen sink was full of dirty dishes that were mostly, if not all, mine. My stray hairs were pasted in a tangled-rope fashion across his shower walls. But now everything is spotless, and I'm forced to admit I have nothing to do. With Ethan back to work and life returning to normal, I realize I have no normal.

Gabby is picking me up when she leaves her office around six. We are heading to her parents' house for dinner. But until then, I've got nothing.

I turn on Ethan's TV and flip through the channels. I check his DVR for anything that piques my interest. I come up empty and turn it off. The silence proves to amplify the voice in my head, telling me I need to get a life.

Flirting and spending your days in bed and eating cinnamon rolls with your old high school boyfriend is a wonderful way to pass the time. But what is going on between Ethan and me doesn't solve the challenges that lie ahead.

I grab a pen and a piece of paper from Ethan's desk and start scribbling down a plan.

I am a fly-by-the-seat-of-my-pants type of person. I am a

see-where-life-takes-you sort of person. But that sort of approach to life isn't yielding results for me. It gets me paying the bills waiting tables and sleeping with married men. I don't want that anymore. I want to try order instead of chaos.

I can do that. I can be an organized person. Right? I mean, I did clean this entire apartment today. It's orderly and contained now. There's no sign that Hurricane Hannah hit. And maybe that's because I don't have to be a hurricane.

I want to build a life here. In Los Angeles. So I'm starting with a list.

Suddenly, I start to feel queasy. My stomach turns sour. But then the phone rings, and my mind is elsewhere.

It's Gabby.

"Hi. Are you ready to be shocked? I'm making a list. An actual, organized life-plan list."

"Who is this, and what have you done with Hannah?" she says, laughing.

"If you want her back, you'll listen to me," I say. "I need a million dollars in unmarked, nonconsecutive bills."

"I'll need time to get together that kind of money."

"You have twelve hours."

"Oh," she says. "I definitely can't do that in twelve hours. Just kill her. It's fine. She'll like heaven." Why did it take me this long to realize I should be in the same city as her?

"Hey!" I say, laughing.

She starts laughing with me. "Ohhhh," she says. "Hannah, it's you! I had no idea."

"Yeah, yeah, yeah," I say. "But don't come crying to me when *you* get kidnapped."

She laughs again. "I called to tell you I'm coming by earlier than I thought. Probably around five, if that works for you. I'll bring you back to my place, and then we can head out to Pasadena to see my parents around seven or so."

"Awesome. I'll hurry up and finish this list," I say, and then we get off the phone.

I look at the piece of paper in front of me. It says "Buy a car." That's the first thing I wrote down. The only thing I wrote down.

I quickly scribble "Get a job," and I waver about whether or not to put down "Find an apartment." The truth is, between Ethan and Gabby, I have plenty of options for where to stay. It seems fair to assume I'll figure something out. But then I decide no, I'm putting it down. I'm not going to see what happens. I'm going to make a plan. I'm going to be proactive.

Car.

Job.

Apartment.

It seems so simple, written out in order. For a moment, as I look at it, I think, *Is that all?* And then I realize that simple and easy aren't the same thing.

By the time Gabby comes to pick me up, I'm standing on the sidewalk waiting for her.

I get into the car, and Gabby starts driving.

She looks at me and shakes her head, smiling. I am grinning from ear to ear.

"Did I call this, or did I call this?" she says.

"Call what?" I ask, laughing.

"You and Ethan."

I shake my head. "It just happened!" I say. "I didn't *know* it was going to happen."

"But didn't I say that it would?"

"Neither here nor there," I say. "The point is, we're together now."

"Together?" Gabby says, laughing. "Like, you're *together*?"

I laugh. "Yes, we're *together*."

"So I can assume that aside from the occasional ride here and there and a few meals, I have lost you to your newfound boyfriend?"

I shake my head. "No, not this time. I'm not seventeen anymore. I have a life to create here. Romance is great. But it's only one part of a well-rounded life. You know?"

Gabby puts her hands to her heart and smiles to herself. I start laughing. I wasn't trying to placate her. I just don't think that having a good boyfriend solves all my problems.

I've still got plenty of problems to solve.

Deanna comes in to bring me my breakfast and check up on me. Shortly after she leaves, Dr. Winters comes in and sits down with Gabby and me to discuss the details of my injury now that I'm a bit more stable. My parents are on their way, and I know they'd want to be here for this, but I can't wait. I have to know.

Dr. Winters explains that the crash severed my femoral artery and broke my right leg and pelvis. I was unconscious and rushed into surgery to stop the bleeding and repair the break. I lost a considerable amount of blood and sustained a pretty significant blow to the head when I fell. As she tells me all of this, she continues to stress the fact that all of my injuries are fairly common in a car accident of this magnitude and that I will be fine. Knowing just how bad it was makes it harder to believe that I will be OK. But I suppose just because something is hard to understand, that doesn't make it any less true.

When Dr. Winters is done going through some memory questions, she tells me that I will be sent home in a wheelchair. I won't be able to walk for a few weeks as my pelvis heals. And even then, I will have to start off very slowly and very gently. I will need physical therapy in order to exercise the muscles that have been damaged, and I'll be in pain . . . well, almost all the time.

"It's a long road ahead," Dr. Winters says. "But it is a steady one. I have no doubt that someday, sooner rather than later, you will be able to go for a run around the block."

I laugh at her. "Well, I've never gone for a run around the block in the past, so now that my legs are immobile, it seems like a good time to start."

"You joke," she says, getting up. "But I've had patients who were complete couch potatoes start training for marathons when they get the use of their legs back. Something about that temporary and jarring loss of mobility can really encourage people to see what they are capable of."

She pats my hand and moves toward the door.

"Make sure you tell the nurses if you need anything. And if you have any other questions, I'm here," she says.

"Thanks," I say, and then I turn to Gabby. "Great. So not only am I unable even to walk myself to the bathroom right now, but if I don't start dreaming of marathons and Nikes, I'm a slacker."

"I believe that is what she said, yes. She said if you don't start training for the L.A. Marathon this very second, your life is a waste, and you might as well pack it in."

"Man, Dr. Winters can be such a bitch," I say, and instantly, there is a knock at the door. For a moment, I'm terrified it's Dr. Winters. I didn't mean it. I was just joking. She's really nice. I like her.

It's Ethan.

"OK for me to sneak in?" Ethan says. "Is now a good time?"

He pulls a large bouquet of lilies from behind his back.

"Hi," I say. I love lilies. I wonder if he remembered that or if it's a coincidence.

"Hey," he says. His voice is gentle, as if speaking too loudly could hurt me. He hasn't moved from the door. "Is this . . . ? Am I . . . ?"

"It's OK," Gabby says. "Come on in. Have a seat." She moves to the other side of me.

He comes closer and hands me the flowers. I take them and smell them. He smiles at me as if I'm the only person in the world.

As I look at him, it comes back to me, almost like a dream at first, and then the more I remember, the more it grabs hold.

I remember Gabby handing me her phone. I remember looking down at it. Seeing Katherine's message.

Going home with Ethan. Is this a terrible idea?

I bury my face in the flowers instead of looking directly at him. In a hospital, where everything is so clinical and unscented, where the air itself is stale, the smell of lilies almost feels as if it could make you high. I breathe in again, stronger, trying to inhale as much of their life and freshness as I can. The irony of the situation isn't lost on me. These are cut flowers. They are, by their very definition, dying.

"Mmm," I say. *He's not serious about us. He's not interested in an "us" if he went home with her. This is Michael all over again. This is me needing to learn that you have to face the truth of a situation head-on. He almost kissed me, and then he went home with another girl.* "They smell great."

"How are you?" he says. He sits down in the chair next to the bed.

"I'm OK," I say. "Really."

He stares at me for a moment.

"Can you take these back?" I say, handing the flowers to Gabby. "I don't have anywhere to really . . ."

"Oh," Gabby says. "Let me go find some water and something to put them in. Sound good?" She's trying to find a reason to leave us alone, and a perfect one just fell into her lap. She slips out the door and smiles at me.

"So," he says, breathing in hard.

"So," I say.

We are both quiet, looking at each other. I can tell he's worried about me. I can tell it's hard for him to look at me and see me in this hospital bed. I also know that it's not his fault I'm upset at the memory of him taking Katherine home. We had no claim on each other, made no promises.

And besides, this memory may be fresh for me because I just remembered it, because it was temporarily lost in the haziness of my brain, but it happened days ago. It's old news to him.

We both speak up at the same time.

"How are you, really?" he asks me.

"How've you been?" I ask him.

He laughs. "Did you just ask me how I've been? How have *you* been? That's the question. I've been worried sick about you."

"I'm OK," I say.

"You scared me half to death," he says. "Do you know that? Do you know how heartbroken I'd be to live in a world you weren't in?"

I know that I should believe him. I know that he's telling the truth. But the fact of the matter is that I worry that I'll believe him too much, that I'll become too easily swayed into believing what I want to believe about him. I don't want to do what I would have done before. I don't want to believe what a person says and ignore what he does. I don't want to see only what I want to see.

I want to be realistic, for once. I want to be grounded. I want to make smart decisions.

So when Ethan smiles at me and makes me feel as if I

invented the world, when he comes close to me and I can feel the warmth of his body and the smell of his laundry detergent just like in high school, I have to ignore it. For my own good.

"I really am OK," I tell him. "Don't worry. It's just some broken bones. But I'm OK."

He grabs my hand. I flinch. He sees me do it and takes his hand back.

"Have they been treating you well?" he says. "I hear hospital food leaves something to be desired."

"Yeah," I tell him. "I could use a good meal. Although the pudding isn't so bad."

"Did they say how long you'll be in here?" he asks. "I want to know when I can take you out on the town again."

I laugh politely. It's this sort of stuff. This sort of flirty, charming stuff. That's the stuff that gets me.

"It's gonna be a while," I say. "You might want to find another girl to paint the town red with."

"No," he says, smiling. "I think I'd rather wait for you."

No, you wouldn't.

I keep hoping Gabby will come back in with the flowers, but she's nowhere to be seen.

"Well," I say, "don't." My tone is polite but not particularly warm. Given the fact that it wasn't a very nice thing to say in the first place, I think I've shown my hand.

"OK," he says. "I should probably get going. You probably need your rest, and I should get to work . . ."

"Yeah," I say. "Sure."

He heads toward the door and turns around. "You know I would do anything for you, right? If you need anything at all . . . ?"

I nod. "Thanks."

He nods and looks down at the floor and then back up at me. He looks as if he's going to say something, but he doesn't. He just taps his hand on the door frame one time and then walks through it.

Gabby comes right back in. "Sorry," she says. "I didn't mean to eavesdrop, but I got back with the flowers a while ago, and I could hear you guys were having a conversation. I didn't want to . . ."

"It's cool," I say as she puts the flowers down on the counter by the door. I wonder where she found the vase. It's nice. The flowers are beautiful. Most men would have brought carnations.

She looks at me. "You're upset about the Katherine thing."

"So you did eavesdrop."

"I never said that I didn't. I just said I didn't mean to."

I laugh. "I'm not *upset* about the Katherine thing," I say, defending myself. "It just confirmed for me that trying something with him again . . . it's maybe not the best idea."

She grabs my hand for a moment. "OK," she says.

I pick up the remote and turn on the TV. Gabby grabs her purse.

"You're leaving?"

"Yeah, I have to get back to the office for a meeting. But your family's almost here. They texted me a few minutes ago saying they were parking. You'll have some time with them, and then I'll leave work, get a change of clothes for tomorrow, and be back here for our nightly slumber party."

"You don't need to stay here tonight," I say.

She frowns at me, as if I'm telling a lie.

"I'm serious," I say, laughing. "My parents can stay. Sarah can stay. No one has to stay. I'm serious. Go home. Spend time with Mark. I'm OK."

My mom pokes her head in. "Hi, sweetheart!" she says. "Hi, Gabrielle!" she adds when she sees her.

"Hi, Maureen," Gabby says, giving her a hug. "I was just taking off." She calls to me from the door. "I'll call you later. We'll discuss it."

I laugh. "OK."

My mom comes in farther. My dad joins her.

"Hi, guys," I say. "How are you?"

"How are we?" my dad says. "How are *we*?" He turns to my mom. "Would you listen to this kid? She gets in a car accident, and when she can talk, the first thing she asks us is how *we* are." He comes to me and gives me a gentle hug. I'm getting called out on this by everyone lately, but *How are you?* is a perfectly reasonable question to ask another human being as a greeting.

"Incredible," my mom says. She comes around my other side.

"Sarah will be up in a minute," my dad says.

"She gets frustrated trying to parallel park," my mom whispers. "She learned how to drive where you park on the left side of the road."

"You can't park in the garage here?" I ask.

My dad laughs. "Clearly, you have never visited someone in the hospital. The rates are maddening."

Good old Mom and Dad. Sarah comes in the door.

"You got it?" my mom asks.

"It's fine," Sarah says. She breathes. "Hi," she says to me. "How are you?"

"I'm OK," I say.

"You look like you feel better than yesterday," my dad says. "You've got some color in your face."

"And your voice sounds good," my mom adds.

Sarah steps closer to me. "I cannot tell you how good it feels to look at you and know you're OK. To hear your voice." She can see that my mom is getting teary. "But the bad news is that your bun is really screwed up," she says. "Here." She takes my head in her hands and pulls my hair out of the elastic.

"Easy now," I say to her. "There's a person attached to that hair."

"You're fine," she says. "Wait." She stops herself. "You are fine, right? Gabby said the damage is all on your lower half."

"Yeah, yeah," I say. "Go ahead."

She drops my hair and walks toward her purse. "You need your hair brushed. Is no one brushing your hair around here?"

She pulls a brush from her purse and starts running it through my hair. It feels nice, except for the moments when she finds deep-rooted tangles at the base of my scalp. I wince as she picks at them, trying to work them free.

"Do you remember when you were little," my mom says as she sits down, "and you used to get those huge knots in your hair from when you would try to braid it yourself?"

"Not really," I say. "But if it felt anything like Sarah yanking at my scalp, I can understand why I blocked it out."

It's not audible, and her face is behind me, but I know for a fact that Sarah is rolling her eyes at me.

"Yeah, you hated it then, too, and I told you to stop playing with your hair if you didn't want me to sit there and detangle it. You told me you wanted to cut it all off. And I told you no.

"Obviously," Sarah says as she puts the brush down and pulls my hair into a high bun.

"Can you do it higher?" I ask. "I don't like it when I can feel it hit the bed." She lets my hair down and tries again.

"OK, well, long story short," my mom says.

"It's a little late for that," my dad jokes. She gives him a look. The look wives and mothers have been giving to husbands and fathers for centuries.

"Anyway," she says pointedly, "you went into the kitchen when I wasn't looking and chopped off your own hair."

"Oh, right," I say, vaguely remembering seeing pictures of my hair cropped. "I think you told me this story before."

"It was so short. Above your ears!" she says. "And I ran into the kitchen and saw what you did, and I said, 'Why did you do that?' and you said, 'I don't know, I felt like it.' "

"A Hannah Savannah sentiment if there ever was one," my dad says proudly. "If that doesn't describe you, I honestly don't know what does. 'I don't know, I felt like it.' " He laughs to himself.

This is exactly the kind of stuff I'm trying to change about myself.

"Yeah, OK, Doug, but that's not the moral of the story," my mom says.

My dad puts his hands up in mock regret. "My apologies," he says. "I'd hate to guess the wrong moral to a story. Call the police!"

"Must you interrupt every story I try to tell?" my mom asks, and then she waves him off. "What I was getting at is that we had to take you to the hairdresser, and they cut your hair into a little pixie cut, which I'd never seen for a little girl. I mean, you were no more than six years old."

That's what I remember, seeing pictures of myself with hair cropped tight to my head.

"Get to the point, Mom," Sarah says. "By the time this story is over, I'll be ninety-four years old."

It's jarring to hear Sarah tease my mom. I would never say something like that to her.

"Fine," my mom says. "Hannah, your hair was gorgeous. Really stunning. Women kept stopping me at Gelson's to ask me where I had the idea to cut your hair like that. I gave them the number of the lady who did it. She ended up moving her business out of the Valley and into Beverly Hills. Last I heard, she cut that *Jerry Maguire* kid's hair once. The end."

"That story was even worse than I thought it was going to be," Sarah says. "There! I'm done."

"How's it look?" I ask my dad and mom.

They smile at me.

"You are one gorgeous girl," my dad says.

"Maybe people will see Hannah's bun and one day I can do Angelina Jolie's bun," Sarah says, teasing my mom.

"The hairdresser wasn't the point!" my mom says. "The point of the story is that you should always have faith in Hannah. Because even when it looks like she's made a terrible mistake, she's actually one step ahead of you. That's the moral. Things will always work out for Hannah. You know? She was born under a lucky star or something."

Sometimes I think my mom's anecdotes should come with Cliffs Notes. Because they're quite good once someone explains them to you.

"I really liked that story," I tell her. "Thank you for telling it. I didn't remember any of that."

"I have pictures of it somewhere," she says. "I'll find them when we get home and send one to you. You really looked great. That's why I'm always telling you to cut your hair off."

"But what would she do without *the bun*?" Sarah asks.

"Yeah," I say. "I am nothing without this bun."

"So fill us in, Hannah Savannah," my dad says. "The doctors said you will recover nicely, but, as is my fatherly duty, I'm worried about how you're feeling now."

"Physically and mentally," my mom says.

"I'm OK," I say. "They have me on a steady amount of painkillers. I'm not comfortable, by any means. But I'm OK." No good would come from telling them about the baby. I put the thought right out of my head. I don't even feel as if I'm keeping anything from them.

"Are you really OK?" my mom asks. Her voice starts to break. My dad puts his arm around her.

I wonder how many times I'll have to say it before anyone believes it. Ugh, maybe it will have to be true first.

"You must have been so scared," my mom says. Her eyes start to water. My dad holds her tighter, but I can see that his eyes are starting to water, too. Sarah looks away. She looks out the window.

All of this joking-around, let-me-do-your-hair, old-family-memories thing is just a song and dance. They are heartbroken and worried. They are stunned and uncomfortable and miserable and sick to their stomachs. And if I'm being honest, something about that soothes me.

I can't remember the last time I felt like a permanent fixture of this group. I have, for well over a decade, felt like a guest in my own family. I barely even remember how we all were when we lived in the same place, in the same house, in the same country. But with the three of them in front of me now, letting the cracks in their armor show, I feel like a person who belongs in this family. A person who is needed to complete the pack.

"I wish you guys lived here," I say as I start to get emotional.

I've never said that before. I'm not sure why. "I feel like I'm on my own so much, and I just . . . I miss you a lot."

My dad comes closer and takes my hand. "We miss you every single day," he says. "Every day. Do you know that?"

I nod. Although I'm not sure yes is the most honest answer.

"Just because you're here and we're there, that doesn't mean we ever stop thinking about you," my mom says.

Sarah nods and looks away and wipes her eyes. And then she puts her hand on my knee. She looks me in the eye and smiles. "I don't know about these guys, but I love you like crazy," she says.

Carl and Tina moved to Pasadena a few years ago. They sold the place they had while we were in high school and downsized to a Craftsman-style house on a quiet street with lots of trees.

It's almost eight by the time Gabby, Mark, and I get to their place. Mark ran late at the office. He seems to run late at the office a lot or works late into the night. I would have thought that being a dentist was kind of predictable. But he always has last-minute stuff come up.

We pull into the driveway and head into the house. Gabby doesn't bother to knock. She goes right in.

Tina looks up from the kitchen and walks toward us with a big, bright smile and open arms.

She hugs Gabby and Mark and then turns to me. "Hannah Marie!" she says, enveloping me in a hug. She holds me tight and rocks me from side to side, like only a mother does.

"Hi, Tina," I say to her. "I've missed you!"

She lets go of me and gives me a good look. "Me, too, sweetheart. Me, too. Go on in and say hello to Carl. He can't wait to get a good look at you."

I walk on, leaving Gabby and Mark with Tina. Carl is in the backyard, pulling a steak off the grill. That's certainly a point for Los Angeles: you can grill twelve months out of the year.

"Do my eyes deceive me?" he asks as he's putting the steak down on a plate and closing the grill. "Could it be *the* Hannah Martin in front of me?"

Carl is wearing a green polo shirt and khakis. He almost always looks as if he's dressed for golf. I don't know if he actually has ever golfed, but he's got the look down pat.

"The one and only," I say, putting my arms out to present myself. He gives me a hug. He's a big man with a tight grip. I almost can't breathe. For a moment, it makes me miss my dad.

I hand Carl the flowers I brought.

"Oh, why, thank you so much! I've always wanted . . . chrysanthemums?" he asks me. He knows he's wrong.

"Lilies," I say.

"I was close," he says, and takes them out of my hand. "I don't know anything about flowers. I just buy them when I've done something wrong." I laugh.

He gestures for me to pick up the plate with the steak on it. I do, and we head inside.

We enter the house through the kitchen. Tina is pouring wine for Gabby and Mark. Carl steps right in.

"Tina, I bought you these lilies just now. You're welcome," he says, and winks at me.

"Wow, honey, so romantic," she says. "It's nice to know that you got them yourself. That you didn't rudely take the flowers that Hannah brought us."

"Yeah," Carl says as he hugs Gabby. He shakes Mark's hand and pats him on the back. "That'd be terrible."

Gabby takes her purse off her shoulder and takes my bag from me. She puts them both down in the hallway. "You can take off your shoes, too," Gabby says. "But just hide them."

I give her a confused look. Tina clears it up. "Barker," she says.

"Barker?"

"Barker!" Carl yells, and down the steps and into the kitchen comes a massive Saint Bernard.

"Oh, my God!" I say. "Barker!"

Gabby starts laughing. Barker runs right to Mark, and Mark backs away.

"I forgot my allergy pills," he says. "Sorry. I should hang back."

"You're allergic to dogs?" I ask.

He nods as Gabby gives me a look. I can't tell what the look is, because in one swift motion, she's down on the floor, rubbing Barker's back. Barker is only too happy to turn over and let her rub his belly.

"So!" Tina announces. "It's a steak-and-potatoes kind of night. Except that Carl has decided to pull out the big guns because you kids are here, so it's steak with *chimichurri* sauce, garlic-and-chive mashed potatoes, and brussels sprouts, because . . . I'm still a mom, and I can't stop myself from making sure you eat your vegetables."

My parents made me eat vegetables until I was about fourteen, and then they gave up. I always liked that about them. When I lived with Carl and Tina, I felt as if I was being force-fed riboflavin on a nightly basis.

Then again, their daughter is a nonprofit executive who married a dentist, so clearly, they were doing something right.

We all sit down at the table, and Carl immediately starts in with dad-like questions.

"Hannah, catch us up on what you've been doing," he says as he cuts the steak.

"Well." I open my eyes wide and sigh. I'm not sure where

to start. "I'm back!" I say, throwing my arms up and flashing my hands for effect. For a moment, I'm hoping this is enough. Clearly, it is not.

"Uh-huh," he says. "And?" He starts serving and passing plates around the table. When I get mine, it's got a lot of brussels sprouts on it. If I don't eat them all, Tina will say something. I just know it.

"And . . . I've mostly been floating from city to city as of late. The Pacific Northwest for a bit. New York, too."

"Gabby said you were living in New York," Tina says, starting to take a bite of her steak. "Was it fabulous? Did you see any Broadway shows?"

I laugh slightly, but I don't mean to. "No," I say. "Not much of that."

I don't want to get into anything about Michael. I don't want to admit to them the mess I got myself in. They may not be my parents, but Carl and Tina are incredibly parental. I care deeply what they think of me.

"New York wasn't for me," I say, sipping the wine they put in front of me and then immediately putting it back down on the table. It smells awful. I don't like it.

Gabby, seeing my discomfort, steps in. "Hannah is a West Coast girl, you know? She belongs back with us."

"Amen to that," Carl says, cutting his steak and taking a bite. He chews with his mouth open sometimes. "I've always said, go where the sunshine is. Anyone who heads for snowier climates is a moron." Tina rolls her eyes at him. He looks at Mark. "Mark, what are you doing drinking wine with a steak like this?"

Mark starts to stumble a little bit. I realize for the first time that Mark is slightly intimidated by Carl. It's not hard to see why. He's a formidable man to have as a father-in-law.

"It's what was in front of me," Mark says, laughing. "I'm not too discerning."

Carl gets up from the table and goes into the kitchen. He comes back and puts a beer in front of Mark.

Mark laughs. "All right!" he says. He seems genuinely much more interested in drinking the beer than the wine Tina gave him, but I don't know if that's just a show for Carl. He's also scratching his wrists and the back of his neck pretty aggressively. Must be Barker.

Carl sits back down. "Men drink beer," Carl says, sipping his own. "Simple as that."

"Dad," Gabby says, "gender has absolutely nothing to do with someone's preference for a drink. Some men like appletinis. Some women like bourbon. It's irrelevant."

"While I admit I have no idea what an appletini is, you're absolutely right," Carl says thoughtfully. "I was being reductionist, and I'm sorry."

Now that I'm back in their home, I remember where it comes from. Where she gets the need to speak clearly and as accurately as possible about gender politics. It's Carl. He will have these antiquated ideas about men and women, but then he routinely corrects himself about them when Gabby brings it up.

"So, Hannah," Tina says, redirecting the conversation, "what's the plan? Are you staying in L.A. for a while?"

I swallow the piece of steak I'm chewing. "Yeah," I say. "I'm hoping to."

"Do you have a job lined up?" Carl asks.

Gabby steps in to defend me. "Dad, don't."

He looks defensive. "I'm just asking a question."

I shake my head. "No," I say, "I don't." I look at the wineglass in front of me. I can't bring myself to drink any more of it. I don't want to have to smell it again. I grab the water next to it and sip. "But I will!" I add. "That's on my list. Car. Job. Apartment. You know, the basic tenets of a functioning life."

"Do you have money for a car?" Carl asks.

"Dad!" Gabby says. "C'mon."

Mark stays out of it. He's too busy scratching his arms. Also, I get the impression that Mark usually stays out of a lot of things.

"Gabby! The girl lived with us for almost two years. She's practically my long-lost daughter. I can ask her if she needs money for a car." Carl turns to me. "Can't I?"

It's a weird relationship I have with the Hudsons. On the one hand, they are not my parents. They didn't really raise me, and they don't check in on me regularly. On the other hand, if I needed anything, I've always known they would step in. They took care of me during one of the most formative times in my life. And the truth is, my parents aren't here. My parents haven't been here for a while.

"It's fine," I say. "I have some money saved. I have enough for a down payment on a car or first, last, and security on an apartment. If I can find a cheap option for each, then I could maybe swing both."

"You're saying you have about five thousand dollars, give or take," Carl says.

Gabby shakes her head. Mark is smiling. Maybe he's just glad the heat is off him for now.

Tina pipes up before I can. "Carl, why don't we save the hard stuff for after dinner?"

"Hannah," he says directly to me, "am I making you uncomfortable? Is this bothering you?"

C'mon! What am I supposed to say to that? Yes, talking about how broke and unprepared for life I am makes me a little uncomfortable. But who on this planet, when asked directly if they are uncomfortable, admits they are? It's an impossible question. It forces you to make the other person feel better about invading your personal space.

"It's fine," I say. "Really."

Carl turns to Gabby and Tina. "She says it's fine."

"OK, OK," Tina says. "Who wants more wine?"

Gabby raises her glass. Mine is untouched. "I'm good," I say.

Tina looks at my plate. "Are you done?" she asks. Everyone else's plate is fairly clean except for a bite here or there. Mine is empty except for all of the brussels sprouts. "I have a fabulous dessert to bring out."

I know it's childish, but I'm honestly worried she will judge me for eating dessert without finishing my vegetables. I start casually eating them quickly. "Sounds great," I say between bites. "I'm almost done."

Tina leaves and heads into the kitchen. Carl has started to ask Mark how the dental practice is going when Tina calls for Carl to help her get another bottle of wine open.

"I'm sorry my dad is hounding you," Gabby says once both Carl and Tina are out of earshot.

I take the last of the brussels sprouts on my fork and cram them into my mouth. I chew quickly and swallow them down. "It's fine," I say. "I'm much less worried about your dad's questions than I am about your mom's judgment if I don't finish my vegetables."

Gabby laughs. "You're right to be worried."

Mark joins in. "One time, I didn't put any of her cooked carrots on my plate, and she pulled me aside later and asked if I was at all concerned about a vitamin A deficiency."

I take another sip of my water. I may have overshot it with the brussels sprouts. My stomach is starting to feel bloated and nauseated.

"I shouldn't have eaten them so quickly," I say, rubbing my stomach. "I suddenly feel . . . ugh."

"Oh, I've learned that one before," Gabby says, laughing.

"No, this is . . . I really don't feel well all of a sudden."

"Queasy or what?" Mark says.

"Yeah," I say. I burp. I actually burp. "Very queasy."

Tina and Carl come out, Tina with wine, Carl with a very large, very gooey, very aromatic batch of cinnamon rolls.

I smile wide as Tina winks at me.

"Do we know Hannah, or do we know Hannah?" Carl says.

He puts it down in front of me. "You get first dibs. I would expect nothing less of you than to pick the one with the most icing."

I inhale deeply, getting the smell of the cinnamon and the sugar. And then, suddenly, I have to get out of here.

I slam my chair out from under me and run toward the hallway bathroom, shutting the door behind me. I'm just in front of the toilet when it all comes back up. I feel faint and a little dizzy. I'm exhausted.

I sit down in front of the toilet. The cool bathroom tile feels good against my skin. I don't know how long I sit there. I'm startled back to reality by Gabby knocking on the door. She doesn't wait for me to answer before she comes in.

"Are you OK?" she says.

"Yeah." I stand up. I feel so much better now. "I'm good." I shake my head in an attempt to snap out of it. "Maybe I'm allergic to brussels sprouts?"

"Oof," she says, smiling. "Wouldn't that be nice?"

In a few minutes, after gathering myself and finding the mouthwash, I make my way back to the table.

"I'm so sorry about that," I say. "I think my body was shocked that I fed it vegetables."

Tina laughs. "You're sure you're OK?"

"Yeah," I assure her. "I'm feeling completely normal."

Gabby grabs her purse and my jacket. "But I'm thinking we should take her home," she announces.

I really do feel as if I could stay, but it's probably smart to head back. Get some sleep.

"Yeah," Mark says, scratching again. "I'm feeling a bit overwhelmed by the dog, too, if I'm being honest."

I don't know if anyone notices it except me, but Gabby rolls her eyes, ever so subtly. She's annoyed with him. For being allergic to dogs. I guess it's the small things in a marriage that grate on you the most.

"Oh, we're so sorry," Tina says. "We'll keep medication for you here from now on. In case you forget another time."

"Oh, thanks," Mark says. "Admittedly, the pills don't help that much." He then proceeds to talk for a full five minutes about all of his symptoms and which ones are and are not helped by allergy pills. The way he talks about it, you'd think being allergic to dogs was like being diagnosed with an incurable disease. Christ, even I'm annoyed with his allergy now.

"Well," Carl says as we move toward the door, "we love having you all here."

"Oh!" Tina says. "Hannah, let me pack up some cinnamon buns for you. Is that OK?"

"I'd love that," I say. "Thank you so much."

"OK, one second." She runs into the kitchen, and Gabby goes with her. Carl and I are standing by the front door. Mark is standing by the steps. He excuses himself to use the restroom. "My eyes are starting to tear," he says by way of explanation.

Carl watches him go and then pulls me over to the side.

"Buy a car," Carl says.

"Hm?"

"Buy a car. Live with Gabby and Mark until you earn some money for a deposit."

"Yeah," I say. "That sounds like the smart way to play it."

"And when you have the car, call my office." He pulls a business card out of his wallet and hands it to me. *Dr. Carl Hudson, Pediatrics.*

"Oh," I say. "I'm not sure I—"

"We have a receptionist," he says. "She's terrible. Absolutely terrible. I have to fire her."

"Oh, I'm sorry," I say.

"She makes forty thousand a year plus benefits."

I look at him.

"When we fire her, we're going to be looking for someone who can answer phones, schedule appointments, and be the face of the office."

"Oh," I say. He's offering me a job.

"If you tell me when you think you could take over, I'll keep her around for a few weeks. Make sure the job is available for you."

"Really?" I ask him.

He nods. "Wouldn't think twice about it. You deserve somebody looking out for you."

I am touched. "Wow," I say. "Thank you."

"When they ask how much you want to be paid, say forty-five. You'll probably get forty-two or forty-three. Full benefits. Vacation time. The whole kit and kaboodle."

"I'm not really trained for working in a doctor's office," I say.

He shakes his head. "You're bright. You'll get it quickly."

Tina and Gabby come out of the kitchen with tinfoil-wrapped cinnamon rolls and Tupperware full of leftovers. Mark comes out of the bathroom.

"Shall we?" Gabby says, heading for the door. She gives me some of the leftovers to carry and opens the front door.

Barker comes running toward us and paws me. I push him down. Mark jumps away from him as if he's on fire.

"You can heat those up in the microwave," Tina says. "Or in the oven at three-fifty."

"And let me know," Carl says, "about what we talked about."

The *thank you* that comes out of my mouth is directed at both of them, but it cannot possibly carry all the emotion I have behind it.

I say it again. "Thank you. Really."

"Anytime," Tina says as she gives me a hug good-bye.

I hug Carl as Tina hugs Gabby and Mark. A few more seconds of good-byes, including a heartfelt one from Gabby to Barker, and we are out the door.

Mark gets into the driver's seat. Gabby takes the passenger seat. I lie down in the back.

"How are you feeling?" Gabby asks.

"I'm fine," Mark says before he realizes she means me. He lets the moment pass.

"I'm good," I say. I mean it. Truly.

When I left the Hudsons' to go to college, it never occurred to me that I could come back.

I kept telling people, "My family is in London, my family is in London," but I should have said, "I also have family in Los Angeles. They live on a quiet, tree-lined street in a Craftsman-style house in Pasadena."

My family left at around nine tonight only after I insisted that they sleep at their hotel. They wanted to stay the night, but the truth is, there isn't anything for anyone to do but sit beside me and stare. And sometimes I need my own space. I need to not have to put on a brave face for a little while. Now I am alone in the peace and quiet. I can hear the hum of electricity, the faint beeping of other patients' machines.

People have been bringing me books left and right. They offer them up as a way to pass the time. Books and flowers. Flowers and books.

I pick up a book from the stack Gabby has made, and I start to read. The book is slow to start, very descriptive. Slow and descriptive would be fine on a normal day, on a day when I'm not trying to quiet my own voice, but that won't work for me right now. So I put it down and pick up another one. I go down the stack until I find a voice quick and thrilling enough to quiet my own.

By the time Henry comes in to check on me, I'm so engrossed that I've temporarily forgotten where I am and who I am. A gift if I've ever been given one.

"Still up?" Henry says. I nod. He comes closer.

I look at his tattoo again. I was wrong before. It isn't *Isabelle*. It's *Isabella*. The image in my head instantly changes from a glamorous blond waif to a voluptuous brunette. Good Lord, I need to get a life.

"Do you ever sleep?" he asks me as he puts a blood-pressure cuff around my arm. "Are you a vampire? What's going on here?"

I laugh and glance at the clock. It's just after midnight. Time means nothing in the hospital. Truly. When I was out in the real world, functioning in everyday society, and someone would say "Time is just a construct," I would roll my eyes and continue to check errands off my To Do list. But I was wrong, and they were right. Time means nothing. Never is that more clear than in a hospital bed.

"No, I'm OK," I say. "Last night, after I saw you, I fell asleep for at least nine hours."

"OK," he says. "Well, keep me posted if that changes. Sleep is an important part of healing."

"Totally," I say. "I hear you."

Henry looks even more handsome today than he did yesterday. He's not the kind of handsome that all women would be attracted to, I guess. His face isn't symmetrical. I suppose his nose is a bit big for his face. His eyes are small. But something about it just . . . works for him.

He puts my chart back into the pocket on my bed.

"Well, I'll see ya—" he says, but I interrupt him.

"Isabella," I say. "Is that your wife?"

I'm slightly embarrassed that I have said this just as he was clearly saying good-bye. But what are you going to do? It happened.

He steps back toward me. Only then do I think to look and see if he has a wedding ring. You'd think I'd have learned this shit by now. No ring. But actually, you know, what I *have* learned is that no ring doesn't mean no wife. So my question still stands.

"No," he says, shaking his head. "No, I'm not married."

"Oh," I say.

Henry doesn't offer who Isabella is, and I figure if he wanted to tell me, he would. So . . . this is awkward.

"Sorry to pry," I say. "You know how it is around here. You get bored. You lose your sense of what's appropriate to ask a stranger."

Henry laughs. "No, no, totally fine. Someone has a huge name tattooed on his forearm, I think it warrants a question. To be honest, I'm surprised people don't ask about it more often."

I laugh. "Well, thank you for checking in on—" I start to say, but this time, it's Henry who talks over me.

"She was my sister," he says.

"Oh," I say.

"Yeah," he says. "She passed away about fifteen years ago."

I find myself looking down at my hands. I consciously look back up at him. "I'm sorry to hear that."

Henry looks at me thoughtfully. "Thank you," he says. "Thanks."

I don't know what to say, because I don't want to pry, but I also want him to know that I'm happy to listen. What do I say, though? My first instinct is to ask how she died, but that seems like bad form. I can't think of anything, so I end up just staring at him.

"You want to ask how she died," Henry says.

I am instantly mortified that I am so transparent and also so tacky. "Yeah," I say. "You caught me. How terrible is that? So morbid and unnecessary. But it was the first thing I thought.

How did she die? I'm terrible." I shake my head at myself. "You can spit in my breakfast if you want. I'll totally understand."

Henry sits down in the chair and laughs. "No, it's OK," he says. "It's such a weird thing, right? Because it's the first thing the brain thinks to ask. *She died? How did she die?* But at the same time, it's, like, sort of an insensitive question to ask."

"Right!" I say, shaking my head again. "I'm really sorry."

He laughs at me. "You didn't do anything wrong. She was sixteen. She hit her head in a pool."

"That's terrible," I say. "I'm so sorry."

"Yeah," he says. "She wasn't supposed to be diving. But she was sixteen, you know? Sixteen-year-olds do things they aren't supposed to do. She was rushed to the hospital. The doctors did everything they could. We actually thought she might survive it, but . . . you know, some stuff you just don't come back from. We kept waiting for her to wake up, and she never did."

"Wow," I say. My heart breaks for him and his family. For his sister.

You spend so much time being upset about being in the hospital in the first place that it is almost jarring to realize how many people don't ever leave. I could have been just like his sister. I could have never woken up.

But I did. I'm one of the ones who did.

I consider for a moment what would have happened if I'd been standing just a little bit farther in the road or a little bit off to the side. What if I'd been thrown to the left instead of to the right? Or if the car had been going five miles per hour faster? I might not have ever woken up. Today could have been my funeral. How weird is that? How absolutely insane is that? The difference between life and death could be as simple and as uncomfortably slight as a step you take in either direction.

Which means that I am here today, alive today, because I made the right choices, however brief and insignificant they felt at the time. I made the right choices.

"I'm so sorry you and your family have had to go through that," I tell him. "I can't imagine what that must feel like."

He nods at me, accepting my sympathy. "It's why I became a nurse, actually. When I was in the hospital, with my parents, waiting and waiting for news, I just felt like I wanted to be in the room, helping, doing something, being involved, instead of waiting for someone else to do something or say something. I wanted to be making sure I was doing my best to help other people in the same position as my family was in back then."

"That makes a lot of sense," I say. I wonder if he knows how honorable it sounds. My guess is he doesn't, that it's genuine.

"It was a few years ago, the tenth anniversary of her death. I was in a daze, really. There was so much I hadn't dealt with that just sort of came out around then. By that point, my parents had divorced, and both had moved back to Mexico, where they are originally from. So I was just sort of dealing with the anniversary myself. Anyway, getting the tattoo made me feel better. So I did it. Didn't think too much past that."

I laugh. "That's my life story!" I tell him. "Made me feel better. So I did it."

"Maybe you should get that tattooed," he says.

I laugh again. "I don't know if I'm a tattoo sort of person. I'm way too indecisive. Although, I admit, yours is striking. It was the first thing I noticed when you walked in here."

Henry laughs. "And not my stunning good looks?"

"My apologies. It was the *second* thing I noticed."

Henry pats his hand on my bed and stands up to leave. "Now I'm running late," he says. "Look what you've done."

"I'm sorry," I say. "I mean, you should be apologizing to me, though. Distracting me from my much-needed rest." I smile.

He shakes his head. "You're right. What was I thinking? A pretty girl asks me a question, and suddenly, I can't keep track of the time. I'll be back to check on you later," he says, and slips out the door.

I find myself unable to hold back the smile that insists on shining through my face. I shake my head at myself, laughing at how ridiculous I'm being. But also, for a moment, I consider staying awake all night. I consider waiting around to see when he comes back.

But that's crazy. He's probably nice to all of his patients. Probably tells all the women they're pretty. I'm just bored and lonely in this place. Desperate for something interesting, something good.

I turn off the light by my bed and slide down a bit until my head rests comfortably on the pillow.

It's not hard to fall asleep once I decide to. That's one thing I've always liked about myself. It's never hard to fall asleep.

By the time we get back to Gabby and Mark's place, I have resolved to take the job. Gabby and Mark talked to me about it the entire way home, and Gabby told me she thought it was without a doubt a great idea. "I know for a fact that he is great to his employees, that their entire practice has a huge emphasis on nurse and staff morale," she said. "And my dad loves you, so you'll be the favorite."

By the time we say good night and retire to our rooms, it's starting to hit me that I have a job offer. I have a shot at a real job. Sometimes I don't realize how weighed down I am by my own worries until they are gone. But I feel much freer tonight than I did this morning.

I call Ethan from my bed to tell him the good news. He's through-the-roof excited for me. And then I tell him about the rest of the evening.

"I must be allergic to brussels sprouts," I tell him. "I barely made it from the table to the toilet before puking up my entire dinner."

"What? Are you still feeling sick? Hold on. I'm going to come get you," he says.

"No," I tell him. "I'm OK here. You don't have to."

"I want to. It's a good excuse to see you. I'm coming. You can't stop me."

I laugh and then realize that I never really thought I was

sleeping here tonight. I think I knew I was just going through the motions until he came to get me. "OK, yeah, yeah, yeah, come get me!" I say. "I'm excited to see you."

"I'll leave now," he says.

So within thirty minutes of us getting home, I am on my way out the door to meet Ethan's car.

When I walk into the living room to grab my bag, I see Gabby in the kitchen in her pajamas, getting a glass of water.

"Headed somewhere?" she asks, teasing me.

"Caught me," I say.

"I called it," she says. "Although I figured you'd have us drop you off at his place, so you lasted longer than I thought."

"At least I'm a little unpredictable."

"I wouldn't go that far," she says as I turn to the door. "Wait."

She pulls the cinnamon rolls off the counter and brings them to me. "Please take these with you. Leave them at Ethan's. I can't look at them without wanting to eat them all."

I laugh. "And you think I can?"

"Yeah, well," she says, "you attract cinnamon rolls everywhere you go. I can't live like that."

I take the cinnamon rolls. "I should send your parents a thank-you note," I say. I hear Ethan's car pull up.

Gabby looks at me as if that's the dumbest idea she's ever heard. "They would be insulted," she says. "It would be like if I sent them one for raising me. Stop."

I laugh.

"But also, go," she says. "Pretty sure he's right outside."

I give her a hug and tell her I'll see her tomorrow.

I walk out the door, and Ethan's car is parked right in front. I watch him for a moment before he knows he's being seen. He's turning the key out of the ignition. He's opening his door.

"You look gorgeous," he says.

I smile and then quickly find myself laughing at the idea that Gabby could have heard him. I can just imagine her opening up a window and calling down to the street, "OK, but that's not where a woman's worth lies!"

I smile at him and walk toward the car as he opens the passenger door for me. I hug him and get in. He gets in on his side and pulls away from the curb.

"Is that an entire batch of cinnamon rolls?" he asks. The smell has filled up the car.

"Yep," I say. "And if you're nice to me, I'll let you have one or five."

"Never a dull, cinnamon-roll-less moment with you."

"Never," I say.

Ethan grabs my hand at a stop sign. He kisses my cheek at a red light.

I feel like myself around him. And I like myself around him. So far, I like who I am in this city. I feel like a long-forgotten version of myself, a version I'm much more comfortable being than the New York me.

Suddenly, a small, wily dog runs out into the middle of the street.

Ethan quickly veers the car to the side of the road to avoid hitting it. The dog continues to make its way across to the other sidewalk. It's late enough that there are no cars coming up behind us yet. Ethan pulls over.

"We gotta get that dog," he says, just as I have my hand on the door handle, about to jump out and chase it down. We both get out of the car and run toward the dog, watching out for any possible oncoming traffic.

I can see it, just up ahead.

"On the right side of the street by the Dumpster," I say. "Can you see it?"

Ethan comes toward me, looking. He starts walking slowly after the dog.

"Hey, buddy," he says when he gets close. The dog prances on down the street, not a care in the world. Ethan creeps up, trying to grab hold, but the moment the dog sees him coming, it runs in the other direction. I run a bit faster and try to cut the dog off on the other side, but I just miss it. The dog is brown and a dingy white, bigger than I thought from far away but still on the smaller side, a terrier of some kind. Shaggy but short-haired, small but feisty.

There's a car coming. Ethan once again gets close and tries to grab the dog but fails. The dog thinks we are playing a game.

The car is now barreling down the road. I start to fill with panic that the dog will run into the street again. I'm a few feet away. The dog is playfully prancing off in the other direction.

I growl at it, loudly. I give it the best animal-like roar I can muster.

It stops in its tracks. I turn away from it and start running, hoping it will chase me. It does. Just as quickly as it was running away from me, it's now running toward me. When it reaches my feet, it jumps up onto me. I quickly bend down and pick it up. The car flies past us. Relief washes over me.

It's a female. No collar. No tags.

Ethan comes running up to meet me. I am holding the dog in my arms.

"Christ," he says. "I honestly thought she was a goner."

"I know," I say. "But she's OK. We got her."

She has curled right into my chest. She is licking my hand.

"Well, clearly, this dog is a trained killer," Ethan says.

I laugh. "Yeah, I have no doubt she's just biding her time until she can attack."

"So no tags," Ethan says. "No leash, no nothing."

"Nope," I say, shaking my head. "My guess is we will have to take her to a vet tomorrow and see if she's chipped. Put some fliers up."

"OK," he says. "In the meantime . . ."

"We can't leave her out on the street," I say. "Do you have room for *two* women to join you this evening?"

Ethan nods. "I'm sure we can find a spot for her."

We both start walking back to the car. When we get there, Ethan opens the door for both of us.

"We should probably name her," I say. "You know, temporarily."

"You don't think we can just call her the Dog?" Ethan says as he goes around to his side.

"No, I think she deserves a noble name. Something epic. Grandiose."

"A big name for a small dog," Ethan offers.

I nod. "Exactly."

Ethan starts driving. We think for a minute, and then I'm convinced I've got it. "Charlemagne," I say. "She's little Charlemagne."

"Charlemagne was a man," Ethan says. "Does that matter?"

"But doesn't it sort of sound more like a woman's name?"

Ethan laughs. "Now that you mention it, yes. All right, well, there you go, Charlemagne it is. Tomorrow, Charlemagne, we're going to find your owner and make someone very happy. But tonight you belong with us."

When we get through the front door of Ethan's apartment, I finally let her go. She immediately starts running around, zipping through the rooms. We watch her, stunned by her energy, until she finally gets a running start and jumps onto the bed. She curls up in the corner.

"I can't keep her," he says to me. "Not that you're saying you think I should, I just . . . want to be clear about that. I can't have pets in my building."

I shake my head. "No, I know. We'll find her real owners tomorrow. Maybe I'll take a bus to a vet first thing."

"I can give you my car," he says. "I could get a ride from someone."

"It's OK," I say. "Since I'm going to take this job with Carl, I have to get a car anyway. I'll turn her in at the vet in the morning and then maybe take a cab or a bus to a few dealerships, see about buying a car."

"You're taking a job," he says. "You're buying a car."

"Yeah," I say.

"You're putting down roots."

"I guess I am."

He smiles at me, holding my gaze much longer than necessary. "With a dog in the bed, I'm guessing we're not gonna get busy," he jokes.

"Probably not."

He shrugs. "Well," he says, his eyes focused on me, "I guess this relationship will have to be about more than just sex. Are you OK with that?"

I smile. I can't help myself. "I suppose I could focus on your mind for once."

He laughs and takes off his shirt. He unzips his pants and flings them onto a chair. "This is as unsexy as I get," he says. "Now, I know it's still really sexy, but . . ."

"I'll try to control myself," I say.

"That'd be best."

Ethan pulls back the covers and gets into bed wearing just his boxers. I undress and pick up his T-shirt from the floor. I slip it over my shoulders and get in next to him.

"You're not sexy at all," Ethan says. "Not one bit."

"No?" I ask doubtfully.

"Pssh, if you think I'm thinking about how great your breasts look in my T-shirt, you are dead wrong. Not having sex with you is the easiest thing I've ever done."

I laugh and curl up into him. Charlemagne is nestled somewhat in the middle. We can barely fit, the three of us. But we make it work.

"Oh, wait," I say just as Ethan turns out the light. "Turn the light back on."

"OK?" he says, and he does.

I hop out of bed and find the list I made earlier this afternoon. I grab a pen and cross out "Get a job."

I hold it up for him. "Only two more to go."

"Ugh," he says, looking at me. "Please get your legs underneath the covers where I can't see them. They're even nicer than your boobs."

I wake up at around two in the afternoon to an unexpected treat.

"Surprise!" Tina says as she and Carl walk into the room. Gabby trails in behind them with an apologetic look on her face. Tina has brought a vase full of some of the nicest flowers I've ever seen.

Flowers, flowers, flowers. Would it kill someone to bring me chocolates?

"They made me promise not to warn you," Gabby says.

Carl rolls his eyes and comes closer to me. "Surprises are better," he says. He leans down and hugs me lightly. Tina is right behind him. As he moves out of the way, she takes position. She smells like vanilla.

"Thank you both for coming."

"Are you kidding?" Tina says. "Gabby has had to hold us back from visiting sooner. If I had my druthers, I'd have been here days ago and not left the room."

She puts the vase of flowers on the table, next to the others.

Carl sits himself right down in the chair next to me. "How are you?" he says. He looks at me intently, with compassion, sympathy, and expertise. I'm not sure if he's asking as a friend, a father figure, or a physician.

"I'm OK," I say.

"Try to move your toes for me," he says, looking intently at the foot of the bed.

"Dad!" Gabby says. "You're not her doctor. Dr. Winters has been doing a fabulous job."

"You can't have too many doctors looking at a patient," Carl says. "Hannah, try to move your toes."

I don't want to try to move my toes.

"Later, Dad," Gabby says. "OK? You're making Hannah uncomfortable."

"Hannah, am I making you uncomfortable?"

What am I supposed to say to that? *Yes, you're making me uncomfortable*? Actually, screw it, yes, life is too short to go around lying.

"Yeah," I say. "A little. It's hell being in this bed, dealing with this body right now. I'd love to just forget about my toes for a few minutes."

Carl looks me in the eye and then nods and looks at Gabby. He puts his hands up. "My apologies! We'll put it on the back burner." I think he's done, but then he speaks up again. "Just make sure you're giving that doctor a challenge now and again. Make sure she's working hard for you, has you as a priority."

"Will do," I say. When he winks at me, I wink back.

"So," Tina says, "has Gabby told you about our dog, Barker? I'm completely in love with this guy. Anywhere I go, I insist that people look at pictures."

She moves toward me with her cell phone and gives Gabby a smile. She doesn't care about me looking at Barker. She is trying to change the subject so Carl doesn't keep going.

"I keep trying to persuade Gabby to get a Saint Bernard just like him," Tina says as she swipes through picture after picture of Barker in various rooms of their house.

"I know," Gabby says, "but Mark's allergic to dogs. It's a whole thing."

We talk for a while, catching up on what I've been up to, what they've been up to, the three of us making fun of Gabby. And then they start to head out. I appreciate that they came but aren't staying long. They seem to understand perfectly the toll that being around other people can take on someone in the hospital.

"When you get out of here," Tina says, "and you're feeling up for it, I want to talk to you about a lawsuit."

"A lawsuit?"

Tina looks to Gabby for permission to continue talking, and Gabby subtly grants it.

"Gabby has filled me in on the situation with the person who hit you, and I talked to a friend of mine who is an ADA."

I don't know whether to be ashamed or proud of the fact that I know that an ADA is an assistant district attorney because of all the *Law & Order* I've been watching.

"OK," I say.

"They have the woman who hit you. She's being charged with a hit-and-run."

"Well, that's good, right?"

"Yeah," Carl says, nodding. "Very good."

"But we wanted to put something in your head. Your medical bills are going to be significant," Tina says. "I'm sure you've spoken to your parents about this, and we don't want to step on anyone's toes, but we want you to know that we will help you, if you need help paying for them."

"What?" I say.

"Only if you need it," Carl says. "We just want you to know that we're here, as a resource, if you need us."

"And," Tina says, "we will help you file a lawsuit against this woman if that's what you decide to do."

I'm overwhelmed by the generosity and thoughtfulness of the Hudsons. "Wow," I say. "I'm . . . I don't know what to say."

Tina grabs my hand. "Don't say anything. It was just important to us that you knew. We will always have your back."

"As far as we're concerned, you're an honorary Hudson," Carl says. "But you already know that, right?"

I look at him and nod, with full honesty.

Carl and Tina go to the door, and Gabby walks them out. When she gets back into the room, I'm staring at the ceiling, trying to process all of it. I hadn't thought about medical bills. I hadn't thought about the person who did this to me.

Someone *did this* to me.

Someone is to blame.

Someone made me lose the baby I didn't know I had.

"You OK?" Gabby asks.

I look at her. I shake it off. "Yeah," I say. "I am. Your parents are . . . I mean, they're . . . they're incredible."

"They love you," Gabby says, sitting down in the chair.

"Do you really think I should sue?"

Gabby nods. "Yeah," she says. "No doubt about it."

"I'm not the suing type," I say, although what do I think that means, exactly?

"I saw it happen, Hannah. That lady hit you while you were in the crosswalk with a walk signal. There was no mistaking what happened. She knew she hit someone. And even then, she did not stop. She kept driving. So knowing that this woman drove away from the scene of a crime that could have been deadly, knowing that she made no attempt to help you or call an ambulance, I think she deserves not just to go to jail but also to make personal amends for what she has done." Gabby's angry. "If you ask me, she can go fuck herself."

"Jesus, Gabby."

She shrugs. "I don't care how it sounds. I hate her."

For a moment, I try to put myself in Gabby's shoes. She watched me get hit by a car. She watched me fall to the ground. She watched me pass out. And she probably thought I might die right there in front of her. And suddenly, I hate that woman, too. For putting her through that. For putting me through this. For all of it.

"OK," I say. "Will you look into it? Or, I mean, tell your mom that I said it was OK?"

"Sure," she says.

"It's a shame *Law & Order* doesn't cover civil suits. Then I'd probably be so well versed in it I could represent myself."

Gabby laughs and then gets up as she sees my parents and Sarah come in. Sarah is dressed in black linen pants with a cotton T-shirt and a gauzy sweater. Even if she didn't have a suitcase with her, you'd know she was headed to the airport.

"All right," Gabby says, kissing me on the cheek. "You're in good company. I'll be back tomorrow." She hugs my family and takes off.

My family didn't tell me they were flying back to London today, so it's a bit of a surprise. But if I'm being completely honest, it's also an immense relief. I love my family. It's just that having them around takes energy I simply don't have right now. And the idea of spending tomorrow without having to entertain company, just Gabby and myself, feels as close to a good day as I'm going to get.

"You guys are off?" I ask. My tone is appropriately sorrow-ful. I make an effort not to allow my inflection to go up at the end of the question, weighing it down so the words stay even.

My mom sits down next to me. "Just Sarah is, honey," she says. "Your father and I aren't going anywhere."

I can feel my smile turn to a frown, and I catch myself. I smile wider. I am a terrible daughter, wanting them to go. "Oh, cool," I say.

Sarah leaves her suitcase by the door and comes around to the other side of me. My father is looking up at the TV. *Jeopardy!* is on.

"I'm so sorry I have to leave," Sarah says. "I've already taken so much time off, and I can't miss any more. I'll lose my part."

"Oh, it's totally fine," I tell her. "I'm going to be fine. There's no need for anyone to stay."

Hint.

"Well, your mother and I certainly aren't leaving anytime soon," my dad says as he finally pulls his attention away from the TV. "We're not leaving our little Hannah Savannah while she's still healing."

I smile, unsure what to say. I wonder if he still calls me Hannah Savannah, as if I were a child, because he really only knows me as a child. He doesn't know me very well as an adult. Maybe it's his way of convincing himself I haven't changed much since they left for London, as if time stood still and he didn't miss anything.

"My flight leaves in a few hours, but I still have time to hang out for a little bit," Sarah says.

Jeopardy! begins Double Jeopardy, and my dad takes a seat, enraptured.

We all listen as one of the contestants chooses the topic "Postal Abbreviations."

"Ugh, so boring," Sarah says.

I wish they would change the channel. I don't want to watch *Jeopardy!* I want to watch *Law & Order.*

Alex Trebek's voice is unmistakable. "This Midwestern state is the only one whose two-letter postal abbreviation is a preposition."

At this, my father throws his hand up and says, "Oregon!"

My mother shakes her head. "Doug, they said Midwestern. Oregon is in the Pacific Northwest."

I'm tempted to mention that *or* is not a preposition, but I don't.

"What is Indiana?" the contestant answers.

"That is correct."

My father slaps his knee. "I was close, though."

He wasn't close. He wasn't close at all. He's so clueless sometimes. He's so absolutely clueless.

"Yeah, OK, Dad," Sarah says.

And the way she says it, the effortlessness of their interactions, as if they are all comfortable saying whatever comes into their own heads, highlights how out of place I feel in my own hospital room when they are here.

I just . . . can't do this. I don't want my family to stay here with me. I want to be left in peace, to heal.

I'm supposed to take it easy in the hospital. I'm supposed to rest. But being with them is not easy, and this is not rest.

Sarah's car is ready to take her to the airport shortly after *Jeopardy!* ends. She grabs her bag and comes over to me, hugging me gently. It's a halfhearted hug, not because she doesn't mean it but because I can't really hug anyone at the moment.

Then she turns to my parents. She hugs them each goodbye.

"You have your passport accessible?" my mom asks her.

"Yeah, I'm good."

"And George is picking you up at Heathrow?" my dad asks.

"Yeah."

There's a stream of questions about logistics and *Did you remember* type things, followed by *I'll miss yous* and *I love yous* all around.

Then she's gone. And it's just my parents and me.

It's never just my parents and me.

And right this second, looking at them as they look back at me, I realize I have nothing to say to them. I have nothing to talk about, nothing I want to do, nothing I need from them, nothing to give them.

I love my parents. I really, really do. But I love them the way you love the grandmother you aren't as close to, the way you love your uncle who lives across the country.

They are not my support system.

And they need to go.

"You guys should feel free to go home, too," I say, as kindly as my voice will allow.

"Nonsense," my mother says, sitting down. "We're here for you. We're going to be with you every step of the way."

"Yeah," I say. "But I don't need you to be." As much as I try to make it sound casual, it comes out raw and heavy.

The two of them look at me, unsure how to respond, and then my mom starts crying.

"Mom, please don't cry," I say. "I didn't mean—"

"No," she says. "It's fine." She wipes her tears. "Would you excuse me for a moment? I just . . . need to get some water."

And then she's gone. Out into the hallway.

I should have kept my mouth shut. I should have just pretended for a little while longer.

"I'm sorry," I say to my dad. He's not looking at me. He's looking down at the floor. "I really am. I'm sorry I said that."

He shakes his head, still not looking at me. "No, don't be."

He looks up and meets my eye. "We know you don't need us. We know you have a whole life you've managed to create for yourself without us."

Some life.

"I—"

"You don't have to say anything. Your mom has a harder time facing all of this than I do, but I'm glad you said something, honestly. We should talk about it freely, be honest with each other more." He comes closer to me and grabs my hand.

"We screwed up, your mother and I. We screwed up." My dad has strikingly gorgeous green eyes. He's my dad, so I don't often notice, but when he looks at you with the intensity he's looking at me with now, it's hard to ignore. They are green the way blades of grass are green, the way dark emeralds are green. "When we got to London and moved in, both your mother and I realized we had made a huge mistake not bringing you with us. We never should have let you stay in Los Angeles. Never should have left you."

I look away. His green eyes are now starting to glass over. His voice is starting to quiver. I can't handle it. I look at my hands.

"Every time we called you," he continues, "the two of us would get off the phone and cry. But you always seemed fine. So we kept thinking that you were fine. I think that was our biggest mistake. Taking you at your word and not wanting to tell you what to do. I mean, you seemed happy with the Hudsons. Your grades were good. You got into a good school."

"Right," I say.

"But looking back on it now, I can see that doesn't mean you were fine."

I wait, trying to see if he will elaborate.

"It's a hard thing," he says. "To admit you have failed your child. You know, so many of my friends nowadays are empty-nesters, and they say that the day you realize your kids don't need you anymore is like a punch to the gut. And I never say it, but I always think to myself that knowing your kid doesn't need you may hurt, but knowing your kid did, and you weren't there . . . it's absolutely unbearable."

"It was only a couple of years," I say. "I would have gone to college anyway and left home then."

"And it would have been on your own terms, your own choice. And you would have known that no matter what happened, you could come home. I don't think we ever made that clear to you. That we were your home."

I can't help but cry. I want to hold the tears in. I'm trying so hard to keep them to myself, not to let them bubble over. I do OK for a moment. But, as with a well-matched arm wrestle, one of us eventually goes down. And it's me. The tears win.

I grab my father's hand and squeeze it. It is, I think, the first time in a long time that I don't feel self-conscious around him. I feel like myself.

He pats my hand and looks up at me. He wipes a tear from my eye and smiles. "There's something that your mother and I have been discussing, and we were going to broach it with you when you were feeling better," he says. "But I want to talk to you about it now."

"OK . . ."

"We think you should move to London."

"Me?"

He nods. "I have no doubt that almost losing your life in a car accident makes you assess your life, and let me tell you, almost losing your daughter in a car accident puts things in perspective real quick. We should be a proper family again. I'm lucky to be your father, lucky to have you in my life. I want *more* of you in my life. Your mother thinks the same. We should have asked you years ago, and we just assumed you knew we'd want you there. But I'm no longer assuming anything. I'm asking you to come. Please. We're asking you to move to London."

It's all too much. London. And my dad. And my mom crying out in the hall. And the hospital bed. And . . . everything.

I look down, away from his eyes, and I hope that when I look back up, I'll know how to respond. I just have to look away long enough to figure out what to say.

But nothing comes to me.

So I do what I always do when I'm lost. I deflect. "I don't know, Dad, the weather is better here."

He laughs and smiles wide at me. "You don't like constant clouds and rain?"

I shake my head.

"Promise me you'll think about it?"

"I promise," I say.

"Who knows, maybe London's the city you were meant for all along."

He's joking. He has no idea the significance something like that might have for me.

And then I realize just how odd it is that I've never come up with that idea myself. In all of my traveling, all of my city hopping, I never once set my sights on the city my family lived in. Does that mean it's not the right place for me? Or is it a sign that this is exactly what I needed to finally see, that London is where I should be? I want to follow my fate, but I also sort of don't want to go to London.

"I'm going to ask you a question," he says. "And I need you to be completely honest with me. Don't worry about how you're going to make your mother and me feel. I want you to worry only about you and what you need."

"OK," I say.

"I'm serious, Hannah."

"OK."

He speaks with a gravity that takes me by surprise. "Would it be easier on you if we left?"

There it is. What I want. In my lap. But I'm not sure I'm capable of reaching out and grabbing it. I don't know if I can bear to say it out loud, to tell my father that I need him to leave, especially after the conversation we've just had.

My dad interjects before I can formulate a response. "I'm not worried about my feelings or your mom's feelings. I'm worried about you. You are my only concern. You are all I care about. And all I need from you is enough information to make the right decision for my daughter. What do you need? Do you need some peace and quiet for now?"

I look at him. I can feel my lip quiver. I can't say it. I can't bring myself to say it.

My dad smiles, and with that smile, I know that he's not going to make me say it. He nods, taking my nonresponse as an answer. "So, it's good-bye for now," he says. "I know it doesn't mean you don't love us."

"I do love you," I say.

"And we love you."

We've said it many times to each other, but this time, this particular time, I can feel it in my chest.

"All right, let me go break the news to your mother."

"Oh, I'm so sorry," I say, putting my hands to my face. I feel terrible.

"Don't be. She's tougher than she realizes sometimes. And she just wants what's best for you."

He slips out into the hallway. Momentarily alone, I find myself tense and tearful.

Soon the door opens, and my parents come in. My mom can't say anything. She just looks at me and runs to me, wrapping her arms around my shoulders.

"We're gonna go," she says.

"OK," I say.

"I love you," she says. "I love you so much. The day you were born, I cried for six hours straight, because I had never loved anyone that much in my life. And I never stopped. OK? I never stopped."

"I know, Mom. I love you, too."

She wipes her tears, squeezes my hand, and lets my father hug me.

"I'm proud of you," he says. "Proud of the person you are."

"Thanks, Dad."

And then that's it. They walk to the door.

My dad turns back to me. "Oh," he says, "I almost forgot."

He picks up a box he left on the counter when he walked in. He hands it over to me.

I open it. It's a cinnamon roll from Primo's. The glaze is stuck to the box, and the dough has started to unravel.

"You remembered," I say. It's such a thoughtful gift, such a tender gesture, that I know I'm going to start crying again if he doesn't leave this minute.

He winks at me. "I'd never forget a thing like that."

And then he's gone out the door, to join my mother and sister. They'll take a cab to LAX and then fly across the country, over the Atlantic, and land at Heathrow.

And I'll stay here.

And I can honestly say that until this moment, I never realized how much my parents have always, always loved me.

Since Ethan left for work, I've been sitting here with Charlemagne trying to figure out what vet to take her to and what bus route to use.

I puked again this morning, shortly after he left. I was feeling sort of queasy when I woke up, and then I thought I felt better, so I opened his fridge to see if there was anything for breakfast. I picked up a package of bacon, and the smell made me sick to my stomach. I threw up and ended up feeling much better. Suddenly, I was starving, which was when I remembered the cinnamon rolls.

I grabbed one for me and one for Charlemagne, but I thought better of it. She's a little thing, after all. So I ripped hers in half, giving one half to her on the floor and adding the other to my plate. I wolfed all of it down in three big bites. Then I ate another one.

In college, during the few times I got so drunk I puked, I always immediately felt hungry afterward. It was as if my body had gotten rid of everything bad and wanted to replace it with something delicious. I'd get up in the morning, go to Dunkin' Donuts, and inhale a cinnamon cake doughnut, the closest thing they had to what I wanted. Some things don't change, I guess.

Now Charlemagne and I are on the couch. She's cuddled up in my lap as I'm leaning over her, trying to figure out if dogs are allowed on public buses. I don't see anything definitive on the Web site, so I close my computer and decide just to take on the day and see where it leads me. If they won't let her on the bus, I'll figure something out.

I lock Ethan's apartment door and head outside. First things first. Charlemagne needs a collar and a leash if I'm going to get her across town. I walk to Target, which isn't all that far from Ethan's place. I have Charlemagne bundled in my arms. I expect someone to stop me here in the store, but no one even bats an eyelash. I had this whole plan to claim she was a service animal, but it isn't necessary. I grab a collar and a leash and head to the register. The cashier looks at me sideways but doesn't say anything. I act as if it's perfectly normal to be holding a dog in a store. In general, I find that when you are doing something you are not supposed to be doing, the best course of action is to act as if you are absolutely supposed to be doing it.

Once I put a collar on her and attach the leash, I decide to go with the same tactic on the bus. I act confident as I wait for the bus to arrive. When it does, I get on during a rush of people, hoping this will distract the bus driver.

No such luck.

"You can't have that dog on here," the bus driver says.

"She's a service dog," I say.

"Doesn't have a service tag," the driver says.

I start to answer, but he cuts me off.

"Wouldn't matter anyway. No dogs."

"OK," I say. I want to debate this a bit and see if I can persuade him to let us on, but my mind is blank, and I'm holding up the line. "Thanks," I say as I get off.

I'm getting this dog to the animal hospital if it's the last thing I do.

I walk back to Target. I go in, again with my head tall, holding Charlemagne in my arms. I head right for the school supplies and buy a backpack. I go back to the same cashier, the one I know won't say anything, and I have her ring me up.

"You're not supposed to have dogs in here," she says. "That'll be fourteen eighty-nine."

"Thanks," I say, pretending I didn't hear that first part. I quickly head out, walk around the corner, and put the bag down on the sidewalk. I lift Charlemagne and put her into the bag, and then I zip it up, leaving a hole at the top for her to breathe.

I walk around to the bus station and wait for another bus. When it comes, I walk on as if I have a backpack full of books, not filled with a tiny terrier. Between my attitude and the fact that Charlemagne doesn't bark, we're golden. I take a seat in the far back. I gently put the bag down at my feet and unzip it a bit more. She waits quietly at the bottom of the backpack. She doesn't make a sound.

I keep her at my feet. She sleeps for most of the ride, and when she's not sleeping, she's just looking up at me sweetly, with her kind face and her huge eyes. Her face is shaggier than the rest of her. She needs a bath. I'm glad she's not begging to be let out of the backpack, glad she's not trying to sit in my lap or play. She has the sort of face that makes you want to jump through hoops to please her, and I don't want us to get kicked off the bus.

We pass street after street, and we've been on the bus for quite a while. Just when I think I've gotten on the wrong bus, that this all has been for nothing, I see the animal hospital up ahead.

I hit the button to request the stop, and soon the bus is

starting to pull over. I stand up, picking up the backpack gently and heading for the double doors in the back of the bus. I'm standing there, waiting for them to open, when Charlemagne starts barking.

I stare at the doors, willing them to open. They don't. Everyone is staring. I can feel their eyes on me, but I refuse to look at anyone to confirm.

I see the driver start to turn around to find the source of the noise, but the doors open up, and I run off the bus. Once we are on the sidewalk, I grab Charlemagne out of the bag. Some of the people on the bus watch us through the window. The bus driver glares at me. But then the bus is off again, crawling down the streets of Los Angeles at a snail's pace, while Charlemagne and I are standing free as birds, just a block from the animal hospital.

"We did it!" I say to her. "We fooled them all!"

She puts her head down on my shoulder and then reaches up and licks my cheek.

I put her down, her leash firmly in my hand, and we make our way toward the building and into the lobby.

There are dogs everywhere. It smells like a kennel in here. Why do cats and dogs have that same musky odor? Individually, they aren't so bad, but the minute you get a group together, it's . . . pungent.

"Hi," I say to the receptionist.

"How can I help you?" she asks.

"I found a dog on the street last night, and I wanted to find out if she's chipped."

"OK," she says. "We are a bit tied up at the moment, but sign in here, and I'll see if we can get that done sooner rather than later." She points me toward a clipboard. Under *Dog's Name,* I put "Charlemagne," and under *Pet Owner* I put my own name, even though her name's probably not really Charlemagne and I'm not really her owner.

"Ma'am?" the receptionist calls to me.

"Yes?"

"No one will be able to help you until six," she says.

"Six?"

"Yeah," she says. "I'm sorry. We've had a few unexpected procedures. We're backed up all afternoon. You're welcome to take the dog home and come back."

I think about putting Charlemagne back into the bag, getting onto the bus, and then doing it all over again this evening. I have no doubt that Charlemagne and I would put up a good fight, but eventually, the bus drivers of Los Angeles are going to be on to us.

"Can I leave her here? And meet the doctor here at six?" It makes me sad to think that she'd be here without me. But that's sort of the point, right? I'm trying to find out who Charlemagne belongs to. Because she *doesn't* belong to me.

The receptionist is already shaking her head. "I'm sorry. We can't do that. People in your position often come and leave the dog, and then they don't come back, and we end up having to put the dog in a shelter."

"OK," I say. "I get it."

She whispers softly to me, "If you leave a large deposit, even a credit card, I can often persuade the vet techs to make room in the kennels. I mean, since we know you'll be coming back."

"You're saying you want collateral?" I ask her, a joking tone to my voice.

She nods, very politely, demurely.

I pull out my wallet and take out my credit card. The receptionist stands up and puts her hands out, ready to take Charlemagne, but I find her much harder to part with than my MasterCard.

"It's OK," the receptionist says to Charlemagne. "We're gonna take good care of you for a few hours while Mommy runs some errands."

"Oh," I say. "Sorry. I'm not her . . . mommy." The word is almost laughable, the thought that I am anyone's, anything's, *mommy*.

"Oh, I know," she says. "But you're her person at the moment, so . . ."

"Still," I say, "I don't want to confuse her."

And then I pick up my wallet and walk out the front door without looking anyone in the eye, because that is the stupidest thing I've ever said. The problem is not that I don't want to confuse the *dog*. The problem is that I don't want to confuse *myself*.

I walk outside and grab my phone. I look for car dealerships in the area. No sense in wasting time. There is a cluster of three dealerships just a mile and a half down the road. I start walking.

I'm going to cross one more thing off my list today.

Soon I might just be a functioning human being.

I called Gabby right after my family left. I told her my dad said I should move to London.

She asked me how I felt about it, and I told her I wasn't sure.

Even though I haven't lived in the same place as Gabby for very long, I somehow can't imagine living that far away from her again.

"You have a lot going on right now," Gabby said. "Just try to get some sleep, and we can go over the pros and cons when you're ready."

When I put down the phone, I did exactly what she said. I fell asleep.

I woke up a little bit ago and looked at the clock: two a.m.

"You're up," Henry says as he walks into my room. "You were asleep earlier."

"Snoring better or worse than Gabby was the other night?"

"Oh, worse," he says. "Definitely worse."

I laugh. "Well, can't you people do something about that? Some sort of surgery?"

"I wouldn't worry too much about it," he says, coming toward me. "You've been through enough, don't you think?" He marks things down on my chart.

"How am I doing?" I ask.

He pops the chart back down and clicks his pen. "You're

good. I think tomorrow they'll put you in the wheelchair and get you mobile."

"Wow!" I say. "Really?" How quickly in life you can go from taking walking for granted to one day being amazed that someone might let you sit in a wheelchair.

"Yeah," he says. "So that's exciting, right?"

"You bet your ass it is," I say.

"Somebody bring you a pastry?" Henry says. His deep blue scrubs are a flattering color. I don't mean that they specifically flatter him. I just mean I've noticed most of the nurses wear a sort of rose pink or light blue. But the navy blue he has is just much more attractive. If I were a nurse, I'd wear dark blue scrubs, sunup to sundown.

"Yeah," I say. I can't believe I forgot. I immediately grab the box. "My dad brought me a cinnamon roll."

"Oh, man, my weak spot," Henry says. "I don't have much of a sweet tooth, but I love a good cinnamon roll."

I am so eager to express my own love for cinnamon rolls that I stumble over my words. "That's what . . . I am . . . you love? . . . Me, too."

He laughs at me.

"I mean, I love cinnamon rolls. I have a cinnamon roll problem," I say.

"No such thing," he says.

Now that we are talking about it, I'm finding it impossible not to eat some of it right now. I open the box and pull off a piece. "You want some?" I ask.

"Oh, that's OK," Henry says.

"You sure? My dad got this from Primo's. I'd argue it's one of the best cinnamon rolls in all of Los Angeles."

He puts his pen into his shirt pocket. "You know what? OK. I'd actually love a bite."

I hand him the box. He picks off a small piece.

"Oh, come on," I say. "Take a real piece."

Henry laughs and takes a bigger piece. "I'm pretty sure this is How to Interact with Patients 101: Do Not Take Their Food."

I laugh. "Nobody's perfect."

"No," he says, chewing. "I suppose not." And then he adds, "Damn, that's good."

"Right? I don't want to brag, but I consider myself a cinnamon roll connoisseur."

"I'm starting to believe it," he says.

"Maybe I should start dropping hints to my visitors that I want more cinnamon rolls. I can probably get us a pretty good stash."

"Tempting," he says. "You feeling OK?"

The minute he says it, I remember who we really are, why we are really here, and I fall back down to earth just the littlest bit.

"Yeah," I say. "I am. Each day feels a little bit better."

"Think you'll feel ready to get into the wheelchair tomorrow? It can be painful, moving around for the first time, being lifted, all of that. You up for it?"

"Are you kidding me? I'm up for anything."

"Yeah," he says. "That's what I thought."

He heads toward the door and then stops. "If you love cinnamon rolls as much as I do, then I'll bet you also love churros. Have you had a churro?"

I give him an indignant look. "Are you kidding me? Have *I* had a churro? I'm from Los Angeles. I've had a churro."

"Oh, well, excuse me . . . Sassypants."

I start laughing. "Sassypants?"

He laughs, too. "I don't know where that came from. It just popped out of my mouth. I'm as stunned as you are."

I start laughing so hard that my eyes water. My whole body is convulsing. You realize when your body is broken just how much of it you use to laugh. But I can't stop laughing. I don't want to stop laughing.

"I guess it was a little weird of me to say," he says.

"A little?" I say between breaths.

He laughs at himself with me.

And then, suddenly, there's a shooting pain down my leg. It is sharp, and it is deep, and it is gut-wrenching. My laughter stops immediately. I cry out.

Henry rushes toward me.

The pain doesn't stop. It hurts so badly I can't breathe. I can't talk. I look down at my feet and see that the toes on my right foot are clenched. I can't unclench them.

"It's OK, you're OK," he says. He moves toward my IV. "You're gonna be OK in a second, I promise." He comes back to me. He grabs my hand. He looks into my eyes. "Look at me," he says. "C'mon, look at me. The pain is gonna go away in a second. You're having a spasm. You just have to bear through it. It's gonna be OK."

I move my gaze to his face. I focus on him through the pain. I look into his eyes, and he stares into mine.

"You got this," he says. "You got this."

And then the pain begins to fade away.

My toes straighten.

My body relaxes.

I can breathe easily.

Henry moves his hands out of mine. He slides them up my arms to my shoulders. "You OK?" he says. "That had to hurt."

"Yeah," I say. "Yeah, I'm OK."

"It's good we are going to get you up and moving soon. Your body needs to be up and about."

"Yeah," I say.

"You did great."

"Thanks."

"You gonna be OK? On your own?"

"Yeah," I say. "I think so."

"If it happens again, just hit the button, and I'll be here." He takes his hands off me. With one swift motion, so subtle I'm almost not sure it happened, he moves a fallen hair out of my face. "Get some rest. Tomorrow is going to be a big day."

"OK," I say.

He smiles and heads out the door. At the very last second, he pops his head back in. "You're badass, you know that?"

I say, "You probably say that to all your patients," and then when he leaves, I think, *What if he doesn't? What if he only says that kind of stuff to me?*

"Ma'am," the dealer says to me. We are sitting at his desk. I've already made my decision. "Are you sure you don't want a *new* car? Something fun? Something a bit more . . . your style?"

I'm considering a used Toyota Camry. The dealer keeps trying to get me to look at this bright red Prius. Admittedly, I'd rather have the bright red Prius. There might have been a time in my life when I would have said "Screw it" and used all my money on the down payment for the Prius, forcing myself to figure out the rest when it came time. Because I love that red Prius.

But I'm trying to make new decisions so that they lead me to better places.

"The Camry's fine," I say. I already test-drove it. I've asked all the right questions. They want ninety-five hundred dollars for it. I tell him I'll give him seventy-five hundred. We go back and forth. He gets me up to eight. He keeps going to his manager to get new negotiating numbers. Eventually, the manager comes over and whines about how little I am willing to pay for the car.

"If I sell it to you for less than eighty-five hundred, I won't make any money off the deal," he says. "You know, we need to make money. We can't just be giving cars away."

"OK," I say. "I guess we can't make this work." I get up out of the chair and grab my purse.

"Sweetheart," the manager says, "don't be crazy."

This is why Gabby has to keep talking about women's rights and gender equality. It's because of dipshits like this.

"Look, I told you I'd pay eight thousand even. Take it or leave it."

Carl is an excellent negotiator. Really cutthroat. When I was a senior, Carl would take either Gabby or me to do all of his negotiating so we learned how to haggle. Mechanics, salesmen, plumbers, you name 'em, Carl made us negotiate prices with them directly. When Carl's Jeep needed a new set of wheels, he stood out around the corner from the shop as I went in and tried to talk the guy down on his behalf. When I'd go back out to him to report the new price, Carl would shake his head and tell me I could do better. And I always did. I was especially proud when the tire guy threw in a free car detailing after my prodding. Gabby once got the guy repairing the hot-water heater to come down five hundred bucks. Carl and Tina took us out to Benihana that night to celebrate the victory.

Carl has always said that people who don't haggle are suckers. And we aren't suckers.

"I'm buying a car today. Doesn't have to be from you," I say to the manager.

The manager rolls his eyes. "All right, all right," he says. "Eighty-one hundred, and it's a deal."

I shake his hand, and they start drawing up the paperwork. I put three thousand down and drive off the lot with a car. There goes most of my money. But it's OK. Because I have a plan.

When I get far enough from the dealership, I pull over to the side of the road and start hitting my hands against the steering wheel, yelling into the air, trying to get out all the nervous energy that's in me.

I'm doing this. I'm making a life for myself. I am *doing* this.

I call Carl at his office.

"Hello!" he says, his voice buttery and pleased to hear from me. "Tell me you're taking the job."

"I'm taking the job."

"Outstanding. I'm going to put you on the phone with Joyce, our HR person here. She will talk to you about a start date, salary, benefits, all of that good stuff. If you don't talk her up to at least forty-two, I'm going to be disappointed in you."

I laugh. "I just paid eighty-one hundred for a ninety-five-hundred-dollar car. I got this. I promise."

"That's what I want to hear!" he says.

"Carl, seriously, thank you for this."

"Thank *you*," he says. "Honestly. This worked out perfectly. Rosalie showed up an hour and a half late this morning and didn't even bother with an excuse. She denies it, but a patient told me last week that she swore at them. So I'm eager to let her go, and I'm just glad we don't have to go through résumés to replace her."

I laugh. "All right," I say. "I'm excited to start working with you . . . *boss*."

He laughs and puts me through to Joyce. She and I talk for about thirty minutes. She says she's going to give Rosalie notice. So my start date will be in two weeks. But if Rosalie decides not to stay the two weeks, the job could start sooner. I tell her I'm OK with that.

"That's why sometimes it really is best to hire someone you know," Joyce says. "I know I'm in HR and I'm supposed to say that you should vet all the applicants, but the truth is, when you have a personal connection, it just makes it easier to be flexible."

She offers me forty thousand, and, hot off the trail of my car purchase, I talk her up to forty-four. I get full health benefits. "And the good news," she says, "is that we cover the rest of your family at a very low cost."

"Oh," I say. "Well, it's just me."

"Oh, OK," she says. "And you'll have two weeks' paid vacation a year and, of course, maternity leave if necessary."

I laugh. "Won't be necessary," I say.

She laughs back. "I hear you."

We finish discussing odds and ends, and soon everything is settled.

"Welcome to Hudson, Stokes, and Johnson Pediatrics," she says.

"Thank you," I say. "Glad to join."

I know he's still working, but I find it impossible not to call Ethan.

"What's up, buttercup?" he says. I'm surprised he answered.

"Do you have a minute?"

"Sure," he says. "Let me just step outside."

I can hear him walk through a door, and the background quiets down.

"What's up?"

"You'd better not ever try to negotiate with me," I tell him. "Because I just talked the car salesman *down* fourteen hundred dollars, and I talked the human resources lady *up* four thousand. So basically, I'm a force to be reckoned with."

Ethan laughs. "A car owner and a job . . . haver."

"You're damn right."

"And did you find Charlemagne's home?"

"They can't see her until six," I say. "So I bought the car, and now I'm headed back. I'm thinking I'll just kill some time in the waiting room, see if the doctor doesn't free up early."

"Six?"

"Yeah. She's there now. I had to leave a credit card so they'd keep her there until I get back."

Ethan laughs again. "What, like collateral?"

"That's exactly what I said!"

He laughs. "Listen, I'm leaving here in a half hour. What part of town are you in? I'll come meet you."

"Oh, that would be awesome!" I say. "I'm in West L.A. The vet is off of Sepulveda."

"Jesus, that's far from my house," he says. "You took a bus there?"

"Yeah," I say.

"With Charlemagne?"

"I may or may not have hidden her in a backpack."

Ethan laughs. "Why don't I come meet you and we can grab an early dinner? Find a happy hour somewhere. I know of a Mexican place close to the animal hospital. I could buy you a celebratory burrito!"

"I'm in!"

I get lost more than once on my way there. Then I try to take an alley, only to realize there is a big truck coming at me from the opposite direction. I have to reverse out slowly and blindly back onto the street and find another way. But I get there eventually. That's me in a nutshell. I'll get there eventually.

I pull into the parking lot of the restaurant, and Ethan is waiting for me by the entrance.

"Is this the new car?" he says dramatically. "I like it. Unexpected. I thought for sure you'd pull up in something cherry red."

I laugh at him. "I'm way more into practical decisions nowadays," I say. "Stable guys, full-time jobs . . ."

"Stray dogs," he adds.

I laugh and correct him. "I am merely helping Charlemagne find her true family," I say as we head into the restaurant. "But the stable guy and the full-time job, those are . . ." I find myself intending to finish the sentence by saying "for keeps," but I quickly realize I don't want to do that.

It's too early to be talking about how serious Ethan and I are or may be in the future. We have a history together, and we have potential to be something very real, but we just started dating again. I think the best thing to do is allow myself to imagine the future in my head but not put it into words just yet.

Which is to say that I think it's very possible that Ethan is the one for me. But I'd rather be dead than say it out loud.

Luckily, Ethan appears to be on the exact same page, because he looks at me, grabs my hand, squeezes it, and says, "I hear you."

The hostess asks if we want to be seated in the dining room or at the bar, and we go for the bar. As we sit down, Ethan orders guacamole.

"I'm very proud of you," he says when the waitress leaves.

"Thank you," I say. "I'm proud of me, too. I mean, I didn't like where my old habits got me, you know? And I feel really motivated to turn over a new leaf."

I think things have been working out for me so far partly because I have people believing in me. Gabby and the Hudsons and Ethan are so encouraging that it makes me feel I can do all the things I set out to do. In other cities, I never had a true support system. I had plenty of friends and, at times, caring boyfriends. But I don't know that I ever had someone truly believing in me even when I didn't. Now I do. And I think maybe I need someone in my corner in order to thrive. I think I am one of those people who need people. Because my family left and I was OK with it, I always thought that I was more of a lone wolf. I guess I thought I didn't need anyone.

"Well, I admire it," Ethan says.

The waiter sets the guacamole down in front of us. I grab a chip and dip in. But before I can even bring it to my lips, it smells awful. I put the chip down.

"Oh, God," I say. "Is it rancid or something?"

"Uh," Ethan says, genuinely confused. "The guacamole?"

"Smell it," I say. "It smells funky."

"It does?" He dips a chip in, brings it to his nose, and eats it. "It's fine. It tastes great."

I smell it again and can't stand it. I hold my stomach.

"Are you OK?" Ethan asks.

"Yeah," I say. "I just need to get away from that."

"You look really pale. And you're sweating. On your forehead a bit."

Just like last night, a wave of nausea runs through me. My throat constricts and turns sour. I'm not sure I'll be able to hold this in very long. I run at full speed to the bathroom, but I don't make it to the toilet. I puke in the sink. Luckily, it's a private bathroom.

Ethan comes in and closes the door behind us.

"This is the ladies' room," I tell him.

"I'm worried about you," he says.

"I'm fine," I say, although I am seriously starting to doubt that.

"You said you puked last night, too," he says.

"Yeah," I tell him. "And this morning."

"Do you think maybe you have the flu? Should you see a doctor? I mean, why else would you be puking all the time?"

The minute he asks the question, I know I don't have the flu.

I understand perfectly now why everything in my life has been going so well. The universe is just lining everything up in perfect order so that I can roll through and ruin it the way I always do.

Classic Hurricane Hannah.

I'm pregnant.

I wake up to the sound of someone fumbling around in the dark. But I don't see anyone. I only hear them.

"Henry?" I ask.

A figure pops up from the floor.

"Sorry," he says. "I can't find my cell phone. I thought I might have dropped it in here."

"It's weird to think that you're here, hovering over me when I'm sleeping," I tell him.

"I wasn't *hovering,*" he says. "I was crawling."

I laugh. "Much worse."

"You didn't see it, right? My phone?" he asks me.

I shake my head.

"Dammit," he says, and I watch as he absentmindedly pulls at a few hair ties around his wrist.

"You told me you'd explain the hair ties," I say. I point to my own head. The one he gave me is the one I'm still using to keep my bun together. Luckily, I can now do it myself with little fanfare. But I still don't have a mirror, so I can't be sure it looks good.

He laughs. "Good memory. A lot of car accident patients struggle to remember basic details."

I shrug. "What can I say? I've always been ahead of the rest."

"I started finding hair ties all over the hospital where I worked back in Texas," he says. I find myself smiling as he sits down. I like that he sits down. I like that he is staying. "And I didn't want to throw them away, because they seemed like they would be useful to somebody, so I started collecting them. But then no one ever asked for one, so they just kept piling up. And then, one day, my boss asked me to do something, and I didn't have a piece of paper to write on, so I put a hair tie around my wrist to remind me, sort of like someone might do with a rubber band. Then I started to do it all the time. And then I started to do it for more than one thing at a time. So if there were four things I needed to remember, four hair ties. If I had two things to do and someone gave me a third task, another hair tie."

"How many times have you stood staring at your wrist trying to remember what one of the hair ties was for?"

He laughs. "Listen, it's not a perfect system." He bends down for a moment. I assume he thinks he sees his cell phone.

He stands back up. He must have been wrong. "Anyway," he says, "that's my hair tie organizational system."

"And the plus is, you have a hair tie for any woman who needs one."

"Right," he says. "But no one has ever asked for one but you."

I smile at him.

"How are you feeling?" he asks me. "OK? No more spasms?"

"No more spasms."

"Good," he says as he looks around the room some more for his phone.

"We could call it," I offer. "Your phone, I mean." There is a hospital phone next to me, on the bed table. I pull it toward me and pick up the receiver. "What's the number?"

I can't quite interpret the look on his face.

"What did I do?" I ask him.

"I can't give you any personal contact information," he says. "It's against the rules."

I am feeling ever so slightly embarrassed. I put the receiver back in the cradle to save face. "Oh, OK. Well, you can dial yourself," I say. "I'll close my eyes."

He laughs and shakes his head. "It won't do much good anyway," he tells me. "The ringer's off."

I can tell that both of us want to change the subject. We just aren't sure how.

"I tried that Find My Phone app," Henry offers.

"Oh, that's great!" I say.

"It said the phone is located at Angeles Presbyterian."

I laugh. "How helpful," I say.

"Well," he says, "if you see it . . ."

"If I see it, I'll ring my little nurse bell."

"And I'll come running," he says.

Neither of us has anything left to say, and yet he doesn't leave. He looks at me. We hold each other's gaze for just a second longer than normal. I look away first. I'm distracted by a dull blueish light that starts flashing in a slow rhythm.

"Eureka!" he says.

I start laughing as he ducks down. When he pops back up with his phone, he's not at the foot of the bed, where he was before. He's by my side. "I knew I'd find it," he says.

Instinctually, I find myself reaching out toward him, to touch him the way I might a friend. But I quickly remember that he's not my friend, that to touch his arm or hand tenderly might be weird. So I pretend I'm going for a high-five. He smiles and enthusiastically claps my hand.

"Nice work," I say.

For a moment, I wonder how things would be different if

I could walk. And we weren't in a hospital but in a bar somewhere. If I'd worn my favorite black shirt and tight jeans. I wonder how this all might be different if there was a beer in my hand, and the lights were low because people were dancing, not because people were sleeping.

Is it crazy to think he would say hello and introduce himself? Is it crazy to think he would ask me to dance?

"Anyway, I should be going," he says. "But I'll come check on you soon. I don't like to go too many hours without making sure you're still breathing." And he leaves before I can say good-bye.

I don't know. Maybe, just maybe, if Henry and I met at a dinner party, we'd spend the entire night talking, and when the night wound down, he'd offer to walk me to my car.

What is it?" Ethan asks me. "What's the matter? Are you going to vomit again? What can I do?"

"No," I say, slowly shaking my head. "I'm totally fine now."

I got my period before I left for L.A. I remember getting it. I remember thinking that I was glad it ended a day sooner than normal. I remember that. *I remember that.*

"Totally good," I tell him. "I think maybe those brussels sprouts are still messing with me."

"OK," he says. "Well, maybe we should head home."

I shake my head. "Nope," I tell him. "Let's hang out until we can go talk to the vet about Charlemagne."

"You're sure?"

I look at my phone. I want to run out of here and buy a pregnancy test, but there is no way I could just up and ditch Ethan without him asking what is going on. And I can't share this with him. I can't even bring up the possibility until it's no longer simply a possibility.

"All right," he says. "If you really are feeling OK."

"I am." The lying begins.

"I'll head out first," he says. "Just so no one thinks we were doin' it in here."

His joke catches me off guard, and I find myself laughing out loud. "OK," I say, smiling.

He ducks out, and I stay in the bathroom for a minute.

I breathe in and out, trying to control my brain and my body. And then I pick up my phone and Google the one thing that could convince me I'm wrong about this. The one piece of evidence I have that maybe I'm not pregnant.

can i be pregnant if i got my period

"You cannot have a menstrual period while you are pregnant . . ." My heartbeat slows. I start to calm. This might all just be OK. "But some women do have vaginal bleeding during pregnancy."

I click on another one.

"My cousin didn't know she was pregnant for four months because she got her period all during her pregnancy."

I click again.

"You may still get your period at the beginning of your pregnancy due to what is called implantation bleeding when the egg implants in the uterus."

Crap.

"Typically, the bleeding will be lighter and shorter than a normal period."

I turn off my phone and slump down on the floor.

Despite every piece of common sense available to me, I got pregnant. And it isn't by the handsome, charming, perfect man I'm starting to believe is the one.

It's by the asshole with a wife and two kids in New York City.

I get hold of myself. No good comes from imploding or exploding right now. I breathe in. I open the door. I walk out of the bathroom and join Ethan at the table.

"How should we kill the time?" he asks. "Should we get away from this horrible guacamole and go find you a cinnamon roll?"

He's going to leave me. My perfect person. The man who

jumps at the chance to get me a cinnamon roll. He's going to leave me.

I shake my head. "You know what?" I say. "Let's just order some burritos and chow down."

"Sounds like heaven," he says as he flags down a waiter.

We order. We talk about his job. We make jokes. And we eat tortilla chips.

With every chip I eat and every joke I make, I push the news further into the recesses of my mind. I bury my problems and focus on what is in front of me.

I am great at pretending everything is fine. I am great at hiding the truth. I almost believe it myself for a minute. By the time our burritos have come and gone, you'd think I'd forgotten.

We head to our cars and plan to meet up at the vet.

"You're perfect," Ethan says as he shuts my car door for me. "You know that?" When he says it, it becomes clear just how much I *haven't* forgotten.

"Don't say that," I tell him. "It's not true."

"You're right," he says. "You're too pretty. I need a girl less pretty."

~

When we get back to the animal hospital, the vet is ready to talk to us.

He pulls us into an exam room, and one of the vet techs brings out Charlemagne. She runs right to me.

"There you are!" I say to her. I pick her up and hold her in my arms.

"So you are the ones who found her?" the vet asks us.

"Yeah," Ethan says. "Running through the street."

The vet looks dismayed. "Well, she's not chipped. She is also not spayed. And she's undernourished. She should be about two or three pounds heavier," he says. He is tall, with a thick gray beard and gray hair. "That may not sound like a lot, but on a dog this size . . ."

"Yeah," Ethan says. "It's a considerable deficit."

"Any idea how old she is?" I ask.

"Well, her teeth aren't fully in yet, so she's still a puppy."

"How young, do you think?"

"No more than four months, maybe five," he says. "My guess is that she lives with someone who isn't paying too much attention . . ."

"Right," I say.

"Or it's possible she's been on the street for a while."

I find it hard to believe she's been on the street for a while. Dogs that live out on the street wouldn't run into the middle of the road. That seems to defy the very concept of survival of the fittest. If you are a dog that runs into the middle of the road, especially in the dark of night, then you are probably not going to last long on the mean streets of . . . anywhere.

"A lot of times, people don't spay their dogs," the vet continues, "and are surprised when they end up pregnant."

Ha!

"Caring for a nursing dog and a litter of puppies, when you don't expect to, can be overwhelming."

I'll say.

"Sometimes people keep them until they can't deal with it anymore and put the puppies out on the street."

Good God.

I look at Ethan, who, not knowing how uncomfortably close

this man is hitting the nail on the head, seems disturbed by all of it. Which makes sense. I am, too. I know that people are awful and do terrible things, especially to things that are helpless, especially to animals that are helpless. But when I look at Charlemagne, it's hard to comprehend. I barely know her, and I'm starting to think I'd do anything for her.

"So we have no real recourse," Ethan says. "In terms of finding out who she belongs to."

The vet shrugs. "Well, not through this route, at least. You could put fliers up around where you found her or go door-to-door. But either way, if you are at all considering keeping her, I might recommend you do that instead of tracking down an original owner, if there is one."

"Oh," Ethan says, "we weren't—"

"And if we did," I say, interrupting him, "would we just schedule an appointment with you guys to get all of that stuff taken care of? Get her spayed and chipped?"

"Yeah," the vet says. "And she'll need a series of shots. We can help you with fattening her up, too. Although, assuming she has consistent access to food, she'll probably take care of that one on her own."

"All right," Ethan says. "Thank you very much for your help." He extends his hand for a handshake. The vet reciprocates. I do the same.

"My pleasure," he says. "She's a sweetheart. I hope you guys can help her find a good home. If not, contact the front desk, and we can help you try to get her into a no-kill shelter. It's not easy. There are already so many other dogs in the city taking up spots, but we try to help."

By the time we leave the animal hospital, the sun has set, and the air is crisp. I have Charlemagne in my arms, her leash wrapped around my hand. She's shaking a bit, maybe because of the cold. I can't help but wonder if it's because she knows her fate is uncertain.

"What are you thinking?" I ask him.

"I don't know," Ethan says. We are standing by our cars. For a moment, I'm stunned that I bought the car just this afternoon. Feels like a lifetime ago. "I can't really have a dog at my place."

"I know," I say.

"I mean, I want to help her, and I don't want her on the street, but I had no intention of adopting a dog," he says. "And I don't know how you can adopt her, you know? Because . . ."

"Because I don't have a place just yet."

"Right."

He looks at me. I look at Charlemagne. I'm not bringing her to a shelter. I'm not doing it. With everything that has happened today, my fate is uncertain, too. Charlemagne and I are kindred spirits. We are both directionless idiots, the kind of girls who run out into the street without thinking.

I may make a lot of mistakes, and I may act without thinking, and I may be the sort of woman who doesn't even realize she's pregnant when it should be blatantly obvious, but I also know that sometimes I get myself into messes and then get myself out of them. Maybe I can get Charlemagne and me out of this mess by throwing us into it.

Charlemagne and I rode a city bus today with just a backpack and a smile. We are a team. She is mine.

"I'm not letting her go back to people who mistreat her," I say. "Not that we could find them even if we wanted to. And I'm certainly not leaving her out on the street or headed to a kill shelter."

Ethan looks at me. I can tell he understands where I'm

coming from but doesn't necessarily get where I'm heading. "OK . . ." he says. "So what do we do?"

"I'm going to keep her," I say. "That's what I'm going to do."

She's not his problem. She's my problem. I'm *choosing* to take care of her.

The parallels do not escape me. And maybe that's part of the reason I am doing this. Maybe it's a physical manifestation of what I'm going through emotionally right now.

I have a baby that's not his. I'm taking on a dog he didn't ask for. I'm not going to make these things his problem.

"OK," he says. "Well, she can stay at my place for tonight, and then tomorrow we can figure out a long-term plan."

He says "we." *We can figure out a long-term plan.*

"That's all right," I tell him, moving toward my car. "I should sleep at Gabby's tonight."

"You're not going to stay with me?"

I shake my head. "I should really sleep there. She won't mind Charlemagne for the night." Yes, she will. Mark is allergic to dogs. Taking Charlemagne back to their apartment is kind of a crappy thing to do. But I need space away from Ethan. I need to be on my own.

"She can be at my place," he says. "For tonight. Really."

I shake my head again, moving away from him. I open my car door. I put Charlemagne on the passenger's seat and shut her in.

"No," I tell him. "It's fine. This is the better plan."

"OK," he says. He is clearly dejected. "If that's what you want."

"I'll call you tomorrow," I tell him.

All he says is "Cool." He says it looking at my feet instead of my face. He's upset, but he doesn't want to show it. So he nods and gets into his car. "I'll talk to you tomorrow, then," he says out his window. Then he turns on his lights and drives off.

I get into my car. I look at Charlemagne. Suddenly, the tears that have been waiting under the surface all night spring forth.

"I screwed it all up, Charlemagne," I tell her. "I ruined it all."

She doesn't respond. She doesn't look at me.

"It was all going to be perfect. And I ruined it."

Charlemagne licks her paw, as if I'm not even talking.

"What do I do?" I ask her. If you were watching us from the outside, you might think I expect her to answer. That's how sincere my voice is, how desperate it sounds. And maybe, on some level, it's true. Maybe if, all of a sudden, she started talking and told me what I need to do to fix this, I would be more relieved than shocked.

Alas, she remains a normal dog instead of a magical one. I put my head on the steering wheel of my brand-new used car, and I cry. And I cry. And I cry. And I cry.

And I wonder when I have to tell Michael.

And I wonder when I have to tell Ethan.

And I wonder how I'm going to afford a baby.

And I wonder how I could be so goddamn stupid.

And I wonder if maybe the world hates me, if maybe I am fated to always be screwing up my life and never getting ahead.

I wonder if I'll be a single mom forever. If Ethan will ever talk to me again. If my parents will come meet my kid or if I'll have to fly internationally with a baby on holidays.

And then I wonder what Gabby will say. I imagine her telling me it will all be OK. I imagine her telling me this baby was meant to be. I imagine her telling me that I'm going to be a great mother.

And then I wonder if that's true. If I will be.

And then . . . finally . . . I wonder about my baby.

And the realization hits me.

I'm going to have a baby.

I find myself smiling just the tiniest bit through my heavy, fearful tears.

"I'm going to have a baby," I say to Charlemagne. "I'm going to be a mom."

This time, she hears me. And while she doesn't start magically talking, she does stand up, walk over the center console, and sit in my lap.

"It's you and me," I say. "And a baby. We can do that, right?"

She curls into my lap and goes to sleep. But I think it speaks volumes that I believe if she could talk, she'd say yes.

It's early in the morning when I hear a knock on my door. I'm alone in my room. I've been up for only a few minutes. My bun is half undone around my shoulders.

Ethan peeks his head in. "Hey," he says, so quiet it's almost a whisper. "Can I come in?"

"Of course," I say. It's nice seeing him. I may have gotten a bit infatuated with the idea that he and I have something romantic left between us, but I can see now that we don't. I will probably always love him on some level, always hold a spot for him in my heart. But dating again, being together, that would be moving backward, wouldn't it? I moved to Los Angeles to put the past behind me, to move into the future. I moved to Los Angeles to change. And that's what I'm going to do.

But that doesn't mean that we can't still mean something to each other, that we can't be friends.

I pat the side of the bed, inviting him to sit right here next to me.

He does. "How are you feeling?" he asks. He has a bakery box in his hand. I'm hoping I know what it is.

"Is that a cinnamon roll?" I ask him, smiling.

He smiles back and hands it over.

"You remembered," I say.

"How could I forget?"

"Wow!" I say as I open the box. "This is a huge one."

"I know," he says. "I saw them a few years ago at this bakery on the Westside, and I thought of you. I knew you'd love them."

"This is so exciting! I mean, I'll have to eat this with a knife and fork." It's way too big for me to eat on my own. I resolve to wait and share it with Henry tonight. I hand it back to Ethan. "Can you put it on the table?"

"You don't want it now?"

I do sort of want it now, but I'd rather wait for Henry. I shake my head.

"You didn't answer my question," he says. "About how you are feeling."

I wave him off. "I'm OK. I'm feeling good. There are some ups and downs, but you've caught me at an up moment. Word on the street is I get to try out my wheelchair today." I watch as the look on Ethan's face changes. I get a glimpse, just for a moment, of how sad it must be to hear me excited about a wheelchair. But I refuse to be brought down about this. This is where I'm at in life. I need a wheelchair. *That's OK*. Onward and upward.

Ethan looks off to the side and then down at the floor. He's looking everywhere but at me.

"What's up?" I ask. "What's bothering you?"

"It just all seems so senseless," he says, looking up at me. "The idea of you being hit by a car. Almost losing you. When I heard what happened to you, I immediately thought . . . you know, she should have been with me instead. If I had been able to persuade you to stay out with me, you wouldn't have been standing in the middle of the road when . . . I mean, what if this all could have been prevented if I'd . . . done something different?"

It's sort of absurd, isn't it? How we grab on to facts and consequences looking to blame or exonerate ourselves? This has nothing to do with him. I chose to go home with Gabby and Mark because that's the choice I made. Nine billion choices I've made over the course of my life could have changed where I am right now and where I'm headed. There's no sense focusing on just one. Unless you want to punish yourself.

"I've looked at this problem up, down, and sideways," I tell him. "I've lain in this bed for days wondering if we were all supposed to do something different."

"And?"

"And . . . it doesn't matter."

"What do you mean, it doesn't matter?"

"I'm saying things happen for a reason. I'm saying there's a point to this. I didn't stick around with you that night because I wasn't supposed to. That wasn't what I was meant to do."

He looks at me. He doesn't say anything.

"You know," I continue, "maybe you and I would have gone out that night and stayed out partying and drinking until the early morning. And maybe we could have walked around the city all night, talking about our feelings and rehashing old times. Or maybe we would have left that bar and gone to another bar, where we ran into Matt Damon, and he would say that we seemed like really cool people and he wanted to give us a hundred million dollars to start a cinnamon roll factory."

Ethan laughs.

"We don't know what would have happened. But whatever would have happened wasn't *supposed* to happen."

"You really believe that?" Ethan says.

"I think I have to," I tell him. "Otherwise, my life is an absolute disaster."

Otherwise, my baby is gone for no reason.

"But yes," I say. "I really do believe that. I believe I'm destined for something. We are all destined for something. And I believe that the universe, or God, or whatever you want to call it, I believe it keeps us on the right path. And I believe I was supposed to choose Gabby. I wasn't supposed to stay with you."

Ethan is quiet. And then he looks up at me and says, "OK. It wasn't . . . I guess it wasn't meant to be."

"Besides," I say, trying to make a joke, "let's be honest. If I'd stuck around with you, we'd just have ended up making out and ruining everything. This way is better. This way, we can finally be friends. Good, real friends."

He looks at me, looks me right in the eye. We don't say anything to each other for a moment.

Ethan finally speaks up. "Hannah, I—"

He stops halfway through his sentence when Henry comes walking in the door.

"Oh, sorry," Henry says. "I didn't know you had visitors."

I feel myself perk up at the sight of him. He's wearing the same blue scrubs from last night.

"I thought you were night shift," I say. "Deanna is my day nurse."

"I'm covering," he says. "Just for this morning. I'll come back if I'm interrupting."

"Oh," Ethan says.

"You're not interrupting anything," I say over him.

Ethan gathers himself and looks at me. "You know what? I should be getting to work," he says.

"OK. You'll come visit me again soon?"

"Yeah," he says. "Or maybe you'll be out of here in a few days."

"Yeah," I say. "Maybe."

"Anyway," he says, "enjoy the cinnamon roll."

Henry laughs. "This is a girl who loves her cinnamon rolls," he says.

Ethan looks at him. "I know," he says. "That's why I brought her one."

I took three pregnancy tests in the bathroom of the CVS just down the street from Gabby's place. I could have left Charlemagne in the car, but I felt terrible doing that, even with the windows cracked, so I put her in the backpack and brought her with me. She yipped in the bathroom once or twice, but no one seemed to care.

All three sticks were positive. And there wasn't a single part of me that was surprised.

Now it's almost nine p.m., and I'm pulling up in front of Gabby's. She must hear my car, because she looks out the window. I see her and laugh. She looks like a crotchety old lady. I'm half expecting her to call out, "What's all that racket?"

By the time I open her front door, Charlemagne trailing behind me on the leash, Gabby is standing on the other side of the door. I feel bad about what I'm doing, by the way. I feel bad about bringing a dog into Mark's house. I know he's allergic, and I'm doing it anyway. But I couldn't stay with Ethan. And I couldn't abandon Charlemagne. So here we are.

"You bought a car?" Gabby says. She's in her pajamas.

"Where's Mark?" I ask her. Charlemagne is behind me. I don't think Gabby can see her.

"He's working late again," Gabby says.

"I have some news," I tell her.

"I know, you bought a car."

"Well, I have more news."

Charlemagne yips. Gabby looks at me askance.

I pull Charlemagne around to the front.

"You have a dog?"

"I am adopting her," I tell her. "I'm really sorry."

"You are adopting a dog?"

"Is it OK if she stays here just for tonight? I bought Mark a whole bunch of allergy pills." I take the five packages of medication that I got in the over-the-counter antihistamine aisle.

Gabby looks at me. "Uh . . . I guess?"

"Great. Thank you. I have news."

"You have more news?"

I nod, but Gabby continues to stare at me. I stare back, unsure if she's really prepared for this. Unsure if I'm really prepared for this.

"We should maybe sit down," I tell her.

"I need to sit down for this?"

"*I* need to," I tell her.

We move over to her couch. I pick up Charlemagne and put her in my lap. Quickly, Charlemagne moves off me and sits on the sofa. I see Gabby waver about whether she wants a dog on her sofa, so I pick up Charlemagne and put her on the floor.

"I'm pregnant."

Hearing it out loud, hearing the words come out of my mouth, brings forth a flood of emotions. I start to cry. I bury my head in my hands.

Gabby doesn't say much at first, but soon I feel her hands on my wrists. I feel her pull my hands away from my face. I feel her take her fingers and put them on my chin, forcing me to face her.

"You know it's going to be OK, right?" she says.

I look at her through my tears. I nod and do my best to say "Yes."

"Does Ethan know?" Gabby asks.

I shake my head. "No one does. Except you. And Charlemagne."

"Who is Charlemagne?" she asks me.

I look at the dog and point to her.

"Oh," Gabby says. "Right. Makes sense. I didn't think we were still naming people Charlemagne."

I start crying again.

"Hey," she says. "Come on. This is good news."

"I know," I say through my tears.

"It's Michael's," she says, as if it's just dawning on her.

"Yeah," I say. Charlemagne starts whining and jumping, trying to join us on the couch. Gabby looks at her and then picks her up and puts her in my lap. She curls up and closes her eyes. I do feel better, honestly, having her in my lap.

"OK, stop crying for a minute," Gabby says.

I sniffle and look at her.

"We are going to handle this, and we are going to be fine."

"We?"

"Well, I'm not going to let you go through this alone, you moron," she says. The way she says the word *moron* makes me feel more loved than I've felt in a long time. She says it as if I'd be a complete idiot to think I was ever alone. And to know that the idea is absolutely absurd to her, to know that it's so far-fetched as to make me a moron, it's a nice feeling. "You know, years from now, you're going to look back on this as the best thing that ever happened to you, right?"

I snort at her. "I'm having a baby with a married man, and

I'm pretty sure it's going to ruin my relationship with my new old boyfriend."

"First of all," she says, "let's not go assuming things. You never know what Ethan will say."

"You know what I'm pretty sure he's not going to say? 'Hey, Hannah, I'm super excited to take on the responsibilities of raising another man's baby.' "

I'm right, of course. Which is why Gabby changes the subject. "You are going to love this baby," she says. "You know that, right? You are such a loving person. You have so much love to give, and you are so loyal to the people you love. Do you have any idea what a great mom you are going to be? Do you have any idea how loved this kid is going to be? The love it will have from its Aunt Gabby will eclipse the sun."

I laugh, despite myself.

"Hannah, you can do this. And one day soon, you're not going to imagine how you ever found meaning in your life before you did." Maybe she's right.

"What if your dad fires me before I'm even hired? 'Hi. Hello. You gave me this job when you thought I wasn't pregnant, and now you're stuck with me.' "

"This is why you puked at dinner," Gabby says.

"Should have been your dad's first clue." To be honest, it probably should have been my first clue.

"Would you listen to yourself? We're talking about my dad. The man who picked up the boutonnieres for our dates to the prom. My dad once sat there with a pair of tweezers pulling tiny pieces of glass out of your foot when you dropped my mom's favorite crystal vase."

"Oh, don't remind me," I say.

"But that's my point. My dad loves you. Not like 'Oh, I'm

telling you my dad loves you.' I mean, he has love in his heart for you. My father loves you. Both my parents do. They like being there for you. My dad's not going to fire you when he finds out you're pregnant. He and my mom are going to jump for joy and tell everyone who will listen that the generation of grandchildren is finally arriving."

I laugh.

"Also, he can't fire you for being pregnant. It's illegal. That's Human Resources 101."

The minute she says "human resources," I remember talking to Joyce. I remember her telling me I have insurance and maternity leave. For a flash, I almost feel as if Gabby is right. That things will be OK.

"OK," I say. "So I still have a job."

"And you still have me, and my parents, and Mark, and . . ." She looks at the dog and smiles. "And Charlemagne."

"I have to call Michael and tell him, right?"

"Yes? No?" she says. "I have no idea. But I'll think about it with you. We'll weigh the pros and cons."

"Yeah?"

"Yeah. And we will come up with an answer. And then you'll do it."

She makes it sound so easy.

"And Ethan might not leave me?"

"He might not," she says, although I can tell by her voice that she has less confidence in this one. "But I can tell you, if he does, it's because it wasn't meant to be."

"You think things are meant to be?" I ask her. For some reason, I think I'll feel better if things are meant to be. It gets me off the hook, doesn't it? If things are meant to be, it means I don't have to worry so much about consequences and mistakes. I can take my hands off the wheel. Believing in fate is like living on cruise control.

"Are you kidding? I absolutely do. There is a force out there, call it what you will. I happen to believe that it's God," she says. "But it pushes us in the right direction, keeps us on the right path. If Ethan says he can't handle the fact that you're pregnant, he's not the one for you. You were meant for someone else. And we will handle *that* together, too. We will handle all of this together."

I close my eyes briefly, and when I open them, the world seems a little brighter. "So what do I do now?"

"Tomorrow morning, we're getting you prenatal vitamins and making an appointment to see an OB/GYN so we can figure out how far along you are."

"It would have to be at least eight weeks," I tell her. "I haven't slept with Michael in a while."

"OK," she says. "So we know that. Still, we'll make the appointment."

"Oh, no," I say out loud. "I had a beer. Last week at the bar."

"It's OK," I hear her say. "It's going to be fine. It happens. You weren't wasted. I saw you."

I am a terrible mother. Already. Already I am a terrible mother.

"You're not a terrible mother if that's what you're worried about," Gabby says, knowing how my brain works almost better than I do. She picks Charlemagne up off my lap and gestures for me to get up. She leads the two of us into my bedroom. "It happens. And it's OK. And starting tomorrow morning, you're going to learn all the things you have to stop doing and all of the things you have to start doing. And you're going to be phenomenal at all of it."

"You really think that?" I ask her.

"I really think that," she says.

I put on my pajamas. She gets in on one side of the bed. Charlemagne lies down with her.

"She's a cute one, this little Charlemagne," Gabby says. "How did she end up at my house?"

I laugh. "It's a long story," I say. "In which I make a snap decision that I now realize was probably hormone-driven."

Gabby laughs. "Well, she's precious," she says. "I like having her around."

I look at Charlemagne. "Me, too."

"I hate Mark's stupid dog allergy," she says. "Let's keep her in here all night and see if he itches. I bet you he won't. I bet you it's all in his head."

I laugh and get into bed next to Gabby. She holds my hand.

"Everything is going to be great, you know," she says.

I breathe in and out. "I hope so."

"No," she says. "Say it with me. Everything is going to be great."

"Everything is going to be great," I say.

"Everything is going to be great," she says again.

"Everything is going to be great."

You know, I almost believe it.

Gabby turns the light off.

"When you wake up in the middle of the night, terrified because you remember that you're pregnant," she says, "wake me. I'm here."

"OK," I say. "Thank you."

Charlemagne snuggles up between the two of us, and I wonder if maybe it's actually Gabby, Charlemagne, and me who were meant to be.

"Mark and I have started talking about when to have a baby," she says.

"Wow, really?" Even though I'm actually having a baby, I can't quite wrap my brain around people having babies.

"Yeah," she says. "Maybe soon. I could hurry up and get pregnant. We could have kids the same age."

"We'd force them to be best friends," I say.

"Naturally," she says. "Or maybe I'll just leave Mark. You and I could raise your baby together. That way, I don't even need to have one. Just me and you and the baby."

"With Charlemagne?" I ask.

"Yeah," she says. "The world's most adorable lesbian couple."

I laugh.

"Only problem is, I'm not attracted to you," she says.

"Ditto," I tell her.

"But just think of it. This baby would be raised by an interracial lesbian couple. It would get into all the good schools."

"Think of the pedigree."

"I've always said God made a mistake making us straight women."

I laugh and then correct her. "I'm trying to believe that God doesn't make mistakes."

Henry checks some stuff and puts the clipboard down.

"Dr. Winters says we can try the wheelchair," he tells me. His voice is solicitous. As if we're doing something taboo.

"Now?" I say. "Me and you?"

"Well, the female nurses can't bench-press as much I can. So yeah, I'll be the one lifting you into the chair."

"You never know," I say. "Maybe every single one of those nurses can bench the same as you, and you don't know because you never asked."

"Well," he says, "regardless of who can bench-press what, it's my job to lift you. But before I do, we've got some stuff to cover."

"Oh," I say. "OK, go for it."

He tells me it may hurt. He tells me it's going to be an adjustment. We can't do much at first, just get into the wheelchair and learn to move around a bit. Simply moving into the chair initially might wear me out. Then Henry starts unhooking me from a few of the machines that have come to feel like my third and fourth arms. He leaves the IV in. He tells me that while I'm in the hospital, that's coming with us.

"Do you feel ready?" he asks me once everything is set up and I'm all that's left to deal with.

"As I ever will," I tell him.

I'm scared. What if this hurts? What if this doesn't work? What if I have to stay in this bed for the rest of my life, and I can never move, and this is it for me? What if my life is sugar-free Jell-O and dry chicken dinners? I'll just lie here in a hospital gown that doesn't close in the back for the rest of my waking days.

Oh, God. Oh, God. This gown doesn't close in the back.

Henry is going to see my ass.

"You're going to see my butt, aren't you?" I ask as he moves toward me.

To his credit, he doesn't laugh at me. "I won't look," he says.

I'm not sure that answer is good enough.

"I'm a professional nurse, Hannah. Give me a little credit. I'm not gonna sneak a peek at your tush for kicks."

I can't help but laugh as I consider my choices. Which is to say that I consider that I don't really have a choice at all if I want to get out of this bed.

"Cool?" he says.

"Cool," I say.

He takes my legs and spins me. I inch myself toward him.

He gets up close to me. He puts his arm around my back, his other arm under my legs.

"One," he says.

"Two," I say with him.

"Three!" we say as he lifts me, and then, within seconds, I'm in the wheelchair.

I'm in a wheelchair.

Someone just had to lift me into a wheelchair.

I was going to have a baby, and now I'm not.

"OK?" Henry says.

"Yeah," I say, shaking my head and pushing the bad thoughts out of my mind. "Yes!" I add. "I'm excited about this! Where are we going?"

"Not much of anywhere this go-around," he says. "Right now, we just want to get you comfortable in the chair and familiar with it. Maybe just wheel around the room a bit."

I turn and look at him. "Oh, come on," I say. "I want out of this room. I've been peeing in a bedpan for days. I want to see something."

He looks at his watch. "I'm supposed to check on other patients."

I get it. He has a job. I'm a part of his job. "OK," I say. "Tell me how it works."

He starts showing me how to push the wheels and how to stop. We roam around the room. I push myself so hard that I crash into the wall, and Henry runs toward me and grabs me.

"Whoa, there," he says. "Take it slow."

"Sorry," I say. "Got away from me."

"I guess we know you probably won't ever be a race-car driver."

"Pretty sure I ruled that out when I got hit by a car."

Henry could, at this moment, feel bad for me. But he doesn't. I like that. I like that so much.

"Well, don't be a pilot, either," he says. "Or did you already cross that one off because you were hit by a plane?"

I look up at him, indignant. "Do you talk to all of your patients this way?" I ask him. There it is. The question I've been pondering for days. And I said it as if I didn't care about his answer in the slightest.

"Only the bad ones," he says. Then he leans down and grabs

the arms of my wheelchair. His face is in mine, so close that I can see the pores on his skin, the specks of gold in his eyes. If this were any other man in any other situation, I'd think he was going to kiss me. "If you happened to roll yourself out of this room," he says with a sly smile across his face, "I'm sure it would take a minute before I caught up with you and wheeled you back in here."

Henry slowly takes his arms off my chair, clearing the way.

I don't look at the door. I stare at him. "If I just happened to scoot my wheels this way," I say, "and push myself right out into the hallway . . ."

"I might not notice until you'd had a nice breath of air out there."

"So this is OK?" I say, looking at him but heading for the door.

He laughs. "Yeah, that's OK."

"And if I get to the threshold?"

He shrugs. "We'll see what happens."

I keep rolling myself forward. My arms are already tired from pushing myself. "If I just roll on right past it?"

He laughs. "You should probably take your eyes off me and watch where you're going," he says, just as I ram a wheel into the door frame.

"Oops," I say, backing up and then straightening. And then I roll myself right out into the hallway.

It's busier than I would have thought. There are more stations, more nurses, than I get a glimpse of in my room. And I'm sure it's the very same air I breathe from my hospital bed, but it seems fresher somehow out here. The hallway is even blander, more banal, than what I imagined from my bed. The floor underneath my wheels is squeaky clean. The walls on either side of me are an innocuous shade of oatmeal. But in some ways, I might as well have landed on the moon. That's how novel and foreign it feels for a split second.

"All right, Magellan," Henry says, grabbing the handles on the back of my chair. "Enough discovering for one day."

When we cross through the doorway back into my room, I thank him. He nods at me.

"Don't mention it."

He wheels me back to my bed.

"You ready?" he says.

I nod and brace myself. I know it's going to hurt when he picks me up, when he puts me down. "Go for it," I say.

He puts his arms underneath my legs. He tells me to put my arms around his neck, to hold on to him tightly. He leans over me, putting his other arm around my back. My forehead grazes his chin, and I can feel his stubble.

I land back on my bed with a thud. He helps me move my legs straight and puts my blanket back on me.

"How are you feeling?" he asks.

"I'm good," I say. "Good."

The truth is, I feel as if I am about to cry. I am about to break down into tears the size of marbles. I don't want to be back in this bed. I want to be up and moving and living and doing and seeing. I have tasted the glory of sitting in the hallway. I don't want to be back in this bed.

"Good," he says. "So I think Deanna is taking over for me in an hour or so. She'll be in to check on you and see how you're doing. I'll tell Dr. Winters that it went well today. I bet they will have you headed for physical therapy in no time. Keep it up."

I know that a nurse telling a patient to "keep it up" is normal. I know that. I think that is what bothers me about it.

Henry is by the door, heading out.

"Thanks," I call to him.

"My pleasure," he says. "See you tonight." And then he seems to suddenly feel nervous. "I just mean . . . if you're awake."

"I know what you mean," I say, smiling. I can't help but feel as if he's looking forward to seeing me. I suppose I could be wrong. But I don't think I am. "See you tonight."

He smiles at me, and then he's gone.

I'm so jittery that I can't sit still, and yet sitting still is all I'm capable of. So I turn on the TV. I sit and wait for something interesting to happen. It doesn't.

Deanna comes in a few times to check on me. Other than that, nothing happens.

The hospital is a boring, boring, boring, quiet, sterile, boring place. I turn the TV off and turn onto my side as best I can. I try to fall asleep.

I don't wake up until Gabby comes in around six thirty. She's got a pizza in her arms and a stack of American magazines.

"You snore so loud," Gabby says. "I swear I could hear you down the hall."

"Oh, shut up," I say. "The other night when you slept here, Henry compared you to a bulldozer."

She looks at me and puts the pizza and magazines down on the table. "Who is Henry?"

"The night nurse guy," I say. "Nobody."

The fact that I call him nobody makes it seem as if he's somebody. I realize that now. Gabby raises her eyebrow at me.

"Honestly," I say, my voice even. "He really is just the night nurse."

"OK . . ." she says.

And then I slump over and bury my red face in the palms of my hands. "Ugh," I say, looking back up at her. "I have a massive, embarrassing, soul-crushing crush on my night nurse."

I am eleven weeks pregnant. The baby is healthy. Everything looks good. The doctor, Dr. Theresa Winthrop, assured me that I am not the only woman who has gotten almost out of her first trimester before figuring out she was pregnant. I feel a little bit better about that.

On the way back to the car, Gabby stops me. "How are you feeling about all of this? You know that if you don't want to, you don't have to do this. Eleven weeks is early."

She's not telling me anything I don't know. I've been pro-choice my entire life. I believe, wholeheartedly, in the right to choose. And maybe, if I didn't believe I could give a child a home or a good life, maybe I'd avail myself of my other options. I don't know. We can't say what we would do in other circumstances. We can only know what we will do with the ones we face.

"I know I don't have to do this," I tell her. "I am choosing this."

She smiles. She can't help herself. "I have some time before I have to go back to the office," she says. "Can I buy you lunch?"

"That's OK," I tell her. "I want to get home before Charlemagne pees all over your house."

"It's fine," she says. "Mark didn't say anything this morning about feeling itchy, by the way. I'm convinced it's all in his head. I'm already planning to persuade him that we should keep both you and Charlemagne with us. We're near his office, actually. Should we go surprise him for lunch and begin our campaign? Plus, I want to see the look on his face when you tell him where we've been this morning."

"I'm honestly concerned that my dog is ruining your home."

"What's the point of owning your own place if you can't get a little pee on it?" Gabby says.

"OK. But don't come crying to me when she stains the hardwood."

We get into the car and drive only a few blocks before Gabby pulls into an underground lot and parks. I've never seen Mark's office before. It occurs to me that I also haven't been to the dentist in a while.

"You know, while we're here," I say, "I really should make an appointment to get my teeth cleaned."

Gabby laughs as we get into the elevator. She presses the button for the fifth floor, but it isn't responding. The doors close, and we somehow end up going down to the lowest level of the garage. The doors open, and an elderly woman gets in. It takes her about thirty years.

Gabby and I smile politely, and then Gabby hits the fifth-floor button again, which now lights up, a bright and inviting orange.

"Which floor?" she asks the elderly lady.

"Three, please."

We head up, and the door opens again on the floor we got in on. Gabby turns to me and rolls her eyes. "If I knew it was going to be ten stops on the elevator, I would have suggested we go eat first," she whispers to me. I laugh.

And there is Mark.

Kissing a blond woman in a pencil skirt.

Gabby left at around ten tonight to go home to Mark. I haven't seen Mark since I've been in the hospital. It's not weird necessarily, because Mark and I were never particularly close. But it seems strange that Gabby is so often here on nights and lunch breaks and Mark hasn't even stopped by. Gabby keeps saying that he's been working late a lot. Apparently, he had to attend a dental conference in Anaheim this week. I don't know much about the life of a dentist, but I always figured dentists were the kind of people who were home in time for dinner. I guess that's not the case with Mark. Either way, his working benefits me greatly, since Gabby spends her time with me instead, which is really all I want anyway.

Since she left, I've just been reading the magazines she brought. I like these magazines much better than the British ones. Which is good, because I slept through most of the day today, so I know I won't be tired for quite some time.

"I knew you'd be up," Henry says when he comes into the room. He's pushing a wheelchair.

"I thought you'd take the night off," I say.

He shakes his head. "I went home this morning. Slept my eight hours, had some dinner, watched some TV. I got in a little while ago."

"Oh," I say.

"And I checked on all my other patients, and they are all sleeping and not in need of my assistance."

"So . . . another lesson?" I ask.

"I'd call this more of an adventure." He has a wild look in his eye. As if we are doing something we shouldn't be doing. It's exciting, the idea of doing something I shouldn't be doing. All I've been doing is healing.

"All right!" I say. "Let's do it. What do I need to do?"

He pulls the rail down on my bed. He moves my legs. We move the same way we moved this morning, only faster, easier, more familiar. I'm in the chair within a few seconds.

I look down, my legs in front of me, in the chair. Henry grabs my blanket and puts it in my lap.

"In case you get cold," he says.

"And so I don't flash anyone," I say.

"Well, that, too, but I didn't want to say it." He stands behind me, attaches my morphine bag to my chair, and pushes me forward.

"Where are we going?" I ask.

"Anywhere we want," he says.

We get out into the hallway.

"So?" he says. "Where first?"

"Cafeteria?" I say.

"Do you really want more cafeteria food?" he asks.

"Good point. How about a vending machine?" I offer.

He nods, and away we go.

I'm outside of my room! I'm moving!

Some doctors and nurses stand outside a room or two, but for the most part, the halls are empty. It's also quiet except for the occasional regulatory beeping.

But I feel as if I'm flying down a California freeway with the top down.

"Favorite movie," I say as we make our way around one of the many corners of the hospital.

"*The Godfather,*" he says with confidence.

"Boring answer," I tell him.

"What? Why?"

"Because it's obvious. Everyone loves *The Godfather.*"

"Well, sorry," he says to me. "I can't love a different movie just because everyone loves the movie I love."

I turn back to look at him. He makes a face at me. "The heart wants what it wants, I guess," I say.

"I guess," he says. "You?"

"Don't have one," I say.

Henry laughs. "You can't make me pick one if you don't have one."

"Why not? It's a fair question. I just don't happen to have an answer."

"Just pick one at random. One you like."

"That's the problem. My answer is always changing. Sometimes I think my favorite movie is *The Princess Bride*. But then I think, no, *Toy Story* is obviously the best movie of all time. And then, other times, I'm convinced that no movie will ever be as good as *Lost in Translation.* I can never decide."

"You think too much," he says. "That's your problem. You're trying too hard to find the perfect answer when *an answer* will do."

"What do you mean?" I ask. We're stopped in front of a soda vending machine, but this isn't what I meant. "Wait, I meant a snack machine. Not a Coke machine."

"My apologies, Queen Hannah of the Hallway," he says, and pushes us forward. "If someone asks you your favorite movie, just say *The Princess Bride*."

"But sometimes I'm not sure it *is* my favorite movie."

"But it will do, is what I'm saying. It's like when I asked you what kind of pudding you liked, and you named all three flavors. Just pick a flavor. You don't need to find the perfect thing all the time. Just find one that works, and go with it. If you had, we'd be on to favorite colors by now."

"Your favorite color is navy blue," I say.

"Yep," he says. "But you can tell that from my scrubs, so you haven't convinced me you're telepathic."

"What's mine?" I ask him. I can see a vending machine at the end of the hall. I also really hope Henry has money, because I didn't bring any.

"I don't know," he says. "But I bet you it's between two colors."

I roll my eyes at him, but he can't see me. He's right. That's what's frustrating.

"Purple and yellow," I say.

"Let me guess," he says in a teasing voice. "Sometimes you like yellow, but then, when you see purple, you think maybe that's your favorite."

"Oh, shut up," I say. "They are both pretty colors."

"And," he says as we reach the machine, "either of them would suffice."

He pulls a dollar out of his pocket.

"I have one buck," he says. "We have to share."

"Some date you are," I joke, and immediately wish I could take it back.

He laughs and lets it go. "What will it be?"

I search the machine. Salty, sweet, chocolate, peanut butter, pretzels, peanuts. It's impossible. I look back at him.

"You're gonna be mad," I say.

He laughs. "You have to pick one. I only have a dollar."

I look at all of them. I bet Henry likes Oreos. Everyone likes Oreos. Literally every human.

"Oreos," I say.

"Oreos it is," he says. He puts the dollar into the slot and punches the buttons. The Oreos fall just in front of me, at my level. I pull them out of the drawer and open them. I give him one.

"Thank you," he says.

"Thank *you*," I say. "You paid for them."

He bites it. I eat it whole. "There's no wrong way to eat an Oreo," he says.

"That's Reese's. There's no wrong way to eat a Reese's," I correct him. "Oh, man! We should have gotten Reese's."

He pulls another dollar out of his scrubs and puts it into the machine.

"What? You said you only had a dollar! You lied!"

"Oh, calm down. I was always going to buy you two things," he says. "I'm just trying to help you be decisive."

He laughs at me as he says it, and I open my mouth wide, outraged. I hit him on the arm. "Jerk," I say.

"Hey," he says. "I bought you *two* desserts."

The Reese's fall. I grab them and give him one again. "You're right," I say. "And you took me on a journey into the hallway. Which you probably weren't supposed to do."

"It wasn't specifically sanctioned, no," he says, biting his peanut butter cup. Mine is already gone. I practically swallowed it whole.

I could ask him, right now, why he's being so nice to me. Why he's taking so much time with me. But I'm afraid if I call attention to it, it will stop happening. So I don't say anything. I just smile at him. "Will you take me the long way back?" I ask.

"Of course," he says. "Do you want to see how far you can wheel yourself before your arms get tired?"

"Yeah," I say. "That sounds great."

He's a great nurse. An attentive listener. Because that is truly all I want in this world. I want to try to do something myself, knowing that when I have nothing left, someone will take me the rest of the way.

He turns me around to face the right direction, and he stands behind me. "Go for it," he says. "I got you."

I push, and he follows me.

I push.

And I push.

And I push.

We get through two big hallways before I need a rest.

"I'll take it from here," he says, grabbing the back of my chair and pushing me forward. He leads us to an elevator and pushes the call button. "You sleepy? You want to head back?"

I turn as best I can to look at him. "Let's say I'm not sleepy, what would we do?"

He laughs. The elevator opens. He pushes me in. "I should have known you wouldn't choose sleep."

"You didn't answer my question. What would we do?"

He ignores me for the moment and pushes the button for

the second floor. We descend. When the door opens, he pushes me out and down a long hallway.

"You're really not going to tell me?"

Henry smiles and shakes his head. And then we turn a corner, and he opens a door.

The cold, fresh air rushes over me.

He pushes me through. We are on a smoking patio. A tiny, dirty, dingy, sooty, beautiful, refreshing, life-affirming smoking patio.

I breathe in deeply.

I can hear cars driving by. I can see city lights. I can smell tar and metal. Finally, there are no walls or windows between me and the spinning world.

Despite my best efforts, I feel myself tearing up.

The air funneling in and out of my lungs feels better, brighter, than all the air I've inhaled since I woke up. I close my eyes and listen to the sounds of traffic. When a few of my tears fall from my eyes, Henry crouches down next to me.

He is on my level. Once again, we are face-to-face.

He pulls a tissue out of his pocket and hands it to me. And right then, as his hand grazes mine and I catch his eye, I don't need to wonder what would happen if he and I met at a dinner party. I know what would happen.

He would walk me home.

"Ready?" he says. "To go back?"

"Yeah," I say, because I know it's time, because I know he has a job to do, because I know we aren't supposed to be out here. Not because I'm ready. I'm not ready. But as he pushes me through that door and it closes behind us, I am, for the first time, so full of joy to be alive that I'd be happy going just about anywhere.

"You're a great nurse," I tell him as we head back. "Do you know that?"

"I hope so," he says. "I love my job. It's the only thing I've ever really felt I was meant for."

We get back to my room. He puts my wheelchair by my bed.

He puts his arms underneath me. "Put your arms around my neck," he says. And I do.

He lifts me and holds me there for a moment, the full weight of my body in his arms. I am so close to him that I can smell his soap on his skin, the chocolate still faintly on his breath. His eyelashes are longer and darker than I noticed before, his lips fuller. He has a faint scar under his left eye.

He puts me down in my bed. I swear he holds on to me just a moment longer than he needs to.

It is perhaps the most romantic moment of my life, and I'm in a hospital gown.

Life is unpredictable beyond measure.

"Excuse me," comes a stern voice from the hallway. Both Henry and I look up to see a female nurse standing in the doorway to my room. She is older and a bit weathered. She has her light-colored hair pulled up in a butterfly clip. She is wearing pale pink scrubs and a patterned matching scrub jacket.

Henry pulls away from me abruptly.

"I thought Eleanor was covering for you the second half of the night," the nurse says.

He shakes his head. "You might be thinking of Patrick. Patrick needs his shift covered until seven."

"OK," she says. "Can I speak to you when you're done here?"

"Sure," Henry says. "I'll be right there."

The nurse nods and leaves.

Henry's demeanor changes. "Good night," he says as he moves to leave.

He's almost out the door when I call to him. "Thank you," I say. "I really—"

"Don't mention it," he says, not looking back at me, already out the door.

Gabby is throwing things around the house. Big things. Porcelain things. They are crashing and shattering. Charlemagne is by my feet. We are standing at the door to the guest room. I'm trying to stay out of it. But I'm pretty much in it.

Gabby never went back to work. I drove us home while she stared straight ahead, virtually oblivious to the world. She didn't say much all afternoon. I kept trying to ask her if she was all right. I kept trying to offer her food or some water, but she kept refusing. She's been as responsive as a statue all afternoon.

And then, the second Mark came through the door and said, "Let me explain," that's when she reanimated.

"I'm not interested in anything you have to say," Gabby said.

And he had the gall to say, "C'mon, Gabby, I deserve a chance to—"

That's when she threw a magazine at him. I couldn't blame her. Even I would have started throwing things at him then, when I heard those stupid words come out of his mouth. She started by throwing whatever was nearby. More magazines, a book that was on the coffee table. Then she threw the remote control. It cracked, and the batteries went flying. That's when Charlemagne and I hightailed it to safer ground.

"Why is there a dog here?" Mark asked. He started scratching his wrists slowly. I don't even think he knew he was doing it.

"Don't ask about the fucking dog!" Gabby said. "She was here all night, and you didn't even notice. So just shut the fuck up about the dog, OK?"

"Gabby, talk to me."

"Screw you."

"Why were you at my office today?" he asked her.

"Oh, you've got to be kidding me! You've got a lot worse problems than how you got caught!"

That's when she walked into the kitchen and started breaking big stuff. Porcelain stuff.

Which brings us to now.

"Who is she?" Gabby screams.

Mark doesn't answer. He can't look at her.

She pauses ever so briefly and looks around at the mess. Her shoulders slump. She can see me off to the side. She catches my eye. "What am I doing?" she says. She doesn't say it to me or Mark, really. She says it to the room, the house.

I take advantage of the moment and walk, through the shards, to put my arms around her. Mark moves toward us, too.

"No," I say abruptly and with force. "Don't you touch her."

He backs away.

"You're going to move out," Gabby says to him as I hold her. I start rubbing her back, trying to soothe her, but she pushes me away. She gathers her strength. "Get your shit and leave," she says.

"This is my place, too," Mark says. "And I'm just asking for a few minutes to talk this out."

"Get. Your. Shit. And leave," Gabby says. Her voice is strong and stoic. She is a force to be reckoned with.

Mark considers fighting back more; you can see it on his face. But he gives up and goes into the bedroom.

"You're doing the right thing," I tell her.

"I know that," she says.

She sits down at the dining-room table, catatonic once again.

Charlemagne starts walking toward us, but Gabby sees her before I do.

"No!" she shouts at the dog. "Be careful."

She stands up and gently walks over to Charlemagne and picks her up. She carries her in her arms over the broken plates. She sits back down at the table with Charlemagne in her lap.

Mark flies through various rooms in the house, getting his things. He slams doors. He sighs loudly. Now seems like the time to start realizing that I never liked him.

This goes on for at least forty-five minutes. The house is silent except for the sounds of a man moving out. Gabby is practically frozen still. The only time she moves is to reposition Charlemagne in her lap. I stand by, close, ready to move or to speak at a moment's notice.

Finally, Mark comes out into the living room. We stare at him from the dining-room table. "I'm leaving," he says.

Gabby doesn't say anything back.

He waits, hoping for something. He gets nothing from her.

He walks to the front door, and Charlemagne jumps down onto the floor.

"Charlemagne, no," I say. I have to say it twice before she stays put.

Mark looks at her, clearly still confused about why there is a dog named Charlemagne in the house, but he knows he won't get any answers.

He opens the front door. He's almost gone by the time Gabby speaks up.

"How long has this been going on?" she asks him. Her voice

is strong and clear. It does not waver. It does not break. She is not about to burst into tears. She is fully in control. At least for this moment.

He looks at her and shakes his head. He looks up at the ceiling. There are tears in his eyes. He rubs them away and sniffs them back up. "It doesn't matter," he says. His voice, too, is strong. But it is full of shame; that much is clear.

"I said, how long has this been going on?"

"Gabby, don't do this—"

"How long?"

Mark looks at his feet and then at her. "Almost a year," he says.

"You can go," she says.

He turns away and does just that. She goes to the window to watch him leave.

When he's finally gone, she turns to me.

"I'm so sorry, Gabby," I say to her. "I'm so sorry. He's an asshole."

Gabby looks at me. "You slept with somebody's husband," she says. She doesn't need to draw any direct conclusions from this. She doesn't need to say out loud what I know she's thinking in her head.

"Yep," I say, both owning my actions and feeling deep shame for them. "And it was wrong. Just like this was wrong."

"But I told you it didn't mean you were a bad person," she says. "I told you that you could still be a wonderful, beautiful person."

I nod. "Yeah, you did."

"And you did this to somebody."

I want to claim that the situation is different. I want to say that what I did with Michael isn't as bad as what this other woman has done with Mark. I want to, once again, hide behind the fact that I didn't *know*. But I did know. And what I did was no different from this.

I slept with someone's husband. I shouldn't have done that.

And now I'm having a baby by that man. And I'm going to raise that baby.

Pretending this child isn't the result of a mistake I made doesn't make it any less true.

And I know now that I have to face things. I have to admit things in order to move forward.

"Yes," I say. "I did a terrible thing. Just like Mark and that woman did a terrible thing to you."

Gabby looks at me. I pull her over to the sofa, and I sit us both down.

"I made a mistake. And when I did, you saw that I was still a good person, and you reserved your judgment, because you had faith in me. That was a wonderful gift. Your belief in me. It's made me believe in myself. It's made me start to change the things I've needed to change. But you don't have to do that for them. You can just hate them."

I swear, she almost smiles.

"We can both just hate them for as long as we need to, and then, one day, when we feel stronger, we'll probably forgive them for being imperfect, for doing a terrible thing. One day, sooner than you think, I bet we'll go so far as to wish them the best and not give them another thought, because we'll have moved on with our lives. But you don't have to believe that right now. You can just hate him. And I can hate him for what he did to you. And maybe one day, he'll change. He'll be a person who did something in the past that he would never, ever, ever do again."

She looks at me.

"Or he'll just be shitty forever, and you're better off being as far away from him as possible," I tell her. "There's that theory, too."

She smiles a smile so small and so quick that I start to question if I really saw it. "I'm sorry," she says finally. "I didn't mean to bring you into this. I'm just . . . I'm sorry."

"Don't give it another thought," I say.

Gabby cries into her hands and then collapses into my arms. "He's not even allergic to dogs," she says. "I've wanted a dog for years, and I couldn't because of him, but I swear, it's all in his head. I bet you he's not even allergic to them."

"Well, now you've got one," I say. "So there's a silver lining. Why don't we just sit here and think of silver linings for right now? What's another one? Did he always forget to take out the trash? Did he leave his wet towel on the bed?"

She looks up at me. "His penis is small," she says. "Seriously, like a golf pencil." And then she starts laughing. "Oh, it feels good to admit that. I don't have to keep pretending his penis isn't small."

I start laughing with her. "That wasn't exactly where I thought you were going to go with this, but OK! That's a good one."

Gabby laughs. It's a deep belly laugh. "Oh, God, Hannah," she says. "The first time I saw it, I thought, *Where's the rest of it?"*

I laugh so hard when she says this that I have to struggle to breathe. "You are making this up," I say.

"Nope," she says, her hands up in the air as if she's swearing to God. "He just has a terrible penis."

Both of us are laughing so hard that tears are coming out

of our eyes. And then, abruptly, it is time to stop. I can see the mood change much the same way you can feel summer turn to fall. One day, everything's sunny, and then, suddenly, it's not.

"Oh, Hannah," she says, burying herself into my chest. Charlemagne sits at our feet.

"Shhh," I say, rubbing her back. "It's OK. It's going to be OK."

"I'm not sure that's true," she says into my chest.

"It is," I say. "It is true."

She looks up at me, her eyes now bloodshot and glassy. Her face is splotchy. She looks desperate and sick. I've never seen her like this. She's seen me like this. But I've never seen her like this.

"I know it's going to be OK, because you are Gabrielle Jannette Hudson. You are unstoppable. You are the strongest woman I've ever known."

"Strongest person," she says.

"Hm?" I'm not sure I quite heard her.

"I'm the strongest *person* you know," she says, wiping her eyes. "Gender is irrelevant."

She's absolutely right. She is the strongest person I know. Her gender is irrelevant. "You're right," I say. "Just one more reason I know you are going to get through this."

She starts heaving tears. She's hyperventilating. "Maybe he had a good reason. Or there is something I misunderstood."

I want to tell her that she could be right, that maybe there is some piece of information that makes all of this better. I want to tell her that because I want her to be happy. But I also know it's not true. And part of loving someone, part of being the recipient of trust, is telling the truth even when it's awful.

"He was cheating on you for almost a year," I tell her. "He didn't make a one-time mistake or get confused."

She looks up at me and starts crying again. "So my marriage is over?"

"That's up to you," I say. "You have to decide what you will tolerate and what you can live with. Why don't you try to relax and I'll get you some dinner?"

"No," she says. "I can't eat."

"Well, what can I do for you?"

"Just sit here," she says. "Just sit next to me."

"You got it," I tell her.

"Charlemagne, too," she says. I get up and pick up Charlemagne. The three of us sit here on the couch.

"My husband is cheating on me, and you're pregnant by a married man," Gabby says.

I close my eyes, taking it in.

"Life sucks," she says.

"Sometimes, yeah," I tell her.

We are both quiet.

"It hurts," she says. She starts crying again. "It hurts so bad. Deep in my gut, it hurts."

"I know," I tell her. "You and I are a team, right? Whatever you face in life, I'll face it with you. Everything that you were prepared to do for me last night, I'm prepared to do for you today. So count on me, OK? Let's get through this together. Lean on me. Squeeze my hand."

She looks at me and smiles.

"When it hurts so bad you don't think you can stand it," I say, "squeeze my hand." I put my hand out for her, and she takes it.

She starts crying again, and she squeezes.

And I think to myself that if, by being here, I have taken away one one-hundredth of the pain that Gabby feels, then maybe I have more of a life's purpose than I ever thought.

"Divide the pain in two," I tell her. "And give half of it to me."

Gabby comes in on Saturday morning, and before she can even get into the room, I tell her to stop. Deanna is standing by my bed.

"Wait," I say to Gabby. "Wait right there."

Deanna smiles and puts out her hand. "You ready?" she says. I nod. Deanna helps me get my feet on the ground. I push my weight onto Deanna's hands, and she helps me put weight on my feet. I'm standing up. Actually standing up. Not without resting on another human being, but still. I'm standing up. She and I have been practicing all morning.

"OK," I say, "I gotta sit down." Deanna helps rest me back on the bed. The relief is immense.

"Oh, my God!" Gabby says, clapping for me as if I'm a child. "Look what you did! This is nuts!"

I smile and laugh. My energy and Gabby's excitement must be infectious, because Deanna is laughing and smiling with us.

"It's crazy, right?" I say. "I've been practicing as much as possible. This morning, Dr. Winters was giving me some tips on how to steady myself. I can't move just yet, really. But I can stand."

"Wow," Gabby says, putting down her purse.

She moves toward us. Deanna helps me get back into bed.

"I am so impressed," Gabby says. "You're ahead of schedule."

"I'll come by to check on you soon," Deanna says. "Good job today."

"Thank you," I tell her as she leaves.

When she's gone, I tell Gabby about last night.

"Henry took me outside," I say.

"You walked outside?"

"No," I say. "In a wheelchair. He took me out on the smoking patio."

"Oh," she says.

This is not sounding nearly as romantic as it felt.

"Oh, never mind," I say. "You had to be there."

She laughs. "Well, I'm proud of you that you stood up today."

"I know! Before you know it, I'll be crawling and eating solid foods."

"Well, don't do it when I'm not here!" she says. "You know I like to get that stuff on videotape."

I laugh. "Just be glad you don't have to change my diaper," I tell her. I'm just making a joke, but it hits a little too close to home. I still can't get to the bathroom on my own. "How are you?" I ask, inviting her to sit down. "How is Mark?"

"He's good," she says. "Yeah."

Something seems off. "What's on your mind?" I ask her.

"No, nothing," she says. "He seems very . . . I don't know. I think the accident, all of this craziness, maybe it jolted something in him. He's been very sweet, very attentive. Bringing me flowers. He bought me a necklace the other day." She starts playing with the one around her neck. It's a string of gold with a diamond at the center.

"That one?" I say, leaning forward. I take the diamond in my hand. "Wow, is that a real diamond?"

"I know," she says. "I made a joke when he gave it to me, like 'OK, what did you do wrong?' "

I laugh. "On TV, it's always that a man comes home with

flowers and jewelry when he invites his boss over for Thanksgiving dinner without asking you first or something."

"Right," she says, laughing. "Maybe he's cheating on me. I'll have to go home and look at all of his shirt collars for lipstick stains, right?"

"Yeah," I say. "If soap operas are any indication, you will find bright red lipstick stains on his collar if he's cheating."

Gabby laughs.

For a moment, I know we are both thinking of the fact that I was once the woman wives watch out for. That I lost a married man's baby. Sometimes I wonder if this accident wasn't a clean slate. If it wasn't permission to start again, to do better.

And then I wonder, if it is a clean slate, what am I going to do with it?

"Well, what are you doing here?" I ask her. "Don't hang out with your lame best friend. Go hang out with your thoughtful, romantic husband. I mean, he could be buying you cashmere and chocolate right now."

"No, right now, I'd rather be here. I'd rather be with you. Besides, Mark said he had to go into work today. Said he'd be unavailable until late tonight. There were billing problems at work, I guess."

"He doesn't have an office manager or someone to do that stuff?"

Gabby thinks it over. "Well, no, he does," she says. "But he says lately, he needs more time to look over their work. So what should we do today? Should I get us a book to read together? Are we watching *Law & Order*?"

I shake my head. "Nope. We're going on an adventure," I tell her.

"Where are we going?"

"Wherever we want," I tell her, and I point to the wheelchair in the corner.

She brings it over, and I skooch myself closer to the edge of the bed.

"Can you pull the railing down?" I ask her. "It's that button there, and then you just press down."

She's got it.

"Now, just move the wheelchair to the side, just to the . . . yeah."

I swing my legs down off the bed.

"Sorry, one last thing. Can you just grab me around my waist? I can do this. I just need a little bit of help."

She grabs me under my arms. "Ready?" she says.

"Yep!" I say, and at the same time Gabby lifts me, I push myself up.

It's not graceful. It's actually quite painful, very noisy, and I end up with my ass half hanging out of my gown, but I'm in the seat. I'm mobile.

"Can you . . ." I say, gesturing toward the half of my gown.

"Oh, right," Gabby says, and she moves it as I try to lift myself just a little to get situated.

"Thanks," I say. "Now, can you take my morphine bag and put it on my chair here?"

She does.

"Ready?" I ask her.

"Ready," she says.

"Oh!" I say, right before I start to push. "Do you have dollar bills?"

"Yeah," she says. "I think I have one or two. Why, are we going to a strip club?"

I laugh as she grabs her purse.

And then we are off.

I see Deanna in the hallway, and she tells me not to go too far. I lead us down the hallway and to the right, just as Henry led me the other day.

"Do you have a favorite movie?" I ask Gabby. If I had to guess, I'd say her favorite movie is *When Harry Met Sally . . .*

"*When Harry Met Sally . . .*" she says. "Why do you ask?"

"I don't know what my favorite movie is," I say.

"Why does that matter? Lots of people don't have a favorite movie."

"But, like, even for the purposes of the conversation, I can't just *pick* one. I can't just decide on a movie to say is my favorite."

"I hope it isn't news to you that you're indecisive."

I laugh. "Henry says that you don't need *the* answer. You just need *an* answer."

"Henry, Henry, Henry," Gabby says, laughing at me. We come to an intersection in the hallway, and I veer left. I'm pretty sure the vending machines are to the left.

"Hardy-har-har, but I'm asking an honest question," I tell her. I'm still pushing myself down the hall. I've still got the strength to keep going.

"What are you actually asking me?"

"Do you think it's true that you don't need the perfect answer but just, you know, *an* answer?"

"To your favorite movie, yes. But sometimes there is only one answer. So I don't think this is a universal philosophy."

"Like what?"

"Like who you marry, for one. That's the biggest example that comes to mind."

"You think there is only one person for everyone?"

"You don't?" The way she asks me this, it's as if it has never occurred to her that I might not. I might as well have said, "You think we're breathing oxygen?"

"I don't know," I say. "I know I did think that at one time. But . . . I'm not sure anymore."

"Oh," she says. "I guess I never considered the alternative. I just assumed, you know, God or fate or life or whatever you want to call it leads you to the person you were meant to be with."

"That's how you feel about Mark?"

"I think Mark is the person life led me to, yeah. He's the only one for me. If I thought there was someone else better suited for me, why would I have married him? You know? I married him because he's the one."

"So he's your soul mate?"

She thinks about it. "Yes? I mean, yeah. I guess you'd say that's a soul mate."

"What if you two end up getting divorced?"

"Why would you say a thing like that?"

"I'm just asking a hypothetical. If there is only one person for everyone, what happens when soul mates can't make it work?"

"If you can't make it work, you aren't soul mates," she tells me.

I hear her out. I get it. It makes sense. If you believe in fate, if you believe something is pushing you toward your destiny, that would include the person you're supposed to spend the rest of your life with. I get it.

"But not cities," I say.

"Huh?"

"You don't have to find the perfect city to live in. You just have to find one that will work."

"Right," she says.

"So I can just pick one and leave it at that," I say. "I don't have to test them all out until something clicks."

She laughs. "No."

"I think I've been jumping from place to place thinking that I'm supposed to find the perfect life for myself, that it's out there somewhere and I have to find it. And it has to be *just so*. You know?"

"I know that you've always been searching for something, yeah," Gabby says. "I always assumed you'd know it when you found it."

"I don't know, I'm starting to think maybe you just pick a place and stay there. You pick a career and do it. You pick a person and commit to him."

"I think as long as you're happy and you're doing something good with your life, it really doesn't matter whether you went out and found the perfect thing or you chose what you knew you could make work for you."

"Doesn't it scare you?" I ask her. "To think that you might have gone in the wrong direction? And missed the life you were destined for?"

Gabby thinks about it, taking my question seriously. "Not really," she says.

"Why not?"

"I don't know. I guess because life's short? And you just kind of have to get on with it."

"So should I move to London or not?" I ask her.

She smiles. "Oh, I see where this is going. If you want to go to London, you should. But that's as much as you'll get from me. I don't want you to go. I want you to stay here. It rains a lot there. You know, for what it's worth."

I laugh at her. "OK, fair enough. We have a bigger problem than London anyway."

"We do?"

"We're lost," I say.

Gabby looks left and then right. She can see what I see. All the hallways look the same. We're in no-man's-land.

"We're not near the vending machines?" she asks.

"Hell if I know," I say. "I have no idea where we are."

"OK," she says, taking hold of my chair. "Let's try to get ourselves out of this mess."

Gabby insisted on going to work today. I tried to persuade her to stay home, not to put extra pressure on herself, but she said that the only way she could feel remotely normal was to go to work.

Ethan called me twice yesterday, and I didn't call him back. I texted him telling him that I couldn't talk. I fell asleep last night knowing I'd have to face him today. I mean, if I keep avoiding him, he'll know something is up.

So I woke up this morning, resolved to work this out. I called Ethan and asked if he was free tonight. He told me to come by his place at around seven.

Which means I have the rest of the day to call Michael. I want to have answers for Ethan's questions when he asks. I want to have all of my ducks in a row. And this is a big duck.

I take a shower. I take Charlemagne for a walk. I stare at my computer, reading the Internet for what feels like hours. When it's six o'clock in New York, when I know Michael will be leaving work, I pick up my phone. I sit down on my bed and dial.

It rings.

And rings.

And rings.

And then it goes to voice mail.

On some level, I'm relieved. Because I don't want to have to have this conversation at all.

"Hi, Michael. It's Hannah. Call me back when you have a minute. We have something we need to talk about. OK, 'bye."

I throw myself backward onto the bed. My pulse is racing. I start thinking of what I'll do if he never calls me back. I start imagining that maybe he will make this decision *for* me. Maybe I'll call him a few times, leave a few messages, and he will just never call back. And I will know that I tried to do the right thing but was unable to. I could live with that.

My phone rings.

"Hannah," he says, the moment I say hello. His voice is stern, almost angry. "We're done. You said so yourself. You can't call me. I finally have things back on track with my family. I'm not going to mess that up again."

"Michael," I say to him. "Just hold on one minute, OK?" Now I'm pissed.

"OK," he says.

"I'm pregnant," I tell him finally.

He's so quiet I think the line has gone dead. "I'll call you back in three minutes," he says, and then he hangs up.

I pace around the room. I feel a flutter in my stomach.

The phone rings again.

"Hi," I say.

"OK, so what do we do?" he asks. I can hear that he's in a closed space. His voice is echoing. He sounds as if he's in a bathroom.

"I don't know," I say.

"I can't leave my wife and children," he says adamantly.

"I'm not asking you to," I tell him. I hate this conversation. I have been working to put this behind me, and now I'm right back in the middle of it.

"So what are you saying?" he asks.

"I'm not saying anything except that I thought you should know. It seemed wrong not to tell you."

"I can't do this," he says. "I made a mistake, being with you. I can see that now. It was my fault. I shouldn't have done it. It was a mistake. Jill knows what I did. We're finally in a good place. I love my children. I cannot let anything ruin that."

"I'm not asking anything of you," I say to him. "That's the truth. I just thought you should know."

"OK," he says. He is quiet for a moment and then, timidly, asks me what he's probably wanted to ask me since I brought this up. "Have you considered . . . not having the baby?"

"If you're going to ask me to have an abortion, Michael, you should at least say the word." Such a coward.

"Have you considered having an abortion?" he asks.

"No," I tell him. "I'm not considering having an abortion."

"What about adoption?"

"Why do you care?" I ask him. "I'm having the baby. I'm not asking for your money or your attention or support, OK?"

"OK," he says. "But I don't know how I feel about having a baby out there."

These are the sorts of things that people should really be thinking about before they have sex, but I'm one to talk.

"Well, then, step up to the plate and deal with it or don't," I say. "That's your business."

"I suppose it's no different from donating sperm," he says. He's not talking to me. He's talking to himself. But you know what? I don't want him to help me raise this baby, and he doesn't want to help me. Clearly, he's just looking to absolve himself of any guilt or responsibility, and if that's what it takes to make this simple, then I will help him do just that.

"Think of it like that," I tell him. "You donated sperm."

"Right," he says. "That's all it is."

I want to tell him he's a complete ass. But I don't. I let him tell himself whatever he needs to. I know that this baby could ruin his family. I don't want that. That's the truth. I don't want to break up a family, regardless of who is right and wrong. And I don't need him. And I'm not sure that my child is better off having him around. He hasn't shown himself to be a very good man.

"OK," I say.

"OK," he says.

Just as I am about to get off the phone, I say one thing, for my unborn kid. "If you ever change your mind, you can call me. If you want to meet the baby. And I hope that if he or she wants to meet you one day, you'll be open to it."

"No," he says.

His answer jars me. "What?"

"No," he says again. "You are making the choice to have this baby. I do not want you to have it. If you have it, you have to deal with the child not having a father. I'm not going to live my life knowing that any day a kid could show up."

"Classy" is all I say.

"I have to protect what I already have," he says. "Are we done here?"

"Yeah," I tell him. "We're done."

We are lost in the maternity ward, and we can't seem to find our way out. First, we were stuck in the delivery department. Now we're outside the nursery.

The last thing I want to do right now is look at beautiful, precious babies. But I notice Gabby is no longer behind me. She's staring.

"We are going to start trying soon," she says. She's not even looking at me. She's looking at the babies.

"What are we going to start trying to do?"

She looks at me as if I'm so stupid I'm embarrassing her. "No, Mark and I. We're going to try to have a baby."

"You want to have a kid?"

"Yeah," she says. "I was going to ask what you thought when you got here, but I didn't get a chance before the accident, and . . . and then, when you woke up . . ."

"Right," I say. I don't want her to say it out loud. The inference is enough. "But you think you're ready? That's so exciting!" My own ambivalence about a baby doesn't, for a minute, take away from the joy of her having one. "A little half Gabby, half Mark," I add. "Wow!"

"I know. It's a really exciting thought. Super scary, too. But really exciting."

"So you'll be . . . doing the ol' . . . actually, is there even a popular euphemism for trying to have a baby?"

"I don't know," she says. "But yes, we'll be doing the ol' . . ."

"Wow," I say again. "I just can't believe that we are old enough to the point where you're going to actually *try* to get pregnant."

"I know," she says. "You spend your whole life learning how *not* to get pregnant, and then, one day, you suddenly have to reverse all of that training."

"Well, this is awesome," I say. "You and Mark are so good together. You're going to be great parents."

"Thank you," she says, and squeezes my shoulder.

A nurse comes up to us. "Which one are you visiting?" she asks.

"Oh, no," Gabby says. "Sorry. We are just lost. Can you point us back to general surgery?"

"Down the hall, take your first right, then your second left. You'll see a vending machine. Follow that hall to the end, take a left . . ." The directions go on and on. Clearly, I took us much farther away than I meant to.

"OK," Gabby says. "Thank you." She turns to me. "Let's go."

We go past what looks like a neonatal unit, maybe intensive care. And then we go through double doors and find ourselves in the children's ward.

"I don't think this is the right way," I say.

"She said there was a left up here somewhere . . ."

I look over at the nurses and then peek through the windows as we move farther down the hall. It's mostly toddlers and elementary-school-age kids. I see a few teenagers. Almost all of them are in hospital beds, hooked up to machines, as I have been. A lot of them wear stockings or caps. It occurs to me that they are covering their bald heads.

"OK," Gabby says. "You're right. We're lost."

I pull over to the side of the hallway.

"I'm just going to go ask a nurse for a map," Gabby says.

"OK," I say.

From my vantage point, I can see into one room with two kids in it. The kids are talking. Two preteen girls in separate beds. A doctor is standing to the side, talking to a set of parents. Both parents look confused and distraught. The doctor leaves. As he does, I can see there is a nurse standing with them. The nurse starts to leave, too, and the parents catch her at the door. They are close enough to me now that I can make out the conversation.

"What did all of that mean?" the mom says.

The nurse speaks gently. "As Dr. Mackenzie said, it's a bone cancer mostly found in adolescents. It can sometimes occur in families. It's rare, but possible, that multiple siblings may develop it. That's why he wants to see your younger daughter, too. Just to be sure."

The mom starts crying. The dad rubs her back. "OK, thank you," the dad says.

The nurse doesn't leave then, though. She stays. "Sophia is a fighter. I'm not telling you anything you don't know. And Dr. Mackenzie is an exceptional pediatric oncologist. I mean, exceptional. If it was my daughter here—my daughter is eight, her name is Madeleine—I'm telling you, I'd be doing exactly what you are doing. I'd put her in the hands of Dr. Mackenzie."

"Thank you," the mom says. "Thanks."

The nurse nods. "If you need anything, if you have any questions, just page me. I'll answer any I can, and if I can't"—she looks them in the eye, assuring them—"I will get Dr. Mackenzie to explain. In simple terms, if he can manage it," she says, making a joke.

The dad smiles. The mom, I notice, has stopped crying.

They end their conversation just as Gabby comes back with the map. Both Gabby and the nurse can now tell I've been eavesdropping. I quickly look away, but it doesn't matter. I've been caught.

Gabby pushes my chair down the hallway.

"I can do it," I say. I take the wheels. When we are far enough away, I ask her, "Was that the kids' cancer ward?"

"It says 'Pediatric Oncology Department,'" she says. "So yeah."

I don't say anything for a moment, and neither does she.

"We're actually not that far from your room," she says. "I just missed a left."

"Being a nurse . . . seems like a hard job. But fulfilling," I say.

"My dad has always said it's the nurses who provide the care," she says. "I always thought it was kind of a cheesy double entendre, but his point always made sense."

I laugh. "Yeah, he could just say, 'Nurses might not be the ones who cure you, but they certainly make you feel better.'"

Gabby laughs. "Tell him that, will you? Maybe he'll use that one from now on."

I don't know what you're supposed to wear to tell your new boyfriend, who used to be your ex-boyfriend and is the man you are pretty much convinced is the love of your life, that you are having a baby with another man.

I decide on jeans and a gray sweater.

I brush my hair so many times it develops a shine to it, and then I put it up in my very best high bun.

Before I head out the door, I offer, one more time, to stay home with Charlemagne and Gabby.

"Oh, no," Gabby says. "Absolutely not."

"But I don't want to leave you alone."

"I'll be fine," she says. "I mean, you know, I won't be fine. That was a lie. But I'll be fine in the sense that I'm not going to burn the house down or anything. I'll be just as sad when you get back. If it's any consolation."

"It is not," I say. I take my hand off the doorknob. I really don't feel good about leaving her by herself. "You shouldn't be alone."

"Who's alone?" she says. "I have Charlemagne. The two of us are going to watch television until our eyes fall out of our heads and then go to sleep. We might take an Ambien." She corrects herself. "I mean, I might take an Ambien." She continues to look at me. "Just to be clear," she says, "I'm not going to drug the dog."

"I'm staying," I say.

"You're going. Don't use me as an excuse to avoid your own problems. You and I have a lot of adjusting to do, and it's better for everyone if we know where things stand with Ethan as soon as possible."

She's right. Of course she's right.

"The new you tackles life head-on, remember?" she says. "The new you doesn't run from her problems."

"Ugh," I say, opening the front door. "I hate the new me."

Gabby smiles as I head out. It is the first smile I've seen in two days. "I'm proud of the new you," she says.

I thank her and walk out the door.

It's ten to seven when I park my car outside Ethan's apartment. It took me three times around the block before I found a spot, but then I saw a car pulling out of a space right in front of his place. I was both frustrated and thrilled at the experience. I suddenly wonder what driving in Los Angeles will be like with a child. Will it take me a half hour getting in and out of the car because I'll never truly figure out how to hook up a car seat? Will I have to circle the block over and over accompanied by the soothing sounds of a baby crying? Oh, God. I can't do this.

I have to do this.

What do you do when you have to do something you can't do?

I get out of the car and shut my door. I breathe in sharply, and then I breathe out slowly.

Life is just a series of breaths in and out. All I really have to do in this world is breathe in and then breathe out, in succession, until I die. I can do that. I can breathe in and out.

I knock on Ethan's door, and he opens it wearing an apron that says "Mr. Good Lookin' Is Cookin." It has a picture of a stick-figure man with a spatula.

I can't do this.

"Hey, you," he says. He grabs me in his arms, tightly, and I wonder if it's too tight for the baby. I don't know the first thing about being pregnant! I don't know anything about being a mom. What am I doing? This is all going to end in a terrible disaster. I am Hurricane Hannah, and everything I touch turns to shit.

"I missed you," he tells me. "Isn't that ridiculous? I can't go one day not seeing you, after years without you."

I smile at him. "I know what you mean."

He leads me into the kitchen. "I know we mentioned going out to dinner, but I decided to make you a proper meal."

"Oh, wow," I say, trying to muster up enthusiasm, but I'm not sure I'm doing a good job.

"I Googled some recipes at work and just got home from the store a few minutes before you got here. What you're looking at is chicken *sopa seca*." He pronounces it with an affected Spanish accent. He is silly and sweet and sincere, and I decide, right this second, that I'm not going to tell him tonight.

I love him. And I think I have always loved him. And I'm going to lose him. And just for tonight, I want to experience how it feels to be his, to be loved by him, to believe that this is the beginning of something.

Because I'm pretty sure it's the end.

Just like that, I become the version of myself that I was just two days ago. I am Hannah Martin, a woman who has no idea that she is pregnant, no idea that she is about to lose the one thing she might have wanted her entire adult life.

"Fancy!" I say to him. "It looks like it takes quite a bit of prep."

"Actually, I just have a few more steps, and then everything goes in the oven," he says. "I think. Yeah, I think it goes in the oven."

I start laughing. "You've never made this before?"

"Chicken *sopa seca*? When in my life would I have ever had reason to make chicken *sopa seca*? I didn't even know what it was until a few hours ago. I make grilled cheese. I bake potatoes. When I'm feeling really fancy, I'll make myself a pot of chili. I don't go around wooing girls with chicken *sopa seca*." He is chopping vegetables and putting them into a pot. I hang back and sit down on the stool by the kitchen.

"What is chicken *sopa seca*?" I ask him.

"I'm still a bit unclear on that," he says, laughing. "But it involves pasta, so . . ."

"You've never even had it?"

"Again, Hannah, I ask you, when do you think I have occasion to have chicken *sopa seca*?"

I laugh. "Well, why are you making it?" I ask. He is pouring broth into the pot. He looks like a natural.

"Because you are the kind of person who deserves a fuss made over her. That's why. And I'm just the guy to do that."

"You could have just made me a cinnamon roll," I tell him.

He laughs. "Considered and dismissed. It's too obvious. Everyone gets you cinnamon rolls. I wanted to do something unexpected."

I laugh. "Well, if you aren't making cinnamon rolls, then what's for dessert?"

"Ah!" he says. "I'm glad you asked." He pulls out a cluster of bananas.

"Bananas?"

"Bananas Foster. I'm gonna light these babies on fire."

"That sounds like a terrible idea."

He laughs. "I'm kidding. I bought fruit and Nutella."

"Oh, thank God," I say.

"How's Charlemagne?" Ethan asks. Charlemagne, the baby, Gabby and Mark—I want to leave all of it at the door. I don't want to bring any of that here.

"Let's not talk about Charlemagne," I say. "Let's talk about . . ."

"Let's talk about how kickass you are," Ethan says. "With a new job starting and a new car and a dog and a handsome boyfriend who makes world-class cuisine."

This is when I should say something. This is my opening.

But his eyes are so kind and his face so familiar. And so much else in my life is scary and new.

He kisses me. I immediately sink into him, into his breath, into his arms.

This is all going to be over. This is ending.

He picks me up off the stool, and I wrap my arms around him.

He brings me into the bedroom. He pulls my T-shirt off. He starts to unfasten my bra.

"Wait," I say.

"Oh, no, it's fine," he tells me. "The *sopa seca* has to simmer on low for a while. It's not going to burn."

"No," I say. I sit up. I look him in the eye. I put my shirt back on. "I'm pregnant."

Dr. Winters comes in to check on me toward the end of the day. Gabby has gone home.

"So," she says, "I've heard you've been galavanting around the hospital in your wheelchair." She smiles. It's a reproach but a kind one.

"I'm not really supposed to be doing that, huh?" I ask.

"Not really," she says. "But I have bigger fish to fry, so to speak."

I smile, appreciative.

"You are healing nicely. We're almost out of the woods here, in terms of risk of complications."

"Yeah?"

"Yeah," she says, looking down at my chart. "We should talk about your next steps."

"OK," I say. "Tell me."

"One of our physical therapists is going to come in tomorrow, around eleven."

"OK."

"And he and I will assess what sort of mobility you have, what you can expect in a reasonable amount of time, what you should know going forward."

"Great."

"And we will come up with a program and a tentative timeline for when you can expect to begin walking unaided."

"Sounds good," I tell her.

"This is a long road ahead. It's one that can be very frustrating."

"I know," I say. I've been sitting in a bed for a week, leaving only rarely and only with help.

"It will only get more frustrating," she says. "You are going to have to learn how to do something you already know how to do. You will get angry. You will feel like giving up."

"Don't worry," I say. "I'm not going to give up."

"Oh, I know that," she says. "I just want you to know that it's OK to *want* to give up. That it's OK to reach a breaking point with this stuff. You have to have patience with yourself."

"You're saying I'm going to have to relearn how to walk," I tell her. "I already know that. I'm ready."

"I'm saying you're going to have to relearn how to live," she says. "Learn how to do things with your hands for a while instead of your legs. Learn how to ask for help. Learn when you have reached your limit and when you can keep going. And all I'm saying is that we have resources at your disposal. We can help you get through all of it. You will get through all of it."

I felt I had this under control, to a certain degree, before she walked in here, and now she's making me feel like everything is a disaster.

"OK," I say. "I'll let that marinate."

"OK," she says. "I'll come check on you tomorrow morning."

"Great," I say. I only half mean it.

It's four o'clock in the afternoon, but I know that if I go to sleep now, I'll wake up in time to see Henry. So that's what I do. I go to bed. I only have a few more nights in this hospital. I'd hate to waste one sleeping.

~

I'm awake by eleven, when he comes in. I'm prepared for him to make a joke about me being nocturnal or something, but he doesn't. He just says, "Hello."

"Hi," I say.

He looks down at my chart. "So you're going to be taking off pretty soon," he says.

"Yeah. I guess I'm just too healthy for this place."

"A blessing if I've ever heard one." He gives me a perfunctory smile and then checks my blood pressure.

"Would you want to help me practice standing?" I ask. "I want to show you how well I'm doing. I stood up almost entirely on my own this morning."

"I have a lot of patients to get to, so I don't think so," he says. He doesn't even look at me.

"Henry? What is going on with you?"

He looks up.

"Henry?"

"I'm being switched to days on another floor. You'll have a nice woman, Marlene, taking care of you for the remaining nights that you're here." He pulls the cuff off my arm and steps back from me.

"Oh," I say. "OK." I feel rejected, somehow. Rebuffed. "Can you still stop by just to say hi?"

"Hannah," Henry says. His voice is now more somber, more serious. "I shouldn't have been so . . . friendly with you. That is my fault. We can't keep joking around and goofing off."

"OK," I say. "I get it."

"Our relationship has to stay professional."

"OK."

"It's nothing personal." The phrase hangs there in the air.

I thought this *was* personal. Which I guess is the problem.

"I should go," he says.

"Henry, c'mon." I find myself getting emotional; I hear my voice cracking. I try desperately to get it under control. I know that letting him know how badly I want to see him again will only serve to push him further away. I know that. But sometimes you can't help but show the things you feel. Sometimes, despite how hard you try to fight your feelings, they show up in the glassiness of your eyes, the downward turn of your lips, the shakiness of your voice, and the lump in your throat. "We're friends," I say.

He stops where he is. He walks toward me. The look on his face is gentle and compassionate. I don't want gentle and compassionate. I am so goddamn sick of gentle and compassionate. "Hannah," he says.

"Don't," I say. "I get it. I'm sorry."

He looks at me and sighs.

"I probably misinterpreted everything," I say finally.

"OK," he says. And then he leaves. He actually leaves. He just turns on his heels and walks out the door.

I don't fall asleep, even though I'm tired. It's not that I can't fall asleep. I think I can. But I keep hoping he will check on me.

At two a.m., a woman in pale blue scrubs comes in and introduces herself as Marlene. "I'll be taking care of you at night from here on out," she says. "I'm surprised you're awake!"

"Yeah," I say somberly. "Well, I slept all afternoon."

She smiles kindly and leaves me be. I close my eyes and tell myself to go to sleep.

Henry's not coming. There's no reason to wait up.

You know what? I don't think I misinterpreted a goddamn thing.

I *like* him. I like being around him. I like being near him. I like the way he smells and the way he never shaves down to the skin. I like the way his voice is sort of rocky and deep. I like his passion for his job. I like how good he is at it. I just like him. The way you like people when you like them. How he makes me laugh when I least expect it. How my legs don't hurt as much when he's looking directly at me.

Or . . . I don't know. Maybe that's all nursing stuff. Maybe he makes everyone feel that way.

I turn off my side light and close my eyes.

Dr. Winters said earlier today that I might try to walk tomorrow.

I try to focus on that.

If I can survive being hit by a car, I will get over having a crush on my night nurse.

Hearts are just like legs, I guess. They mend.

"It's not yours," I tell Ethan. He knows this, of course, based on timing alone. But I have to make it crystal clear.

"It could be, though, right?" he asks me. "I mean, maybe last week . . ."

I shake my head. "I'm eleven weeks. It's not yours."

"Whose is it?"

I breathe in and then out. That's all I have to do. In and then out. The rest is optional. "His name is Michael. He and I dated in New York. I thought it was more serious than it was. He and I were careless toward the end. He doesn't want another child."

"Another child?"

"He's married, with two children," I tell him.

He sighs loudly, as if he can't quite believe what I'm saying. "Did you know he had a family?"

"It's sort of hard to explain," I say. "I didn't know at first. For a long time, I assumed I was the only one he was with. But then I should have known better and, let's just say, I . . . made some mistakes."

"And now he doesn't care that you're pregnant?" Ethan stands up, furious. His emotions are just starting to set in, reality just starting to grab on to him. It's easier for him to be mad at Michael than it is to be mad at me or at the situation. So I let him, for a moment.

"He doesn't want the baby," I say. "And that's his right." I believe in a man's decision not to have a baby as much as I believe in a woman's.

"And you're just going to let this asshole treat you like this?"

"He doesn't want the baby. I do. I'm prepared to go it alone."

That word, the word *alone*, brings him back down to earth. "What does this mean for us?" he asks.

"Well," I say, "that's up to you."

He looks at me. His eyes find mine and hold on. And then he looks away. He looks down at his hands, which are placed firmly on his knees. "Are you asking me to be someone's father?"

"No," I say to him. "But I'm also not going to tell you that this doesn't change things. I'm pregnant. And if you're going to be with me, that means you'll be going through this with me. My body will be going through a lot. I'll have mood swings. When it gets time to have the baby, I'll be scared and confused and in pain. And then, once the baby is born, there will be a child in my life, at all times. If you want to be with me, you'll be with my child."

He listens, but he doesn't speak.

"I know you didn't ask for any of this," I say.

"Yeah, you can say that again," he snaps. He looks at me with remorse.

"But I wanted you to know so you could make a decision about your future."

"Our future," he says.

"I guess," I say. "Yeah."

"What do you want?" he asks.

Oh, boy. How do I even begin to answer that question? "I want my baby to be healthy and happy and have a safe, stable childhood." I suppose that's the only thing I know for sure.

"And us?"

"I don't want to lose you. I think you and I really have something, that this is the beginning of something with huge potential for us . . . But I would never want to put you in the position to do something you aren't ready for."

"This is a lot," he says. "To process."

"I know," I say. "You should take all the time you need." I stand up, ready to leave, ready to give him time to think.

He stops me. "You're really ready to be a single mother?"

"No," I say. "But this is the way life has worked out. And I'm embracing it."

"But I mean, this could be a mistake," he says. "What if you just made a mistake one night with this guy? Are you ready to live with the consequences of that for your entire life? Do I have to live with the consequences of that for mine?"

I sit back down. "I have to think that there is a method to all of this madness," I tell Ethan. "That there is a larger plan out there. Everything happens for a reason. Isn't that what they say? I met Michael, and I fell in love with him, even though I can clearly see now that he wasn't who I thought he was. And one night, everything happened just so, and I got pregnant. And maybe it's because I'm supposed to have this baby. That's how I'm choosing to look at it."

"And if I can't do it? If I'm not ready to take all of this on?"

"I suppose it would follow that if you and I come to a place we can't get past, then we aren't meant to be. Right? Then we aren't right for each other. I mean, I think I have to believe that life will work out the way it needs to. If everything that happens in the world is just a result of chance and there's no rhyme or reason to any of it, that's just too chaotic for me to handle. I'd have to go around questioning every decision

I've ever made, every decision I will ever make. If our fate is determined with every step we take . . . it's too exhausting. I'd prefer to believe that things happen as they are meant to happen."

"So you and I finally have the timing worked out, we can finally be together, be what we suspected we always were. And in the middle of that, it turns out you're pregnant with another man's baby, and you're saying *que será será*?"

I want to cry. I want to scream and shout. I want to beg him to stay with me during all of this. I want to tell him how scared I am, how much I feel I need him. I want to tell him how the night I reconnected with him, the night we spent together, was the first time I've felt at ease in years. But I don't. Because it will only drag this thing out further. It will only make things worse. "Yeah. *Que será será*. That's what I'm saying."

I get up and walk out into the living room. He follows me. I can smell dinner. I wish, just for a moment, that I hadn't told him. Right now, we'd be in his bedroom.

And then I think, if I'm wishing for things, maybe I should wish that I'm not pregnant at all. Or that it's his baby. Or that I never left Los Angeles. Or that Ethan and I never broke up.

But I wonder how different my world would be if any of those things had happened. You can't change just one part, can you? When you sit there and wish things had happened differently, you can't just wish away the bad stuff. You have to think about all the good stuff you might lose, too. Better just to stay in the now and focus on what you can do better in the future.

"Ethan," I tell him, "the minute I saw you again, I just knew that you and I were . . . I mean, I'm pretty sure you and I are . . ."

"Don't," he says. "Just . . . not right now, OK?"

"OK. I'll leave you with your *sopa seca*." I smile tenderly and then open the door to leave. He sees me out and shuts the door.

When I get to the last step, he calls my name. I turn around.

He's standing at the top of the stairs, looking down at me. "I love you," he says. "I don't think I ever really stopped."

I wonder if I'll be able to make it to my car before I burst into tears, before I cease to be a human being and become just a puddle with big boobs and a high bun.

"I was going to tell you that tonight," Ethan says. "Before all of this."

"And now?" I say.

He gives me a bittersweet smile. "I still love you," he says. "I've always loved you. I might never stop."

His gaze falls to the ground, and then he looks back up at me. "I just thought you should know now . . . in case . . ." He doesn't finish his sentence. He doesn't want to say the words, and he knows I don't want to hear them.

"I love you, too," I say, looking up at him. "So now you know. Just in case."

Luckily for everyone involved, my physical therapist is not my type.

"OK, Ms. Martin," he says. "We are—"

"Ted, just call me Hannah."

"Right, Hannah," Ted says. "Today we're going to work on standing with a walker."

"Sounds easy enough." I say it because that's what I normally say to everything, not because it actually sounds easy enough. At this stage in my life, it sounds quite hard.

He puts my feet on the floor. That part I've gotten good at. Then he puts the walker in front of me. He pulls me up onto him, resting my arms and chest on his shoulders. He is bearing my weight.

"Slowly, just try to ease the weight onto your right foot," he says. I hang on to him but try to back off just a little. My knees buckle.

"Slow," he says. "It's a marathon, not a sprint."

"I don't know if you should be using running terms to someone who can't walk," I tell him.

But he doesn't spit something back at me. Instead, he just smiles. "Good point, Ms. Martin."

When people are nice and sincere and they don't fire back with smart-ass remarks, it makes my harmless sarcastic words seem downright rude.

"I was just joking," I tell him, immediately trying to take it back. "Use all the sports analogies you want."

"Will do," he says.

Dr. Winters comes in to check on us. "Looking good," she says.

I'm half standing up in a hospital gown and white knee socks, leaning over a grown man, with my hands on a walker. The last thing I am is "looking good." But I decide to say only nice things, because I don't feel that Dr. Winters and Ted the physical therapist are up for my level of sarcasm. This is why I need Henry.

Dr. Winters starts asking questions directly to Ted. They are talking about me and yet ignoring me. It's like when I was little and my mom's friends would come over and say something like "Well, isn't she precious" or "Look at how cute she is!" and I always wanted to say, "I'm right here!"

Ted moves slightly, pushing more of my weight onto my own feet. I don't feel as if I have balance, per se, but I can handle it.

"Actually, Ted," I say, "can you . . ." I gesture at the walker, asking him to bring it right in front of me, which he does. I shimmy off him and put both arms on the walker. I'm holding myself up. I don't have my hands on a single person.

Dr. Winters actually claps. As if I'm learning how to crawl.

There is only so long you can be condescended to before you want to jump out of your skin.

"Let me know when you want to sit back down, Ms. Martin," Ted says.

"Hannah!" I say. "I said call me Hannah!" My voice is rough and unkind. Ted doesn't flinch.

"Ted, why don't you leave Hannah and me alone for a minute?" Dr. Winters says.

I'm still standing with the walker on my own. But no one is cheering anymore.

Ted leaves and shuts the door behind him.

Dr. Winters turns to me. "Can you sit down on your own?" she asks.

"Yeah," I tell her, even though I'm not sure it's true. I try bending at my hips, but I can't seem to get control properly. I land on my bed with more force and bounce than I mean to. "I should apologize to Ted," I say.

She smiles. "Eh," she says. "Nothing he hasn't heard before."

"Still . . ."

"This is hard," she says.

"Yeah," I tell her. "But I can do it. I just want to *do* it. I want to stop being treated with kid gloves or having people cheer because I can feel my toes. I know it's hard to do, but I want to do it. I want to start walking."

"I didn't mean it was hard to walk," she says. "I mean that it's hard not to be able to walk."

"You sort of tricked me," I tell her, laughing. "Your sentence was misleading."

Dr. Winters starts laughing, too. "I know what I'm talking about," she says. "This stuff is frustrating. But you can't rush it."

"I just want to get out of here," I tell her.

"I know, but we can't rush that, either—"

"Come on!" I say, my voice rising. "I've been lying in this bed for days. I lost a baby. I can't walk. The only time I can get up is when someone pushes me around the hideous hallways. Something as mundane as walking by myself to the other side of the room is unimaginable to me. That's where I'm at right now. The mundane is unimaginable. And I have absolutely no control over anything! My entire life is in a tailspin, and I can't do anything about it." And Henry. Now I don't even have Henry.

Dr. Winters doesn't say anything. She just looks at me.

"I'm sorry," I say, getting a handle on myself.

She hands me a pillow. I take it and look at her. I'm not sure I know where this is going.

"Put the pillow up to your face," she says.

I'm starting to think Dr. Winters is nuts.

"Just do it," she says. "Indulge me for a second."

"OK," I say, and put the pillow up to my face.

"Now, scream."

I pull the pillow away from my face. "What?"

She takes the pillow in her hand and gently puts it up to my face. I take it from her. "Scream as if your life depends on it."

I try to scream.

"C'mon, Hannah, you can do better than that."

I try to scream again.

"Louder!" she says.

I scream.

"C'mon!"

I scream louder and louder and louder.

"Yeah!" she says.

I scream until there is no more air in my lungs, no more force in my throat. I breathe in, and I scream again.

"You can't walk," she says. "And you lost a baby."

I scream.

"It's going to be months until you fully recover," she says.

I scream.

"Don't hold it in. Don't ignore it. Let it out."

I scream and I scream and I scream.

I'm angry that I can't walk yet. I'm angry that Dr. Winters is right to clap for me when I stand up with a walker, because standing up on my own, even with a walker, is really, really hard.

I'm angry about the pain.

And about that lady just driving away. As if I was nothing. Just kept on driving down the street while I lay there.

And I'm angry at Henry. Because he made things better, and now he's gone. And because he made me feel stupid. Because I thought he cared about me. I thought that maybe I meant something to him.

And I'm angry that I don't.

I'm angry that I ended up pregnant with Michael's baby.

I'm angry at myself for falling in love with him.

I'm angry that my parents come and go out of my life.

Right now, in this moment, it feels as if I'm angry at the whole goddamn world.

So I scream into the pillow.

When I'm done, I take the pillow away from my face, put it back on the bed, and turn to Dr. Winters.

"Are you ready?" she says.

"For what?" I ask her.

"To move forward," she says. "To accept that you cannot walk right now. And to be patient with yourself and with us as you learn how to do it again."

I'm not sure. So I take the pillow, and I put it up to my face. I scream one last time. But my heart's not in it. I don't have anything left to yell about. I mean, I'm still angry. But it's no longer boiling to the surface. It's a simmer. And you can control a simmer.

"Yeah," I say. "I'm ready."

She stands in front of me. She helps me stand up. She calls Ted into the room.

And the two of them stand with me, help me, coach me, walk me through the art of balancing on two feet.

When I get home, Charlemagne runs toward me, and I hear Gabby get out of her bed.

She comes down the stairs and looks at me. She can see from my face that it didn't go well. I can tell from hers that she's been crying.

"You're home early."

"Yeah," I say.

"You told him?"

"Yeah."

She gestures to the sofa, and we both walk over and sit down. "What did he say?"

"Nothing? Everything? He's going to think about it." Then I ask about her. "Did Mark call again?" Mark has called at least ten times since he left. Gabby hasn't answered any of them.

"Yeah," she says. "But I didn't answer again. It's not time to talk right now. I have to get myself together and get ready for it. I'll hear him out. I'm not writing him off entirely, I suppose."

"Got it," I say.

"But I'm also being realistic. He was having an affair for a long time. I can't think of an explanation he could have that would change my mind about getting a divorce."

"You're not tempted to answer the phone and scream at him?"

She laughs. “Definitely. I am definitely tempted to do that. I will probably do that soon.”

“But not right now.”

“What does it get me?” she says, shrugging. “At the end of the conversation, I’ll still be me. He’ll still be him. He’ll still have cheated on me. I have to accept that.”

“So at least we’re facing our problems head-on,” I tell her.

She looks at me and smiles sadly. “At least we have that.”

“We make quite a pair, don’t we?”

Gabby huffs. “I’ll say.”

“I couldn’t do any of this without you.”

“Ditto,” she says.

“I kind of want to just feel sorry for myself and cry,” I tell her. “Maybe for the foreseeable future.”

She nods. “Honestly, that sounds great.”

We both slump down on the couch. Charlemagne joins us.

The two of us quietly cry on and off for the rest of the night, taking turns being the one crying and the one consoling.

I think that through our wallowing, we are able to release some of our fear and pain, because when we wake up the next day, we both feel stronger, better, more ready to take on the world, no matter what it throws at us.

We go out for breakfast and try to make jokes. Gabby reminds me to take my prenatal vitamins. We walk Charlemagne and then go buy her a dog bed and some chew toys. We begin to potty train her by bringing her to the front door when she pees. Every time she looks as if she has to pee, we pick her up and bring her to the front door, where we have a wee-wee pad. Gabby and I high-five each other with an unmatched level of excitement when Charlemagne goes straight to the wee-wee pad on her own.

When Mark calls that night, Gabby answers. She calmly listens to what he has to say. I don't eavesdrop. I try to give her space.

It's hours until she comes to find me in my room.

"He apologized a million times. He says he never meant to hurt me. He says he hates himself for what he's done."

"OK," I say.

"He says he was going to tell me. That he was working up the courage to tell me."

"OK . . ." Her voice is shaky, and it's making me nervous.

"He loves her. And he wants a divorce."

I sit up straight in bed. "*He* wants a divorce?"

She nods her head, just as stunned as I am. "He says I can keep the house. He won't fight me on a settlement. He says I deserve everything he can give me. He says he loves me, but he's not sure he was ever in love with me. And that he's sorry he wasn't brave enough to face that fact earlier."

My mouth is agape.

"He says, looking back on it, he should have handled it differently, but he knows this is right for both of us."

"I'm going to kill him," I tell her.

She shakes her head. "No," she says. "I'm kind of OK."

"What?"

"Well, I think I'm in shock, first of all," she says. "So take this with a grain of salt."

"OK . . ."

"But I always just had this feeling that maybe there was someone better out there."

"Really?"

"Yeah," she says. "I mean, we've been together since we were in college, and then we both went on to more school, and who has time to really focus on dating then? Right? So I stayed with him because . . . I didn't really see a reason not to. We were comfortable around each other. We were happy enough. And then, you know, I got to the age where I felt I should get married. And things have been fine between us. Always fine."

"But just fine?"

"Right," she says.

"I mean, I don't know," she says. "I just sometimes hoped that I could have something more than just fine. Someone who made me feel like I hung the moon. But I sort of stopped believing that existed, I think. And I figured, why not marry a guy like Mark? He's a nice guy."

"Questionable."

She laughs. "Right. Now it's questionable. But at the time, I didn't think twice about it. You know? I was in a good relationship with a stable man who wanted to marry me and buy a house and do all the things you're supposed to do. I didn't see any reason not to take him up on that just because I felt like he was a B-plus. And I was perfectly happy. I mean, I doubt, if this hadn't happened, that I ever would have verbalized any of this. It just wasn't on my mind. I was happy enough. I really was." She starts crying again.

"Are you OK?" I ask.

"No," she says, getting hold of herself. "I'm absolutely devastated. But—"

"But what?"

"When he told me, I just kept thinking that if I met someone out there who was better for me, who I felt passionately for, I'd want to leave Mark. That's the truth. I'd want to leave. I don't think I would have done what he did. But I'd have wanted to."

Charlemagne comes into the room and curls up in a ball.

"So what now?" I ask.

"Now?" Gabby says. "I don't know. It's too hard to think long-term. I'm heartbroken and miserable and sort of relieved and embarrassed and sick to my stomach."

"So maybe we take it one step at a time," I say.

"Yeah."

"I'm really craving cinnamon rolls," I tell her.

She laughs. "That sounds great," she says. "Maybe with a lot of icing."

"Who wants a cinnamon roll with only a little icing?" I ask her.

"Touché."

"Maybe right now, all we have to do is go get cinnamon rolls with a lot of icing."

"Yeah," she says. "Me and the pregnant lady, putting back a half dozen cinnamon rolls."

"Right."

She leaves to go put on her shoes. I put on a jacket and flip-flops. You can do that in Los Angeles.

We get into the car.

"Ethan hasn't called you, right?" Gabby says.

I shake my head. "He will when he knows what he wants to do."

"And until then?" she asks.

"I'm not going to wait around for some man to call," I say, teasing her. "My best friend wouldn't stand for that."

She shrugs. "I don't know," she says. "Extenuating circumstances."

"Still," I tell her, "if he wants to be with me, he'll be with me. If he doesn't, I'm moving on. I have a baby to raise. A job to start. I'm going through a lot. I don't know if I told you this, but my best friend is getting divorced."

Gabby laughs. "You're telling me! Mine is pregnant with a baby that isn't her boyfriend's."

"No shit!" I say.

"Yeah!" Gabby says. "And she came home the other day with a dog she decided to adopt out of the blue."

"Wow," I tell her. "Your friend sounds nuts."

"Yours, too," she says.

"Think they'll be OK?" I ask her.

"I know I'm supposed to say yes, but the truth is, I think they're doomed."

The two of us start laughing. It's probably much, much funnier to us than it would seem to anyone else. But the way she says we're doomed makes it clear just how *not* doomed we are. And that feels like something to let loose and laugh about.

After eleven days in this hospital, I'm leaving today. I'm going to end up right back here in forty-eight hours, albeit in the outpatient center. I'll be seeing Ted, the earnest physical therapist, several times a week for the foreseeable future.

Dr. Winters has been prepping me for this. She has gone over all the details with me, and I know them backward and forward.

Gabby is here helping me pack up my things. I've got enough on my plate just trying to get to the bathroom on my own. But I'm making my way there slowly. I want to brush my teeth.

I use my walker to get close enough to the sink.

I stand in front of the mirror, and I truly see myself for the first time in almost two weeks. I have a faint bruise on the left side of my face, near my temple. I'm sure it was a doozy when I got here, but now it's not too bad. I look pale, certainly. But if I had to guess, I'd say that's as much from being inside the same building day after day as it is from any health concerns. My hair is a mess. I haven't taken a proper shower in what feels like forever.

I'm looking forward to sleeping in a real bed and bathing myself, maybe blow-drying my hair. Apparently, preparations have to be made to make that work, too. Mark installed a seat in the shower. Oh, to clean myself unaided! These are the things that dreams are made of.

Now that I'm leaving the hospital, I am starting to realize just how much this has set me back. Weeks ago, I would have guessed that by now I'd at least have gone out and bought a car or started looking for a job. Instead, I'm not where I started but even further behind.

But I also know that I've come a long way in my recovery and as a person. I've faced things I might not have faced otherwise. And as I stare at myself in the mirror for the first time since I got here, I find myself ready to face the ugliest of truths: it might, in fact, be a merciful act of fate that I stand here, unencumbered by a budding life inside me.

I am not ready to be a mother.

I am nowhere near it.

I slowly brush my own teeth. They feel clean and slick when I am done.

"Why is there always pudding in your room?" Gabby asks me. I turn myself around in slow spurts of energy.

She has a chocolate pudding cup in her hand. I don't know when it got here. But I know it was Henry.

He left me pudding at some point in the past day. He left me chocolate pudding. Doesn't that *mean* something?

Gabby is over the pudding. She has moved on to other things. "Dr. Winters should be here soon to check you out," she says. "And I read all the documents. I've even been doing research on physical therapy rehabilitation—"

You don't just leave pudding for someone you don't care about.

"Can you get me the wheelchair?" I ask her.

"Oh," she says. "Sure. I thought you were going to try to use the walker until it was time to go."

"I'm going to find Henry," I tell her.

"The night nurse?"

"He started working days on another floor. I'm gonna find him. I'm going to ask him out on a date."

"Is that a good idea?" she says.

"He left me pudding," I say. That is my only answer. She waits, hoping I have more, but I don't. That's all I've got. *He left me pudding.*

"Should I come with you?" she asks me once she realizes I'm not going to change my mind.

I shake my head. "I want to do this on my own."

I sit down on my bed. The act takes a full thirty seconds to complete. But once I do, I instantly feel better. Gabby pulls the wheelchair around next to me.

"You're sure I can't come with you? Push you, maybe?"

"I'm already going to need you to help me into the shower. My level of dignity is fairly low, so I'm just hoping to spare myself the experience of you watching me tell someone I have feelings for him when, you know, he will probably turn me down."

"This seems like something that maybe you should wait and think about," she says.

"And tell him when? What am I gonna do? Call him on the phone? 'Hello, hospital. Henry, please. It's Hannah.' "

"That's a lot of *Hs*," she says.

"You can only muster up this type of courage a few times in your life. I'm just stupid enough to have it now. So help me into the damn wheelchair so I can go make a fool out of myself."

She smiles. "All right, you got it."

She starts helping me into the chair, and pretty soon I'm rolling. "Wish me luck!" I say, and I head for the door and then brake abruptly, as I've learned to. "Do you think sometimes you can just *tell* about a person?"

"Like you meet them and you think, this one isn't like the rest of them, this one is something?"

"Yeah," I tell her. "Exactly like that."

"I don't know," she says. "Maybe. I'd like to think so. But I'm not sure. When I met Mark, I thought he looked like a dentist."

"He *is* a dentist," I tell her, confused.

"Yeah, but when we were in college, when I was, like, nineteen, I thought he looked like the kind of guy who would grow up to be a dentist."

"He seemed stable? Smart? What? What are you trying to say?"

"Nothing," she says. "Never mind."

"Did you think he looked boring?" I ask her, trying to get to the bottom of it.

"I thought he looked bland," she says. "But I was wrong, right? I'm just saying I didn't get those feelings you're talking about with my husband. And he's turned out to be a great guy. So I can't confirm or deny the existence of being able to just *tell*."

I think you can. That's what I think. I think I've always thought that. I thought it the first time I met Ethan. I thought there was something different about him, something special. And I was right. Look at what we had. It turned out not to be for a lifetime, but that's OK. It was real when it happened.

And I feel that way about Henry now.

But I don't know how to reconcile that with what Gabby is saying. I don't want to say that I believe you can tell when you meet someone who's right for you and then acknowledge that by that logic, Mark's not the one for her.

"Maybe some people can tell," I offer.

"Yeah," she says. "Maybe some people can. Either way, you believe you feel it. That's what's important."

"Yeah," I say. "Right. I gotta tell him."

"What are you gonna say?" she asks me.

"Yeah," I say, turning my wheelchair back to her. "What *am* I going to say?" I think about it for a moment. "I should practice. You be Henry."

Gabby smiles and sits down on the bed, taking on an affected manly pose.

"No, he's not like that," I say. "And he'd be standing."

"Oh," she says, standing up. "Sorry, I just wanted it to be easier because you're . . ."

"In a wheelchair, right," I say. "But don't coddle me. If I'm wheeling through the halls trying to find him, most likely he's going to be standing, and I'll be sitting."

"OK," she says. "Go for it."

I breathe in deeply. I close my eyes. I speak. "Henry, I know this sounds crazy—"

"Nope," she says. "Don't start with that. Never start with 'I know this sounds crazy.' Come from strength. He'd be lucky to be with you. You've got an extraordinary attitude, a brilliant heart, and an infectious optimism. You are a dream woman. Come from strength."

"OK," I say, and then I look down at my legs. "I don't know, Gabby. This isn't my strongest moment."

"You're Hannah Martin. Your weakest moment is a strong moment. Be Hannah Martin. Let's hear it."

"OK," I say, starting over. And then it just comes out of me. "Henry, I think we have something here. I know I'm a patient and you're a nurse, and this is all very against the rules and everything, but I truly believe we could mean something to each other, and we owe it to ourselves to see. How often can you say that about somebody and really mean it? That the two of you have potential for something great? I want to see where we end up. There's something about you, Henry. There's something about us. I can just tell." I look at Gabby. "OK, how was that?"

Gabby stares at me. "Is that how you really feel?"

I nod. "Yeah."

"Go find him!" she says. "What the hell are you doing practicing on me?"

I laugh. "What do you think he'll say?"

"I don't know," she says. "But if he turns you down, he's such a massive idiot that I'm pretty sure you'll have dodged a bullet."

"That doesn't make me feel better."

She shrugs. "Sometimes the truth doesn't," she says. "Now, go."

And so I do.

I wheel myself out of my room and speed down the hall to the nurses' station. I ask where Henry is, and they tell me they don't know. So I get into the elevator, and I go to the top floor, and I start wheeling the halls. I won't stop until I find him.

It's Saturday night. Gabby and I are watching a movie. Charlemagne is lying in her dog bed at our feet. We ordered Thai food, and Gabby is eating all the pad Thai before I can even get my hands on it.

"You know I'm pregnant, right? I should at least get a chance to eat some of the food."

"My husband cheated on me and then left me," she says. She's not even looking up. She's just shoveling noodles into her mouth with her eyes glued to the television. "I don't have to be nice to anyone right now."

"Ugh, fine, you win."

The phone rings, and I look at the caller ID, stunned. It's Ethan.

Gabby pauses the movie. "Well, answer it!" she says.

I do. "Hi," I say.

"Hey," he says. "Is now a good time?"

"Sure. Yeah."

"I was thinking I would come over," he says. "Now, if that's OK. I can stop by."

"Yeah," I tell him. "Absolutely. Come by."

I hang up the phone and stare at Gabby. "What is he going to say?" I ask her.

"I was just going to ask you. What *did* he say?"

"He said he wants to come over. He said he'll stop by."

"Which was it? Come over or stop by?"

"Both. First he said one, then the other."

"Which one was first?"

"Come by. I mean, come over. Yeah, then he said 'stop by.' "

"I don't know if that's good or bad," she says.

"Me, neither." Suddenly, I am overwhelmed by desperation. What is about to happen? "Do you think it's possible he's up for all of this? That I might not lose him?"

"I don't know!" she says. She's just as stressed out about this as I am.

"People shouldn't be possibly breaking up with their boyfriends while they are pregnant," I say. "All of this anxiety can't be good for the baby."

"Are you gonna change?" Gabby asks.

I look down at myself. I'm wearing black leggings and a huge sweatshirt. "Should I?"

"Politely, yes."

"OK," I say. "What do I wear?" I get up and head to my room, thinking of what to put on.

"How about that red sweater?" she calls up the stairs. "And just jeans or something. Super casual."

"Yeah, OK," I say, peeking my head back out to talk to her. "Casual but nice."

"Right," she calls to me. "Also, fix your bun. It's falling over."

"OK."

The doorbell rings when I'm putting on mascara.

"I'll get the door!" Gabby says, and I hear her run up the stairs, away from the front door and toward me. "Before I do, though . . ." she says when she's standing outside my room.

"Yeah?"

"You're amazing. You're smart, and you're loving, and you are the best friend I've ever had, and you are just the best best best person in the universe. Don't ever forget that."

I smile at her. "OK," I say.

And then she turns away and runs down to get the door. I hear her greet him. I come out of my room and down the stairs.

"Hi," I say to him.

"Hi," he says. "Can we talk?"

"Sure."

"You guys take the living room," Gabby says. "I was going to take Charlemagne for a walk anyway."

Ethan bends down and pets Charlemagne as Gabby grabs the leash and slips on a pair of shoes. Then she and Charlemagne are out the door.

Ethan looks at me.

We don't have to talk about anything. I can tell just by the sorrowful look on his face what he's here to say.

It's over.

All I have to do is get through this. That is all I have to do. And when he's gone, I can cry until I'm a senior citizen.

"We can sit down," I tell him. I am proud of how even my voice sounds.

"I can't do it," he says, not moving.

"I know," I tell him.

His voice breaks. His chin starts to spasm, ever so slightly. "I've thought, for so many years now, that I just needed to get you back, and everything would be fine." He's so sad that I don't have any room to be sad.

"I know," I say. "Come sit down." I lead him over to the sofa. I sit so he will sit. Sitting helps sad people, I think. Later, when he is gone, when I am the sad one again, I will sit. I will sit right here.

"I messed this all up. We never should have broken up in college. We should have stayed together. We should have . . . we should have done this all differently."

"I know," I say.

"I'm not ready for this," he says. "I can't do it."

I knew this was what he was going to say, but hearing the words still feels like I'm being punched in the lungs.

"I completely understand," I tell him, because it's true. I wish I didn't understand. Maybe then I could be angry. But I've got nothing to be angry about. All of this is my doing.

"I've been trying for days now to get on board with the idea. I keep thinking that I'll get used to it. That it will all be OK. I keep thinking that if someone is right for you, nothing should get in the way of that. I keep trying to convince myself that I can do this."

"You don't have to—"

"No," he says. "I love you. I meant that when I said it, and I mean it now. And I want to be with you through everything in your life. And I want to be the kind of man who can say, 'OK, you're pregnant with someone else's baby, and that's OK.' But I am not that man, Hannah. I'm not ready to have my own child yet. Let alone raise someone else's. And I know you say that I wouldn't be the dad. I know that. But how can I love you and not share this with you? How could I not be there for all of it? It would drive a wedge between us before we've even gotten this thing off the ground."

"Ethan, listen, I get it," I tell him. "I am so sorry to have put you in this position. I never wanted to do this to you. To make you choose between the life you want and being with me."

"I want a family of my own someday. And if I say yes to you right now, if I say I think we can be together when you're having this baby, I feel like I'd be committing to a family with you. I absolutely believe that we could have a great future together. But I don't think we are ready for this, for having a baby together. Even if it *were* mine."

"Well, you never know what you're ready for until you have to face it," I say. I'm not trying to convince him of anything. It's just something I've learned recently.

"If I had come to you last week and said, 'Hannah, let's have a baby together,' what would you have said?"

"I would have said that was insane." I hate that he's right. "I would have said I'm not ready."

"I'm not prepared to take on another man's baby," he says. "And I'm ashamed of that. I truly am. Because I want to be the man you need. How many times have I told you that there was nothing we could do to mess this up?"

I nod knowingly.

"I want to be the right man for you," he continues. "But I'm not. I can't believe I'm saying this, but . . . I'm not the right man for you."

I look at him. I don't say anything. Nothing I could say would change the way either of us feels. I much prefer problems with solutions, conflicts where one person is right and the other is wrong, and all you have to do is just figure out which is which.

This isn't one of those.

Ethan reaches his hand out and grabs mine. He squeezes it.

And in that one motion, he is no longer the sad one. I am the sad one.

"Who knows?" he says. "Maybe I'll end up a single dad in a

couple of years, and we'll find each other again. Maybe it's just the timing. Maybe now is not our time."

"Maybe," I say. My heart is breaking. I can feel it breaking.

I swallow hard and get hold of myself. "Let's leave it at this," I say. "Just like in high school, this isn't our time. Maybe one day, we'll get the timing right. Maybe this is the middle of a longer love story."

"I like that idea."

"Or maybe we just weren't meant to be," I say. "And maybe that's OK."

He nods, ever so slightly, and looks down at his shoes. "Maybe," he says. "Yeah. Maybe."

Henry's not on my floor or any of the floors above mine. I checked in with nurses, administrators, three doctors, and two visitors of patients whom I mistook for staff. I rolled over three different feet on two different people, and I knocked over a trash can. I'm not sure that pushing yourself around in a wheelchair is that difficult. I think I might just be that uncoordinated.

When I give up on the sixth floor, I get back into the elevator and head down to the fourth, the floor below mine. It's my last shot. According to the elevator buttons, the first three floors hold the lobby, the cafeteria, and administrative offices. So he's got to be on the fourth. It's the only one left.

The elevator opens, and there's a man waiting for it. I start to roll myself out, and he holds the elevator open for me as I pass by. He smiles and then slips into the elevator. He's handsome in an unconventional way, maybe in his late forties. For a moment, I wonder if he smiled at me because he thinks I'm cute, but then I realized he just felt bad for me, wanted to help me out. The realization stings. It is not unlike the time I thought people were checking me out at the grocery store because I was having a great hair day, only to realize later that I'd had a booger. Except this is worse, to be honest. The booger incident was less condescending.

I shake it off the way I shake off everything else that plagues me, and I breathe in deeply, ready to roll my way to Henry. I'm stopped in my place by a nurse.

"Can I help you?" she asks me.

"Yes," I tell her. "I'm looking for Henry. He's a nurse here."

"What's the last name?" she asks. She is tall and broad-shouldered, with short, coarse hair. She looks as if she's been doing this job for a long time and might be sick of it.

I don't actually know Henry's last name. None of the other nurses brought it up, but that's probably because there were no Henrys on that floor anyway. The fact that she's asking is a pretty good indication that he's here.

"Tall, dark hair, brown eyes," I tell her. "He has a tattoo. On his forearm. You know who I'm talking about."

"I'm sorry, Miss, I can't help you. What floor are you a patient on?" She hits the up button on the elevator. I think it's for me.

"What? The fifth floor," I say. "No, listen to me. Henry with the tattoo. I need to speak to him."

"I can't help you," she says.

The elevator in front of us dings and opens. She looks at me expectantly. I don't move. She raises her eyebrows, and I raise mine back. The elevator closes. She rolls her eyes at me.

"Henry isn't here today," she says. "He starts on my service tomorrow. I've never met him, so I'm not sure that it's the Henry you're talking about, but the Henry I know was transferred to me because his boss felt he was getting too close to a patient." She can see my face change, and it emboldens her. "You can see my hesitance," she says. She hits the button again.

"Did he get in trouble?" I ask her, and the minute it comes out of my mouth, I know it's the wrong thing to say.

She frowns at me, as if I have confirmed her worst fears about myself and that I also just don't seem to get it.

"I retract my question," I tell her. "You're probably not open to helping me find him outside of the hospital, right? No last name, no phone number?"

"That's correct," she says.

I nod. "I hear you," I say. "Could I leave a message? With my phone number?"

She's stoic and stone-faced.

"I'm gonna guess that even if I did, you'd probably just throw it away."

"I wouldn't waste much thought about it," she says.

"OK," I say. I can finally see now that it's not going to happen today. Even if I could get past this woman, he's still not here. Unless . . . maybe she's lying? Maybe he is here after all?

I hit the up button on the elevator. "OK," I say. "I read you loud and clear. I'll get out of your hair."

She looks at me sideways. The elevator dings and appears again. I start rolling myself into it and wave good-bye. She walks away. I let the elevator doors close, and then I hit the button for the same floor I'm on.

The doors open, and I take off. I wheel myself in the opposite direction from where she's looking, past the nurses' station. I'm at the corner before she sees me.

"Hey!" she says. I take the corner and push with all of my might toward the end of the hall. My arms feel weak, and my heart is pumping faster than it has in days, but I keep going. I turn back to see her briskly walking toward me. Her face looks pissed, but I get the impression she's trying not to cause a scene.

In front of me are two double glass doors. They don't open from my side, so I'm stuck. I'm dead-ended. The evil nurse is coming for me. On the opposite side of the doors, I see a doctor coming through. Any second now, he's going to open the doors, and I can roll in. Maybe.

I'm not sure what's possessed me to do this. Maybe it's my desire to find Henry. Maybe it's the fact that I've been cooped up in a room for so long with everyone on the planet telling me what to do. Maybe it's the fact that I almost died, and on some level, that has to make you fearless. Maybe it's all three.

The door opens, and the doctor walks by me. I roll myself through, praying the doors close before Nurse Ratched gets to me. But I don't have time to stop and look. I keep rolling, looking in each room for Henry. I get right to the end of the hall. I turn left around the corner, and then I feel the grip of two hands on the back of my chair. Abruptly, I come to a complete stop.

Caught.

I turn and look at her. "What can I say so that you don't arrest me?"

She pushes me forward, but she doesn't answer my question. Suddenly, with my adrenaline now fading, I'm realizing that my stunt was stupid and fruitless. He's really not here. And unless I come back to this hospital tomorrow and try this again, I'm probably never going to find him.

"I can push myself," I tell her.

"Nope," she says.

I laugh nervously. "This sort of thing probably happens all the time, I bet," I say, trying to lighten the mood.

"Nope."

We get to the elevator. She hits the button. I can't look at her. The elevator opens.

"Well," I say, "I guess this is good-bye."

She stares at me and then puts her hands back on my chair. "Nope."

She pushes the two of us into the elevator and hits the button for the fifth floor.

I sit in silence, staring forward. She stands next to me. When the elevator opens, she pushes me toward the nurses' station.

"Hi, Deanna," she says. "Can you tell me what room this patient belongs in?"

"I can tell you," I say to her. "I'm right over here."

"If it's all right with you, Wheels, I'd like to hear it from Deanna," she says to me.

Deanna laughs. "Hannah's right. She's just right there." Deanna points to my door, and Nurse Ratched pushes me all the way to my room, where Gabby is waiting.

Gabby sees the two of us and isn't quite sure what to make of it. "What happened?"

Nurse Ratched pipes up before I can. "Look," she says directly to me, "everyone makes bad decisions sometimes, and this is probably a crazy time in your life, so I'm going to let this go. But you will not come down to my floor again. Are we clear?"

I nod, and she starts to leave.

"Nurse," I say, and then I realize I shouldn't call her Nurse Ratched to her face. "Sorry," I say. "What was your name?"

"Hannah," she says.

"For heaven's sake! I'm trying to apologize. I'm just asking your name."

"I know," she says. "My name is Hannah."

"Oh," I say. "Sorry."

Hannah looks at Gabby. "Is she always this charming?"

"This appears not to be her best day," Gabby says. I think

that's as close as she can come to defending me. So I appreciate it.

"I just wanted to say I'm sorry for giving you trouble. I was wrong to do it."

"Well, thank you," she says. She turns to leave.

"Hannah," I say.

She turns back to me.

"I'm a stalker."

"Excuse me?"

"It's not Henry's fault," I tell her. "That we got too close, I mean. He was nothing but professional, and I basically stalked him. He kept making it clear that we had a professional relationship and nothing more. And I kept pressing the issue, trying to get him to change his mind. It's me. He's not . . . I'd hate for him to be considered unprofessional because of the way I behaved. It was me."

She nods and leaves. I'm not entirely sure if she believes me, but my actions today sort of support the claim that I'm at least a little delusional. So I have that going for me.

I turn to Gabby. "He wasn't there, and I caused a scene."

"No big speech?"

I shake my head. "There was a chase, though."

"Well, I guess that's enough drama for one day. Dr. Winters came while you were gone. She says we're good to go."

"So we're leaving?" I ask her.

"Yep."

"What do I do about Henry?" I ask her. "I can't leave knowing I'll never see him again."

"I don't know," she says. "Maybe you'll run into him sometime? Here at the hospital, during a physical therapy appointment?"

"Maybe," I say.

"If it's meant to be, you'll find each other," she says. "Right?"

"Yeah," I tell her. "I don't know. I guess."

Instinctually, from muscle memory, I put my hands on the armrests of the wheelchair, as if I think I'm going to stand up. And then I remember who I am. And what is going on.

Deanna comes in. "You ready to go?" she says.

"Yes, ma'am," I tell her.

Gabby has my things. Deanna pushes me to the elevator. She stays with us as we start to move down. I wonder if Deanna is doing this because it's protocol or because I'm a flight risk. The elevator opens for a minute on four, as an older woman gets in. I can see Nurse Hannah standing at the nurses' station talking to a patient. She looks at me and then looks away. I swear I see a smile crack on her face, but I see what I want to see sometimes.

When we get to the lobby, Deanna tells me that the wheelchair is mine to keep. For a moment, I think, *Cool, free wheelchair*, and then I remember the hard road ahead. *Shake it off.*

"Thanks, Deanna," I say as we exit onto the street. She waves and heads back in.

Mark pulls up with the car. He gets out and runs toward me. I realize it's the first time I've seen him since the accident. And that's sort of weird, isn't it? Shouldn't he have visited me? I would have visited him.

Gabby and Mark put my stuff into the car, and I wheel myself to the door. I try to open it myself, but it's harder than I think. I wait patiently for one of them to come around to the side, and as I do, I look up at the building.

I may never see Henry again.

Gabby opens my door and helps me into the backseat. Mark puts my wheelchair into the trunk. We drive away.

If I'm meant to find him, I'll find him. I guess I do believe that.

But sometimes I wish *I* got to decide what I was meant to do.

Gabby left early this morning to go spend the day with her parents. Mark is coming later to pick up the rest of his things, and she doesn't want to be here.

Mark has only come by one other time since he left, to grab a few suits and some odds and ends. Neither Gabby nor I was here, and it was a bit creepy, to be honest, coming home to see the house picked through. Gabby changed the locks after that. So now Mark needs one of us to be here while he moves his stuff out. It seems quite obvious that I am the woman for the job.

In his e-mail, he said he'd be here by noon, but it's early enough that I figure I've got some time to kill. I decide now is the time to call my parents and tell them the news. At this hour, I can probably grab them before they head out for dinner in London.

I dial their landline, prepared to tell them I'm pregnant the moment one of them picks up. I'm just going to blurt it out before I start to worry what they will say.

But the voice I hear on the other end of the line, the voice that says "Hello?" isn't my mother or my father. It's my sister.

"Sarah?" I ask. "What are you doing at Mom and Dad's?"

"Hannah!" she says. "Hi! George and I are here for the week-end." She pronounces it "wee-KEND." I find myself rolling my eyes. I can hear my dad in the background, asking who is on the phone. I hear my sister's voice turn away from the handset. "It's Hannah, Dad. Chill out . . . Dad wants to talk to you," she says.

"Oh, OK," I say back, but she doesn't give up the phone.

"I want to know when you're coming to visit," she says. "You didn't come last Christmas like you normally do, so I think we're owed."

I know she's joking. But it irritates me that she assumes I should always go there. Just once, I'd like to be important enough to be the visited instead of the visitor. Just once.

"Well, I'm in L.A. now," I tell her. "So the flight is a bit longer. But I'll get there. Eventually."

"OK, OK," she says to my dad. "Hannah, I have to go." She's gone before I can even say good-bye.

"Hannah Savannah," my dad says. "How are you?"

"I'm good, Dad. I'm good. How are you?"

"How am I? How am I? That is the question."

I laugh.

"No, I'm fine, sweetheart. I'm fine. Your mother and I are just sitting here discussing whether we want to order Italian or Thai takeaway for dinner. Your sister and George are trying to get us to go out someplace, but it's pouring out, and I'm just not in the mood."

My plan to blurt it out has failed.

Or has it?

"That's nice. So, Dad, I'm pregnant."

. . .

. . .

. . .

I swear to God, it sounds as if the line has gone dead. "Dad?"

"I'm here," he says, breathless. "I'm getting your mother."

I hear another voice on the phone now. "Hi, Hannah," my mom says.

"Can you repeat what you said, Hannah?" my dad says. "I'm afraid that if your mother hears it from me, she will think I am playing a joke on her."

I have to blurt it out twice?

"I'm pregnant."

. . .

. . .

. . .

Silence again. And then a high-pitched squeal. A squeal so loud and jarring that I pull the phone away from my ear.

And then I hear my mother scream, "Sarah! Sarah, get over here!"

"What, Mom? Good Lord. Stop screaming."

"Hannah is pregnant."

I hear the phone being rustled from person to person. I hear them all fighting over the handset. I hear my mother win.

"Tell us everything. This is marvelous. Tell us about the father! I didn't know you were seeing someone serious."

Oh, no.

My mom thinks I got pregnant on purpose.

My mom thinks I'm ready to have a baby.

My mom thinks there's a father.

My mom, my own mother, is so unaware of who I truly am and what my life is like that she thinks I planned this baby.

That is one of the funniest things I have ever heard. I start laughing, and I keep laughing until the tears in my eyes fall to my cheeks.

"No father in the picture," I say between fits of laughter. "I'll be a single mother. Entirely accidental."

My mother quickly adjusts her tone. "Oh," she says. "OK."

My dad grabs the phone from her. "Wow!" he says. "This is shocking news. But great news! This is great, great news!"

"It is?" I mean, it is. It is. But they think it is?

"I'm going to be a grandpa!" he says. "I am going to be a phenomenal grandfather. I'm going to teach your kid all kinds of grandpa things."

I smile. "Of course you will!" I say it, but I don't mean it in the slightest. He's not here. He's never here.

Sarah grabs the phone from my dad and starts talking about how happy she is for me and how it doesn't matter that I'm raising the baby on my own. And then she corrects herself. "I mean, it matters. Of course it *matters*. But you're going to be so great at it that it won't *matter*."

"Thanks," I say.

And then my mother steals the phone from Sarah, and I can hear the background din changing as she moves into another room. I hear the door shut behind her.

"Mom?" I say. "Are you OK?"

I hear her brace herself. "You should move home," she says.

"What?" I ask her. I don't even understand what she's talking about.

"We can help you," she says. "We can help you raise a baby."

"You mean I should move to London?"

"Yeah, here with us. Home with us."

"London is not my home," I tell her, but this doesn't faze her in the slightest.

"Well, maybe it should be," she says. "You need a family to

raise a baby. You don't want to do it on your own. And your father and I would love to help you, love to have you here. You should be here with us."

"I don't know . . ." I say.

"Why not? You just moved to Los Angeles, so you can't tell me you've built a life there. And if there is no father in the picture, there is no one to hold you back."

I think about what she's saying.

"Hannah," she says. "Let us help you. Let us be your parents. Move into the guest room, have the baby here. I've always said you should have moved to London with us a long time ago." She has never said that. Never once said that to me.

"I'll think about it," I tell her.

I hear the door open. I hear her talk to my father.

"I'm telling Hannah it's time for her to move to London."

"Absolutely, she should," I hear him say. Then he grabs the phone. "Who knows, Hannah Savannah, maybe you were always meant to live in London."

Until this very moment, it never even occurred to me that I might belong in London. The city my own family lives in, and I never considered moving there.

"Maybe, Dad," I say. "Who knows?"

By the time I get off the phone, my parents are convinced I'm moving there as soon as possible, despite the fact that I very clearly promise only that I will consider it. In order to get them off the phone, I have to promise to call them tomorrow. So I do. And then they let me go.

I lie there on my bed, staring at the ceiling for what feels like hours. I daydream about what would happen if I left Los Angeles, if I moved to London.

I consider what my life might look like if I lived in my parents' London apartment with a new baby. I think about my child growing up with a British accent.

But mostly, I think about Gabby.

And everything I'd miss if I left here.

It's noon before Mark shows up.

I answer the door quickly, my hands jittery and nervous. I'm not nervous because he intimidates me or I don't know what to say to him. I'm nervous because I'm scared I might say something I'll regret.

"Hi," he says. He's standing in front of me, wearing jeans and a green T-shirt. As I hoped, he's alone. He has broken-down boxes under his arm.

"Hi," I say. "Come on in."

He steps into the house, lightly, as if he doesn't belong here. "The moving van is coming in a half hour," he says. "I got a small one. That's sounds right, right? I don't have a lot of stuff, I guess."

"Right," I tell him.

I watch as his gaze travels down to Charlemagne, the two of them foes in the most conventional sense of the word. The house isn't big enough for the two of them.

Mark rubs his eyes and then looks at me. "Well," he says, "I'll get to packing, I guess. Excuse me."

He's more uncomfortable about this than I am. His vulnerability eases me. I'm less likely to scream at a repentant man.

I sit on the sofa. I turn on the TV. I can't relax while he's here, but I'm also not going to stand over him.

The movers ring the bell soon after, and he rushes to answer the door.

"If you guys are going to be in and out," I tell him, "I'll keep Charlemagne in the bedroom."

"Great," he says. "Thanks." The movers come in, and Charlemagne and I stay in my room.

I feel like crying for some reason. Maybe it's my hormones. Maybe it's because I never wanted Gabby to have to go through this. I don't know. Sometimes it's hard to tell anymore what's my real reason for crying, laughing, or standing still.

When he's done, he knocks on my door. "That's the last of it," he says.

"Great," I say back.

He looks down at the floor. Then up at me. "I'm sorry," he says. "For what it's worth."

"It's not worth very much," I tell him. Maybe it's because he has the audacity to try to apologize that I no longer feel for him.

"I know," he says. "This situation isn't ideal."

"Let's not do this," I tell him.

"She's going to end up with someone better for her than me," he says. "You, of all people, should know that's good news."

"Oh, I *know* she's going to end up with someone better than you," I tell him. "But that doesn't change the fact that you acted like a chickenshit about it, and instead of being honest, you lied and you cheated."

"You know, when you meet the love of your life, it makes you do crazy things," he says in his own defense. As if I couldn't possibly understand what he's been through because I haven't met my soul mate. As if being in love is an excuse for anything. "I didn't want to love Jennifer this way. I didn't mean for it to happen. But when you have that kind of connection with someone, nothing can stand in its way."

I don't believe that being in love absolves you of anything. I no longer believe that all's fair in love and war. I'd go so far as to say your actions in love are not an exception to who you are. They are, in fact, the very definition of who you are. "Why are you trying to convince me you're a good guy?"

"Because you're the only one Gabby will listen to."

"I'm not going to defend you to her."

"I know that—"

"And more to the point, Mark, I don't agree with you. I don't think meeting the love of your life gives you carte blanche to ruin everything in your path. There are a lot of people out there who find the person they believe they are supposed to be with, and it doesn't work out because they have other things they have to do, and instead of being a liar and running from their responsibilities, they act like adults and do the right thing."

"I just want Gabby to know that I never meant to hurt her."

"OK, fine," I tell him, so that he will leave. But the truth is, it's not OK. It's not OK at all.

It doesn't matter if we don't mean to do the things we do. It doesn't matter if it was an accident or a mistake. It doesn't even matter if we think this is all up to fate. Because regardless of our destiny, we still have to answer for our actions. We make choices, big and small, every day of our lives, and those choices have consequences.

We have to face those consequences head-on, for better or worse. We don't get to erase them just by saying we didn't mean to. Fate or not, our lives are still the results of our choices. I'm starting to think that when we don't own them, we don't own ourselves.

Mark moves toward the front door, and I follow him out.

"So I guess that's it, then," he says. "I guess I don't live here anymore."

Charlemagne comes out of the bedroom and runs over to him. He's skittish around her, scared. Maybe that's why she pees on his shoe. Or maybe it's because he's standing at the door, where we normally put her wee-wee pads.

Either way, I watch as she squats down and pees right on him.

He makes a face of disgust and looks at me. I stare back at him.

He turns around and walks out.

When Gabby comes home later that day, Charlemagne and I rush to the door. I greet her by telling her what Charlemagne did.

Gabby laughs a full belly laugh and leans over to give Charlemagne a hug.

The three of us stand there, laughing.

"My parents want me to move to London," I say. "They said they'll help me with the baby."

Gabby looks up at me, surprised. "Really?" she says. "What do you think of that? Think you'll go?"

And then I say something that I've never said before. "No," I say. "I want to stay here." I start laughing suddenly.

Gabby looks at me as if I have three heads. "What is so funny?" she says.

Between the laughter, I say, "It's just that I ruined things with the only man I think I've ever really loved. I'm pregnant with a baby I didn't plan for, as a result of sleeping with a married man, who won't even be in my child's life. I'm fatter than I've ever been. And my dog is still peeing inside the house. And yet, somehow, I feel like my life here is so good I couldn't possibly leave it. For the first time in my life, I have someone I feel like I can't live without."

"Is it me?" Gabby says suspiciously. "Because if it's not, this is a weird story."

"Yeah dude," I say to her. "It's you."

"Awww, thanks, bro!"

I'm sitting in the backseat of the car, looking out the open window. I'm inhaling the fresh air as we drive through the city. It's possible that from an outside perspective, I look like a dog. But I don't care. I'm so happy to be out of the hospital. To be living out in the real world. To see sunshine without the filter of a windowpane. Everything in the world has a smell to it. Outside isn't just the smell of fresh-cut grass and flowers. It's also smoke from diners and garlic from Italian restaurants. And I love all of it. It's probably just because I've spent so much time inhaling inorganic scents in a sterile hospital. And maybe a month from now I won't appreciate it the way I do right now. But that's OK. I appreciate it now.

I turn my head away from the window for a moment when I hear Mark sigh at a red light. I notice now that it is eerily quiet in the car. Mark seems to be getting more and more nervous the closer we get to their house. As I pay more attention, I can tell that he's out of sorts.

"Are you OK?" Gabby asks him.

"Hm? What? No, yeah, I'm fine," he says. "Just focusing on the road."

I can see his hands twitching. I can hear the shortness of his breath. And I'm starting to wonder if I'm missing something, if maybe he really doesn't want me living with them, if he sees it as a burden.

If he did, if he told Gabby that he didn't want to take on the responsibility, she'd fight him on it. I know that. And she'd never let on to me. I know that, too. So it's entirely possible that I'm imposing and I don't even know it.

We pull up to the side of the road in front of their place, and I can see that Mark installed a ramp for me to get up the three small steps to their door. He gets out of the car and immediately comes around to my side to help me out. He opens my door before Gabby can even get to me.

"Oh," he says. "You need the chair." Before I can answer, he's opened the trunk and is pulling it out. It drops to the ground with a thud. "Sorry," he says. "It's heavier than I thought."

Gabby moves toward him to help him open it up, and I see him flinch at her touch.

It's not me he's uncomfortable around. It's her.

"Are you sure you're OK?" she asks.

"Let's just get inside, OK?" he says.

"Um, OK . . ."

The two of them help me into the chair, and Mark grabs my bags. I wheel myself behind Gabby as she makes her way to the front door.

When she opens it and the three of us walk through the door, the tension is palpable. There is something wrong, and all three of us know it.

"I installed a seat in the shower and took the door off. It's just a curtain now. That should make it easy for you to get in and out on your own," Mark says.

He's talking to me, but he's looking at Gabby. He wants her to know all the work he did.

"I also moved all of your things into the first-floor office.

And put the guest bed in there so you don't have to go up and down the stairs. And I lowered the bed. You can try it."

I don't move.

"Or later, I guess."

Gabby looks at him sideways.

"You should be able to rest down on it to sit and then swing your legs over, as opposed to having to use your pelvis to sit or stand."

"Mark, what is going on?" Gabby asks.

"I bought a two-way pager system, so if you're in bed, you can just talk into it, and Gabby will know to come get you. And the dining-room table was too high, so this morning I had one delivered that is lower to the ground so your chair can reach."

Gabby whips her head around the corner, surprised. "You did that this morning? Where did our table go?"

Mark breathes in. "Hannah, could you give us a minute? Maybe you could confirm that your bed is the right height?"

"Mark, what the hell is going on?" Gabby's voice is tight and rigid. There is no bend in it, no patience.

"Hannah," he pleads.

"OK," I say, and I start wheeling myself away.

"No!" Gabby says, losing her patience. "She can barely move herself from place to place. Don't ask her to leave the room."

"It's fine, really," I say, but just as I say it, Mark blurts it out.

"I'm leaving," he says. He looks at the ground when he says it.

"To go where?" Gabby asks.

"I mean I'm leaving you," he says.

She goes from confused to stunned, as if she's been slapped across the face. Her jaw goes slack, her eyes open wide, her head shakes subtly from side to side, as if incapable of processing what she's hearing.

He fills in the gaps for her. "I've met someone. And I believe she is the one for me. And I'm leaving. I've left you with everything you two could need. Hannah is taken care of. I'm leaving you the house and most of the furniture. Louis Grant is drafting the paperwork."

"You called our attorney before you talked to me?"

"I was just asking him for a referral when he explained he could do it himself. I didn't mean to go behind your back."

She starts laughing. I knew she was going to start laughing when he said that. I wonder if the second it came out of his mouth, he thought, *Oh, crap, I shouldn't have said that*. I want to wheel out of the room very badly, but I also know that my wheelchair squeaks, and we are three people in one room. If one of us leaves, the other two are going to notice. And I'm not even sure they are registering that I'm here. I don't want to bring attention to the fact that I'm here by not being here anymore.

"You have got to be kidding me," she says.

"I'm sorry," he says. "But I'm not. We should talk about this in a few days, when you've had time to adjust to the information. I'm truly sorry to hurt you. It was never my intention. But I am in love with someone else, and it no longer seems fair to keep going the way we have been."

"What am I missing?" she asks. "We were talking about having a baby."

Mark shakes his head. "That was a . . . that was wrong of me. I was . . . pretending to be someone I'm not. I have made mistakes, Gabrielle, and I am now trying to fix them."

"Leaving me is fixing your mistakes?"

"I think we should talk about this at a later date. For now, I have moved my clothes and other things to my new place."

"Did you take my dining-room table?"

"I wanted to make sure you and Hannah had what you needed, so I took the table to my new home and bought you both a table that would work better for Hannah's situation."

"She's going to be walking eventually. I want my table back."

"I did what I thought was best. I think I should go now."

She stares at him for what feels like hours but is probably only thirty seconds. And then she erupts like I have never seen her before.

"Get out of my house!" she screams. "Get out of here! Get away from me!"

He heads for the door.

"I never should have married you," she says, and you can tell she means it. She deeply, deeply means it. She doesn't say it as if it's just occurring to her or as if she wants to hurt his feelings. She says it as if she is heartbroken that her worst fears came true right in front of her very eyes.

He doesn't look back at her. He just walks out the door, leaving it open behind him. It strikes me as cruel, that small gesture. He could have shut the door behind him. It's almost instinctual, isn't it? To shut the door behind you? But he didn't. He let it hang open, forcing her to close it.

But she doesn't. Instead, she crumples to the ground, yelling from the base of her lungs. It's throaty and deep, a grunt more than a scream. "I hate you!"

And then she looks up at me, remembering that I am here.

She gathers herself as best she can, but I wouldn't say she succeeds. Tears are falling down her face, her nose is running, her mouth is open and overflowing. "Will you get his key?" she says. She whispers it, but even in attempting to whisper, she cannot control the edges of her voice.

I spring into action. I wheel myself out the front door and down the ramp. He's getting into the car.

"The key," I say. "Your key, to the house."

"It's on the coffee table," he says. "With the deed. I signed over the townhouse," he says, as if it is a secret he has been waiting to tell, like a student excited to tell the teacher he did the extra credit.

"OK," I say, and then I turn my chair around and head back toward the front door.

"I want her to be OK," he says. "That's why I gave her the house."

"OK, Mark," I say.

"It's worth a lot of money," he says. "The equity in the townhouse, I mean. My parents helped us with the down payment, and I'm giving it to her."

I turn the chair around. "What do you want me to say, Mark? Do you want a gold medal?"

"I want her to understand that I'm doing everything in my power to make this easier on her. That I care about her. You get it, don't you?"

"Get what?"

"That love makes you do crazy things, that sometimes you have to do things that seem wrong from the outside but you know are right. I thought you'd understand. Given what Gabby told me happened between you and Michael."

If I hadn't just been in a car accident where I almost lost my life, maybe I'd be hurt by something as small as a sentence. If I hadn't spent the past week learning how to stand up on my own and use a wheelchair, maybe I'd let myself fall for this sort of crap. But Mark has the wrong idea about me. I'm no longer a person willing to pretend the things I've done wrong are justifiable because of how they make me feel.

I made a mistake. And that mistake is part of what has led me to this moment. And while I neither regret nor condone what I did, I have learned from it. I have grown since. And I'm different now.

You can only forgive yourself for the mistakes you made in the past once you know you'll never make them again. And I know I'll never make that mistake again. So I let his words rush past me and off into the wind.

"Just go, Mark," I tell him. "I'll let her know the house is hers."

"I never meant to hurt her." He opens his car door.

"OK," I say, and I turn away from him. I roll myself up the ramp. I hear his car leave the street. I'm not going to tell her any of that. She can see the deed to the townhouse on her own and form an opinion about it. I'm not going to try to tell her he didn't mean to hurt her. That's absurd and meaningless.

It doesn't matter if we don't mean to do the things we do. It doesn't matter if it was an accident or a mistake. It doesn't even matter if we think this is all up to fate. Because regardless of our destiny, we still have to answer for our actions. We make choices, big and small, every day of our lives, and those choices have consequences.

We have to face those consequences head-on, for better or worse. We don't get to erase them just by saying we didn't mean to. Fate or not, our lives are still the results of our choices. I'm starting to think that when we don't own them, we don't own ourselves.

I roll back into the house and see Gabby, still lying on the floor, nearly catatonic. She's staring at the ceiling. Her tears spill from her face and form tiny puddles on the floor.

"I don't know if I've ever felt pain like this," she says. "And I think I'm still in shock. It's only going to get worse, right? It's only going to get deeper and sharper, and it's already so deep and so sharp."

For the first time in what feels like a long time, I'm higher up than Gabby. I have to look down to meet her eyeline. "You won't have to go through it alone," I tell her. "I'll be here through every part of it. I'd do anything for you, do you know that? Does it help? To know that I'd move mountains for you? That I'd part seas?"

She looks up at me.

I move one foot onto the ground and lean over. I try to get my hands onto the floor in front of me.

"Hannah, stop," she says as I push my center of gravity closer to her, trying to lie down next to her. But I don't have the mechanics right. I don't have the right strength just yet. I topple over. It hurts. It actually hurts quite a bit. But I have pain medication in my bag and things to do. So I move through it. I scoot next to her, pushing the wheelchair out of the way.

"I love you," I tell her. "And I believe in you. I believe in Gabby Hudson. I believe she can do anything."

She looks at me with gratitude, and then she keeps crying. "I'm so embarrassed," she says between breaths. She's about to start hyperventilating.

"Shhh. There's no reason to be embarrassed. I can't go to the bathroom on my own. So you have no right to claim embarrassment," I tell her.

She laughs, if only for the smallest, infinitesimal second, and then she starts crying again. To hear it makes my heart ache.

"Squeeze my hand," I tell her as I take her hand in mine. "When it hurts so bad you don't think you can stand it, squeeze my hand."

She starts crying again, and she squeezes.

And at that moment, I realize that if I have taken away a fraction of her pain, then I have more purpose than I have ever known.

I'm not moving to London. I'm staying right here.

I found my home. And it's not New York or Seattle or London or even Los Angeles.

It's Gabby.

That night, Gabby and I decide to take Charlemagne for a long walk. At first, we were just going to walk around the block, but Gabby suggests getting out of the neighborhood. So we get into the car and drive to the Los Angeles County Museum of Art.

Gabby says it's beautiful at night. There is a light installation that shines brightly in the dark. She wants to show me.

We stop at Coffee Bean and get tea lattes. Mine is herbal because Gabby read an article that said pregnant women shouldn't have any caffeine. There are about ten others that say caffeine is fine in moderation but Gabby is very persuasive.

We park the car a few blocks from the museum, put Charlemagne on the sidewalk, and start walking. The air is cool; the sun set early tonight, and it's quiet on the streets of L.A., even for a Sunday night.

Gabby doesn't want to talk about Mark, and I don't really want to talk about the baby. Lately, it seems as if all we do is talk about Mark and the baby. So we decide instead to talk about high school.

"Freshman year, you had a crush on Will Underwood," Gabby says. She sips her drink right after she says it, and I look at her to see her eyes giving a mischievous glance. It's true, I did have a crush on Will Underwood. But she also knows that just mentioning it is enough to make me mortified. During our freshman year, Will Underwood was a senior who was completely cheesy and dated freshman girls. When you are a freshman girl, you don't understand what's so unlikable about guys who are interested in freshman girls. Instead, I very much hoped he'd notice me. I wanted to be one of those girls. He's now a shock jock on an FM station here.

"Well, I've never had good taste," I say, laughing at myself, and then I point at my belly. "As evidenced here by my baby with no daddy."

Gabby laughs. "Ethan was a good one," she says. "You were smart enough to choose Ethan."

"Twice," I remind her as we keep walking. Charlemagne pulls on the leash, leading us toward a tree. We stop.

"Well, I'm no better at choosing, clearly," Gabby says, and it occurs to me that when you're going through a divorce or when you're having a baby, there is no not talking about it. It shades everything you do. You have to talk about it, even when you aren't talking about it. And maybe that's OK. Maybe what's important is that you have someone to listen.

Charlemagne pees beside the tree and then starts scratching away at the grass, trying to cover it up. This is a pet peeve of Gabby's, because Gabby appreciates a nicely landscaped curb.

"Charlemagne, no," Gabby says. Charlemagne stops and looks up at her, hoping to please. "Good girl," Gabby says, and then she looks at me. "She's so smart. Did you think dogs were this smart?"

I laugh at her. "She's not that smart," I tell her. "Earlier today, she ran into the wall. You just love her, so you think she's smart. Rose-colored glasses and what have you."

Gabby cocks her head to the side and looks at Charlemagne.

"No," she says. "She's really smart. I just know it. I can tell. I mean, yes, I do love her. I love her to pieces. I honestly don't know what I was doing without a dog this whole time. Mark ruined all the good stuff."

Obviously, Mark didn't actually ruin every good thing in the world, but I don't contradict her. Anger is a part of healing. "Yeah," I say. "Well, actually, you did have good taste in men once. Remember how in love you were with Jesse Flint all through high school? And then senior year? You guys went out on the one date?"

"Oh, my God!" Gabby says. "Jesse Flint! I could never forget Jesse Flint! He was an actual dream man. I still think he's the most handsome guy I've ever seen in my life."

I laugh at her. "Oh, come on! He was tiny. I don't even know if he was taller than you."

She nods. "Oh, yes, he was. He was one inch taller than me and perfect. And then stupid Jessica Campos got back together with him the day after our date, and they ended up getting married after college. The major tragedy of my young life."

"You should call him," I say.

"Call Jesse Flint? And say what? 'Hey, Jesse, my marriage is over, and I remember one nice date with you when we were seventeen. How's Jessica?' "

"They got divorced, like, two years ago."

"What?" Gabby says. She stops in place. "No more Jesse and Jessica? Why did I not know about this?"

"I assumed you did. It was on Facebook."

"He's divorced?"

"Yeah, so maybe you two can talk about what divorce is like or something."

She starts walking again. Charlemagne and I walk with her. "You know something embarrassing?"

"What?"

"I thought about Jesse on my wedding day. How uncool is that? As I was walking down the aisle, I specifically thought, *Jesse Flint is already married. So he isn't the one you were meant to be with*. It made me feel better about my decision. I think I figured, you know, Mark really was the best one out there for me that was available."

I can't help it. I start laughing. "It's like you really wanted to get Count Chocula, but someone took the last box, and all they had was Cheerios, so you told yourself, 'OK, Cheerios is what I was meant to have.'"

"Mark is totally Cheerios," Gabby says. But she doesn't say it as if she's in on the joke. She says it as if it's a Zen riddle that has blown her mind. "Not Honey Nut, either. Straight-up, heart-healthy Cheerios."

"OK," I tell her. "So one day, when you're ready, probably a bit far off into the future, you call Count Chocula."

"Just like that?" she asks.

"Yep," I say. "Just like that."

"Just like that," she says back to me.

We walk for a little while, and then she points to a series of lights shining in long rows.

"That's the Urban Light installation I was telling you about," she says.

We walk closer to it and stop just in front of it, across the street. I have a wide view.

It's made up of old-fashioned streetlights, the kind that look as if they belong on a studio lot. The lights are beautiful, all clustered together in rows and columns. I'm not sure I understand the meaning behind it, exactly. I don't know if I get the artist's intention. But it is certainly striking. And I'm learning not to read too much into good things. I'm learning just to appreciate the good while you have it in your sights. Not to worry so much about what it all means and what will happen next.

"What do you think?" Gabby asks me. "It's pretty, right?"

"Yeah," I say. "I like it. There's something very hopeful about it."

And then, as quickly as we came, we turn around and walk back toward the car.

"You're going to find someone great one day," I say to Gabby. "I just have this feeling. Like we're headed in a good direction."

"Yeah?" she says. "I mean, all signs sort of point otherwise."

I shake my head. "No," I say. "I think everything is happening exactly as it's supposed to."

It's early in the morning, and Gabby and I have been lying on the floor all night. The sun is starting to break through the clouds, into the windows, and straight onto my eyes. It gets bright so early now.

"Are you awake?" I whisper. If she's sleeping, I want her to sleep. If she's awake, I need her to help me get up and pee.

"Yeah," she says. "I don't think I slept all night."

"You could have woken me up," I tell her. "I would have stayed up with you."

"I know," she says. "I know you would have."

I turn my head toward her and then push my torso up using my arms, so I'm sitting down. My body feels tight, tighter than it ever felt in the hospital.

"I have to pee," I tell her.

"OK," she says, getting up slowly. It's clumsy, but she's up. I can see now that her eyes are red, her face is swollen. She's not doing well. I suppose that's to be expected.

"If you can get me up and bring me my walker, I can do it," I tell her. "I want to do it on my own."

"OK," she says. She gets the walker from where we left it by the front door yesterday. She unfolds it and locks it into place. She puts it in front of me. And then she puts her arms under mine and lifts me. It's sounds so simple, standing up. But it's incredibly hard. Gabby bears almost my entire weight. It can't be easy for her. She's so much tinier than I am. But she manages to do it. She leans me on my walker and then lets go. Now I'm standing on my own, thanks to her.

"OK," I say. "I'll just be anywhere from three to sixty minutes. Depending on whether I manage to fall into the toilet."

She tries to laugh, but her heart isn't in it. I move myself slowly, step by step, in the right direction. "You're sure you don't want help?" she asks.

I don't even turn around. "I got it," I tell her. "You just take care of you."

It feels as if the bathroom is a million miles away, but I get there, one tiny, tentative step at a time.

When I get back to the living room, I'm feeling cold, so I shuffle over to my things that Gabby brought home from the hospital. I rummage through the bag, looking for my sweatshirt. When I finally see it and pull it out, an envelope drops to the floor. The front simply says "Hannah." I don't recognize the handwriting, but I know who it's from.

Hannah,

I'm sorry I had to trade your care to another nurse. I can't keep treating you. I enjoy your company too much. And my coworkers are starting to take notice.

I'm sure you know this, but it's highly unprofessional of any of us on the nursing staff to have a personal relationship with a patient, no matter the scope. I'm not allowed to exchange any personal contact information with you. I'm not allowed to try to contact you after you leave the hospital. If we were to run into each other on the street, I'm not even supposed to say hello to you unless you say hello first. I could be fired.

I don't have to tell you how much this job, this work, means to me.

I've been thinking about breaking the rules. I've been thinking about giving you my number. Or asking for yours. But I care too much about my work to compromise it by doing something I've sworn not to do.

All of this is to say that I wish we had met under different circumstances.

Maybe one day we will end up at the same place at the same time. Maybe we'll meet again when you aren't my patient and I'm not your nurse. When we are just two people.

If we do, I really hope you say hello. So that I can say hello back and then ask you out on a date.

Warmly,
Henry

"He left me the house," I hear from the couch. I tuck the letter away in my bag and turn to see Gabby crying, looking at the coffee table. She has the deed to the house in her hands.

"Yeah," I say.

"His parents paid for the down payment. A lot of his own money went into the mortgage."

"Yeah."

"He feels bad," she says. "He knows what he's doing is screwed up, and he's still doing it. That's what's so strange about this. That's not like him."

I set the walker in front of the couch and slowly let myself down. I really hope we aren't moving from this couch anytime soon, because I think that's all the energy I have for a while.

Gabby looks at me. "He must really love her."

I look at her and frown. I put my hand on her back. "It

doesn't justify what he did," I tell her. "His timing, his selfishness."

"Yeah," she says. "But . . ."

"But what?"

"He did everything he could except stay."

I hold her hand.

"Maybe he just has a feeling about her," Gabby says, echoing my sentiments from yesterday morning. Although, I'll tell you, it feels like a decade ago. "Maybe he can just *tell*."

I don't know what to say to that, so I don't say anything.

"I was never sure he was the one. Even when you asked me the other day, I could sort of feel myself sugarcoating what I really thought. I just thought Mark was a smart decision. We'd been together for a long time, and I just figured that's what you do. But I never had the moment when I just *knew*. You," she says to me, "have that feeling."

I dismiss her. "I've had that feeling before, though. For a long time, I had that feeling about Ethan. Now I have it about Henry. I mean, maybe it doesn't count, if you have it for more than one person."

"But I *never* had it. About him. He never had it about me. And maybe he has it now. It makes me feel a little better," she says. "To think that he left me because he met the one."

"Why does that make you feel better?" I cannot possibly conceive of how that could make her feel better.

"Because if I'm not his soul mate, then that means he's not mine. There's someone else out there for me. If he found his, maybe I'll find my own."

"And that makes you feel better?"

She holds her index finger and thumb together to form the

smallest gap. "Ever so slightly," she says. "So much it's almost nonexistent."

"Invisible to the naked eye," I add.

"But it's there."

I rub her back some more as she digests all of this.

"You know who I thought of yesterday? When you were talking about that feeling? The only one I think I might have felt that with?"

"Who?"

"Jesse Flint."

"From high school?"

She nods. "Yeah," she says. "He ended up marrying that girl Jessica Campos. But I—I don't know, until then, I always figured we would have something."

"They got divorced," I tell her. "A few years ago, I think. I saw it on Facebook."

"Well, there you go," she says. "Just that little piece of information gives me hope that there's somebody out there who makes me feel the way Henry makes you feel."

I smile at her. "I can promise you, there is someone better out there. I'd write it in stone."

"You have to find Henry," she says. "Don't you think? How do we do it? How are you going to find Henry?"

I tell her about the letter and then I shrug. "I might not find him," I say. "And that's OK. If you'd told me a month ago that I was going to get hit by a car and Mark was going to leave you, you'd never have been able to convince me that things would be OK. But I got hit by a car, and Mark left you, and . . . we're still standing. Well, you can stand. I'm sitting. But we're still alive. Right? We're still OK."

"I mean, things are pretty crappy, Hannah," she says.

"But they are OK, aren't they? Aren't we OK? Don't we both still have hope for the future?"

"Yeah." She nods somberly. "We do."

"So I'm not going to go around worrying too much," I tell her. "I'm just going to do my best and live under the assumption that if there are things in this life that we are supposed to do, if there are people in this world we are supposed to love, we'll find them. In time. The future is so incredibly unpredictable that trying to plan for it is like studying for a test you'll never take. I'm OK in this moment. To be with you. Here. In Los Angeles. If we're both quiet, we can hear birds chirping outside. If we take a moment, we can smell the onions from the Mexican place on the corner. This moment, we're OK. So I'm just going to focus on what I want and need *right now* and trust that the future will take care of itself."

"So what is it, then?" Gabby asks.

"What is what?"

"What is it you want out of life *right now*?"

I look at her and smile. "A cinnamon roll."

THREE WEEKS LATER

I am now firmly in my second trimester. I've gained enough weight that I look big but not enough that it's clear I'm pregnant. I'm just big enough to look like I have a beer belly. I'm sure I'll be complaining when I'm the size of a house, but I'm inclined to think this part is worse, at least for my ego. Some days, I feel good. Other days, I have a backache and eat three sandwiches for lunch. I'm convinced that I have a double chin. Gabby says I don't, but I do. I can see it when I look in the mirror. There's my chin and then a second chin right there below the first one.

Gabby comes to a lot of my doctor's appointments and birthing classes. Not all of them but most of them. She has also been reading the books with me and talking things through. Will I have a natural birth? Will I use cloth diapers? (My instinct tells me no and no.) It's nice to have someone in my corner. It makes me more confident that I can do this.

And I am finally finding my confidence. Sure, this is all very scary, and sometimes I want to crawl under the blankets and never come out. But I'm a woman who has been desperately looking for purpose and family, and I found both. Never has it been more clear to me that I have family around me in unconventional places, that I have always had more purpose than I have ever known.

I no longer feel a rush to leave this city and head for greener pastures, because there are no greener pastures and there is no better city. I am grounded here. I have a support system here. I have someone who needs me to put down roots and pick a place.

My parents were disappointed to learn that I wasn't going to join them in London, but the moment they resigned themselves to my decision, they suggested that the two of them and Sarah come out to L.A. when the baby is born. *They* are going to come and visit *me*. Us.

I just started working at Carl's office, and it has been both hugely stabilizing and really eye-opening. I see mothers and fathers every day who are in our office because they have a sick kid or a new baby or they are worried about one thing or another. You see how deeply these parents love their children, how much they would do for them, how far they are willing to go to make them happy, to keep them healthy. It's really made me think about what's important to me, what I'd be willing to lose everything for, not just as a friend or as a parent but also as a person.

I'm enjoying it so much that I'm thinking about working in a pediatrician's office long-term. Obviously, this is all very new, but I can't remember the last time a job made me this excited. I like working with kids and parents. I like helping people through things that might be scary or new or nerve-racking.

So this morning, while Gabby is taking Charlemagne to the vet, I have found myself Googling nursing schools. I mean, it seems completely absurd to have a job, go to nursing school, and have a child, but I'm not going to lct that stop me. I'm looking into it. I'll see if there is any way I can make it work. That's what you do when you want something. You don't look for reasons why it won't work. You look for reasons why it will. So I'm searching, I'm digging, for ways to make it happen.

I'm looking into the local community college when my phone rings.

It's Ethan.

I hesitate for a moment. I hesitate for so long that by the time I decide to answer, I've missed the call.

I stare at the phone, stunned, until I hear his voice.

"I know you're home," he says, teasing me. "I can see your car on the street."

I whip my head toward the entry, and I can see his forehead and hair through the glass at the top of the door.

"I didn't get to the phone in time," I tell him as I stand up and walk to the door.

There is a part of me that doesn't want to open it. I've been thinking lately that maybe I am meant to raise this baby on my own, to be on my own, until my kid is in college and I'm pushing fifty. Sometimes, when I'm lying awake at night, I imagine a middle-aged Ethan knocking on my door, years in the future. He says he loves me and can't live without me anymore. And I tell him I feel the same way. And we spend the second half of our lives together. I have told myself on more than one occasion that the timing will work out one day. I've told myself this so many times that I've started to believe it.

And now, knowing he's on the other side of the door, it feels wrong. This wasn't a part of my new plan.

"Will you open the door?" he asks. "Or do you hate me that much?"

"I don't hate you," I say. "I don't hate you at all." My hand is on the knob, but my wrist doesn't turn.

"But you're not going to open the door?"

It's polite to open the door. It's what you do. "No," I say, and then I realize the real reason I don't want to open it, and I figure the best thing to do is to tell him. "I'm not ready to see you," I say. "To look at you."

He's quiet for a moment. Quiet so long that I think he might have left. And then he speaks. "How about just talking to me? Is that OK? Talking?"

"Yeah," I say. "That's OK."

"Well, then, get comfortable," he says. "This may take a minute." I see his hair disappear from view, and I realize he's sitting down on the front stoop.

"OK," I say. "I'm listening."

He's quiet again. But this time, I know he hasn't left. "I broke up with you," he says.

"Well, I don't know about that," I tell him. "I didn't leave you much choice. I'm having a baby."

"No," he says. "In high school."

I smile and shake my head, but then I realize he can't see me, so I give him the verbal cue he's looking for. "No shit, Sherlock."

"I think I wanted to pin it on you because I didn't want to admit that I might have avoided this whole thing if I'd acted differently back then."

"Avoided what? Me being pregnant?" I don't want to avoid being pregnant. I like where life has led me, and if he can't handle it, that is not my problem.

"No," he says. "Being without you for so many years."

"Oh," I say.

"I love you," he says. "I'm pretty sure I loved you from the moment I met you at Homecoming and you told me you listened to Weezer."

I laugh and work my way down to sit on the floor.

"And I broke up with you because I thought I was going to marry you."

"What do you mean?"

"I was nineteen and a freshman in college, and I thought, I have already met the girl I'm going to marry. And it scared me, you know? I remember thinking that I'd never sleep with anyone else. I'd never kiss another girl. I'd never do any of the things my friends at school were doing, things I wanted to do. Because I'd already met you. I'd already met the girl of my dreams. And you know, for one stupid moment in college, I thought that was a bad thing. So I let you go. And if I'm being completely honest, even though it makes me sound like a total jerk, I always thought I'd get you back. I thought I could break up with you and have my fun and be young, and then, when I was done, I'd go get you back. It never occurred to me that you have to hold those things sacred."

"I didn't know that," I tell him.

"I know, because I never told you. And then, of course, I realized that I didn't want any of those stupid college things, I wanted you, but when I came home for Christmas to tell you, you were already dating someone else. I should have blamed myself, but I blamed you. And I should have fought for you, but I didn't. I felt rejected, and I turned to someone else."

"I'm sorry," I say.

"No," he says. "You shouldn't be sorry. I'm sorry. I'm sorry I keep chickening out. I see what I want, and I'm too scared to do what it takes to have it. I'm too much of an idiot to sacrifice the small stuff in order to have the big stuff. I love you, Hannah. More than I have ever loved anyone else. And I told you, when I got you back, that I would never again let anything get in the way."

I nod to myself, even though I know he can't see me.

"And what do I do? At the first sign of trouble, I back out."

"It's not that simple, Ethan. We started dating again, and within two weeks, I told you I was having another man's baby. These are extenuating circumstances."

"I don't know," he says. "I'm not sure I believe in extenuating circumstances, not when it comes to this."

"You said it yourself," I tell him. "Sometimes the timing just doesn't work out."

"I'm not sure I believe in that anymore, either," he says. "Timing seems like an excuse. Extenuating circumstances is an excuse. If you love someone, if you think you could make them happy for the rest of your life together, then nothing should stop you. You should be prepared to take them as they are and deal with the consequences. Relationships aren't neat and clean. They're ugly and messy, and they make almost no sense except to the two people in them. That's what I think. I think if you truly love someone, you accept the circumstances; you don't hide behind them."

"What do you mean?"

"I mean I love you, and I want to be with you, and if you want to be with me, then nothing is going to stop me. Not timing, not babies, nothing. If you want to do this, if you want to be with me, I will take you in whatever form I can have you. I will love you just as you are. I won't try to change a single thing about you."

"Ethan, you don't know what you're saying."

"I do," he says. With my back against the door, I can feel that he has stood up. I stand up with him. "Hannah, I believe you are the love of my life, and I'd rather live a life with forty babies that aren't mine than be without you. I have missed you every day since I last saw you. I've missed you for years. I'm not saying this is an ideal situation. But I am saying that it's one I'm on board for, if you'll have me."

"What happens when my baby is born?" I ask him.

"I don't know," he says. "I know I said that I wasn't ready to be a father. But I keep thinking to myself, what if it was my baby? Would I behave differently? And I would. If you were pregnant by me, accident or not, I'd *get* ready."

"And now?" I ask him through the door. "When it's not your kid?"

"I'm not sure I see much of a difference anymore," he says. "What you love, I love."

I stare down at the floor. My hands are shaking.

"We can figure out how you want to play it," he says. "I can be a dad or a stepdad or a friend or an uncle. I can help with all the classes and be there when you give birth, if you'll let me. Or I can hang back, if that's what you want. I'll follow your lead. I'll be the person you need me to be. Just let me be a part of this, Hannah. Let me be with you."

I put my hands on the door to steady them. I feel as if I might fall down. "I don't know what to say," I tell him.

"Say how you feel," he says.

"I feel confused," I say. "And surprised."

"Sure," he says.

"And I feel like maybe we can do this."

"You do?"

"Yeah," I say. "I feel like maybe this was how it was supposed to go all along."

"Yeah?" he says. I can feel the joy in his voice as it vibrates through the door.

"Yeah," I say. "Maybe I was meant to have this baby. And I was meant to be with you. And everything is happening the way it's supposed to." What I believe to be fated seems to fall perfectly in line with what I want to be true at any given moment. But I think that's OK. I think that's hope. "It's messy," I tell him. "You said earlier that it's messy, and you're right. It's messy."

"Messy is OK," he says. "Right? We can do messy."

"Yeah," I say, tears now falling down my face. "We can do messy."

"Open the door, sweetheart, please," he says. "I love you."

"I love you, too," I say. But I don't open the door.

"Hannah?" Ethan says.

"I'm fat now," I tell him.

"That's OK."

"No, really, I'm growing a double chin."

"I have back acne," he says. "Who cares?"

I laugh through my tears. "Pretty soon I won't be able to reach my feet."

"Then I'll put your socks on. What did I tell you? There's nothing you can do to get rid of me," he says.

"And you meant it?"

"I meant it."

I open the door to see Ethan standing on the stoop. He is wearing a light blue T-shirt and dark jeans. His eyes are glassy, and his mouth is smiling wide. He has a box of cinnamon rolls in his hand.

"You're the most gorgeous woman I've ever seen," he says, and then he steps into the house, and he kisses me. And for the first time in my life, I know I have done everything right.

THREE MONTHS LATER

I can walk now. Without a walker. On my own. I use a cane sometimes, when I'm tired or sore. But it never holds me back. Sometimes I walk to the convenience store down the street to get a candy bar, not because I want the candy bar but because I appreciate the walk to get one.

Gabby's still not ready to date, still skittish from the shock of it all, but she's moving on. She's happy. She got us a dog. A Saint Bernard just like Carl and Tina have. She named him Tucker.

The woman who hit me proved also to be responsible for another hit-and-run two years ago. She didn't hit a person then, but she did hit a car and drive off. Between insurance payouts and the lawsuit, I'll have enough money to be comfortable on my feet.

When I got to the point where I could get myself from place to place, I bought a car. It's a cherry-red hatchback. You can see me coming from miles away, which I like. I think it's a very "me" car.

Then, once I had a car, I started looking for a job.

I told Carl and Tina that I've been thinking about going to nursing school. After the money comes in, I'll be able to afford it, and I keep thinking about the nurses who helped me during my hospital stay. In particular, I think of Nurse Hannah and how well she handled me at my most annoying. And I think of

Deanna and that pediatric nurse who helped those parents on the oncology floor.

And of course, I think of Henry.

Nurses help people. And I'm starting to think there's nothing more important I can do with my time than that.

When you almost lose your life, it makes you want to double down, to do something important and bigger than yourself. And I think this is my thing.

Carl offered me a job at his pediatric office until I figure out what I want to do. He says that his practice has a program to help staff members go to night school if they meet certain financial criteria. When I reminded him that I probably won't meet those criteria, he laughed at me and said, "Good point! Just come take the job for the experience and living wage, then. Spend your money on school."

So I took him up on it. It's early still, I've only been working there a few weeks, but it's confirming what I already know: I'm headed in the right direction.

I told my parents that I wasn't moving to London, and they were sad but seemed to take it well. "OK," my mom said, "we get it. But in that case, we need to talk about a good time for us to visit."

And then my dad pulled the phone away from her and said he was coming in July, whether I liked it or not. "I don't want to wait until Christmas to see you again, and to be honest, I'm starting to miss Fourth of July barbecues."

A few weeks later, my mom called to say they were considering buying a condo in Los Angeles. "You know, just a place where we could stay when we come to visit from now on," she said. "That is, if you're staying in Los Angeles . . ."

I told her I was. I said I wasn't going anywhere. I said I was here to stay. I didn't even think twice about it. I just said it.

Because it was true.

Ethan has started dating a really nice woman named Ella. She's a high school teacher and a pretty intense cyclist. He bought a bike last month, and now they are on some three-day trek raising money for cancer research. He seems incredibly happy. The other day, he told me that he can't believe he's gone so many years living in Los Angeles without seeing it from a bike. He has bike shorts now. Hilariously tight little bike shorts that he wears with a bike shirt and a helmet. We had dinner the other night, and he biked there from his place, a thirty-minute drive away. The smile on his face when he walked in the door rivaled the sun.

And he's been great to me. He texts me whenever he sees a place with a cinnamon roll that I haven't tried. When I could walk upstairs on my own, he came over and helped Gabby and me move my stuff back up to the second floor. Even he and Gabby have become close in their own right. The point is, Ethan is a great friend. And I'm glad I didn't ruin it by thinking we had anything left between us. We are better this way.

I'd be lying if I said I never think about the child I might have if I hadn't been hit. Occasionally, I'll be doing something completely arbitrary, like taking a shower or driving home, and I'll think about it, the baby. The only way I can make any peace with it is to know that I wasn't ready to be a mother then. But one day, I will be. And I try not to busy my mind with too many thoughts about the past or what could have been.

I wake up most mornings feeling refreshed and well rested,

with an excitement about the day. And as long as you can say that, I think you're doing OK.

I woke up early this morning, so I figured I'd get into the car and head to Primo's. It's a habit I've started for myself, a small treat when I find the time. I often call my dad while I'm there. It's not the same as when he would take me as a child, but it's close. And I'm finding that, at least with my parents, the more we talk on the phone, the better I feel.

I call him now as I'm driving, but he doesn't pick up. I leave a message. I tell him I'm on my way to Primo's and I'm thinking of him.

I pull into the crowded Primo's parking lot and park the car. I grab my cane from the backseat and walk around to the front of the store. I stand in line and order a cinnamon roll and a buttermilk doughnut for Gabby.

I pay, and I'm handed an already-greasy bag.

And then I hear a familiar voice speak to the cashier. "A cinnamon roll, please."

I turn and look. For a moment, I don't recognize him. He's wearing jeans and a T-shirt. I've only seen him in navy-blue scrubs.

I look down at his arm, to make sure I'm not crazy, to confirm that I'm not seeing things.

Isabella.

"Henry?" I say. But of course it's him. And I'm surprised just how familiar he looks, how natural it seems that he would be standing in front of me.

Henry.

"Hello," I say to him. "Hello, hello. Hi."

"Hi," he says, smiling. "I thought I might see you here one of these days."

The man behind the counter gives Henry his cinnamon roll, and Henry hands over some cash.

"All the cinnamon roll joints in all the world, and you had to walk into mine," I say.

He laughs. "By design, actually," he says.

"What do you mean?"

"I figured if I was ever gonna meet you again, run into you, and start a conversation like two normal people, I knew my best bet was a place with good cinnamon rolls."

I blush. I know I'm blushing, because I can feel the warmth on my cheeks.

"Can we talk outside?" he says. The two of us are holding up the line.

I nod and follow him out. He sits down at one of the metal tables. I put down my food. Both of us pull out our cinnamon rolls. Henry takes a bite of his first.

"Did you get my letter?" he asks me when he's done chewing.

I chew, closing my eyes and nodding. "Yeah," I say finally. "I looked for you for a while. On street corners and in stores. I kept looking at men's arms."

"For the tattoo?" he asks.

"Yeah," I say.

"And you never found me."

"Until today," I say.

He smiles.

"I'm sorry if I caused any problems for you at work," I say.

He waves me off. "You didn't. Hannah didn't love the stunt you pulled after I left, though," he says, laughing. "But she also said you seemed like a stalker. And that I was clearly not to blame."

I blush so hard I have to put my head in my hands. "Oh, I'm so embarrassed," I say. "I was on a lot of medication."

He laughs. "Don't be embarrassed," he says. "It made my day when I found out about it."

"It did?" I ask him.

"Are you kidding me? Prettiest girl you've ever seen rolls herself through a hospital desperately trying to find you? Made my week."

"Well," I say. "I . . . wanted to say a proper good-bye, I guess. I felt like we . . ."

Henry shakes his head. "You don't need to explain anything to me. Are you free tonight for dinner? I want to take you on a date."

"You do?" I say.

"Yes," Henry says. "What do you say?"

I laugh. "I say yeah. That sounds lovely. Oh, but I can't tonight. I have plans with Gabby. But tomorrow? Could you do tomorrow?"

"Yep," he says. "I can do whenever you can do. What about now? What are you doing now?"

"Now?"

"Yeah."

"Nothing."

"Will you go for a walk with me?"

"I would love that," I tell him. I wipe the sugar off my hands and grab my cane. "I hope you don't mind that I have to use my cane."

"Are you kidding me?" he says. "I've been going to bakeries for months hoping to find you. Something as small as a cane isn't going to put me off."

I smile. "Plus, if I didn't need this cane, I probably would never have met you. Although, who knows, maybe we could have met another way."

"As a man who has been trying to run into you for months, let me assure you how rare it is that two specific people's paths will cross."

He takes my hand in his, and I have waited for it for so long, have believed so strongly that it may never happen, that it proves as intimate a gesture as any I have ever experienced.

"To car accidents, then," I say.

He laughs. "To car accidents. And to everything that has led up to this."

He kisses me then, and I realize I was wrong about the hand holding. It now feels teenager-ish and quaint. This is what I'd been waiting for.

And as I stand there, in the middle of the city, kissing my night nurse, I know, for the first time in my life, that I have done everything right.

After all, he tastes like a cinnamon roll, and I've never kissed anyone who tasted like a cinnamon roll.

THREE YEARS LATER

Gabby hates surprises, but Carl and Tina insisted that it had to be a surprise party. I told them I would go along with their plan, and then I spilled the beans to Gabby last week so she'd know what to expect. I just knew that if it were me, I'd want the heads-up. So here we are, at her thirty-second birthday, me, Ethan, and fifty of her closest friends, huddled in her parents' living room, completely in the dark, waiting to surprise someone who won't be surprised.

We hear her parents' car pull into the driveway. I give one last warning to everyone to be quiet when I see their headlights go out.

We hear them walk up to the door.

We see the door open.

I turn on the lights, and the entire room of us yells, "Surprise!" just as we are supposed to.

Gabby's eyes go wide. She's a good faker. She looks genuinely terrified. And then she turns immediately into Jesse's chest. He laughs, holding her.

"Happy birthday!" he says, and then he spins her back around to look at all of us.

Tina decorated the room tastefully. Champagne and a dessert bar. White and silver balloons.

Gabby makes her way to me first. "Thank God you told me,"

she whispers. "I don't know if I could have handled all of this without a warning."

I laugh. "Happy birthday!" I tell her. "Surprise!"

We laugh.

"Where's Gabriella?"

"I left her with Paula," I say. Paula is our go-to babysitter, maybe more of a nanny. She's an older woman I worked with in Carl's office. She retired and then found herself really bored, so she looks after Gabriella during the day when I am at work or anytime Gabby, Ethan, and I aren't around. Gabriella loves her. Ethan and I have always jokingly called Gabby the third parent, so it was only natural that we started calling Paula the fourth. For a woman who felt as if her parents weren't around, I've certainly given my kid a plethora of them.

"Did you tell Paula yet?" Gabby asks in a clandestine whisper. "About the *thing*?" I can only assume that she's referring to the fact that Ethan and I have, just this month, started trying to have a second child.

"No," I whisper. "You're still the only one who knows."

"Seems better just to let everyone know once we've succeeded," Ethan says. "But Hannah has forgotten to tell you the best part about tonight."

"I have?"

"Paula said she'd spend the night, so it's party time, as far as I'm concerned!" Ethan says, standing beside me. "And happy birthday! That, too." He hands Gabby a bottle of wine that we picked up for her.

"Thank you!" she says. She gives him a big hug. "I love you guys. Thank you so much for all of this."

"We love you, too," I say. "Have you seen the Flints? They're in the back." I point, but she's already moving toward them. I watch her as she hugs her soon-to-be in-laws. You can tell they love her.

"Nice try, kiddo," Carl says, coming up to me. "You two almost fooled me."

I act mock-confused. "I have no idea what you're talking about."

"She knew. I know my daughter, and she knew. And I know Jesse didn't tell her, because he's still too scared of me. You're the only one brave enough to defy me."

I laugh. "She hates surprises," I say in my own defense.

Carl shakes his head and then looks at Ethan. "Is this what serves as an apology with your wife?"

Ethan laughs and puts his hands up in surrender. "I'm staying out of it."

"I'm sorry," I say to Carl sincerely.

He waves me off. "I'm teasing. As long as she's happy, I don't care. And it appears she is."

Tina fights her way through the crowd to talk to us. She gives me a big hug and then goes straight for the kill. "When are you leaving the office to start school full-time?"

"Next month," I say. "But I'm still not sure about this."

I look to Carl. So far, I have put myself through school by working just under full-time for him and taking advantage of his practice's tuition-reimbursement program. It's been an amazing opportunity, but with Gabriella and the possibility of a second child, I want to finish my certification faster. Ethan and I discussed it, and I'm leaving my job to go to school full-time. But if Carl wants me to stay longer, I'll stay longer. I'd do anything for him. Without him, without the Hudsons in general, I don't know where I'd be.

"Would you stop? Get your certification. And when you're done, at least give me the first option to hire you. That's all I can ask."

"But you two have done so much for me. I don't know how I could ever repay you."

"You don't *repay* us," Tina says. "We're your family."

I smile and put my head on Carl's shoulder.

"I do need a favor of you tonight, though," Carl says. "If you'll oblige me."

"Of course," I say.

"Yates has been on me to hire someone from his old office. A nurse, I guess, who's here with him. I swear, Yates is like a dog with a bone. He just will not let up when he wants something."

Dr. Yates is a new doctor at the practice. Carl and Dr. Yates don't see eye to eye on a lot of stuff, but he's a good guy. I invited him to the party even though Carl thought it wasn't necessary. But Carl also wanted to invite the entire office *except* Yates. So . . . I think I was right about this.

"And you know me," Carl continues. "I'm not good talking business at a party. Or, rather, I hate talking business at a party." Carl is perfectly fine talking business anywhere. He just doesn't want to talk to Yates.

"I'll do a quick screening for you if I run into them," I say.

"I'm going to go check on Gabriella," Ethan says. He steps into the kitchen, and I watch as he calls Paula. He always does this. He talks a big game about leaving her for a night, and then he calls every two hours. He has to know how she is, what she's eaten. For someone who didn't know if he was ready to be a parent, he is the most conscientious parent I've ever seen.

He officially adopted Gabriella last year. Ethan wanted us all to have the same name. "We're a family," he says. "A team."

She is now Gabriella Martin Hanover. We are the Martin Hanovers.

And sure, maybe Gabriella and Ethan aren't related by blood, but you'd never know it to look at them, to hear them talk to each other. They are family as much as any two people can be. The other day at the grocery store, the cashier said Gabriella and Ethan had the same eyes. He smiled and said thank you.

"I know, sweetheart, but Daddy needs to talk to Paula," I can hear him saying into the phone. "If you go to bed when Paula asks you to, Mama and I will come in and give you a kiss when we get home, OK?" Gabriella must have given the phone back to Paula, because the next thing I hear out of Ethan's mouth is "OK, but you got the marble out of her nose?"

We are tired a lot of the time. We don't go on dates as often as we'd like. But we love each other madly. I'm married to a man who became a father because he loved me and now loves me because I made him a father. And he makes me laugh. And he looks handsome when he dresses up, which he has done tonight.

He comes back into the room, and soon the place is so loud we can barely hear each other speak. Just when the party seems to hit its peak, someone asks Jesse to tell the story of how he and Gabby met. Slowly but surely, the entire house quiets down to listen. Jesse stands at the base of the fireplace so he can be seen and heard by everyone. He's too short to be seen on his own.

"First day of geometry class. Tenth grade. I looked to the front of the classroom and saw the most interesting girl I'd ever laid eyes on."

Jesse has told this story so many times I could tell it myself at this point.

"And, to my delight, she was shorter than me."

Everyone laughs.

"But I didn't ask her out. I was too nervous. Three weeks into school, another girl asked me out, and I said yes because I was fifteen and was going to take it wherever I could get it."

The crowd laughs again.

"Jessica and I dated for a long time and then broke up senior year. And of course, when we broke up, I immediately found Gabby and asked her out. And we had this great date. And then, the next morning, my girlfriend called me, and she wanted to get back together. And . . . we did. Jessica and I spent college together, got married after, yada yada yada . . ."

He always says "yada yada yada."

"Jessica and I split up after two years of marriage. It just wasn't working. And then, a few years later, I get a Facebook request from Gabby Hudson. *The* Gabby Hudson."

That's my favorite part. The part where he calls her *the* Gabby Hudson.

"And I got really nervous and excited, and I started Facebook-stalking her and wondering if she was single and if she would ever date me. And the next thing I know, we're out to dinner at some hip restaurant in Hollywood. And I just had this feeling. I didn't tell her then, because I didn't want to be creepy, but I felt like I finally understood why people get married a second time. When I got divorced, I wasn't sure if I'd ever be up for it again. But then it all clicked into place, and I understood that my marriage failed the first time because I picked the wrong person. And finally, the right person was standing in front of me. So I waited the appropriate amount of months of dating, and I told her how I felt. And then I asked her to marry me, and she said yes."

That's usually the end of his story, but he keeps talking.

"I was reading a book about the cosmos recently," he says, and then he looks around and goes, "Hold on, trust me, this relates."

The crowd laughs again.

"And I was reading about different theories about the universe. I was really taken with this one theory that states that everything that is possible happens. That means that when you flip a quarter, it doesn't come down heads *or* tails. It comes up heads *and* tails. Every time you flip a coin and it comes up heads, you are merely in the universe where the coin came up heads. There is another version of you out there, created the second the quarter flipped, who saw it come up tails. This is happening every second of every day. The world is splitting further and further into an infinite number of parallel universes where everything that could happen *is* happening. This is completely plausible, by the way. It's a legitimate interpretation of quantum mechanics. It's entirely possible that every time we make a decision, there is a version of us out there somewhere who made a different choice. An infinite number of versions of ourselves are living out the consequences of every single possibility in our lives. What I'm getting at here is that I know there may be universes out there where I made different choices that led me somewhere else, led me to *someone* else."

He looks at Gabby. "And my heart breaks for every single version of me that didn't end up with you."

I'm embarrassed to say that I start crying. Gabby catches my eye, and I can see she's teary, too. Everyone is staring in rapt attention. Jesse is done speaking, but no one can turn away. I know that I should do something, but I'm not sure what to do.

"Way to make the rest of us look bad!" a guy shouts from the back of the room.

The crowd laughs and disperses. I turn and look behind me, trying to find the man who spoke, but I don't see him. Instead, I see Dr. Yates. I turn to Ethan.

"Dr. Yates is back there," I say. "I'm going to go say hi. I'll be back in a second."

He nods and walks over to the desserts. "I'll get you some cheesecake," he says. "Unless I see a cinnamon roll."

I head over to Dr. Yates.

"Hannah," he says. "Quite a party."

I laugh. "So it is."

"Listen, I want to introduce you to someone." He gestures to the man standing next to him. The man has a large tattoo on his forearm. I can't quite make out what it is. I think it's some sort of cursive script. "This is Henry. I'm trying to persuade him to leave Angeles Presbyterian and come work with us."

"Well, it's a great place to work," I say.

"And Henry is one of the best nurses I've ever worked with," Dr. Yates says.

"Quite a recommendation!" I say to Henry.

"Well, I paid good money for him to say that," he says.

I laugh.

"Would you two excuse me?" Dr. Yates says. "I want to say hello to Gabby."

He walks off, and I am left with Henry, unsure what to say.

"Did you see the dessert bar?" I ask.

"Yeah," he says. "I was gonna grab something, but honestly, I like breakfast sweets much better. Cheese danishes, for instance. Or cinnamon rolls."

"I am obsessed with cinnamon rolls," I say.

"Rightfully so," he says. "They are delicious. I'd take a cinnamon roll over a brownie any day."

I laugh. "It is like you are stealing the words right out of my mouth."

He laughs, too. "Are you from around here?"

"Yeah," I say. "I am. You?"

He shakes his head. "No, I moved out from Texas about eight years ago."

"Oh, whereabouts in Texas?" I ask.

"Just outside of Austin."

I smile. "I lived in Austin for a little while," I say. "Great area."

"Yeah," he says. "Hot as hell, though."

"Yes," I say. "Amen to that."

"So are you a nurse, too?" he asks me.

"Trying to be," I say. "I'm about to leave the practice to go to school full-time. I'm eager to be done with school and start working."

"I remember when I officially became an RN." He laughs to himself. "Seems like ages ago."

"Well, I'm a little bit behind," I say.

"Oh, no," he says. "That's not what I meant at all. I just meant I feel like eons have passed since I started."

"Did you always want to work in health care?" I ask him. Since we're on the subject, no sense in wasting the opportunity to find out more about him and see if he's right for the office.

He nods. "Yeah, more or less. My sister died when I was young."

"I'm so sorry," I say.

He waves me off. "Not necessary, but thank you. I just remember being in the hospital as a kid and seeing how much the nurses were doing to take care of her, to make her comfortable, to make all of us comfortable, and, I don't know, I guess I just always wanted to do that." Aaaaaand there's no way I would ever say no to this guy, with a story like that.

"For me, it was when I was pregnant with my daughter and I had just started working in the office," I say. "I could see how scared some of the parents were sometimes and how much they needed someone who understood what they were going through, and I just really wanted to be that person. And then, once I had my daughter, I felt that fear. I felt how much you ache at the thought of anything happening to them. I just wanted to help soothe the anxiety, you know?"

He smiles. It's a nice smile. There's something very calming about it. "Yeah, I hear you," he says.

If Jesse is right and there are other universes out there, I've probably met Henry before in one of them. We might work together somewhere. Or we would have met in Texas years ago. Maybe in line for a cinnamon roll.

"Well, I'm sure I'll be seeing you," I say. "Some way or another."

"Yeah," he says. "Or maybe in another life."

I laugh and excuse myself as Ethan comes and finds me. He brings me a bite-sized cheesecake.

"What do you say we leave early?" he says.

"Early?" I say. "I thought we were partying all night. Paula will sleep at our place."

"Yeah," he says. "But what if we left the party and went . . . to a *hotel*?"

My eyebrows go up. "Are you suggesting what I think you're suggesting?"

"Let's make a baby, baby."

I put down my glass of water and pop the cheesecake into

my mouth. I scoot over to the corner of the room, where I see Carl, Tina, Gabby, and Jesse talking.

"Carl, he seems great. Henry, I mean. You should hire him. For sure. Gabby, I love you. Happy birthday. If you'll excuse Ethan and me, we have to go home."

Gabby and Tina give me a hug. Ethan shakes hands with Carl and Jesse.

Ethan and I walk out the front door. It started to rain sometime during the evening. I'm chilly, and Ethan takes off his jacket and puts it around my shoulders.

"We could stay up all night, you know," he says, teasing me. "Or we could have sex once, turn on the TV, and fall asleep peacefully."

I laugh. "That last one sounds great," I say.

I get into the car, and I am overwhelmed by gratitude.

If there are an infinite number of universes, I don't know how I got so lucky as to end up in this one.

Maybe there are other lives for me out there, but I can't imagine being as happy in any of them as I am right now, today.

I have to think that while I may exist in other universes, none is as good as this.

Gabby hates surprises, but I couldn't persuade Carl and Tina to go about this any other way, and I wasn't going to be the one who told her. So here we are, at her thirty-second birthday, me, Henry, and fifty of her closest friends, huddled in her parents' living room, completely in the dark.

We hear her parents' car pull into the driveway. I give one last warning to everyone to be quiet when I see their headlights go out.

I hear them walk up to the door.

I see the door open.

I turn on the lights, and the entire room of us yells, "Surprise!" just as we are supposed to.

Gabby's eyes go wide. She's genuinely terrified for a moment. And then she turns immediately into Jesse's chest. He laughs, holding her.

"Happy birthday!" he says, and then he spins her back around to look at all of us.

The living room is full of beautiful decorations. Champagne flutes and Moët. A dessert bar. Henry and I went all over Los Angeles today to find linen tablecloths to match the décor. Henry loves Gabby. Would do anything for her.

Gabby makes her way to me first. "Are you mad?" I ask as she hugs me. "I toyed with the idea of telling you."

She pulls away from me. You can tell from her face that she's still startled. "No," she says. "I'm not mad. Overwhelmed, maybe. I'm sort of shocked that between you and Jesse, no one let it slip."

"We made a pact," I tell her. "Not to say anything. It was really important to your parents."

"They did all this?" she says.

I nod. "All their idea."

"Happy birthday," Henry says. He hands her a glass of champagne. She takes it and gives him a hug.

"And I suppose you won't be having any?" Gabby says, looking at my belly. I'm seven months pregnant. It's a girl. We're naming her Isabella, after Henry's sister. Gabby doesn't know that we've talked about naming her Isabella Gabrielle, after her.

"Nope," I say. "But I'll be drinking with you in spirit. Have you seen the Flints?" I ask her. "They are . . ." I look around until I find them in the back, waving at her and talking to Jesse. She's already moving toward them.

I watch her as she hugs her soon-to-be in-laws. They love her—that much is clear.

"Well done, kiddo," Carl says to me. "I wasn't sure you'd be able to pull it off."

"I'm not great with keeping secrets," I tell him. "But I figured this was an important one. So . . . ta-da!" I lift my hands up in the air, as if I've performed a magic trick.

Carl looks at my hands and then at Henry. "You let your wife attend parties without a wedding ring, son?"

Henry laughs. "You can get into that with her," he says. "I don't tell her what to do."

"I had to take it off," I tell Carl, defending myself. "My fingers are the size of sausages."

Carl shakes his head, teasing me. "Not even married a year, and already she's coming up with reasons to take off the ring. Tsk-tsk."

"You're right. I'm liable to run off at any minute," I say, pointing down to my belly.

Carl laughs, and Tina fights her way through the crowd to talk to us.

"Look at you. About to be a mother and a nurse," she says, by way of hello.

I will finish my nursing degree in a year or so, but that seems like a lifetime from now. All I can think about these days is the baby I'm about to have.

"I'm starting to get nervous about juggling it all when the baby comes," I tell her. "I mean, I know I can do it. Plenty of women do it. I think I'm just anxious about everything changing."

"You're gonna be great," Tina says, smiling at me.

"How many times do I have to ask you to come back and work for me once you're done with school?" Carl says.

"I don't want you to feel like you have to offer me a nursing spot," I say. "I want to earn it on my own."

"I'd give you the shirt off my back if you needed it," Carl says. "But that's not why I'm offering you a job."

"It isn't?"

"No. I think you're going to be a great nurse, and I want you at my office."

"Plus, this little baby girl is the closest thing we've got to a grandchild," Tina says. "I'd like to keep you as close by as possible."

"Everybody wants access to the kid," Henry says.

"When you two have been married as long as we have," Carl tells him, "and your children are grown, and you're bored as hell, you're gonna want access to grandkids, too. Trust me. Do you know how much television I watch? It's shameful. I need a distraction."

Gabby and Jesse come back and join us.

"What are we talking about?" Gabby asks.

"Grandchildren," Tina says, looking at Gabby and Jesse with intent.

"Oh, no!" Jesse jokes. "Gabby, turn away slowly, and maybe they won't see us."

Gabby mimes trying to leave, but Tina pulls her and Jesse back.

"Hannah and Henry seem to have found a way to have a baby," Tina says. "And I'm not getting any younger. It wouldn't kill you to *try*."

"Tina," Jesse says, "I promise you, the minute your daughter and I are happily wed, it will be the first thing on my To Do list."

Ethan and Ella join us. They must have just come through the door.

"Sorry we're late," Ella says. "I was stuck at work, and you know how it is! Happy birthday!" she says to Gabby. She hugs her and then turns to Ethan, who hugs Gabby and smiles. He shakes Henry's hand, gives Jesse a pat on the back, and then hugs me.

"We did bring a present," Ethan says. "To make up for it."

It's a box of Godiva chocolates. The moment I see them, I want to shove them all into my mouth. I figure I can take them from Gabby later if I really want them. Or get some of my own. I know that if I say I want them, Henry will stop on the way home. He always gets me any food I want, at any time of night. He says that's his job. He says it's the least he can do. "You carry the baby. I'll get the food." His morning breath is terrible, and he's cheap as hell, but I feel like the luckiest woman in the entire world.

The party goes on, all of us hopping from person to person, talking and sharing stories about Gabby. Just when the party seems to hit its peak, someone asks Jesse to tell the story of how he and Gabby met. Slowly but surely, everyone quiets down to listen in. Jesse stands at the base of the fireplace so he can be seen and heard by everyone.

"First day of geometry class. Tenth grade. I look to the front of the classroom and see the prettiest girl I've ever laid eyes on." Jesse has told this story about nine thousand times, and each time starts the same. "Although Gabby would say that's not the first thing that I should have noticed about her." He looks over at her, and she smiles. "But you'd have to notice it about her. She was gorgeous. And, to my delight, she was also short. So I figured I had a shot."

The whole crowd laughs.

"But I didn't ask her out, because I was a chicken. Three weeks into school, another girl asked me out, and I said yes, because when you're fifteen and a girl asks you out, you say yes."

The crowd laughs again.

"Jessica and I dated all through high school, and we broke up senior year. So what do I do? I go right out and find Gabby and ask her out. And we have this great date. And then the next morning, my ex-girlfriend calls me, and she wants to get back together. And . . . long story short, I married Jessica. Anyway, eventually, Jessica and I split up. We had to split up. We weren't right for each other. And once I could see that, there was no turning back. So we divorced. And then, a few years later, I get a Facebook request from Gabby Hudson. *The* Gabby Hudson."

That's my favorite part. The part where he calls her *the* Gabby Hudson.

"And I get way ahead of myself, and I start Facebook-stalking her and wondering if she's single and if she'd ever date me, and yada yada yada, the next thing I know, we're at lunch on the beach in Santa Monica. She refused to let me pay and said going dutch was the most appropriate thing to do. And we started walking back to my car, and I didn't tell her this then, because I knew it would freak her out, but I felt like I finally understood why people get married again. You get your heart broken, you fail at marriage, you're not sure you'll ever be up for it a second time. And then it all clicks into place, and you see that you failed the first time because you picked the wrong person. And now the right person is standing in front of you. So I waited the appropriate amount of months of dating, and then I told her how I felt. And she said she felt the same way. And now we're getting married. And I'm the luckiest guy alive."

That's usually the end of his story, but he keeps talking.

"I was reading a book about the cosmos recently," he says, and then he looks around and goes, "Hold on, trust me, this relates."

The crowd laughs again.

"And I was reading about different theories about the universe. I was really taken with this theory that some very credible physicists believe in called the multiverse theory. And it states that everything that is possible happens. That means that when you flip a quarter, it comes down heads *and* tails. Not heads *or* tails. Every time you flip a coin and it comes up heads, you are merely in the universe where the coin came up heads. There is another version of you out there, created the second the quarter flipped, who saw it come up tails. Every second of every day, the world is splitting further and further into an infinite number of parallel universes, where everything that could happen is happening. There are millions, trillions, or quadrillions, I guess, of different versions of ourselves living out the consequences of our choices. What I'm getting at here is that I know there may be universes out there where I made different choices and they led me somewhere else, led me to *someone* else." He looks at Gabby. "And my heart breaks for every single version of me that didn't end up with you."

Maybe it's the moment. Maybe it's the hormones. But I start crying. Gabby catches my eye, and I can see that she's teary, too. Jesse is done speaking, but no one can turn away. Everyone is staring at Gabby. I know I should do something, but I'm not sure what to do.

"Way to make the rest of us look bad," Henry says loudly.

The crowd laughs and disperses. I look at him, and he wipes the tears from my eyes.

"I love you as much as that show-off loves her," he jokes. "I just didn't watch the same *Nova* special."

"I know," I tell him. "I know." Because I do know. "Do you think that theory is true?" I ask Henry. "Do you think there are versions of us out there who never met?"

"Maybe one where you didn't get into an accident and you ended up married to a cinnamon roll chef?" he says.

"Everything that is possible happens . . ."

"Do you wish you were married to a cinnamon roll chef?"

"I certainly wish you were better at making cinnamon rolls," I say. "But no, this universe is OK with me."

"You sure? We can try to defy space and time and go find another for you."

"No," I tell him. "I like this one. I like you. And her." I point to my belly. "And Gabby. And Jesse. And Carl and Tina. I'm excited to get my nursing degree. And I'm OK with the fact that sometimes when it rains, my hip aches. Yeah," I say. "I think I'll stay."

"OK," he says, kissing me. "Let me know if you change your mind."

He slips off to the bathroom, and I start to head toward Gabby and Tina, standing by the mini-cheesecakes. I'm mostly interested in the mini-cheesecakes, but I am stopped in place behind a linebacker of a man. I ask him to move, but he doesn't hear me. I am about to give up.

"Sir," I hear from behind me. "Can she get through?"

The linebacker and I both turn around to see Ethan standing there.

"Oh, I'm so sorry," the linebacker says. "I'm a glutton for cheesecake. When I'm in front of it, everything around me is a blur."

I laugh and fumble through. Ethan steps up with me.

"Six months now?" he asks. He takes a piece of banana cream pie.

"Seven," I say, taking a piece of cheesecake.

"What is this? No cinnamon rolls for you?"

"It is a nighttime party," I say. "So it's OK. But I've been eating them pretty much nonstop lately. Henry says you can smell cinnamon in my hair."

Ethan laughs. "I believe it. I'm sure I told you that after we broke up, I couldn't smell a cinnamon roll without getting depressed."

"You never told me that," I say, laughing. "How long did that last? Until Thanksgiving break?"

He laughs back. "Fair enough," he says. "It is true, though."

"Well, you shouldn't have broken up with me, then," I tell him.

He guffaws. "You broke up with me, OK?"

"Oh, please," I say. "Go sell it to somebody else."

"Well," he says, "whoever broke up with whom, my heart was broken."

"Ditto," I tell him.

"Yeah?" he says, as if this information makes him feel better.

"Are you kidding? I didn't sleep with anyone else for years afterward, because I kept thinking of you. I bet you can't say the same."

He laughs. "No," he says. "I definitely slept with people. But that's . . . that didn't mean anything."

"I always thought we'd get back together at some point," I say. "It's funny how the teenage brain works."

He shrugs, eating his pie. "Not that funny. I thought it, too. From time to time. I almost . . ."

"What?" I ask.

"When you came back to L.A., right before the accident, I thought maybe . . ."

I think back to that time. That was a rough period. I kept a happy face through all of it. I tried really hard to keep it together, but looking at it now, I think of how heartbreaking it all was. I think of the baby I lost, and I wonder if . . . I wonder if I had to lose that baby to get to where I am now. I wonder if I had to lose that baby to have this one.

"I think I thought maybe, too," I say.

"Just didn't work out that way, I guess," he says.

"I guess not." I see Henry coming back from the bathroom. I see him stop and talk to Carl. He loves Carl. If we could have a bronze bust of Carl in our living room, he'd do it. "Who knows?" I tell Ethan. "If Jesse's theory is right, about the universes, maybe there's one out there where we figured out a way to make it work."

Ethan laughs. "Yeah," he says. "Maybe." He lifts his pie as if to make a toast. I lift my cheesecake to meet it. "Maybe in another life," he says.

I smile at him and leave him by the dessert table.

I miss my husband.

He's now standing in a circle with Gabby, Jesse, Carl, and Tina. I join them.

"I see you found the cheesecake," Gabby says.

"The pregnant lady always finds the cheesecake," I tell her. "You know that."

Henry moves closer to me as he continues to talk to Carl. He puts his arm around me. He gives me a squeeze. He opens his mouth wide, and I smile at him. I feed him the cheesecake.

It's on his face.

"I love you," he says with his mouth full. I can barely make out the words individually. But there's no doubt what he said.

He kisses me on the forehead and grazes his hand against my belly.

One Saturday night in my late twenties, I was hit by a car, and that accident led me to marry my night nurse. If that's not fate, I don't know what is.

So I have to think that while I may exist in other universes, none of them are as sweet as this.

ACKNOWLEDGMENTS

I am fortunate enough to have more than one Gabby in my life, and for that I am grateful every day. Thank you to Erin Fricker, Julia Furlan, Sara Arrington, and Tamara Hunter for being such phenomenal people and close friends. This book is dedicated to you, because your friendship has kept me going at times when I wasn't sure I could take another step. And to Bea Arthur, Andy Bauch, Katie Brydon, Emily Giorgio, Jesse Hill, Phillip Jordan, Tim Paulik, Ryan Powers, Jess Reynoso, Ashley and Colin Rodger, Jason Stamey, Kate Sullivan, and all the rest of my incredibly supportive and wonderful friends, I am so lucky to know all of you and have you in my life.

To Carly Watters, the world's most wonderful agent, I often thank the fates (or mere chance) for bringing me to your blog back in 2012 and driving me to query you. That I got so lucky as to be repped by someone I *like* so much is either the very definition of destiny or a wonderful coincidence. I am equally thankful to Brad Mendelsohn and Rich Green. Thank you, Brad, for understanding me and getting my work the way you do, and Rich, I'm so excited about what we've done.

Greer Hendricks, it's impossible to imagine a universe where you are any more lovely. Thank you for being such a pleasure to talk to and for being so incredibly good at what you do. My work could not be in better hands. The same goes to Sarah Cantin, Tory Lowy, and the rest of the Atria team.

To the Hanes and Reid families, thank you. To Rose and Warren, Sally and Bernie, Niko and Zach: When I tell my friends how much I love my in-laws, I'm pretty sure they all roll their eyes at me as if I'm a student reminding the teacher that she forgot to assign homework—but I'll keep saying it until I'm blue in the face. I'm lucky to have married into such a wonderful family. I love you all.

To the Jenkins and Morris families, thank you. To my mother, Mindy, and my brother, Jake, I love you. I am so fortunate to have you in my corner. Thank you for always believing in me and for always being game to talk through ideas about life and humanity.

To my grandmother, Linda, words will never express what you mean to me. I feel humbled just to have known you, let alone to have been so lucky as to be your granddaughter. Thank you for every single moment of our time together. I am who I am because I have grown up trying to make you proud. Consider this my solemn promise to remember to stop and smell the roses.

And finally, to Alex Reid: This book isn't about us. But there's one line that I wrote just for you. "I know there may be universes out there where I made different choices and they led me somewhere else, led me to *someone* else. And my heart breaks for every single version of me that didn't end up with you."

MAYBE IN ANOTHER LIFE

TAYLOR JENKINS REID

At the age of twenty-nine, Hannah Martin still has no idea what she wants to do with her life. She has lived in six different cities and held countless meaningless jobs since college, but on the heels of a disastrous breakup, she has finally returned to her hometown of Los Angeles. To celebrate her first night back, her best friend, Gabby, takes Hannah out to a bar—where she meets up with her high school boyfriend, Ethan.

It's just past midnight when Gabby asks Hannah if she's ready to go. Ethan quickly offers to give her a ride later if she wants to stay.

Hannah hesitates.

What happens if she leaves with Gabby?

What happens if she leaves with Ethan?

In concurrent storylines, Hannah lives out the effects of each decision. Quickly, these parallel universes develop into surprisingly different stories with far-reaching consequences for Hannah and the people around her, raising questions including: Is anything meant to be? How much in our life is determined by chance? And perhaps most compellingly: Is there such a thing as a soul mate?

Hannah believes there is. And, in both worlds, she believes she's found him.

QUESTIONS AND TOPICS OF DISCUSSION

1. Hannah opens the novel needing to find a sense of home, and a renewed, stronger sense of self. Does she find both of these things by the novel's conclusion? Are they different in each ending, or more or less the same?

2. Hannah has a complicated and somewhat distant relationship with her family after they move to London. Hannah's dad admits, "Your mother and I realized we had made a huge mistake not bringing you with us. We never should have let you stay in Los Angeles. Never should have left you" (page 125). What do you think about this statement? What does Hannah's reaction to this confession indicate to you?

3. Why do you think Gabby makes such an effort to spell out her feminism?

4. There are some choices that Hannah faces in both of her stories. Can you identify these? Discuss whether her ultimate decisions differ or are the same in each plot thread. What is their significance?

5. Turn to p. 194 and reread the conversation Hannah has with Ethan from her hospital bed. What do you make of her statement, "Whatever would have happened wasn't *supposed* to happen" (page 165)? Do you agree with Hannah that believing we're all destined for something makes it easier to bear the harder moments?

6. Hannah says, "I'm starting to think maybe you just pick a place and stay there. You pick a career and do it. You pick a person and commit to him" (page 210). Is this idea—that sometimes, you just have to make a decision and stick with it—mutually exclusive with any notion of fate or destiny?

7. Reread Gabby and Hannah's conversation about soul mates (pages 208–210). Do you agree with Hannah when she says that sometimes you can just *tell* about a person? Have you ever had a person about whom you felt you could just *tell*?

8. While on the surface, the novel may seem to focus on which man Hannah will end up with, there are several types of love explored in *Maybe in Another Life*. Discuss these as a group. Which of the many relationships depicted was your favorite? How did they change and grow in each storyline?

9. Mark tries to defend his decision to leave Gabby by saying, "I didn't mean for it to happen. But when you have that kind of connection with someone, nothing can stand in its way" (page 273). What do you think about this? Do you agree with Hannah's belief that "your actions in love are not an exception to who you are. They are, in fact, the very definition of who you are" (page 274)? How does this jibe with the idea that sometimes you can just *tell* someone is right for you?

10. Did you believe in fate when you started the novel? Did the novel change, challenge, or uphold your opinion?

11. Certainly some of the characters, including Hannah at times, believe in fate. Do you think the book itself suggests that fate exists? What about soul mates?

12. Did you find yourself rooting for one ending versus the other? Do you have an opinion on whether Hannah should have ended up with Henry or with Ethan? If you were Hannah, which ending would you have wanted for yourself?

13. Think about the statement that Jesse makes at the end of the novel: "Everything that is possible happens" (page 330). If that's true, what do other versions of your life look like?

ENHANCE YOUR BOOK CLUB

1. Hannah has a special love for cinnamon rolls. In honor of her, make (or buy from your favorite bakery) some cinnamon rolls for your book club.

2. The 1998 movie *Sliding Doors* (starring Gwyneth Paltrow) takes a similar premise as *Maybe in Another Life*, and examines how one woman's life differs based on whether or not she catches a train. Watch the film as a group, and discuss how its portrayal of two possible outcomes for one woman's life differs from Hannah's story. Are the two projects making the same point or contrasting ones?

3. Taylor Jenkins Reid is the author of two other novels, *Forever, Interrupted* and *After I Do*. Pick one to read as a group and compare and contrast it with *Maybe in Another Life*. What do Reid's earlier books have to say about fate and soul mates?

Praise for *Forever, Interrupted*

"Touching and powerful . . . Reid masterfully grabs hold of the heartstrings and doesn't let go. A stunning first novel."

—*Publishers Weekly*, starred review

"You'll laugh, weep, and fly through each crazy-readable page."

—*Redbook*

"A moving novel about life and death."

—*Kirkus*

"A poignant and heartfelt exploration of love and commitment in the absence of shared time that asks, what does it take to be the love of someone's life?"

—Emma McLaughlin and Nicola Kraus,
#1 *New York Times* bestselling authors

"Moving, gorgeous, and at times heart-wrenching."

—Sarah Jio, *New York Times* bestselling author

"Sweet, heartfelt, and surprising. These characters made me laugh as well as cry, and I ended up falling in love with them, too."

—Sarah Pekkanen, internationally bestselling
author of *The Opposite of Me*

"This beautifully rendered story explores the brilliance and rarity of finding true love, and how we find our way back through the painful aftermath of losing it. These characters will leap right off the page and into your heart."

—Amy Hatvany, author of *Safe with Me*

ALSO BY TAYLOR JENKINS REID

Forever, Interrupted

AFTER I DO

~ *A Novel* ~

TAYLOR JENKINS REID

WASHINGTON SQUARE PRESS

New York London Toronto Sydney New Delhi

W

Washington Square Press
A Division of Simon & Schuster, Inc.
1230 Avenue of the Americas
New York, NY 10020

First Washington Square Press trade paperback edition July 2014

For information about special discounts for bulk purchases, please contact Simon & Schuster Special Sales at 1-866-506-1949 or business@simonandschuster.com.

The Simon & Schuster Speakers Bureau can bring authors to your live event. For more information or to book an event, contact the Simon & Schuster Speakers Bureau at 1-866-248-3049 or visit our website at www.simonspeakers.com.

Manufactured in the United States of America

40 39 38

Library of Congress Cataloging-in-Publication Data

Reid, Taylor Jenkins.
After I do : a novel / Taylor Jenkins Reid.
pages cm
1. Marriage—Fiction. 2. Separation (Psychology)—Fiction. 3. Self-realization—Fiction. 4. Domestic fiction. 5. Psychological fiction. I. Title.
PS3618.E5478A69 2014
813'.6—dc23
2013046056

ISBN 978-1-4767-1284-0
ISBN 978-1-4767-1285-7 (ebook)

To Mindy Jenkins and Jake Jenkins
(May this serve as the final word that I
have the best feet in the family.)

flagrant, *adj*

I would be standing right there, and you would walk out of the bathroom without putting the cap back on the toothpaste.

The Lover's Dictionary

part one

WHERE DOES THE GOOD GO?

We are in the parking lot of Dodger Stadium, and once again, Ryan has forgotten where we left the car. I keep telling him that it's in Lot C, but he doesn't believe me.

"No," he says, for the tenth time. "I specifically remember turning right when we got here, not left."

It's incredibly dark, the path in front of us lit only by lampposts featuring oversized baseballs. I looked at the sign when we parked.

"You remember wrong," I say, my tone clipped and pissed-off. We've already been here too long, and I hate the chaos of Dodger Stadium. It's a warm summer night, so I have that to be thankful for, but it's ten P.M., and the rest of the fans are pouring out of the stands, the two of us fighting through a sea of blue and white jerseys. We've been at this for about twenty minutes.

"I don't remember wrong," he says, walking ahead and not even bothering to look back at me as he speaks. "You're the one with the bad memory."

"Oh, I see," I say, mocking him. "Just because I lost my keys this morning, suddenly, I'm an idiot?"

He turns and looks at me; I use the moment to try to catch up to him. The parking lot is hilly and steep. I'm slow.

"Yeah, Lauren, that's exactly what I said. I said you were an idiot."

"I mean, you basically did. You said that you know what you're talking about, like I don't."

"Just help me find the goddamn car so we can go home."

I don't respond. I simply follow him as he moves farther and farther away from Lot C. Why he wants to go home is a mystery to me. None of this will be any better at home. It hasn't been for months.

He walks around in a long, wide circle, going up and down the hills of the Dodger Stadium parking lot. I follow close behind, waiting with him at the crosswalks, crossing at his pace. We don't say anything. I think of how much I want to scream at him. I think of how I wanted to scream at him last night, too. I think of how much I'll probably want to scream at him tomorrow. I can only imagine he's thinking much of the same. And yet the air between us is perfectly still, uninterrupted by any of our thoughts. So often lately, our nights and weekends are full of tension, a tension that is only relieved by saying good-bye or good night.

After the initial rush of people leaving the parking lot, it becomes a lot easier to see where we are and where we parked.

"There it is," Ryan says, not bothering to point for further edification. I turn my head to follow his gaze. There it is. Our small black Honda.

Right in Lot C.

I smile at him. It's not a kind smile.

He smiles back. His isn't kind, either.

ELEVEN AND A HALF YEARS AGO

It was the middle of my sophomore year of college. My freshman year had been a lonely one. UCLA was not as inviting as I'd thought it might be when I applied. It was hard for me to meet people. I went home a lot on weekends to see my family. Well, really, I went home to see my younger sister, Rachel. My mom and my little brother, Charlie, were secondary. Rachel was the person I told everything to. Rachel was the one I missed when I ate alone in the dining hall, and I ate alone in the dining hall more than I cared to admit.

At the age of nineteen, I was much shier than I'd been at seventeen, graduating from high school toward the top of my class, my hand cramping from signing so many yearbooks. My mom kept asking me all through my freshman year of college if I wanted to transfer. She kept saying that it was OK to look someplace else, but I didn't want to. I liked my classes. "I just haven't found my stride yet," I said to her every time she asked. "But I will. I'll find it."

I started to find it when I took a job in the mailroom. Most nights, it was one or two other people and me, a dynamic in which I thrived. I was good in small groups. I could shine when I didn't have to struggle to be heard. And after a few months of shifts in the mailroom, I was getting to know a lot of people. Some of them I really liked. And some of those people really liked me, too. By the time we broke for Christmas that year, I was excited to go back in January. I missed my friends.

When classes began again, I found myself with a new

schedule that put me in a few buildings I'd never been in before. I was starting to take psychology classes since I'd fulfilled most of my gen eds. And with this new schedule, I started running into the same guy everywhere I went. The fitness center, the bookstore, the elevators of Franz Hall.

He was tall and broad-shouldered. He had strong arms, round around the biceps, barely fitting into the sleeves of his shirts. His hair was light brown, his face often marked with stubble. He was always smiling, always talking to someone. Even when I saw him walking alone, he seemed to have the confidence of a person with a mission.

I was in line to enter the dining hall when we finally spoke. I was wearing the same gray shirt I'd worn the day before, and it occurred to me as I spotted him a bit farther up in the line that he might notice.

After he swiped his ID to get in, he hung back behind his friends and carried on a conversation with the guy running the card machine. When I got up to the front of the line, he stopped his conversation and looked at me.

"Are you following me or what?" he said, looking right into my eyes and smiling.

I was immediately embarrassed, and I thought he could see it.

"Sorry, stupid joke," he said. "I've just been seeing you everywhere lately." I took my card back. "Can I walk with you?"

"Yeah," I said. I was meeting my mailroom friends, but I didn't see them there yet anyway. And he was cute. That was a lot of what swayed me. He was cute.

"Where are we going?" he asked me. "What line?"

"We are going to the grill," I said. "That is, if you're standing in line with me."

"That's actually perfect. I have been dying for a patty melt."

"The grill it is, then."

It was quiet as we stood in line together, but he was trying hard to keep the conversation going.

"Ryan Lawrence Cooper," he said, putting his hand out. I laughed and shook it. His grip was tight. I got the distinct feeling that if he did not want this handshake to end, there was nothing I could do about it. That's how strong his hand felt.

"Lauren Maureen Spencer," I said. He let go.

I had pictured him as smooth and confident, poised and charming, and he was those things to a certain degree. But as we talked, he seemed to be stumbling a bit, not sure of the right thing to say. This cute guy who had seemed so much surer of himself than I could ever be turned out to be . . . entirely human. He was just a person who was good-looking and probably funny and just comfortable enough with himself to seem as if he understood the world better than the rest of us. But he didn't, really. He was just like me. And suddenly, that made me like him a whole lot more than I realized. And that made me nervous. My stomach started to flutter. My palms started to sweat.

"So, it's OK, you can admit it," I said, trying to be funny. "It's *you* who have actually been stalking *me*."

"I admit it," he said, and then quickly reversed his story. "No! Of course not. But you have noticed it, right? It's like suddenly you're everywhere."

"*You're* everywhere," I said, stepping up in line as it moved. "I'm just in my normal places."

"You mean you're in *my* normal places."

"Maybe we're just cosmically linked," I joked. "Or we have similar schedules. The first time I saw you was on the quad, I think. And I've been killing time there between Intro to Psych and Statistics. So you must have picked up a class around that time on South Campus, right?"

"You've unintentionally revealed two things to me, Lauren," Ryan said, smiling.

"I have?" I said.

"Yep." He nodded. "Less important is that I now know you're a psych major and two of the classes you take. If I was a stalker, that would be a gold mine."

"OK." I nodded. "Although if you were any decent stalker, you would have known that already."

"Regardless, a stalker is a stalker."

We were finally at the front of the line, but Ryan seemed more focused on me than on the fact that it was time to order. I looked away from him only long enough to order my dinner. "Can I get a grilled cheese, please?" I asked the cook.

"And you?" the cook asked Ryan.

"Patty melt, extra cheese," Ryan said, leaning forward and accidentally grazing my forearm with his sleeve. I felt just the smallest jolt of electricity.

"And the second thing?" I said.

"Hm?" Ryan said, looking back at me, already losing his train of thought.

"You said I revealed two things."

"Oh!" Ryan smiled and moved his tray closer to mine on the counter. "You said you noticed me in the quad."

"Right."

"But I didn't see you then."

"OK," I said, not clear what he meant.

"So technically speaking, you noticed me first."

I smiled at him. "Touché," I said. The cook handed me my grilled cheese. He handed Ryan his patty melt. We took our trays and headed to the soda machine.

"So," Ryan said, "since you're the pursuer here, I guess I'll just have to wait for you to ask me out."

"What?" I asked, halfway between shocked and mortified.

"Look," he said, "I can be very patient. I know you have to work up the courage, you have to find a way to talk to me, you have to make it seem casual."

"Uh-huh," I said. I reached for a glass and thrust it under the ice machine. The ice machine roared and then produced three measly ice cubes. Ryan stood beside me and thwacked the side of it. An avalanche of ice fell into my glass. I thanked him.

"No problem. So how about this?" Ryan suggested. "How about I wait until tomorrow night, six P.M.? We'll meet in the lobby of Hendrick Hall. I'll take you out for a burger and maybe some ice cream. We'll talk. And you can ask me out then."

I smiled at him.

"It's only fair," he said. "You noticed me first." He was very charming. And he knew it.

"OK. One question, though. In line over there," I said as I I pointed to the swiper. "What did you talk to him about?" I was asking because I was pretty sure I knew the answer, and I wanted to make him say it.

"The guy swiping the cards?" Ryan asked, smiling, knowing he'd been caught.

"Yeah, I'm just curious what you two had to talk about."

Ryan looked me right in the eye. "I said, 'Act like we are having a conversation. I need to buy time until that girl in the gray shirt gets up here.'"

That jolt of electricity that felt small only a few moments earlier now seared through me. It lit me up. I could feel it in the tips of my fingers and the furthest ends of my toes.

"Hendrick Hall, tomorrow. Six P.M.," I said, confirming that I would be there. But by that point, I think we both knew I was dying to be there. I wanted *then* and *there* to be *here* and *now*.

"Don't be late," he said, smiling and already walking away.

I put my drink on my tray and walked casually through the dining hall. I sat down at a table by myself, not yet ready to meet my friends. The smile on my face was too wide, too strong, too bright.

• • •

I was in the lobby of Hendrick Hall by 5:55 P.M.

I waited around for a couple of minutes, trying to pretend that I wasn't eagerly awaiting the arrival of someone.

This was a date. A real date. This wasn't like the guys who asked you to come with them and their friends to some party they heard about on Friday night. This wasn't like when the guy you liked in high school, the guy you'd known since eighth grade, finally kissed you.

This was a date.

What was I going to say to him? I barely knew him! What if I had bad breath or said something stupid? What if my mascara smudged and I spent the whole night not realizing I looked like a raccoon?

Panicking, I tried to catch a glimpse of my reflection in a window, but as soon as I did, Ryan came through the front doors into the lobby.

"Wow," he said when he saw me. In that instant, I was no longer worried that I might be somehow imperfect. I didn't worry about my knobby hands or my thin lips. Instead, I thought about the shine of my dark brown hair and the grayish tint to my blue eyes. I thought about my long legs as I saw Ryan's eyes drift toward them. I was happy that I'd decided to show them off with a short black jersey dress and a zip-up sweatshirt. "You look great," he continued. "You must really like me."

I laughed at him as he smiled at me. He was wearing jeans and a T-shirt, with a UCLA fleece over it.

"And you must be trying really hard to not show how much you like *me*," I said.

He smiled at me then, and it was a different smile from earlier. He wasn't smiling at me trying to charm me. He was charmed *by* me.

It felt good. It felt really good.

• • •

Over burgers, we asked each other where we were from and what we wanted to do with the rest of our lives. We talked about our classes. We figured out that we'd both had the same teacher for Public Speaking the year before.

"Professor Hunt!" Ryan said, his voice sounding almost nostalgic about the old man.

"Don't tell me you liked Professor Hunt!" I said. No one liked Professor Hunt. That man was about as interesting as a cardboard box.

"What is not to like about that guy? He's nice. He's complimentary! That was one of the only classes I got an A in that semester."

Ironically, Public Speaking was the only class I got a B in that semester. But that seemed like an obnoxious thing to say.

"That was my worst class," I said. "Public speaking is not my forte. I'm better with research, papers, multiple-choice tests. I'm not great with oral stuff."

I looked at him after I said it, and I could feel my cheeks burning red. It was such an awkward sentence to say on a date with someone you barely knew. I was terrified he was going to make a joke about it. But he didn't. He pretended not to notice.

"You seem like the kind of girl who gets straight As," he said. I was so relieved. He had somehow managed to take this sort of embarrassing moment I'd had and turned it around for me.

I blushed again. This time for a different reason. "Well, I do OK," I said. "But I'm impressed you got an A in Public Speaking. It's actually not an easy A, that class."

Ryan shrugged. "I think I'm just one of those people who can do the public speaking thing. Like, large crowds don't scare me. I could speak to a room full of people and not feel the slightest bit out of place. It's the one-on-one stuff that makes me nervous."

I could feel myself cock my head to one side, a physical indication of my curiosity. "You don't seem the type to be nervous talking in any situation," I said. "Regardless of how many people are there."

He smiled at me as he finished his burger. "Don't be fooled by this air of nonchalance," he said. "I know I'm devilishly handsome and probably the most charming guy you've met in your life, but there's a reason it took me so long before I could find a way to talk to you."

This guy, this guy who seemed so cool, he liked *me. I* made him nervous.

I'm not sure there is a feeling quite like finding out that you make the person who makes you nervous, nervous.

It makes you bold. It makes you confident. It makes you feel as if you could do anything in the world.

I leaned over the table and kissed him. I kissed him in the middle of a burger place, the arm of my sweatshirt accidentally falling into the container of ketchup. It wasn't perfectly timed, by any means. I didn't hit his mouth straight on. It was sort of to the side a bit. And it was clear I had taken him by surprise, because he froze for a moment before he relaxed into it. He tasted like salt.

When I pulled away from him, it really hit me. What I had just done. I'd never kissed someone before. I had always *been* kissed. I'd always kissed *back*.

He looked at me, confused. "I thought *I* was supposed to do that," he said.

I was now horribly, terribly mortified. This was the sort of thing I'd read about in the "embarrassing moments" section of *YM* magazine as a girl. "I know," I said. "I'm sorry. I'm so . . . I don't know why I—"

"Sorry?" he said, shocked. "No, don't be sorry. That was perhaps the single greatest moment of my life."

I looked up at him, smiling despite myself.

"All girls should kiss like that," he said. "All girls should be exactly like you."

When we walked home, he kept pulling me into doorways and alcoves to kiss me. The closer we got to my dorm, the longer the kisses became. Until just outside the front door to my building, we kissed for what felt like hours. It was cold outside by this point; the sun had set hours ago. My bare legs were freezing. But I couldn't feel anything except his hands on me, his lips on mine. I could think of nothing but what we were doing, the way my hands felt on his neck, the way he smelled like fresh laundry and musk.

When it became time to progress or say good-bye, I pulled away from him, leaving my hand still in his. I could see in his eyes that he wanted me to ask him to come back to my room. But I didn't. Instead, I said, "Can I see you tomorrow?"

"Of course."

"Will you come by and take me to breakfast?"

"Of course."

"Good night," I said, kissing his cheek.

I pulled my hand out of his and turned to leave. I almost stopped right there and asked him to come up with me. I didn't want the date to end. I didn't want to stop touching him, hearing his voice, finding out what he would say next. But I didn't turn around. I kept walking.

I knew then that I was sunk. I was smitten. I knew that I would give myself to him, that I would bare my soul to him, that I would let him break my heart if that's what it came to.

So there wasn't any rush, I told myself, as I got into the elevator alone.

When I got to my room, I called Rachel. I had to tell her everything. I had to tell her how cute he was, how sweet he was. I had to tell her the things he said, the way he looked at me. I had to relive it with someone who would understand just how exciting it all was.

And Rachel did understand; she understood completely.

"So when are you going to sleep with him? That's my question," she said. "Because it sounds like things got pretty steamy out there on the sidewalk. Maybe you should put a date on it, you know? Like, don't sleep with him until you've been dating this many weeks or days or months." She started laughing. "Or years, if that's the way you want to play it."

I told her I was just going to see what happened naturally.

"That is a terrible idea," she told me. "You need a plan. What if you sleep with him too soon or too late?"

But I really didn't think there *was* a too soon or too late. I was so confident about Ryan, so confident in myself, that something about it seemed foolproof. As if I could already tell that we were so good together we couldn't mess it up if we tried.

And that brought me both an intense thrill and a deep calm.

• • •

When it did happen, Ryan and I were in his room. His roommate was out of town for the weekend. We hadn't told each other that we loved each other yet, but it was obvious that we did.

I marveled at how well he understood my body. I didn't need to tell him what I wanted. He knew. He knew how to kiss me. He knew where to put his hands, what to touch, how to touch it.

I had never understood the concept of making love before. It seemed cheesy and dramatic. But I got it then. It isn't just about the movement. It's about the way your heart swells when he gets close. The way his breath feels like a warm fire. It's about the fact that your brain shuts down and your heart takes over.

I cared about nothing but the feel of him, the smell of him, the taste of him. I wanted more of him.

Afterward, we lay next to each other, naked and vulnerable but not feeling as if we were either. He grabbed my hand.

He said, "I have something I'm ready to say, but I don't want you to think it's because of what we just did."

I knew what it was. We both knew what it was. "So say it later, then," I said.

He looked disappointed by my answer, so I made myself clear.

"When you say it," I told him, "I'll say it back."

He smiled, and then he was quiet for a minute. I actually thought he might have fallen asleep. But then he said, "This is good, isn't it?"

I turned toward him. "Yeah," I said. "It is."

"No," he said to me. "This is, like, perfect, what we have. We could get married someday."

I thought of my grandparents, the only married couple I knew. I thought of the way my grandmother cut up my grandfather's food sometimes when he was feeling too weak to do it himself.

"Someday," I said. "Yeah."

We were nineteen.

ELEVEN YEARS AGO

Over summer break, Ryan went home to Kansas. We talked to each other every day. We would send e-mails back and forth in rapid fire, waiting impatiently for the other to respond. I would sit on my bed, waiting for him to get home from his internship and call me. I visited him early in the summer, meeting his parents and sister for the first time. We all got along. They seemed to like me. I stayed for a week, the two of us hanging on each other's every word, Ryan sneaking into the guest room to see me every night. When he drove me to the airport and walked me up to the security gate, I thought someone was ripping my heart out of my chest. How could I leave him? How could I get on the plane and fly so many miles away from the other half of my soul?

I tried to explain all of this to Rachel, also home for the summer after her freshman year at USC. I complained to her about how much I missed him. I brought him up in conversation more often than he was really relevant. I had a one-track mind. Rachel mostly responded to these overdramatic testaments of my love by saying, "Oh, that's great. I'm really happy for you," and then pretending to vomit.

My brother, Charlie, meanwhile, had just turned fourteen and was about to enter high school, so he wanted nothing to do with Rachel or me. He didn't even pretend to listen to anything I had to say that summer. The minute I started talking, he would put on his headphones or turn on the TV.

A few weeks after I got home from visiting him, Ryan insisted that he visit me. It didn't matter that the tickets were expensive or that he wasn't making any money. He said it was worth it. He had to see me.

When he arrived at LAX, I watched him come down the escalator with the other passengers. I saw him scan the crowd until he saw my face. I saw it register. I saw in that moment how much I was loved, how relieved he was to have me in his eyesight. And I could recognize all of those emotions because I felt the same way about him.

He ran to me, dropping his bag and picking me up in one fell swoop. He spun me around, holding me tighter than I had ever been held. As devastated as I'd been to leave him weeks ago, I was that thrilled to be with him again.

He put me down and grabbed my face in his hands, kissing me. I opened my eyes finally to see an older woman with kids watching us. I caught her eye by accident, and she smiled at me, shyly looking away. The look on her face made it clear that she had been me before.

My family caught up to us then, finally done parking the car. They had all insisted on coming, in part, I think, because it was so clear that I did not want them to come.

Ryan dried his sweaty hand on the back of his jeans and offered a handshake to my mother.

"Ms. Spencer," he said. "It's nice to see you again." They had met once before, only briefly, when Mom came to move me out of the dorms.

"Ryan, I told you to call me Leslie," my mom said, laughing at him.

Ryan nodded and gestured to Rachel and Charlie. "Rachel, Charlie, nice to meet you. I've heard a lot of good things."

"Actually," Charlie said, "we prefer to be called Miss and Mr. Spencer."

Ryan chose to take him seriously. "Excuse me, Mr. Spencer, my mistake. Miss Spencer," he said, tipping his imaginary hat and bowing to Rachel. Then he extended his hand in a firm handshake to Charlie.

And maybe because someone was taking him seriously, Charlie chose to lighten up.

"OK, fine," Charlie said. "You can call me Charles."

"You can call him Charlie," Rachel interjected.

We all headed to baggage claim. And as much of a spoilsport as Charlie wanted to be, I couldn't help but notice that he talked Ryan's ear off the entire way home.

NINE AND HALF YEARS AGO

Spring break of our senior year, Ryan and I both decided to stay in Los Angeles. But at the last minute, my mom found a deal on flights to Cabo San Lucas and decided to splurge. That's how the five of us—my mom, Rachel, Charlie, Ryan, and I—found ourselves on a flight to Mexico.

Oddly enough, Charlie was perhaps the most excited about this idea. As we took our seats on the plane—Mom, Ryan, and I on one side of the aisle, Rachel, Charlie, and a strange bald man on the other—Charlie kept reminding my mom that the drinking age was eighteen.

"That's nice, sweetheart," she said to him. "That doesn't change the fact that you're still sixteen."

"But it would be less illegal," he said, as he clipped in his seat belt and the flight attendants walked up and down the aisles. "It's less illegal for me to get drunk in Mexico than here."

"I'm not sure there are degrees of illegal," Rachel said, scrunching herself tightly in the middle seat so as not to touch the bald man. He had already fallen asleep.

"Although I think prostitution is legal in Mexico," I said. "Right? Is it?"

"Well, not for minors," Ryan said. "Sorry, Charlie."

Charlie shrugged. "I don't look sixteen."

"Is weed legal in Mexico?" Rachel asked.

"Excuse me!" my mom said, exasperated. "This is a *family* vacation. I didn't bring you all to Mexico to get high and hire hookers."

And of course, all of us laughed at her. Because we had all been joking. At least, I thought we had all been joking.

"You're too gullible, Mom!" Rachel said.

"We were kidding," I added.

"Speak for yourself!" Charlie said. "I was serious. They might actually serve me alcohol at this place."

Ryan laughed.

It really struck me then just how different Charlie was from Rachel and me. It wasn't just in the superficial stuff, either, like the difference between brothers and sisters, high-schoolers versus college students. He was markedly different from the two of us.

Rachel and I were a little more than a year apart. We experienced things together, through a similar lens. When our dad left, I was almost four and a half years old, and Rachel had just turned three. Mom was still pregnant with Charlie. Rachel and I may not really remember our dad, but we had time with him. We knew his voice. Charlie entered this world with only my mother to hold him.

I sometimes wondered if Rachel and I were so close, if we meant so much to each other, that it prevented us from really letting Charlie in. By the time he was born, we had our own language, our own world. But the truth was, Charlie simply wasn't that interested in us. As a little kid, he did his own thing, played his own games. He didn't want to do the kind of stuff Rachel and I were doing. He didn't want to talk about what Rachel and I talked about. He was always forging his own path, rejecting the one we had laid out for him.

But as much as we had our differences, it was staggering how the three of us had grown up to look exactly alike. Charlie may not have been similar to Rachel and me in temperament or personality, but he couldn't distance himself from us genetically.

We all shared the same high cheekbones. All three of us got our dark hair and blue eyes from our mother. Charlie was taller and lankier, Rachel was petite and daintier, and I was broader, curvier. But we belonged together, that much was clear.

The plane took flight, and we started talking about other things. When the seat-belt sign went off, my mom got up and went to the bathroom. That's when I saw Ryan lean over the aisle to whisper something to Charlie. Charlie smiled and nodded.

"What did you just say to him?" I asked. Ryan smiled wide and refused to tell me. "You're not going to tell me?"

"It's between Charlie and me," Ryan said.

"Yeah," Charlie piped in. "It's between us."

"You can't buy him alcohol at this place," I said. "Is that what you were talking about? Because you can't." I sounded like a narc.

"Who said anything about anyone buying anyone alcohol?" Ryan said, perhaps a bit too innocently.

"Well, then, why can't I know what you're talking about?"

"Some things don't involve you, Lauren," Charlie said, teasing me.

My jaw dropped. Mom was on her way toward us, back from the bathroom.

"You are!" I said, somehow yelling and whispering. "You are going to get my sixteen-year-old brother drunk!"

Rachel, finally having enough of all this, said, "Oh, Lauren, cut it out. Ryan leaned over and said, 'Let's see if I can get your sister to freak out over nothing.'"

I looked at him for confirmation, and he started laughing. So did Charlie.

"I swear," Rachel said. "You're as gullible as Mom."

A LITTLE MORE THAN NINE YEARS AGO

I graduated magna cum laude. I missed summa cum laude by a fraction, but Ryan kept telling me not to worry myself over it. "I'm just graduating," he said. "Not a single Latin word after it, and I'm going to be fine. So you're going to be better than fine."

I couldn't argue about my prospects. I already had a job. I had accepted a position in the alumni department of UCLA. I wasn't sure what I wanted to do with my psychology degree, but I figured it would come to me in due time. The alumni department seemed like an easy, reliable place to start out.

On graduation day, Ryan and I were at opposite ends of the auditorium, so we only spoke in the morning and then made faces at each other during the ceremony. I spotted my mom in the audience with her huge camera, Rachel and Charlie next to her. Rachel was waving at me, giving me a thumbs-up. A few rows back, I saw Ryan's parents and his sister.

As I sat there, waiting for the moment when they called my name, it occurred to me that this was the end of so many things, and more to the point, it was the beginning of my adult life.

Ryan and I had rented a studio apartment in Hollywood. We were moving in the next week, on the first of the month. It was an ugly little thing, cramped and dark. But it would be ours.

The night before, Ryan and I had fought about what furniture to buy. He thought all we needed was a mattress on the floor. I figured that since we were adults, we should have a bed frame. Ryan thought all we needed were a few cardboard boxes for our clothes; I was insistent that we have dressers. It got heated. I said he was being cheap, that he didn't understand how to be an adult. He said I was acting like a spoiled brat, expecting money to grow on trees. It got bad enough that I started crying; he got upset enough that his face turned red.

And then, before we knew it, we were at the part where we both admitted we were wrong and begged each other's forgiveness with a passion unlike anything since the last time we'd fought. That was always the way it was with us. The *I love you*s and *I'm sorry*s, the *I'll never do that again*s and the *I don't know what I'd do without you*s always eclipsed the thing we were fighting about in the first place.

We woke up that morning with smiles on our faces, holding each other tight. We ate breakfast together. We got dressed together. We helped each other put on our caps and gowns.

Our life was starting. We were growing up.

I stood up with my row and followed the path up to the podium.

"Lauren Spencer."

I walked up, shook the chancellor's hand, and took my diploma. Out of the corner of my eye, I saw Ryan. He was holding a sign so small only I could see it. "I Love You," it said. And at that moment, I just knew adulthood was going to be great.

SEVEN AND A HALF YEARS AGO

For the fourth anniversary of when we met, Ryan and I went camping in Yosemite.

We had been out of school for a year and a half. I was making a decent salary in the alumni department. Ryan was doing OK himself. We were just starting to get ahead of our bills a bit, starting to save, when we decided that a trip to Yosemite wouldn't put us back too much. We had borrowed camping equipment from my mom and packed food from home.

We got there late Friday afternoon and pitched our tent. By the time it was properly set up, the sun was setting and it was getting cold, so we went to bed. The next morning, we woke up and decided that we should hike up Vernal Fall. The visitor's guide said that Vernal Fall was a hard hike but that the view from the top was like nothing you could imagine. At that, Ryan said, "I'm in the mood to see something I could never imagine." So we put on hiking boots and got into the car.

I knew that he had called my mother the week before our trip and asked for her blessing. I knew that he had told her he had a ring picked out. My family doesn't keep secrets. We try to, but we're all too excited to keep anything good to ourselves. It bursts out of us, overflowing like a ruptured pipe. So on some level, I was expecting to get to the top of Vernal Fall and find him on one knee.

However, the guidebook was pretty misleading. Vernal Fall wasn't just a hard hike. It felt impossible. I kept thinking it would end, that we were close to the top. But the way the path snaked up the mountain, you'd turn a corner and realize you had hours more work ahead of you. There were treacherous paths, steep climbs, areas where you couldn't rest. At one point, I cut myself on one of the rocks, a deep gash torn into my ankle. Despite the fact that it was bleeding into my sock, there was nothing I could do. I just had to keep moving.

And yet somehow during this entire hike, there were groups of people ahead of us and behind us who seemed to be doing just fine. There were even people coming down the mountain with smiles on their faces, proud of themselves for making it up there. I wanted to grab their shirts and demand that they tell me what lay ahead. But what was the point? Maybe if I didn't know what I was in for, I wouldn't know to give up.

By the second hour, Ryan and I were standing on stairs built into the mountain, stairs so rickety and steep that you couldn't fit your whole foot on them at once. There was a waterfall nearby, and I remember thinking to myself, *This is a beautiful waterfall, but I don't even care because I'm so exhausted*. I felt as if I'd never get up that mountain, and this view that I supposedly couldn't imagine, well, I didn't care to imagine it anymore. My hair was sticking to my forehead. My shirt was soaked through with sweat. My face was as red as a tomato. This wasn't the way to get engaged. And I wasn't even sure that was Ryan's intention. It was starting to seem that maybe it wasn't.

I figured I'd ask Ryan if he wanted to turn around, and if he said yes, I probably wasn't spoiling anything anyway. If he said no, I'd do it. I'd climb the rest of the mountain, and I'd see what happened.

"Wanna turn around?" I said. "I don't know if I can do this."

Ryan could barely catch his breath. He was a few stairs behind me. He was more fit than I was, but he insisted on staying behind so he could catch me if I slipped.

"Sure," he said. "OK."

Suddenly, I was crestfallen. I didn't realize how much I'd been waiting for him to propose to me until I heard him say we could turn back. It was like when you aren't sure what you want for dinner and someone suggests Chinese, and only then do you realize how badly you wanted a burger.

"Oh, OK," I said, starting slowly to back my feet up and turn my body back. This moment felt like a failure on two accounts. I thought of all those people I had seen making their way down the mountain. They seemed victorious. As I started to turn down the mountain, I knew that I would seem victorious to all the people I would pass on the way down. It just goes to show how alike failure and success can appear. Sometimes only you know the truth.

"Oh, wait," Ryan said. He bent down to readjust his backpack, and I got scared because he was so perilously close to the edge of the stairway. He looked as if he could slip right into the waterfall.

But he didn't. He reached his hand out and carefully rested one knee on an unreliable stair. He looked at me and said, "Lauren, I love you more than I've loved anything in my life. You are the reason I was put on this earth. You make me happier than anything I've ever known. I cannot live without you." He was smiling, and yet the edges of his mouth were starting to pull in and quiver. His voice started to lose its confidence. It became shaky. I noticed the group ahead of us had turned around. The pack of kids a few stairs behind Ryan had stopped and were waiting.

"Lauren," he said, now barely hiding his emotion, "will you marry me?"

That waterfall suddenly felt like the most gorgeous waterfall I'd ever seen in my life. I ran down the steps to him and whispered "Yes" into his ear. There wasn't a moment of hesitation. There was nothing except my absolute and irrevocable answer. *Yes. Yes. Yes. Are you crazy? Yes.*

Ryan hugged me, and I wept. I suddenly had the energy of ten men. I knew if we kept going, I could get up those stairs. I could make it to the top of that damn mountain.

Ryan turned and yelled, "She said yes!" People started clapping. I could hear Ryan's voice echoing through the canyon. A woman shouted, "Congratulations!" I swear it felt as if all of Yosemite was in on it.

We pushed forward, and within an hour, we had made our way to the top. Vernal Fall was more gorgeous than anything I could have imagined. Ryan and I stayed up there, putting our feet in the wide stream, letting the rushing water clean us, watching the squirrels eat nuts and the birds soar overhead. We talked about the future as we ate the sandwiches we had packed for ourselves. We talked about potential wedding dates, about when we'd have kids, if we'd buy a house. The wedding, we figured, could be in a year or so. The kids could wait until we were thirty. The house we'd have to play by ear. Maybe it was because I was high up in the clouds physically, or figuratively, but I felt that the sun shone brighter that afternoon, that the world was mine for the taking. The future seemed so easy.

When we finally left, it was with heavy hearts. This thing that I felt I couldn't do, this thing that wasn't worth it, had started to feel like the only important thing I'd ever done.

A LITTLE MORE THAN SIX YEARS AGO

Two months before the wedding, we went shopping for a new bed. We intended to get a queen-size. With the mattress, box spring, bed frame, and sheets, a queen was cheaper. It was practical. But when we got to the mattress store and started to look at the beds, we were tempted to go for broke. We were looking at two mattresses set up next to each other, one king, one queen. Ryan was standing behind me, his arms wrapped around my shoulders, and he whispered into my ear, "Let's spring for the big one. Let's make all of our sex hotel sex." My heart fluttered, and I blushed, and I told the man we'd take the king.

SIX YEARS AGO

We had a July wedding. It was outdoors on the wide lawn of a hotel just outside of Los Angeles. I wore a white dress. I threw my bouquet. We danced all night, Ryan spinning me around, holding me close, and showing me off. The morning after the festivities were over, we got into the car and headed out for our honeymoon. We had considered places like Costa Rica or Paris, maybe a cruise through the Italian Riviera. But the truth was, we didn't have that kind of money. We decided to take it easy. We'd drive up to Big Sur and stay in a cabin in the woods, where no one could find us for a week. A fireplace and a beautiful view seemed like all the luxury we needed in the world.

We got on the road early in the morning, hoping to make good time by beating midday traffic. We stopped for breakfast and again later for lunch. We played Twenty Questions, and I fiddled with the radio, tuning in to local stations as we passed through towns. We were in love, high on the novelty of marriage. The words *husband* and *wife* felt as if they had a shine to them. They were simply more fun to say than all the other words we knew.

We were two hours outside of Big Sur when the tire blew. The loud bang scared us both out of our newlywed daze. Ryan quickly pulled over to the side of the road. I hopped out first; Ryan was a second behind me.

"Fuck!" he said.

"Calm down," I told him. "It's going to be OK. We just

have to call Triple A. They will come out here and solve the whole thing."

"We can't call Triple A," he said.

"Sure we can," I told him. "I have the card in my wallet. Let me get it."

"No," he said, shaking his head and pulling his hands up onto the back of his neck in a resigned position. "I forgot to pay the renewal fee."

"Oh," I said. The disappointment was clear in my voice.

"It came last month, and it said on it that we had to pay it by the fifteenth, and . . . with the wedding and everything going on at work, I just . . ." He shrugged, and his voice got defensive. "I forgot, OK? I'm sorry. I forgot."

I wasn't mad at him. He made a mistake. But I was very concerned with what we were going to do about it. I was frustrated that I was in this position. If you do not have the ability to call Triple A, how do you fix a tire? We were not the sort of people who knew how to do that on our own. We were the sort of people who needed Triple A. I didn't like that about us at that very moment. In fact, I was starting to think we were two useless idiots on the side of the road.

"You don't know how to fix a tire, right?" I asked him. I knew he didn't. I shouldn't have asked.

"No," he said. "I don't. Thank you for highlighting that."

"Well, shit," I said, the polite cushion around my voice fading and exposing my irritation. "What should we do?"

"I don't know!" he said. "I mean, it was an accident."

"Yeah, OK, so what do we do? We're on the side of the road in the middle of nowhere. How are we going to get to the cabin?"

"I don't know, OK? I don't know what we're gonna do. I think there is a spare tire in the trunk," he said, walking back there to confirm it. "Yeah," he said as he lifted the bottom out. "But there's no jack, so I don't know what we would even do."

"Well, we have to think of something."

"You could think of something, too, you know," he said to me. "This isn't only up to me."

"I never said it was, all right? Geez."

"Well? What's your bright idea, then?"

"You know what?" I said. "I . . . Why are we even fighting right now? We're on our honeymoon."

"I know!" he said. "I know that! Do you have any idea how upset I am that this is happening on our honeymoon? Do you have any idea how heartbroken I am that I fucked up this thing that we have been looking forward to for months?"

I found it completely impossible to be angry with Ryan when he was angry at himself. I melted like a popsicle the minute I suspected he might blame himself for anything. It was part of the impracticality of fighting with him. I would fight until he admitted he'd done something wrong, and then I'd spend the entire rest of the night trying to take it all away, trying to convince him he was nothing short of perfect.

"Baby, no," I said. "No, you didn't mess anything up. This is going to be fine. I swear. Totally fine." I hugged him, burying my head in his chest and holding his hand by the side of the road.

"I'm sorry," he said, meaning it.

"No!" I said. "Don't be sorry. It's not just your job to pay the Triple A bill. It could have happened to either of us. We had so much stuff going on with the wedding. C'mon," I said, lifting his chin. "We're not gonna let this get us down."

Ryan started laughing. "We aren't?"

"Hell no!" I said, trying to cheer him up. "Are you kidding? I, for one, am having a great time. As far as I'm concerned, the honeymoon has already started."

"It has?"

"Yep," I said. "We'll make it a game. I'll try to flag down the next car that comes down the road, OK? If they stop and they have a jack and they let us borrow it, I win. Next car, you go. Whoever gets the jack wins."

Ryan laughed again. It was so nice to see him laugh.

"Neither of us knows how to use a jack," he pointed out.

"Well, we'll figure it out! How hard could it be? I'm sure we can Google it."

"OK, you're on, sweetheart," he said.

But he never got a chance. I flagged down the first car that came down the road, and they let us use their jack. They even taught us what to do and helped us get the donut on.

We were back on the road in no time, no trace of anger or frustration. I buried my head in his shoulder, my back bent awkwardly over the center console. I just wanted to be near him, touching him. It didn't matter if it wasn't comfortable.

The donut got us all the way to the lodge in Big Sur. Trees surrounding us to our right, massive cliffs dropping off into the Pacific to our left. The sky above us was just turning from blue to a rosy orange.

We checked in, yet another honeymooning couple in the cabins of Big Sur. The woman at the front desk looked as if she'd seen it all before. There was nothing new about us to her, and yet everything about this was new to us.

Our hotel room was small and cozy, with a gas fireplace on the far wall. When we put our bags down, Ryan joked that our bed at home was bigger than the bed in the cabin. But everything felt so intimate. He was mine. I was his. The hard part was over: the wedding, the details, the planning, the families. Now it was just us, starting our life together.

We were on the bed before our bags were unpacked. Ryan slid on top of me. His weight pressed against me, weighing me down, pushing me further into the mattress. I had chosen a masculine man, a strong man.

"Baby, I'm so sorry," he said to me. "I'll renew the Triple A membership as soon as we get home. Now, even! I can do it now."

"No," I said. "Don't do it now. I don't want you to do it now. I don't want you to ever leave this spot."

"No?"

"No," I said, shaking my head.

"Well, what should we do, then?" Ryan asked. He used to ask this when he wanted to have sex. It was his way of making me say it. He always loved making me say the things he wanted to say.

"I don't know," I teased him. "What *should* we do?"

"You look like you have something on your mind," he said, kissing me.

"I have nothing on my mind. My mind is blank," I said, smiling wide, both of us knowing everything that wasn't being said.

"No," he said. "You're thinking about having sex with me, you perv."

I laughed loudly, so loudly it filled the tiny room, and Ryan kissed my collarbone. He kissed it tenderly at first and then started to lick further up my neck. By the time he reached my earlobe, nothing seemed funny anymore.

THREE YEARS AGO

I had just started a new job, still in the alumni department but now at Occidental College.

My former coworker, Mila, recommended me for the position. We'd worked together in the alumni department at UCLA, and she'd left for Occidental the previous year. I was excited by the idea of working with her again and eager to branch out. I loved UCLA, but I'd been there my entire adult life. I wanted to learn a new community. I wanted to meet new people. Plus, it didn't hurt that Occidental's campus was breathtaking. If you're looking for a change of scenery, choose beautiful scenery.

And since I was making more money, Ryan and I decided to find a new place. When we saw a house for rent in Hancock Park, we pulled over. Sure, it looked too big for us. It looked too expensive for us. And we technically didn't need a second bedroom or a yard. But we wanted it. So Ryan picked up the phone and dialed the number on the sign.

"Hi, I'm standing outside your property on Rimpau. How much are you renting it for?" Ryan said, and then he listened intently.

"Uh-huh," he said. I couldn't hear what the other person was saying. Ryan was pacing back and forth. "And is that including utilities?"

I was eager to hear what number this person had given him.

"Well, we can't do that," Ryan said. I sat on the hood of our car, disappointed. "I've noticed, though, that this sign has been out for a while." He was bluffing. Ryan knew no such thing. "So I'm wondering what your wiggle room is." He listened and then looked at me, and I smiled at him. "OK, is it open now? Can my wife and I take a look?"

Ryan directed his eye to a drainpipe. "Yeah, I see it. We'll take a look, and I'll call you back." He hung up, and we ran to the front door. Ryan got the key from the drainpipe and let us in.

While so much of Los Angeles is crowded roads and cramped buildings, Hancock Park is almost entirely residential, full of long, wide streets and houses set far back from the curb. Most of the neighborhood was built in the 1920s, and this place was no exception. The house was old, but it was gorgeous. Rough stucco exterior, dramatic interior archways, hardwood floors, checkered tile kitchen. The rooms were small and tight but perfect for us. I saw my life in there. I saw where our couch would go. I saw myself brushing my teeth over the prewar porcelain sink.

"We can't afford this, can we?" I asked him.

"I will make this work, if you want it," Ryan said to me, standing in the middle of the house. It was so empty that his voice traveled quickly, finding its way into the farthest corners of the room. "I will get this woman down to something we can afford."

"How?" I asked. I wasn't sure what the starting number was, and Ryan wasn't telling, which said to me that it was much higher than the figure we had in mind.

"Just . . . Do you want it?" he asked me.

"Yes, I want it. Bad."

"Then I'm gonna get it for you." Ryan left the house through the front door and walked back to the sidewalk. I walked through the kitchen and opened the sliding glass doors that led to the backyard. It was small and useless, a patch of grass and a few bushes. But there was an old lemon tree in the corner. Lemons were scattered around the trunk, most of them rotting where the peel touched the earth. It looked as if no one had taken care of the lemon tree. No one had watered it or pruned it. No one cared about it. I walked out and reached high above my head to a lemon still on the branch. I twisted it off the tree and smelled it. It smelled fresh and clean.

I took it out to the front yard to show Ryan. He was still on the phone, pacing up and down the sidewalk. I stared at him, trying to decipher how the conversation might be going. Finally, he looked up at the sky and smiled, pumping his fist into the air and looking at me as if we'd won the lottery. "September first? Yeah, that works."

When he hung up the phone, I ran into his arms, jumping up and wrapping my legs around his waist. He laughed.

"You did it!" I said. "You got me the house!" I handed him the lemon. "We have a lemon tree! We can make fresh lemonade and lemon bars and . . . other lemon stuff! How did you do it?" I asked him. "How did you talk her down?"

Ryan just shook his head. "A magician never tells."

"No, but seriously, how did you?"

He smiled, evading me. For some reason, I liked it better not knowing. He had made the impossible possible. And I liked that I didn't know his secret. It made me think that maybe other impossible things were possible. That maybe all I needed was to want it badly enough, and I really could have it.

That night, I was already looking at paint colors and thinking about packing up our stuff. I was so committed to our new house that I could no longer stand the sight of our current apartment.

I was on my computer, mentally decorating and online shopping, when Ryan walked over to me and closed my laptop.

"Hey!" I said. "I was looking at that!"

He smiled. "Well, looks like you can't use the computer anymore," he said. "So what should we do to pass the time?"

"Huh?" I asked. I knew what he was getting at.

"I'm just saying . . . it's late, and we should probably get into bed. What should we do when we get in there?" He wanted to have sex. He wanted me to say it.

"I was looking at that, though!" I told him. My voice had bounce to it, but the truth was, I really wasn't in the mood.

"You sure you don't have anything on your mind? Anything you want to do?"

Maybe if he'd said what he wanted, I might have given it to him. But it wasn't what I wanted to do. And I wasn't going to pretend it was.

"Yeah, I know exactly what I want to do," I said. "I want to continue looking at curtains!"

Ryan sighed and opened my computer back up. "You are no fun," he said, laughing and kissing me on the cheek before leaving the room.

"But you still love me, right?" I joked, calling out to him in the other room.

He popped his head back in. "Always will," he said. "Until the day I die." Then he threw himself onto the floor, lying on the ground with his tongue out and his eyes shut, pretending to be dead.

"Are you dead?" I teased him.

He was silent. He was freakishly good at remaining perfectly still. His chest didn't even rise and fall with his breath.

I got on the floor next to him and playfully poked at him.

"Looks like he's really dead," I said out loud. "Ah, well." I sighed. "That just means more time for me to look at curtains."

That's when he grabbed me and pulled me toward him, burying his fingers into my armpits, making me laugh and scream.

"So how about now, huh?" he said, when he was done tickling me. "What do you want to do now?"

"I told you," I said, standing up and smiling at him. "I want to look at curtains."

• • •

The day after we moved in, I was still unpacking boxes and considering painting the bedroom when Ryan came in and said, "What would you say if I told you I think we should get a dog?"

I threw the clothes that were in my hand back into their box and started walking into the hallway to get my shoes. "I'd say it's Sunday morning, there might be dog adoptions right now. Get your keys."

I was half joking, but he didn't stop me. We got into the car. We drove around looking for signs. We came home with Butter, a three-year-old yellow Lab. He peed and pooped all over the house, and he kept us up all night scratching his neck with his hind leg, but we loved him. The next morning, we renamed him Thumper.

Ryan and I installed a doggie door a few weeks later, and the minute we were done, Thumper jetted into the backyard. We watched as he ran around and around, jumped on the fence, and then settled on a spot to lie out in the sun.

I was sitting on the floor, stretching, when he finally came back into the house. He walked right in and sat in my lap. He was done playing outside. He wanted to be near me.

I cried for a half hour because I couldn't believe I could love a dog so much. When I finally gathered myself, I noticed there was sticky dirt in my lap and all over his paws. He smelled clean and sweet.

It turned out Thumper liked playing with lemons.

TWO YEARS AGO

I was washing the sheets one evening and decided that it was probably time to wash the mattress pad. So I pulled everything off the bed and threw it all in the laundry.

When I went to put the mattress pad back on the bed, I noticed a huge, well-worn, darker spot in the middle. It was oblong and graying where everything else was bright white.

I laid it on the bed and showed it to Ryan.

"Weird, right?" I said. "What is that from?"

Ryan gave it a good look, and as he did, Thumper came into the room. He hopped onto the bed and fit his furry tan body right into the faded gray stain, his big, dirty paws crossed over his black nose, his big, dark eyes looking at the two of us. Mystery solved. We had found the culprit.

We looked at each other and started laughing. I loved watching Ryan laugh that hard.

"That's how dirty he is," Ryan said. "He can permanently stain layers of fabric."

Thumper barely looked at us. He wasn't concerned with being laughed at. He was blissfully happy in the middle of the bed.

We kicked him off briefly so we could put the sheets on. We gathered the pillows and blankets. We got into bed, and then we told Thumper he could get back in.

He jumped right back into his spot.

Ryan turned out the light.

"I feel like this," I said, as I gestured to Ryan and me with Thumper in the middle, "is enough. Is that bad? I mean, I feel like the three of us, you and me and this dog, are all we need. I don't feel like I'm aching to add a kid to this. That's bad, right?"

"Well, we always said thirty," Ryan said, as if thirty was decades away.

"Yeah, I know," I said. "But you're twenty-eight. I'll be twenty-eight soon, too. We're two years from thirty."

Ryan thought about it. "Yeah, two years doesn't really seem like a long time."

"Do you really think we'll be ready for kids in two years? Do you feel like we are there yet?"

"No," he said plainly. "I guess I don't."

It was quiet for a while, and since we'd already turned out the lights, I wasn't sure if maybe we were done talking, if we were on our way to falling asleep.

I had started to fade a bit, started to dream, when I heard Ryan say, "That was just a guess, though, when we said thirty. We could do thirty-two, maybe. Or thirty-four."

"Yeah," I chimed in. "Or thirty-six. Plenty of people have kids when they are past forty, even."

"Or not at all," Ryan said. It wasn't loaded. His voice wasn't pointed. It was just a fact. Some couples don't have kids at all. There's nothing wrong with that. There's nothing wrong with not being ready, not knowing if you are up for it.

"Right," I said. "I mean, we can just play it by ear. Doesn't have to be thirty just because we planned on thirty."

"Right," he said. The word hung in the air.

We had plenty of time to decide what we wanted. We were still young. And yet I couldn't help but feel a type of disappointment that I'd never felt before: a sense that the future might not turn out exactly the way we pictured it.

"I love you," I said into the darkness.

"I love you, too," he said, and then we fell asleep, Thumper in between us.

A YEAR AND A HALF AGO

I was reading a magazine in bed. Ryan was watching television and petting Thumper. It was almost midnight, and I was tired, but something was nagging at me. I put my magazine down.

"Do you remember the last time we had sex?" I asked Ryan.

He didn't look over from the television, nor did he turn it down or pause it.

"No," he said, not giving it another thought. "Why?"

"Well, don't you think that's . . . you know . . . not great?"

"I guess," he said.

"Can you pause the TV for a second?" I asked him, and he did, begrudgingly. He looked at me. "I'm just saying, maybe it's something we should work on."

"Work on? That sounds awful." Ryan laughed.

I laughed, too. "No, I know, but it's important. We used to have sex all the time."

He laughed again, but this time, I wasn't sure why. "When was this?" he teased.

"What? All the time! You know, there were times we would do it, like, four times a day."

"You mean, like the time we did it in the laundry room?" he asked.

"Yes!" I said, sitting up, excited that he was finally agreeing with me.

"Or the time we did it three times in forty-five minutes?"

"Yes!"

"Or the time we had sex in the backseat of my car parked on a side street in Westwood?"

"This is exactly what I'm talking about!"

"Baby, those all happened in college."

I looked at him, keeping his gaze, trying to remember if that was true. Was all of that in college? How long ago was college, anyway? Seven years ago.

"I'm sure we've done crazy stuff since then, haven't we?"

Ryan shook his head. "Nope, we haven't."

"Surely we have," I said, my voice still sounding upbeat.

"It's not a big deal," he said, grabbing the remote and turning the TV back on. "We've been together for almost ten years. We were bound to stop having sex all the time."

"Well," I said, talking over the TV, "maybe we should spice it up."

"OK," he said. "So spice it up, then."

"Maybe I will!" I said, joking with him and turning off the light. But . . . you know, I never did.

A YEAR AGO

It was a Friday night in the middle of the summer. We were in the height of long, sunny days. I knew Ryan was meeting a few friends after work and wouldn't be home for a while, so instead of going straight home, I drove into Burbank and went to IKEA. I had been meaning to buy a new coffee table. Thumper had chewed through a leg on our old one.

After picking out a new table and paying for it, it was later than I thought. I got on the freeway to head home and found that it was backed up for what looked like miles. I flipped through the talk-radio stations until one of them announced that there was a three-car accident on the 5. That's when I knew I'd be there for a while.

It was about forty-five minutes until traffic started to pick up, and when it did, I felt my mood markedly improve. I was flying across the freeway when I saw a number of cars in front of me hit their brakes. Once again, traffic came to a complete stop.

I slowed down just in time, and then, instantaneously, I felt something slam into me. The entire car lurched forward.

My heart started to race. My brain started to panic. I looked in my rearview mirror and saw, in the twilight, a dark blue car veering away.

I started to pull over to the side of the freeway, but by the time I got there, the car that hit me had sped down the shoulder, out of sight.

I called Ryan. No answer.

I got out and stood on the shoulder, slowly maneuvering

my way to look at the back of my car. The entire back right half had been smashed. My brake lights cracked, my trunk crumpled in.

I called Ryan again. No answer.

Frustrated, I got back into the car and drove home.

When I got there, Ryan was sitting on the couch, watching television.

"You've been here the whole time?" I asked.

He turned off the TV and looked at me. "Yeah, we rescheduled drinks," he said.

"Why didn't you answer the phone when I called you? Twice?"

Ryan made a vague hand gesture to his phone across the room. "Sorry," he said. "I guess the ringer must be off. What's the matter?"

I finally put my purse down. "Well, I was hit in a hit-and-run," I said. "But I'm fine."

"Oh, my God!" Ryan said, running toward the window to take a look at the car. I'd said I was fine. But it still bothered me that he didn't run to take a look at *me*.

"The car is in bad shape," I said. "But I'm sure insurance will cover it."

He turned to me. "You got the license plate of the person who hit you, right?"

"No," I said. "I couldn't. It all happened too fast."

"They aren't going to cover it," Ryan said, "if you can't tell them who did it."

"Well, I'm sorry, Ryan!" I said. "I'm sorry someone slammed into me and didn't bother to hand me their license-plate number."

"Well, you could have gotten it as they sped away," Ryan said. "That's all I meant."

"Yeah, well, I didn't, OK?"

Ryan just looked at me.

"I'm fine, by the way. Don't worry about me. I was in a car accident, but who cares, right? As long as I can square it all with the insurance company."

"That's not what I meant, and you know it. I know you're OK. You said you were OK."

He was right. I did say that. But I still wanted him to ask. I wanted him to hug me and feel bad for me. I wanted him to offer to take care of me. And also, deep down, I was truly, truly pissed off that he had been sitting there watching a movie while I stood on the shoulder of the 5 South, not knowing what I should do.

"OK," I said, after it was quiet for a while. "I guess I'll call the insurance company."

"Do you want me to do it?" he asked.

"I got it, thanks," I said.

The woman I filed the claim with asked me how I was. She said, "Oh, you poor baby." I'm sure that's just what they say to everyone in an accident. I'm sure they are taught to act very concerned and understanding. But still, it felt nice. After I reviewed all of the information with her, she told me that the insurance company would cover it after all. We just had to pay the deductible.

When I got off the phone, I walked into the living room and joined Ryan.

"They will pay for it," I said. I was trying to keep my tone polite, but the truth was, I wanted him to know that he had been wrong.

"Cool," he said.

"We just have to pay a deductible."

"Got it. Sounds like it would have been better if we'd gotten the license plate. I guess we know for next time."

It took everything I had not to call him an asshole.

SIX MONTHS AGO

"Where do you want to go for dinner?" I asked Ryan. He was twenty minutes late coming home from work. He seemed to always be late coming home from work. Sometimes he'd call, sometimes he wouldn't. But regardless, I was always starving by the time he got home.

"I don't care," he said. "What do you want to eat? I just don't want Italian."

I groaned. He would never just pick a place. "Vietnamese?" I said, standing by the front door, grabbing my coat. As soon as we agreed on a place, I wanted to get moving.

"Ugh," he said. His voice was grumpy. He didn't want Vietnamese.

"Greek? Thai? Indian?"

"Let's just order pizza," he said. He took off his jacket when he said it. He was deciding that we would stay home. But I wanted to go out.

"You just said you didn't want Italian," I said.

"It's pizza." His tone was a little bit pointed. "You asked me what I wanted. I want pizza."

"Sorry, did I do something?" I asked him. "You seem frustrated with me."

"I was going to say the same to you."

"No," I said, trying to back off, trying to seem pleasant. "I just want to eat dinner."

"I'll get the pizza menu."

"Wait." I stopped him. "Can't we go out? I feel like I've been eating such junk lately. I'd love to go out someplace."

"Well, call Rachel, then. I'm sorry. I've had a long day at work. I'm exhausted. Can't I sit this one out?"

"Fine," I said. "Fine. I'll call Rachel."

I picked up my phone and walked out the door.

"Do you want to get dinner?" I asked her before she said hello.

"Tonight?" Rachel asked me, surprised.

"Yeah," I said. "Why not tonight?" Sure, I had seen her for lunch the day before, and we went out for drinks two nights before that, but c'mon. "I can't see my own sister three times in four days?"

Rachel laughed. "Well, no, I mean, you know very well I'd see you *seven* times in four days. *Eight. Nine. Ten* times in four days. I just mean, it's Valentine's Day. I assumed you and Ryan had plans."

Valentine's Day. It was Valentine's Day. I found myself unable to admit, even to my own sister, that Ryan and I had forgotten.

"Right, no, totally, but Ryan has to work late," I said to her. "So I thought maybe we could get dinner, you and me."

"Well, obviously, I'm up for it!" she said. "I am, as always, sans Valentine. Come on over."

FOUR MONTHS AGO

Ryan was supposed to go to San Francisco for work one week. He was going to be gone from Monday night to Saturday morning.

He asked me if I wanted to go with him.

"No," I said, without hesitation. "Better to save the vacation time."

"Got it," he said. "I'll tell the travel department it's just me, then."

"Yeah, sounds good."

The weeks went by, and I found myself desperately looking forward to time alone. I thought about it the way I thought about going to Disneyland as a kid.

And then a week before he was supposed to leave, he called me at work and told me the trip was canceled.

"Canceled?" I asked.

"Yeah," he said. "So I'll be home all next week."

"That's great!" I said, hoping my voice was convincing.

"Yeah," Ryan said. His voice was not.

THREE MONTHS AGO

I lost my wallet. I'd had it when we were at the store. I remembered pulling my credit card out to pay for the dress I was buying. Ryan was in the men's section at the time.

Then we walked around a bit more, got into the car, and came home. And that's when I realized it was gone.

We searched the living room, the couch cushions, the car, and the driveway. I knew I had to go back to the mall. I had to retrace our steps from the store to the car.

"I guess we have to go back to the store," I said. My voice was apologetic. I felt bad. This wasn't the first time I'd lost my wallet. In fact, I probably lost it about once every six months. Only three times had I never found it again.

"You go," Ryan said, heading back into the house. We had just finished checking the car. "I'm going to stay here."

"You don't want to come?" I said. "We could get dinner while we are out."

"No, I'll just grab something here."

"Without me?" I asked.

"Huh?"

"You're gonna eat dinner without me?"

"I'll wait, then," he said, as if he was doing me a favor.

"No, it's OK. You seem mad, though. Are you mad?"

He shrugged.

I smiled at him, trying to warm him up. "You used to think it was cute, remember? How I always lost my wallet? You said my lack of organization was endearing."

He looked at me, impatient. “Yeah, well,” he said to me, “it gets old after eleven years of it.”

And then he went inside the house.

When I got into the car and started driving away, my wallet slid out from underneath the passenger’s seat.

Didn’t matter, though. I cried anyway.

SIX WEEKS AGO

It was Ryan's thirtieth birthday. We spent the night out with his friends, going from sports bar to sports bar.

When we got home, Ryan started undressing me in the bedroom. He unbuttoned my shirt, and then he took the tie out of my hair, letting it fall onto my shoulders. I had a flash of how this would all go. He would kiss my neck and push us onto the bed. He would do the same things he always did, say the same stuff he always said. I'd stare up at the ceiling, counting the minutes. I wasn't in the mood. I wanted to go to sleep.

I held on to the sides of my open shirt and pulled them closer. "I'm not up for it," I said, moving away from him toward my pajamas.

He sighed. "It's my birthday," he said, keeping his hands on my shirt, staying close to me.

"Just not tonight, I'm sorry, I'm just . . . my head hurts, and I'm so tired. We've been out at the smoky bar all night, and I'm feeling . . . not very sexy."

"We could get in the shower," he said.

"Maybe tomorrow," I offered, putting on my sweatpants, ending the discussion. "Would that be OK? Tomorrow?"

"Lauren, it's my birthday." His tone wasn't playful or pleading. He was letting me know he expected me to change my mind. And suddenly, that enraged me.

I looked at him, incredulous. "So what? I owe you or something?"

LAST WEEK

Ryan asked me where his leftover burger was from the night before.

"I fed it to Thumper for dinner," I said. "I added it to his dog food."

"I was going to eat that," he said, looking at me as if I'd stolen something from him.

"Sorry," I said, laughing at how serious he was being. "It was pretty nasty, though," I added. "I don't think you would have wanted it."

"Like you have any idea what I want," he said, and he grabbed a bottle of water and walked away.

RIGHT NOW

The ride home from Dodger Stadium is cold and lonely despite it being eighty degrees out and that there are two of us in the car. We use the radio to gracefully ignore each other for a little while, but it eventually becomes clear that there is nothing graceful about it.

When we pull into the driveway, I am relieved to be able to get away from him. By the time we get to the front of our house, we can hear Thumper whimpering at the door. He is fine being alone, but the minute he can hear us, and I swear he can hear us from blocks away, he suddenly becomes overtaken with dependence. He forgets how to live without us the minute he knows we are there.

Ryan puts his key in the lock. He turns toward me and pauses. "I'm sorry," he says.

"No, me, too," I say. But I don't really know what I am even sorry for. I feel as if I've been sorry for months now without a reason. What am I really doing wrong here? What is happening to us? I've read books on it. I've read the articles that show up in all the women's magazines about marital ruts and turning the heat up in your marriage. They don't tell you anything real. They don't have any answers.

Ryan opens the door, and Thumper runs toward us. His excitement only highlights our own misery. Why can't we be more like him? Why can't I be easy to please? Why can't Ryan be that happy to see me?

"I'm going to take a shower," Ryan says.

I don't say anything back. He heads to the bathroom, and

I sit down on the floor and pet Thumper. His fur soothes me. He licks my face. He nuzzles my ear. For a minute, I feel OK.

"Goddammit!" Ryan calls from the bathroom.

I close my eyes for a moment. Bracing myself.

"What?" I call to him.

"There is no fucking hot water. Did you call the landlord?"

"I thought you were calling the landlord!"

"Why do I always have to do that stuff? Why is it always up to me?" he asks. He has opened the bathroom door and is standing there in a towel.

"I don't know," I say. "You just normally do. So I assumed you were going to be the one to handle it. Sorry." It is clear by the way I say it that I am not sorry.

"Why don't you ever do what you say you're going to do? How hard is it to just pick up the goddamn phone and call the landlord?"

"I never said I was going to do it. If you wanted me to do it, you should have said something. I'm not a mind reader."

"Oh, OK. Got it. My apologies. I thought it was clear that if we have no hot water, someone needs to call the landlord."

"Yeah," I say. "That is obvious. And it's normal for me to assume that you will do it. Since you are the person who normally does that. Just like I am the one who does all the fucking laundry in this house."

"Oh, so you do the laundry, and that makes you some sort of saint?"

"Fine. You can do your laundry, then, if it doesn't matter who does it. Do you know how to use the washing machine?"

Ryan laughs at me. No, he scoffs at me.

"Do you?" I say. "I'm not being funny. I'll bet you a hundred bucks you don't know how it works."

"I'm sure I could figure it out," he says. "I'm not as much of a complete moron as you make me out to be."

"I don't make you out to be anything."

"Oh, yes, Lauren. Yes, you do. You act like you're the most perfect person in the whole world and you're stuck with your stupid husband who can't do a damn thing but call the landlord. You know what? I'll be the one who gets the hot water fixed. Since you do all the complicated stuff for smart people, like the laundry." He starts angrily putting his clothes back on.

"Where are you even going?" I say to him.

"To see if I can fix the fucking thing!" he says, putting on his shoes with equal parts anger and haste.

"Now? It's almost midnight. You need to stay here and talk to me."

"Let's drop it, Lauren," Ryan says. He walks to the front door. His hand is on the doorknob, getting ready to leave. Thumper is resting at my feet, no idea what he's in the middle of.

"We can't drop it, Ryan," I say. "I'm not going to drop it. We've been 'dropping it' for months now."

That's what's really concerning about all of this. We aren't fighting about the hot water or the Dodger Stadium parking lot. We aren't fighting about money or jealousy or communication skills. We are fighting because we don't know how to be happy. We are fighting because we are not happy. We are fighting because we no longer make each other happy. And I think, at least if I'm speaking for myself, I'm pretty pissed off about that.

"We have to deal with this, Ryan. It's been three straight weeks of bitching at each other. Out of the past month, I think we have spent maybe one evening in a good mood. The rest of it has been like this."

"You think I don't know that?" Ryan says, his hand gesticulating wildly. When he gets angry, his normally confident and controlled demeanor becomes unrestrained and forceful. "You think I don't know how miserable I am?"

"Miserable?" I say. "Miserable?" I can't argue with what he is saying. It's really about how he says it. He says it as if I'm the one making him miserable. As if I'm the one who's causing all of this.

"I'm not saying anything you didn't just say yourself. Please calm down."

"Calm down?"

"Stop repeating everything I say as a question."

"Then try being a bit more clear."

Ryan sighs, moving his hand to his forehead, covering it with his thumb and fingers as if they were the brim of a baseball cap. He's rubbing his temples. I don't know when he became so dramatic. Somewhere along the way, he went from being this super calm, collected person to being *this* guy, this guy who sighs loudly and rubs his temples as if he's Jesus on the cross. It's as if the world is happening *to* him. I can tell he wants to say something, but he doesn't. He starts to, and he stops himself.

I'm not sure what it is about me that insists that he say every little thing in his head. But when we fight like this, I can't stand to see him hold back. You know why? I know why. It's because if you're really holding back, you don't even start to say it. But that's not what he does. He does this little song and dance where he pretends he's not going to say something, but it's clear that eventually, he's going to say something.

"Just say it," I say.

"No," he says. "It's not worth it."

"Well, clearly, it is. Because you can barely stop yourself. So get on with it. I don't have all fucking night."

"Why don't you take it down a notch, OK?"

I shake my head at him. "You are such a dick sometimes."

"Yeah, well, you're a bitch."

"Excuse me?"

"Here we go. Her Royal Highness is offended."

"It's not hard to be offended by being called a bitch."

"It's no different from you just calling me a dick."

"It is, actually. It's much different."

"Lauren, get over it. OK? I'm sorry I called you a bitch. Pretend I called you whatever you want to be called. The point is, I'm sick of this. I'm sick of every little thing being a disaster of epic proportions. I can't even go to a goddamn Dodgers game without you moping through every inning." Thumper moves from my feet and heads toward Ryan. I try not to worry that he's choosing sides.

"If you don't want me to be upset, then stop doing things to upset me."

"This is exactly the problem! I'm not doing things to upset you."

"Right. You just get tickets to the Dodgers game even when I tell you I don't feel like going. That's not to upset me, that's because . . . why, exactly?" I move toward the dining-room table, getting a better angle at him, looking at him even more directly, but I'm not doing a great job of paying attention to the speed and force of my body. I hit the table so hard with my hip that I almost knock over the vase in the middle of the table. It wobbles, ever so slightly. I steady it.

"Because I want to see the Dodgers, and I really don't fucking care if you're there or not. I got the extra ticket to be nice, actually."

I cross my arms. I can feel myself crossing them. I know it's terrible body language. I know it makes things worse. And yet there is no other way for my arms to be. "To be nice? So you wanted to spend Friday night by yourself at the Dodgers? You didn't even want me to go with you?"

"Honestly, Lauren," Ryan says, his voice now perfectly calm, "I did not want you to go with me. I haven't wanted you to go someplace with me in months."

It's the truth. He's not saying it to hurt me. I can see that in his eyes, in his face, in the way his lips relax after he says it. He doesn't care if it hurts me. He's just saying it because it's true.

Sometimes people do things because they are furious or because they are upset or because they are out for blood. And those things can hurt. But what hurts the most is when someone does something out of apathy. They don't care about you the way they said they did back in college. They don't care about you the way they promised to when you got married. They don't care about you at all.

And because there is just the tiniest part of me that still cares, and because his not caring enrages that tiny part of me, I do something I have never done before. I do something I never thought I would ever do. I do something that, even as I'm doing it, I can't believe is actually happening.

I pick up the vase. The glass vase. And I throw it against the door behind him. Flowers and all.

I watch Ryan duck, yanking his shoulders up around his neck and ears. I watch Thumper jump to attention. I watch as the water flies into the air, the stems and petals disperse and fall to the ground, and the glass shatters into so many pieces that I'm not sure I even remember what it used to look like.

And when all of the shards have landed, when Ryan looks up at me stunned, when Thumper scurries out into the other room, the tiny part of me that cared is gone. Now I don't care anymore, either. It's a shitty feeling. But it beats the hell out of caring, even the tiniest bit.

Ryan stares at me for a moment and then grabs his keys off the side table. He swipes the water and glass out of his way with the shoes already on his feet. He walks out the front door.

I don't know what he's thinking. I don't know where he's going. I don't know how long he'll be gone. All I know is that this might, in fact, be the end of my marriage. It might be the end of something I thought had no ending.

• • •

I stare at the door for a while after Ryan leaves. I can't believe that I have thrown a vase at the wall. I can't believe that the crushed mess of glass on the floor is because of me. I wasn't intending to hurt him. I didn't throw it *at* him. And yet the violence of it startles me. I didn't know I was capable of it.

Eventually, I stand up and go to the kitchen and get the broom and the dust pan. I put on a pair of shoes. I start to sweep it all up. As I do, Thumper comes running into the room, and I have to tell him to stop where he is. He listens and sits, watching me. The *clink* of the pieces against one another as they hit the trash can are almost soothing. *Brush. Brush. Clink.*

I grab a few paper towels and run them over the area to mop up any remaining shards and water, and then I vacuum. I'm hesitant to stop vacuuming, because I don't know what I'm going to do after I'm done. I don't know what to do with myself.

I put everything away and lie down on the bed. I am reminded of when we bought it, why we bought it.

What happened to us?

I can hear a voice in my head, speaking crisply and clearly. *I don't love him anymore.* That's what it says. *I don't love him anymore.* And maybe more heartbreaking is the fact that I know, deep down, he doesn't love me, either.

It all clicks into place. That's what all of this is, isn't it? That's what the fighting is. That's why I disagree with everything he says. That's why I can't stand all the things I used to stand. That's why we haven't been having sex. That's why we never try hard to please each other. That's why we are never pleased with each other.

Ryan and I are two people who used to be in love.

What a beautiful thing to have been.

What a sad thing to be.

Ryan must have returned late at night or early in the morning. I don't know which. I didn't wake up when he came home.

When I do wake up, he is on the other side of the bed, Thumper in between us. Ryan's back is facing me. He is snoring. It scares me that we are able to sleep during this sort of turmoil. I think of the way it used to be, the way fights used to keep us up all night and into the morning. The way we couldn't sleep on our anger, couldn't put it on hold. Now we are on the verge of defeat and . . . he's snoring.

I wait patiently for him to wake up. When he finally does, he doesn't say anything to me. He stands up and walks to the bathroom. He goes to the kitchen and brews himself a cup of coffee and gets back into bed. He is next to me but not beside me. We are both in this bed, but we are not sharing it.

"We're not in love anymore," I say. Just the sound of it coming out of my mouth makes my skin crawl and my adrenaline run. I am shaking.

Ryan stares at me for a moment, no doubt shocked, and then he pulls his hands to his face, burying his fingers in his hair. He is a handsome man. I wonder when I stopped seeing that.

When we got married, he was almost prettier than I was on our wedding day. Our wedding pictures, where he is smiling like a young boy, his eyes crinkled and bright like stars, were beautiful, in part, because he was beautiful. But he no longer seems exceptional to me.

"I wish you hadn't said that," Ryan says, not looking up, not moving his head from his hands. He is frozen, staring at the blanket beneath him.

"Why?" I ask him, suddenly eager to hear what he thinks, desperate to know if maybe he remembers something I don't, to know if he thinks I am wrong. Because maybe he can convince me. Maybe I *am* wrong. I want to be wrong. It will feel so good to be wrong. I will wallow in my wrongness; I will swim in it. I will breathe it in and let it overtake my lungs and my body, and I will cry it out, heavy tears so full of relief they will be baptismal.

"Because now I don't know how we keep going," he says. "I don't know where we go from here."

He finally looks up at me. His eyes are bloodshot. When he pulls his fingers out of his hair, they leave it in disarray, scattered every which way across his head. I start to say, *What do you mean?* but instead, I say, "How long have you known?"

Ryan's face drops into an expression that isn't so much miserable but, rather, lifeless. "Does it matter?" he asks me, and honestly, I'm not sure. But I press on.

"I just figured it out," I say. "I'm just wondering how long you've known you weren't in love with me."

"I don't know. A few weeks, I guess," he says, staring back at the blanket. It is striped and multicolored, and for that, I am thankful. It will keep his attention. Maybe he won't look at me.

"Like a month?" I ask.

"Yeah." He shrugs. "Or like a few weeks, like I said."

"When?" I say. I don't know why I get out of bed, but I do. I have to stand up. My body has to be standing.

"I just told you when," he says. He doesn't move from the bed.

"No," I say, my back now up against our bedroom wall. "Like, what happened that made you realize it?"

"What happened that made *you* realize it?" he asks me. The blanket's stripes have failed to do their job; he looks at me. I flinch.

"I don't know," I say. "It just sort of flew into my head. One moment, I didn't know what was going on, and then suddenly, I just . . . got it."

"Same here," he says. "Same thing for me."

"But, like, what day? What were we doing?" I don't know why I need to seek this information out. It just feels like something I don't know—his side of this. "I'm just trying to get some context."

"Just lay off it, OK?" Back to the stripes.

"Just be honest, would you? We're clearing the air here. Just let it out. It's all about to come out anyway, every last ugly piece of this. Just let it out. Just let it—"

"I'm not in love with another woman, if that's what you're asking," he says.

That wasn't what I was asking at all.

"But I just . . ." He continues. "I noticed that I am seeing them differently."

"Women?"

"Yeah. I look at them now. I never used to look at them. I was looking at one of them, and I just . . . I realized that I don't think of you the way I think of them."

"Women?"

"Yeah."

I let it sink in. Thumper gets off the bed and walks over to me. Can he sense what's happening? He sits at the door by my feet and looks at Ryan. My heart starts to crack. This might all end in me losing Thumper.

"So what does this mean?" I ask quietly, gently. By saying

the words out loud, I have changed our fate. I have set us in motion. I am ripping us out of this comfortable prison once and for all. I am going to solve this problem. I have a lot of other problems, and I know this is going to cause a whole new set of problems, but living with someone I don't like isn't going to be one of them. Not anymore.

Ryan steps toward me, and he holds me. I want it to feel better than it does. His voice is just as quiet and calm as mine. "This can't be the end, Lauren. This is just a rough patch or something."

"But," I say, looking up at him, finally ready to say the last of what had been in my heart for so long, "I can't stand you."

It feels like such a sweet and visceral release, and yet the minute it comes out of my mouth, I wish I never said it. I wish I was the sort of person who doesn't need her pain to be heard. I want to be the type of person who can keep it to herself and spare the feelings of others. But I'm not that person. My anger has to take flight. It has to be set free and allowed to bounce off the walls and into the ears of the person it could hurt the most.

Ryan and I sink to the floor. We rest our backs against the wall, our knees bent in front of us, our arms crossed, our posture perfectly matched. We have spent enough years together to know how to work in sync, even if we don't want to. Thumper sits at my feet, his belly warming them. I want to love Ryan the way I love Thumper. I want to love him and protect him and believe in him and be ready to jump in front of a bus for him, the way I would for my dog. But they are two completely different types of love, aren't they? They shouldn't even have the same name. The kind that Ryan and I had, it runs out.

Eventually, Ryan speaks. "I have no idea what we are going to do," he says, still sitting with me, his back now slouched, his posture truly defeated, his gaze directed firmly at the wayward nail in our hardwood floor.

"Me, neither," I say, looking at him and remembering how much I used to melt when I smelled him. He is so close to me that I quietly sniff the air, seeing if I can inhale him, if I can feel that bliss again. I think maybe if I can breathe deeply enough, his scent will flow through my nose and flood my heart. Maybe it will infect me again. Maybe I can be happy again if I just smell hard enough. But it doesn't work. I feel nothing.

Ryan starts laughing. He actually manages to laugh. "I don't know why I'm laughing," he says, as he gains his composure. "This is the saddest moment of my life."

And then his voice breaks, and the tears fall from his eyes, and he truly looks at me for maybe the first time in a year. He repeats himself, slowly and deliberately. "This is the saddest moment of my life."

I think, for a moment, that we might cry together. That this might be the beginning of our healing. But as I go to put my head on his shoulder, Ryan stands up.

"I'm going to call the landlord," he says. "We need hot water."

"I wrote down 'couple's counseling,' 'living separately,' and 'open marriage,'" I say, sitting at our dining-room table. I have a piece of paper in front of me. Ryan has a piece of paper in front of him. I am not open to the idea of open marriage. I am just spitballing. But I know, I am positive, that an open marriage is not on the table.

"Open marriage?" Ryan asks. He is intrigued.

"Ignore that last one," I say. "I just . . . I didn't have any other ideas."

"It's not a bad idea," Ryan says, and the minute he says it, I hate him. Of course, he would say that. Of course, that would be the one he jumped on. Leave it to Ryan to ignore that I said "couple's counseling" but jump at the chance to screw someone else.

"Just . . ." I say, annoyed. "Just say what you wrote down."

"OK." Ryan looks down at his paper. "I wrote 'date again' and 'trial separation.'"

"I don't know what those mean," I say.

"Well, the first one is kind of like your thing about living apart. We would just try to see if maybe we lived in different places and we just went on a few dates and saw each other less, maybe that would work. Maybe take some pressure off. Make it more exciting to see each other."

"OK, and the second one?"

"We break up for a little while."

"You mean, like, we're done?"

"Well, I mean," he starts to explain, "I move out, or you

move out, and we see how we do on our own, without each other."

"And then what?"

"I don't know. Maybe some time apart would make us . . . you know, ready to try again."

"How long would we do this? Like, a few months?"

"I was thinking longer."

"Like, how long?"

"I don't know, Lauren. Jesus," Ryan says, losing his patience at all of my questions. It's been a few weeks since we told each other we didn't love each other anymore. We've been tiptoeing around each other. This is the beginning of pulling the Band-Aid off. A very large, very sticky Band-Aid.

"I'm just asking you to clarify your suggestion," I say. "I don't think you need to act like this is the Spanish Inquisition."

"Like, a year. Like, we take a year apart."

"And we sleep with other people?"

"Yeah," Ryan says, as if I'm an idiot. "I think that's kind of the point."

Ryan has made it clear that he no longer thinks of me the way he thinks about other women. It hurts. And yet when I try to break down why it hurts, I don't have an answer. I don't really think of him in that way, either.

"Let's talk about this later," I say, getting up from the table.

"I'm ready to talk about this now," Ryan says. "Don't walk away."

"I'm asking you nicely," I say, my tone slow and pointed, "if we can please discuss this later."

"Fine," Ryan says, getting up from the table and throwing his sheet of paper into the air. "I'm getting out of here."

I don't ask him where he is going. He leaves often enough now that I know his answer will be harmless. I resent him so much for being predictable. He'll go to a bar and get a drink.

He'll go to the movies. He'll call his friends to play basketball. I don't care. He'll come back when he feels like it, and when he does, the air in the house will be sharpened and tightened, so much that I will feel I can barely breathe.

I lie on the couch for hours, contemplating a year without my husband. It feels freeing and terrifying. I think about him sleeping with another woman, but the thought quickly transforms into the thought of me sleeping with another man. I don't know who this man is, but I can see his hands on me. I can feel his lips on me. I can imagine the way he will look at me, the way he will make me feel like the only woman in the room, the most important woman in the world. I imagine his slim body and his dark hair. I imagine his deep voice. I imagine being nervous, a type of nervous I haven't been in years.

When Ryan finally does come home, I tell him I think he is right. We should take a year apart.

Ryan sighs loudly, and his shoulders slump. He tries to speak, but his voice catches. I walk over to him and wrap my arms around his shoulders. I start crying. Once again, finally, we are on the same team. We wallow in it for a while. We let ourselves feel the relief we have given each other. That's what it feels like, ultimately: immense relief. Like cold water on a burn.

When we disengage, Ryan offers to move out. He says I can keep the house for the year. I take him up on it. I don't argue. He's offering me a gift. I'm going to take it. We sit quietly next to each other on the sofa, holding hands, not looking at each other for what feels like hours. It feels so good to stop fighting.

Then we realize we both thought we were the one keeping Thumper.

We fight about the dog until five in the morning.

Most of Ryan's things are packed. There are boxes all over the living room and bedroom with words like "Books" and "Bathroom Stuff" scribbled in black Sharpie. The moving truck is on its way. Ryan is in the bedroom packing shoes. I can hear each one land on the cardboard as it is chucked.

I grab a few of my things and prepare to leave. I can't stay here for this. I can't watch it happen. I am glad he is leaving. I really am. I keep telling myself that over and over. I keep thinking of my new freedom. But I realize that I don't really know what it means—freedom. I don't know anything of the practical ramifications of my actions. We have covered only the basics in terms of our preparation. We haven't talked about what it would feel like or what our new life would look like. We've stuck to numbers and figures. We've talked about how to divide our bank account. We've talked about how to afford two rent payments. How to keep him on my insurance. Whether we need to file legally. "We'll cross that bridge when we come to it," Ryan said, and I let it go. That answer was good with me. I certainly don't want any of this in writing.

I told Ryan last night that I didn't want to be here to see him leave. He agreed that it might be best if I left for the weekend and gave him his space to move out as he wished. "The last thing I need is you critiquing the way I pack my toothbrush," Ryan told me. His voice was jovial, but his words were sincere. I could feel the tension and resentment underneath. The smile on his face was the sort of smile car salesmen have, pretending everybody's having a good time when, really, you're at war.

I pick up my deodorant and my face wash. I pick up only the most necessary pieces for my makeup bag. I grab my toothbrush and put it in my travel case, snapping the toothbrush cap over the bristles so they won't get dirty. Ryan usually stuffs his in a plastic bag. He is right to be defensive about the way he packs toothbrushes. He does it wrong. I put all of it in my bag and zip it up. For better or worse, I am ready to go.

My plan is to drive straight to Rachel's house. Rachel knows that things with Ryan and me aren't going well. She has noticed how tense I've been. She has noticed how often I criticize him, how rarely I have anything nice to say. But I have been insisting that things were fine. I don't know why I've had such a hard time admitting it to her. I think, in some ways, I hid it because I knew telling Rachel made it real. I had already told Mila about all of this. The tension, the fighting, the loss of love, the plan to separate. For some reason, in my mind, Mila could know, and that didn't seem tantamount to carving it in stone. But with Rachel, it would be official. A witness. I can't turn around and pretend it never happened. Maybe that's the difference between a friend and a sister: a friend can just listen to your problems in the present, but your sister remembers and reminds you of everything in the past. Or maybe it's not a difference between friends and sisters. Maybe it's the difference between Mila and Rachel.

But this really *is* happening. The moving truck is coming. And if I am going to deal with this, I need Rachel. Rachel, who will hold my hand and tell me it is going to be OK. Rachel, who will believe in me. I have to admit to her that my marriage is failing. That *I* am failing. That I am not the successful and together older sister I have been pretending to be. That I am no longer the one with her shit together.

I find Ryan in the bedroom, grabbing boxes of clothes. We have already split up the furniture. We are both going to have to go shopping on our own. I now need a new TV. Ryan is going to need pots and pans. What had seemed like a whole is now two halves.

"OK," I say. "I'm going to go and leave you to it." Ryan has friends coming over to help. He doesn't need me.

He doesn't need me.

"OK," he says, looking into the closet. Our closet. My closet. He finally looks up at me, and I can see he has been crying. He breathes in and out, trying to control himself, trying to take control of his feelings. Suddenly, my heart swells and overtakes me. I can't leave him like this. I can't. I can't leave him in pain.

He does need me.

I run to him. I put my arms around him. I let him bury his face in me. I hold him as he lets it out, and then I say, "You know what? This is stupid. I'm going to stay." This whole idea has been far-fetched and absurd. We just needed a wake-up call. And this is the wake-up call. This is what we needed to see how foolish we've been. Of course, we love each other! We always have. We just forgot for a little while but we are going to be OK now. We have pushed ourselves to the brink and learned our lesson. We don't have to go through with this. It is over. We can end this strange experiment right here and go back to the way things were. Marriages aren't all roses and sunshine. We know that. This was silly. "Forget this," I say. "You're not going anywhere, sweetheart. You don't have to go anywhere."

He is quiet for some time longer, and then he shakes his head. "No," he says, drying his tears. "I need to leave." I stare at him, frozen with my arms still around him. He pushes his point further. "You should go," he says, wiping his own tears away. He is back to business.

That's when I fall apart. I don't melt like butter or deflate like a tire. I shatter like glass, into thousands of pieces.

My heart is truly broken. And I know that even if it mends, it will look different, feel different, beat differently.

I stand up and grab my bag. Thumper follows me to the front door. I look down at him with my hand on the knob, ready to turn it. He looks up at me, naive and full of wondering. For all he knows, he is about to go for a walk. I am not sure whom I feel worse for: Ryan, Thumper, or myself. I can't bear it a second longer. I can't pet him good-bye. I turn the knob and walk out the front door, shutting it behind me. I don't stop to take a breath or get my bearings. I just get into the car, wipe my eyes, and set out for Rachel's house. I am not strong enough to stand on my own two feet.

I need my sister.

part two

NOVEMBER RAIN

I just need you to hear what I'm about to say and not try to talk me out of it. Don't judge me. Or say I'm making a mistake, even if you think I am. Making a mistake, I mean. Because I probably am. But I just need you to listen and then tell me everything is going to be OK. That's what I need, basically. I need you to tell me everything is going to be OK, even if it probably isn't."

"OK." Rachel agrees immediately. She doesn't really have a choice, does she? I mean, I've shown up on her doorstep unannounced at nine A.M. on a Saturday, screaming, "Don't judge me!" So she just has to go with it. "Do you want to come in? Or—" she starts to ask me, but I don't wait for her to finish.

"Ryan and I are splitting up."

"Oh, my God," she says, stunned. She stares at me for a moment and then unfreezes, opening the door wide for me to step in. I do. She's still in her pajamas, which seems reasonable. She probably just woke up. Chances are, she was having a perfectly nice dream when I rang her doorbell.

Once I walk past her and she shuts the door behind me, she can see I've packed a bag. It's all coming together for her.

She takes the bag from my shoulder and puts it down on the couch. "What did you—I mean, how did this—how did the two of you—are you OK? That's what's important. How are you feeling?"

I shrug. Most of the time when I shrug, it's because I'm indifferent. And yet now, even though my shrug means a million things at once, none of them is indifference.

"Do you want to talk about why you're splitting up?" Rachel says calmly. "Or should I just make you some . . . I don't know. What do people eat when they are divorcing?"

"We're not divorcing," I say, moving past her and taking a seat on her couch.

"Oh," she says, taking a seat beside me. "You said you were splitting up, so I just assumed . . ." She curls her feet in, sitting cross-legged and facing me. Her pajama pants are white with blue and salmon-colored stripes. Her tank top is the same salmon as the stripes on the bottom. She must have bought them as a set. My sister is exactly the person who wears the set together. I am exactly the person who cannot find a single matching pair.

"We're breaking up," I say. "Like, we are not going to be seeing each other for a while, but then, you know, we're going to give it another shot."

"So you're separating, then? It's a trial separation?"

"No."

"So . . . Lauren, what am I missing here?"

"You aren't supposed to judge."

"I'm not judging," she says, taking my hand. "I'm trying to understand."

"We're going on a break. We can't live in the same place anymore. We can't stand each other." The look on her face confirms that she's known this for a while, but I don't acknowledge it.

"But you're not getting a divorce because . . . ?" she asks me. Her voice is gentle. I think that's maybe the thing I need most right now. I'm functioning pretty similarly to a dog, in that, really, the words themselves don't matter. I'm just listening for high-pitched tones, sounds that are smooth and soothing. "I mean, if you guys have been having problems for a while, if it's bad enough that you don't want to live together, then what is stopping you from just breaking up altogether?"

I take a moment and think about how to answer. I mean, the word *divorce* never came up.

Obviously, it was in my head. I thought about saying it. But I never wrote it down on that sheet of options. And while I can't imagine that Ryan didn't think of it, didn't consider it, didn't *almost* say it, something stopped him, too.

I think that's important. Neither of us suggested it. Neither of us said that this thing we have together, this thing that we have broken and is no longer working, neither of us said that we should throw it away.

"I don't know why," I say when I finally answer her. "Because I made a promise, I guess. Or, I don't know, I'm hoping there's a third option for us besides living unhappily or giving up entirely."

Rachel considers this. "So how long is this break?" She says "break" as if it's a new word that I made up. "So how long is this flarffensnarler?" That's how she says it.

I breathe in. I breathe out. "One year." My resolve starts to melt away. My composure starts to crack. The true pain of what I'm doing starts to slowly seep in, not unlike the way the sun shines brightly enough to break up a cloudy day.

Rachel can see I'm starting to cry before the tears actually form in my eyes, and it further softens her into exactly the Rachel I need. She does not need to know the details. She wants only to hold me and tell me everything will be OK, even if it won't be. So that's what she does; she holds me, and she runs her hands through my hair. And she says what I've been waiting all morning to hear.

"It really will be OK," she says, her voice almost cooing to me. "I know you told me to say it. But it's actually true. This will all be OK."

"How do you know?" I shouldn't ask her things like this. I told her to say something. She said it. I can't press her on it. I can't try to get her to say things I haven't scripted for her. But she seems so confident right now, so sure that I will be OK, that I want to know more about this version of me she sees. How is the Lauren in her head going to be OK? And how can I be more like that Lauren?

"I know it will be OK because everything is OK in the end. And if it's not OK, it's not the end."

I pull back and look at her. "Isn't that from one of your mugs?"

Rachel shrugs. "Just because it's on a mug doesn't mean it's not true."

"No," I say, lying down, my head in her lap. "I guess you're right."

"You know what else I know?" she says.

"What?"

"I know you have a really great year ahead of you."

"I find that hard to believe. I'm turning thirty, and I'm on the verge of divorce."

"I thought you weren't getting divorced?" Rachel says.

I roll my eyes at her. "It's hyperbole, Rachel. A rhetorical device." I am at my most condescending when I'm at my least secure. I guess the problem is that I don't know how much of a hyperbole it is. I'll insist to everyone, my sister included, that it's not going to happen. But what if it does? I mean, what if it does?

"No, I'm serious," she says. "This part is hard. But I know you, and you don't do things that you shouldn't do. You don't take this stuff lightly. Neither does Ryan. He's a good man. And you're a good woman. If the two of you decided this was a good idea, that's because it's a good idea. And good ideas are never a bad idea."

It's quiet for a minute before we both start laughing.

"OK, that last part didn't make a whole lot of sense, but you know what I meant."

I look up at her, and she looks down at me. I always know what she means. We've always had a way of understanding each other. Maybe more to the point, we've always had a way of believing in each other. I need to be believed in right now.

"I'm glad you're here," Rachel says to me. "Not under these circumstances, obviously. But I'm glad you're here."

"Yeah?"

"Yeah, it's nice to see you, just you."

"With no Ryan?"

"Yeah," she says. "I love Ryan, but I love you more. It will be nice to have a year of just you."

She's better with words than she thinks she is, because for the first time, I can see something to look forward to this year. It will be nice to have a year of just me.

• • •

"So, delicate question, I guess," Rachel says to me. We are at her kitchen table. She has made Cinnamon Toast Crunch–encrusted French toast with fresh whipped cream. I want to take a picture, it looks so gorgeous and decadent. She puts the plate in front of me as she speaks, and I immediately stop listening to whatever she is saying. I know this will taste even better than it looks. Which is saying a lot. But this is Rachel's forte. She makes Oreo pancakes. She makes red velvet crepes with cream cheese filling. She cannot make a casserole or an egg dish to save her life, but anything that requires a bag of sugar and heavy cream, and she's your woman.

"This looks incredible," I say to her, grabbing my fork. I press the end of it against the corner of the bread and grind it against the plate until I've set my piece free. It tastes exactly like I imagined. It takes like everything is fine. "Oh, my God," I say.

"I know, right?" Rachel has absolutely no qualms about admitting that what she has made tastes great. She does it in a way that implies she had nothing to do with it. You can tell her that her pumpkin spice cake is the most delicious thing you've ever tasted, and she will say something like, "Oh, tell me about it. It's sinful," and you get the impression that she is complimenting the recipe instead of herself.

"Anyway," I say, after I have finished chewing, "what is your delicate question?"

"Well," she says, licking the whipped cream off her fork. "Who gets . . ." She pauses and then sort of gives up. She doesn't know how to say it.

"Thumper," I say, so that she doesn't have to. "Who gets Thumper?"

"Right, who gets Thumper?"

I take a deep breath. "I get him for the first two months just so everything doesn't change at once for him." I feel stupid when I say this. Ryan and I act as if Thumper is a child, and it comes out in the smallest and most embarrassing ways. But Rachel doesn't bat an eyelash.

"And then Ryan gets him?"

"Yeah, for two months after that. That brings us to January, and we will renegotiate."

"Got it."

"It sounds stupid, right?" I say. The truth is, I was eager to agree to the idea when Ryan came up with it. It meant that no matter what, we would see each other in two months, and that gave me a sense of security. It felt like training wheels on a bike.

"No," Rachel says, not even looking at me. She continues to eat her breakfast. "Not at all. Everyone has their own way of doing things."

"Well, what, then?" I ask.

Rachel looks . . . I don't know. There is something going on with her face. She seems to be holding something back. "What do you mean?" she asks.

"What are you thinking that you're not saying?"

"I thought I was supposed to be supportive!" Rachel says, half laughing and completely defensive. "I can't tell you every little thought in my head and tell you everything you want to hear at the same time."

I laugh. "Yeah, OK," I say.

We are quiet for a minute. I have scarfed down all of my food. There is nothing left to do but stare at my white plate. I try to move the crumbs around with my fork.

"But what is it, though?" I say. I want to know. I'm not sure why. Maybe I need the truth more than I need to hear what I want to hear. Maybe there is almost never a time when you don't need the truth. Or maybe it's just that you need the truth the most at the times you think you don't want to hear it. "Just tell me. I can handle it."

Rachel sighs. "I just . . ." she starts. She looks up at me. "I feel bad for Ryan."

I'm not sure what I thought she was going to say, but it wasn't that. I expected something about how I'm taking the Thumper thing too seriously. I expected something about how maybe Ryan and I should give it another try. I expected that maybe she was going to say the one thing that I fear is actually true: that I'm being a whiny-ass baby and that every marriage is hard, and I should just shut up and go home and quit this bullshit, because not being happy is not a real problem.

But she doesn't say that. She actually tears up and says, "I just . . . he lost his wife, his house, and his dog on the same day."

I don't say anything to her. I just kind of look at her. I let it sink in.

She's right. I used to love that man so much. I used to be the person who made sure he had everything he wanted. When did I become the person who took it all away?

I start to cry. I put my head down on the table, and Rachel rushes to my side.

"I'm sorry," she says. "I'm sorry! See? I'm not good at this. I suck at it. I'm the shittiest person at this. You are a good person, and you're doing the right thing."

"Thumper is just for two months," I say. "The whole thing is only for a year."

"I know!" Rachel says, holding me, squeezing my shoulders. "Ryan is fine. I know he's fine. He's one of those guys, you know, who's always fine."

"You think he's fine?" I ask her, lifting my head off the table. It is somehow awful to think that he is fine. It is almost as awful as thinking about him being miserable. I cannot stand the thought that he is OK or not OK.

"No," Rachel says. I can sense her desperation to get out of this conversation. She can't say the right thing, and she knows it, and maybe she's a little annoyed at the situation I've put her in. "Ryan is fine, as in 'He will be fine.' Not like 'He's totally fine.'"

"Right," I say, composing myself. "We will both be fine."

"Right," she says, grasping for the calm tone in my voice. "Fine."

So that's what I aim for. I aim for fine.

I am fine.

Ryan is fine.

We will be fine.

One day, this will all be fine.

There is a big difference between something that is fine and something that *will be* fine, but I decide to pretend, for now, that they are the same.

"You know you have to tell Mom soon, right?" Rachel says to me.

"I know," I say.

"And Charlie," she says. "But who knows with Charlie? That could go either way."

I nod, already lost to my imagination. I think about telling them. I think about how Charlie will crack some joke. I think about whether my mom will be disappointed in me. If she'll feel the same way I do, that I've failed. After a minute, I recognize that this line of thinking is going nowhere fast. "You know what?" I say.

"What?"

"They'll be fine."

Rachel smiles at me. "Yes, they will. They will be fine."

I go home on Sunday night at seven o'clock, the time that Ryan and I agreed on. I knew he would be gone. That was the whole point. But as I open the door to my empty house, the fact that he is gone really hits me. I am alone.

My house looks as if I was robbed. Ryan didn't take anything that we hadn't discussed ahead of time, and yet it feels as if he has taken everything we owned. Sure, the major furniture is there, but where are the DVDs? Where is the bookshelf? Where is the map of Los Angeles that we had mounted and framed? It is all gone.

Thumper runs toward me, his floppy tan ears bouncing on his head, and I fall down when his paws hit me right on my hips, knocking me off balance. I hit the hardwood with a thud, but I barely feel it. All I can feel is this dog loving me, licking my face, jumping all over me. He nudges my ears with his nose. He looks so happy to see me. I am home. It doesn't look the way it used to. But it is my home.

I walk to the back of the house and feed Thumper. He stands there, looking up at me for a moment, and then chows down.

I turn on the light in the dining room, and I see a note that Ryan has left. I wasn't anticipating that he would leave anything. But seeing the note there, I want to run to it and tear it open. What is there left to say? I want to know what there is left to say. My hands rip apart the envelope before my brain has even told them to.

His handwriting is so childish. Men's handwriting is rarely

identifiable by any sense of masculinity. It's only identifiable by the lack of sophistication. They must decide in sixth grade to start worrying about other things.

Dear Lauren,

Make no mistake: I do love you. Just because I don't feel the love in my heart doesn't mean I don't know it's there. I know it's there. I'm leaving because I'm going to find it. I promise you that.

Please do not call or text me. I need to be alone. So do you. I am serious about this time away. Even if it's hard, we have to do it. It's the only way we can get to a better place. If you call me, I will not answer. I don't want to back down from this. I will not go back to what we had.

In that spirit, I wanted to wish you a Happy Birthday now, even though I'm a few weeks in advance. I know thirty is going to be a hard year, but it will be a good year, and since I won't be talking to you on the day, I wanted to let you know I'll be thinking of you.

Be good to my boy, Thumper. I'll call you in two months to discuss the handoff. Maybe we can meet at a rest stop like a pair of divorced parents—even though we are neither.

Love,
Ryan

P.S. I fed the beast dinner before I left.

I look down at Thumper, who is now standing at my feet, looking up at me.

"You little trickster," I say to him. "You already ate."

I read the letter again and again. I break apart the words. They hurt me and fill me with hope. They make me cry, and they make me angry. Eventually, I fold the letter back up and throw it in the trash. I stare at it in there on the top of the pile. It feels wrong to throw it away. As if I should keep it. As if it should be kept in a scrapbook of our relationship.

I go into the bedroom and look for the shoebox I keep on the very top shelf. I can't reach it on my own. I go into the hallway closet and get the step stool. I go back into the bedroom closet and strain my fingers to reach the edge of the box. It falls down onto the closet floor, busting open. Papers fan across the carpet. Ticket stubs. Old Post-it notes. Faded photos. And then I see what I'm looking for.

The first letter Ryan ever wrote me. It was a few weeks after we met in the college dining hall. He wrote it on notebook paper. The page has been folded over so many times it now strains to stay flat enough to read.

Things I Like About You:

1. *When I say something funny, you laugh so loud that you start to cackle.*
2. *How, the other day, you actually used the phrase "Shiver Me Timbers."*
3. *Your butt. (Sorry, these are the facts.)*
4. *That you thought chili con carne meant chili with corn.*
5. *That you're smarter, and funnier, and prettier, and greater than any girl I know.*

A few weeks after I got the letter, he noticed that I had kept it. He found it in my desk in my dorm room. And when I wasn't looking, he crossed out *Like* and replaced it with *Love*. *Things I Love About You*.

He added a sixth reason underneath in a different-colored pen.

6. *That you believe in me. And that you feel so good. And that you see the world as a beautiful place.*

It was the reason I started a shoebox. But . . . I can't put the letter he left for me tonight in this shoebox. I just can't. It has to stay in the trash.

I put everything back in the box. I put the box away. I brush my teeth. I put on pajamas. I get into bed.

I call for Thumper. He comes running and lies right down next to me. I turn off the light and lie there in the darkness with my eyes wide open. I'm awake so long my eyes adjust to the night. The darkness seems to fade; what was opaque blackness turns to a translucent gray, and I can see that while I have a warm body next to me, I am alone in this house.

I'm not sad. I'm not even melancholy. I'm actually scared. For the first time in my life, I am alone. I am the single woman home alone in the middle of the night. If someone tries to break in, it's up to a friendly Labrador and me. If I hear a strange noise, I'm the one who has to investigate. I feel the same way I felt as a kid at campfires hearing ghost stories.

I know I'm OK. But it sure doesn't feel like it.

I go back to work on Monday morning, and I'm surprised at how much I don't have to talk about all of this. People know I'm married, but really, it rarely comes up. Questions like "How was your weekend?" or "Do anything fun?" are easily answered honestly while keeping the important facts to myself. "It was good. How about yours?" and "Oh, I got to spend a lot of time with my sister. What about you?" seem to get the job done. By noon, I've already learned that you can stop almost all questions about your personal life by being the person who asks the most questions.

But Mila knows me. Actually knows me. She's been my sounding board for months. She knows it all. So as we get into the car to go get lunch, her voice drops low, and she gets real.

"So," she says as she puts the car into drive, "how are you doing?"

"I am . . . fine," I say. "I really am. This weekend sucked, and I cried a lot. I spent all of Saturday night in my sister's bed, crying, while she watched some show about zombies. But then I got home last night, and . . . I'm OK."

"Uh-huh," Mila says. "Did you stretch out in bed? Pour some wine and take a bath without anyone bothering you?"

Mila's been with her partner, Christina, for five years. They have three-year-old twin boys. Something tells me these are her fantasies.

"Not exactly," I say. "I just . . . got home and went to bed, mostly."

She pulls into a spot close to the entrance, and we head in.

"If it was me," she says, "I would be relishing this. A year seems like a long time, but it's going to go so fast. You have your freedom now! You have a life to live. You can make everything smell good. You can have a floral bedspread."

"Christina won't let you have a floral bedspread?"

"She hates floral anything. Loves flowers. Hates florals."

It seems silly, but the floral bedspread feels, suddenly, like something I have to have. I have never lived alone as an adult. I have always shared a bedroom with this man. But now I can buy a blanket with huge flowers across it. Or a bow. Or, I don't know, what's girlie that men don't like? I want it. I want to relish my girliness. I want to buy something pale pink just because I can. I don't have to justify the expense to anyone. I don't have to advocate for why I need a new duvet. I can just go buy one.

"What the hell have I been doing?" I say to Mila, as we stand in line to order. "Why on earth didn't I redecorate the minute he left?"

"I know!" Mila says. "You have to go shopping straight after work. Buy all the crap you always wanted that he thought was stupid."

"I'm gonna do it!" I say.

Mila high-fives me. We eat our sandwiches, and we manage to talk about other things. We don't bring Ryan up again until Mila is parking the car back on campus.

"I am so jealous," she says. "If Christina was gone, I would light a vanilla candle in every room in the house. I would walk into each room and go"—she sniffs and releases—"ahhhh." And then, as if it had just occurred to her, "You don't have to wear sexy uncomfortable panties anymore. You can live in big, comfy underwear."

I laugh. "You don't wear comfortable underwear?"

"I wear a lace bra and panty set every day," Mila says. "I

keep my woman *happy*." She then backpedals. "I didn't mean that you didn't keep . . . Sorry. I was just making a joke."

I laugh again. "It's fine. I'm still reeling from the surprise that you wear sexy underwear every day."

Mila shrugs. "She likes it. I like that she likes it. But man, I am so jealous that you can wear granny panties now."

"I don't even know if I own granny panties," I tell her. "I mean, I just wear normal-people underwear every day. Oh, wait," I say, remembering. "I do have this one pair that I never wear anymore because Ryan used to always make fun of them. He used to call them my parachute panties."

"Super huge? Full coverage? Feels like wearing a cloud?"

"I loved them!"

"Well, go home and put them on, girl! This is your time."

My time. Yeah, this is my time.

After work, I go shopping and buy a big, fluffy white pillow, two striped throws, and a rose-colored bedspread with the outline of an oversized poppy flower on it. I look at the bed, and I think it looks as if it's straight out of a magazine. It looks so pretty.

I take a shower, using all the hot water, singing my heart out because no one can hear me. After I get out, I dry myself off with a towel and head into the bedroom. I dig into the back of my top drawer, past the bikini briefs and the occasionally necessary thongs, and I find them. My parachute panties.

I put them on and stand there in the middle of my bedroom. They aren't quite as magical as I remember them. They feel like normal underwear. Then I catch a glimpse of myself in the mirror. I can see what Ryan was talking about. They sag in the butt and the crotch. Between that and the thick waistband just below my navel, I might as well be wearing a diaper.

I look at the bed with fresh eyes. I don't even like floral patterns. What am I doing? I like blue. I like yellow. I like green. I don't like pink. I have never, in my life, liked pink. This "freedom" quickly starts to feel like such a small thing. This is what I was excited about? Buying a floral blanket? Wearing saggy underwear?

Mila can't light a candle in the house because Christina doesn't like candles and keeping Christina happy is more important than lighting the goddamn candles. That's the truth of it. She's not handcuffed to her. She wants to be with her. She'd rather be with her than light the candles. She'd be heartbroken without her, and the candles would be nothing more than a silver lining. That's all this is. It's a silver lining.

It's just a small, good thing in a situation that totally fucking sucks.

Charlie calls late one night. It's just late enough that it seems unusual for someone to call. I jump for the phone, my heart racing. My mind is convinced that it's Ryan. I am in a T-shirt and my underwear. There's a coffee stain on my shirt. It's been there for days. When you don't have anyone to witness how dirty you are, you find out how truly dirty you are willing to be.

When I look at the phone and realize it's Charlie and not Ryan, I am surprised at how sad it makes me. It makes me really sad. And then I instantly get worried. Because Charlie never calls. He's not even in our time zone.

Charlie left L.A. the minute he had a chance. He went north to Washington for school. He went east to Colorado after that. Somehow in the past year, he's found himself in Chicago. I'm sure soon he'll tell us he's moving to the farthest tip of Maine.

"Charlie?" I answer.

"Hey," he says. Charlie's voice is gruff and gravelly. He spent his teenage years hiding cigarettes from us. When Rachel and I figured it out, sometime around when he was seventeen, we couldn't believe it. Not only that he was smoking but that he didn't tell us. We understood not telling Mom, but us? He wouldn't even tell us? He stopped a few years ago. "Did I wake you?"

"No," I say. "I'm awake. What's going on? How are you?"

"I'm good," he says. "I'm good. How about you?"

"Oh," I say, breathing in deeply as I decide what I want to

say and how I want to say it. "I'm fine," I say. I guess I don't want to say it at all.

"Fine?"

"Yeah, fine."

"Well, that's not what I heard. I heard you're getting a D-I-V-O-R-C-E."

Fucking Rachel.

"Rachel told you?"

"No," Charlie says, starting to explain.

"Rachel had to have told you. No one else knows."

"Chill out, Lo. Ryan told me."

"You talked to Ryan?"

"He *is* my brother-in-law. I assumed it was OK to talk to him."

"No, I just—"

"I called him, and he told me that you guys are getting D-I-V-O-R-C-E-D."

"Why do you keep spelling it? And we're not getting divorced. Did Ryan say that? Did he say we were getting a divorce?" I can hear that my voice sounds panicked and frantic.

"He said that you are taking a break. And when I asked if it was a trial separation, he said, 'Sure.'"

"Well, it's a bit more nuanced than that, you know? It's not, like, a formal separation."

"Lauren, do you know a single couple that has been separated and then got back together? They all get divorced."

"What do you want, Charlie? Or are you just calling to make me want to die?"

"Well, two things. I wanted to call and see if you were OK. If there was anything I could do."

"I'm fine. Thank you," I say. "What was the second thing?"

"Well, this is where things get more complicated."

"That sounds promising," I say. I am now back in bed.

"Part of the reason I called Ryan in the first place was because Mom has decided to throw you a surprise party."

This is just a weird joke he's playing. "Hilarious," I say.

"No, dude. I'm serious."

"Why would she do that?" I'm now up and out of bed again. I pace the floor when I'm nervous.

"She feels like we don't do enough traditional stuff, I guess. And she wanted to host a party."

"At her house?"

"At her house."

"And where do you come into all of this?"

"Well, she's flying me in."

"You're flying in from Chicago just to go to my thirtieth birthday party?"

"Trust me, I wouldn't do it if I was paying for the ticket."

"You're so sweet."

"No, I mean, you hate birthdays. I know that. I tried to tell Mom. She won't listen. And you're lucky I caught her before she called Ryan herself. She told me she was going to call him tomorrow, so I told her I'd do it since I had been meaning to call him anyway. Which, it turns out, was a good thing, but I'm pretty sure you don't want Mom to find out about this the way I just did."

"Does Rachel know yet?"

"About the party?"

"Yeah."

"I doubt it. Mom just told me a few hours ago. She said it all hinged on whether I could fly in and Ryan could get you to her place without you finding out, hence why I brought it up with him."

"That must have been such an awkward conversation," I say, something in me finally calming down. "With Ryan, I mean."

"It wasn't the best, no. He did ask about you, though."

"He did?"

"Yeah, he asked how you were doing. And I had to be, like, 'Bro, I didn't even know you two broke up. How would I know?'"

We laugh for a bit, and then I feel the need to clarify. "We didn't break up," I say.

"Yeah, all right," Charlie says. "Just listen. You gotta tell Mom before the party. She's gonna wonder where Ryan is, and it's gonna be all weird, and anyway, I wanted to give you the heads-up. I mean, you've got three weeks to do it. So that gives you some time."

"Right," I say. "Well, hey, that's exciting that you're coming home."

"Yeah," he says. "It will be nice to see you guys." It's quiet for a moment before he adds, "Also, Lauren, I get that you have Rachel and everything, but . . . you have me, too. I'm here for you, too. I love you, you know."

The fact that my brother can be such a dick is part of the reason he's able to make you feel so much better. When he says he loves you, he means it. When he says he'll always be there for you, he means it.

"Thanks," I say to him. "Thank you. I'll be OK."

"Are you kidding me? You're gonna be fine," he says, and it feels better than all the other times I've heard it.

We get off the phone, and I get back into bed. I turn off the light and grab a hold of Thumper and start to doze off, but my phone rings again. I know who it is before I even look at the screen.

"Hey, Rach," I say.

"Mom is throwing you a surprise party," she says. Her voice is not just laced with schadenfreude, it is made of it. Schadenfreude is all there is.

"I know," I say. "I just talked to Charlie."

"She's flying Charlie home so he can be there."

"I know," I say. "I just talked to him."

"She's flying Grandma Lois out, too. And Uncle Fletcher."

"Now, that I didn't know."

"Apparently, she wants everyone to meet her new boyfriend."

"She has a new boyfriend?"

"Do you even call Mom anymore?"

Admittedly, I have not spoken to my mom in weeks. She lives thirty minutes away, but it's very easy to avoid talking to someone if you never answer the phone.

"His name is Bill. He's apparently a mechanic."

"Is he her mechanic?"

"I don't know," Rachel says. "Why does that matter?"

"I don't know," I say. "I just can't see Mom, like, picking up her mechanic."

"She says he's hot."

"Hot?"

"Yeah, she says he's hot."

"This is all very weird."

"Oh, it's totally, amazingly, delightfully weird."

"I'm going to bed," I say. "I need to let my dreams sort out all of this."

"OK," Rachel says. "But you gotta tell Mom you're separated, right? I mean, you have to before the party. Otherwise, this is going to be a disaster."

"When was the last time Mom threw a party?" I ask Rachel.

"I have no idea. It was definitely the early nineties, though."

"Precisely. So this is going to be a disaster no matter what I do."

"Do you think she'll have a punch bowl?"

"What?"

"Isn't it just like Mom to have a punch bowl?"

And for some reason, this is the funniest thing I've heard all day. My mother will totally have a punch bowl.

"OK, I'm really going to sleep this time."

"Streamers. I bet you there will be streamers."

"I'm going to bed."

"You want over/under on streamers?"

"I don't think that makes sense. You have to have numbers in order for the over/under thing to work."

"Oh, right. OK, five bucks says there are streamers."

"I'm going to bed," I remind her one last time.

"Yeah, fine. I'm just saying . . . five bucks says there are streamers. Are you in or out?"

"What is the matter with you?"

"In or out?"

"In," I say. "I'm in. Good night."

"Good night!" Rachel finally says, and gets off the phone. I lay my head down and smell Thumper. He smells awful. Dogs smell so awful, and yet smelling Thumper is wonderful. He smells heavenly to me. I close my eyes, and I drift off to sleep, where my brain tries to make sense of all this news. I dream that I get to my birthday party and everyone yells, "Surprise!" I see Mom making out with a guy dressed as a race-car driver. Rachel and Charlie are there. And then, just as the yelling dies down, I look through the crowd, and I see Ryan. He makes his way to me. He kisses me. He says, "I could never miss your birthday."

When I wake up, I know it's a dream. But I can't help but hope, maybe, just maybe, it's a premonition.

"So, honey, what are your plans for your birthday? The big three-oh is coming up!" my mother says when I finally pick up the phone. Her voice is cheerful. My mother is always cheerful. My mother is the type of woman who rarely admits she's unhappy, who thinks you can fool the whole world with a smile.

"Uh," I say. Do I have a chance to prevent this calamity? I could tell her that I have plans, and then she might give up on this whole thing. But she's already bought Charlie's ticket. Uncle Fletcher is coming. "No, nothing. I'm free," I say, somewhat resigned.

"Great! Why don't you and Ryan come over, and I'll make you dinner?" She says it as if the world's problems have just been solved. My mom didn't really make dinner when we were younger. There simply wasn't time. Between working a full-time job as a real estate agent and doing her best to get the three of us to and from school and finished with our homework every night, we ordered a lot of pizzas. We had a lot of babysitters. We watched a lot of TV. It wasn't because she didn't love us. It was because you can't be two places at once. If my mother could have solved that physical impossibility, she would have. But she couldn't. So even though I know she's not actually going to be making dinner, that this is all a ruse, the idea of a home-cooked meal by my mother sounds sort of nice. Not in a nostalgic way but rather in a novel way. Like if you saw a duck wearing pants.

"OK, sounds good," I say. I know that this is my moment. I

should mention that it will be just me. Here is my opportunity to start the conversation.

"Oh, I wanted to ask you," my mom jumps in. "Would it be OK if I invited my boyfriend, Bill?"

Hearing my fifty-nine-year-old mother use the word *boyfriend* is jarring. We need a new word for two older people who are dating. Shouldn't our vocabulary grow with the times? Who is taking care of this problem?

"Uh, no, that's fine. I was going to say, actually, that Ryan won't be joining us."

"What?" My mother's voice has become sharp where it was once carefree.

"Well, Ryan is—"

"You know what? Whatever works for you two works for me. I know I sometimes get greedy with wanting to see the two of you all the time."

"Yeah," I say. "And I know that Ryan—"

"I'm really eager for him to meet Bill, too," my mom says. "When he gets the chance. I know you two are busy. But one of Bill's boys is married to just this shrew of a woman, and I've been telling Bill about how I really hit the jackpot with Ryan. I guess it's different, sons-in-law versus daughters-in-law, but Ryan is such a good addition to the family. It does make me worry, though. Who will Rachel choose? Or worse! Charlie. I swear, the boy's probably got ten kids in six states, and we'd never know it. But you, my baby girl, you chose so well."

This is one of the things my mother says to me most often. It is her way of complimenting both Ryan and me at the same time. When Ryan and I first got married, he used to tease me about it. "You chose so well!" he would say to me on the way home from her house. "So well, Lauren!"

"Yep," I say. "Yeah."

And in those two affirmative words, I dig myself deeper into the hole. I can't tell her now. I can't tell her ever.

"So what does Ryan have to do that is more important than his wife's birthday?" my mom asks, it suddenly dawning on her that this situation I'm presenting is a bit odd.

"Huh?" I say, trying to buy myself time.

"I mean, how could he miss your birthday?"

"Right, no. He has to work. It's a big project. Super important."

"So you two are celebrating on another night?"

"Yep. Yeah."

"Well, that's great news for me!" she says, becoming delighted. "I get you all to myself. And you'll get to meet Bill!"

"Yeah, I'm excited about that. I didn't know you were dating anyone."

"Oh," my mom says. "You just wait. You will just die. He is so charming." I can practically hear her blushing.

I laugh. "That's great."

"So me, you, and Bill, then?" my mom confirms.

"Well, how about Rachel?" I say. I don't know why I'm playing this game. I know everyone on God's green earth is going to be there.

"Sure," my mom says. "That sounds lovely. My girls and my man."

Ugh. My mom has no idea how she sounds when she says stuff like that. I mean, maybe she does know how she sounds, but she doesn't know how she sounds to me. So gross.

"Let's tone down the 'my man' stuff there," I say, laughing.

She laughs, too. "Oh, Lauren," she says. "Let loose a little!"

"I'm loose, Mom."

"Well, get looser," she says to me. "And let me sound ridiculous. I'm in love."

"That's awesome, Mom. I'm really happy for you."

"Tell Ryan he has to meet Bill soon!"

"Will do, Mom. I love you."

I put down the phone and drop my head into my hands.

I'm a liar, liar, liar. Pants on fire.

The next couple of weeks are hard. I don't go out anywhere. I stay in bed, mostly. Thumper and I go on a lot of walks. Rachel calls me every night around six to ask me if I want to get dinner. Sometimes I say yes. Sometimes I say no. I don't make plans with friends.

I watch a lot of television, especially at night. I find that leaving the TV on as I fall asleep makes it easier to forget that I'm alone in this house. It makes it easier to drift off. And then, when I wake up, it doesn't feel quite so stark and dead in the morning if I'm accompanied by the sounds of morning television.

I wonder, constantly, about what Ryan is doing. Is he thinking of me? Does he miss me? What is he doing with his time? I wonder where he is living. Numerous times, I pick up the phone to text him. I think to myself that nothing bad can come from just letting him know I'm thinking about him. But I never send the text. He asked me not to. I'm not sure if never hitting send is a hopeful or cynical thing to do. I don't know if I'm not talking to him because I believe in this time apart or if I think that a simple text won't matter anyway. I don't know.

I imagined that by the time a few weeks had passed, by the time Thumper and I had gotten into a rhythm with our new life, I would have made a few, some, any observations or realizations. But I don't feel as if I know anything more now than I did before he left.

To be honest, I think I was hoping that Ryan would leave and I'd instantly realize that I couldn't live without him, and he'd realize he couldn't live without me, and we'd come running back to each other, each of us aching to be put back together. I imagined, in my wildest dreams, kissing in the rain. I imagined feeling how it felt when we were nineteen.

But I can see that it's not going to be that easy. Change, at least in my life, is more often than not a slow and steady stream. It's not an avalanche. It's more of a snowball effect. I probably shouldn't pontificate about my life using winter metaphors. I've only seen real snow three times.

All of this is to say that I have to be patient, I guess. And I can be patient. I can wait this out. Four and a half weeks done. Forty-seven and a half to go. Then maybe I will get my moment in the rain. Maybe then my husband will come running back to me, loving me the way he did when we were nineteen years old.

The night of my birthday, Rachel rings my doorbell promptly at six thirty.

"Well," she says, stepping into the house. "Uncle Fletcher is staying on Mom's couch. Grandma Lois apparently refused to crash at Mom's and instead decided she's staying at the Standard."

"The Standard? The one in West Hollywood?" I ask. Rachel nods. The Standard is a very hip hotel on the Sunset Strip. It has clear plastic pods hanging from the ceiling instead of chairs. The pool is packed year-round with twenty-year-olds in expensive bathing suits and more expensive sunglasses. Behind the check-in desk is a large glass case built into the wall where they pay young models to lie there by themselves and have people stare at them. You heard me.

"What on earth is Grandma doing at the Standard?" I ask Rachel.

She can't stop laughing. "Are you going to be ready to go soon?"

"Yeah," I say, heading off to look for my shoes. I call to her from the bedroom. "But seriously, how did she end up there?"

"Apparently, a friend of Grandma's just told her about Priceline," Rachel says.

"Uh-huh," I call to her as I look under my bed for the other sandal I'm missing.

"And she went to the Web site and clicked on an area of the map that looked like it was halfway between us and Mom's." Rachel lives close to me in Miracle Mile, and my mother, once we all moved out of the house and she could downsize, found a place in the hills. Grandma could have easily stayed with any of us. We're always within a twenty-five-minute car ride if you take back roads. And we always take back roads. I'd go so far as to say that finding the most esoteric way to get from one place to another is our family's biggest competition. As in "Oh, you took Laurel Canyon the whole way? It's faster to cut through Mount Olympus."

"OK," I say. I found the sandal! I walk out to the living room.

"And then she said what she was willing to spend."

"Right."

"And she agreed to stay at whatever hotel would be that cheap."

"OK, but the Standard is kind of expensive."

"Well, she must have been willing to pay a lot. Because that's where they put her."

"She was expecting, like, a Hilton or something, right?"

"That is my guess."

I start laughing hard. My grandmother is a fairly hip lady. She knows what's what. But she has the most delightfully curmudgeonly attitude toward things she calls "farcical." The last time I saw her, I told her about how Ryan and I order pizza using an app on our phones, and she said to me, "Sweetheart, that's farcical. Pick up the darn phone."

"She's not gonna like the lady in the glass wall."

"No, she is not," Rachel says, laughing.

"OK, I'm ready. Let's get this over with." I open the front door for Rachel, and then I wave to Thumper as I go.

"Happy Birthday, by the way," Rachel says to me as we head to her car.

"Thank you."

"Did you get my birthday voice mail?" she asks me.

"Yep," I say. "Voice mail, text, e-mail, and Facebook post."

"I'm nothing if not thorough."

"Thank you," I say to her as we get into the car.

It felt good to be bombarded with her happy thoughts all day. I had e-mails from friends. Mila took me out for Thai food. Mom called. Charlie called. It was a good day. But my brain was focused almost exclusively on how Ryan did not call. It shouldn't have been a surprise. It shouldn't still be a surprise. He told me he wasn't going to call. But it's all I can think about. Each time my phone beeps or I get a new e-mail, I hope. Maybe he won't be able to resist. Maybe he'll have to call. Maybe he'll want to hear my voice.

It doesn't feel like a birthday without him. He was supposed to wake me up by saying, "Happy Birthday, Birthday Girl!" like he does every year. He was supposed to take me out to breakfast. He was supposed to send flowers to work. He was supposed to come to my office and take me out to lunch. He used to put so much effort into my birthday. Specifically because he knew I hated birthdays. I don't like the pressure to have fun. I don't like to get older. And so he would distract me all day with special presents and thoughtful ideas. One year, he sent me to work with eight birthday cards so I could read one for every hour I was there.

Ryan should be making me dinner tonight. He is supposed to make me Ryan's Magic Shrimp Pasta, which is, from what I can tell, just shrimp scampi. But it always tastes great. And we only ever have it on my birthday. And he always makes it so that I will look forward to my birthday. Because I get to eat Ryan's Magic Shrimp Pasta.

He was able to take me out of my own head. He was able to make me happier, to change me into a happier person. And where is he now?

It occurs to me, however, briefly, that maybe he's there.

Maybe he's at the party. Maybe everyone knows but me. Maybe he's waiting for me.

Rachel turns on the radio, in effect blaring my own thoughts out of my head. I'm thankful. When we get off the main road, Rachel turns the music down.

"This isn't going to be that bad," she says, when she pulls into my mother's neighborhood.

"No, I know," I say. "It will be sort of like watching bad improv comedy. It's unbearable but entirely nonthreatening."

"Right, and if it's any consolation, everyone is here because they love you."

"Right."

Rachel pulls up in front of my mother's house. She turns the wheels in and yanks the emergency brake. The streets are steep and full of potholes. You have to watch where you park and where you step. I look out my window at my mom's place. My mother couldn't throw a surprise party to save her life. I can already see the shape of Uncle Fletcher's bald head through the living-room curtains.

"All right," I say. "Here goes!"

Rachel and I walk to my mom's front door and ring the doorbell. I guess that's the code. Everyone quiets inside. I don't know how many people are in her house, but it's enough to make a big difference when they quiet down.

I hear my mom come to the door. She opens it and smiles at me. I don't know why I was getting so sentimental in the car. Ryan hasn't made me Ryan's Magic Shrimp Pasta the past two birthdays. We got into a fight about whether the shrimp was fully cooked, and he hasn't made it since.

Rachel and my mother look at me expectantly, and then it happens, louder and more aggressive than I could have ever imagined.

"SURPRISE!"

I was expecting it, and yet it shocks me. There are so many people. It's overwhelming. There are so many eyes on me, so many people staring. And none of them, not one of them, is Ryan.

I start to cry. And somehow, maybe because I know I can't cry, because it will just ruin everything if I cry, I stick my head up, and I smile, and the tears recede. And I say, "Oh, my God! I can't believe this! I feel like the luckiest girl in the whole world!"

• • •

When the fanfare dies down, it gets easier to process. People stop looking at me. They turn toward each other and talk. I go over to the kitchen to get myself a drink. I am expecting perhaps wine and beer, but right in front of me, on the kitchen counter, is a punch bowl.

Charlie comes up behind me. "I spiked it," he says. I turn around to look at him. He looks much the same as when I saw him a few months ago. He's filled out since he was a teenager, grown out instead of up. He appears to have become lax about shaving, and his greasy hair implies he may have become lax about shampooing, too, but his ice-blue eyes shine brightly. It feels so nice to see my brother's face in front of mine. I hug him.

"I'm so glad to see you," I say. "If this weird party had to happen, I'm glad it at least brought you home."

"Yeah," Charlie says. "How are you doing?"

"I'm OK," I say, nodding my head the way I do. It's still uncomfortable to be the one in crisis. Charlie is normally in some sort of dramatic trouble. I'm supposed to listen to his problems. Not the other way around.

"OK," he says. He seems content to let that be it. He may feel just as awkward being supportive as I do feeling supported.

"So how was the flight?" I ask.

Charlie opens the fridge and grabs another beer for himself. He doesn't really look at me directly. "Fine," he says, as he twists off the cap and snaps it directly into the trash. Sometimes I worry that he is too good at flinging bottle caps where he wants them to go. It's something that requires practice, and I worry about how often he practices.

"You're hiding something," I say. I pull the ladle out of the punch bowl and put some punch in a clear plastic cup. I'm pretty sure my mom shopped for this party at Party City.

"No, nothing. The flight was good. Did you see the streamers in the dining room?"

"Are you kidding me?" I say, defeated. "Now I owe Rachel five bucks." I take a sip of the punch. It's strong. It's absolutely dreadful. "Oh, my God, you actually spiked this."

"Of course I did. That's what I told you." Charlie pushes his way through the doors of the kitchen and heads back into the living room. I take another sip, and it burns going down. But for some reason, I keep the drink in my hand, as a line of defense against the litany of questions I'm in for. And then I barge through the doors myself.

It begins.

• • •

"So where is Ryan?" asks my mom's best friend, Tina. I make up something about work.

Then my second cousin Martin chimes in with "How are things with you and Ryan?" I tell him they are fine.

There don't seem to be many of my friends here. No one invited Mila, for instance. It's just my mom's friends and almost our entire family. I spend a half hour deflecting birthday wishes and questions about Ryan's whereabouts as if they are bullets. But I know that Grandma Lois is the real person to fear. She has the most frightening question to ask me. If all of these well-wishers are evil mushrooms and turtles I must jump over and stomp on, Grandma is King Koopa, waiting for me at the end. What I find comforting about this analogy is that Rachel and Charlie are my Luigis. They will have to go through all of this on their own sometime in the future. Maybe they'll do it differently from how I have, but most likely, the end will be the same.

Regardless, I figure I'd better get it all over with, so I go looking for Grandma. When I find her, she is sitting on the sofa by herself. I take an extra big gulp of punch before I sit down next to her. It stings on the way down.

"Hi, Grandma," I say, hugging her. She can barely lift herself off the couch, so I do most of the work. It seems to me, when you get older, your body goes one of two ways: pleasantly plump or spritely skinny. My grandmother went pleasantly plump. Her face is round and gentle. Her eyes still twinkle. If it sounds like I'm describing Santa Claus, that's because there is a bit of a resemblance. Her hair is wild and bright white. Her belly, however, does not shake when she laughs like a bowl full of jelly. And I think that's an important distinction.

I sit down a bit too close to her, and the couch starts to sink in the middle. We're both gravitating toward the center. But it seems rude to move over.

"Honey, move over," Grandma says to me. "You're dragging me down off the couch."

"Oh, sorry, Grandma," I say, as I slide to the middle. "How are you?"

"Well, the cancer's coming back, but other than that, I'm fine." My grandmother always has cancer. I don't actually know what this means. She's never really clear on it. She just says she has cancer, and then, when you ask her about it, she won't pin down what type of cancer or whether she's actually been diagnosed. It started after my grandfather died six years ago. At first, we would get up in arms every time she said it, but now we just let it go. It's a weird family quirk that I don't even notice until there's another witness to it. A few Thanksgivings ago, we invited Ryan's friend Shawn to join us, and as we all got into the car on the way home, Shawn said, "Your grandmother has cancer? Is she OK?" And I realized that it probably seemed absurd to him that she had announced she had cancer again and no one batted an eyelash. I get the distinct feeling she is hoping for cancer so that she can be with my grandfather.

"And things are good at home? With Uncle Fletcher?" I ask.

"Things are fine. I'm boring, Lauren. Stop asking about me. What I want to know is—" Here it comes. The moment I have been dreading. Here it comes. "When are you and that handsome grandson-in-law of mine going to give me a great-grandkid?"

"Well, you know how it is, Gram," I say, sipping the punch to buy myself some time.

"No, honey, I don't know how it is. You're thirty years old. You don't have all day."

"I know," I say.

"I'm not trying to be a pain. I just think, you know, I'm not going to be around forever, and I'd like to meet the bundle of joy before I go."

Whether she has cancer or not, my grandmother is eighty-seven. She may not be around for many more years. It suddenly occurs to me that I am the only way she will ever meet a great-grandchild. Uncle Fletcher doesn't have any kids. Rachel isn't going to have one anytime soon. Charlie? Please. And because my marriage is a colossal failure, because I'm so disconnected from my own husband that I don't even know where he lives, she may never get that chance. Me. I'm the reason she won't meet the next generation. I could give that to her, if only I'd been good at being married, if only I'd succeeded.

"Well," I say, drinking the last of the punch in my cup, "I'll talk to Ryan."

"You know, your grandfather said he wasn't ready for kids."

"Yeah?" I say, relieved that she is talking about anything other than me. "And how did that go?"

"What could he do?" my grandmother says. "It was time to have kids."

"Just that simple, huh?"

"Yep." Grandma pats my knee. "Things are a lot simpler than you kids make them out to be. Even your mother. Sometimes, I swear."

"Mom seems to be doing OK," I say. I look across the room and see her talking to an older gentleman. He's tall and handsome in a silver fox sort of way. He's looking at her as if she has a secret and he wants to know what it is. "That isn't Bill, is it?"

Grandma squints. "I don't have my glasses," she says. "Is it a handsome man?"

"Yeah," I say. "In an older sort of way."

"You mean a younger sort of way," she jokes.

"Yeah," I say. "That's what I meant."

"If he's looking at her like she's a hamburger and he's on a diet, then yes. That's Bill. I met him earlier today, and he kept staring at your mother like they were teenagers."

"Oh," I say. "That's cute!"

Grandma waves me off. "Your mother is almost sixty years old. She's no teenager."

"Do you believe in love, Gram?" Why am I doing this? I'm feeling a bit buzzed, to be honest—that's probably why I'm doing this.

"Of course I do!" she says. "What do you take me for? Some sort of coldhearted monster?"

"No, I just mean . . ." I look at my mother again. She looks really happy. "Isn't that great? How in love they seem?"

"It's farcical," my grandmother says. "She's almost eligible for social security benefits."

"Did you love Grandpa the whole time?" Maybe she didn't. Maybe I'm just like her. Maybe she's just like me. Ending up like my Grandma would not be so bad.

"The whole time," she says. "Every day." OK, so maybe not.

"How?" I ask her.

"What do you mean, how? I had no choice. That's how."

I look up at my mom, a woman I respect and admire. A woman with three kids and no husband but, at fifty-nine, a new boyfriend. My mother is going to have sex tonight. She's going to have the kind of sex that makes you feel like you invented sex. And my grandmother is going to lie in her hotel room, convinced she has cancer, so that she can one day soon be with the man she had no choice but to love, the man who took care of her and stood beside her until the day he died, the man who gave her children and came home every day and kissed her on the cheek.

I don't know where I fit in. I don't know which one of these women I am. Maybe I'm neither. But it would be nice to feel as if I was one of them. That way, I'd have a road map. I'd be able to know what happens next. I'd be able to ask someone what I should do, and they could answer me, truly answer me.

If I'm not one of them, if I'm my own person, my own version of a woman, in my own marriage, then I have to figure it out for myself.

Which I really don't want to do.

• • •

I'm just coming out of the bathroom when I finally see Rachel again.

"You owe me five dollars for the streamers," she says.

"I'm good for it," I say.

"How are you holding up?"

"You mean with the charade?"

"Yeah," she says. "And the rest of it."

I breathe in deeply. "I'm good," I say. I don't know what the actual answer is. I don't think it's that I'm good, though.

"Have you met Bill yet?"

"No." I shake my head "But he seems nice from afar."

"Oh, he's totally nice. And he treats Mom like she's a princess. It's kind of weird. I mean, it's great. But then also you're, like, 'Ew, Mom.' And Mom just eats. It. Up. Ugh, you know how she is, you know? It's like, she just loves the attention."

"Well, you know Mom," I say. "I'm going to get another drink."

Rachel and I head into the kitchen. When we burst through the double doors, we catch my mom and Bill kissing. Bill pulls away, and Mom blushes. I'm nearly positive that his hand was up her shirt. Rachel and I just stand there for a moment as Charlie comes bounding in from the living room and crashes into the back of us. Mom starts fixing her hair. Bill is trying to act normal. It's easy for Charlie to put together what he's just missed. It's entirely PG-13. But it's a mother and her boyfriend being walked in on by three adult children, so it's uncomfortable.

"Hi, kids," my mom says, as if she had been doing the dishes.

Bill puts his hand out to introduce himself to me. "Bill," he says, grabbing my hand and shaking it hard. His eyes are green. His hair is salt-and-pepper gray, although more salt than pepper. He's got one of those megawatt smiles.

"Lauren," I say, making eye contact and smiling, like I've been taught to do.

"I know!" Bill says. "I've heard a lot about you."

"Ditto."

"Rachel, will you help me bring this cheese platter out into the living room?" my mom says.

"Yeah, OK," Rachel says, smiling and taking so much delight in the awkwardness of this that you'd think she'd have brought popcorn. She picks up a tray and heads out with my mother.

"I just came in for a beer," Charlie says, grabbing another one out of the fridge and heading back out. He doesn't even take the time to snap the cap in the trash. He's out of here in two seconds flat. Now it's just Bill and me.

"Happy Birthday," Bill says.

"Oh, thank you very much," I say. Why is this so awkward? I guess I don't usually meet any of my mother's boyfriends. I mean, I know she's had them, but they don't often last long enough to get invited to a birthday party. "So you're a mechanic?" I ask. I don't know what else to ask.

"Oh, no," Bill says. "We met at the mechanic. That's probably where the wires got crossed. No, I'm a financial adviser."

"Oh," I say. "I'm sorry, I didn't realize. That's funny. What a random thing to think you were."

"No problem," Bill says. "I'd love to think of myself as a mechanic. I can't fix a goddamn thing."

"Not a leaky-faucet-fixing kind of guy?"

"I can help with your taxes," he says. "That's the kind of guy I am."

Bill puts his arms behind him on the counter and rests against it. The way he relaxes makes me relax but also makes me realize that he wants to talk to me for a while. He's getting comfortable. This is . . . I think he's trying to get to know me.

"And you work in alumni relations, right? That's what your mom told me."

"Yeah," I say. "I like it a lot."

"What do you like about it?"

"Oh, well, I like interacting with the former students. You meet a lot of people who graduated recently and are looking for guidance from older alumni, and then you also get people who graduated years and years ago and are looking to mentor someone. So that's fun."

"You're inspiring me to call my own alma mater," he says, laughing. "Sounds like you're doing some good work."

I'm going to go out on a limb here and say Bill was married for a long time and my mom is his first, or one of his first, girlfriends since his wife passed away. This is all very new to him.

"So you have kids of your own?" I ask him.

He nods, and his face brightens. "Four boys," he says. "Men, really. Thatcher, Sterling, Campbell, and Baker."

Oh. My. God. Those are some of the worst names I have ever heard. "Oh, great names," I say.

"No," he says. "Their names suck. But they are family names. My wife's family. My late wife, rather. Anyway, they are good kids. My youngest just graduated from Berkeley."

"Oh, that's great," I say. We talk about Rachel and Charlie, and then, predictably, we get to the topic of my mother.

"She's really something," Bill says.

"That she is," I say.

"No, I'm serious. I'm not . . . I'm not well versed in the dating pool. But your mom really gives me hope. She makes me excited again. Is that OK to say? Is that weird that I said that?"

"No," I say, shaking my head. "It's nice to hear. She deserves somebody who feels that way about her."

"Well," he says, "you know what that is, right? From what your mom tells me, you and Ryan are quite the pair."

It's all too much. My mother in love. This man baring his soul to me for no good reason. Ryan not being here. It's all too much. I walk over to the punch bowl and pour myself a cup.

It's almost full, the punch bowl. My mom must keep refilling this thing. Get a grip, Mom. No one likes the punch. I take a sip, instantly remembering how strong and foul it is. I chug the whole thing, forcing it down and putting the cup back on the counter.

Bill looks at me. "You OK?" he says.

"I'm fine, Bill." Everyone needs to stop asking me that question. My answer isn't going to change.

• • •

I've had two more cups of punch by the time the cake comes out. My breath, at this point, seems flammable. As my mother and the rest of my family join around the cake, the candles sending shadows flickering high above, I look around and have this moment where I feel as if I can see very clearly what a shit show my life has become.

I am turning thirty. I am thirty. And I'm celebrating, not with the man I have loved since I was nineteen, but with Uncle Fletcher, who is staring at me from across the table. He just wants the cake. This isn't what thirty is supposed to look like. It's not what thirty is supposed to feel like. By thirty, you're supposed to have things figured out, aren't you? You're not supposed to be questioning everything you've built your life on.

I blow out the candles, and things start to get a bit hazy. My mom starts passing out cake. Uncle Fletcher takes the biggest piece. I accidentally drop mine on the floor, and since no one seems to notice, I just leave it there. It's a terrible thing to do, but I get the feeling that if I bend down, my mind will go all woozy.

Eventually, Rachel comes and finds me. "You don't look so great," she says.

"That's not a pleasant thing to hear," I say.

"No, I'm serious," she says. "You look kinda pale."

"I'm drunk, girl," I say. "This is what drunk looks like."

"What were you drinking?"

"The punch! That deliciously horrendous punch."

"You drank that?"

"Wasn't everyone drinking it?"

"No," Rachel says. "I couldn't get even a sip down. It was nasty. I don't think anyone here was drinking that."

I look around the room and notice for the first time that no one is holding anything other than glasses of water or beer bottles.

"It did seem weird that it was always full," I say.

Rachel calls for Charlie. He strolls over as if it's a favor.

"What did you spike the punch with?" she asks him.

"Why?"

"Because Lauren has been drinking it all night."

"Uh-oh," he says playfully.

"Charlie, what did you put in it?" Rachel's voice is serious now, and at the very least, I can tell she doesn't think this is funny.

"In my defense, I was just trying to liven up what we all knew would be a rather lame party."

"Charlie," Rachel says sternly.

"Everclear," he says. The word hangs there for a little while, and then Charlie asks me, "How much did you drink?"

"Four glasses-ish." It would be a hard word to say if I felt entirely in control of my faculties. As it is, it comes out with a lot more "sh" sounds than I mean for it to.

Both Charlie and Rachel join together, albeit by accident, to say, "Shit."

Charlie follows up. "I honestly thought some people might have a glass or two, tops."

"Dudes, what is Everclear? Why is this a dig beal?" I'm

not entirely sure I said that correctly just now, but also, I'm starting to feel like if I did mess it up, it's funny, and I should keep doing it.

"It's not even legal in every state. That's how strong it is," Rachel says to me. Then, to Charlie, she adds, "Maybe we should take her home."

For once, Charlie doesn't disagree. "Yep." He nods. "Lauren, when was the last time you puked from drinking?"

"From huh?"

"From drinking."

"I have no idea."

"I'm going to tell Mom you aren't feeling well," Rachel says. "Charlie, will you get her into the car?"

"You guys are being such dillyholes." Whoa. Not a word. But should be. "Someone write that down! D-I-L-L-Y—"

Rachel leaves as Charlie takes my arm and directs me toward the door. "I'm really sorry. I swear, I thought people would realize that it was strong and not drink that much. I thought maybe Uncle Fletcher would have a glass or two and start dancing on the table or something. Something fun."

"Dudes, this was totally fun."

"Why do you keep calling me dudes?" Charlie asks.

I look at him and really think about it. And then I shrug. When we get to the front door, my mother and Rachel cut us off.

"Mom, I'm just gonna take her," Rachel says.

But my mother is already feeling my forehead. "You look clammy, sweetheart. You should get some rest." She looks at me a moment longer. "Are you drunk?"

"Yep!" I say. This is hilarious, isn't it? I mean, I'm thirty years old. I can be drunk!

"I spiked the punch," Charlie says. You can tell he feels bad.

"With what?" my mom asks him.

Rachel cuts in. "It was strong, is the point. And Lauren didn't know. And now she's had a bit too much, and I think we should bring her home."

"Charlie, what the fuck?" my mom says. When my mom swears, you know she means business. It's sort of like how you know to be scared of other moms when they use your full name.

"I thought it would be funny," he says. "No one was drinking it."

"Clearly, someone was drinking it."

"I can see that, Mom. I said I was sorry. Can we drop it?"

"Just get her home," my mom says. My mom doesn't really yell. She just gets really disappointed in you. And it's heartbreaking sometimes. I feel bad for Charlie. He tends to get it more than the rest of us. "When will Ryan be home to take care of you?" my mom asks.

Rachel cuts in. "I'll stay with her, Mom. She's just drunk. It's not a big deal."

"But Ryan will be there, right? He can make sure you're on your side, you know? So you don't choke on your own vomit." My mom doesn't really drink that often, and because of that, she thinks everyone who does is Jimi Hendrix.

"Yeah, Mom, he'll be there," Rachel says. "I won't leave until he gets there."

"Well, then, you are going to be there for a looooooooooong time," I say.

"What?" my mom asks.

Rachel and Charlie try to stop me with "Come on, Lauren," and "Let's go, Lauren."

"No, it's cool, guys. Mom can know."

"Mom can know what?" my mom asks. "Lauren, what is going on?"

"Ryan left. Vamoosed. He lives somewhere else now. Not

sure where. He said not to call him. I got Thumper, though! Woo-hoo!"

"What?" My mother's shoulders slump. Rachel and Charlie shut the front door, dejected. We were almost out of here scot-free.

"He left. We don't live together anymore."

"Why?"

"Mostly because the love died," I say, laughing. I look around, expecting to see everyone else laughing, but no one is laughing.

"Lauren, please tell me you're joking."

"Nopes."

"How long ago was this?"

"A few weeks or so. Coupla weeks. But did you hear the part about how I got Thumper?"

"I think we should take Lauren home," Rachel says, and my mom looks as if she's about to argue with her but then doesn't.

She kisses me on the cheek. "One of you will stay with her?"

Both Charlie and Rachel volunteer. So cute. Cutest little siblings.

"All right," my mom says. "Good night."

They both say good night, and as I'm just out the door, I call to my mom, "I accidentally dropped some cake into the corner over there."

But I don't think she hears me.

Charlie and Rachel put me in the backseat, and I can feel just how tired I've been this whole time. We hit a red light, and I hear Charlie tell Rachel to take Highland to Beverly Boulevard, and then he turns toward me and suggests I get some sleep. I nod and close my eyes for a minute, and then . . .

I wake up to the sound of my doorbell ringing. The world seems cloudy and heavy, as if I can feel the air around me and it's weighing me down. I start to stand up and realize that Rachel is lying in bed next to me. Thumper is in the corner coiled into a ball.

The doorbell rings again, and I hear someone go to open the door. My head feels like a bowling ball balancing on a wet noodle. I wade through my house until I see my brother and my mother standing on either side of my front door. Charlie must have slept on the couch.

"Hey," I say to them. I can feel the sound of my voice pulsating through my head. It vibrates in my eyes and jaw. They both look at me. My mother has a cardboard drink tray of four coffees in her hand. Rachel comes up right behind me.

"Oh, good," my mom says, stepping into the house. Thumper hears her and comes running, too. "You're all up," she says.

She hands Charlie one of the cups. "Americano," she says, and she hands it to him.

He takes it and smiles at her. "Thanks, Mom."

Mom then holds out a cup for Rachel, and Rachel walks up to her. "Skim latte," my mom says.

With two more cups in the tray, my mom takes hers out and rests it on the table by the door and then takes the last one and gestures toward me.

"Double espresso," she says. "I figured you'd need to wake up."

I gently take it from her hands. "Thanks, Mom."

She shuts the door behind her, and the chill in the air ceases a bit. I know that by this afternoon, it will be sweltering and hot, but the September mornings tend to be overcast and a bit chilly. My hands are cold, and the hot cup feels great in my palms.

"No coffee for Thumper, huh?" I say, making a joke, and my mother, what a mother, puts her hand into her purse and pulls out a sandwich bag with bacon in it.

"I had some extra bacon from breakfast," she says. Thumper comes running toward her. My mom crouches down and feeds it to him, rubbing his head and letting him lick her face.

I am overwhelmed with love for my mom right now. She always knows just what to do. When do you learn that in life? When do you learn what to do?

My mom stands back up and looks at Rachel and Charlie. "Why don't you guys go for a walk?" she says.

Charlie starts to decline, but Rachel intercedes. "Yeah," she says. "We'll take Thumper." By the time Rachel grabs the leash, Thumper is so excited that to deny him would be cruel.

Charlie rolls his eyes and then resigns himself to it. "Yeah, all right."

Within moments, they are out the door, the opening and closing of which send a chill back into the house. My mom looks at me the way you'd look at a dying bunny. "I think we need to talk," she says.

"Yeah, OK," I say, and I walk back to my bedroom and get into bed. It's warm there, underneath the blankets. I can see my mother looking at my place and noticing all the things that are gone. She doesn't mention it.

"So," she says, sitting down next to me, pulling the tab of her coffee lid back, and blowing on the steam as it rises. "Tell me what happened."

At first, I try to tell her the facts. When he left. Where

everything went. I tell her about the fight at Dodger Stadium. I tell her about not feeling like I love him anymore. I tell her about the conversation about what to do. I tell her as much as I remember, as much as I can bear to think about.

But she wants more. She wants to know not just the when and the where but the how and the why. I spend so much time not thinking about these things that it's hard to start thinking about them again.

"Why didn't you tell me?" she asks.

"I don't know," I say, directing my gaze to my bedside lamp.

"Yeah, you do," she says. "You know why."

"Why?" I say. She sounds as if she knows the answer.

"No, *I* don't know," she says. "But I know you know."

"It just didn't come up naturally, I guess," I say.

"That would never come up naturally. Were you waiting for me to ask you if you and Ryan were still together? And then you could say, 'Actually, Mom . . .'?"

"I didn't want to disappoint you. I didn't want you to think that I . . . screwed it up, you know? I can fix this. I can fix it. It's not broken. I can still do this."

"Do what?"

"Be married. I can still do it."

"Who says you aren't doing it?"

"Well, I'm not currently doing it. But I can do it."

"I know you can do it, sweetheart," she says. "You, of anyone I know, can do anything you set your mind to."

"No, but, like, I don't want you to think I failed. Yet."

"If your marriage does not work out—" she says, and she stops me from interrupting before I even decide to. "Which it will, I know it will. But if it doesn't, it doesn't mean you failed."

"Mom," I say, my voice starting to crack. "That is exactly what it means."

"There is no failing or winning or losing," she says. "This is life, Lauren. This is love and marriage. If you stay married for a number of years and you have a happy time together and then you decide you don't want to be married anymore and you choose to go be happy with someone else or doing something else, that's not a failure. That's just life. That's just how love is. How is that a failure?"

"Because marriage is about a commitment to something else. It's a commitment to stay together. If you can't stay together, you fail at it."

"Good Lord, you sound like Grandma."

"Well, isn't that the truth of it, though?"

"I don't know," my mom says. "I don't know anything about marriage, obviously. I was only married for a few years, and where is he now?"

Where *is* my father now? Honestly, that's a question I rarely think about. He could have a family in North Dakota, or maybe he's living on a beach in Central America. Or he could be in the phone book. I have no idea. I've never checked. I haven't ever searched for him, because I've never felt as if anything was missing. You only seek answers when you have questions. My family has always felt complete. My mother has been all I've needed. I forget that sometimes. I take for granted her ability to guide me, to guide our family, as its one true leader.

"But the way I see it," she continues, "your love life should bring you love. If it doesn't, no matter how hard you try, if you are honest and fair and good, and you decide it's over and you need to go find love somewhere else, then . . . what more can the world ask of you?"

I think about what she's said. I don't really know what I think, I guess. "I just don't want you to dislike Ryan," I say.

"Honey, I love that boy as if he was my own child. I'm serious about that. I love him. I believe in him. I want him to be happy, just as much as I want you to be happy. And I could never fault anyone for doing anything in the name of their own truth." Sometimes my mom speaks as if she's a guest on *Oprah*. I think it's because she spent twenty years watching guests on *Oprah*. "When you first started dating Ryan, I liked him because I could tell he was a good person. I learned to love him because he always put you first, and he treated you well, and I trusted him to do right by you. I still believe he does what he believes is the right thing for both of you. That doesn't change because you two say you're not in love anymore. That's always been who he is."

"So this isn't the sort of thing where when we get back together, you won't like Ryan anymore?"

My mom laughs and sighs at the same time. "No," she says. "This isn't one of those things. All I care about is that the two of you are happy. If only one of you can be happy, I have to go with blood on this one and choose you. But I want you both to be happy. And I believe you're doing what it takes to be happy. Whether I understand it or would do the same thing in your shoes, or any of that, that doesn't matter. I believe in the two of you."

It's weird how words from the right mouth at the right time can bolster you up and make you strong. They can change your mind. They can cheer you up. I'm glad Charlie spiked the punch. I'm glad I told my mom.

I can hear Charlie and Rachel come back in through the front door, and I assume that means that this conversation is over, but my mom calls out, "Give us another minute, OK?"

I hear Rachel call out, "Yup," from the living room and then start talking to Charlie. Charlie's voice carries louder than any of ours. Our voices might bounce off the walls, but his penetrates through them. I can hear his muffled laughing as I listen to the rest of what my mother has to say.

"Now, the one thing I am going to tell you, Lauren, is that

you cannot hide this, OK? You need to be strong and be you and stop caring what people think and tell the goddamn truth. Be confident and proud of what you and Ryan are trying to do."

"What are we trying to do?" I say. "I don't understand what there is to be proud of."

"You're trying to stay married," she says. "And be happy doing it. I've never accomplished it. So to me, that's brave. To me, you are brave."

It feels weird to hear, because this whole time, I've just been waiting for someone to call me a coward.

"OK," my mom calls out. "You can come in now."

Rachel comes to the door. Charlie is there behind her, and Thumper is at her feet. As I look at them in my house, I realize that it's been a long time since we were all a family, just us. Ryan has been such a part of me that he became a part of this. But maybe it's OK that he's not a part of this right now. It's nice to look at the faces around the room and see . . . my family.

My mom waves her hand to let them know that they are welcome. They all come sit on the bed, Thumper pushing his way into the middle, trying to get the attention of all of us.

"Everything OK?" Rachel says.

"Everything is good," I say, and that seems to work as enough of a segue to get the conversation away from my marital troubles and toward other things, like what Charlie is going to do with his life. (He has no idea.) If Rachel is dating anyone (Whom would she be dating?) and whether Thumper may need another dose of flea medication. (Yes.) Charlie's flight leaves tonight, and I think it's making my mother sentimental.

"Can we do dinner at my house tonight?" she asks. "As a family?"

"My flight leaves at ten," Charlie says.

"We can take you," I tell him, referring to Rachel and myself. "We will just leave Mom's around eight."

"I could serve dinner around six?" she offers.

"Serve dinner?" Rachel asks. "Like, you're gonna make our dinner?"

My mom frowns at her. "Why do you kids act like I've never made a meal?"

The three of us look at one another and start laughing. As much as we are all a family, we are also three siblings with a mother. Sometimes it is three against one.

"I have made dinner before, you know," my mother continues, ignoring our laughter. "You'll see. I'll make something great."

I appear to be the one feeling the most charitable. "OK, Mom. You got it. We'll be there at six. Ready to eat a home-cooked meal."

"Oh, you kids have made me so happy! I can't even tell you. All three of you at my house for Sunday dinner." She gets up off the bed. "Grandma and Fletcher are leaving in a few hours, so I should go have lunch with them. Then I'll go grocery shopping. Not sure what I'm going to make," she says. "But this is going to be great." She nods to herself. "Just great."

She gathers her things and says good-bye to all of us. I walk her out to her car to thank her for talking to me earlier.

"Honey, you do not need to thank me," she says, getting into the front seat of her SUV. "I have three grown children. To be honest, it's a relief to be needed."

I laugh and hug her through the car window. I didn't even realize I needed her until she just said it. How stupid is that? "We'll see you tonight," I say.

"Six o'clock!" she calls out as she pulls out of the driveway.

I nod and wave. I watch her drive away. I watch as her car, so big and fast, is eventually so far away that it looks small and slow.

Dinner is burnt, but I don't think my mom actually realizes it. Despite the charred chicken and lumpy potatoes, all of the elements seem to click. No one really mentions Ryan. We make fun of Rachel. We ask about Bill. Charlie seems happy to be there. No one acknowledges how terrible the cooking is. To be honest, I don't think any of us really care.

Mom made too much food. Or maybe we just couldn't stand to eat very much of it. Either way, there are plenty of leftovers. By the time we have taken in all the dishes and put all the extras into Tupperware containers, it is time to head out.

"Well, who wants to take the chicken? Charlie? Will you eat it on the plane?"

"You want me to bring half a roasted bird carcass on a plane?"

Mom frowns at him and hands the chicken to Rachel. "You'll eat it, right?"

"Sure," she says. "Thanks, Mom." Then she looks at Charlie and shakes her head. My mom pawns the green beans and carrots off on me and then thrusts the container of sweet potatoes at Charlie.

"You can take the potatoes, at least," my mom says, but Charlie isn't having it. He won't relent. That's part of what I've never understood about him, or what he's never understood about life. Sometimes you should just take the potatoes and say thank you and then throw them in the trash when Mom's not looking.

We say our good-byes and then head out on the road. Rachel has agreed to drive, because I'm still hungover from last night. I feel as if it will be days until I'm OK to operate heavy machinery. Charlie grabs the front seat, so I sit in the back.

I hate driving to the airport. LAX is a nightmare, but it's more than that. The route is such an unattractive view of Los Angeles. You don't see beaches and sunsets. You don't see palm trees and bright lights. You see strip malls and parking garages.

So I don't bother looking out the window and instead close my eyes and listen as Charlie and Rachel debate whether to take the freeway or La Cienega Boulevard. Rachel wins because she's driving and because she's right. The freeway will be clear at this time of night.

When we get to the terminal, Rachel turns left into the parking garage.

"Why are you parking the car? Just drop me off," Charlie says. It doesn't make a lot of sense, but our family doesn't really drop people off. We pay the money to park the car. We walk across the lanes of traffic. We see you off at the security checkpoint. I'm not sure why.

"Stop, Charlie," Rachel says. "We're walking you in."

Charlie rolls his eyes and starts to bitch about it and then stops himself. "OK," he says. "All right." So maybe he has learned to take the potatoes sometimes.

We park and walk out. Truth be told, we don't have much to talk about. But when Charlie checks in and walks to the gate, when it's time to say good-bye, I'm suddenly sad to see my little brother go. He's ornery, and he's kind of a jerk. He doesn't say the things you should say to people. He spikes punch with Everclear. But he's a good guy, with a kind heart. And he's my little brother.

"I'm going to miss you," I say to him as I hug him.

"Me, too," he says. "And I'm proud of you, or whatever. You know, for what it's worth."

I don't press him on it, the way I want to. I don't sit him down and say, *What makes you say that? What do you really think of what I'm doing? Do you think I can fix this? Do you think Ryan will come back to me? Is my life over?* I just say, "Thanks."

Rachel hugs him, too, and then he takes off, up the escalator and back home to Chicago, where people have seasons and cold air. I've never understood it. People come from all over the country to experience our sunny winters and mild summers. Charlie got out as soon as he could, looking for snow and rain.

As Rachel and I are walking back to the car, we get lost and end up on the floor below at Arrivals. It occurs to me that Arrivals is a much nicer place to be than Departures. Departures is good-bye. Arrivals is hello.

I happen to look toward the revolving doors. I see dads coming home to their families. I see men and women in business suits finding their drivers. I see a young woman, probably a college student, run toward the young man waiting for her. I see her wrap her arms around him. I see him kiss her on the lips. I see, on their faces, that feeling I once knew so well. I see relief. I see joy. I see that look people get when the thing they have been dreaming of is finally in front of them, able to be touched with the tips of their fingers and the length of their arms. I think I stare for a second too long, because she turns to look at me. I smile shyly and look away. I think of when it was me, when I was the one waiting at Arrivals for that one person I ached for. Now I'm the lady looking.

For a moment, I think that if I saw him right now, if Ryan were here, I'd have the same look on my face as this couple has. I want him in my arms that badly. But how long would it last? How long before he said something that pissed me off?

When Rachel and I finally get headed in the right direction, we walk out onto the street level and wade our way through people hailing cabs and hopping into their friends' cars. We are standing at the crosswalk, waiting to cross the street, when I see two people waiting for a shuttle. As quickly as I would recognize my own face in the mirror, I know what I am looking at. There is absolutely no doubt in my mind that I am looking at the back of Ryan's head.

It doesn't even register as weird at first; my brain simply processes it as a normal, everyday occurrence. Oh, here is that person who's always around. Here he is. Except this time, he is holding the hand of a slim, tall brunette. And now he's bending down to kiss her.

My heart drops. My jaw drops. Rachel starts crossing the street, but I just stand there, frozen. Rachel turns around to see me there, and her eyes catch mine. She follows my gaze, and she sees it, too. Ryan. Ryan at Arrivals. Ryan. At Arrivals. Kissing a woman. My heart starts beating so fast that I almost feel I can hear it. Is it possible to hear blood pulsing through you? Does it sound like a quiet, violent gong?

Rachel grabs my hand and doesn't say anything. She is determined to get me out of this situation. She wants me to cross the street. She wants me to get into the car. But we have missed the walk signal, and we can't just run through this steady stream of cars, as much as, right now, that feels like the only thing to do.

It's good that she's holding me. I fear that I lack the self-control not to go over there and knock him down. I want to pummel him to the ground and ask him why he would do this. Ask him how he looks at himself in the mirror. I swear to

God, it's as if I can physically feel the pain. It's a physical pain. And it's searing through me. And then the light turns, and the white walk sign is on, and I put one foot in front of the other, and I move forward, and I think of nothing but how much this hurts and which foot goes where. When we get to the other side of the street, when the walk sign turns into a red hand, I turn around and look at him. We are now separated by a sea of speeding cars.

When my eyes find him again, when they fixate on the front of his face, I can plainly see that I was wrong. It's not him. It's not Ryan.

I can spot Ryan in a crowd. I can recognize his scent from another room. Just a few months ago, we were separated at the grocery store, and I found him by recognizing his sneeze from a few aisles away. But at this airport, this time, I got it wrong. It's not Ryan. All of that fear and jealousy and hurt and pain so sharp I thought it could cut me—it wasn't real. It was entirely imaginary. It's stunning, really, what I can do to myself with only a misunderstanding.

"It wasn't him," I say to Rachel.

She slows down and looks. "Wait, are you serious?" she says, squinting. "Oh, my God, you're right."

"It wasn't him," I say, stunned. My pulse slows, my heart relaxes. And yet I am still overstimulated and jumpy. I slow down my breathing.

Rachel puts her hand on her chest. "Oh, thank God," she says. "I did not want to have to talk you down from that."

We get into the car. I put on my seat belt. I roll down the window. *It's OK*, I tell myself. *It didn't happen*.

But it will someday.

He's going to kiss someone else, if he hasn't already. He's going to touch her. He's going to want her in a way that he no longer wants me. He's going to tell her things he never told me. He's going to lie there next to her, feeling satisfied and happy. She's going to remind him of how good it can feel to be with a woman. And while all of this is happening, he's not going to be thinking about me at all. And there's not a thing I can do to stop it.

Over the course of the next few days, it is all I can think about. I am seething with jealously over something that I have no evidence of. It consumes me to the point where I can't sleep night after night. By Friday, I can't keep all this angst to myself. I ask Mila's advice.

"Do you think he's already slept with someone?" I ask her when we're getting tea from the office kitchen.

"How should I know?"

"I just mean, do you think that he has?"

"Why don't we talk about this at lunch?" Mila says, looking around the kitchen in the hopes that no one is listening.

"Yeah, OK," I say.

Mila and I go out for Chinese food, and she brings it up. It takes her about four minutes. Which is four minutes longer than I wanted to wait, but I didn't want to seem like a crazy person.

"Do you want the truth?" she says.

I'm not clear on how to answer, because it's entirely possible that I want to be lied to.

"Yes," she says. "I think he probably has."

It's a knife in my chest. I've never been the jealous type with Ryan. It was always so clear that he wanted no one but me. For so much of our relationship, it was obvious that he loved me and desired me. I never felt threatened by any woman. He was mine. And now I've set him free.

"Why?" I say. "Why do you think that?"

"Well, first of all, he's a man. That's the biggest piece of evidence. Second of all, you said yourself you two were not having all that much sex. So it's probably been pent up inside of him. He probably slept with the first woman who looked at him the right way."

I take a long sip of my soda. It becomes a gulp and then sort of a chug. I put my cup down. "Do you think it's with someone prettier than me?"

"How on earth would I know that?" Mila says. "You have to stop torturing yourself. Accept that it has probably happened. The stress of questioning whether it has or has not happened is too much. You have to just assume that it has happened and start to deal with it. He slept with someone else. What are you going to do?"

"Die, mostly," I say. Why does this feel so awful? Why does it feel so much more awful than when he left? Deciding to separate was hard. Actually separating was hard. But this? This is something entirely different. This is devastating. This is . . . I don't know. It feels as if I will never feel better in my entire life.

Mila grabs my hand. "You're not going to die. You are going to live! That is the point here. C'mon! You were not happy with him. Let's not sugarcoat the past. You were deeply unhappy. You said yourself that you didn't love him. You two are going your separate ways. If anything, this should just show you that it's time for you to find your own way."

"What does that mean, though?" I say. Isn't that what I've been doing?

Mila puts down her fork and clasps her hands, getting down to business. "What are you doing this weekend?" she asks me pointedly. "Do you have plans for tonight?"

"Well, I got a new book from the library," I say. Mila makes a face but doesn't interrupt me. "And then I heard LACMA is free tomorrow, so I thought maybe I'd check that out. Haven't been in a while." I made that last part up. I have absolutely no plans to go to LACMA. I haven't gone to an art museum since college. Probably not going to start now. I just didn't want to admit that I have no plans at all.

"Uh-huh." Mila is not impressed.

"What?" I say.

"That sounds pretty close to what I'm going to do, except instead of LACMA, I'm going to take Brendan and Jackson to get their hair cut."

"OK . . . ?" I say.

"I'm in a committed relationship with twins, and you're single."

Single? No. I am not single. "I am not single," I say. "I'm . . . married but . . ."

"Estranged?"

"Oh, that's an awful word." I don't know why it's such an awful word. There's just something about how all the vowels and consonants come together that I don't care for.

"You're single, Lauren. You live alone. You have no one who expects you to be anywhere at any given time."

"Well, Rachel sometimes . . ." I don't even finish the sentence. "Fine, I'm single," I say. "What is the point?"

"Get out of the house! Go get drunk and screw someone you don't know."

"Oh, my God!" I don't know why I find it so shocking. I guess it's that she's talking about me. Me! I mean, I know that is what people do. They go out to bars, and they meet strangers, and they have casual sex with them after a few dates or no dates or however many dates they feel they need to justify what they want to do. I get that. But I have never done that. I never really had the opportunity. And now, I guess, I do have the opportunity, but it feels as if I've missed the starting line for that sort of thing; that race took off without me. I gather myself and look at Mila, but her face doesn't change.

"I'm serious," she says. "You need to get out there. You need a love affair or something. You need to get laid. By someone who isn't Ryan. You need to see what it's like with someone else. Have you even ever slept with someone besides Ryan?"

"Yeah," I say, somewhat defensively. "I had a boyfriend in high school."

"That's it?"

"Yes!" I say, now definitely defensive. "What is the big deal?"

"It just isn't enough people."

"It is!" I say.

Mila shakes her head and puts down her fork. She tries another approach. "Do you remember what it was like the first time you kissed Ryan?"

"Yeah," I say, and within a second, I feel as if I'm back there. I'm leaning across the table, over my burger and fries. I'm kissing him. And then I remember how it felt when he kissed me back. When he kissed me on the way home. When he kissed me good-bye. Even after kissing became a thing we did like breathing, without thinking, without care, I held on to those first kisses. I relished the way my heart stopped for a second whenever our lips met.

"Remember how good it felt to be kissed for the first time? How it felt electric? Like you could power a whole house off your fingertips?"

"You've really thought about this."

"I just love the beginnings of relationships," Mila says wistfully. "The first time Christina kissed me . . . nothing compares to that. Now I kiss her, and it's like, 'Hey, how are you? What smells? Is it the trash?'"

We both start laughing.

"Anyway, I can't help but be excited for you, knowing that you have the chance to have that feeling again. You can meet someone and feel those butterflies again, if you want to."

"No, I can't," I say. "I have a husband to go back to."

"Yeah, in ten and a half months. Some marriages don't even *last* ten and a half months. You can have a love affair, Lauren. One that makes you feel like you did when you were nineteen. If it were me, that's what I would be doing."

I let this settle for a minute as I think about it. It does sound nice, in a lot of ways, and it also sounds terrifying and messy. How can I have a love affair when I'm married? How can I juggle those two huge relationships? An active romance and an inactive marriage?

"Do you think Ryan is having a love affair?" I ask Mila.

Mila loses her patience. "That's what you're taking from this?"

"No," I say. "I get your point. I do. I'm just . . . if he was . . . what would that mean?"

"It would mean absolutely nothing."

"Nothing?"

"Nothing. Did you love your high school boyfriend?"

I shrug. "Yeah, I did."

"Do you give a shit about him now?"

"No," I say, shaking my head.

"Well, that's a love affair for you."

• • •

Despite Mila's advice, I continue to obsess. I think about it on the drive home. I think about it as I'm feeding Thumper. I think about it while I'm watching TV, while I'm reading a book, while I'm brushing my teeth. It drives me mad. My brain replays the same imagined images over and over. It falls down a rabbit hole of *what ifs*. I just want to know what is going on in his life. I just want to hear his voice. I just want to know that he's OK and he's still mine. I can't have lost him yet. He can't be someone else's yet. I can't do this. I can't live like this. I can't live without him. I can't. I have to know what he's thinking. I have to know how he is.

I want to call him. I have to call him. I have to. I pick up the phone. I push the icon next to his name, and then I immediately hang up. It didn't even get a chance to ring. I can't call him. He doesn't want me to call him. He said not to call him. I can't call him.

My laptop is right in front of me. It's easy to grab. When I open it up, I'm not sure what I'm looking for. I'm not sure what I'm doing. And then, opening the browser, I know exactly what I'm doing. I know exactly what I'm looking for. I don't bother trying to hide it from myself. I have gone into the deep end. I have lost control.

I sign into Ryan's e-mail.

His in-box loads, and it's empty. I stop myself. This is wrong. It's incredibly, very, super, really, totally, completely, and absolutely wrong. I move my cursor to the menu, and I hover over where it says "Sign out." This is where I should click. This is what I should do. I can turn around. I can pretend I never did this. I don't have to be this person. For a second, it feels so easy. It seems so clear. *Just log out, Lauren. Just log out.*

But before I click it occurs to me that he never changed his password. He could have, right? It would make sense if he had. But he hasn't. Does that mean something?

I notice the number seven by his drafts folder. He has seven unsent e-mails. I don't even think, really, it's just an impulse. I drag the cursor down and click the folder open. There I see seven e-mail drafts, all addressed to me. All with the subject "Dear Lauren."

They are addressed to me. They are for me. I can click on these. Right?

• • •

August 31

Dear Lauren,

Leaving the house today sucked. I don't know why we did this. When I wrote you that letter, it took everything I had not to rip it up and sit down and just stay there until you came home and we could sort this all out.

But then I thought about the last time you were happy to see me when I got home, and I couldn't remember when that was. And thinking about that made me so mad that I picked up the last of my things and I walked out the door.

I didn't say good-bye to Thumper. I couldn't do it. It makes me sick to think about sleeping in this stupid apartment tonight. I don't have a bed yet. I don't have much of anything yet except our TV. My friends have helped me put everything where it sort of belongs, and they left about an hour ago.

I'm miserable. I'm fucking miserable about this. I was glad when my friends left, because I didn't have it in me to pretend to be OK anymore. I'm not OK. I feel sick. I've lost my wife and my dog. I've lost my home.

I don't know. I don't know why I'm writing this. I don't even know if I'm going to send it. Part of me thinks that you and I have been so dishonest with each other lately that a little honesty, a little discourse, might improve things. I have spent so long saying, "Sure, I'll go to the mall with you to pick out new lipstick," when I didn't want to. Saying, "Yeah, Greek food sounds great," when it doesn't, that I hate you for it now. I hate Greek food, OK? I hate it. I hate how we can never just get a hamburger anymore. Why does every dinner have to be a tour of the world? And if so, why can't we just stick with Italian and Chinese?

Ah. See? This is why I know that it's good that I left. I hate you for liking falafel. I don't think that's healthy.

But also, I don't know that it's so unhealthy that it means I have to sleep alone tonight on this shitty carpet.

But then I think about going home. I think about walking through the door and you not even getting up off the couch. I think about how you'll just look at me and say, "Pho for dinner?" and I want to punch the wall.

So, fine. I'm here. I'm alone. I'm miserable. And I know it makes me a terrible person, but I really hope you're miserable, too. That's the truth. That's how I feel right now. I really, really hope that you're miserable, too.

Love,
Ryan

• • •

September 5

Dear Lauren,

I know I told you not to call me, but sometimes I can't believe you aren't calling me. I can't believe you're able to just live your life like I was never there. How can you do that? It makes me furious to think about sometimes. You're probably just going to work and acting like everything is fine.

I told my parents about us today. It wasn't easy. They were not happy. They got really mad at you, which I thought was weird. I tried to explain to them that this isn't about one or the other of us. I tried to tell them that it was a joint decision. But they weren't listening. I think, you know how they are, they have such a narrow view of marriage. And they are disappointed in me. They made that clear. They kept saying, "This is not how you should be handling your problems, Ryan." And they kept saying they were upset at you for taking my house and my dog. They can't see clearly, I don't think. They think we should split it up so that one of us gets Thumper and the other one gets the house. Neither of us should get both. I don't know. I don't agree with them. I don't see it that way. It doesn't feel right to take the house from you, and it doesn't feel right to take Thumper away from his home so abruptly.

I know I said that I wanted to date other people, but now that I'm out in the real world, it feels really strange to think about. Very unnatural. How is that even supposed to work? It doesn't make sense. To think about kissing someone other than you? I almost feel like I don't remember how to do it. There is a new girl at work who keeps flirting with me, and sometimes I think that I'm supposed to jump on it, go for it or whatever. I don't know. I don't even want to talk about it.

I'm still not sure if I'm going to send these to you. Sometimes I think I will. There is a part of me that feels like years ago I stopped fighting with you. It just became easier to agree with you or ignore you. I feel like I just said whatever you wanted to hear. And I stopped being honest. I stopped telling you what I really thought. What I really wanted. And so maybe if I tell you all of this now, maybe we can clear the air, maybe we can start again. The other part of me thinks that if we do tell each other everything, if I send you this stuff, we might not survive it. So I don't know what I'm going to do.

I'm not sure you'd care, anyway. I mean, sometimes I think you don't really see me anymore. I know you see me, see me. But I'm talking about the fact that sometimes I don't think you listen when I say things. Sometimes I think you just assume you know what I'm going to say next, or what I'm going to do next, or what I'm going to feel next, and your eyes glaze over as if I'm the most boring person you've ever met.

You didn't use to think that, though. I remember in college, one of the reasons it was so nice to be around you was that you made me feel like I was the most interesting person in the room. You made me feel like I made the funniest jokes and told the best stories. And I don't know, I don't think that was fake. I think you really thought that.

And now I don't think you think that at all. I think I'm like looking at the back of a cereal box for you. I'm just something you sit and stare at because I'm there.

This is getting sad. I hope you are doing OK. Sometimes I think I should send you these just so you might write back and I can hear how you are. I wonder how you are all the time.

Love,
Ryan

• • •

September 9

Dear Lauren,

Do you remember when we moved in with each other for the first time? Right after we graduated from college? And it was such a hot day, and we moved into the shithole apartment in Hollywood, and it was way too small, and the kitchen smelled like some sort of weird chemical? And you almost started crying because you didn't want to live in such a crappy apartment? But it was all we could afford. I was living off of the last of my parents' graduation gift money, and you were starting your job in the alumni department. And I remember thinking, as we crammed into that small bed that first night, that I was going to take care of you. I was going to work hard and get you a better apartment. And I was going to be the man who gave you the life you wanted. And I mean, things don't really work out exactly how you think. You were the one who made enough money so that we could afford to move out of that place and into Hancock Park. But I mean, I negotiated with the landlord. I did everything I could to convince her, because I wanted you to have everything you wanted. I really did think I did a good job of taking care of you. I always wanted you to feel safe with me, to feel loved by me, supported by me.

I learned how to stop trying to solve your problems and just let you vent about them. I learned that you need a few minutes in the morning before you can talk to somebody. I learned that you never leave yourself enough time to get somewhere and then you freak out about being late. And I loved it about you.

Why wasn't that enough?

Doesn't it seem like it should have been enough?

Back then, moving in together, lying in that tiny bed, I just thought that my job was clear. All I had to do was support you and love you and listen to you and take care of you. And it all seemed so easy back then.

Now it seems like the hardest thing in the world.

What am I doing sitting here writing to you? I'm wasting my time.

Ryan

• • •

September 28

Dear Lauren,

The last time we had sex was in April. Just in case you were wondering. Which you're not. But you never seemed to care very much, and I do care. So if I ever do send these to you, I think you should know that the last time we had sex was almost five months before I moved out. That's four months before you told me you didn't love me anymore. Four months of us living in the same house, pretending to be good to each other, pretending to be happy, and not laying a hand on each other. I figured I'd wait until you noticed. And you never noticed. So, you know, in case you ever notice and you want to know. It was April. And it sucked.

• • •

September 29

Dear Lauren,

Happy Birthday! I know that you're at a surprise party. Charlie called me a few weeks ago before he knew we were whatever we are. Anyway, I know your family is with you. I know you're probably having a blast. It's nine o'clock right now, so you're probably living it up as I type this. I'm hanging out here at my apartment. There is only so much you can do to distract yourself from the fact that it's your wife's thirtieth birthday and you're not with her. You know?

I gave up on that about a half hour ago, and now I've just been nursing a beer and thinking about you.

I almost got up off the couch and drove over to your mom's place to be there.

But I figured that was a bad idea.

Because what happens? We see each other and we admit how hard this is and we end this crazy experiment, and then what? In two months, we're back where we were. We haven't changed. So nothing would change. You know?

So instead, I'm sitting here, doing nothing.

I just want you to know that I thought about it. I thought about showing up at the house with two grocery bags, ready to make you Ryan's Magic Shrimp Pasta.

I didn't do it, but yeah, I guess I just want you to know that I thought about it.

Happy Birthday,
Ryan

• • •

October 1

Is Thumper doing OK? It's killing me being away from him. It's so stupid, but I was in the grocery store the other day getting dinner for myself, and I remembered that I needed laundry detergent, so I went into the aisle to get it, and it was also where they kept the pet food, and I thought, "Oh, do we need food for Thumper?" and, you know, it just flashed into my mind for a split second before I remembered that I don't live with him anymore.

Love,
Ryan

• • •

October 9

Dear Lauren,

I'm not going to take Thumper. This pain of living without both of you, it's too hard. It's too lonely. It's too sad. I can't do that to you.

Love,
Ryan

• • •

I can't see through my tears anymore. Looking at these is sort of like standing in a burning-hot shower and seeing how long I can bear it. I'm way past the point of worrying about whether this is wrong. I know it's wrong. I know he isn't sure whether he wants me to see these. But I also know that I have to read them. They matter too much. I care too much. It's too much.

These letters are the evidence of how ugly our marriage has become and yet proof that we are tied to each other. We can hate and love, miss and loathe each other all within the same breath. We can never want to see each other again while never wanting to let go.

He hates me as much as he loves me. I hate these letters as much as I love them. The pain and the joy are locked together, tightly bound. I read the letters over and over again, hoping to separate one from the other, hoping to discern whether love or hate wins out in the end. But it's like pulling on the ends of a finger trap. The more I try, the tighter they cling to each other.

When I finally get hold of myself, eyes dry, nose running, light-headed, I go into the kitchen and pull a piece of bacon out of the fridge. I put it in a pan. I wait for it to sizzle and pop. When it does, I put it in Thumper's bowl. He comes running as he hears the sound of the bacon hitting the stainless steel. He eats it within half a second. I pull out another piece and put it in the pan as he waits. That's when I really put the pieces together. If Ryan sends me that e-mail about me keeping Thumper, then I won't see him in a few weeks. I really will be on my own for the foreseeable future.

On a scale of one to ten, how bad is it to log into someone's e-mail without them knowing?" I ask Rachel over the phone. I'm sitting at my desk at work. I've read the e-mails tens of times. Some parts I even know by heart.

"I guess I'd need to know the particulars," she says.

"The particulars are that I logged into Ryan's e-mail and read some of his e-mails."

"Ten. That is a ten out of ten. You should not have done that."

"In my defense, they were addressed to me."

"Did he send them to you?"

"They were in his drafts folder."

"Still ten. That's really bad."

"Wow, you're not even going to try to see my side of it?"

"Lauren, it's really bad. It's dishonest. It's rude. It's disrespectful. It completely undermines—"

"OK, OK," I say. "I get it."

I know what I've done is wrong. I guess I'm not really wondering if it's wrong. I know it's wrong. What I'm looking for is for Rachel to say something like, *Oh, yeah, that's wrong, but I would have done the same thing, and you should keep doing it.*

"So I should not keep doing it?" I ask her. Maybe if I go about this directly, I can get the answer I'm looking for.

"No, you absolutely should not."

"Oh, for fuck's sake!" I say. I should not have done it. But what can I do? I already did it. And does it really matter if I keep doing it? I mean, it's already done. If he asks, *Have you logged into my e-mail account and read my personal e-mails that were addressed to you?* I will have to answer yes whether I did it once or one hundred times.

"Let's say he addresses another one to me, though," I say. "Then it's OK to look."

"It's not OK to be checking in the first place," Rachel says. "I have to get back to work," she adds. "But you better cut it out."

"Ugh, fine." It's quiet for a moment before I ask my final question. "You're not judging me, right? You still think I'm a good person?"

"I think you're the best person," she says. "But I'm not going to tell you what you're doing isn't wrong. It's just not my style."

"Yeah, fine," I say, and I hang up the phone.

I walk over to Mila's desk.

"On a scale of one to ten, how bad is it to log into someone's e-mail without them knowing?"

She looks up from her computer and frowns at me. She picks up her coffee cup and crosses her arms.

"Is the person you? And the other person Ryan?"

"If it was . . ." I say.

She considers it. "I can see where you'd think I was the person to help you justify this, because really, I would probably read them if I were in your position," she says, swiveling back and forth in her chair. A victory! "But that doesn't mean it's OK." Short-lived.

"He's writing to *me*, Mila. He's writing *to* me."

"Did he send them to you?"

"WHY IS EVERYONE SO PREOCCUPIED WITH THAT?"

Everyone turns and looks in my direction. I switch to a whisper.

"The letters are *for* me, Mila," I say. "He didn't even change his password. That's basically like he's admitting he wants me to read them." I'm now too close to her face, and my whisper is breathy. I'm pretty sure she can tell I had an onion bagel for breakfast.

Mila politely backs away a bit. "You don't have to whisper. Just don't shout. A normal tone of voice is fine," she says in an exemplary normal tone of voice.

"Fine," I say, a bit too loudly, and then I find my rhythm again. "Fine. All I'm asking is that if you were me and you knew that he was writing to you, baring his soul to you, saying the things that he never said when you were married, saying things that broke your heart and made you cry and made you feel loved all at the same time—if that was happening, are you telling me you wouldn't read them?"

Mila considers it. Her face turns from stoic to reluctant understanding. "It would be tempting," she says. I already feel better just hearing that. "It would be hard not to read them. And you have a halfway decent point about the password."

I pump my fists in the air. "Yes!" I say.

"But just because something is understandable doesn't mean it's the right thing to do."

"I miss him," I say to Mila. It just comes out of my mouth.

Mila's resolve fades. "If it was you writing the letters, would you want him to read them even if you didn't send them?"

My gut answer is yes. But I take my time and really think about it. I stand and look at Mila and consider her question. I put myself in Ryan's shoes. The answer that keeps coming back is yes.

"Yes," I say. "I know that answer seems self-serving, but I really mean it. He said in his letters that he feels like he often didn't tell me how he really felt. That he kept a lot of stuff inside just to make things easier, and then he started to resent me. I did that, too! I would sometimes choose to just go along with what he wanted or what he said so that I didn't cause a fight. And somewhere along the way, I started to feel like I couldn't be honest. Does that make sense? Things became so tense, and I started to resent him so much that I was suddenly furious about everything, and I didn't know where to start. I think he feels the same way. This could be an opportunity for us. This could be what we need. If it were me writing to him, trying to bare my soul, trying to show the real me, I would want him to read it." I shrug. "I would want him to see the real me."

Mila listens, and when I'm done, she smiles at me. "Well, then, maybe it is the right thing for the two of you," she says. "But you're taking a huge risk. You need to know that. This *could* be exactly what he wants. He may be happy to know that you can understand him better and that you know the deepest parts of his soul and you accept him for that. That might be what he's hoping for." From her tone, I can tell that she's not done, but I wish that was the end of the sentence. "But he also might be furious." Here we go. "He might be livid that you betrayed his trust. He might not trust you again. It could be a terrible way to start off this new chapter in your lives together. When the year is over and he comes back, how can you tell him all that you know? Are you going to admit what you did? And do you really, truly, in your heart, feel like he is going to say, 'OK, sounds good'?"

"No," I say. "But I do think that more good will come from it than bad."

Mila looks unconvinced.

"I feel like I have an opportunity to learn who my husband is in a whole new way. I have an opportunity to get to know him without a filter. I can learn what I did wrong. I can start to understand what he needs from me. What I can do better the next time around. I'm going to learn how to love him again. I'm going to learn how to be a better wife to him, how to give him what he needs, how to tell him what I need. This is good. I have good intentions. This is coming from a good place."

I set out to convince Mila. I just wanted someone to tell me that it was OK to do something I knew wasn't OK. But in doing so, I've convinced myself somehow.

"Well, I wash my hands of it, then," she says. "It sounds like you know what you're doing."

I nod and head back to my office. I have no idea what I'm doing.

Mila calls to me just as I'm almost out of earshot. "Mexican?" she says.

I look at the clock. It's twelve forty-seven. "Give me five minutes."

When we get into the elevator to head downstairs, I ask Mila if she likes Persian food.

"Yeah, it's all right."

"Greek food?"

She shrugs. "It's OK."

"Vietnamese?"

"Don't think I've ever had it. Is it like Thai?"

"Sort of," I say. "It's like pho, which is a soup. Or banh mi. Sometimes stuff is served with a fish sauce."

"Fish sauce? A sauce made of fish or a sauce for fish?"

"No, it's made of fermented fish. It's delicious."

"I don't know. I really want Mexican," she says as we get off the elevator.

I nod my head. It's that simple. Why didn't Ryan ever just say, *I really want Mexican*. Why sit through all of those foods he didn't like? I would have gone out for a burrito instead. I wouldn't have even minded. Why didn't he know that?

"You know," Mila says. She's walking a bit ahead of me

and trying to find her keys in her purse. "If you think Ryan will be happy with you reading his e-mails and spying on his most vulnerable moments, then it's only fair that you subject yourself to the same."

"What do you mean?"

"What scares you? What do you want?"

"I don't know. I guess I—"

"Don't tell me," she says. "Put it in an e-mail."

That night, I check his e-mail drafts one more time before going to bed.

• • •

October 15

Dear Lauren,

It's sex. Honestly, it's sex. It's the one thing that, I think, I couldn't tolerate being broken and the one thing that just completely broke down. That's what this is all about for me. I think I could have had more patience with you in other areas if you'd just been a little bit more interested in actually having sex. I think I could have been more thoughtful toward you. I think I could have been happier to spend time with you. I think I could have been better at listening to you. If I hadn't been so pissed at you for never, ever, EVER WANTING TO HAVE SEX.

What the fuck? It's not even that difficult, Lauren. I wasn't asking you to become some sort of sex queen. It just would have been nice to have sex twice a week. Twice a month? It would have been nice to have you initiate it maybe once a year.

It always felt like you were doing me a favor. As if I was asking you to do the dishes.

And I don't know why I never screamed at you about it. Because I screamed at you in my head. Sometimes I'd get so pissed off after you said "Not tonight" for the twentieth night in a row that I would go and take a cold shower and scream at you in my mind. I would actually have a full-on fight with you in my head, anticipating the things you would say and screaming my responses to myself. And then I'd towel off and get into bed next to you and never say any of it out loud. You would just sit there with your fucking book in your hand, acting like everything was fine.

Why didn't I just tell you that nothing was fine?

I can't be a husband to you if you treat me like a friend.

I need to HAVE SEX, LAUREN. I NEED TO HAVE SEX WITH MY WIFE FROM TIME TO TIME. I NEED TO FEEL LIKE SHE LIKES HAVING SEX WITH ME.

I can't spend months of the year masturbating quietly in the bathroom because you "aren't up to it tonight."

Ryan

• • •

I want to scream at him. I want to tell him that if he wanted me to like having sex with him, then he probably should have tried a bit harder to make it good for me. I want to tell him that it's a two-way street. That he wasn't the only one who was going to bed unsatisfied. I want to tell him that the only difference between him and me was that at least I gave him an orgasm every couple of months. But then there's another, huge, big, aching part of me that wants to say, *Come home, come home. We can fix everything now that I know this.*

I get into bed and try to get some sleep. I toss and turn. I stare are the ceiling, but sometime in the night, my brain finally shuts down, and I fall asleep.

When I wake up, I have so much I am dying to say.

• • •

October 16

Dear Ryan,

Here are some things I think you should know:

The couch no longer smells faintly of sweat, because no one goes running and then doesn't take a shower before they lie on it.

I have really been enjoying the act of throwing away my receipts. I no longer have to account for every single penny that goes in and out of the bank account. Sometimes I go to the store, realize I forgot my coupon, and then just buy the thing anyway. Why? Because fuck you. That's why.

I tip twenty percent every time. Every. Time. I no longer care that you think eighteen is standard.

I am really looking forward to an entire Dodgers season going by without a single trip to the clusterfuck that is Dodger Stadium.

Do you understand how a broom works?

I have always hated eating at that stupid Chinese restaurant on Beverly Boulevard that you love so much. It's not that good.

That joke you tell about the nuns washing their hands at the Pearly Gates is totally gross, not funny at all, and fucking embarrassing.

Men who have beards are supposed to trim them. You can't just let it grow and think it looks nice. It takes upkeep.

And speaking of hair, you need to learn to trim your pubic hair. I don't know how much clearer I could possibly make this. Apparently, buying you a beard trimmer and saying, "Ha ha ha, I think this also works on pubes," was not clear enough.

If you're looking for reasons why our sex life was an unmitigated disaster, maybe you should consider the fact that you haven't put in a modicum of effort since, I don't know, senior year of college. Do you even understand how women experience pleasure? Because it's not through relentless, rhythm-less pounding.

I stop typing and look at what I've written. I want so badly to delete those last parts. It's all so embarrassing and uncomfortable. What if he really read this? What if he really saw it?

I delete it. I have to delete it. I can't say that stuff.

But then I remember that I told Mila that I want to be honest. I told her that the reason I thought I should read Ryan's e-mails was that I needed to hear his honesty. I needed him to be unfiltered. How can I justify reading his honest thoughts if I delete my own?

So I press control-Z. It reappears on the screen.

It has to stay there. I have to do this right. He's probably not ever going to read this. So really, I'm typing to myself. Maybe that's the problem; maybe I'm nervous to admit some of this stuff, even to myself.

That's why I have to do it.

I hit save and get redirected to my in-box. Where I now see I have one new e-mail.

From Ryan. He actually sent me an e-mail. He pressed send on one of them.

• • •

October 16

Dear Lauren,

I'm not going to take Thumper. I think it's best he stay there.

Take care,
Ryan

Before I can take a breath, hit the reply button, and type "Fine," I think better of it. I type "OK." I hit send.

So that's it, then. The training wheels are off. I have no firm plans to see my husband again. I probably won't see him for almost a year.

I stand up. I get into the shower. I get dressed. I feed Thumper. I go to work. I go through the motions of my day. When I get home, before I feed Thumper or take my shoes off, I sign in to his e-mail again.

There's a new draft I haven't read before.

• • •

October 16

Dear Lauren,

I've met someone.

Ryan

The sound that comes out of my mouth, it's not a cry or a sob.

It's not a scream, either.

It's a whimper.

I print it out. I go into the hallway closet. I get the step stool. I go to the bedroom closet. I grab the shoebox. I open it and put the letter in.

I let the paper sit there in the box of memories. It sits on top of the ticket stub from when we took the train to San Diego and spent the weekend lying on the beach. It sits on top of the photo of us at the Crab Shack in Long Beach, where we went with my family for his twenty-third birthday. It sits on top of Thumper's first collar, the bright pink one we bought him on the way home because Ryan said he refused to "cater to gender norms for dogs, and this one is on sale." It sits on top of the dried flower petals from my wedding bouquet.

It sits on top of all of that. Because I can't pretend this isn't happening anymore. I can't pretend this isn't part of our story.

I take off my wedding ring and put it in the box. It is, for now, better kept with the other mementos.

After that, Ryan stops writing to me altogether.

For a week or two, I check his drafts folder every day, hoping to see something. But he never writes.

Halloween comes, and I buy a big variety pack of candy for trick-or-treaters, but when I get home, I find myself wondering if Ryan and his mystery girl are dressing up together, doing a couple's costume. I distract myself by turning my front light out and eating the candy myself. I give the nonchocolate ones to Thumper.

After a few weeks of sulking, I resolve to just check his e-mail every once in a while. I take up hobbies to distract me. Thumper and I start going for hikes in Runyon Canyon. We walk up the mountain until we can barely move, until we think we can't go one more step, and then we keep going. We never let the mountain win.

After a while, Rachel starts coming with us. She also encourages me to start running. So I do. I run every other day. As the weeks go by, the temperature starts to get cold in Los Angeles, so I buy a tight-fitting fleece. My shins start to hurt, so I buy proper shoes. I push myself farther and farther down the street. I run longer. I run faster. I run until one day, my face looks thinner and my stomach feels tighter. And then I keep running. It quiets the voices in my head. It calms my nerves. It forces me to think of no one, nothing, but the sound of my breath, the banging of my heart inside my chest, and the fact that I must keep going.

Eventually, I don't check Ryan's e-mail at all.

part three

THAT'S THE WAY LOVE GOES

It's a Sunday morning in late November, and even though it was only sixty degrees yesterday, it is eighty-five today.

"This weather makes no sense to me," Mila says. "Not that I'm complaining. I'm just saying that it makes no sense to me."

Christina is watching the kids. Mila's only request for the morning was, "I don't care where we go. Just get me away from children and moms." So I figured the Rose Bowl flea market would be fun. She seemed to be in a pretty bad mood when I picked her up, but she perked up once we got on the road. Now that we're here, she seems much more like herself. The only issue is that neither of us is really shopping for anything in particular, so we are just aimlessly wandering through the aisles.

A booth of dream catchers draws Mila in, and she starts looking. "What do dream catchers even do?" she asks.

"I'm going to avoid the obvious answer of 'catch dreams,'" I say.

"Yeah, but what does that actually mean? Catch dreams?"

"No idea," I say. I don't want to talk loudly enough that the booth owner hears us and insists on giving us a ten-minute lesson. I made this mistake once with a guy selling antique chamber pots. As I see the owner coming over, I aim to change the subject by saying, "Let's change the subject."

Mila walks away from the dream catchers and heads further in. "OK," she says. "How about we discuss me setting you up on a blind date?" She turns to me and makes an overly excited face, as if her abundance of excitement about this idea might sway me at all.

"That's a no. That's actually an 'absolutely not,'" I say.

"Oh, stop," she says. "You need to meet somebody! Have a good time!"

Do I think it would be nice to meet somebody? Sure, yeah. Sometimes I do. But a blind date? No. "It's just not my style."

"What *is* your style? Meeting people in study hall?"

I open my mouth wide to indicate that I am insulted. "It was the *dining* hall, for your information."

"Look, you haven't been in the dating world for a long time, so I think it's important that you understand that people don't meet people standing in line at the pharmacy or when they go to reach for the same magazine at the bookstore."

"Then how do they meet them?"

"Blind dates!" she says. "Well, also online, but you're not ready for that. It's all about blind dates."

That's absurd. Obviously, people meet people other ways. Although the truth is, I don't really know how anybody meets anybody outside of college. And I don't know that I want to find out just yet. "I'm just not sure if I'm ready," I say. I head toward a booth selling silver jewelry and start trying on rings.

"Suit yourself," she says. "Christina says he's cute, though."

"You have someone in mind already? What, do the two of you sit at home snuggled up in your matching pajamas talking about my sad life?"

Mila joins me at the ring booth. "First of all, we have never worn matching pajamas. We're lesbians, not twins," she says. "And second of all, no, we do not snuggle and talk about your sad life. We do, however, sometimes get bored and try to meddle where we don't belong. I see it as a public service."

"A public service?"

"You think you're the first person I set up on a blind date?

My sister and her husband? Me. Christina's boss and her boyfriend? Me."

"Didn't you also set up Samuel in admissions with Samantha in the housing office?"

Mila waves it off. "That one was a mistake. I thought the Sam/Sam thing was adorable, and it clouded my vision. But Christina says this guy is really cute. He's recently divorced. Mid-thirties. Eighth-grade social studies teacher, so you know he's probably a sweetheart."

"I don't know," I say. "It sounds complicated. I'm not looking for anything serious. I don't know. I just . . . I don't think so."

"OK," she says, falsely resigned. "I'll just have Christina tell him it's a no go."

I put down the ring I was looking at. "She already talked to him?"

"Yeah," Mila says, shrugging. "It's a shame, too, because he was excited about it. She showed him your picture, and he said you were beautiful."

I look up at her, skeptical. "You're not making this up?"

She puts her hand up as if swearing an oath. "Hand to God."

I smile at her, despite myself.

Mila smiles back at me. She got further than she thought she would.

I walk past her to the booth next to us. It's a man selling hats. Half of them are Dodgers caps. It's enough to make me wonder where my husband is at this very moment. He stopped writing me long ago. I have no idea what his life is like. He could be in bed with a blond woman. He could be making her breakfast. He could be in love. He could be having sex with her this very minute. That man who stood on the steps of Vernal Fall and told me he couldn't live without me . . . I wonder what he's doing right now, living without me.

"You OK?" Mila asks me, when she finally gets my attention. "You look distracted."

"Yeah," I say. "I'm fine." It's not the full truth, exactly. But it's much less of a lie than it used to be.

After work on Monday, I'm at the Farmers Market at the Grove when my phone starts to ring. I put down the gourmet jam I'm looking at and dig into my purse to try to find my phone.

It's Charlie.

"Hey," I say.

"Hey, do you have a minute?"

I walk away from the stand and find a place to sit. "I've got nothing but time," I say. I say this to be kind, but also, I actually have nothing but time. Being single leaves you a lot of time to spare. "What's up?"

"I'm going to come home for Christmas," he says.

"That's great! We are all going to Mom's, and I think there is talk of Bill joining us. And Grandma is coming. Not sure about Uncle Fletcher, but I would assume so. So it will be nice to have it with—"

Charlie cuts me off. "Listen, I need your help with something."

"OK . . ."

"I have some news to tell everyone, and I'm not sure how to do it. And so I was wondering what you thought first."

"OK," I say. This is a novel feeling, Charlie caring what I think. But I'm also cautiously terrified. If Charlie is seeking out my advice, if he doesn't think he can handle it himself, then this has got to be big, right? It's got to be bad.

"You're sitting down? Or I mean, you have time to talk?"

"Oh, my God, Charlie, what is it?"

He breathes in, and then he says it. "I'm going to be a dad."

"You're going to see Dad?" How does he even know where Dad is? Did Dad call him?

"No, Lauren. I'm having a baby. I'm going to *be* a dad."

There are people walking past me, shoppers haggling over tomatoes and avocados, kids calling for their mothers. There are cars whizzing by in the distance. Butchers selling various cuts of meat to women on their way home from work. But I can't hear any of that. I just hear my own breathing. All I can hear is my own deafening silence. What do I say? I decide to go with, "OK, and how do you feel about that?"

Charlie's voice starts to brighten. "I think it's great, honestly. I think it's the best news I've gotten in my entire life."

"You do?"

"Yeah. I'm twenty-five years old. I have a job I don't care about. I live across the country from my family. My friends are . . . whatever. But what am I doing? What have I done that's so great? I keep moving from place to place, thinking I'm going on these adventures, and nothing ever comes of it. And then I happen to meet Natalie, and two months later, I get a call saying that I'm . . . This is good. I really think this is good. I can be a father to someone."

This is surreal. "And how is it going to work with this Natalie person?" I'm sticking to logistical questions, because I'm out of my league, emotionally.

"Well, that's part of what makes this complicated but possibly really fortuitous."

"OK," I say.

"Natalie lives in L.A., so . . . I'm moving home."

Whoa. My mom is going to have a grandchild to play with. My grandmother will have a great-grandchild. Charlie solved the problem. He took the pressure off of me. It's not up to me anymore. That's good, right? "Wow, this is a lot to take in!" I say.

"I know. But here is the thing. She's an amazing woman. And I really think she is someone I can try to make it work with. She's smart, and she's funny. We have a great time together."

"How did you two meet?

"We met on an airplane," he says. "And we . . . hooked up. And I didn't think anything of it. So, you know, that part is a hard sell."

"An airplane?" I say, but I'm putting the pieces together faster than I can talk. My brother slept with a woman he met on the plane when he came home for my birthday. That's what we're talking about. "Ew, Charlie!" I say, laughing. "Was it, like, *on* the airplane?"

"In an attempt to protect the dignity of myself and my child's mother, I decline to answer." So yes, it was.

"Holy crap," I say, marveling at just how sudden and insane this all is. "So you are moving in with someone named Natalie. And you two are having a baby."

"Yep. We've been talking every night after work, calling each other, e-mailing. I really like her. We get along very well. We have the same ideas so far about how we want to handle this."

"That's great," I say. "When is she due?"

"End of June."

"Well, Charlie," I say, "congratulations!" Admittedly, there is a part of me that feels leapfrogged, passed over, rendered irrelevant.

Charlie sounds relieved. "Thank you. I'm pretty scared to tell Mom."

"No," I say. I can feel myself shaking my head. "Don't be. You sound happy. And Natalie sounds great. And this is, like, the best news Mom could hope for. You're moving home, and she gets a grandchild. I'm telling you, she's gonna be so happy."

"You think so? I feel like most moms probably don't want to hear their sons say, 'So I knocked up this girl.'"

"Right, it will be a shock, for sure. But that's also not what you're saying. You have a plan. You feel good about it. If you feel good about it, she's going to feel good about it. Have you told Rachel?"

"No," he says. "I just wanted to get your take on whether I should call now or do it in person at Christmas. I feel like Rachel can be a bit judgmental about these things. She's kind of defensive about being single. It's been so long since she even dated anyone, you know? I want to be sensitive to that."

"So you figured you'd call your almost-divorced sister," I say, teasing him.

He laughs. "Oh, come on, you and Ryan will be fine. You said so yourself. I'm not worried about you," Charlie says. "If anything, I called you because you're the one who always knows what to do."

In a time when I feel as if my whole life is in shambles, when I feel as if the last thing I know is *what to do*, it swells my heart to think that my little brother might look up to me. But if I tell him any of that, if I let on how much it means to me, I'll lose it right here in the Farmers Market. So instead, I keep a lid on it. "I think your instincts are right to do it in person," I say. "If you're coming home for Christmas, maybe just give Mom the heads-up and tell her that you're going to bring a friend or something? I'm assuming you'll be staying with Natalie?"

"Yeah," Charlie says. "So I guess I should maybe let Mom know I won't be staying with her, that I'll be staying with someone else. That will trigger her suspicions that something is up, but I'll just keep it under wraps until I see her. Better to tell her in person, you're right."

"Yes, exactly," I say. "And don't worry. She really will be happy."

"Thank you," Charlie says, and for the first time, I feel the usual edge to his voice is gone.

"I'm so curious," I say. "So you meet her, and you, you know, wherever you, you know. And how does she track you down? When she finds out she's pregnant and she knows it's yours, how does she find you all the way in Chicago?"

"I gave her my number," Charlie says, as if the answer is perfectly obvious.

"You gave your number to a woman you barely know, who you had sex with once on an airplane?"

"I always give my number to one-night stands," Charlie says. "Condoms are only ninety-eight-percent effective."

And that, right there, is my little brother. He somehow manages to be just as thoughtful as he is cynical. And now he's going to be someone's dad.

And I'm going to be someone's aunt.

"Hey, Charlie?" I say.

"Yeah?"

"You're gonna be a great dad."

Charlie laughs. "You think so?"

I don't actually have any idea. I have no evidence whatsoever. I just choose to believe in him. And for a second, I understand why everyone thinks my marriage will be OK. They don't have any evidence. They just choose to believe in me.

Mila comes into the office the next morning with bloodshot eyes and a deep-seated frown.

"Whoa, are you OK?" I ask her.

"I'm fine," she says, putting her keys down on her desk and taking her purse off her shoulder. It drops with a thud.

"You're sure you're good?"

She looks up at me. "Do you want to go grab coffee?" she asks. Ours isn't the sort of office where people often just leave to go get coffee the minute they come in, but I doubt anyone will really notice.

"Sure," I say. "Let me get my wallet."

Mila puts her purse back on her shoulder as I run to my desk and grab my bag. We are quiet until we hit the elevator bank. I press the down button, the elevator *dings*, and luckily, there is no one on it.

"I didn't sleep last night," she says, as the doors close.

"At all?"

"Nope. And I got about four hours the night before but only about two the night before that." Her posture is that of a defeated woman. She's got her arm propped on her hip, as if it's supporting her.

"Why?"

We unexpectedly stop on the fourth floor. A woman in a black skirt suit steps in and presses the button for the second floor. It's clear we were talking. It's also clear that we are now not going to talk because she's in here. It's an uncomfortable fifteen-second flight for all of us. When the elevator finally stops again, the woman steps out, the doors slowly close, and in perfect synchronicity, our conversation continues.

"Because Christina and I have been fighting all hours of the night lately," she says.

"Fighting about what?"

Ding.

We are on the first floor, making our way through the lobby, heading toward the coffee stand. Mila and I never come here, because we don't like weak coffee and stale bagels. But sometimes you need to go get coffee more than you actually need coffee. And this is one of those times.

"We fight about everything. You name it! The kids, who should feed the dog, if we should be looking for a bigger place, when the right time to buy a house is, whether or not we should have sex."

"Do you guys have sex a lot?" I ask. I think, on some level, I'm looking for empirical evidence that I am normal. That all couples have trouble with sex. Maybe they don't have sex that often, either. "Is it sort of a problem with you two?"

"No, we have plenty of sex," she says. "That's rarely the issue. It's more like should we when the kids are awake?"

So there goes that theory. The cheese stands alone.

She steps up to the coffee stand. "Hazelnut latte, please," Mila says to the man running the place.

"Ma'am, I'm sorry, we are out of milk," he says to her. He said he was sorry, but he doesn't seem the slightest bit concerned.

"You're out of milk?"

"Yes, ma'am."

"So you just have black coffee?"

"And sugar," he adds.

This is what happens when people will buy your coffee regardless of the quality. If your location is good enough, you don't even have to have anything to sell.

"OK," she says. "Regular coffee, black. You want anything?" she asks, gesturing to me.

I wave my hand to say no. The man hands Mila a cup of coffee and charges her two bucks.

"So you guys are just fighting about a lot of stuff?" I ask, getting us back on track. Mila sits down on a bench in the lobby, and I sit down next to her.

"Yeah, and then, when we're done fighting, one of the twins gets up, and I can't go back to sleep."

"Jesus," I say. "What do you think is going on?"

"With the fighting?"

"Yeah."

Mila looks despondent. "I don't know. I honestly don't know. We didn't used to fight that often. A squabble here or there, you know? None of this scream-until-you-see-the-sunrise crap."

"Has anything happened that might have put you two on edge?"

She shrugs, sipping her coffee cautiously. "Raising kids is hard. Taking care of a family is hard. And I think sometimes it gets to one or the other of us. Right now, it's getting to both of us at the same time. Which is not good."

Her purse beeps, and she fishes through it to find her cell phone. I'm assuming it's a text from Christina, because her face grows furious.

"I swear to God," she says, shaking her head, "I'm going to kill her. I am going to *kill* her."

"What did she do?"

She shows me the text message. It just says, "Can't pick up Brendan and Jackson from day care. You do it?" It seems relatively harmless, and yet I know there is a context that turns that text into an infuriating betrayal. I can imagine when you add up the sleepless nights and the unkind words, the history, and the resentments, that simple text might be enough to break the camel's back.

"What are you gonna do?" I ask.

Mila breathes in deeply, takes a sip of coffee, and stands up. "I'm going to get over it," she says. "That's what I'm going to do. I'm going to drink about five of these," she says, gesturing to the coffee, "to get me to five o'clock, then I'm gonna pick up my kids, I'm going to find a way to be nice to my partner, and I'm going to go to bed. That's what I'm going to do."

I nod. "Sounds like a plan."

We head back toward the elevators, and as we do, I wonder why I couldn't do that. Why couldn't I find the answer in five cups of coffee and being nice when I got home? I don't know. I don't know that I'll ever know. Maybe part of it is that I'm not Mila. Maybe part of it is that Ryan's not Christina. Maybe part of it is that we don't have kids. Maybe if we had kids, we would have fought through this all differently. I don't know why Ryan and I are different. I just know that it's OK that we are.

Because I don't want to go home tonight and work hard at being nice to somebody. I just don't feel like it right now. I like that I get to go home and do whatever I want. I get to watch what I want on TV. I get to take a really long shower. I get to order Venezuelan food. Thumper and I will get into bed around midnight, and we will sleep soundly, a luxurious amount of room between us in our bed.

And I think if you like your evening plans, you're not allowed to regret what led you to them. I think that should be a rule.

When Mila and I get into the elevator, she thanks me for listening. "I feel better. Much better. I just needed to vent, I think. How are you? Let's talk about you."

I laugh. "Nothing much to report," I say. "Things are fine."

"That's good," she says.

It's quiet, and I try to fill the silence. "You can do it," I say. "You can set me up on that date."

I don't know why I say it. I guess I'm trying to make her feel better.

Mila pushes the stop button on the elevator, and it halts, forcing me to push off of the wall for balance.

"Are you just doing this to make me feel better?" she asks me.

"No," I say. "I just . . . I think it's time I had some fun." I guess that's true. I do think it might be kind of fun. Sort of.

She smiles wide. "Oh, this is going to be great!"

Mila hits the button again, and we start to ascend.

"I'm proud of you," she says.

"You are?" I ask her, as the doors open and we start walking.

"Yeah," she says. "This is a big step for you."

It is? Ah. I guess it is. I think I should have thought about this more.

A few hours later, she comes into my office with a smile on her face and more coffee in her hand. "Can you do Saturday night?"

"This Saturday night?" I thought this was some far-off idea. I did not think we were talking Saturday night.

"Yeah."

"Um . . ." I say. "Sure. Yeah. I guess I can do Saturday."

"I'll give him your number," Mila says, and then she comes over to my desk and takes over my computer. "Do you want to see a picture of him?"

"Oh, yeah, totally," I say, remembering that I'm supposed to be attracted to this person.

She pulls up a photo.

He's handsome. Light brown hair, square jaw, glasses. In

the photo, he's planting a tree with some kids. He has on a T-shirt and jeans, with gardening gloves and a huge shovel in his hand.

I look at the picture. I really consider it. I could kiss him, I think. You know, maybe. Maybe he is a person I could kiss.

I spend my Saturday morning cuddled in bed with Thumper. We watch a lot of reality television, and then I read magazines until noon.

I start to call Rachel to tell her that I've agreed to a blind date tonight, but as I dial her, my phone starts ringing at the same time. The dialing and ringing all at once knock me for a loop, and I manage to hang up on everyone after somehow leaving a voice mail of myself going, "Uh, what? Wait, Ah!" for Rachel.

Just as I go to check my missed calls to see who called, it rings again, and I answer. "Hello?"

"Lauren?"

"Yeah."

"Hi, it's David."

I'm nervous. The good kind. I remember this kind. It doesn't feel exactly like butterflies in your stomach. It's more like hummingbirds in your chest. Either image, though, taken literally, is entirely frightening. "Oh, hey, David," I say, "How are you?"

His voice is friendly and calming. It's a nice voice. "I'm good, you?"

"Yeah, I'm good."

It's quiet for a moment, and my mind races through options of things to say, but ultimately, I come up empty. *Someone say something.*

"I was thinking maybe seven o'clock? There's a great Greek place on Larchmont if you like Greek. I mean . . ." He starts to stumble. He sounds kind of nervous. "I mean, some people don't like Greek. Which is fine."

This might be easier than I thought.

"Greek sounds great. Were you thinking of Le Petit Greek?" When it comes to Greek food, I know what's where.

"Yes!" he says, excited. "Have you been there?"

I used to make Ryan take me there when I wanted moussaka. I should have noticed he only ever ordered the steak. He doesn't even really like steak.

"I have, yeah," I say. "I love it. Great choice."

"OK, so seven o'clock," David says. "You'll know it's me because I'll be wearing a red rose on my lapel."

"Nice," I say. I'm not sure if he's joking, so I don't want to laugh at him.

"That was a joke," he says. His tone is eager to clarify. "Maybe I should do something like that, though. I'll wear a black shirt. Or . . . yeah, a black shirt." He might be more nervous about it than I am.

"Cool," I say. "You have yourself a date." I immediately find myself embarrassed for hitting the nail too closely on the head. It's embarrassing, right? To call a date a date?

"OK," David says. "Looking forward to it."

I hang up and put the phone on the table. I look at Thumper, who is now sitting under the table at my feet. I have to duck underneath the table to see him, to really look him in the eye.

"It's not weird that he didn't offer to pick me up, is it?" I ask Thumper. He cocks his head slightly. "It's just, like, the way people do things, right?"

I take his yawn as a yes.

My phone rings again and startles me. Rachel.

"What the hell did you leave on my voice mail?" she asks me, laughing.

"I got confused."

"Clearly."

"I have a date tonight," I tell her.

"A date?" she says. "Like, with a man?"

"No, it's with a panda bear. I'm really excited."

"You think you're ready for that? With a man, I mean? I understand you're not actually dating a panda bear."

I sigh. "I don't know. I mean, Ryan's dating someone."

"If Ryan jumped off a cliff, would you?"

Is it bad that there was a time in my life when I might have considered saying yes to that? I'm inclined to think it's beautiful that I once believed in someone that much, that completely, and without reservation.

David has parsley in his teeth, and I'm not sure how to tell him.

"Anyway, so I took a job teaching social studies to eighth-graders in East L.A., and I thought it would be for a year or two, but I just really like it," he says. He laughs at himself a bit, and it's really charming. It is. But he has parsley on his front tooth. And it's a big piece. It's not so much that I mind. I mean, parsley is not the measure of a person. It's just that I know he's going to go to the bathroom at some point, and he's going to look in the mirror, and he's going to see it. And he's going to come back out and say, "Why didn't you tell me there was a huge piece of parsley in my teeth?" And I'm going to have to sit here and shrug like an idiot.

"You have a—" I start, but he accidentally speaks over me.

"I mean, in college, I was convinced I would graduate with my political science degree and next stop, the Senate! But, you know, life had other plans," he says. "What about you?"

"Kind of the same thing," I say. "I work in the alumni department at Occidental."

"That sounds like it could be fun."

"Yeah," I say. "It's a good job. Same as what you're talking about. It's not what I set out to do. I was a psych major. I just assumed I'd be a psychologist, but I found this, and I don't know, I really like it. I find myself getting really excited when we are putting together the newsletters, planning reunions, that sort of thing."

David takes a sip of his white wine, and when he does, the parsley manages to wash away.

"Isn't it nice," he says, "once you've outgrown the ideas of what life should be and you just enjoy what it is?"

Of all the things people have said to me about my marriage, none has resonated like this does. And he's not even talking about my marriage.

I lift my glass to toast.

"Here's to that," I say. David *clinks* his wineglass to mine and smiles at me. You know what? Without the parsley there to distract you, it's quite a smile. It's bright white and streamlined. His face is handsome in a conventional way, all cheekbones and angles. He's not so attractive that you'd stop traffic to look at him. But neither am I. He's just a humbly good-looking guy. Like, if he were the new doctor in a small town in the Midwest, all the local women would schedule an appointment. He's that kind of attractive. His glasses sit comfortably on his nose, as if they have earned the right to be there.

"So what kind of stuff are you into?" David asks me. "I mean, when you're not at work, what are you doing?"

"Uh . . ." I say, unsure of how to answer the question. I read books. I watch television. I play with my dog. Is that the stuff he means? It doesn't seem very interesting. "Well, I just recently started hiking and running. I like taking my dog out in the sun. I always feel good about myself when he gets tired before I do. It's rare, but it does happen. I guess, other than that, I hang out with my family, and I read a lot."

"What do you read?" He takes a bite of his salmon as he listens to me.

"Fiction, mostly. I'm getting into thrillers lately. Detective stories," I say. The truth is, I've stopped reading anything with a love story in it. It's much less depressing to read about murder. "What about you?"

"Oh, nonfiction, mostly," he says. "I stick to the facts."

It's quiet for a moment. Admittedly, it is hard to keep up a conversation with a stranger and pretend he is not as much of a stranger as he is. I try to come up with something to say. I talked to him about his job already. What do I ask?

"Sorry," he says. "This is my first date in a very long time. I'm sorry if it's awkward."

"Oh!" I say. "Me, too. First time on a date in a while. I have no idea what I'm doing."

"I haven't dated anyone since Ashley," he says, and then confirms what I already have deduced. "My ex-wife. Christina keeps trying to set me up with people. But I never . . . this is the first time I've agreed to it."

I laugh. "Mila was really pushing it."

"So I take it you are also a victim of the institution?" he says, smiling. "Divorced?"

"Well," I say, "I'm separated. My husband and I. We're separated."

"Well, I'm sorry to hear that," David says.

"No, me, too," I say. "About yours."

David laughs to himself. "Well, we never separated. I found her sleeping with one of her coworkers. I filed for divorce as fast as I could."

"That's awful," I say, putting my hand to my chest. I've known David for, like, an hour. But I can't believe someone would do that to him.

"You don't even know the half of it," he says. "But I won't get into that. I told myself, 'Don't talk about Ashley at dinner.'"

I laugh knowingly. "Oh, trust me. Same here. I'm relearning how to talk to people since Ryan left. Honestly, this is my first date since I was nineteen. I have a whole list of things I've told myself not to do."

"Let me guess. Don't talk about your ex. Don't talk about

how lost you feel being alone again. Don't talk about how weird and awkward it is to sit across the table from someone *other* than your ex."

I add a few myself. "Don't eat off his plate, just because you're used to being able to do that. Don't admit you haven't been on a date in eleven years."

David laughs. "We're doing better with some than with others." He tips his wineglass toward me, and I reciprocate. Our glasses *clink*, and we drink.

We laugh our way through dinner. We order more wine than we should. As buzzed becomes tipsy, the filter of what to say and not say starts to wash away. We tell each other the things we don't tell other people.

He tells me he wakes up sometimes thinking he should just take her back. I tell him Ryan is dating someone else and that when I think about it, I think my heart might implode. I tell him I'm not sure I ever had much of a life outside of Ryan. He nods knowingly and tells me that in his darkest hours, he wishes he never caught her. That he just never found out. That he could live his whole life being the guy who didn't know that his wife was cheating. He tells me he liked life better then. I tell him I'm starting to wonder who I even am without Ryan. I tell him I'm not sure I ever knew.

It's the first time I've told someone the uglier truths about how much it hurts. It's the first time someone has been able to tell me they hurt, too. It is comforting when you share your pain with someone, and they say, "I can't even begin to understand how difficult that must be." But it is better when they can say, "I understand completely."

When dinner ends, he walks me to my car. We walk down Larchmont Boulevard past the closed shops and cafés, all decorated with wreaths and lights in preparation for Christmas next week. It would be a romantic moment if we hadn't spilled our guts to each other, exposing our wounds and washing away all mystery. When we get to my car, David kisses me on the cheek and smiles at me.

"Something tells me we've friend-zoned each other," he says.

I laugh. "I think so," I say. "But a friend is a good thing to have."

"It's too bad we're so clearly not ready," he says, laughing. "You're a beautiful woman."

I blush, and yet I am relieved. I'm not ready to go on a date that ends with passion. I'm just not ready. I grab David's hand. "Thank you," I say, opening my car door and getting into the front seat. "Keep my number, will you? Feel free to call me when no one else gets it."

He smiles that nice smile. "Ditto," he says.

Charlie calls me the night before he's supposed to get into town.

"It's all set, I guess. Mom knows I'm staying with someone else. That went over like a lead balloon."

"She'll be fine, trust me."

"Yeah, and Natalie is a little nervous."

"Oh, yeah, I would be, too. It's a scary thing." Am I nervous? To meet her? I think I kind of am.

"I told her, though, everyone loves pregnant ladies. Especially ones carrying my kid."

My kid. My little brother just said "my kid." It still doesn't entirely make sense to me. But it is happening. I need to remember that. Just because it's been a secret and I haven't had anyone to talk to about it doesn't mean that it's not real. It's real, and it's about to become realer.

"OK, so you'll just meet us at Mom's, then?"

"Yeah," he says. "What time is dinner again?"

"Dinner is at five, but I think we are opening presents around one or two."

"That means two."

"Huh?"

"Mom told you one or two so that you get there at one and she has more time with you, but really, she's planning on two."

"Why are you saying it like it's some diabolical plan?"

"I'm not."

"Well, there's nothing wrong with your family wanting to spend more time with you."

"I know," Charlie says. "But we'll be there at two instead of one. That's all I'm saying." He's being precious with his time because he has someone he wants to spend time with. He wants to be alone with Natalie. He doesn't want to spend his entire day with his family. Me? I'll happily spend the entire day with my family. What else would I be doing?

"OK, then, I'll tell Mom you'll be there at two."

"Cool."

"And Charlie?"

"Yeah?"

"You got Mom a gift, right?"

"We're still doing that?"

"Yes, Charlie, we're still doing that. I gotta go. Rachel is calling on the other line."

"Cool. OK, 'bye. And don't tell her yet!"

"I won't. I got it." I hit the button to change calls, and I drop Rachel. What the hell? How hard is it to navigate two phone calls on the same phone at the same goddamn time? I call her back.

"Learn how to use your phone," she says.

"Yeah, thanks."

"So we have a problem."

"We do?"

"Well, I do. And I'm inclined to make you help me, so it's sort of your problem, too."

"OK," I say. "Let's hear it."

"Grandma read an article that says white sugar is linked to cancer."

"OK," I say. "So I'm going to guess that Mom is insisting that all of the desserts you make be sugar-free."

"Have you even heard of such a ridiculous thing?" Rachel is the one being ridiculous here. We live in Los Angeles. It would take me five minutes to go out and find a gluten-free, sugar-free, dairy-free, vegan cupcake if I wanted.

"You can do it," I say. "Dessert is like breathing to you. You have got this."

"She doesn't even have cancer," Rachel says. "You know that, right? I mean, we never talk about it, but I think it's clear the woman is cancer-free."

I start to laugh. "You seem to have forgotten that that's good news," I say.

Rachel laughs. "No!" she says. "I love that she's cancer-free, I'm just not sure why that means I have to make sugar-free pumpkin pie."

"All right, how about this?" I ask. "You look at recipes now and find some you think will be good. Send me the list of ingredients that you don't already have. I'll go to the grocery store tomorrow and get them all. And then I'll come over and help you cook every last one of them."

"You would really do that?"

"Are you kidding? Absolutely. Mom didn't ask me to bring anything this year. I should pull my own weight."

"Wow," Rachel says, her voice lighter. "OK, thank you." Then she adds, "You have to get to the store before five or six, I bet. Just letting you know. The stores are gonna close early for Christmas Eve."

"I will. I promise."

"And will you also get some of that fake snow stuff?"

"What stuff?"

"They have it at the grocery store sometimes in the Christmas aisle. The stuff that you spray on the windows and it looks like snow?"

I know what she's talking about. Mom used to spray it

on all the windows around the house when we were little. She'd light a candle that smelled like firewood and sing "Let It Snow." My mother has always put a big emphasis on showing us a proper Christmas. One year, Charlie started crying because he'd never seen snow, so my mom put ice in a blender and then tried to sprinkle it on top of him. I wonder if Charlie remembers that. I wonder if he's going to put ice in a blender for his own snow-deprived child.

"You got it. You just give me a list, and I'll get it all," I say.

I hang up and put the phone down.

I look around the house. I don't have anything to do.

I decide to text David. I don't know why. I guess because it is something to do. Someone to talk to.

Ever think that the real problem with living without your spouse is that you're sometimes just really bored?

I figure he may not answer. Or he may not see it until later. But he texts me back right away: *Soooooo bored. I underestimated how much time being married takes up in a day.*

I text him back: *It's like I resent the lack of distraction now. And I hated how much he distracted me before.*

He responds: *The worst is at work! I used to IM with her when the kids were taking tests or watching a movie. Now I just read* CNN.

Me: *It's Dullsville.*

Him: *Ha ha ha. Exactly.*

And that's it. That's all we say to each other. But . . . I don't know. I feel better.

Can you hand me that?" Rachel calls to me. She has on a polka-dot apron, her hair in a high bun. She has flour on her face. The pumpkin pie is in the oven.

Now she's started on sugar-free sugar cookies. I made a joke earlier: "I guess they are just called *cookies*, then, huh?" She laughed, but I could tell her heart wasn't in it. We've been at this since eight thirty this morning, when I showed up with everything on the list she sent me. I expected that list to include weird chemicals, but it was really just honey and Stevia.

"Hand you what?"

"That." Rachel isn't even looking at me. She's not even pointing. "The . . ." She makes an empty gesture with her hand. "The . . ."

Somehow, with her waving hand and the large lump of dough she has in front of her, I figure out what she needs. "The rolling pin?" I pick it up and hand it to her. Its weight causes it to land with a *thump* in her hand.

She stops and pauses for a second. "Thank you," she says. "Sorry, I'm doing too many things at once."

She puts flour on the rolling pin and starts to roll. "Have you heard this thing about Charlie bringing a date to Christmas?"

"Hm?" I say. God, I'm bad at lying to my sister. We don't keep secrets from each other. It's not what this family does. So I don't really know how to do it. What should I say, exactly? Should I be noncommittal? Like never really say anything either way? Plausible deniability? Or do I just outright lie to her face, say something entirely untrue with such conviction that I almost believe it myself? This stuff is just not my strong suit.

"Charlie is bringing a date to Christmas," she says. The dough is flat, and now Rachel is searching around her kitchen for something. Not in there, I guess. Or there. There she goes. She's got it. "Check these out!" she says proudly. She pulls out cookie molds in the shapes of finely intricate snowflakes.

"Those are so cool!" I say. "But they look really difficult to use."

Rachel shrugs. "I practiced last week. We're good."

I go to her refrigerator and grab a bottle of seltzer water. The cap won't turn, I can't get it to open, and so I hand it to her. She wordlessly cracks the seal and hands it back to me. "You should quit your job," I say.

"What?" She's only half paying attention. She's starting to place the cookie molds on the dough.

"I'm serious. You are so good at this stuff. You make the most decadent desserts and awesome breakfasts. You should open a bakery."

Rachel looks up at me. "I can't do that."

"Why not?"

"With what money?"

"I don't know." I shrug. "How does anyone start a business? Business loan, right?"

Rachel puts the mold down. "It's not realistic."

"So you've thought about it?"

"I mean, sure. Everyone thinks about trying to make money doing the things they love."

"Yeah, but not everyone has such a passion and talent for something you *can* really make money from," I say. Rachel works in HR, which always struck me as an odd match. She's a right-brained person. I always imagined her doing something more traditionally creative.

"There are way more talented bakers than me," she says.

"I don't know," I say. I'm entirely serious. "You are really, really good. And look at you, you practice using snowflake cookie molds in your spare time. How many people can say that?"

"I'm not saying I don't love it."

"Think about it," I say. "Just think about it."

"It's just not realistic."

I put my hands up. "I'm just saying think about it."

After a few hours, Rachel and I gather up the cookies and the pie. We gently move the gingerbread house she made last night into the back of my car. I grab the two cans of snow and throw them into my purse. As I get into the front, Rachel has the key in the ignition, but she is looking down, almost in a daze. I expect her to start the car, but she doesn't.

"Yoo-hoo," I say, as I wave my hand in the air to get her attention.

She looks up. "Sorry," she says, turning the key. Then she looks at me. "You really think I'd be good at it, though? The bakery thing?"

I nod my head. "Better than good. Seriously."

She doesn't respond, but I can see she takes it to heart. "Merry Christmas, by the way!" she says as we hit the freeway. "I can't believe I forgot to say that this morning."

"Merry Christmas!" I say back to her. "I think it's gonna be a good one."

"Me, too," she says. Her gaze is straight ahead at the road, but her mind isn't on this freeway.

My phone buzzes, and I look down at it. I think, for a split second, that it might be Ryan. Maybe on Christmas, we can bend the rules.

But it's not Ryan. Of course it's not.

It's David.

Merry Christmas, new friend.

I text back: *Merry Christmas to you, too!*

It's not from Ryan, but I'm smiling nonetheless.

Merry Christmas!" my mother calls to us before she even opens the door. You can hear the thrill in her voice. This is always the happiest day of her year. Her children are home. She gets to give us presents. We're all on our best behavior. In general, she gets to treat us as if we are still kids.

She opens the door wide, and Rachel and I both say "Merry Christmas!" in unison. When we get inside, Grandma Lois is sitting on the couch. She goes to get up, and I tell her she doesn't have to.

"Nonsense," she says. "I'm not an invalid."

She takes a look at the desserts on the table. "Oh, Rachel, they are so gorgeous. Look at the detail on those cookies. I'm sorry to say I can't have any. I read recently that they have done studies correlating white sugar to cancer."

"No, Mom," my mom says. "Rachel made it all sugar-free." She turns to Rachel for confirmation. "Right?"

"Yep," Rachel says, suddenly proud of herself. "Even the sugar cookies!"

"So I guess they're just *cookies*, then?" my mom jokes, and she is not much of a joker, so you can see her eyes start to crinkle as she holds back a smile, waiting for other people to laugh.

"Good one, Mom!" I say, and high-five her. "I tried that one earlier today."

Everyone starts to talk about the things you talk about at Christmas. What is cooking, when it will be done, how good everything smells. Grandma usually takes over Mom's kitchen every Christmas, making everything from scratch, but this year, my mother lets us know, she pitched in.

"I made the sweet potatoes *and* the green beans," she says proudly. Something about her childlike pride reminds me of the can of snow.

"Oh!" I say, "Look, Mom! Rachel and I brought spray snow." I pull out the cans. "Awesome, right?"

She grabs them from my hands and shakes them immediately. "Oh, this is great! Do you guys want to spray, or should I?"

"Let them do it, Leslie," my grandmother says to my mother. The way she says it, the way it's a suggestion that should be heeded, the way it's laced with love and derision, makes me realize that my grandmother is sort of a bossy mom. I always think of my grandmother as *my* grandmother. I never think about the fact that she is my mother's mother. My mom isn't at the top of the totem pole, which is what it often feels like. Rather, she's just one piece of a long line of women. Women who first see themselves as daughters and then grow to be mothers and eventually grandmothers and one day great-grandmothers and ancestors. I'm still in phase one.

My grandmother sneaks a piece of sugar cookie and eats it, but it's not a very stealthy move, because we all see her.

"Oh, my!" she says. "These are fantastic. You're sure you didn't use any sugar?"

Rachel shakes her head. "Nope, none."

"Leslie, try this," she says to my mother.

My mother takes a bite. "Wow, Rachel."

"Wait, are they that good?" I say. I was with her all morning; you'd think I'd have tried one. I take a bite. "Jesus, Rachel," I say, and my grandmother slaps the back of her hand against my arm.

"Lauren! Don't take the Lord's name in vain on Christmas!"

"Sorry, Grandma."

"Where is Uncle Fletcher?" Rachel asks, and my mom starts shaking her head and waving her hands behind Grandma's back. The classic "Don't ask" signal, signaled classically too late.

"Oh." Grandma sighs. "He decided not to come after all. I think, maybe, you know, he needs some time to himself."

"Oh, that makes sense," I say, trying to ease the conversation along. This seems to have made my grandmother a little sad.

"No," she says, nodding. "I think I'm realizing that your uncle is a little . . ." She lowers her voice to a whisper. "Weird."

She says it as if being "weird" is a thing people don't speak about. Uncle Fletcher has never been in a relationship. He lives at home with his mother. He makes his living selling things on eBay and taking temp jobs. I'm pretty sure that if they release a computer game good enough, he will die playing it in his underwear.

"You just figured this out now, Grandma?" Rachel asks. I'm surprised she's feeling bold enough to say that—none of us talks about Uncle Fletcher's eccentricities—but it seems to make my grandmother laugh.

"Sweetheart, I once believed your grandfather when he told me you don't get pregnant the first time you do it. That's how we got Uncle Fletcher in the first place. So I've never been the sharpest tool in the shed."

If we don't talk about Uncle Fletcher's weirdness, we definitely don't talk about my grandparents having sex. So after the comment sits in the air a bit, waiting for us all to realize it has actually been said, it cracks us open. My mother, Rachel, and I are laughing so hard we can't breathe. My grandmother follows suit.

"Grandma!" I say.

Grandma shrugs. "Well, it's true! What do you want from me?" We all catch our breath, and Grandma keeps the conversation going. "So where is Ryan today? Surely he's not working on Christmas."

I just assumed that my mother would have done my dirty work for me and told my grandmother about what was happening. In fact, I assumed she told her months ago. I was sort of surprised that Grandma never called me to bring it up. And when I called her on Thanksgiving, I was pleasantly surprised when she didn't mention anything. But it's plain to see that she has no idea. Oh, the naiveté of wishful thinking.

I look to Rachel, but she starts paying more attention to the cookies than necessary, averting everyone's gaze, especially mine. My instinct is to make something up, to avoid this conversation and put it off for another day, but my mother is giving me a look that makes it clear she's expecting a braver version of her oldest daughter. So I try to be that daughter.

"We . . ." I start. "We split up. Temporarily. We are separated. I guess that's the term."

Grandma looks at me and cocks her head slightly, as if she can't quite believe what she's hearing. She looks at my mother, her face saying, *What do you have to say about this?* And my mother gestures back to me, her arms saying, *If you have a problem, you tell her yourself.* My grandmother looks back to me and takes a breath. "OK, what does that mean?"

"It means that we reached a point where we were no longer happy, and we decided that we wanted more out of . . . marriage than that. So we split up. And I'm really hoping that after we spend this time apart, we will find a way to . . . make it work."

"And you think being apart will do that?"

"Yes," I say. "I do. I think we sort of pushed each other to the brink, and we both need some air."

"Did he cheat on you? Is that what's happened?"

"No," I say. "Absolutely not. He wouldn't do that."

"Did he hit you?"

"Grandma! No!"

She throws her hands up in the air and back down on the counter. "Well, I don't get it."

I nod. "I thought you might not, which is why I haven't broached it with you." Rachel is so clearly avoiding being a part of this conversation, she might as well be whistling off to the side.

"So you just decided you weren't 'happy'?" She uses air quotes when she says "happy," as if it's mine alone, a word I made up, a word that doesn't belong in this conversation.

"You don't think being happy is important?"

"In a long-term marriage?"

"Yes."

"Not only is it not the most important thing, but I would argue that it's not even all that possible."

"To be happy at all?"

"To be happy the whole time."

It's so confusing, isn't it? I mean, why fill our minds with everlasting love and then berate us for believing in it?

"But don't you think that it's something to strive for? To try to be happy the whole time? To try to not just grin and bear your marriage but to thrive in it?"

"Is that what you think you're doing?"

"I believe this to be the best way to learn how to love my husband the way I want to. Yes."

"And is it working?"

Is it working? Is it working? I have absolutely no idea if it's working. That's the whole problem. "Yes," I tell her. I say it with purpose and with confidence. I say it as if there is no other answer. Maybe I say yes because I want her approval, because I want her to back off, because I want to put her in her place. But I think I say yes because I believe, on some level, that thoughts become words, and words become actions. Because if I start saying it's working, maybe in a few days or a few months, I'll look back and think, *Absolutely. This is absolutely working.* Maybe that conviction has to start right here, with a little white lie. "Yes, I do believe it's working."

"How?"

"How?"

"Yes, how?"

Now my mother and Rachel are not pretending to do anything else. They are listening intently, their ears and eyes aimed toward me.

"Well, I have missed him far more than I ever realized I would. When he left, I thought I wasn't in love with him anymore, but I didn't realize just how much I *did* still love him. I do still love him. The minute he left, I felt the hole in my life that he filled. I couldn't have done that without missing him, without losing him."

"One might argue that you can get that kind of perspective from a long weekend away. You got anything else?"

I want to prove to her that I know what I'm doing. "I mean, I don't know if it's anything to talk about here," I say.

"Oh, please, Lauren. Let's hear it."

I'm exasperated. "Fine. Fine. I can see now, now that he is gone, and I have real worries that he might be with someone else, I mean, I think he is with someone else. I know he is. And I'm jealous. At first, I got seethingly jealous. I realized that I had stopped seeing him as someone who, you know, was attractive, I guess. I was taking him for granted in that way. And now that I know that he is dating, it's very clear to me what I had when I had it."

"So what you're saying is that you forgot your husband was

desirable, and now that you can see another woman desiring him, you remember?"

"Sure," I say. "You can say that."

"Do you have cocktail parties?"

"Grandma, what are you talking about?" Rachel says, finally interjecting. I know my grandmother loves me. I know she wants what's best for me. I know she has very specific ideas of what that is. So while I do feel defensive, I don't entirely feel attacked.

"I'm asking her a serious question. Lauren, do you have cocktail parties?"

"No."

"Well, if you did, and you invited some young women, and you left your husband's arm for a minute, you'd notice that he'd end up talking to a number of very pretty young ladies, who would be glad to take him off your hands. And you'd go home to have the best sex of your life." She puts up her hand to wave us off before we ever start. "Excuse me for being vulgar. We're all ladies here."

"That's what worked for you, Grandma," I say, pushing the image of my late grandfather flirting with young women and then having sex with my grandmother out of my mind. "Don't you respect that something else might work for me?"

My grandmother considers me. My mom looks at me, impressed. Rachel is staring at us, desperate to see what happens next. My grandmother grabs my hand. "Make no mistake, I respect *you*. But this is stupid. Marriage is about commitment. It's about loyalty. It's not about happiness. Happiness is secondary. And ultimately, marriage is about children." She gives me a knowing look. "If you had a baby, no matter how unhappy you were together, you'd have stayed together. Children bind you. They connect you. That's what marriage is about."

Everyone just sort of looks at her. Not saying anything. She can see that no one is going to agree with her. So she eats a cookie and wipes the crumbs off her fingers.

"But you know, you kids these days. You do what you do. I can't live your life for you. All I can do is love you."

That's as much of a victory as anyone gets from Lois Spencer. I'll take it.

"You're sure you still love me?" I ask, teasing. I have always, always, always already known the answer to that one.

She smiles at me and kisses my cheek. "Yes, I most certainly do. And I admire your spirit. Always have."

I blush. I love my grandmother so much. She's so cranky and such a know-it-all, but she loves me, and that love may be fierce and opinionated. But it is love.

"One thing," she says. "And this goes for all of you, actually."

"You've got our attention, Mom," my mother says.

"I'm old. And maybe I'm a traditionalist. But that doesn't mean I don't know what I'm talking about."

"We know, Grandma," Rachel says.

"What I'm saying is, I can try to respect the way you do things, but don't forget that the old way works, too."

"What do you mean?" I ask her.

"I mean, if you had hosted a cocktail party, and you had left him to his own devices, and you had flirted with other men and he'd seen it, or he had flirted with other women and you'd seen it, if you had spent a few weekends apart from each other sometimes, given each other some space now and again, maybe you wouldn't need a whole year apart now. That's all I'm saying."

The doorbell rings, and it ends the conversation. In mere moments, Charlie will be walking through the door with the mysterious Natalie. But long after my grandmother and I are done talking, her words stay in my mind. She might very well be right.

• • •

Natalie is gorgeous. She's not gorgeous in a hot, sultry way. Or even a skinny, supermodel sort of way. She's gorgeous in that way where she just looks healthy and happy, with a beautiful smile, in a pretty dress. She looks like she works out, eats well, and knows what clothes look good on her. Her laugh is bright and loud. She listens to you; she really looks at you when you're speaking. And she's thoughtful and well mannered, judging from the poinsettia she gives my mother. I know she had sex with my little brother in the bathroom of an airplane, but it's hard to reconcile that with the person I see in front of me. The person in front of me brought Rocky Road fudge to Christmas.

"I made it this morning," she says.

"Is it sugar-free, sweetheart?" my grandmother says, and Natalie is understandably confused.

"Oh, no, I'm sorry," she says. "I . . . didn't know that that was . . ."

"It's fine," my mom says. "My mother is being absurd."

"It's not absurd to want to ward off any further cancer," my grandmother says. "But thank you so much, dear, for bringing it. We can give it to the dog."

Everyone stares at one another; even Charlie is at a loss for words. My mom doesn't even have a dog.

"I was joking!" Grandma says. "You all are so thick it's farcical. Natalie, thank you for bringing the fudge. Sorry that this family can't take a joke."

When Grandma turns her head, Charlie mouths "Sorry" to Natalie. It's sweet. I think he may be trying to impress her. I've never seen Charlie try to impress anyone.

"It's so nice to meet you all," Natalie says.

"Come," my mom says. "Let's put the presents down by the tree. Can I get you two anything? Charlie, I know you probably want a beer. Natalie, I have some mulled wine?"

"Oh." Natalie shakes her head casually. "Water is fine."

Eventually, we all sit down by the tree.

"So Natalie, tell us about yourself," Rachel says.

And Natalie, kind, sweet, naive Natalie, tries to answer, but Charlie steps in.

"That's such an annoying question, Rachel. What does that mean?"

"Sorry," Rachel says, shrugging defensively, as if she's been falsely accused of a heinous crime. "I'll try to be more specific next time."

The doorbell rings again, and my mother stands up to get it. She comes back in with Bill by her side.

"Merry Christmas!" Bill announces to the room. He has gifts in his hands, and he puts them down at the tree. Everyone gets up and hugs. Mom gets him a beer.

The small talk begins. People start asking one another questions. None of them is interesting. I learn that Natalie works in television casting. She's from Idaho. In her spare time, she likes to pickle things. When she asks me if I'm married, Charlie interrupts.

"Awkward topic," he says, immediately sipping his beer. The entire family hears, and each one of them laughs. Every one of the sons of bitches laughs. And then I laugh, too. Because it's funny, isn't it? And when things are funny, it means they are no longer only sad.

So Merry Christmas to me.

• • •

I've eaten far too much. Too much ham. Too much bread. Too many spoonfuls of sweet potatoes. When the sugar-free sugar cookies get passed around, I squeeze a few into the nooks and crannies of my stomach, and then I'm ready to pass out.

My mother has had enough glasses of mulled wine to stain her teeth a faint purple. She's getting a bit snuggly with Bill at the table. My grandmother is on her second piece of pie, sneaking her spoon into the sugar-laden whipped cream when she thinks we aren't looking. Charlie, meanwhile, appears stoic and sober. Natalie is smiling. Rachel is accepting compliment after compliment on her cookies, with a false modesty rivaled only by Miss Piggy. Charlie stands up.

So here we go, here it is. Oh boy oh boy oh boy.

"So . . ." he starts. "Natalie and I have some news."

That's all my mom needs. That's it. She's crying. I don't think she even knows why she's crying, what she thinks Charlie is going to say, or whether she's happy or sad.

Rachel looks up at Charlie as if he's a mental patient and she's not sure which way he's going to veer today.

Natalie is still smiling, but it's starting to buckle at the corners.

"We are going to be having a baby together."

Waterfalls. My mother's eyes are like two waterfalls. And not the kind that trickle from a little stream, either. These are the kind that gush, the kind that, were I white-water rafting, I would see up ahead and go, "Oh, shit."

Rachel's jaw has dropped. Bill isn't sure which way this is all going. And then my grandmother starts clapping.

She starts clapping! And then she stands up and she walks over to Charlie and Natalie, and she gives them huge, wet kisses on their cheeks, which has to be so very weird for Natalie, and she says, "Finally! Someone's giving me a great-grandchild!"

Charlie thanks her for being so great about it, but all attention is on Mom.

"Do you two have a plan?" she asks.

"Yep." Charlie nods. "I'm moving back here to L.A., in with

Natalie. We're raising the baby together. I feel like the luckiest man in the world, Mom. I really do."

"And what about a job?"

"I have a few interviews lined up next month."

That's all she needs to know, I guess. Because the tears that could have been from joy or sadness only a few seconds ago now only make their way to her chin if they can get past her giant smile. She runs to Charlie and hugs him. She holds on to him, clinging to him. She is sloppy in her movements, operating from gut, moving out of emotion. She hugs Natalie.

Natalie stands up, clearly overwhelmed but doing her best, and hugs my mom back, squeezing her tight. "I'm so glad you're happy," Natalie says.

"Are you kidding me? I'm going to be a grandmother!"

"It's a nice club to be in," Grandma says, and she winks at me. It's a sweet moment. I have forgotten how special a wink can make you feel.

When the commotion has died down, attention falls to Rachel. "I'M GONNA BE A FUCKING AUNT?" she yells, running toward them and hugging them so hard that she rocks them from side to side.

"Rachel!" Grandma says.

"Sorry, Grams. Sorry." She turns to Natalie, putting her hands on Natalie's upper arms. "Natalie, welcome to the Spencer family! We are so, so, so excited to have you!"

When everyone looks at me, I realize that I'm supposed to react, too. "Oh!" I say, "AHHHHHH!" and then hug them both. We all stand there, around them, suffocating them, overwhelming them, wanting to take part in their joy. It's then that I realize this is really happening. Our lives are changing. One of us is growing up. Everyone thought it would be me. And it's not. It's Charlie.

The truth is, it makes me feel like a failure, in some small way. It makes me feel as if I've veered off the path, as if I've been treading water while Charlie swam the race. But that's a tiny piece of me. The rest of me can't believe my baby brother is growing up to be a strong, solid man. The rest of me can't believe I'm going to have a little baby in my life to shower with presents. The rest of me can't believe that my grandmother is finally going to get that great-grandchild she's been asking for, that she has gotten news so great it has silenced her usual judgments.

It's a good day. And it's a wonderful Christmas. And I wish Ryan were here to see it. I wish he and I were going home to the same place. I wish we were going to get into bed tonight and gossip about the rest of them, the way we used to. It's at moments like this that I remember how much a part of all this he was.

The five of us—Rachel, Mom, Grandma, Natalie, and myself—surround Charlie, and maybe he's looking for an escape. Maybe he needs a breath of fresh air. He looks at Bill, and Bill stands up and puts out his hand. Charlie breaks away from us to shake it.

"Congratulations, young man," Bill says. "Best decision you'll ever make."

Charlie looks down at the floor, ever so briefly, and then he looks Bill in the eye and says, "Thanks." I think maybe every man wants to get a pat on the back when he shares the news that he's becoming a father. I'm just glad Bill is here to give it to him.

• • •

"So when are you getting married?" Grandma asks, as Natalie helps Mom and me with the dishes. Rachel, Charlie, and Bill are still at the table. Natalie and I are stacking plates. Grandma and Mom are loading the dishwasher.

"Oh," my mom says. "Lay off her, Mom. They don't have to get married just because they are having a baby."

"Well," Natalie says, "probably July, actually."

"July? I thought you said the baby was due in June," my mom says.

"For the wedding," Natalie says. "The baby will be born by then. It seems easier than trying to fit into a wedding dress."

"*After* the baby is born?" my grandmother asks.

But at the same time, my mother is using the exact same tone and inflection to say, "Wait, you're getting married?"

"Yeah." Natalie catches herself. "Wait, did we not say that?"

"You said nothing about a wedding," I say, as Rachel comes into the kitchen with a few empty serving bowls.

"Whose wedding?" Rachel asks.

"You said you were living together," my mom says. She says it slowly, approaching the sentence as if it's a bomb that might detonate at any second.

"We are getting married," Natalie says. "I'm sorry we didn't mention that part! Charlie!" she calls out. She's right to call in the reserves.

Charlie pops in through the door, and we all stare at him. All five of us. His sisters. His mother. His grandmother. His . . . fiancée?

"You're getting married?" I ask him.

"Yeah," says Charlie, as if I asked him if he likes chicken. "Of course. We're having a baby."

"Finally, someone makes sense in this family!" my grandmother says.

"Mom, will you go into the dining room and keep Bill company?" my mom asks her.

Grandma must be feeling charitable, because she puts down the dish in her hand and walks out.

"Having a baby doesn't mean you have to get married," Mom says.

Natalie inches toward Charlie. I think, perhaps, we are no longer doing a very good job of making her feel welcome. My mom notices the shift in her body language.

"I mean, it's great news," my mom says. "We're just surprised is all."

"How is marrying the mother of my child a surprise?" Charlie asks. Charlie really should learn to leave well enough alone.

"No, you're right," my mother says, backing off. This backing off is entirely for Natalie's benefit. Once Natalie is out of earshot, she'll say how she really feels. That's how you know that Natalie isn't really family just yet. "It shouldn't have been a surprise. You're absolutely right."

"It will be an awesome wedding," Rachel adds lamely.

But she's trying, so I try, too. "Congratulations, new sister!" I say. It comes out so forced and unnatural that I resolve to shut up.

"Thanks," Natalie says, clearly very uncomfortable. "I think I'll go see if there is anything else to bring in."

We all know there isn't a single thing to bring into this kitchen. But none of us says anything. When Natalie is finally gone, my mother starts speaking very gently.

"You don't have to do this," she says. "It's not the nineteen fifties."

"I want to do it," Charlie says.

"Yeah, but why not take your time to think about it?" Rachel says.

"Why are you assuming I haven't?"

"How long have you two even known each other?" my mom asks.

"Three months."

"And she's three months pregnant?" my mom asks.

"Yes."

"Got it," my mom says, starting to wash dishes. She's frustrated, and she's taking it out on the pots and pans.

"Don't judge me, Mom."

"Who's judging?" she says, moving the plates into the sink and running the water over them. "I'm just saying, take your time. You have your whole life to decide whom to marry."

"What are you talking about? Natalie is pregnant. We are moving in together. She is going to be my wife."

"But moving in together doesn't mean she has to be your wife. You can raise a child together and see how the relationship goes," I say.

"Lauren, you're supposed to be on my side here," Charlie says, and it makes me feel . . . included somehow. As if I am in possession of something extra that makes Charlie and me a team. Charlie isn't on a team with anyone. So the fact that he thinks I'm on his side, well, it makes me want to be on his side.

"I am on your side," I say. "I'm just saying that you have never been married before, Charlie. You don't know what it really entails."

"Neither do you!" Charlie says. His tone is uncontrolled and defensive, as if we've cornered a rat. "I just mean that everyone is figuring it out, right? Mom, you tried it your way, and that didn't work for you. Lauren, you're not sure how to do it. Who's to say mine won't work just because it doesn't look like yours?"

Rachel chimes in. "I guess I'm not needed in this conversation."

"Of course you're needed," Charlie says. "I want you all to be on board with this. I really like this woman. I think I can make this work for us."

"You can't just make a marriage work because you want it

to work, Charlie." My mom says it, but I might as well have said it myself.

"But you had no problem when I said we were raising a baby?" he asks.

"They are two totally different things," she says. "If you two don't work out, you can co-parent."

"I don't want to co-parent!" Charlie says. "I want a family."

"Co-parenting is a family. Single-parent homes are families." My mom is starting to take this as an indictment of her, and I can understand why. I think it's about to become one.

"No, Mom. That's not the kind of family I want. I don't want to live across town from my kid. I don't want to meet Natalie in the parking lot of a Wendy's on Sunday afternoons to drop him off, OK?"

This is something that Charlie learned from television. Our dad never took us for the weekend. He didn't live across town. He just left.

"OK," my mom says, trying to keep herself calm. "You have to do what you think is right for your children."

"Thank you," Charlie says.

"But I have to do what is right for my children," she says. "And so I'm going to tell you that marriage is hard work. No matter how hard I tried, I could not succeed. It was impossible for me. Can you think of another thing that I have ever told you was impossible?"

Charlie listens and then shakes his head. "No," he says quietly.

"And your sister," my mom says, as she gestures toward me, "is a very smart woman, a loving woman, who means well and almost always does the right thing." I stole a Capri Sun from the grocery store when I was eleven. I swear she's never forgiven me.

"I know," says Charlie.

"And even *she* isn't sure how to make one work."

"I know," Charlie says.

"So listen to us when we say that marriage is not to be taken lightly."

"Once again, no one cares about my opinion!" Rachel says bitterly. How quickly we all regress when we're in the same room.

"Oh, for heaven's sake, Rachel," my mom says, losing her temper. "So you don't have a boyfriend. Big deal. No one's treating you like a leper."

"When every conversation is about someone's boyfriend or husband, then I do think—" Rachel shuts herself up. "Whatever. It's not about me. Sorry."

My mom puts her arm around her and squeezes her into the crook of her body. Rachel resigns into it. My mom keeps going, looking directly at Charlie. "You don't have to marry Natalie to prove you're not your father. Do you get that? You couldn't be your father in a million years."

Charlie doesn't say anything. He looks at the floor. It must be so different being a boy without a dad instead of a girl without a dad. I should stop assuming they are the same thing.

"You have a lot of options," Mom says. "And all we want you to do is think about them."

"Fine," Charlie says.

"Are you going to think about them?" she asks him.

"Already have," he says. "I've made up my mind. I want to marry Natalie."

"Do you love her?" Rachel asks.

"I know I will," Charlie says. "I know I want to."

His tone makes it clear that we have reached the end of the conversation. A part of me feels like saying, *You can lead a horse to water, but you can't make him drink,* and the other part of me thinks that if anyone can out-stubborn marriage, it's Charlie. If anyone can trip and fall into a happy marriage, it's my baby brother. And also, in the deepest part of my heart, I think he's right. I may be married, but I don't know a damn thing about marriage. So who's to say Charlie's way is any worse than anyone else's?

"July it is, then," my mom says, smiling. She gestures for Charlie and me to come toward her and Rachel. Charlie looks at me, and I cock my head to say, "Come on, a hug won't kill you."

The four of us bear-hug. "The rest of them out there, they're fine and all. But this . . ." My mom squeezes the three of us tight. It's more of a metaphorical gesture now; we're too old to fit anymore. "This is my family. You guys are my meaning of life."

We're so squished together that now I'm having trouble breathing. I figure Charlie will be the first one to break the huddle, but he doesn't.

"I love you guys," he says.

From deep inside the belly of the pack comes Rachel's muffled voice, "We love you, too, Charlie."

When it gets late and Grandma starts complaining that she's tired, we all start packing our things. I gather my own pile of new sweaters and socks. Rachel grabs her new slow cooker. We throw all the wrapping paper away. Charlie and Natalie start saying good-bye to everyone.

"Welcome to the family," my mom says to Natalie, as they make their way to the front door. She hugs her. "We couldn't be happier to have you." She hugs Charlie for a long time, holding him tight. "So you're flying out tomorrow?" she asks. "And then when do we have you back for good?"

"I'm packing up my stuff over the next few weeks, and then I should be moved into Natalie's place by mid-January."

My mom laughs. "Oh, Natalie, I think you're going to be

my favorite kid. You're giving me a grandchild and bringing my son home!" She puts her hand on her heart and frowns the way people do when they are really, really happy.

They head to their car. I know they are going to talk about us. I know Natalie is going to ask how things went. I know Charlie is going to tell her that everyone loved her. He's not going to tell her what we said, but she's going to know the gist of it anyway. I know at some point, Natalie is going to ask Charlie if Grandma really has cancer. And Charlie is going to have to explain how all of this works.

When Rachel and I start to head out, I offer to drive. Rachel hands me the keys, and when she does, Grandma asks us for a ride. "Oh," I say. "I thought you were staying here."

"No, dear. I'm staying at the Standard."

Rachel starts laughing.

"Again?" I say.

"They have a lady who sits in a glass box behind the check-in desk. It's a riot!" Grandma says.

Rachel, Grandma, and I give Mom a kiss good-bye amid cheers of "Merry Christmas!" and "Thanks for the socks." We leave the house to her and Bill. From the look on Bill's face, I get the distinct impression he's got some weird Santa sex costume waiting for her or something. Gross.

We get into the car, and before I even turn on the ignition, Grandma starts in. "What do we think about this Bill guy?" she says.

Rachel turns her head and then her shoulders toward Grandma in the backseat. "I like him," she says. "You don't like him?"

"I'm just asking what you think," Grandma says diplomatically.

I keep my eyes on the road, but I join the conversation. "I think he seems really taken with Mom. I think that's nice."

"You two are a far cry from when you were little. You used to hate every man she dated."

"No, we didn't," Rachel says.

"We didn't even meet that many of them," I say.

"She stopped introducing you," Grandma says. "Because you used to get so upset."

I don't remember any of this.

"Are you sure? You're not thinking of Charlie or something?" Rachel asks.

"Honey, I remember it like it was yesterday. You hated every man who walked in that house. Both of you did. I remember she used to call me up and say, 'Mom, what do I do? They can't stand any of them.'"

"And what did you say?" I ask.

"I said, 'Stop introducing them, then.'"

"Huh," Rachel says, turning forward.

Huh.

"Sweetheart, don't take Sunset," my grandmother says when I get over the hill into the city.

"Grandma, you don't even live here!" Rachel says.

"Yeah, but I pay attention to the way your mother goes. Take Fountain, and then cut up Sweetzer. It's better."

I spend late Christmas night with Thumper, reading a mystery about a family murdered in a small Irish town. The detective is on the outs with the department and really has to solve this one to prove he's got what it takes. With Thumper next to me, his head resting on my stomach, I admit, this is a great way to end a holiday.

My phone rings around eleven. It's David.

"Hi," he says. His voice is soft and shy.

"Hi," I say. I can feel myself smiling wide. "How was your Christmas?"

"It was nice," he says. "I spent the day with my brother and his wife and kids."

"That sounds fun," I say.

"It was fun," he says. "His kids are four and two, so it's cute to see them open a playhouse and get all excited."

"And then you spent the rest of the day trying to put it together for them," I offer.

David laughs. "I'll tell you, those instruction booklets are torture. But it's nice to be able to do that."

"I'm going to be an aunt myself, actually," I say. "So I'm looking forward to all of that stuff."

"Oh, wow, congrats!" he says.

I thank him, and there is a long pause.

"Well, yeah," David says. "I don't know why I called, I guess. I just wanted to see how your Christmas went. I was thinking about you. And . . . you know . . . holidays can be lonely, so I just . . . wanted to see how you were . . . faring."

Sometimes you want to forget the fact that you're alone, and instead, you want to relish the feeling that someone understands you, someone is fighting the same battle that you are. Also, you know, sometimes you just want to feel wanted and desired. Sometimes you want to feel what it feels like with someone new. Sometimes you forget about whether you're *ready* to do something, and you just let yourself *do* it.

"David," I say warmly. "Would you like to come over?

There is a brief pause. "Yes," he says. "Yes, I would."

• • •

"Oh, my God!" I am yelling. Or maybe I'm not. I don't know. "Oh, my God!" Oh, my God. Oh, my God.

God, yes.

Oh, God.

Oh. God.

Oh. God.

Oh. God. Oh God. Oh God. Yes. Yes. Yes. Yes. Yes. Yes. Yes.

YES.

And then I fall on top of him.

And he thanks me as he catches his breath. And he says, "I needed that."

And I say, "Me, too."

• • •

The next morning, I wake up to hear Thumper scratching at the door. He's not usually shut out of the bedroom.

I open the door and let him in. He jumps on David, smelling him, investigating. He's wary. David wakes up to Thumper's snout in his armpit.

"Excuse me, Thumper," David says groggily. Then he turns and looks at me. "Good morning." He smiles.

"Good morning." I smile back.

He rubs his eyes. He looks vulnerable without his glasses, as if I'm seeing the real him that not everyone gets to see. He squints at me.

"Do you need your glasses?" I laugh.

"That would be great. I just can't . . . well, I can't see them anywhere. Because I can't see without them," he says, as he feels for them.

I pick them up off the nightstand on his side. In doing so, I lean over him, my body brushing his. I can feel how warm he is to the touch.

"Sorry," I say. "Here you go."

He kisses me before he takes them out of my hand. The kiss is deep and passionate. I forget who I am, who he is, for a second.

He takes his glasses out of my hand, but he doesn't put them on. He puts them back on the nightstand. And he kisses me again, pulling me down on top of him. I guess the weirdest part about all of this is how it doesn't feel weird at all.

"Mmm," he says. "You feel good."

My hips fall onto his hips. My legs fall to the side. He moves his pelvis, pushing and pulling us tighter.

"Thumper," he says, looking right at me. "Get out of here, would you?"

Thumper ignores him. I laugh.

"Thumper," I say, "Go!"

And Thumper goes.

I melt into him.

At first, I am doing the things I know I should do. I am arching my back, I am grinding my hips, but somewhere along the way, I forget to do the things you're supposed to do.

I just move.

When I'm naked and underneath him, when I'm moaning

because he's doing all the right things, he breathes into my ear. "Tell me what you want."

"Hm?" I manage to get out. I don't know what he means, what he wants me to say.

"Tell me what to do to you. What do you like?"

I don't even know how to answer him. "I'm not sure," I say. "Give me some options."

He laughs and lifts my hips off the bed, running his hands down the length of me.

"Yes," I say. "That."

• • •

After David leaves, I go to my computer and open an e-mail draft. For the first time in a long time, I have something to say.

Dear Ryan,

How come you never asked me what I wanted? How come you never cared about what I needed in bed? You used to pay attention, you know? You used to spend hours touching me, finding things that made me tingle. When did you stop?

Why did it become easier for me to just satisfy you and then move on to something else? Why didn't you stop me and say that it was my turn? Why didn't you offer more of yourself to me? You never asked me what I liked. You never asked me my wildest fantasies.

David asked me last night what I wanted, and I didn't know how to answer him. I don't even know what I want. I don't know what I like.

But I can tell you that I'm going to figure it out. And I'm going to learn to ask for it.

If you come home, if we make this work, sex has to be about me, too. It has to. Because I remember what it's like, now, to be touched as if your pleasure is the only thing that matters. And I'm not going to let anyone make me forget again.

Love,
Lauren

My grandmother calls me from her hotel room later that day.

I pick up the phone. "Hey, Grams," I say. "What's up?"

"I had a thought."

"Oh?"

"About your problem, you and Ryan."

"OK . . ."

"Have you ever read Ask Allie?"

"What is that?" Good Lord, is she about to recommend an advice column?

"It's an advice column." Yep, she is.

"Oh, OK," I say. "Not sure about that."

"It's a really good one! This woman has the best advice. Last week, a lady wrote in about how she doesn't know how to deal with the fact that her son wants to become a Mormon."

"Uh-huh," I say.

"And Allie said that it's not about what religion he chooses but that the lady should be proud of having a son who thinks for himself and takes an active role in his spirituality. But she just said it so beautifully! Oh, it was beautiful."

"It sounds like it," I say. I don't know. I guess it sounds like it.

"Well, I think you should write to her!"

"Oh, no, no, no. Sorry, Grandma. I don't think that's for me."

"Are you kidding? I'm sure Allie would have something to say about it."

"Well, yeah, but—"

"Don't decide now. I'll send you some of her columns. You'll see."

"I can just Google it."

"No, I'll send them."

"OK, sounds good."

"You are going to be impressed with her, though. And maybe she could really shed some light on what you guys are going through. You might even be able to help people going through the same thing. I'm sure there are plenty of people your age dealing with the same challenges." She pauses for a moment. "I guess what I'm saying is that maybe she could offer some insight."

"Thanks, Grandma," I say to her. There is a small lump in my throat, but I swallow it down.

"Of course, sweetheart," she says. "Of course." She sounds as if she might be swallowing the lump in her throat, too.

I think we should throw Natalie a baby shower," Rachel says as we're hiking through Runyon Canyon the next Saturday morning. Thumper is, as always, leading the charge.

"Yeah, that would be nice," I say. "We should do everything we can to make sure she feels welcome. We sort of botched it the other day."

"Right," Rachel says. "We blew that one. But I do really like her. She seems awesome."

"I hope their baby has her coloring. Can you imagine? What a gorgeous baby that will be."

Thumper has stopped to smell something, and Rachel and I stop with him. We're standing off to the side waiting for him as we talk.

"You knew, right?" Rachel says. "He told you ahead of time?"

I can't look directly at Rachel until I decide what I'm going to say. I pretend to look at whatever Thumper is smelling, and in pretending, I actually notice that he's about to step in mud. I yank his collar, but he steps right in it anyway. Now both his front paws are covered in it. I should just come clean.

"Yeah," I say. "I did. He told me a bit before." I really feel like shit about this. Our family always spills the beans about everything, and this time, I kept the beans.

I watch as Rachel's face starts to lose resolve. She doesn't look me in the eye for a few moments. She stares at the gravel path beneath our feet.

"You OK?" I ask.

"Yeah," she says, her voice cracking and her eyes looking

forward. She starts walking ahead, and so I follow her, dragging Thumper along.

"You don't sound OK," I say.

"Why didn't he tell me?" she asks. "Did he say why he didn't want me to know ahead of time?"

What do I do? Do I tell her the truth and possibly hurt her feelings? Or do I keep yet another secret from her? I opt to split the difference. "I think he was afraid that you wouldn't take the news well."

"But why? I love Charlie! I'm always happy for Charlie. I'm always happy for everybody."

"I think sometimes we worry that you can't handle some of the love talk. We all have some sort of love life to discuss, for better or worse, in my case." I shrug. "But you know, you haven't been able to find a relationship, and I think . . . maybe . . . it's hard to . . ."

"I seem bitter," Rachel says.

"Yeah, a little."

"You know, it's funny. I swear, I don't even think about being single that much."

I look at Rachel as if she's trying to sell me the Brooklyn Bridge.

"No, I'm serious!" she says. "I really like my life. I have a perfectly fine job. I can afford to live on my own. I have the best sister in the world." She vaguely gestures to me, but it's clear she's not saying it to flatter me. She's saying it because she thinks it's true, and it's one of the things in her life that she's happy about. Ironically, that's even more flattering. "My mom is doing well. I get to spend my nights and weekends with people I love. I have plenty of friends. And the best part of my week is every Sunday morning when I wake up around seven thirty, go into the kitchen, and bake something completely new from scratch while listening to *This American Life*."

"I didn't know you did that," I say. We have stopped moving again. Our feet just sort of gave up on moving forward and instead planted themselves firmly in their places.

"Yeah," she says. "And to be honest, I don't really feel like anything is missing."

"Well, isn't that—" I start to say, but Rachel isn't done.

"But that's not how the rest of you all live," she says.

"What do you mean?"

"I mean, Mom always has someone. Even if we don't meet him and it's not as serious as she's been with Bill, she's always talking about meeting some guy."

"Right," I say.

"And Charlie is always dating someone. Or impregnating them, as the case may be."

"Right," I say, laughing.

"And you," she says. She doesn't need to extrapolate further. I know what she means.

"Right."

"That was part of why I was so excited for you to have time away from Ryan, you know?"

"Sure."

"It just seemed like maybe you could have my kind of life, too."

"Living alone?"

"Living alone and being on your own and finding your Sunday morning hobby. I was excited about the idea that I'd have someone to talk to and it wasn't always about boyfriends or husbands or girlfriends."

"Right." Even separated from my husband, I am still preoccupied with the opposite sex. Maybe not all the time. But still. On some level, my love life is a defining factor in my life. I've never been a person who had a career passion, really. I like my job at Occidental in part because it affords me a life outside of work that I really enjoy. I make enough money to have the things I need and want. I have time to spend with my family and, in the past, with Ryan. Love is a big part of who I am. Is that OK? I wonder. Is it supposed to be that way?

Rachel is quiet for a moment. "I just . . . I don't feel like I'm missing out on love, really."

"You don't?"

"No," she says. "Honestly, the problem is that I just feel like I don't fit in."

I never thought about it that way. Rachel just always seemed as if she was jealous or unhappy being single. I didn't realize that perhaps it was the way the rest of us considered her singleness that really bothered her.

"I want to meet someone," Rachel says. "Don't get me wrong."

"OK."

"But if that doesn't happen until I'm forty or fifty, I think I'm OK with that. I have other things I'm interested in."

"And if you don't have kids?"

"I don't want to have kids," Rachel says. "That's the other thing." She's never said this before. We don't talk about it that often, I guess. And I suppose I never asked her. I just assumed that she did. How hetero-normative of me. "I love kids. I'm excited for Charlie's kid. I'm excited for when you have kids. But you know? I just haven't ever felt that longing to have my own. I look at new moms sometimes, and I immediately feel stressed out for them. I saw this family the other day at the mall. It was these two parents and then these two kids. The boy was a teenager, the girl was maybe ten, and I just . . . I felt this very clear sense of 'I don't want that.'"

"Well, you might," I say. In my head, I'm thinking that she'll feel it once she meets someone, and then I realize, Jesus Christ, it's so ingrained in me that I can't get it out of my brain, even when I'm consciously trying to get it out of my brain. Marriage and kids. Marriage and kids. Marriage and kids.

"Sure," she says. "I might. But listen, you and Charlie, you want that normal family life so bad. You wanted it so bad you met someone at nineteen and never looked back. Charlie wants it so bad that he's going to marry a woman he barely knows." She shrugs. "I don't need it."

My sister and I are alike in so many ways, and it is that similarity where I have always found comfort. But the truth is, we are two distinct women, with two distinct sets of wants and needs. This basic difference between us was always there. I just never saw it, because I was never looking.

"I'm really glad this came up, actually," I say. "I'm happy you said all of this."

"Thanks," she says. "I think it's been on my mind for a while."

"I forget sometimes that you're not me," I say. "You seem so much like me that I just assume you think all the same things I do."

"We're still pretty similar," she says. "You know me better than I know myself sometimes."

"I do?"

"Yeah," she says, nodding. "I have an appointment with a bank on Tuesday."

"You do?"

"I'm looking into a small-business loan."

"For the bakery idea?"

She smiles, embarrassed. "Yeah."

I high-five her. "Oh, my God! This is such great news!"

"You don't think it's a disaster waiting to happen?"

"I really don't. I swear. I really think you would be so good at it."

"I was thinking of doing a line of sugar-free stuff, too, seeing as how the sugar cookies went over so well."

I laugh. "Finally, Grandma's cancer does us a favor."

Rachel nods and laughs. "I knew it would be good for something!"

We move on to talk about other things, but on the car ride home, one thing just keeps playing over and over in my mind. *You want that normal family life so bad. You wanted it so bad you met someone at nineteen and never looked back.*

I couldn't see it until she said it, and yet now it seems so blazingly clear that it's all I can see. It's amazing the things that have been written across your forehead for so long that even when you're looking in the mirror, you don't see them.

At home, there's an envelope waiting in my mailbox from one Mrs. Lois Spencer of San Jose, California.

Here they are, sweetheart. A few of Ask Allie's columns. Think about it. Love, Grandma.

She printed them out from the Internet and mailed them to me. I laugh to myself as I look them over and then stick them in a box of miscellaneous stuff. I tell myself that I'll sit down and read them soon. Then David calls asking if he can come over, and I say yes. I jump into the shower.

By the time I'm dressed and dry, I've already forgotten where I put the Ask Allie articles. They simply aren't on my mind. I'm not thinking about what advice I need to fix my marriage. I'm not reflecting on what my grandmother thinks of what I'm doing.

I'm not reflecting at all, really.

I'm starting to just live.

In January, I help Charlie move into his apartment with Natalie. The entire family goes out for a big Italian dinner at Buca di Beppo, the plastic checkered tablecloths and old-timey photos reminding us all of when we came here as kids, when Mom would order two extra bowls of pasta and tell us it was our lunches for the week.

In February, I help Rachel put together her business prospectus. I help her research possible bakery locations. I help her learn the ins and outs of applying for a small-business loan. She asks me if I'd be willing to cosign, and I tell her I can't think of another person I'd be ready to vouch for more than her.

In March, Charlie and Natalie decide to have the wedding at the house of one of Natalie's friends in Malibu. Their house apparently backs up onto the beach. I determine that Natalie must have obscenely rich friends. The save-the-dates go out. The caterer is hired. Charlie's only job is to choose a DJ. So that won't be done until June.

By the beginning of April, Natalie is in her third trimester. And my mom is struggling with how to handle her relationship with Bill. He thinks they should move in together. She does not.

And meanwhile, I sneak texts with David. I open my door to him late at night. We call each other when we need a friendly ear or want an understanding touch. I like David a lot, and I know he likes me. But he's still in love with the woman who cheated on him. And I . . . am in no position to be loving anyone. So we are good to each other and good for each other, and we are, essentially, that thing I've heard about from teenagers: friends with benefits. And there is something freeing about having sex with a man you don't see a future with. It's all butterflies and orgasms. There's no politics or unspoken words. And when he's going too fast, you just say, "Slower."

When Mila asks me if Ryan has been writing to me, I tell her the truth. "I have no idea," I say. "I haven't checked in months."

part four

MOST OF THE TIME

Rachel, Mom, and I have been planning Natalie's baby shower. When we asked Natalie if we could throw it for her, she seemed really overjoyed and flattered. We asked her what sort of theme she wanted or what she'd like to do, and she just said that she was sure she would love whatever we came up with. She tries so hard to be accommodating and kind, and it's really sweet, but sometimes I want to grab her by the shoulders and say, "Tell us the truth! Do you like the color yellow?" So at least we know.

Rachel, Mom, and I are sitting at this pizza place, trying to come up with a theme, but somehow the conversation evolves—or devolves, I guess, depending on how you look at it—into whether Mom should let Bill move in.

"I just don't think I'm ready for something like that," my mom says, as the waiter puts our pizzas on the table. The minute it's in front of them, both my mom and Rachel start damping their slices with napkins to soak up the grease. I just bite right into mine.

"You guys have been dating for a while now," Rachel says.

"Yes, but right now, on the nights that he doesn't stay with me, I miss him."

"Right," I say. "Which is why you would ask him to move in . . ." I'm speaking with my mouth full, which my mother normally abhors, but she's too focused on her own problem to notice me.

"No!" my mom says. "I like missing people. You know when

you call someone just to hear their voice? Or you wait all day until you can see them that night? If Bill lives with me, he stops being this person I can't wait to see, and he becomes the man who leaves his dirty dishes in the sink."

"But you can't sustain this part," I say. "The natural process is that the relationship becomes more serious as time goes on." Of course, there are exceptions to this.

"Yeah, or it fizzles out," my mom says. "I don't need a life partner. I'm not interested in a partnership. Someone to share the bills. Someone to raise children with. I did all of that, and I did it on my own. I make my own money. I pay my own bills. I want love and romance. That's all."

"But after a while, relationships become more about partnership and less about romance. That's just how it works. It's the nature of love. If you want to stay with Bill, he's eventually going to stop bringing you flowers," I say.

My mom shakes her head. "This is why I don't want to commit to Bill."

"Wait, what?" Rachel asks. "You are in love with Bill, right?"

"Right. *Right now*, I'm in love with Bill. And eventually, we will grow tired of each other."

"And when that happens?" I ask.

"We'll break up," she says, shrugging. "I want romance in my life. That's what I want. And I don't need anything else from a man. I've lived my whole life, or, I guess, my life since you guys were little, dating for fun. If the romance dies, I want to be able to leave, is what I'm saying. I want to be able to have that feeling again with someone else. It's how I've been living my life for a long time. It works."

"So you'd never get married again?" I say.

"You just chew 'em up and spit 'em out?" Rachel adds.

"You two are ridiculous. All I'm saying is that I'm not looking for all of the work that comes with a long-term relationship. The best part of a relationship is the falling-in-love part. And there's nothing wrong with admitting that."

"You don't think Bill's different? You don't think there is a way to have a long-term relationship that is worth the work?" Rachel says.

My mom starts to answer, but I jump in. "I guess if romance is your primary goal, then you can't let him move in. I get it. Romance fades. It just does. If you don't like the other stuff, then I get why you'd have to have an exit strategy."

"I still think romance and commitment don't have to be mutually exclusive," Rachel says, but she says it in a wistful way, as if she's pontificating on the theory of love instead of the practicality of it.

I think back to when Ryan made my stomach flip, the way he used to look at me. The way his attention was enough to lift me off the ground. The way it felt as if anything could happen.

What if I never have that feeling again? That sense where your nerve endings are so raw that you can physically feel everything that he says? That feeling where your head is light, your stomach is empty, and your legs are on fire?

Ryan is supposed to come home in three months so that we can decide if we want to spend the rest of our lives together. I mean, the goal here is to spend the rest of our lives together. If I really feel that romance doesn't last, if I really think that's true, am I ready to never feel that tingle again? Was I ever ready?

"Let's talk about something else," my mom says. "Lauren looks like she's about to cry."

"No, I'm sorry," I say. "I was trapped in my own mind for a second. But we should get back to Natalie's shower, right? What else do we have to go over?"

"Well, actually, before we get back to that, I just remembered that I need a copy of your social security card to add to my loan package as the cosigner," Rachel says.

"Oh, sure. When do you need it?"

"Thursday?"

"Yeah, that's fine. I'll find it. It's in my house somewhere."

"I am so proud of you," my mom says to Rachel. "This is such a brave thing you're doing."

"It's stupid, right?" Rachel says. She still can't fully believe in herself just yet. But I know she must believe in herself a great deal when she's alone, working out what to do. Because you don't go to the bank and discuss a small-business loan unless you're serious. You don't scout out bakery locations unless you believe in yourself at least a little bit.

"If no one ever did anything stupid, I wouldn't have you girls and Charlie," my mom says.

It's supposed to be encouraging, but Rachel says, "So you do think it's stupid."

And then she and I start laughing before my mom can defend herself.

"Oh, you two are such a pain in the ass," she says. "I swear."

My desk is full of clutter. I used to sit down and actually do work at this desk in years past. I remember when Ryan and I first moved in and we had the extra space, and I would make a big show of sitting down at my desk to do things because it felt so fancy to have an extra room for things like desks. And then slowly, I got over the desk and started using it as storage for stuff that didn't have a home.

I start searching through drawers for my social security card. It could be anywhere. I am not a person who labels files. One time, I labeled a file folder "Important Files." That's how lazy I am when it comes to organizing. I dig through the bottom drawer first, front to back. Oh, here is it. Here is my "Important Files" file. I open it, hoping to find the card, because, really, if you have an "Important Files" file, wouldn't that be a good place to have put your social security card?

I have my birth certificate. I have my diploma. I have my old student-loan contracts. The title to my car. I even have the court order for my change of name from when my mom changed our last names after our dad left. She changed them all back to Spencer, her maiden name. Until I was about six years old, we were Lauren, Rachel, and Charles Prewett. I look at the document for longer than I realize. My eyes are focused on it, but my brain is elsewhere. I'm momentarily mesmerized, thinking about the life of Lauren Prewett. Would things have turned out differently if I'd kept my father's name? Would I have met some nice young boy with the last name Proctor or Phillips in homeroom, the two of us seated next to each other thanks to the work of alphabetizing? Would my heart have held out for my dad longer if I'd kept his name? I don't know. There's nothing to know, really, because none of those things happened. But I'm thankful to my mother for changing it, for taking the time to go down to the courthouse and change our fates, for rightfully claiming us as her own.

I finish with the folder, and there's no social security card. I put it back in the drawer. I shuffle through the things on the top of my desk, and that's when I find Grandma's Ask Allie columns. I glance at them, and one or two words catch my eye. I find myself sitting back, putting my feet up, and reading.

One man's wife has been diagnosed with Parkinson's, and he's scared about how their life is going to change. He calls himself "Worried in Oklahoma."

A mother writes in to say that she and her husband know their son is gay, because he has told his two siblings. But he hasn't come out to them yet. She wants to know how to let their son know that he can be honest with them. She signs her letter "Eager to Be Supportive."

There's a woman who thinks her mother shouldn't be driving anymore and needs advice on how to broach the subject with her. She calls herself "Hoping to Be Gentle."

Allie tells "Worried in Oklahoma" that it's OK for him to be scared and to find people other than his wife to talk about his fears with. "Talk about them so much with other people," she says, "that by the time your wife is ready to talk about what scares her, you have answers. Above all else, find someone who can say to you, 'Me, too.'"

Allie tells "Eager to Be Supportive" that it sounds as if she's concerned that her son doesn't know she loves him unconditionally. "Don't be. You've spent twenty-three years unintentionally telling him this with every fiber of your being. That love has shown through everything you've said and done. Unconditional love is the freedom to follow your heart and still have a home. You have given that to your son, and now all you have to do is sit back, be patient, and wait for him to use it."

Allie tells "Hoping to Be Gentle" that she can try to be as gentle as she likes, but the underlying message is going to hurt her mother. But that hurt is necessary in love, because "if your family won't tell you the truth, who will? Be the daughter your mother needs. Be the daughter who does ugly stuff for the right reasons. That's where the deep, beautiful, mystifying love of family truly kicks in."

She's not talking to me or about me or with me or for me, and yet everything she says resonates. Allie is good. Allie is real good.

Mila comes into the office in the morning with a latte for me.

"To what do I owe this gift?" I say, happily taking it. I didn't get much sleep last night.

"They gave me the wrong one by mistake, so I took a sip, realized it was the wrong one, and they had to let me keep both," she says.

"Well, thank you," I say. "I needed this." The coffee is still hot in the cup, so hot that it's burned my tongue. I'm now going to have that annoying numbness for the rest of the morning.

"Up late?" Mila asks, her voice implying something salacious.

"Are you asking me if I was up late having sex with David?"

Mila laughs. "Wow, you really don't understand subtlety."

"I'd argue you don't understand it as much as you think you do," I say.

She hits me with the back of her hand. "So you were, then?" she asks.

"No, actually," I tell her. "I stayed up reading the backlog of posts from this advice columnist."

Mila's shoulders slump. "I'm bored now. I was interested when I thought you were getting laid."

I laugh. "You know, you never cared about my sex life when I was with Ryan. Now, with David, suddenly, you're fascinated."

"I'm not *fascinated*," she says. "I don't wanna know, like, what you guys *do* and stuff. I just like living vicariously through you. New love. The fun of sleeping with someone you're just getting to know. It's fun, isn't it?"

"Yeah," I say, nodding my head. "It is. It is fun."

"I don't have that anymore," she says wistfully. "And that's fine. I'm not complaining. I love Christina more than anything. I feel like the luckiest woman in the world to have her."

"But things slow down after a while," I say. "I get it."

"I mean, we haven't been together all that long. Five years is long, I guess. But not that long. It's the kids. Things slow down with kids. It's like she's not just this beautiful woman for me to explore and discover. She's my kids' mom. She's my partner raising them. It's . . ."

"Boring?"

"Yeah. And boring is great. I love boring. It's just . . ."

"Boring."

Mila smiles at me. "Right." She takes a sip of her coffee. "Hence why I need to get my thrills from your sex life, even if it is with a man. I can overlook that."

"You know," I say to her, my voice escalating to a wild idea, "you could write to Ask Allie."

"Who?"

"The advice columnist I've been reading. She's great. Oh, God, I was reading one last night, about this woman who can't get over the trauma of being mugged at gunpoint years ago, and Allie said the most beautiful thing—"

Mila puts her hand up. "I'm going to stop you right there."

I look at her.

"You sound like a loony."

I start laughing. I think it's because she said "loony." "I do not sound like a loony!" I say.

"Oh, yes, you do. You sound exactly like a loony." Now she's laughing, too.

"Maybe *you're* the loony," I ask her.

Mila shakes her head. "That's exactly what a loony would say."

"Stop saying the word *loony*, please."

Mila smiles and starts walking back toward her desk. "Enjoy your coffee," she says. "Loony."

Admittedly, I floated the idea to Mila in part because I'm considering doing it myself. I wasn't hoping to be called a loony, but maybe I don't care if it makes me a loony. Maybe.

April 18

Dear Ryan,

I'm considering writing to one of those advice columnists about us. That's how confused I still am.

When we started this, I thought that I just needed some time away from you. I just needed time to breathe. I needed a chance to live on my own and appreciate you again by missing you.

Those first few months were torture. I felt so lonely. I felt exactly what I wanted myself to feel, which was that I couldn't live without you. I felt it all day. I felt it when I slept in an empty bed. I felt it when I came home to an empty house. But somehow, one day, it just sort of became OK. I don't know when that happened.

I thought at one point that maybe if I learned who you truly are, then I could love you again. Then I thought maybe if I learn who I really am, what I really want, then I could love you again. I have been grasping at things for months, trying to learn a lesson big enough, important enough, all-encompassing enough that it would bring us back together. But mostly, I'm just learning lessons about how to live my life. I'm learning how to be a better sister. I'm learning just how strong my mother has always been. That I should take my grandmother's advice more often. That sex can be healing. That Charlie isn't such a little kid anymore.

I guess what I'm saying is that I've started focusing on other things. I don't feel all that desperate to figure us out and fix this. I feel sort of OK that it's not fixed.

That's not the direction this is supposed to go, is it?
Love,
Lauren

• • •

I read the letter over and over. I change a word here and there. I add commas and spaces. On some level, I think maybe I'm delaying the moment when I hit save, trying to make sure I want my words taking up space somewhere out there in the ether of the Internet. But I'm not willing to delete them. So eventually, I stop preening, and I hit the button. Save.

I get up and decide to go for a run. I put on my shorts. My sports bra. My T-shirt. My running shoes. I say good-bye to Thumper. I hide my keys under the doormat. I take off.

As my heels round the pavement, as my heart starts to pump faster, as my body wants to slow down and I push it forward, all I can do is think about what I wrote. Is it true? Do I not feel any closer to knowing how to fix my marriage? Am I not sure I want to?

I go home and take a shower. And I think about my letter. I make myself dinner, and I think about my letter.

If I mean what I wrote, then doesn't that mean that I have to face the idea of the end? Could this be the beginning of the end of *us*?

What would I do with my life?

I'm not sure what possesses me. It's almost an instinct rather than an action. I grab my computer and log into Ryan's e-mail. I don't know what I'm expecting to find. I guess I'm expecting to find that he has forgotten me. That he has moved on. That he doesn't think about me. But I look at the number next to his drafts folder. There are three more letters.

I open the folder. They are all to me. All from within the past three weeks. Ryan has started writing to me again.

• • •

March 31

Dear Lauren,

I had to get away from you. I had to stop writing to you. I had to stop telling you everything that was going on. I noticed how I was talking to you throughout the day, in my head, even when I was mad at you, even when I wanted nothing to do with you. I had to stop doing that. I had to stop seeing you as someone to talk to.

So I stopped writing.

And writing to no one, talking to no one, felt lonely. So I had to stop being lonely.

At first, there was Noelle. Noelle is a perfectly nice woman, and she was very sweet to me and very patient with my reservations about everything, but I just wasn't that into her.

And then there was Brianna, and that was fine.

And then I met Emily. And Emily is somehow different enough from you that she doesn't remind me of you but not so different that I feel like I'm dating the opposite of you on purpose. And because of that, I think I was able to stop thinking about you so much. I just started thinking about Emily. I don't mean to hurt you when I say this, but I looked forward to seeing Emily as much as possible, and I forgot about you. As much as a person can forget about his wife, I guess. I really felt like I was able to be present and engaged with her. We've even gone away together a few times, and each time, I've felt like Emily's boyfriend, as opposed to your husband.

And I just really needed that.

And then yesterday was her birthday. And I thought that maybe I should make her something, you know? So I made her Ryan's Magic Shrimp Pasta. Which didn't even feel weird. I know it was our thing, but I don't know. It seemed like a perfectly reasonable thing to do.

And I made it, and she ate it, and she said thank you, and then we went out to a bar with some of her friends. And that should have been enough. That should have been fine.

But I just kept thinking about the first time I made it for you, the way you gushed over it. The way you ate so much more than you should have and you almost made yourself sick. I kept thinking about the way your eyes lit up every year when I said I would make it. I don't think Ryan's Magic Shrimp Pasta was about you, I realized. I think it was about me. I think I thrived on your approval. It was like a battery that kept me going. I looked forward to your birthday as much as you did. And it was because I knew that on your birthday, I was the one who made the day worthwhile. It made me feel like I mattered. It made me feel like I was doing something right.

But Emily just ate the Ryan's Magic Shrimp Pasta and said thank you and wiped her mouth and asked if I was ready to go. She didn't get it. And this feels so silly to put into words, but it really felt like in not getting Ryan's Magic Shrimp Pasta, she didn't get me.

And it made me miss you. Not you, my wife. Or you, the woman who has been with me since I was nineteen years old. You. Lauren Maureen Spencer Cooper. I missed you.

And it wasn't a passing feeling. It was real. I truly felt there was a hole in my life and the only thing that could fill it was you.

I think this is working, Lauren. I think we're gonna be OK.

Love,
Ryan

• • •

April 3

Dear Lauren,

I drove by the house this evening. I didn't mean to. I had a dinner I had to go to in downtown, and I took Olympic back across town. I was listening to the radio. They were doing a piece about this serial killer in Colombia, and I was so fascinated I think I stopped paying attention to my driving.

When I got to the corner of Olympic and Rimpau, I should have gone straight, but my hand flicked on my turn signal, and I took a right, leading me to the wrong home. It was muscle memory. You make a right turn day after day after day for years, and . . . you know how it is.

I realized I had made a mistake just as I hit the stop sign on Rimpau and 9th, but it was too late. I was going to have to drive by if only to turn around.

When my car got up to our driveway, I admit, I slowed down. I saw the light was on. And then I noticed another car parked in the driveway. I heard Thumper bark. I swear I heard him. I came to a complete stop, I'm embarrassed to say, and I looked into the window a few seconds. I don't know what I was hoping to see. You and Thumper, probably. But what I saw was you and someone else. Someone, I'm assuming, you're dating.

I turned off the car. I actually turned the key and pulled it out of the ignition. I undid my seat belt, and I had my hand on the door handle. That's how close I came to walking into my own house and punching that guy in the fucking face.

But two things stopped me. The first was that I knew it was the wrong thing to do. I knew, as I sat there with my hand on the handle, that it was wrong and I shouldn't do it. That it would jeopardize everything. That it would make you feel spied on. I didn't want you to feel that way.

And the second thing was that I was supposed to be at Emily's in twenty minutes. And how could I explain to her where I was? How could I have explained to you why I had to leave?

I put my seat belt back on, I put the key back in the ignition, and I high-tailed it out of there. I ran through the stop sign. I almost slammed into someone when I hit the red light onto Wilshire. I was ten minutes late to Emily's, and when she asked, I told her I hit traffic.

So I guess what I'm saying is that I'm a hypocrite. And when I come home, we need curtains for the front window.

Love,
Ryan

• • •

April 17

Dear Lauren,

Charlie just called me and told me that he's having a baby? With some woman named Natalie? And he lives in Los Angeles now? And they are getting married?

I'm going to be an uncle, and I didn't know. I understand why you didn't tell me. I understand why you didn't call. I told you not to. I brought that on myself.

But I wish we could talk about this. I wish we could have talked about this. There's a lot to say, and you're the only one to say it to. Part of me thinks if I saw you today, I'd fall in love with you all over again. And another part of me thinks that I would feel something entirely different. Better, even. Because you're not just the girl I'm infatuated with, you're not the girl I just met. You're you. You're me.

This year has been a success, for me. I know it's not over. I know the hard part, getting back to a good place together, finding ways to make it work again, I know all of that is still ahead. But I am bursting with the energy to do whatever it takes. Does that make sense?

I'm ready to tackle this marriage. I was missing the energy before. And I have the energy now.

Love,
Ryan

• • •

I crumble to the floor.

In all of the possible scenarios, I always assumed the question was whether or not I would end up brokenhearted.

It never even occurred to me that I might end up breaking a heart.

"You have got to be kidding me." I am standing on Charlie's doorstep at eight fifteen in the morning, and that's how I open the conversation. As much as Ryan's letters left me in tears, they also made me furious at Charlie for calling him behind my back in the first place.

I slept on it. Well, really, I stewed on it. And when I woke up this morning, I was somehow angrier, even more convinced that I had been the victim of a deep and ugly betrayal. So I drove over to Charlie's house and rang the doorbell. He opened the door, and that's what I said, "You have got to be kidding me."

Now he's just sort of staring at me, deciding what to say.

"You talked to Ryan, I guess," he says, as he leaves the door open and leads me into the living room. His tone is defensive and personally disappointed. He's wearing chinos and a white undershirt. I'm interrupting his morning routine getting ready for work.

"Excellent work, detective," I say. Now's not the time to explain my hacking habit.

"Look, I had a very good reason," he says.

"You don't get to decide things about my marriage," I say. "Leave Ryan out of this."

"It's not about your marriage, Lauren. Jesus."

Natalie has been sitting on the couch, her hands over her swollen belly. She's wearing thin sweatpants and a sweatshirt. "I'm going to go into the bedroom," she says.

"I'm really sorry," I say to her, somehow able to extract the anger from my voice long enough to speak politely to her. "I didn't mean to ruin your morning."

Natalie waves her hand. "It's totally fine. I thought this moment might come. I'll be in the bedroom."

Charlie gives Natalie a look that says both *Thank you* and *I'm sorry*.

When she's gone, I lay into him again. "Do you have no loyalty?"

Charlie shakes his head and tries to remain calm even while I let my voice fly. "Lauren, just hear me out."

I cross my arms and frown at him. It's my way of hearing him out and finding him guilty at the same time.

"Ryan is the baby's uncle."

"Through me!" I say. "He's the baby's uncle because I am the baby's aunt. By blood."

"I know. But still. It's an important distinction, don't you think? Not just your husband but also the baby's uncle."

"So what?"

"So . . . look around, Lauren. Do you see any other men in my life?"

I don't say anything, I just stare at him.

"We have no brothers," Charlie says. "Just me."

"OK," I say, agreeing with him in order to push the conversation forward.

"And clearly no dad," Charlie says.

"OK," I say again.

"And Grandpa's dead," he says.

"OK."

"All of my close friends are back in Chicago. I live with my fiancée. I spend most of my time with her, at work, or with my mom and two sisters."

I'm still angry, but I can recognize that this is not a line of conversation I can really disagree with. "OK," I say, this time more gently than all the previous times. I shift my body language to be less confrontational.

Charlie looks at me for a while, considering something. I can see him start to get emotional. He lowers his voice. "I'm having a son, Lauren. I'm having a boy."

Thoughts fly through my head so fast I can't choose one and hold on to it. That's great news! My family will be so happy! I didn't know they were finding out the sex of the baby beforehand! I'm so excited to have a nephew! A nephew!

"I'm going to have a nephew?" I say to him. The anger has retreated; it no longer bubbles on the surface. Part of it is the shock of finding out something I thought I wouldn't find out for a few months. Part of it is that my little baby brother, who clearly feels he has so much to prove, is getting a chance to prove it.

"Yeah," he says. I can see his eyes get glossy. "What do I know about raising a son? About being a dad? I have no idea. I have absolutely no idea. I mean, I know I'm going to figure it out but fuck, talk about making it up as you go along. My son needs an uncle, OK? I know things are strained between the two of you, I get it, but Ryan has had my back since I was fourteen. He was the first guy I really looked up to. And . . . I want my son to know him. I want him to be a part of my son's life. To be honest, I need someone to call and admit to that I have no idea what I'm doing."

"You have me," I say. "You have Rachel."

"You two don't have dads, either. We don't know anything about dads. And I'm sorry, this just . . . this isn't a thing a woman can help me with. It just isn't."

"OK," I say. I mean, what else can I say? I don't think I was wrong for being upset, but I think it would be juvenile and selfish to continue being upset in light of all this. "I get it. I wish you had talked to me first. But . . . no, I get it."

"Well, I did wait to talk to you, really," he says. "Because there is something that I would like to do, but I want your blessing before I do it."

"Uh," I say. "OK . . ."

"I'd like to invite Ryan to the wedding."

"Absolutely not." It flies out of my mouth like a bullet leaving a gun.

"Please think about it."

"No, Charlie. I'm sorry. Ryan and I said, in no uncertain terms, that we are not seeing each other or speaking until we have been apart for an entire year. That year is up at the end of August. Not July. And I haven't spent the last eight months resisting the urge to call him just to blow it all early. He won't want to break the deal, either, Charlie."

Charlie looks hurt by what I've said, and I'm not sure which part, exactly, is more hurtful to him. Is it that his own sister won't make an exception for his wedding? Or that I said the only man Charlie looks up to probably wouldn't want to come? Goddammit. You know, when you marry a man, you marry his family, and vice versa. They tell you that. But they don't tell you that when you leave a man, you leave his family. When your husband moves across town and starts dating someone named Emily, he breaks your brother's heart, too.

"Just let me invite him," Charlie says. "That's all I'm asking."

"Charlie, I really don't want him there."

"This isn't about you."

"Charlie—"

"Lauren, did it ever occur to you that my wedding is going to have family pictures? That we are going to put them around the house? That Mom is going to have one on her mantel? And years from now, you're going to look at them and see the hole this year has left in the family? You're going to taint my wedding with your bullshit because you can't see past it right now."

"There is not a hole in the family," I say.

"Yeah, there is. Ryan isn't just someone you love. He's a part of this family."

"Well, no one else seems to have a problem with it except you."

"Wrong again. Mom misses him. Mom told me a few months ago that she had to delete his number from her phone because it was too hard not to call him and check in on him and make sure he was OK."

"Well, Rachel's fine with it," I say.

"That's because Rachel thinks only of you. But I bet if you asked her, she'd say she wants to know how he is."

I can feel my pulse begin to quicken and the blood rush to the surface of my cheeks. I am starting to grow furious. "I made him a part of this family," I say. "And he's a part of this family on my terms."

"I know that you want that to be true. But it's not. You don't own Ryan. You brought him into this family, and you asked us to love him. And we do. And you can't control that."

I try to think of myself in a similar position, but the truth is, I can't. I don't know Natalie all that well. She will be a sister to me one day, but that takes time. It takes history and shared experiences. We don't have that yet. And she's the closest I've come. I was never all that close with Ryan's family, so I don't miss them. I don't know how I'd feel if I was Charlie in this situation. I've never been Charlie in this situation. And maybe that's the problem. Maybe I'm so very much *me* in this situation that I cannot see anyone else or anything else. And maybe I should take that as a sign that I might be wrong. That is, of course, most often the reason people are wrong when they are wrong, isn't it? When they can't understand anything but their own point of view?

I start to talk, to tell him that I will think about it. I open my mouth with the intention of saying, *You're right. I should give it some thought.* But Charlie speaks over me.

"This is so stupid. You two are getting back together in, what, August? What's a few weeks going to matter?"

"I have no idea if we are getting back together at all! I don't even know if—"

"What are you talking about? You said in the beginning that was the whole plan. You spend this time apart, and you get back together."

"Yeah, and you told me then that people rarely get back together. Most of the time, when people separate, it's just a stop on the way to divorce."

Charlie shakes his head at me. "Stop this. You're being dramatic. I'm sorry I said that. I was being a dick. Listen, I want him there. And it's my wedding, and I really do think of him as the baby's uncle, as my brother. Isn't that enough? Isn't that important enough?"

I look at him, thinking about what he has said. Son of a bitch. Life is not just about me. Even my marriage is not just about me.

"Go ahead," I say. "Invite him."

"Thank you," Charlie says.

"No plus one," I say. "Please."

"No plus one," Charlie says, placing his palms up and out in surrender.

"If Ryan is the man you're closest to, who is your best man?" I ask him. I'm suddenly heartsick thinking that my little brother has no best man.

"Oh," he says. "I was going to ask Wally, back in Chicago. But I'm not sure he's going to be able to come in the first place. Natalie and I discussed not having a wedding party at all, actually. I think that might be what we do."

"Not Ryan?" I ask him. I'm so late for work at this point that it's sort of silly to try to speed this up.

"I know what I'm asking you by inviting Ryan," he says. "It doesn't seem fair to ask for more."

So often I am convinced that my brother is a thoughtless jerk, and so often he proves that the thoughtless jerk is me.

"It's OK," I say. "Ask him."

Charlie holds back a smile. He manages to keep his face serious. "I don't want to put you in any more of a weird spot than I already have," he says.

"It's fine," I tell him. "You should do it. He'll say yes. I know he'll say yes."

"You think so?" Charlie asks, letting his excitement show just a little bit.

"Yeah," I say. "He will."

We hug, and Charlie looks at his watch. "Holy shit, I'm late," he says. "You know what? Fuck it." Charlie calls out to the bedroom. "Natalie, are you able to take the day off?"

"What?" I hear from the other room.

"Could you take the day off?"

"Um . . . I guess? I was going to leave early for a doctor's appointment anyway," she says, her voice getting closer as she joins us.

"How about you?" Charlie says to me. "Can you take the day off? We can go see a movie or something?" Natalie is now standing next to him, her arm draped around his waist, her head tucked into his arm. Look at them. Look at my brother. A pregnant woman at his side.

"Oh," I say. I start formulating an answer.

"Wait a minute," Charlie says. "If you and Ryan agreed not to talk for a whole year, how did you know I told him about the baby?" Charlie's voice isn't the least bit suspicious. It's curious and lively.

But I feel as if I've been caught red-handed, the criminal in the interrogation room under the hot lights.

"I should get to work, actually. I'm already an hour late, and traffic is going to be murder. You two have a nice, romantic day!" I say. I'm already heading for the door.

April 20

Dear Lauren,

Charlie called me today and said he spoke with you and that it was OK with you if he asked me to be his best man.

What is happening in the world? I remember when he used to beg me to play Grand Theft Auto with him when you and I would visit on weekends from college. I didn't even like that game, but I used to do it just to get him to shut up. And the whole time, he would just talk about girls. The. Whole. Time. And he was so stupid about girls. It baffled me. For a boy living in a house with three women, you'd think he knew how to talk to girls, but he just had no idea. And so I told him about how I asked you out. I told him that whole thing about how I pretended that it was you who was asking me out. And how it's normal to be nervous, but you just have to do it anyway, because the girls are usually nervous, too, and they don't notice that you're nervous, and just stupid shit like that.

And now he's getting married and having a baby. With someone he really seems to like.

And you and I aren't speaking.

Thank you for saying it was OK. I miss your family a lot. That phone call from Charlie, it made my day. Hell, it might have made my year. This year has been so hard and so confusing, and when I heard Charlie's voice on the phone, it really reminded me of what I've been missing.

I'm looking forward to this wedding. If only because I know I'll get to see you again.

Love,
Ryan

Natalie is wearing a maxidress. She's the sort of pregnant that makes you want to offer your seat to her on the bus. Due in six weeks, she is glowing, but when you tell her that, she says, "It's sweat. Trust me. I'm sweating like the house is on fire."

I didn't tell anyone it's going to be a boy, so we stuck with yellow as the shower theme. My mother insisted on hosting it, and she's gone a little over the top. There are yellow balloons and yellow streamers. There are gifts wrapped in yellow. And a yellow cake, courtesy of Rachel. I think perhaps there is also an unspoken theme of ducks that I didn't get the memo about. The buffet table and the coffee table are covered in rubber duckies. Rachel even made a rubber ducky out of fondant and put it on the top of the cake.

"Guess it's more of a fondant ducky," I say when she shows us.

My mom laughs. "That's what I said, but she didn't seem to think it was funny."

"This cake is beautiful," Natalie says. "Rachel, I can't thank you enough. It looks professionally done."

I know that Rachel has baked this same cake five times, decorating it just this way, to be sure that she could do it. I know that she was up until the early hours of the morning getting the duck right. But she acts as if it was a breeze. "Oh, please," she says. "It's my pleasure." Rachel has on a cute short red dress with a square collar. She was wearing high heels for the occasion but kicked them off about ten minutes ago, well before anyone was even here. "Although I did take a picture of it for my portfolio." She's supposed to hear news on the loan any day now.

Mom comes out from the kitchen with a platter. "OK, you three girls will tell me if I've overdone it," she says. "But look! How cute, right?" My mother shows us a plate of cucumber sandwiches.

"It's not high tea, Mom," Rachel says. "It's a baby shower."

My mom frowns, but Natalie turns it right around. "They are adorable, Leslie. Really. Thank you so much. And my friend Marie, who is coming, is a vegetarian and always worries that there won't be things for her to eat. So it's perfect."

"Thank you, Natalie. I'm relishing this time before you feel as comfortable around me as my daughters do. This is when I still get compliments and not things like 'It's not high tea, Mom.'" My mother's impression of Rachel sounds absolutely nothing like Rachel and everything like Minnie Mouse.

Natalie laughs. "I really do like them, though!" she says.

"OK, Natalie," I say. "You've proven your point. She likes you best."

My mom laughs and puts the platter down and goes back into the kitchen to get more.

"Do you need help?" Natalie asks.

Rachel puts her arm out to stop Natalie from saying any more. "Relax," she says. "You're the pregnant one," she says. "We are the ones who should be offering to help Mom, and we aren't."

"Yeah, so don't make us look bad," I say.

Natalie laughs and sits down on the couch, crossing one leg underneath her and smoothing out her dress. "Well, since I have you two, I actually wanted to ask you a favor," she says. "As I know you know, Charlie asked Ryan to be his best man."

Rachel's jaw drops, and she whips her head at me. "What?" she says.

I shrug. "It's what Charlie wants. What was I going to say?"

"And you're OK with it?" Rachel asks. "How have we not talked about this?"

"It's fine," I say to Rachel. I don't want to get into it and complicate things in front of Natalie.

Natalie looks at me. "I want to say thank you for that," she says. "It has made Charlie really happy, and obviously, I'm not as well versed in the details of you and Ryan, but I would imagine it takes a big person to . . . just . . . thank you."

I nod at her. It's such a complex issue, with so many feelings involved, I fear that if I speak, even if only to say *You're welcome*, I'll start crying, and I won't even know exactly why.

"Anyway, Ryan is Charlie's best man, and it turns out his friend Wally is going to be able to make it to the wedding, so Charlie wanted him to be up there with him, too," Natalie says. "Which means I've got two spots on my side, and I'd love it if you two would be my bridesmaids."

"Wow," Rachel and I both say at the same time.

Rachel continues. "Are you kidding? That is so thoughtful of you."

"I know that it's short notice," Natalie says. "I wasn't sure what was happening with Charlie's side, but now that it's all settled, I really do think it worked out perfectly. I would love to have you two up there with me."

"Are you sure?" I ask. "I mean, our feelings won't be hurt if you have friends you'd like to ask."

"No," Natalie says. "I mean, I have people I could ask. I have girlfriends I love. But you guys are family. I love the idea of being a part of a big family. My family is just me and my parents. I'm excited to have sisters." Natalie tiptoes around the word *sisters* as if she's not sure that it's OK for her to be so presumptuous, and because of that, I feel the need to go overboard in letting her know that I absolutely do want to consider her my sister. That I want her to be a part of our family.

"We are excited, too!" I say, and then try to modulate my enthusiasm to seem less over the top. "Seriously, I feel lucky that Charlie has chosen someone so cool."

"Yeah?" Natalie says. "You'd be my sort of co-maids of honor, I guess. Since there isn't an official one."

"Works for us," Rachel says.

My mom comes back out with pigs in a blanket. "Check these babies out!" she says, laughing to herself. The three of us look at the tray and see that she's put food coloring in the "blankets." Some of them are pink, some of them are blue. "Since we don't know the sex of the baby yet. Get it?"

"So we are going to be eating the babies as an appetizer?" Rachel asks. I start laughing; I can't help it. Natalie tries to stifle hers.

My mom looks down at the plate, frowning. "Oh, no," my mom says. "Do you think people will feel like they're eating babies?"

"You guys are so mean!" Natalie says. "Leslie, they are great. It's a perfect baby shower thing."

"Mom, I was totally kidding," Rachel says, trying to take it back. My mom normally doesn't mind being made fun of, but today she's taking it at least a little bit seriously, and I feel bad about that.

She hasn't put the tray down. She's seriously considering not serving them. "No," she says. "It's weird. Shoot. I should have just left them not colored."

"No," I say. "Please. She really was kidding. It's perfect. It's just like those games where people melt candy bars in diapers to look like poop or bob for nipples, you know? Baby showers are supposed to be a little over the top. It's good!"

"You're sure?" my mom asks all of us.

"Positive," Rachel says.

Natalie nods her head. I walk over to my mom and put my arm around her. "Totally. You've done such a great job. It looks incredible."

"OK," she says, finally putting the tray down. "But I didn't get any nipples to . . . bob for. Is that bad?"

"No," I say. "It was just a suggestion. Is there more stuff in the kitchen? I'll come help you."

We head toward the kitchen, leaving Natalie and Rachel in the living room.

When we are out of earshot, I ask, "You doing OK?"

"Yeah," she says. "This is . . . it's a little stressful!"

"What can I help with?" I ask, standing at the counter, but it looks as if everything is under control.

"No, nothing," my mom says. "It's just . . . it's my first grandbaby."

"I know," I say.

"I always pictured myself throwing a baby shower for my first grandbaby."

"Sure," I say. "I can understand that."

"And I just figured . . ."

I wait for her to finish, but she doesn't. "You thought it'd be for me," I say.

It takes my mom a while to answer. "Yeah," she finally admits. "Which is fine. Your life is your life. I'm so proud of what you're doing with it."

"I know, Mom. But that doesn't mean it's not surprising. Or that things haven't worked out in a way that is stressful or confusing," I say.

"I'm so happy about all of this," my mom says. "I really am."

"But . . . ?" I ask.

"But," she says, taking the bait, "I don't know her. When I was shopping at the store and putting together the menu, I kept stopping and going, 'Does Natalie like olives? Does Natalie like cilantro?' I mean, some people hate cilantro."

"Yeah," I say.

"I just don't know her all that well yet," my mom says. "It's hard to throw a baby shower for someone you don't know that well yet."

"All that matters is that your heart is in the right place," I say. "Natalie is easy to please."

"Yeah, maybe," my mom says, staring at the plate of crab cakes in front of her. "Will you just go out there and casually ask her if she likes cilantro? I put some in the crab cakes, and some people just really hate cilantro."

"Sure, Mom," I say, just as the doorbell rings.

We can hear Rachel open the door, and a group of women's voices begin to chatter. The party has started. Natalie's friends and coworkers will start streaming in. The gift table will begin to pile up. Before you know it, we will be pinning the sperm on the egg and acting as if the Diaper Genie is the most fascinating object the world has ever seen. "You know, one day, it will be me," I say as I leave the kitchen. "And when it is, you can serve all the cilantro you want."

David is lying across my bed. His shirt is off. He's just in his underwear. We've been drinking.

It all started because David said he wanted to make me dinner, and he brought over a bag of groceries and took over the kitchen. And since he brought dinner, I figured I should open one of the bottles of wine that's been taking up space on the credenza. We each had a glass of red wine and then had another. And then another. And then we opened another bottle for some reason. Between the deliciousness of dinner and all the laughing, more drinking seemed like a good idea.

And here we are, stuffed and still drunk. We started kissing in bed. But his watch got caught in my hair, and we started to laugh. And since then, we haven't really recovered. We're just lying next to each other, both half dressed, holding hands and looking up at the ceiling.

"I think Ryan is going to want to get back together," I say to the air.

David doesn't move or look at me. He keeps his focus on the ceiling. "Yeah?" he asks. "Why do you think that?"

"Well, he said as much," I say.

Now he does shift toward me. "I thought you guys weren't talking," he says. David knows the deal. He knows the drill. At this point, he knows about the fights and the resentments. He knows about the lack of sex, the bad sex.

"He writes me letters sometimes," I say. I leave it at that. I don't feel like explaining it.

"Ah," he says. His hand is still in mine. He's starting to massage my hand in his. "Well, how do you feel about that?"

I laugh, because that *is* the question, isn't it? How do I feel about that? "I don't know," I say, and then I sigh. "I'm thinking that I'm not sure I feel the same way. Or, yeah, that's exactly it. I'm not *sure* I feel the same way. It scares me that I'm not *sure* anymore."

"Man," David says, looking back up at the ceiling. "I'm almost envious of you. I wish . . . God, I wish I could stop thinking about Ashley. I wish I could feel *unsure* that I love her or want her."

"It still hurts?" I ask, but I know the answer. I'm just trying to give him space to talk about it.

"Every day. It hurts every day. It kills me not to tell her everything going on in my life. And sometimes I just want to call her and say, 'Let's get dinner. Let's figure this out.'"

"Why don't you?" I ask. I roll onto my stomach, with my elbows out in front of me. Listening pose.

"Because," he says, his voice becoming animated and passionate, "she cheated on me. You can't . . . if someone cheats on you, I mean, the self-respecting thing to do is to leave that person. You can't be with someone who cheats on you."

Normally, I would agree with him. But it really sounds as if he's saying it because he's been told that's what he should think.

"I don't know," I say. "It was one time, right?"

"She says it was one time. But isn't that what all people who cheat say? Anyway, I'm not sure it matters whether it was once or a millions times." He turns over onto his stomach now, too. Our shoulders grazing each other.

"People make mistakes," I say. If I have learned one thing in all of this, it's that we're all capable of more than we think we are, for better or worse. Everyone has the potential to fuck up big when the stakes are high. "I threw a vase at my husband's head."

David turns to me. "You?"

I nod.

Yes, it was me. Yes, I am ashamed I did it. But it also wasn't me. That wasn't me. That person was so angry. I was so angry. I'm not angry anymore.

"The point is, everyone makes mistakes. And I have to think, the way you love Ashley, the way you talk about her, the way you can't get over her, I'm not sure that's all that common of a love. It might be the kind of love that can overcome this sort of stuff."

The fact is, I look at David, I look at how he yearns for his ex-wife, I look at how he is clearly unable to move on from her in any meaningful way, and I'm the one who's jealous. Not of her. Of him. I want to love like that. I want to feel as if I'm not OK without someone, without Ryan. But I *am* OK.

Things aren't perfect right now. But I'm OK.

That can't be good.

David and I keep talking. The conversation drifts in and out but always goes back to Ashley. I'm paying attention. I'm listening. But my mind is elsewhere.

I have something I need to do.

• • •

April 30

Dear Ask Allie,

I have been married for six years. My husband and I met eleven years ago. For most of my adult life, I have believed he was my soul mate. For most of our relationship, I have truly loved him and felt loved by him. But some time ago, for reasons that have only started to become clear to me now, we stopped being good to each other.

When I say that the reasons for this are starting to become clear, I mean I have realized that our marriage suffered from issues of resentment. We resented each other for things like how often we had sex, the quality of the sex we did have, the places we wanted to eat dinner, how we showed affection for each other, all the way down to basic errands like calling the plumber.

I've come to realize that resentment is malignant. That it starts small and festers. That it grows wild and unfettered inside of you until it's so expansive that it has worked its way into the furthest, deepest parts of you and holds on for dear life.

I can see that now.

And the reason I can see all of this now is that my husband and I recognized that we had a problem about nine months ago, and we decided to give each other some space. We agreed to a yearlong break.

The year is not over, and I already feel I have gained a great deal of perspective that I didn't have this time last year. I understand myself better. I understand what I did to contribute to the downfall of my marriage. I also understand what I allowed to happen to my marriage. When this trial period is over, I know I will be a changed woman.

The problem is that in our time apart, I have learned that I can lead an incredibly fulfilling life without my husband. I can be happy without him. And that scares me. Because I think, maybe, you shouldn't spend your life with someone you don't need. Isn't your marriage supposed to be the union of two halves of a whole? Doesn't that necessitate that they cannot be whole themselves? That they must feel as if they are missing a piece when they are apart?

When I agreed to this idea of taking time off, on some level, I thought I'd learn that it wasn't possible. I thought I'd learn that life without my husband was unbearable and that it would be so unbearable that I'd beg him to come home, and when he came home, I'd have learned a lesson about never undervaluing him again. I thought this was a way to shock myself into realizing how much I needed him.

But when the worst happened, when I lost him and he started dating other people, the sun rose the next morning. Life went on. If it's true love, is that even possible?

During our time apart, I've talked to anyone who will listen about my marriage. I've talked to my sister, my brother, my mother, my grandmother, my best friend, a man I'm seeing casually, and all of them have different ideas of what marriage is. All of them have different advice about what to do.

And yet I'm still lost.

So what do you think, Allie?

Do I get back together with the man I used to love?

Or do I start over, now that I know that I can?

Sincerely,
Lost in Los Angeles

I don't reread it. I know that I'll lose my nerve. I just hit send. And off it goes, into the nothingness of the Internet.

I come into the office and head right to Mila's desk.

"I wrote to her, the advice columnist."

Mila looks up at me, smiling. "Well, I guess I have to take back all that stuff I said about it making you a loony."

"You don't think it means I'm crazy?" I say.

Mila laughs. "I find it easier to define 'crazy' by what rational people do rather than my own preconceived ideas. You did it. You're a rational person. Thus, it is not crazy."

My head cocks to the side. "Thank you," I say. I really did think she was going to think I was crazy. I'm glad I was wrong.

"So show me this woman, this Ask Allie," she says. "I want to read up on her. See what you've gotten yourself into."

I take over her computer and type in the Web address. The page pops up. The question at the top is the one I read last night. It's about a man who has been cheating on his wife for years and feels he finally needs to tell her. Ask Allie isn't very nice to him.

"Don't read that one," I say. "Or, I mean, you can, but read this one first."

I pull up the letter she wrote to a woman who placed her daughter up for adoption years ago and now wants to find her but doesn't know if she should. I really like the part where she tells her, *Make yourself available, make yourself easily found, should someone try to find you. Be open, be generous, be humble. You are in a unique position in which you cannot require love and acceptance, but you must give it if your daughter seeks it from you. It may seem hard, almost impossible, to love without the expectation of love in return, but once you have figured out how to do it, you will find that you really are a parent.*

"Let me know what you think," I tell Mila, and then I head back to my office.

Twenty minutes later, Mila is at my desk. "How have I spent my whole life not reading these letters?" she says. "Did you read the one about the gay son? I lost it right at my desk. I was tearing up!" Her voice changes as she sits down. "So what if she reads your letter? What if she answers it?"

"She's not gonna answer it," I tell her. "She's probably not even going to read it."

"She could, though," Mila says. "She might."

"I very much doubt it."

"You wrote to her about Ryan?" she asks.

"Yeah," I say.

"Did you mention the year-apart thing? That could be a good hook."

"You sound like my grandmother!" I say. "I asked her if she thought it made sense to start a marriage over or if . . ."

"If what?"

"If I shouldn't just start over on my own."

"Whoa," Mila says. "That's even an option? You're thinking about that?"

"I don't know what I'm thinking! That's why I wrote her."

"How did you sign it?"

"Oh, come on, that's the most embarrassing part," I say.

"Give it up, Cooper. How did you sign it?"

I sigh and resign myself to admitting it. "Lost in Los Angeles."

Mila nods her head in approval. "Not bad!" she says. "Not bad at all."

"Get out of my office," I say, smiling at her. "Are you free for lunch tomorrow? I need a second set of eyes on a dress fitting."

"What kind of dress?" Mila asks, her hand on the doorframe.

"Bridesmaid."

Mila raises her eyebrow. "What are the wedding colors?"

"Um," I say, trying to remember what Natalie told me. "Coral and pale yellow, I think."

"Sort of like persimmon and poppy?"

"I don't even know what you just said."

"Like grapefruit and lemon?"

"Sure," I say. "That sounds about right." Whatever happened to primary colors?

Mila nods her head approvingly. "Your sister-in-law's got style."

For some reason, I am personally flattered by her compliment. Natalie *does* have style. And she's going to be *my* sister-in-law. I get to have another sister. Maybe one day, we'll be so close that I forget that she was once new and unfamiliar. Maybe one day, I'll love her so much that I momentarily forget she's Charlie's wife or my nephew's mom. She'll just be my sister.

Rachel, Thumper, and I are supposed to go hiking this morning, but for the first time, we truly cannot find a parking space. We circle around the area for about thirty minutes before we all lose our patience.

"Brunch instead?" Rachel asks.

"Sure," I say. Eating brunch is exactly the opposite of hiking, and yet it feels like the natural move. "Where to?"

Rachel pulls up a list in her phone. "Are you up for checking out a bakery?" In her off time, Rachel has been going to every bakery she can find in Los Angeles, trying to figure out what she likes and what she doesn't. Slowly but surely, this bakery idea has become a real thing in her mind. It's something that is going to happen, sooner or later. The sooner or later depending on a small-business loan.

"Absolutely," I say. "Am I headed right or left?"

"Left," she says. "I want to check out this place in Hollywood I heard about. I read about it on a blog, like, a year ago and never made my way over to check it out. Apparently, they serve high-end waffles."

"High-end waffles? Like luxury waffles?"

Rachel laughs, pointing to her right to indicate that I need to turn here. "Like cream cheese waffles, peanut butter banana waffles, bacon waffles. You know, trendy waffles."

"That sounds like a dumb idea for a restaurant," I say. "Because what if I want eggs with my waffles?"

"Look, I just heard that the space was really cool, and I want to see it. We don't even have to eat there. We can eat farther down the block. Just take this until you hit Melrose, and take a left, and then we're gonna take a right."

"Aye-aye, Captain."

"Don't say that," Rachel says. She turns to Thumper, who is waiting patiently in the backseat. "Why does she talk like that, Thumper?" He has no answer.

When we get to Larchmont Boulevard, I park the car along the street, and Rachel, Thumper, and I head toward the storefront, but we can't find it.

"What number did you say it was?" I ask her.

"I don't remember," she says, trying to find it in her phone. She looks down at the screen and frowns, and then she looks straight ahead. We're standing in front of a glass storefront with a sign, "FOR LEASE," written across it in big red capital letters.

"This is it," she says, disappointed.

"It closed?"

"I guess so," she says. She stares into the storefront for a moment and then says, "If Waffle Time can't stay in business, how am I going to stay in business?"

"Well, you're not going to name your place Waffle Time, that's number one."

Rachel drops her arms and looks at me. "Seriously, Lauren. Look at all this place had going for it. Look at the foot traffic here. Everyone stops and walks around Larchmont. Parking is fairly easy. There's a parking lot right there for seventy-five cents. Where else is there a lot for seventy-five cents?"

"Well, it's seventy-five cents for a half hour," I say. "But I see your point."

Rachel puts her head to the glass and peers in, cupping her hands around her eyes to better her vision. She sighs. "Look at this place!"

I do the same, right beside her. There is an exposed brick wall on one side. A long L-shaped counter, a cash register on the small end of the L, built-in stools on the long side. There is a white, faded display case on the back wall. It looks adorable. With a couple of tables and chairs, I imagine it was a really nice place to get a luxury waffle.

"I could do it here," she says. "Right? I could try to lease this place."

"Absolutely," I say. "Does it seem like something in your price range?"

"I barely even know my price range," she says. "But no, not really."

It's been a long time since I've seen her this drawn to something.

I pull out my phone and take down the number on the sign. "You can call," I say, a hopeful tone in my voice. "It never hurts to call."

"No," she says. "You're right. It doesn't hurt to call."

There are two types of people in this world. There is the type of person who, when faced with this predicament, takes down the number but never calls, already assuming the answer is no. And there is the type of person who takes down the number and calls anyway, hoping for a miracle. Sometimes those people end up in the same place. Sometimes the person who calls ends up ahead.

Rachel will call. That is the type of person Rachel is. And that's how I know that her bakery has a real shot. That, and I think she will corner the baby shower market with those fondant duckies.

Friday afternoon, David calls me at work and asks if I'm free that night. "I have a surprise that has landed in my lap, and I'd love to take you," he says.

"Oh?" I'm intrigued.

"The Lakers are playing the Clippers in the playoffs," he says, excited.

"Oh, interesting," I say. Dammit. He wants to go to a basketball game? "I didn't know you were into basketball."

"I'm not, really. But Lakers versus Clippers? Two L.A. teams against each other on their way to the finals? That seems epic. And not the way people use that word now. I mean, an actual epic struggle for the heart of Los Angeles sports fans. Plus, these are great seats."

"OK," I say. "Cool. Go, Lakers!"

"Or Clippers," David says. "We'll have to decide."

I laugh. "I suppose we should be on the same team for this."

"Might make things easier," he says. "So I'll pick you up at your place around six?"

"Sounds good."

When he shows up at my door at ten of six, the sun is out and is only now considering the idea of setting. The heat, which in only a month or two will become as oppressive as a straitjacket, is merely mild and soothing, like a sweatshirt.

We get into the car, and David starts careening through the streets. He navigates with confidence. I am tempted, when he turns onto Pico, to suggest he take Olympic. I stop myself. It's not polite.

And yet Pico gets us there much, much more slowly than Olympic would have. The traffic is aggressive and bumper-to-bumper. People are cutting people off, sneaking into lanes they aren't supposed to, and in general acting like jerks. By the time we are downtown, circling around the Staples Center, I am remembering why I don't go to the Staples Center. I hate crowds of people. I hate congested parking lots. I don't really care about sports.

David pulls into a private lot charging twenty-five dollars to park.

"Are you serious?" I ask. I can't believe it. "Twenty-five dollars?"

"Well, I'm certainly not dealing with the bullshit of trying to get into one of those lots." He points down the street to men with bright flashing batons and flags, offering parking for fifteen. Cars are backed up for blocks to get in.

I nod my head.

We get out of the car. It takes us ten minutes just to cross the street to get to the Staples Center. A sea of people, some in yellow and purple jerseys, some in red and blue, swarms past us.

David takes my hand, which is good, because I have no idea where I am. We make our way into the stadium, entering through what look like the main doors. We hand over our tickets.

The ticket taker, a humorless forty-something man, frowns at us and tells us we are at the wrong door. He says we need to go to the left, around the building.

David is losing his patience now, too. "We can't get in this way?"

"Left and around the building," the man says.

So we go.

We finally find the right door.

We walk in. We are told that our seats are in section 119, which is nowhere near the door we came in. By the time we find our seats, they are inhabited by two teenage boys in Clippers jerseys. We have to ask them to leave, which makes me feel like pretty much the worst person in this stadium, since these boys actually care about this game and I don't care in the slightest.

But regardless, we sit down.

We watch the ball go back and forth.

David turns to me, the stress finally leaving his face. "OK," he says. "Let's root for the Clippers."

"Sounds good. Why Clippers?"

David shrugs. "They seem like the underdog."

It's as good a reason as any. When they score, David and I jump up. When a foul is called against them, we boo. We cheer for the guy trying to make the halftime shot. We pretend to be impressed by the Laker Girls. We stomp our feet in rapid-fire motion when the announcer tells us to make some noise. But my heart is not in it. I don't care.

The Clippers lose, 107 to 102.

David and I leave with the flow of the rest of the stands. We are pushed into the people in front of us. I trip on a stair. We break away from the crowd. We leave the stadium.

The sun set some time ago. I should have brought a sweater.

"Do you remember which way we came in?" David says. "It was this way, right? After we came around the building?"

"Oh, I thought you were paying attention."

"No," he says, his voice strained. "I thought you were."

I realize then that between parking in a random lot and walking all around the stadium to get in, neither of us has any idea where we parked.

And that's when I think, *Jesus Christ. I've done all of this,*

I've spent all of this time, done all of this work, just to end up back here?

Because while it may not look the same as trying to find your car in Lot C of Dodger Stadium, it sure as hell feels exactly like it.

And then I look at David, and I think that if all roads eventually lead here anyway, I'd rather it was with Ryan.

May 14

Dear Lauren,

I broke up with Emily. It wasn't really a serious thing, but I thought it was better to be honest. I've been thinking about you and me so much that it feels wrong to have another woman in my bed. And it felt wrong to do that to her, too. So I broke it off.

I've been thinking about our future. I've been thinking about what life holds for us. I've been thinking of ways I can be a better husband. I made a whole list! Good stuff, I think. Stuff that is actionable. Not just things like "Be nicer" but actual ideas.

I was thinking one of them could be that we have one night a week where we eat some international food you like. For instance, every Wednesday, we go out to dinner for Vietnamese, Greek, Persian, Ethiopian, whatever you want. And I'll never complain. Because the rest of the week, we will compromise. But one day a week, we eat together at some crazy place you love. Because I want you to be happy, and you deserve to have tahdig or pho or a bahn mi sandwich or any of those other things. Also, I'll only make you go to the Chinese place on Beverly once a month. I know you hate it. There is no sense in going there all the time just because I like the orange chicken.

See, honey? Compromise! We can do this!

Love,
Ryan

Rachel calls me when I'm at work, and I have plenty of work to do, but I pick up the phone.

"It's out of my price range," she says. "I went to look at it, and it's perfect. Completely perfect. But it's too much money. Like, not realistic for me but not so expensive that it's outrageous. It's just enough to torture me."

"I'm sorry," I say.

"Thanks. I don't know why I called you to tell you that. I think I just . . . I got kind of excited about the idea? And then I thought maybe this whole thing was going to become real?" She's saying all of these things as if they are a bunch of questions, but it's clear she knows them to be facts. "Yeah," she adds. "I think when I saw that space, I saw it all in my head, you know? 'Batter' written in script above the door. Me with an apron."

"You're calling it Batter?" I ask her.

"Maybe," she says defensively. "Why?"

"No, I like it."

"Oh, well, yeah. Anyway, I think it just seemed real."

"We will find you something," I say. "We can go out again this weekend and look at stuff."

"Yeah, OK. Are you around Friday night, actually? I kind of want to go when they are closed and just peer in. I feel like a spy when I do it to their face."

I start to laugh. "I can't Friday. I have plans."

"With that guy David? I feel like I barely know this guy. You never talk about him," she says.

"Yeah, I don't know, I guess there isn't much to talk about."

The truth is that I asked him to dinner because I want to tell him I think we should stop sleeping together. It's not that I don't care for him or like him. I do. And the night at the Staples Center was frustrating, but that's not it, either.

It's that I need to figure out how I feel about Ryan. I have to make a decision about what I want. And I can't do that if I'm distracting myself with David. David and I aren't going anywhere. And while I've never minded that about us, it's time to start making some life decisions. It's time to stop playing around.

"But I can do Saturday night," I say. "I'll be free Saturday night."

"Actually, forget it," she says. "Forget it. I'm calling the bank. That's where my bakery should be. I'm gonna see if I can increase the loan. I want to lease Waffle Time."

"You sure?" I ask her.

"No," she says.

"But you're going to do it anyway?" I ask.

"Yep," she says with remarkable confidence. And then she gets off the phone.

I asked David to meet me at a bar in Hollywood. We've been having a nice time chatting, but I think it's important that I don't mince words.

"I think we should stop seeing each other," I tell him.

He looks pretty surprised, but he seems to take it in stride. "Is this because I acted like such a dick at the Staples Center? I was just frustrated because we couldn't find the car," he says, smiling.

I laugh. "I just . . . Ryan and I are supposed to 'get back together' soon." I use my fingers to suggest quotations as I say it.

"Totally get it," he says. He puts his arms up in surrender. "I won't look at you seductively anymore."

I laugh. "You're such a gentleman," I say.

The bartender comes over and asks us what we want to drink. I remember him from years ago. Ryan and I came here once for a friend's birthday party. Ryan ended up having a few too many that night as the group of us were huddled around the bar. Around midnight, I grabbed the keys and told Ryan it was time to go home. After we said our good-byes and were headed for the door, Ryan stopped short at the end of the bar. He belligerently got the bartender's attention and said to him, "Excuse me, excuse me, have you ever seen a woman this beautiful?" pointing at me. I blushed. The bartender shook his head. "No, sir, I haven't." I remember thinking then that I was the luckiest woman in the entire world. I remember thinking, after all these years together, he thinks I'm the most beautiful woman in the world. I felt like one of the ones who had it all figured out. Now the same bartender is still serving drinks here, and I'm breaking up with another man.

"So what about you?" I ask David after we order. "What are you gonna do?"

"Me?" He shrugs. The bartender puts down David's beer and my glass of wine. "I'm no closer to figuring any of this out than I ever have been."

"For what it's worth," I offer, "I think you should call her."

"You do?"

"Yeah," I say. "I do. From everything you've told me, she was heartbroken to lose you. You said she dropped to her knees and begged you to forgive her, right?"

"Yeah," David says. "Yeah, she did."

"And you, you're heartbroken, too. After all this time. I think that means something."

David laughs. "You don't think it just means I'm maladjusted?"

I laugh, too. "Maybe. But even if you're maladjusted, you might as well be happy."

He considers it. "You remember she cuckolded me, right? I mean, I'm a cuckold."

I laugh at the word and then shrug. "So you're a cuckold. I mean, that's the reality of it. You leaving her doesn't change it. Maybe it's not what you wanted. But it's what you have. And you can be a cuckold on your own. Or a cuckold with the woman you love." I smile at him. "You're the one who told me that it's nice when you can let go of what you thought life should be and just be happy with what it is."

David looks at me. He really looks at me. He's quiet. And then he says, "OK. Maybe I'll call her."

The bartender comes by and drops off the check at the table. "Whenever you're ready," he says.

Our glasses are half full, but I think we're ready.

"So should I take from all of this newfound wisdom that you know what you want to do about Ryan?"

I smile at him, taking my last sip of wine. "Nope," I say. "Still not a damn clue."

When I get home, I wait for Thumper to come to me, and then I sit with him on the floor. I'm not sure for how long. At some point, I get up and open my e-mail. I start to try to write to Ryan. But nothing comes out. I don't know how I feel. I don't know that I have much to say. I sit there, staring at the blank screen, until the phone rings, jolting me out of my catatonic daze. It's Rachel. I pick up the phone and put it through to voice mail. I'm not up for talking at the moment.

A few seconds later, she calls again. It's not like her, so I pick up.

"Hey," I say.

"Have you talked to Mom?" Her voice is no-nonsense and rushed.

"No, why?" I immediately sit forward; my pulse starts to race.

"Grandma's been admitted to the hospital. Mom just got a call from Uncle Fletcher."

"Is she OK?"

"No." Rachel's voice starts to break down. "I don't think so."

"What happened?"

Rachel is quiet. When she finally does speak, her voice is meek and embarrassed. She sounds as if she's in pain and yet ashamed. "Complications from acute lymphoblastic leukemia."

"Leukemia?"

Rachel is hesitant to admit that I have heard her correctly. "Yes."

"Cancer? Grandma has cancer?"

"Yeah."

"Please tell me you are joking," I say. My voice is brisk and almost angry. I'm not angry at Rachel. I'm not angry at Grandma or Mom or Uncle Fletcher. I'm not even angry at acute whatever-it's-called leukemia. I'm angry at myself. I'm angry at all those times I laughed at her. All those times I rolled my eyes.

"I'm not joking," Rachel says. "Mom booked us flights leaving tomorrow morning. Can you go?"

"Yeah," I say. "Yeah, I'll make sure I can go. Is Charlie going?"

"We aren't sure. Natalie can't fly. He may drive up."

"OK," I say. I don't know what else to add. I have so many questions that I feel lost about which one to ask first. So I just go with the one I'm the most terrified of. "How long does she have?"

"Uncle Fletcher thinks only a few days."

"A few *days*?" I thought we were talking months. I was hoping for years.

"Yeah," Rachel says. "I don't know what to do."

"What time is the flight?" I ask her.

"Seven A.M."

"Is Mom meeting us there?"

"Mom's at the airport trying to get a flight out now."

"OK," I say. "I need to find someone to watch Thumper. Let me make a few phone calls, and I'll just come over once I have everything squared away."

"OK," she says. "I'm going to check in with Charlie. I'll talk to you soon."

"OK," I say. "I love you."

"I love you, too."

Part of me thinks I should call Ryan. He should watch

Thumper. But I also know that I have so much going on in my life right this very second that adding that complication on top of it seems messy. I won't be able to give Ryan the attention he needs in the midst of this. It won't do anyone any good. So I call Mila.

"I'm sorry it's so late," I say when she answers.

"Everything OK?" she asks, her voice muffled and tired. I tell her about my grandmother. I tell her about Thumper.

"Sure, absolutely. We'll watch him. Do you want to bring him over now?"

"Yeah," I say. "I'll see you soon."

I pack up his food and his leash. I put on shoes under my pajama bottoms. The two of us get into the car. I'm at her front door before I know it. I don't even remember how we got here.

Mila invites us in. She and Christina are in sweats. We whisper, because the kids are asleep. I rarely see Christina, but I am reminded now that she has such a kind face. Bright eyes, big cheeks. She gives me a hug.

"No matter what, we are here for you," she says. "Not just Mila but me, too." Mila looks at her and smiles.

"I should be back in a few days," I say. "He is pretty well behaved. If you have any trouble, just call me."

"Don't worry about us," Mila says. "You just worry about you. I'll take care of everything at work. I'll make sure everyone knows you need some time."

I nod and bend down to rub noses with Thumper. "I'll be home soon, baby boy."

When I walk out of the house, knowing I've left my dog, it hurts like a pinch. I get into my car and start crying. The tears stream down my face, clouding my vision. I can barely see. I pull over to the side of the street, and I let it out.

I'm crying for my grandmother. I'm crying for my mom.

I'm crying for Thumper. For Rachel and Charlie and me. And throughout all of it, I am crying over Ryan.

I know I will get through this, even though it will be hard. It will feel impossible, and yet I will do it. I know that. But the voice shouting in my ear, the feeling pulling at my heart and constricting my chest, says that it would be easier if Ryan were here. It would just be that little bit easier to have him by my side. Maybe it doesn't matter if you need someone during the everyday moments of your life. Maybe what matters is that when you need *someone*, they are the one you need. Maybe needing someone isn't about not being able to do it without them. Maybe needing someone is about it being easier if they are by your side.

I pull out my phone and open an e-mail draft.

May 30

Dear Ryan,

Grandma has been admitted to the hospital with leukemia. She doesn't have much time. I keep thinking of all the times I made fun of her behind her back for saying she had cancer. The way we all treated it like some big family joke.

And I keep thinking that it would feel so good if you were here with me. It would feel so nice to hear your voice. You would tell me everything was going to be OK. You would hold me. You would wipe away my tears. You would tell me you understood. Just like you did when we lost Grandpa.

I'm leaving for San Jose in a few hours. We're going to spend her last days with her there. This kind of stuff is why I married you. I married you because you take care of me. Because you make things seem OK when they aren't OK. Because you believe in me. You know I can handle things even when I feel like I won't make it through.

I know that I can do this without you. I've learned that this past year. But I just miss you right now. I just want you near me. You bring out the best in me. And I could use the best of me right now.

I love you.

Love,
Lauren

I almost hit send. It seems important enough to actually send to him. But I don't. I choose to hit save. I put the car into drive, and I move forward.

part five

NOTHING COMPARES 2 U

The flight was fine. It was fine in that there was no turbulence or delays. It's a forty-five-minute flight, so it's not all that torturous. But it was awful in that all Rachel and I did was say, "I really didn't think she had cancer," over and over.

When we get to the hospital, my mom is waiting next to my grandmother's bed. Uncle Fletcher is talking to the doctor. Mom sees us before we get into the room, and she steps outside to prep us.

"She's not doing great in terms of energy," my mom says, her face and voice both stoic. "But the doctors are confident that she's not in much pain."

"OK," I say. "How are you?"

"Terrible," she says. "But I'm not going to deal with it until I have to. I think the best thing for all of us is to buck up. Put on a brave face. Use this time to tell her how much she means to us."

Because we don't have much time left.

"Can we talk to her?" Rachel asks.

"Of course." Mom opens her arm and directs us into the room. Rachel and I sit down on either side of Grandma. She looks tired. Not the sort of tired after you've run a race or the sort of tired after you haven't slept. She looks the sort of tired that you might be after living so long on this earth.

"How are you, Grandma?" Rachel asks.

Grandma smiles at Rachel and pats her hand. There's no answer to that question.

"We love you, Grams," I say. "We love you so much."

She pats my hand this time and closes her eyes.

We all stand around for hours, waiting for her to wake up, seizing the moments when she's lucid and smiling. No one cries. I don't know how we all do it.

Around three, Charlie and Natalie arrive. Natalie looks as if she could burst at any minute. Charlie looks haggard and stressed. He looks at Grandma sleeping. "It's bad?" is all he asks, and Mom nods.

"Yeah," she says. "It's bad."

She takes Charlie and Natalie into the hall to talk to them. Rachel goes with her. It's just me, sleeping Grandma, and Uncle Fletcher. I never have much to say to Fletcher, and now, when it seems there is so much to say, I'm still speechless. He is, too. After a while, he excuses himself, saying he's going to find a nurse. As much as I have nothing to say to him, I also don't want him to go. I don't want to be alone in this room. I don't want to face this alone.

I walk up to the chair next to Grandma that Uncle Fletcher just vacated, and I sit down. I grab her hand. I know she's asleep, but I talk to her anyway. I'm not alone in this room yet, I realize. She's still here.

"You know, I wrote to Ask Allie," I tell her. "I wrote to her about Ryan and me. You were right about a lot of the things you said. About how I could have avoided this year altogether if maybe I'd valued some things differently. And yet I think I needed this year. I think it was in me, and it had to come out, if that makes sense. I think I needed extra time with Rachel. I needed to be able to focus on Charlie. I needed to explore some other things. Or, you know, maybe I didn't need to do it. Maybe there are a number of ways I could have handled my marriage, and this was just . . . this was the way I handled it. Anyway, I wrote to Ask Allie about it. I asked her what she thought I should do. You were right about her," I say, laughing under my breath. "She's good." It's eerily quiet in the room, so I keep talking. "Ryan was here when Grandpa died. And I remember the way he just held me and somehow made it better. Can just anyone do that for you? Can you be held by just anyone? Or does it have to be someone in particular?"

"Someone in particular," she says. Her voice is rough and scratchy. Her eyes are still closed. Her face barely moves when she talks.

"Grandma? Are you OK? Can I get you anything? Should I get Mom?"

She ignores me. "You have that someone. That's all I've been trying to say. Don't give up on him just because he bores you. Or doesn't pick up his socks."

"Yeah," I say. She seems too weak to keep talking, so I don't want to ask her questions. And yet there is so much I want to learn from her. Her eccentricities, the things that felt so silly and laughable before, now seem profound and insightful. Why do we do this? Why do we undervalue things when we have them? Why is it only on the verge of losing something that we see how much we need it?

"I wasn't actually positive that I had cancer," she says. "I hadn't been to the doctor in ages. I kept telling your mother and your uncle that I was going." She laughs. "But I never went. I figured if I did have it, I didn't want anyone trying to cure it. A few times, I walked out the door, telling Fletcher I was going to see my oncologist. I didn't even have an oncologist. I was playing bridge with Betty Lewis and the Friedmans." She laughs again, and then she fades out for a moment and perks back up. "The doctors say this type is fast-moving. Most likely, I just developed it. You guys weren't wrong to make fun of me all those years I kept saying I had it," she says, smiling at me, letting me know she knew what we were saying the whole time. "I was ready to die, and I think that was the only way I could admit it."

"How can you be ready to die?"

"Because my husband is gone, Lauren," she says. "I love you all so much. But you don't need me anymore. Look at all of you. Your mom is doing so well. Fletcher is fine. You three kids are doing great."

"Well . . ."

"No, you are," she says, patting my hand. "But I miss my mom," she says. "I miss my dad. I miss my big sister. I miss my best friend. And I miss my husband. I've lived too long without him now."

"But you were doing OK," I say. "You were getting out of bed. You were making a life without him."

My grandmother gently shakes her head. "Just because you can live without someone doesn't mean you want to," she says.

The words bang around in my brain, knocking into one another, bouncing off the edges of my mind, but they keep rearranging themselves in the same order.

I don't say anything back. I look at her and squeeze her hand. I often think of my grandmother as the old lady at the dinner table. But she's seen generations. She was a child once. She was a teenager. A newlywed. A mother. A widow.

"I'm sorry this has been so hard," I say. "I never thought of how difficult it must have been for you without Grandpa. It's a hard life."

"No, sweetheart, it's not a hard life. I'm just done living."

When she says it, she's also done talking. She falls back asleep, holding my hand. I rest my chin on her arm and watch her. Eventually, Natalie comes back in, needing to sit down.

"It's hard to stay on my feet so long," she says. "It's also hard to sit still for a long time. Or lie down for too long. Or eat. Or not eat. Or breathe."

I laugh. "Is this such a good idea?" I ask her. "I mean, you're due in, like, days, right?"

"I'm due Thursday," she says. Five days away. "But it was never a question. We had to come. This is where we need to be. I'd be uncomfortable sitting at home, you know? This way . . . this is better."

"Can I get you anything?" I ask her. "Ice chips?"

"You know I'm not actually in labor, right?" Natalie laughs at me, and I laugh back.

"Fair enough!" I say. It wasn't when she said she needed to be here for Grandma that she became a sister to me. It was when she made fun of me for offering ice chips. Big gestures are easy. Making fun of someone who's just trying to help you, that's family.

Charlie joins us. Uncle Fletcher comes in with a bag of Doritos. I don't even know if he went to get a nurse. Mom and Rachel come in. Rachel has clearly been crying. I look at her and see the red in her eyes. I give her a hug.

We stand around. We sit. We wait. I'm not exactly sure what we can do to make any of this better. Sometimes we are talking. Sometimes we are quiet. There are too many of us in this small room, and so we take turns walking out into the hall, walking down to the vending machines, getting a glass of water. Nurses come in and out. They change fluids. The doctor comes in and answers our questions. But really, there aren't many questions to ask. Questions are for when you think there is a way to save someone.

I feel a knot start to form in my throat. It gathers strength as it moves up to the surface. I excuse myself. I go out into the hall.

I put my back against the wall. I slide down to the floor. I imagine Ryan sitting next to me. I imagine him rubbing my back, the way he did when my grandfather died. I imagine him saying, *She's going to a better place. She's OK*. I imagine the way my grandfather might have done this for my grandmother when she lost her own mom or her own grandmother. I imagine my grandmother sitting where I am now, my grandfather kneeling beside her, telling her all the things I want to be told. Holding her the way that only someone in particular can hold you. When I'm her age, when I'm lying in a hospital bed, ready to die, whom will I be thinking of?

It's Ryan. It's always been Ryan. Just because I can live without him doesn't mean I want to.

And I don't. I don't want to.

I want to hear his voice. The way it is rough but sometimes smooth and almost soulful. I want to see his face, with his stubble from never shaving down to the skin. I want to smell him again. I want to hold the roughness of his hands. I want to feel the way they envelop mine, dwarfing them, making me feel small.

I need my husband.

I'm going to call him. I don't care about the pact we made. I don't care about the messiness of it. I just need to hear his voice. I need to know that he's OK. I stand up and pull my phone out of my pocket. I don't have any service. So I walk around the floor, trying to get a bar or two. Nothing.

"Excuse me?" I ask at the nurses' station. "Where can I get cell service?"

"You'll have to go outside," she says. "Once you get out the front doors, you should be OK."

"Thanks," I say, and I walk to the elevators. I hit the button. It lights up, but the elevator doesn't come. I hit it again and again. I've waited this long to call Ryan, and now, suddenly, I must talk to him this second. The urge has overtaken me. I need to ask him to move back home. I need to tell him I love him. He has to know right now.

Finally, the elevator *dings*. I get in. I press the ground floor. The elevator drops quickly. It's so quick that my stomach doesn't fall at the same pace as my feet. I'm relieved when I touch ground. The doors open. I walk through the lobby. I walk through the front glass doors and step outside. It's a hot, balmy day. It seems so cloudy in the hospital that I've forgotten that it's actually very sunny and bright. I look at my phone. Full service.

It's loud out here in the front of the hospital. Cars are zooming by. Ambulances are pulling in and out. It occurs to me that I am not the only one losing someone right now. Natalie isn't the only one about to have a baby, either. Charlie's not the only man about to become a father. My mother isn't the only one about to lose her last parent. We are a family of people going through all the things people go through every day. We are not special. This hospital doesn't exist for us. I'm not the only woman about to call her husband and ask him to come home. I don't know why it feels good to know that. But it does. I'm not alone. There are millions of me.

A cab pulls up to the sidewalk, and a man gets out. He has a backpack. He shuts the cab door and turns to face me.

It's Ryan.

Ryan.

My Ryan.

He looks exactly the same as when I left him at our house ten months ago. His hair is the same length. His body looks the same. It's so familiar. Everything about him is familiar. The way he walks. The way he shuffles the backpack onto his shoulders.

I stand still, staring right at him. I can barely move. I'm not sure when it happened, but I have dropped my phone.

He walks toward the sliding doors and then stops once he sees me. His eyes go wide. I know him so well that I know what he's thinking. I know what he's going to do next.

He runs toward me and picks me up, grabbing me, clutching me.

"I love you," he says. He has started to cry. "I love you, Lauren, I love you so much. I've missed you. God, I've missed you."

My face hasn't changed. I'm still stunned. My arms are wrapped around him. My legs are wrapped around him. He puts me down and kisses me. When his lips touch mine, my heart burns. It's like someone lit a match in my chest.

How did he know I needed him? How did he know to find me?

He wipes my tears away. Tears I didn't even know were on my face. He's so gentle about it, so loving, that I wonder how I was able to wipe away my own tears all these past months. In an instant, I have forgotten how to live without him, now that he is here.

"How did you know?" I say. "How did you know?"

He looks me in the eye, preparing me. "Don't be mad," he says. His tone is playful, but the underlying message is serious.

"OK," I say. "I won't." I mean it. Whatever brought him here is a blessing. Whatever brought him here was right to do it.

"I've been reading your e-mail drafts."

I drop to the ground.

I laugh so hard that I lose control of myself. I laugh past the point where my abdomen aches and my back hurts. And because I'm laughing, Ryan starts laughing. And now we're both on the sidewalk laughing. His laugh makes mine seem funnier. And now I'm laughing simply because I'm laughing. I can't stop. And I don't want to stop. And then I see my phone, busted up and broken, from when I dropped it. And that seems hilarious. It's all so perfectly, wonderfully, amazingly, beautifully hilarious, isn't it? When did life get so fucking funny?

"Why are we laughing?" Ryan says, in between breaths.

So it turns out this is how I confess. This is how I tell him what I've done. "Because I've been reading yours, too," I say.

He cackles wildly. He's laughing at me and with me and for me. People are walking by and looking at us, and for the first time in my life, I really don't care what they think. This moment is too intoxicating. It has such a strong hold on me that nothing can bring me back to earth until I'm ready.

When we finally do get control of ourselves, our eyes are wet, our heads are light. I start to sigh loudly, the way people do when they are recovering from fits of laughter. I try to get control of myself, like a pilot landing a plane, slow and steady, readying to hit solid ground. Except instead of feeling the world under my feet, I take off again at the last minute. My sighs turn into tears. Laughing and crying are so intrinsically tied together, spun of the same material, that it's hard to tell one from the other sometimes. And it's easier than you think to go from being so happy you could cry to so devastated you could laugh.

The weeping becomes sobbing, and Ryan puts his arms around me. He holds me tight, right here on the sidewalk. He rubs my back, and when I start to wail, he says, "It's OK. It's OK."

I look at his left hand as it holds mine. He has his wedding ring on.

Ryan and I get up off the sidewalk slowly. He grabs his bag. He picks up the pieces of my dropped cell phone and puts it back together.

"We might need to get you a new phone," he says. "This one appears to have taken a beating."

He grabs my hand as we walk into the hospital. We join the group of people waiting at the bank of elevators. When an elevator finally arrives, all of us cram into it, pushing against one another, spreading out against the three walls. Ryan never lets go of my hand. He squeezes it tight. He holds on for dear life. Both of our hands are sweating into each other. But he never lets go.

When we get to the eighth floor, I lead us off the elevator, and standing in front of us, ostensibly waiting for a down elevator, is Rachel.

"Where have you been?" Rachel asks. "I've been looking all over for you. I called you four times."

I start to answer, but Ryan answers for me. "Her phone is broken," he says, showing Rachel the pieces.

Rachel stares at him, her eyes fixated on him, trying to piece together why seeing him in front of her feels as if it makes perfect sense and yet doesn't make any sense at all. "Um . . ." she says. "Hi, Ryan."

He moves toward her and hugs her. "Hey, Rach. I've missed you. I came as soon as I heard."

Ryan's back is facing me, as Rachel's face is in my direct eye line. She mouths, *Is this OK?* half pointing to Ryan's back.

I give her a thumbs-up. That's all she needs. She just needs a thumbs-up. If I'm thumbs-up, she's thumbs-up. "I'm so glad to see you!" she says. She turns on the charm as if it has a switch, but it's real. She's being entirely genuine.

"Me, too," he says. "Me, too."

"We've missed you around these parts," Rachel says, giving him a sisterly light punch to the arm.

"You don't even know the half of it," he says. "What can I do? How can I help now that I'm here?"

"Well," Rachel says, looking at me now, "we've had a slight hiccup."

"Hiccup?" I say.

"Natalie and Charlie ran down to prenatal."

"Oh," I say.

"When is she due?" Ryan says. "It's soon, right?"

"Thursday," I say.

"Right," Rachel says. "Well, she thinks she has something called Braxton-Hicks."

"What is Braxton-Hicks?" Ryan and I both say at the same time. It's muscle memory, the way we can function as one unit so easily. It's such second nature to be two halves of a whole that after months of not speaking, we are now speaking as one.

"I don't know. Mom explained it. It's something where it seems like you're in labor but you're probably not."

"*Probably* not?" I ask.

"No," Rachel says. "I mean, she's not. But they thought it was best to address it. Apparently, the contractions feel just like real contractions."

"So it's painful?" Ryan says.

Rachel nods and tries not to laugh.

"What?" I ask.

"It's not funny," Rachel says. "It's totally not."

"But?"

"But when the first one came, Natalie grabbed her stomach and said, 'Holy Satan, fuck me.' Even Mom was laughing."

I start laughing along with Rachel. Multiple elevators have come and gone at this point, and we just continue to stand here.

"You guys are mean," Ryan says.

I start to defend myself, but Rachel intervenes. "No, it's just funny because Natalie is the nicest person I've ever met. Truly. When she said it, Mom laughed so hard she blew a huge snot bubble."

I start laughing again; Ryan does, too. My mother has appeared right behind Rachel.

"Rachel Evelyn Spencer!"

Rachel looks at me and rolls her eyes. "Mom heard me, huh?"

I nod.

"Sorry, Mom," she says, turning around.

"Never mind that," my mom says, her face growing serious. "We have a slight hiccup."

"Yeah, Rachel told us," I say.

My mom's line of sight focuses in on Ryan and then my hand, which is still holding his after all this time. "Good Lord, this is all just too much," she says. She sits down in one of the chairs along the hall and puts her head in her hands. "It's not Braxton-Hicks," she says. "Natalie is in labor."

"Please tell me you're joking," Rachel says.

"No, Rachel, I'm not joking. And this is a good thing, remember? We want this baby born."

"No, I know," she says, reprimanded. "I just mean it's a lot at once."

"Can I do anything?" Ryan asks.

My mom looks at him and stands up. She hugs him tight.

She hugs him the way only a mother can hug. It's not a mutual hug, like Rachel and Ryan had. My mother is hugging. Ryan is being hugged. "I'm just so glad to see your face, sweetheart," she says. "So glad to see your face."

Ryan looks at her for a moment, and I think he might lose it. He might actually start crying. But he changes course. "I missed you, Leslie."

"Oh, honey, we all missed you."

"How is Grandma Lois doing?" he asks. "Can I see her?"

"She's sleeping at the moment," my mom says. "I think we should split up. Some people need to go be with Natalie and Charlie, and the rest of us need to be with Grandma."

It's an impossible choice, isn't it? Do you want to be there for the last moments of one life or the first moments of another? Do you honor the past or ring in the future?

"I can't do this," my mom says. "I can't choose. My grandbaby or my mother?"

"You don't have to choose," I say. "Between me, Ryan, Rachel, and Fletcher, we've got everything. You can go back and forth."

"I suppose I'm going to get stuck with Uncle Fletcher?" Rachel says.

I look at her. The look on my face is an apology and a plea.

"Fine," she says. "Everyone has a life event but me. So I'll just go watch Grandma with Uncle Fletcher."

"Thank you," I say.

"When the baby is born, please come get me. Please? Ryan? Will you come get me? Switch with me or something?"

"Absolutely," he says.

"I'll go with you," Mom says to Rachel. "Keep us posted, please," she says to Ryan and me.

"OK," I say. "You got it."

"If she wakes up," Ryan chimes in, "tell her I'm here?"

"Are you kidding?" Mom says. "I don't know if we could keep the news in if we tried!"

Ryan smiles as I hit the elevator down button, and then I hit the up button. I don't know where we're going.

"Mom?" I call out.

She turns around.

"What floor?"

"Five."

The down elevator *dings*. It's here. Here we go. We have been chosen to ring in the future.

It turns out that ringing in the future is not like New Year's Eve when you can count down from ten until the ball drops. Ringing in the future is a lot of waiting. It's a lot of sitting in uncomfortable chairs and walking back and forth to the vending machine. It's a lot of checking regularly with Charlie but not staying in the room itself.

"She's at three centimeters," Charlie says, when we find their room. He's talking to us while looking at Natalie, and it's clear he assumes we are Mom.

"You OK, Natalie?" I ask. She looks like crap. I mean, she looks beautiful, because beautiful people are beautiful even when they look like crap, but all the signs for looking like crap are there. Her hair is disheveled, her face is flushed. She's clearly been crying. And yet, somehow, she's entirely happy.

"Yep," she says. "I'm good. Just don't ask me during a contraction." She looks up at me and sees a strange man standing beside me. Admittedly, I should have thought about the fact that Ryan is a stranger and Natalie is in a hospital gown on a bed with stirrups.

"Uh . . ." she says, looking at him.

Charlie follows her eyes and turns around. His face lights up as if a lightbulb has just gone on above his head. "Ryan!" He steps up, dropping Natalie's hand, and gives Ryan a bro hug. There is a lot of back patting.

"Hey, Charlie!" Ryan says. When they are done hugging, Charlie stands next to him, and Ryan keeps his hand on Charlie's shoulder for just a second longer than a friend would.

They are closer than friends. Charlie starts to introduce Ryan to Natalie, but she starts cringing and gasping for air. Charlie runs to her. He's so quick it looks instinctual. This is a guy my mom has to beg to help with the dishes, but the minute Natalie is in pain, he's there. He's supporting her. Helping her. Being there for her.

"Can I do anything?" I ask. I am hesitant to offer ice chips again, but she did say that they were appropriate for labor. "Ice chips?"

Natalie laughs for a moment through her pain. It is, perhaps, the best laugh I've ever gotten in my entire life.

"Yeah," Charlie says, his hand being squeezed. "Ice chips."

Ryan and I leave to find some. The nurse tells us there is an ice machine at the end of a very long hall. We start walking.

"So I read about this guy David," Ryan says. "Is David still a . . . still a thing?"

"No." I shake my head. "No, not a thing."

"I want to kill him," Ryan says, smiling. It's a dangerous smile. "You know that, right? I've wanted to kill him for months. I sometimes dream about it. Notice I didn't call them nightmares." Our shoes squeak on the hospital floor.

"I'm not too fond of Emily, either," I say. For the first time in months, I allow myself to feel the rage I had when I found out he was seeing other women. I can feel it once again, the way it rises to the surface like a flotation device. The way it keeps bouncing back no matter how hard you push it down.

"Emily never held a candle to you," he says, when we finally get to the ice machine.

I grab a cup and put it underneath the machine. I could say more. I could ask more. But I decide to leave it at that. The machine grumbles, but it spits nothing out. Ryan slams the side of it, throwing his whole body against it. Chips start to flow out into the cup.

We walk back to Charlie and Natalie's room and hand Charlie the ice chips. He thanks us, and even though Natalie appears to no longer be in pain, I figure it's best if Ryan and I go to the waiting room.

"You'll come get us if you need anything?" I ask Charlie, and he nods.

Ryan makes a fist and gives Charlie a pound. "Good luck," he says.

The waiting room is mostly empty, save for a new grandparent or two. So we take a seat in the middle by the wall. Sometimes we talk about a lot of things. Sometimes we don't say anything. Sometimes we are quiet for a long time, and then the conversation takes off again when one of us says something like "I can't believe you don't like Persian food" or "I can't believe you bought me that beard trimmer to get me to shave my pubes. Definitely the most embarrassing thing I've ever read. I read that, and I literally walked straight into the bathroom and trimmed them." Ryan smiles, laughing. He gives a fake shiver. "Mortifying."

"I'm sorry," I say. "I honestly did not think you would ever read that."

"No, but it's good I did, right? A little pinch of embarrassment at first, but now I know. And henceforth my nether regions will be squeaky clean."

I look down at the ground. The hospital carpet is a pattern of diamonds. Diamond after diamond after diamond. I unfocus my eyes a bit and realize that if you look at it a different way, it's a large series of Xs. Or Ws.

"I think if I've learned anything about how to . . . fix this," I say, "it's that I really need to work on telling you what I want."

"Yeah," he says. "Same here. That's a big one for me. I was just going along with what I thought you wanted all the time, and after a while, I think I just grew pissed off about it."

"Yeah," I say, nodding my head. "I assumed that the way to be a good partner to you was compliance."

"Yes!" he says, eager in agreement.

"And so I never asked for the things I needed."

"You expected me to know them."

"Yeah," I say. "And when you didn't know them, or you didn't guess them, I just assumed you didn't care. That I didn't matter. That you were choosing you over me."

"I know exactly what you mean," he says. "Imagine if I had just told you I hate international food."

"Right!" I say. "I don't even care that much about eating Persian food or Greek food or Vietnamese. I really don't. I only ever cared about having dinner with you."

"So that's one of the things we have to do better, Lauren. We have to. We have to be honest."

"Yeah," I say.

"No," Ryan says, turning toward me, grabbing my hand, looking me in the eye. "Brutal honesty. It's OK to hurt me. It's OK to hurt my feelings. It's OK to embarrass me. As long as you do it from love. Nothing you could ever say out of love could hurt as much as it did to look into your eyes and see that you couldn't stand me anymore. I would rather be told to shave my pubes a thousand times than have you look at me the way you had been."

I want to roll around on the floor with him. I want to smell his hair. I want to kiss his neck. I want to sneak into one of those doctor "on call" rooms they have on soap operas and make love to him on the bunk beds. I want to show him what I have missed. Show him what he has missed. Show him what I have learned. I want to lose sight of where I end and he begins.

And we will do that. I know that. But I also have to remember that this is the beginning of the solution. This is the part where we do the work to fix our marriage.

"I love you," I say, my voice quivering. My muscles relaxing. My eyes filling with tears.

"I love you, too," he says, his voice breaking into a cry. It's a controlled cry. His tears barely make their way over the edge of his eyelid.

He kisses me.

And it is now that I understand the true value of the past ten months.

Sure, I have learned things about myself. I've learned what I want in bed. I've learned to ask for what I need. I've learned that love and romance don't have to be the same thing. I've learned that not everyone wants one or the other. I've learned that what you need and what you want are both equally important in love. I've learned a lot. But I could have learned these things with Ryan by my side. I could have sought out these lessons *with* him instead of *away* from him. No, the true value of this year isn't that I've learned ways to fix my marriage. The value of this year has been that I finally *want* to fix my marriage.

I have the energy to do it. I have the passion to do it. I have the drive. And I believe.

I want my marriage to work. I want it to work so bad that I feel it deep in my bones. I know the sun will rise tomorrow if I fail. I know that I can live with myself if we don't make it. But I want it. I want it so bad.

"So you'll stayed married to me?" Ryan asks. It has the weight and vulnerability of when he asked me to marry him, all those years ago.

I smile. "Yes," I say. "Yes!"

He grabs me and kisses me. He holds me. "She said yes!" he says to the waiting room. The few people in here just look at us and smile politely.

"I feel so good right now. I feel alive for the first time in years," he says. "I feel like I could conquer the world."

I kiss him. I kiss him again. He's so cute. And he's so handsome. And he's so smart. And funny. And charming. I don't know how I stopped seeing all of that.

"I never lost faith," he says. "I mean, in the back of my mind, I always hoped. You know that game people play in the car, when you see a car with one headlight out, you make a wish as you—"

"Flick the roof and say 'Pididdle,'" I say.

He nods. "I've only ever wished for one thing. Each time."

"Me?"

"Us."

"Even this whole year?"

"Every time."

We need each other. Whatever that means. We complement each other. We have great potential to make each other better. I was the one who had the strength to be honest about what we were doing to each other. I was the one who was brave enough to break this thing in half in the hopes of putting it back together. But when I lost faith, he's the one who had enough for both of us.

Ryan takes his hand out of mine for the first time in hours. He leans back and puts his arm around me. He pulls me in to him. The arms of the chairs make it slightly uncomfortable, and yet it is entirely comforting. I let my head sink into the crook of his armpit. I breathe in, sighing. He smells. He smells like Ryan. A scent pleasing in its familiarity and yet repulsive in its odor.

"Ugh," I say, not backing away. "You need to wear deodorant. Have you forgotten to keep yourself deodorized?"

"Smell it, baby girl," he says in an overly manly voice. "That's the smell of a man."

"The smell of a man is Old Spice," I say. "Let's invest in some."

That's when my grandmother dies. I mean, I can't be sure. I don't hear about it for another ten minutes. But when I do hear about it, they say it happened ten minutes ago. So I'm pretty sure it happened as I sat here, smelling Ryan's armpit, telling him to use deodorant.

It was supposed to happen after the baby was born. Or when I was with her. Or as she held my hand and told me the meaning of life. It wasn't supposed to happen when I was laughing with Ryan about Old Spice.

Some people love that about life, that it's unpredictable and unruly. I hate it. I hate that it doesn't have the common decency to wait for a profound moment to take something from you. It doesn't care that you just want one picture of your grandmother holding her great-grandchild. It just doesn't care.

• • •

My mom is crying when I get to Grandma's room. Fletcher is hugging her. Rachel is sitting in a chair by herself, head in her hands. Mom asked the nurses to move Grandma's body. It's gone by the time I get there. Thank fortune for small favors. I couldn't have handled that. I simply don't have it in me.

But the empty bed is hard enough. How can you miss someone so much already? My mind is full of all the things I didn't say. It doesn't matter how much I *did* say. There was still so much *left* to say. I want to tell her that I love her. That I will always remember her. That I am happy for her. That I believe she will find Grandpa.

Mom tells me that she told Grandma that Ryan was here. "I told her that he was with you, that he was taking care of you. To be honest, I couldn't tell if she heard me. But I think she did."

We all discuss plans, and we cry in one another's arms.

After a while, after we have squeezed too many tears out of our eyes, my mother tells us we need to "buck up."

"Chins up, people! Look alert! It's a big day for Charlie, OK? A big day for all of us. Grandma would not want this to be a day of sorrow. A baby is coming."

Rachel and I nod, drying our tears with tissues. Ryan has his hands on both of our shoulders.

"Fletch, you can stay here and take care of the details, right?"

Fletcher nods. He isn't crying in front of us, and I get the distinct impression that he's looking forward to being alone so that he can.

"And you come find me down on the fifth floor when you're ready."

My mom claps her hands together like a football coach, as if this is the state championship and we're down by six.

"We can do this!" she says. "There is plenty of time to think about Grandma, but right now, we need to be here for Charlie. We need to push this out of our minds and think about the beautiful little baby that's coming."

Rachel and I nod again.

"Yeah, coach!" Ryan says, giving my mom a high-five.

She looks at him, stunned, for a moment and then laughs. "For Charlie!" she cheers.

"For Charlie!" the three of us say, and Fletcher joins in at the last minute.

"I'll check in on you soon," my mom says to Fletcher, and then we all break for the elevator. When it comes, when we get in, when Rachel pushes the button for the fifth floor, when I feel the elevator drop, all I can think is that my mom has lost her mother today, and she's not crying. She's fighting to make this day right for her son. For her grandchild. Look at the things we are capable of in the name of the people we love.

Jonathan Louis Spencer is born at 1:04 A.M. on June 2. He weighs eight pounds, six ounces. He has a full head of dark hair. He has a squooshed face. He sort of looks like Natalie. If someone squooshed her face.

By sometime around nine in the morning, we've all held him. The nurse has taken him and brought him back, and now Jonathan rests in my mother's arms. She is rocking back and forth. Natalie is half-asleep in the hospital bed.

Charlie looks at me, proud papa written all over his face. "I've only known him for eight hours," he says to me, sitting in a chair, staring straight ahead at his baby boy. "But I could never leave him."

I grab his hand.

"It doesn't make any sense," Charlie says, shaking his head. "How our dad could have left. It doesn't make any sense, Lauren."

"I know," I say.

Charlie looks at me. "No, you don't," he says. It's not accusatory. It's not pointed. He is merely telling me that there is an experience in this world that he understands more intimately than I do. He's letting me know that as much as I think I get it, there is a world of love out there, a world of deep, unending, unconditional dedication that I know not of.

"You're right," I say. "I don't yet."

"I've never loved anything like this," he says, shaking his head again. He looks at Natalie, and he starts to cry. "And Natalie," he says. "She gave it to me."

My brother may not have been in love with Natalie when he asked her to marry him or when he decided to move back here. He may not have been in love with her when he brought his things into her house and started to make a life with her. But somewhere along the way, he learned to do it. Maybe it happened at 1:03 or 1:04 or 1:05 this morning. But there's no doubt it happened. You can see it in his eyes. He loves this woman.

"I'm proud of you, Charlie," Ryan says, patting him on the back. "I'm so happy for you."

Charlie closes his eyes, holding in the tears that want to fall onto his cheeks. "I'm gonna do this," Charlie says. He opens his eyes. He's not talking to me. He's not talking to Ryan. He's not talking to Rachel or Natalie or my mom. He's talking to Jonathan.

"We know you are," my mom says. She's not answering for herself. She's answering for all of us. She's answering for Jonathan.

I look at Jonathan's face. How can something so squooshed be so beautiful?

I look at Ryan, and I can tell what he's thinking. We can do this, too, one day. Not today. Probably not next year. But we can do this one day. Ryan squeezes my hand. Rachel sees it, and she smiles at me.

It's a good day. My mom, Charlie, Natalie, Jonathan, Rachel, Ryan, even me—we made this a good day.

"Wait," I say. "Is Louis for Lois?"

Natalie laughs. "It wasn't, but it is now!"

Charlie starts laughing, and so does my mom. If Charlie and my mom are laughing, then I'm right. It's a good day.

There is a funeral. And a wedding. And in between, a reunion.

At the funeral, Ryan holds my hand. Bill holds my mother. Charlie holds Natalie. Rachel holds Jonathan. Fletcher reads the eulogy.

I'm not going to lie, his eulogy is a little weird. But he does capture the heart of Grandma. He talks about how much she loved Grandpa. He talks about how lucky he felt to live in a home where his parents loved each other. He talks about how his parents are together again, and that brings him great solace. He talks about the right things my grandmother always said at the wrong times. He talks about how we all laughed when she said she had cancer, and he tells it right. He makes it funny and idiosyncratic instead of sad and rueful.

My mom stays quiet. She tries to keep the tears in and mostly succeeds. I am surprised to find that she does not lean on Rachel, Charlie, and me all that much. When she does cry, she turns to Bill.

Once the funeral is over, we all go back to Fletcher's house for food. We talk about Grandma. We coo over Jonathan. We follow Natalie around the room and ask her if she needs anything. She's the star of the family now. She's given us the crown jewel.

When I'm tired and I want to go, when I've had enough talking, enough crying, enough dwelling, I look over at Charlie and Ryan, talking to each other in the corner, each with a beer in his hand.

How did I forget that they are brothers in their own right? They do it so well.

When Ryan and I finally get back to Los Angeles, we don't go to our home or to his apartment. We go to Mila's house.

And waiting for us there is Thumper Cooper.

Ryan doesn't say anything when Thumper runs to him. He doesn't say *Down, boy* or *Hey, buddy* or any of the things you say to an excited dog. He just holds him close. And Thumper, normally excitable and rambunctious, rests comfortably and patiently in his arms.

Mila gives Ryan a hug of her own. "So you're back, huh?" she asks. She knows she'll get the details soon. She's just glad he's here. "Happy to see you," she says, smiling at me.

Ryan laughs. "Happy to be seen."

We thank Mila and Christina, and the three of us get into the car. We drive to our place. We get out of the car. I open the front door. We all walk in.

Here we are. Our tiny family. Nothing's missing anymore.

We're home.

That night, Ryan gets into bed next to me. He holds me. He kisses me. He slides his hand down my body, and he says, "Show me. Show me how to do what you want."

And I do. And it feels better than it did with David. Because I am once again myself with the man I love.

We forgot, for a while, how to listen to each other, how to touch each other. But we remember now.

The next morning, I wake up and open the shoebox in the closet. I dig out my wedding ring. I put it back on.

The wedding is a month later. It's a hot July day. We're at Natalie's friend's beach house in Malibu. What this friend does for a living, I don't know. I would guess, judging from the fact that this house is quite literally on the beach and has one-hundred-eighty-degree ocean views from every floor, that it's something in entertainment. There is a bonfire scheduled for late tonight and a lobster bake picnic scheduled for after the ceremony. Drinks and dancing are on the roof deck. Remind me to start hobnobbing with Hollywood producers. I would like for this to become a regular thing.

The ceremony is starting in a few minutes. Natalie, Rachel, and I are finishing getting ready. Natalie is wearing a Grecian-looking dress, draped around her. Her face is flush. Her boobs are huge. Her hair is long and curled. She is wearing long earrings that are buried in her long, dark hair. Her eyes have so much life behind them.

"Does this look right?" Rachel asks, as she fastens the halter top of her "persimmon" dress behind her neck. I assure her that it does. I know, because mine looks exactly the same.

Natalie's mom is helping Natalie get her shoes on. I thought Natalie's parents would be lithe and vibrant like her, but they look entirely average. Her mom is round in the middle. Her dad is short and hefty. I'm not sure what it is about them that makes it clear that they are from Idaho, but they certainly don't seem to be from around here. Maybe it's the fact that they are some of the nicest, most sincere people I've ever met.

Natalie's dad knocks on the door to come in.

"Just a minute, Harry!" Natalie's mom calls out. "She'll be ready in a second!"

"I want to take a picture, Eileen!"

"Just a second, I said!"

Natalie looks at Rachel and me with a laugh. "Oh!" she says, the thought just coming to her. "The bouquets! I left them in the fridge."

"It's cool," I say. "I got it." I cross out of the room through the shared bathroom and head down the stairs to the kitchen, where I can see my brother standing with Ryan and his friend Wally just outside the sliding glass doors.

Charlie is dressed to the nines in a fitted cream suit. He looks sleek and handsome. He doesn't look nervous. He doesn't look shy. He looks ready. Ryan and Wally are wearing black suits with black ties. Outside on the beach, white chairs line either side of the aisle, facing the light blue sea. People are trickling in. They grab their programs. They take their seats. The minister is standing there, waiting. My mom is sitting in the first row on the right side. She is wearing a navy-blue dress. She's got Jonathan in her arms. Bill is sitting next to her in a gray suit. Mila and Christina are a few rows back. They are having a rare moment alone without their kids. I can see Christina look over and kiss Mila's temple. She smiles at her.

I grab the three bouquets from the refrigerator and shake them out over the sink.

"Any last insights?" I hear Charlie say. "Any words of advice?"

I should head back upstairs, but I want to hear Ryan's answer.

"All you have to do is never give up," he says.

"Simple enough," Charlie says.

Ryan laughs. "It is, actually."

I hear a pat on the back, I'm not sure who is patting whom, and then I hear a third voice, which I'm assuming is Wally's. "Dude, I have zero advice to give. Because I've never been married. But if it makes any difference, I think she's great."

"Thanks," Charlie says.

"You ready?" Ryan asks.

I hear them start walking, and I peek to see their backs as they walk out together, getting ready to take their places.

I run back up to the bedroom to find Natalie. All four of them—Natalie, her parents, and Rachel—are ready to go. I hand Natalie her bouquet and hand one of the smaller ones to Rachel. I keep the third.

"OK," Rachel says. "Here we go."

Natalie breathes in. She looks at her dad. "Ready?"

He nods his head. "If you are."

Her mom snaps a picture.

"OK, I'm going down first," her mom says. "I'll see you in a second." She kisses Natalie on the cheek and leaves before she can start crying.

"Hoo. OK. Here we go," Natalie says. "Any last tips?" She laughs. I assume she's talking to her dad, but she's talking to me. I am now a person people go to for marital advice.

I tell her the only thing there is to tell her. "All you have to do is never give up."

Natalie's dad laughs. "Listen to her," he says. "She's absolutely right."

It's ten o'clock, and the party is still going strong. When Natalie danced with her dad, I got misty. When Charlie danced with Mom, I broke down. The sun set around eight, but it's been a warm night. The wind off the beach is strong and cools us down. Charlie and Natalie put the baby to bed a few hours ago.

Rachel made the cake, and it is the hit of the night. People keep asking about it. Everyone thinks it was from a very expensive bakery somewhere in Beverly Hills. I correct one person who asks Rachel about it. I say, "It's from this great new place opening up called Batter," I say. "Location TBD."

"Location is on Larchmont Boulevard," Rachel says, correcting me. When I give her an inquisitive look, she tells me the bank approved the loan.

"When were you gonna tell me?"

"Well, I just found out, and I didn't want to steal the sunshine from Charlie's wedding," she says.

I whisper, "Congratulations."

"Thanks," she whispers back. "You can pretend you're hearing it for the first time when I tell everyone next week. You're good at that." She smiles at me to let me know she's teasing.

Mom and Bill dance the night away. Later on by the rooftop bar, I point to him across the room, eating shrimp cocktail. "So the romance is alive and well, huh?" I ask Mom.

She shrugs. "I don't know," she says. "Maybe it's OK to stick around a little longer than the honeymoon phase."

"Wow," I say. "I'm impressed. Are you thinking about letting him move in?"

She laughs at me. "I'm thinking about it. All I'm doing is thinking. Have you seen this, by the way?"

"What?" I say, turning my head to look where she's pointing. Over in the far corner of the dance floor, Rachel is now dancing with Wally.

"Interesting, no?"

I think about how Rachel would want me to answer. "Yeah," I say, shrugging. "We'll see what happens."

"Yes, we will."

The music changes. You know the party is reaching its peak when the DJ plays "Shout."

Ryan runs up to me. "Baby! We gotta dance!"

I put my drink down and turn to my mother. "If you'll excuse me," I say.

"Certainly," she says.

We run into the crowd. We surround Charlie and Natalie. We join Rachel and Wally. We sing our hearts out. And because "Shout" is the type of song that brings everyone onto the dance floor, Mom and Bill hop in just as Natalie's parents make their way into the circle. Soon Mila and Christina join us, and even Uncle Fletcher can't resist. We dance together, twisting side-to-side, crouching lower and jumping higher as the song plays on, forgetting to worry about whether we look silly, forgetting to worry about anything at all.

I look at the people in this circle with me—my family, my friends, my husband—and I am overwhelmed with hope for the future.

I don't know if everyone is as thankful for this moment as I am. I don't know if everyone here understands how fragile life and love can be. I don't know if they are thinking about that right now.

I just know that I've learned it for myself. And I'll never forget it.

A few months later, it's a Wednesday night. My night to pick whatever dinner I want. I decide to order from the Vietnamese place down the street and then think better of it. Ryan has had a hard day at work. I'm going to order us a pizza.

But before I do, Ryan waves me over to his computer.

"Uh . . . Lauren?" he says.

"Yeah?" I say, walking toward him.

"Remember when you said you wrote to that woman?"

"What woman?"

"Ask Allie?"

I sit down next to him. Thumper is at his feet. "Yeah," I say.

"Well, it looks like she wrote back to you. Are you 'Lost in Los Angeles'?"

• • •

Dear Lost in Los Angeles,

I'm going to let you in on a little secret. It's a lesson learned by those who have faced the most miserable of tragedies, and it's a secret that I suspect you yourself already know: the sun will always rise. Always.

The sun rises the next day after mothers lose their babies, after men lose their wives, after countries lose wars. The sun will rise no matter what pain we encounter. No matter how much we believe the world to be over, the sun will rise. So you can't go around assessing love by whether or not the sun rises. The sun doesn't care about love. It just cares about rising.

And the other little piece of information that I think you need to know is that there are no rules in marriage. I know it would be easier if there were. I know we all sometimes hope for them; cut-and-dried answers would make the decisions easier. Black-and-white problems would be simpler to solve. But there simply isn't a rule that works for every marriage, for every love, for every family, for every relationship.

Some people need more boundaries, some people need fewer. Some marriages need more space, some marriages need more intimacy. Some families need more honesty, some families need more kindness. There's no single answer for any of it.

So I can't tell you what to do. I can't tell you if you should be with your husband or not. I can't tell you if you need him or want him. Need and want are words we define for ourselves.

Here is what I can tell you. All that matters in this life is that you try. All that matters is that you open your heart, give everything you have, and keep trying.

You and your husband reached a point in your marriage where most people would give up. And you didn't. Let that speak to you. Let that guide you.

Do you have more to give your marriage? If you do, give it everything you've got.

Much love,
Allie

• • •

I print out the letter and put it in the shoebox in the closet. It's the first thing you see when you open it now; it's on top of all the keepsakes and mementos. I think of it as the last piece of advice my grandmother ever gave me.

Ever gave us all.

And I intend to follow that advice.

I don't know if Rachel's bakery is going to succeed.

I don't know if Charlie and Natalie will stay together.

I don't know if my mom will move in with Bill.

I don't know if Ryan and I will celebrate our fiftieth anniversary.

But I can tell you that we are all going to try.

We're all going to give it everything we've got.

ACKNOWLEDGMENTS

This book is dedicated to my mother, Mindy, and my brother, Jake, because I would not be able to write about family without them. Thank you both for being so supportive and encouraging. The same goes for Linda Morris, an extraordinarily exceptional grandmother. And much thanks to the rest of the Jenkins and Morris families.

Thank you to the Reid and Hanes families, including but certainly not limited to the Encino clan of Rose, Warren, Sally, Bernie, Niko, and Zach. Words cannot express my gratitude for your unyielding and sincere support. I could not have married into a more loving family.

I am lucky enough to have far too many supportive friends to name and that alone makes me immensely grateful every day of my life. In addition to the wonderful friends I thanked in my first book, special attention must go to the early readers of this one: Erin Fricker, Colin Rodger, Andy Bauch, Julia Furlan, and Tamara Hunter. I am also hugely thankful to Zach Fricker for answering every medical question I have with a curmudgeonly zeal.

Carly Watters, my cheerleader and first line of defense, I'd be a starving artist without you. You also consistently prove that Canadians are the nicest people in the world.

Greer Hendricks, you make every book infinitely better in ways both big and small. Your expertise and intuition are invaluable. Sarah Cantin, you make being a professional writer feel easy. To the copy editors, cover designers, and publicity team at Atria, thank you. Atria feels like family I only see on the Internet.

I've been blessed with fellow authors who have shared their audience and time with me: Sarah Pekkanen, Amy Hatvany, Sarah Jio, Emma McLaughlin and Nicola Kraus, and many more. Thank you all so much. I feel so lucky to be the recipient of your kindness and support.

To the woman who opened up her heart to me and confided the story of her own beautiful and fragile marriage, I cannot thank you enough for your time and trust.

Special thanks go to my pit bull, Rabbit Reid, for being the apple of my eye. Rabbit, you can't read and you don't speak English, but I think you know how important you are to my every day. I also owe a great deal of thanks to Owl Reid, a dog so noble and good that I honestly believe I'm a better person for having known her. If anyone is thinking about getting a dog, give pit bulls a chance. There is no love quite like it.

And lastly, my husband, Alex Reid: This book is as much yours as it is mine. Every sentence I write is as much yours as it is mine.

AFTER I DO

TAYLOR JENKINS REID

Questions and Topics for Discussion

1. Read through Lauren's flashbacks of her and Ryan's relationship, leading up to the night of the Dodgers game. At what point did you notice a shift in their dynamic? Discuss with the group.
2. Early in the novel, Lauren playfully says of Ryan, "He always loved making me say the things he wanted to say." In what ways does this become a loaded assessment of their relationship?
3. Turn to page 125, when Lauren and her mother are discussing marriage. Lauren says that she doesn't want to fail at her marriage, which her mother dismisses: "If you stay married for a number of years and you have a happy time together and then you decide you don't want to be married anymore and you choose to go be happy with someone else or doing something else, that's not a failure." Do you agree with her?
4. Even though the underlying question of the narrative is whether Lauren and Ryan's marriage will survive, Ryan himself is not an active character for the majority of the novel, and we spend much of our time with other people in Lauren's life. How does observing Lauren in these dynamics enhance our understanding of her? And did you have a favorite supporting character?
5. What do you think Lauren gets out of her relationship with David? Is the fact that he is separated from his wife integral to their dynamic?
6. Did Rachel's revelation on page 225 surprise you? Do you have any relationships like hers and Lauren's in your

life—where the similarities are so clear that the differences can be ignored, sometimes to a fault?

7. Discuss the theme of communication within the novel. To what degree do these characters struggle to express themselves, and how do they find alternative ways of doing so when straight dialogue doesn't suffice?
8. Turn to page 236 and re-read the conversation that Rachel and Lauren have with their mother about romance and long-term relationships. Do you understand Ms. Spencer's perspective that "I don't need a life partner . . . I want love and romance." Can romance be kept alive by forestalling a greater commitment, or is it "the nature of love," as Lauren suggests, for relationships to "become more about partnership and less about romance"?
9. Discuss the role that sex plays in Lauren and Ryan's relationship, and how it relates to the feelings of resentment that she describes on page 272. If romance is, in fact, destined to evolve into more of a partnership, what happens to sex in that equation? Is romance required for a mutually fulfilling sexual relationship?
10. Even though Lauren and Ryan don't have children, the potential demise of their relationship still has collateral damage. Turn to page 257, and the conversation that Lauren has with her brother about inviting Ryan to his wedding. Do you think Lauren has a right to an opinion here? Do you agree with her statement that "I made him a part of this family . . . and he's a part of this family on my terms"?
11. Thinking about Ryan, Lauren says: "We have spent enough years together to know how to work in sync, even when we don't want to." To what extent is a long-term relationship defined by whether the other person is

someone with whom you know how to endure the tough moments of life? Find examples within the novel to support your opinion.

12. Lauren gets relationship advice from a variety of people throughout the novel. Did any of it in particular resonate with you? Pick a favorite line and share why you connected to it with the group.
13. Speaking of advice: the Ask Allie column plays a large role throughout the book. Was Lauren able to take any wisdom from Allie's old columns that perhaps a closer friend or family member couldn't have said to her directly? What did you think of her final letter to Lauren?
14. Consider the romantic partnerships that Lauren has to look to as models: her mother and Bill, Charlie and Natalie, Mila and Christina, even her grandmother and deceased grandfather. What does she take away from each of them?
15. Discuss the portrayal of compromise in the novel, and compare how it is depicted in romantic relationships versus within family dynamics. Do you think of compromise differently when it comes to family members, as opposed to romantic partners? Why or why not?

Enhance Your Reading Group

Read Taylor Jenkins Reid's debut novel *Forever, Interrupted* as a group. How are these love stories different? Having now read two of Reid's novels, what can you identify as distinct qualities of her writing style?

The e-mails that Ryan and Lauren write each other but never send prove to be very cathartic to both of them. If you could write to someone you've been romantically involved with (in the past or currently), knowing that they might read it but that they couldn't confront you about it, what would you say?

The book makes the point that "marriage" is a word that has many different definitions. Whether you are married or unmarried, what does marriage mean to you?

What's the best piece of advice you've ever been given about marriage and family?

FOREVER, INTERRUPTED

ALSO BY TAYLOR JENKINS REID

After I Do

Maybe in Another Life

One True Loves

The Seven Husbands of Evelyn Hugo

FOREVER, INTERRUPTED

~ A Novel ~

TAYLOR JENKINS REID

WASHINGTON SQUARE PRESS

ATRIA

New York London Toronto Sydney New Delhi

ATRIA
An Imprint of Simon & Schuster, Inc.
1230 Avenue of the Americas
New York, NY 10020

This book is a work of fiction. Any references to historical events, real people, or real places are used fictitiously. Other names, characters, places, and events are products of the author's imagination, and any resemblance to actual events or places or persons, living or dead, is entirely coincidental.

First Washington Square Press/Atria Paperback edition July 2013

WASHINGTON SQUARE PRESS/ATRIA Paperback and colophons are registered trademarks of Simon & Schuster, Inc.

Designed by Jill Putorti

Manufactured in the United States of America

29 30 28

Library of Congress Cataloging-in-Publication Data

Reid, Taylor Jenkins.
Forever, interrupted : a novel / Taylor Jenkins Reid.—1st Washington Square Press trade paperback ed.
p. cm.
1. Grief—Fiction. 2. Loss (Psychology)—Fiction. 3. Female friendship—Fiction. I. Title.
PS3618.E5478F67 2013
813'.6—dc23

2012035073

ISBN 978-1-4767-1282-6
ISBN 978-1-4767-1283-3 (ebook)

To Linda Morris
(for reading the murder mysteries of a twelve-year-old girl)

And to Alex Reid
(a man the whole world should fall in love with)

Every morning when I wake up I forget for a fraction of a second that you are gone and I reach for you. All I ever find is the cold side of the bed. My eyes settle on the picture of us in Paris, on the bedside table, and I am overjoyed that even though the time was brief I loved you and you loved me.

—CRAIGSLIST POSTING, CHICAGO, 2009

PART ONE

JUNE

"Have you decided if you're going to change your name?" Ben asks me. He is sitting on the opposite end of the couch, rubbing my feet. He looks so cute. How did I end up with someone so goddamn cute?

"I have an idea," I tease. But I have more than an idea. My face breaks into a smile.

"Really?" he asks.

He seems too sexy to be a husband. He's young and he's tall and he's strong. He's so perfect. I sound like an idiot. But this is how it's supposed to be, right? As a newlywed, I'm supposed to see him through these rose-colored glasses. "I was thinking of going by Elsie Porter Ross," I say to him.

He stops rubbing my feet for a minute. "That's really hot," he says.

I laugh at him. "Why?"

"I don't know," he says, starting to rub my feet again. "I just like the idea of both our names together."

"I like it, too!" I say. "It's kinda hot."

"I told you!"

"That settles it. As soon as the marriage certificate gets here, I'm sending it to the DMV or wherever you have to send it."

"Awesome," he says, taking his hands off of me. "Okay, Elsie Porter Ross. My turn."

I grab his feet. It's quiet for a while as I absentmindedly rub his toes through his socks. My mind wanders, and after some time, it lands on a startling realization: I am hungry.

"Are you hungry?" I ask.

"Now?"

"I really want to get Fruity Pebbles for some reason."

"We don't have cereal here?" Ben asks.

"No, we do. I just . . . I want Fruity Pebbles." We have adult cereals, boxes of brown shapes fortified with fiber.

"Well, should we go get some? I'm sure CVS is still open and I'm sure they sell Fruity Pebbles. Or, I could go get them for you."

"No! I can't let you do that. That would be so lazy of me."

"That is lazy of you, but you're my wife and I love you and I want you to have what you want." He starts to get up.

"No, really, you don't have to."

"I'm going." Ben leaves the room briefly and returns with his bike and shoes.

"Thank you!" I say, now lying across the sofa, taking up the space he just abandoned. Ben smiles at me as he opens the front door and walks his bike through it. I can hear him put the kickstand down and I know he will come back in to say good-bye.

"I love you, Elsie Porter Ross," he says, and he bends down to the couch to kiss me. He is wearing a bike helmet and bike gloves. He grins at me. "I really love the sound of that."

I smile wide. "I love you!" I say to him. "Thank you."

"You're welcome. I love you! I'll be right back." He shuts the door behind him.

I lay my head back down and pick up a book, but I can't concentrate. I miss him. Twenty minutes pass and I start to expect him home, but the door doesn't open. I don't hear anyone on the steps.

Once thirty minutes have passed, I call his cell phone. No answer. My mind starts to race with possibilities. They are all far-fetched and absurd. He met someone else. He stopped off at a strip club. I call him again as my brain starts to think of more realistic reasons for him to be late, reasons that are reasonable and thus far more terrifying. When he does not answer again, I get off the couch and walk outside.

I'm not sure what I expect to find, but I look up and down the street for any sign of him. Is it crazy to think he's hurt? I can't decide. I try to stay calm and tell myself that he must just be stuck in some sort of traffic jam that he can't get out of, or maybe he's run into an old friend. The minutes start to slow. They feel like hours. Each second passing is an insufferable period of time.

Sirens.

I can hear sirens heading in my direction. I can see their flashing lights just above the rooftops on my street. Their whooping alarms sound like they are calling to me. I can hear my name in their repetitive wailing: *El-sie. El-sie*.

I start running. By the time I get to the end of my street, I can feel just how cold the concrete is on the balls of my feet. My light sweatpants are no match for the wind, but I keep going until I find the source.

I see two ambulances and a fire truck. There are a few police cars barricading the area. I run as far into the fray as I can get before I stop myself. Someone is being lifted onto a stretcher. There's a large moving truck flipped over on the side of the road. Its windows are smashed, glass surrounding it. I look closely at the truck, trying to figure out what happened. That's when I see that it isn't all glass. The road is covered in little specks of something else. I walk closer and I see one at my feet. It's a Fruity Pebble. I scan the area for the one thing I pray not to see and I see it. Right in front of me—how could I have missed it?—halfway underneath the moving truck, is Ben's bike. It's bent and torn.

The world goes silent. The sirens stop. The city comes to a halt. My heart starts beating so quickly it hurts in my chest. I can feel the blood pulsing through my brain. It's so hot out here. When did it get so hot outside? I can't breathe. I don't think I can breathe. I'm not breathing.

I don't even realize I am running until I reach the ambulance doors. I start to pound on them. I jump up and down as I try to pound on the window that is too high above me to reach. As I do, all I hear is the sound of the Fruity Pebbles crunching beneath my feet. I grind them into the pavement each time I jump. I break them into a million pieces.

The ambulance pulls away. Is he in it? Is Ben in there? Are they keeping him alive? Is he okay? Is he bruised? Maybe he's in the ambulance because protocol says they have to but he's actually fine. Maybe he's around here somewhere. Maybe the ambulance was holding the driver of the car. That guy has to be dead, right? No way that person survived. So Ben must be all right. That's the karma of an accident: The bad guy dies, the good guy lives.

I turn and look around, but I don't see Ben anywhere. I start to scream his name. I know he's okay. I'm sure of it. I just need this to be over. I just want to see him with a small scrape and be told he's fine to go home. Let's go home, Ben. I've learned my lesson to never let you do such a stupid favor for me again. I've learned my lesson; let's go home.

"Ben!" I shout into the nighttime air. It's so cold. How did it get so cold? *"Ben!"* I shout again. I feel like I am running in circles until I am stopped in my place by a police officer.

"Ma'am," he says as he grabs my arms. I keep shouting. Ben needs to hear me. He needs to know that I am here. He needs to know that it's time to come home. "Ma'am," the officer calls again.

"What?" I yell into his face. I rip my arms out of his grasp and I spin myself around. I try to run through what is clearly a marked-off area. I know that whoever marked this off would want to let me through. They would understand that I just need to find my husband.

The officer catches up to me and grabs me again. "Ma'am!" he says, this time more severe. "You cannot be here right now." Doesn't he understand that this is exactly where I *must* be right now?

"I need to find my husband!" I say to him. "He could be hurt. That's his bike. I have to find him."

"Ma'am, they have taken your husband to Cedars-Sinai. Do you have a ride to get there?"

My eyes are staring at his face, but I do not understand what he is saying to me.

"Where is he?" I ask. I need him to tell me again. I don't understand.

"Ma'am, your husband is on his way to Cedars-Sinai Medical Center. Would you like me to take you?"

He's not here? I think. He was in that ambulance?

"Is he okay?"

"Ma'am, I can't—"

"Is he okay?"

The officer looks at me. He pulls his hat off his head and places it on his chest. I know what this means. I've seen it done on the doorsteps of war widows in period pieces. As if on cue, I start violently heaving.

"I need to see him!" I scream through my tears. "I need to see him! I need to be with him!" I drop to my knees in the middle of the road, cereal crunching underneath me. "Is he all right? I should be with him. Just tell me if he is still alive."

The police officer looks at me with pity and guilt. I've never seen the two looks together before but it's easy to recognize. "Ma'am. I'm sorry. Your husband has . . ."

The police officer isn't rushed; he isn't running on adrenaline like me. He knows there is nothing to hurry for. He knows my husband's dead body can wait.

I don't let him finish his sentence. I know what he's going to say and I can't believe it. I won't believe it. I scream at him, pounding my fists into his chest. He is a huge man, probably six foot four at least, and he looms over me. I feel like a child. But that doesn't stop me. I just keep flailing and hitting him. I want to slap him. I want to kick him. I want to make him hurt like I do.

"He passed away on impact. I'm sorry."

That's when I fall to the ground. Everything starts spinning. I can hear my pulse, but I can't focus on what the policeman is saying. I really didn't think this was going to happen. I thought bad things only happened to people with hubris. They don't happen to people like me, people that know how fragile life is, people that respect the authority of a higher power. But it has. It has happened to me.

My body calms. My eyes dry. My face freezes, and my gaze falls onto a scaffolding and stays there. My arms feel numb. I'm not sure if I'm standing or sitting.

"What happened to the driver?" I ask the officer, calm and composed.

"I'm sorry?"

"What happened to the person driving the moving truck?"

"He passed away, ma'am."

"Good," I say to him. The police officer just nods his head at me, perhaps indicating some unspoken contract that he will pretend he didn't hear me say it, and I can pretend I don't wish another person to have died. But I don't want to take it back.

He grabs my hand and leads me into the front of his police car. He uses his siren to break through traffic and I see the streets of Los Angeles in fast-forward. They have never looked so ugly.

When we get to the hospital, the officer sits me down in the waiting room. I'm shaking so hard that the chair shakes with me.

"I need to go back there," I say to him. "I need to go back there!" I yell louder. I take notice of his name tag. Officer Hernandez.

"I understand. I'm going to find out all of the information that I can. I believe you will have a social worker assigned to you. I'll be right back."

I can hear him talking but I can't make myself react or acknowledge him. I just sit in the chair and stare at the far wall. I can feel my head sway from side to side. I feel myself stand and walk toward the nurses' station, but I am cut off by Officer Hernandez coming back. He is now with a short, middle-aged man. The man has on a blue shirt with a red tie. I bet this idiot calls it his power tie. I bet he thinks he has a good day when he wears this tie.

"Elsie," he says. I must have told Officer Hernandez my name. I don't even remember doing that. He puts out his hand as if I were going to shake it. I see no need for formality in the midst of tragedy. I let it hang there. Before all this, I would never have rejected someone's handshake. I am a nice person. Sometimes, I'm even a pushover. I'm not someone who is considered "difficult" or "unruly."

"You are the wife of Ben Ross? Do you have a driver's license on you?" the man asks me.

"No. I . . . ran right out of the house. I don't . . ." I look down at my feet. I don't even have on shoes and this man thinks I have my driver's license?

Officer Hernandez leaves. I can see him step away slowly, awkwardly. He feels like his job is done here, I'm sure. I wish I was him. I wish I could walk away from this and go home. I'd go home to my husband and a warm bed. My husband, a warm bed, and a fucking bowl of Fruity Pebbles.

"I'm afraid we cannot let you back there yet, Elsie," the man in the red tie says.

"Why not?"

"The doctors are working."

"He's *alive*?" I scream. How quickly hope can come flying back.

"No, I'm sorry." He shakes his head. "Your husband died earlier this evening. He was listed as an organ donor."

I feel like I'm in an elevator that is plummeting to the ground floor. They are taking pieces of him and giving them to other people. They are taking his parts.

I sit back down in the chair, dead inside. Part of me wants to scream at this man to let me back there. To let me see him. I want to run through the twin doors and find him, hold him. What are they doing to him? But I'm frozen. I am dead too.

The man in the red tie leaves briefly and comes back with hot chocolate and slippers. My eyes are dry and tired. I can barely see through them. All of my senses feel muted. I feel trapped in my own body, separated from everyone around me.

"Do you have someone we can call? Your parents?"

I shake my head. "Ana," I say. "I should call Ana."

He puts his hand on my shoulder. "Can you write down Ana's number? I'll call her."

I nod and he hands me a piece of paper and a pen. It takes me a minute to remember her number. I write it down wrong a few times before I write it down correctly, but I'm pretty sure, when I hand over the piece of paper, it's the correct number.

"What about Ben?" I ask. I don't know what exactly I mean. I just . . . I can't give up yet. I can't be at the call-someone-to-take-her-home-and-watch-her phase yet. We have to fight this, right? I have to find him and save him. How can I find him and save him?

"The nurses have called the next of kin."

"What? I'm his next of kin."

"Apparently his driver's license listed an address in Orange County. We had to legally notify his family."

"So who did you call? Who is coming?" But I already know who's coming.

"I will see if I can find out. I'm going to go phone Ana. I'll be back shortly, okay?"

I nod.

In this lobby, I can see and hear other families waiting. Some look somber but most look okay. There is a mother with her young daughter. They are reading a book. There is a young boy holding an ice pack to his face next to a father who seems annoyed. There is a teenage couple holding hands. I don't know why they are here, but judging from the smiles on their faces and the way they are flirting, I can only assume it's not dire and I . . . I want to scream at them. I want to say that emergency rooms are for emergencies and they shouldn't be here if they are going to look happy and carefree. I want to tell them to go home and be happy somewhere else because I don't need to see it. I don't remember what it feels like to be them. I don't even remember how it feels to be myself before this happened. All I have is this overwhelming sense of dread. That and my anger toward these two little shitheads who won't get their smiles out of my fucking face.

I hate them and I hate the goddamn nurses, who just go on with their day like it isn't the worst one of their lives. They make phone calls and they make photocopies and they drink coffee. I hate them for being able to drink coffee at a time like this. I hate everyone in this entire hospital for not being miserable.

The man in the red tie comes back and says that Ana is on her way. He offers to sit down and wait with me. I shrug. He can do whatever he wants. His presence brings me no solace, but it does prevent me from running up to someone and screaming at them for eating a candy bar at a time like this. My mind flashes back to the Fruity Pebbles all over the road, and I know they will be there when I get home. I know that no one will have cleaned them up because no one could possibly know how horrifying they would be to look at again. Then I think of what a stupid reason that is for Ben to die. He died over Fruity Pebbles. It would be funny if it wasn't so . . . It will never be funny. Nothing about this is funny. Even the fact that I lost my husband because I had a craving for a children's cereal based on the Flintstones cartoon. I hate myself for this. That's who I hate the most.

Ana shows up in a flurry of panic. I don't know what the man in the red tie has told her. He stands to greet her as she runs toward me. I can see them talking but I can't hear them. They speak only for a second before she runs to my side, puts her arms around me. I let her arms fall where she puts them, but I have no energy to hug back. This is the dead fish of hugs. She whispers, "I'm sorry," into my ear, and I crumble into her arms.

I have no will to hold myself up, no desire to hide my pain. I wail in the waiting room. I sob and heave into her breasts. Any other moment of my life, I'd move my head away from that part of her body. I'd feel uncomfortable with my eyes and lips being that close to a sexual body part, but right now, sex feels trivial and stupid. It feels like something idiots do out of boredom. Those happy teenagers probably do it for sport.

Her arms around me don't comfort me. The water springs from my eyes as if I'm forcing it out but I'm not. It's just falling on its own. I don't even feel sad. This level of devastation is so far beyond tears, that mine feel paltry and silly.

"Have you seen him, Elsie? I'm so sorry."

I don't answer. We sit on the floor of the waiting room for what seems like hours. Sometimes I wail, sometimes I feel nothing. Most of the time, I lie in Ana's arms, not because I need to but because I don't want to look at her. Eventually, Ana gets up and rests me against the wall, and then she walks up to the nurses' station and starts yelling.

"How much longer until we can see Ben Ross?" she screams at the young Latina nurse sitting at her computer.

"Ma'am," the nurse says, standing up, but Ana moves away from her.

"No. Don't ma'am me. Tell me where he is. Let us through." The man in the red tie makes his way over to her and tries to calm her down.

He and Ana speak for a few minutes. I can see him try to touch Ana, to console her, and she jerks her shoulder out of his reach. He is just doing his job. Everyone here is just doing their job. What a bunch of assholes.

I see an older woman fly through the front doors. She looks about sixty with long, reddish brown hair in waves around her face. She has mascara running down her cheeks, a brown purse over her shoulder, a blackish brown shawl across her chest. She has tissues in her hands. I wish my grief were composed enough to have tissues. I've been wiping snot on my sleeves and neckline. I've been letting tears fall into puddles on the floor.

She runs up to the front desk and then resigns herself to sit. When she turns to face me briefly, I know exactly who she is. I stare at her. I can't take my eyes off of her. She is my mother-in-law, a stranger by all accounts. I saw her picture a few times in a photo album, but she has never seen my face.

I remove myself and head into the bathroom. I do not know how to introduce myself to her. I do not know how to tell her that we are both here for the same man. That we are both grieving over the same loss. I stand in front of the mirror and I look at myself. My face is red and blotchy. My eyes are bloodshot. I look at my face and I think that I had someone who loved this face. And now he's gone. And now no one loves my face anymore.

I step back out of the bathroom and she is gone. I turn to find Ana grabbing my arm. "You can go in," she says and leads me to the man in the red tie, who leads me through the double doors.

The man in the red tie stops outside a room and asks me if I want him to go in with me. Why would I want him to go in with me? I just met this man. This man means nothing to me. The man inside this room means everything to me. *Nothing* isn't going to help losing *everything*. I open the door and there are other people in the room, but all I can see is Ben's body.

"Excuse me!" my mother-in-law says through her tears. It is meek but terrifying. I ignore it.

I grab his face in my hands and it's cold to the touch. His eyelids are shut. I'll never see his eyes again. It occurs to me they might be gone. I can't look. I don't want to figure it out. His face is bruised and I don't know what that means. Does that mean he was hurt before he died? Did he die there alone and lonely on the street? Oh my God, did he suffer? I feel faint. There's a sheet over his chest and legs. I'm scared to move the sheet. I'm scared that there is too much of Ben exposed, too much of him to see. Or that there is too much of him that is gone.

"Security!" she calls out into the air.

As I hold on to Ben's hand and a security guard shows up at the door, I look at my mother-in-law. She has no reason to know who I am. She has no reason to understand what I am doing here, but she has to know I love her son. That much has to be obvious by now.

"Please," I beg her. "Please, Susan, don't do this."

Susan looks at me curiously, confused. By the sheer fact that I know her name, she knows she must be missing something. She very subtly nods and looks at the security guard. "I'm sorry. Give us a moment?" He leaves the room, and Susan looks at the nurse. "You too. Thank you." The nurse leaves the room, shutting the door.

Susan looks tortured, terrified, and yet composed, as if she has only enough poise to get through the next five seconds and then she will fall apart.

"His hand has a wedding ring on it," she says to me. I stare at her and try to keep breathing. I meekly lift up my own left hand to match.

"We were married a week and a half ago," I say through tears. I can feel the corners of my lips pulling down. They feel so heavy.

"What is your name?" she asks me, now shaking.

"Elsie," I say. I am terrified of her. She looks angry and vulnerable, like a teenage runaway.

"Elsie what?" she chokes.

"Elsie Ross."

That's when she breaks. She breaks just like I have. Soon, she's on the floor. There are no more tissues in sight to save the linoleum from her tears.

Ana is sitting next to me holding my hand. I am sitting next to Ben's side, sobbing. Susan excused herself some time ago. The man in the red tie comes in and says we need to clear some things up and Ben's body needs to be moved. I just stare ahead, I don't even focus on what's happening, until the man in the red tie hands me a bag of Ben's things. His cell phone is there, his wallet, his keys.

"What is this?" I ask, even though I know what it is.

Before the man in the red tie can answer me, Susan appears in the doorway. Her face is strained; her eyes are bloodshot. She looks older than she did when she left. She looks exhausted. Do I look like that? I bet I look like that.

"What are you doing?" Susan asks the man.

"I'm . . . We need to clear the room. Your son's body is going to be transferred."

"Why are you giving that to her?" Susan says, more directly. She says it like I'm not even here.

"I'm sorry?"

Susan steps further into the room and takes the bag of Ben's stuff from in front of me. "All decisions about Ben, all his belongings, should be directed to me," she says.

"Ma'am," the man in the red tie says.

"All of it," she says.

Ana stands up and grabs me to go with her. She intends to

remove me from this situation, and while I don't want to be here right now, I can't just be removed. I pull my arm out of Ana's hand and I look at Susan.

"Should we discuss what the next steps are?" I say to her.

"What is there to discuss?" Susan says. She is cold and controlled.

"I just mean . . ." I don't actually know what I mean.

"Mrs. Ross," the man in the red tie says.

"Yes?" Both Susan and I answer at the same time.

"I'm sorry," I say. "Which one did you mean?"

"The elder," he says, looking at Susan. I'm sure that he meant it as a sign of respect, but it's torn right through her.

"I'm not going to give this any more credence," she says to everyone in the room. "She has absolutely no proof that my son even knew her, let alone married her. I've never heard of her! My own son. I saw him last month. He never mentioned a damn thing. So no, I'm not having my son's possessions sent home with a stranger. I won't have it."

Ana reaches toward Susan. "Maybe it's time for us all to take a step back," she says.

Susan turns her head, as if noticing Ana for the first time. "Who are you?" she asks. She asks it like we are clowns coming out of a Volkswagen.

"I'm a friend," Ana says. "And I don't think any of us are in a position to behave rationally, so maybe we can just breathe—"

Susan turns toward the man in the red tie, her body language interrupting Ana midsentence. "You and I need to discuss this in private," she barks at him.

"Ma'am, please calm down."

"Calm down? You're joking!"

"Susan—" I start to say. I don't know how I planned on finishing, but Susan doesn't give a shit.

"Stop," she says, putting her hand up in my face. It's aggressive and instinctual, as if she needs to protect her face from my words.

"Ma'am, Elsie was escorted in by the police. She was at the scene. I have no reason to doubt that she and your son were as she says . . ."

"Married?" Susan is incredulous.

"Yes," the man in the red tie says.

"Call the county! I want to see a record of it!"

"Elsie, do you have a copy of your marriage certificate that you can show Mrs. Ross?"

I can feel myself shrinking in front of them. I don't want to shrink. I want to stand tall. I want to be proud, confident. But this is all too much and I don't have anything to show for myself.

"No, but, Susan—" I say as tears fall down my face. I feel so ugly right now, so small and stupid.

"Stop calling me that!" she screams. "You don't even know me. Stop calling me by my name!"

"Fine," I say. My eyes are staring forward, focused on the body in the room. My husband's body. "Keep all of it," I say. "I don't care. We can sit here and scream all day but it doesn't change anything. So I really don't give a shit where his wallet goes."

I put one foot in front of the other and I walk out. I leave my husband's body there with her. And the minute my feet hit the hallway, the minute Ana has shut the door behind us, I regret walking out. I should have stayed with him until the nurse kicked me out.

Ana pushes me forward.

She puts me in the car. She buckles my seat belt. She drives slowly through town. She parks in my driveway. I don't remember any of it happening. Suddenly, I am at my front door.

Stepping into my apartment, I have no idea what time of day it is. I have no idea how long it has been since I sat on the couch like a cavalier bitch whining about cereal in my pajamas. This apartment, the one I have loved since I moved in, the one I considered "ours" when Ben moved in, now betrays me. It hasn't moved an inch since Ben died. It's like it doesn't care.

It didn't put away his shoes sitting in the middle of the floor. It didn't fold up the blanket he was using. It didn't even have the decency to hide his toothbrush from plain view. This apartment is acting like nothing has changed. Everything has changed. I tell the walls he's gone. "He's dead. He's not coming home." Ana rubs my back and says, "I know, baby. I know."

She doesn't know. She could never know. I walk carelessly into my bedroom, hit my shoulder on the door hinge and feel nothing. I get into my side of the bed and I can smell him still. He's still here in the sheets. I grab his pillow from his side of the bed and I smell it, choking on my own tears. I walk into the kitchen as Ana is getting me a glass of water. I walk right past her with the pillow in my hand and I grab a trash bag, shoving the pillow into it. I tie it tight, knotting the plastic over and over until it breaks off in my hand and falls onto the kitchen floor.

"What are you doing?" she asks me.

"It smells like Ben," I answer. "I don't want the smell to evaporate. I want to save it."

"I don't know if that's going to work," she says delicately.

"Fuck you," I say and go back to the bed.

I start crying the minute I hit my pillow. I hate what this has made me. I've never told anyone to fuck off before, least of all Ana.

Ana has been my best friend since I was seventeen years old. We met the first day of college in line at the dining hall. I didn't have anyone to sit with and she was already trying to avoid a boy. It was a telling moment for each of us. When she decided to move to Los Angeles to be an actress, I came with her. Not because I had any affinity for Los Angeles, I had never been here, but because I had such a strong affinity for her. Ana had said to me, "C'mon, you can be a librarian anywhere." And she was absolutely right.

Here we were, nine years after meeting, her watching me like I'm going to slit my wrists. If I had a better grip on my senses, I'd say this is the real meat of friendship, but I don't care about that right now. I don't care about anything.

Ana comes in with two pills and a glass of water. "I found these in your medicine cabinet," she says. I look in her hand and I recognize them. It's Vicodin from when Ben had a back spasm last month. He barely took any of them. I think he thought taking them made him a wimp.

I take them out of her hand without questioning and I swallow them. "Thank you," I say. She tucks the duvet around me and goes to sleep on the couch. I'm glad she doesn't try to sleep in bed with me. I don't want her to take away his smell. My eyes are parched from crying, my limbs weak, but my brain needs the Vicodin to pass out. I shuffle over to Ben's side of the bed as I get groggy and fall asleep. "I love you," I say, and for the first time, there's no one to hear it.

I wake up feeling hungover. I reach over to grab Ben's hand as I do every morning, and his side of the bed is empty. For a minute I think he must be in the bathroom or making breakfast and then I remember. My devastation returns, this time duller but thicker, coating my body like a blanket, sinking my heart like a stone.

I pull my hands to my face and try to wipe away the tears, but they are flowing out of me too fast to catch up. It's like a Whac-A-Mole of misery.

Ana comes in with a dish towel in her hands, drying them.

"You're up," she says, surprised.

"How observant." Why am I being so mean? I'm not a mean person. This isn't who I am.

"Susan called." She is ignoring my outbursts, and for that, I am thankful.

"What did she say?" I sit up and grab the glass of water on my bedside table from last night. "What could she possibly want from me?"

"She didn't say anything. Just to call her."

"Great."

"I left the number on the refrigerator. In case you did want to call her."

"Thanks." I sip the water and stand up.

"I have to go walk Bugsy and then I'll be right back," Ana

says. Bugsy is her English bulldog. He drools all over everything and I want to tell her that Bugsy doesn't need to be let out because Bugsy is a lazy sack of shit, but I don't say any of this because I really, really want to stop being so unkind.

"Okay."

"Do you want anything while I'm out?" she asks, and it reminds me that I asked Ben to get me Fruity Pebbles. I get right back into bed.

"No, nothing for me. Thank you."

"Okay, I'll be back shortly." She thinks for a minute. "Actually, do you want me to stick around in case you decide to call her now?"

"No, thanks. I can handle it."

"Okay, if you change your mind . . ."

"Thanks."

Ana leaves, and as I hear the door shut, it hits me how alone I am. I am alone in this room, I am alone in this apartment, but more to the point, I am alone in this life. I can't even wrap my brain around it. I just get up and pick up the phone. I get the number from the front of the refrigerator and I see a magnet for Georgie's Pizza. I fall to the floor, my cheek against the cold tile. I can't seem to make myself get up.

DECEMBER

It was New Year's Eve and Ana and I had this great plan. We were going to go to this party to see this guy she had been flirting with at the gym, and then we were going to leave at 11:30 p.m. We wanted to drive to the beach, open a bottle of champagne together, and ring in the new year tipsy and drenched in sea spray.

Instead, Ana got too drunk at the party, started making out with the guy from the gym, and disappeared for a few hours. This was fairly typical of Ana and something that I had come to love about her, namely that nothing ever went as planned. Something always happened. She was a nice reprieve from my own personality. A personality for whom everything went as planned and nothing ever happened. So when I was stranded at the party waiting for Ana to pop out of wherever she'd been hiding, I wasn't angry or surprised. I had assumed things might take this turn. I was only slightly annoyed as I rang in the new year with a group of strangers. I stood there awkwardly, as friends kissed each other, and I just stared into my champagne glass. I didn't let it ruin my evening. I talked to some cool people that night. I made the best of it.

I met a guy named Fabian, who was just finishing med school but said his real passion was "fine wine, fine food, and fine women." He winked at me as he said this, and as I gracefully removed myself from the conversation shortly thereafter, Fabian asked for my number. I gave it to him, and although he was cute, I knew that if he did call, I wouldn't answer. Fabian seemed like the kind of guy who would take me to an expensive bar on our first date; the kind of guy who would check out other girls while I was in the bathroom. That was the kind of guy who found victory in sleeping with you. It was a game to him and I . . . just never knew how to play it well.

Ana, on the other hand, knew how to have fun. She met people. She flirted with them. She had whatever that thing is that makes men fawn over women and lose their own self-respect in the process. Ana had all the power in her romances, and while I could see the point in living like that, from an outside view it never seemed very full of passion. It was calculated. I was waiting for someone that would sweep me off my feet and would be swept up by me in equal parts. I wanted someone who wouldn't want to play games because doing so meant less time being together. I wasn't sure if this person existed, but I was too young to give up on the idea.

I finally found Ana asleep in the master bathroom. I picked her up and cabbed her home. By the time I reached my own apartment, it was about 2:00 a.m. and I was tired. The bottle of champagne intended for our beach rendezvous went unopened and I got in bed.

As I fell asleep that night, eyeliner not fully cleaned off my face, black sequined dress on the floor, I thought about what this year could bring and my mind raced with all of the possibilities, however unlikely. But out of all the possibilities, I didn't think about being married by the end of May.

I woke up New Year's Day alone in my apartment, just like I woke up every other day, and there was nothing in particular that seemed special about it. I read in bed for two hours, I took a shower, I got dressed. I met Ana for breakfast.

I'd been up for about three and a half hours by the time I saw her. She looked like she hadn't been up for five minutes. Ana is tall and lanky with long brown hair that falls far beyond her shoulders and perfectly matches her golden brown eyes. She was born in Brazil and lived there until she was thirteen, and it's still noticeable every once in a while in some of her words, mostly her exclamations.

That particular morning, she was wearing big sweatpants and she had her hair pulled up into a ponytail, a zip-up sweatshirt covering her torso. You could barely tell she wasn't wearing a shirt underneath her sweatshirt, and it occurred to me that this is how Ana does it. This is how she drives men crazy. She looks naked while being entirely covered. And you would have absolutely no indication she does this on purpose.

"Nice shirt," I said, as I pulled my sunglasses off and sat down across from her. Sometimes I worried that my own average body looked oversize compared to hers, that my own plain features only served to highlight how beautiful she was. When I made jokes about it, she would remind me that I am a blond woman in the United States. She'd say blond trumps everything. I've always thought of my hair as dirty blond, almost mousy, but I saw her point.

Even with how gorgeous Ana is, I've never heard her express satisfaction with her own looks. When I would say I didn't like my small boobs, she'd remind me that I have long legs and a butt she'd kill for. She'd always confess how much she hated her short eyelashes and knees, that her feet looked like "troll feet." So maybe we're all in the same boat. Maybe all women feel like "before" photos.

Ana had already made herself comfortable on the patio, having a muffin and an iced tea. She pretended like she was about to get up when I sat down, but just reached for a half hug.

"Are you ready to kill me for last night?"

"What?" I said as I pulled out the menu. I don't know why I even bothered to look at the menu. I ate eggs Benedict every Saturday morning.

"I don't even remember what happened, honestly. I just remember parts of the cab ride home and then you taking my shoes off before you pulled the covers over me."

I nodded. "That sounds about right. I lost you for about three hours and found you in the upstairs bathroom, so I can't speak to how far you and that guy from the gym got, but I would imagine . . ."

"No! I hooked up with Jim?"

I put the menu down. "What? No, the guy from the gym."

"Yeah, his name is Jim."

"You met a guy at the gym named Jim?" Technically, this wasn't his fault. People named Jim should be allowed to go to gyms, but I couldn't shake the feeling this somehow made him ridiculous. "Is that a bran muffin?"

She nodded, so I took some of it.

"You and I might be the only two people on the planet that like the taste of bran muffins," she said to me, and she might have been right. Ana and I often found striking similarities in each other in meaningless places, the clearest one being food. It doesn't matter if you and another person both like tzatziki. It has no bearing on your ability to get along, but somehow, in these overlaps of taste, there was a bond between Ana and me. I knew she was about to order the eggs Benedict too.

"Anyway, I saw you making out with Jim from the gym, but I don't know what happened after that."

"Oh, well I'm going to assume that it didn't get much further because he's already texted me this morning."

"It's eleven a.m."

"I know. I thought it was a bit quick. But it is flattering," she said.

"What can I get for you two?" The waitress who came up to us wasn't our usual waitress. She was older, had been through more.

"Oh, hi! I don't think we've met before. I'm Ana."

"Daphne." This waitress wasn't nearly as interested in being friends with us as Ana might have hoped.

"What happened to Kimberly?" Ana asked.

"Oh, not sure. Just filling in for the day."

"Ah. Okay, well, we'll make this easy on you. Two eggs Benedict and I'll have an iced tea like she has," I said.

"You got it."

Once she left, Ana and I resumed our earlier discussion.

"I've been thinking about resolutions," Ana said, offering me some of her iced tea while I waited for mine to get there. I declined because I knew if I had some of hers, she'd take that as license to drink some of mine when it arrived and she'd drink my whole damn glass. I'd known her long enough to know where to draw my boundaries and how to draw them so she wouldn't notice.

"Okay. And?"

"I'm thinking something radical."

"Radical? This should be good."

"Celibacy."

"Celibacy?"

"Celibacy. Not having sex."

"No, I know what it means. I'm just wondering why."

"Oh, well, I came up with it this morning. I'm twenty-six years old and last night I got drunk and can't be entirely sure if I slept with someone or not. Maybe time to slow it down."

"You could just stop drinking."

"What are you talking about?"

"You know, stop getting drunk."

"At all?"

"Stop it. I'm not saying something preposterous here. There are plenty of people that just don't drink."

"Yeah, Elsie, they're called alcoholics."

I laughed. "Fair enough, drinking isn't the problem. It's the sleeping around."

"Right. So I'm just going to stop sleeping around."

"And what happens when you meet someone you really want to be with?"

"Well, I'll cross that bridge when I come to it. I didn't meet anyone last year worth my time. I can't say I expect that to change this year."

Daphne showed up with two eggs Benedicts and my iced tea. She put them down in front of us, and I didn't realize how hungry I'd been until the food was staring me in the face. I dug right in.

Ana nodded, chewing. When it started to look like she could speak without spitting food, she added, "I mean, if I meet someone and fall in love, sure. But until then, nobody's getting in here." She made an *x* in the air with her utensils.

"Fair enough." The best part about this place was they put spinach in the eggs Benedict, kind of an eggs Benedict Florentine. "This doesn't mean I can't sleep around though, right?" I said to her.

"No, you still can. You won't. But you still can."

Ana was soon on her way back to the other side of town. She was living in Santa Monica in a condo that overlooked the Pacific Ocean. I'd've been jealous enough to resent her if she hadn't offered on a regular basis for me to move in. I always declined, knowing that living with Ana might be the only thing that could teach me to dislike her. I never did understand how Ana could live the way she did on the salary of a part-time yoga teacher, but she always seemed to have enough money for the things she wanted and needed when she wanted and needed them.

After she left, I walked back to my apartment. I knew exactly how I'd be spending my afternoon. It was a new year and I always felt like a new year didn't feel new without rearranging the furniture. The problem was that I had rearranged my apartment so many times in the two years I'd lived there that I'd exhausted all rational possibilities. I loved my apartment and worked hard to afford it and decorate it. So as I moved the couch from wall to wall, ultimately realizing that it really looked best where it was originally, I was still satisfied. I moved the bookcase from one wall to another, switched my end tables, and decided this was enough of a change for me to commemorate the year. I sat down on the couch, turned on the television, and fell asleep.

It was 5:00 p.m. when I woke up, and while it was technically a Saturday night and single people on Saturday nights are supposed to go out to bars or clubs and find a date, I opted to watch television, read a book, and order a pizza. Maybe this year was going to be the year I did whatever the hell I wanted, regardless of social norms. Maybe.

When it started raining, I knew I'd been right to stay inside. Ana called a few hours later asking what I was doing.

"I wanted to make sure you're not sitting on the couch watching television."

"What? Why can't I watch television?"

"It's a Saturday night, Elsie. Get up! Go out! I'd say you should come out with me but I'm going on a date with Jim."

"So much for celibacy."

"What? I'm not sleeping with him. I'm eating dinner with him."

I laughed. "Okay, well, I'm spending the night on my couch. I'm tired and sleepy and . . ."

"Tired and sleepy are the same thing. Stop making excuses."

"Fine. I'm lazy and I like being alone sometimes."

"Good. At least you admitted it. I'll call you tomorrow. Wish me luck keeping it in my pants."

"You'll need it."

"Hey!"

"Hey!" I said back.

"Okay, I'll talk to you tomorrow."

"Bye."

With the phone in my hand, I ordered a pizza. When I called Georgie's Pizza to order it, the woman on the phone told me it would be an hour and a half before it was delivered. When I asked why, all she said was "Rain." I told her I'd be there in a half hour to pick it up.

Walking into Georgie's Pizza, I felt nothing. No part of my brain or my body knew what was about to happen. I felt no premonition. I was wearing bright yellow galoshes and what can only be described as fat jeans. The rain had matted my hair to my face and I'd given up pushing it away.

I didn't even notice Ben sitting there. I was far too involved with the minutiae of trying to buy a pizza. Once the cashier told me it would be another ten minutes, I retired to the small bench in the front of the store, and it was then that I noticed there was another person in the same predicament.

My heart didn't skip a beat. I had no idea he was "it"; it was "he." He was the man I'd dreamed about as a child, wondering what my husband would look like. I was seeing this face I had wondered about my whole life and it was right here in front of me and I didn't recognize it. All I thought was, He'll probably get his pizza before I get mine.

He looked handsome in a way that suggested he didn't realize just how handsome he was. There was no effort involved, no self-awareness. He was tall and lean with broad shoulders and strong arms. His jeans were just the right shade of blue; his shirt brought out the gray in his green eyes. They looked stark against his brown hair. I sat down next to him and swatted my hair away from my forehead again. I picked up my phone to check my e-mail and otherwise distract myself from the waiting.

"Hi," he said. It took me a second to confirm he was, in fact, speaking to me. That easily, my interest was piqued.

"Hi," I said back. I tried to let it hang there, but I was bad with silence. I had to fill it. "I should have just had it delivered."

"And miss all this?" he said, referencing the tacky faux-Italian decor with his hands. I laughed. "You have a nice laugh," he said.

"Oh, stop it," I said. I swear, my mother taught me how to take a compliment, and yet each time I was given one, I shooed it away like it was on fire. "I mean, thank you. That's what you're supposed to say. Thank you."

I noticed that I had subconsciously shifted my entire body

toward him. I'd read all of these articles about body language and pupil dilation when people are attracted to each other, but whenever I got into a situation where it was actually useful (*Are his pupils dilated? Does he like me?*), I was always far too unfocused to take advantage.

"No, what you're supposed to do is compliment me back," he said, smiling. "That way I know where I stand."

"Ah," I said. "Well, it doesn't really tell you much if I compliment you now, does it? I mean, you know that I'm complimenting you because you've asked . . ."

"Trust me, I can still tell."

"All right," I said, while I looked him up and down. As I made a show of studying him, he stretched out his legs and lengthened his neck. He pulled his shoulders back and puffed out his chest. I admired the stubble on his cheeks, the way it made him look effortlessly handsome. My eyes felt drawn to the strength of his arms. What I wanted to say was "You have great arms," and yet, I didn't have it in me. I played it safe.

"So?" he said.

"I like your shirt," I said to him. It was a heathered gray shirt with a bird on it.

"Oh," he said, and I could hear honest to God disappointment in his voice. "I see how it is."

"What?" I smiled, defensively. "That's a nice compliment."

He laughed. He wasn't overly interested or desperate. He wasn't aloof or cool either, he just . . . was. I don't know whether he was this way with all women, whether he was able to talk to any woman as if he'd known her for years, or whether it was just me. But it didn't matter. It was working. "Oh, it's fine," he said. "But I'm not even going to try for your number. Girl compliments your eyes, your hair, your beard, your arms, your name, that means she's open to a date. Girl compliments your shirt? You're getting shot down."

"Wait—that's not—" I started, but I was interrupted.

"Ben Ross!" the cashier called out, and he jumped up. He looked right at me and said, "Hold that thought."

He paid for his pizza, thanked the cashier genuinely, and then came and sat right back down next to me on the bench.

"Anyway, I'm thinking if I ask you out, I'm going to be shot down. Am I going to be shot down?"

No, he was absolutely not going to be shot down. But I was now embarrassed and trying hard not to seem eager. I smiled wide at him, unable to keep the canary feathers in my mouth. "Your pizza is going to get cold," I told him.

He waved me off. "I'm over this pizza. Give it to me straight. Can I have your number?"

There it was. Do-or-die time. How to say it without screaming it with all of the nervous energy in my body? "You can have my number. It's only fair."

"Elsie Porter!" the cashier yelled. Apparently, she had been calling it for quite a while, but Ben and I were too distracted to hear much of anything.

"Oh! Sorry, that's me. Uh . . . just wait here."

He laughed, and I walked up to pay for my pizza. When I came back, he had his phone out. I gave him my number and I took his.

"I'm going to call you soon, if that's okay. Or should I do the wait-three-days thing? Is that more your style?"

"No, go for it," I said, smiling. "The sooner the better."

He put out his hand to shake and I took it.

"Ben."

"Elsie," I said, and for the first time, I thought the name Ben sounded like the finest name I'd ever heard. I smiled at him. I couldn't help it. He smiled back and tapped his pizza. "Well, until then."

I nodded. "Until then," I said, and I walked back to my car. Giddy.

JUNE

I tear the Georgie's magnet off the refrigerator and try to rip it in half, but I can't get it to succumb to my weak fingers. It just bends and stretches. I realize the futility of what I'm doing, as if removing this magnet, destroying this magnet, will ease my pain in any way. I put it back on the refrigerator door and I dial Susan.

She answers on the second ring.

"Susan? Hi. It's Elsie."

"Hi. Can you meet this afternoon to go over arrangements?"

"Arrangements?" I hadn't really thought about what Susan would want to talk about. Arrangements hadn't even occurred to me. Now, as I let it register, I realize that of course there are arrangements. There are things to plan, carefully calculated ways to grieve. You can't even mourn in peace. You must do it through American customs and civilities. The next few days will be full of obituaries and eulogies. Coffins and caterers. I'm shocked she's even contemplating me being a part of them.

"Sure. Absolutely," I say, trying to inject some semblance of get-up-and-go into my voice. "Where should I meet you?"

"I'm staying at the Beverly Hotel," she says and she tells me where it is, as if I haven't lived in Los Angeles for years.

"Oh," I say. "I didn't realize you were staying in town." She lives two hours away. She can't at least stay in her own city? Leave this one to me?

"There's a lot to take care of, Elsie. We can meet at the bar downstairs." Her voice is curt, uninterested, and cold. I tell her I will meet her there at three. It's almost one. "Whatever is convenient for you," she says and gets off the phone.

None of this is convenient for me. What would be convenient for me is to fall asleep and never wake up. That's what would be convenient for me. What would be convenient for me is to be at work right now because everything is fine and Ben will be home tonight for dinner around seven and we're having tacos. That's convenient for me. Talking to the mother-in-law I met yesterday about funeral arrangements for my dead husband isn't convenient for me no matter what time it happens in the afternoon.

I get back in bed, overwhelmed by everything I need to do before I meet with her. I'll need to shower, to get dressed, to get in the car, to drive, to park. It's too much. When Ana comes back, I'm in tears with gratitude because I know she will take care of everything.

I arrive at the hotel a few minutes late. Ana goes to park the car and says she'll be in the lobby. She says to text her if I need her. I walk into the bar area and scan for Susan. It's cold in this bar despite being warm outside. I hate air-conditioning. I moved here to be warm. The room is brand-new but made to look old. There's a chalkboard menu behind the bar that's too clean to be from the era the decorator would like you to believe. The stools are reminiscent of a speakeasy, but they aren't cracked and worn. They look pristine and unused. This is the age we live in; we are able to have nostalgia for things made yesterday. I would have loved this bar last week, when I liked things cool and clean. Now I hate it for being false and inauthentic.

I finally spot Susan sitting at a high table in the back. She is reading the menu, head down, hand covering her face. She glances up and spots me. As we look at each other for a moment, I can see that her eyes are swollen and red but her face means business.

"Hi," I say as I sit down. She does not get up to greet me.

"Hi," she says as she adjusts herself in her seat. "I stopped by Ben's apartment last night to try to—"

"Ben's apartment?"

"Off Santa Monica Boulevard. I talked to his roommate and he told me that Ben moved out last month."

"Right," I say.

"He said Ben moved in with a girl named Elsie."

"That's me," I say, excited by the prospect of her believing me.

"I gathered as much," she says drily. Then she pulls a binder from the floor and puts it in front of me. "I received this from the funeral home. It's a list of options for the service."

"Okay," I say.

"Decisions will need to be made regarding flowers, the ceremony, the obituary, et cetera."

"Sure." I don't entirely know what the "et cetera" is. I've never been in this situation before.

"I think it's best you tend to those duties."

"Me?" Yesterday she didn't even believe I had a right to be at the hospital. Now she wants me to plan his funeral? "You don't want to have any input?" I say, dubious.

"No. I won't be joining you. I think it's best you take care of this yourself. You want to be his next of kin . . ."

She trails off, but I know how she was going to end it. She was going to say, "You want to be his next of kin, you got it." I ignore her attitude and try to keep Ben—my Ben, her Ben, our Ben—in mind.

"But . . . his family should be involved."

"I am the only family Ben has, Elsie. Had. I am all he had."

"I know. I just meant . . . you should be involved in this. We should do this together."

She is quiet as she gives me a tight and rueful smile. She looks down at the utensils on the table. She plays with the napkins and saltshaker. "Ben clearly did not want me involved in his life. I don't see why I should be intimately involved in his death."

"Why would you say that?"

"I just told you," she says. "He clearly did not care enough to tell me he was getting married, or moving in with you, or whatever you two were to each other. And I . . ." She wipes a tear away with a tissue, delicately and with purpose. She shakes her head to clear it. "Elsie. I don't care to discuss this with you. You have a list of things to do. All I ask is that you inform me as to when the service will be and what will be done with his ashes."

"Ben wanted to be buried," I say. "He told me he wanted to be buried in sweatpants and a T-shirt so he'd be comfortable."

At the time, when he told me, I thought this was sweet. It didn't occur to me that I wouldn't be senile by the time he passed away, that it would be within months of that very conversation.

Her face scrunches itself around her eyes and mouth, and I can tell she's mad. The lines around her mouth become pronounced, and for the first time I can see evidence that she is an older woman. Does my mom have these lines? It's been so long since I've seen her, I don't know.

Maybe Susan doesn't realize what she's doing. Maybe she thinks she's strong enough to cut off her nose to spite her face here, to give me this funeral arranging as a punishment, but she's not. And she's already bothered.

"Everyone in our family has been cremated, Elsie. I never heard Ben say he wanted otherwise. Just tell me what is going to be done with the ashes." She looks down at the table and sighs, blowing air out of her mouth and onto her lap. "I should be going." She gets up from the table and leaves, not looking back at me, not acknowledging my existence.

I grab the binder and head toward the lobby, where Ana is

waiting patiently. She drives us home and I walk right up the front steps to my door. When I realize I've left my keys inside, I turn around and start crying. Ana soothes me as she pulls my spare key off her key ring and hands it to me. She hands it to me as if it will make everything okay, as if the only reason I'm crying is I can't get into the apartment.

JANUARY

I woke up the morning after meeting Ben to a text message from him.

"Rise and Shine, Elsie Porter. Can I take you to lunch?"

I jumped out of bed, shrieked like an idiot, and hopped in place compulsively for at least ten seconds. There was so much energy in my body I had no other way of getting it out.

"Sure. Where to?" I texted back. I stared at the phone until it lit up again.

"I'll come pick you up. Twelve thirty. What's your address?"

I sent him my address and then ran into the shower as if it was urgent. But it wasn't urgent. I was ready to go by 11:45 and I felt entirely pathetic about that. I put my hair up in a high ponytail and shimmied into my favorite jeans and most flattering T-shirt. Sitting around my house for forty-five minutes dressed and ready to go made me feel silly, so I decided to get out of my house and go for a walk. And in all of my glee and excitement, I locked myself out.

My heart started beating so fast I couldn't think straight. I'd left everything inside, my phone, my wallet. Ana had my spare key, but that wasn't going to do me much good without a phone to call her. I walked up and down the street looking for change so that I could ultimately call her on a pay phone, but it turns out, people don't really leave quarters on the ground. You'd think they would because quarters are small and sort of meaningless most of the time, but when you really need one, you realize just how ubiquitous they aren't. Then I decided to find a pay phone anyway since maybe I could rig it to call for free or there'd be a quarter stuck in the little change box. After scouring the neighborhood, I couldn't find a single one. Which left me no viable option I could think of other than breaking into my own apartment.

So that's what I tried to do.

I was on the second story of a duplex, but you could kind of get to the patio from the front stairs; so I walked up the stairs, climbed onto the railing, and tried to grab on to the rail of my patio. If I could get my hand on it and swing a leg around, I was pretty confident I could get onto the patio without much chance of falling to my death. From there, it was just a matter of crawling through the little doggie door in the screen that had been put there by the tenants before me. I had hated that damn doggie door until that very moment, when I was convinced it was my salvation.

As I continued my attempts to grab on to the patio rail, I realized that this might actually be an incredibly stupid plan, in which I was sure to be injured. If it was taking me this long to grab the rail in the first place, why on earth did I think I could easily swing my leg onto it once I reached it?

I made one final and valiant attempt to grab on before I got the cockamamie idea that it was best to go leg first. I was leg first when Ben found me.

"Elsie?"

"Ah!" I almost lost my footing, but I managed to get my leg back onto the steps, only slightly falling over in the process. I caught myself. "Hi, Ben!" I ran down the steps and hugged him. He was laughing.

"Whatcha doin' there?"

I was embarrassed, but somehow not in any threatening way.

"I was trying to break into my own apartment. I locked myself out without a phone or a wallet or anything."

"You don't have a spare key?"

I shook my head. "No. I did, at one point, but then it seemed smarter somehow for me to give it to my friend Ana, so she had it in case of emergency."

He laughed again. It didn't feel like he was laughing at me. Although, I think technically he was.

"Got it. Well, what do you want to do? You can call Ana from my phone now if you want. Or we can go get lunch and then you can call her when we get back?"

I started to answer, but he cut me off.

"Or, I'm also happy to break into your house for you. If you haven't given up on that idea yet."

"Do you think you can swing your leg over this rail onto that one?" I said. I was joking, but he wasn't.

"Absolutely, I can."

"No, stop. I was kidding. We should go get lunch."

Ben started taking off his jacket. "No, I insist you let me do this. It will look brave of me. I'll be considered a hero."

He walked closer to the rail and judged the distance. "That's actually quite far. You were going to try to do that?"

I nodded. "But I have little regard for my own safety," I said. "And a very bad sense of distance."

Ben nodded. "Okay. I'm going to jump this thing, but you have to make me a promise."

"Okay. You got it."

"If I fall and hurt myself, you won't let them call my emergency contact."

I laughed. "Why is that?"

"Because that's my mother and I blew her off for lunch today so I could see you."

"You blew off your mom for me?"

"See? It doesn't make you look very good either, letting me do it. So do we have an agreement?"

I nodded firmly. "You got it." I put out my hand to shake. He looked me in the eye and dramatically shook it, as a smile crept back onto his face.

"Here we go!" he said, and he just jumped it, like it was nothing, pulled his legs up and out, grabbed on to the patio rail, and swung his leg over.

"Okay! Now what?" he asked.

I was mortified to admit the next part of my plan. I hadn't considered how he would fare against the doggie door.

"Oh. Well. Hmm. I was just gonna . . . I was going to crawl in through the doggie door there," I said.

He looked behind him and down. Seeing it through his eyes, I realized it was even smaller than I'd thought.

"This doggie door?"

I nodded. "Yeah. I'm sorry! I should have mentioned that part first maybe."

"I cannot fit through that door, I don't think."

"Well, you could try to help me get over there," I said.

"Right. Or I could jump back over and we could call your friend Ana."

"Oh! That too." I had already forgotten that option.

"Okay, well. I might as well try once now that I'm here. Hold on."

He bent down and peeked in. His head fit in fine and he kept trying to push through. His shirt got caught in the door and was pulled up around his chest. I could see his stomach and the waistband of his underwear. I realized how physically attracted I was to him, how masculine he was. His abs looked solid and sturdy. His back was tanned and defined. His arms, flexed as he lifted himself through, looked strong and . . . capable. I had never before been attracted to the idea of being protected by someone, but Ben's body looked like it could protect me and I was surprised at the reaction it elicited in me. I wondered how I got here exactly. I barely knew this man and I was objectifying him as he broke into my apartment. He finally got both shoulders through and I could hear muffled tones of "I think, actually, I can do it!" and "Ow!" His butt disappeared and his legs slid inside. I walked around to my front door as he opened it, beaming, arms wide. I felt traditional and conventional, a damsel in distress saved by the strapping man. I thought that women who were attracted to that were stupid, but I also did, just for a moment, feel like Ben was my hero.

"Come on in!" he said. It was such a surreal reversal of how I imagined our lunch would start that I couldn't help but feel a bit exhilarated. I couldn't possibly predict what would happen next.

I stepped inside, and he looked around my apartment.

"This is a really nice apartment," he said. "What do you do?"

"Those two sentences in a row mean 'How much money do you make?'" I said. I wasn't being bitchy; at least I didn't feel like I was. I was teasing him, and he was teasing me back when he said, "Well, it's just hard for me to imagine that a woman could afford such a nice place on her own."

I gave him a look of mock indignation, and he gave me one right back.

"I'm a librarian."

"Got it," he said. "So you're doing well. This is good. I've been looking for a baby mama."

"A baby mama?"

"Sorry. Not a baby mama. What's it called when a woman pays for all the stuff for the man?"

"A sugar mama?"

He looked mildly embarrassed, and it was so charming to see. He had seemed so in control up until that moment, but seeing him even the slightest bit vulnerable was . . . intoxicating.

"Sugar mama. That's what I meant. What's a baby mama?"

"That's when you aren't married to the woman who is the mother of your child."

"Oh. No, I'm not looking for one of those. People do look for sugar mamas, though, so watch out."

"I'll be on guard."

"Shall we go?" he said.

"Sure. Let me just grab my—"

"Keys."

"I was going to say wallet! But yes! Keys too. Can you imagine if I'd forgotten those again?" I grabbed them off the counter, and he took them delicately out of my hand.

"I'm going to be in charge of the keys," he said.

I nodded. "If you think that's best."

JUNE

I wake up to the ugly, disgusting world over and over again, each time closing my eyes tightly when I remember who I am. I finally get up around noon, not because I feel ready to face the day but because I can no longer face the night.

I walk into the living room. "Good morning," Ana says as she sees me. She's sitting on the couch and she grabs my hand. "What can I do?"

I look her in the eye and tell her the truth. "You can't do anything. Nothing you could possibly do would make this any easier."

"I know that," she says. "But there must be something I can do just to . . ." Her eyes are watering. I shake my head. I don't know what to say. I don't want anyone to make me feel better. I can't even think past this very moment in time. I can't think forward to this evening. I don't know how I'll make it through the next few minutes, let alone the next few hours. And yet, I don't know anything anyone can do to make those minutes easier. No matter how Ana acts, how hard she scrubs my house clean, how gentle she is with me, no matter if I take a shower, if I run down the street naked, if I drink every ounce of alcohol in the house, Ben is still not with me. Ben will never be with me again. I suddenly feel like I might not make it through the day, and if Ana isn't here to watch me, I don't know what I'll do.

I sit beside her. "You can stay here. Stay near me. It won't make it easier, but it will make me believe in myself more, I think. Just stay here." I'm too emotional to cry. My face and body are so consumed with dread, there's no room left to produce anything.

"You got it. I'm here. I'm here and I won't leave." She grabs me, her arm around my shoulders, squeezing me. "Maybe you should eat," she says.

"No, I'm not hungry," I say. I don't anticipate ever being hungry again. What does hunger even feel like? Who can remember?

"I know you're not hungry, but you still have to eat," she says. "If you could have anything in the whole world, what could you manage to get down? Don't worry about health or expense. Just if you could have anything."

Normally, if someone asked me that, I'd say I wanted a Big Mac. I always just want a Big Mac, the largest container of fries McDonald's has, and then a pile of Reese's peanut butter cups. My palate has never been trained to appreciate fine foods. I never crave sushi or a nice chardonnay. I crave fries and Coca-Cola. But not now. To me right now, a Big Mac might as well be a staple gun. That is how likely I am to eat it.

"No, nothing. I don't think I could keep anything down."

"Soup?"

"No, nothing."

"You have to eat at some point today. Promise me you'll eat at some point today?"

"Sure," I say. But I know I won't. I'm lying. I have no intention of carrying through on that promise. What's the point of a promise anyway? How can we expect people to stick to their word about anything when the world around us is so arbitrary, unreliable, and senseless?

"You need to go to the funeral home today," she says. "Want me to call them now?"

I hear her and I nod. That's all I can do. So it's what I do.

Ana picks up her phone and calls the funeral home. Apparently, I was supposed to call yesterday. I can hear the receptionist say something about "being behind." Ana doesn't dare pass this information along to me, but I can tell by her tone on the phone that they are giving her a hard time. Let them come at me. Just let them. I'd be happy to scream at a group of people profiting from tragedy.

Ana drives me to the office and parks the car in front, on the street. There is a parking garage underneath the building, but it's $2.50 every fifteen minutes and that's simply absurd. I refuse to encourage those overpriced assholes by using their service. This has nothing to do with my grief, by the way. I have a lifelong hatred of price gouging. It says on the sign that it's free with validation from Wright & Sons Funeral Home, but that seems awfully tacky on everyone's part. "Yes, we would like him embalmed. By the way, could you validate this for me?"

Ana finds a spot on the street easily enough. I check the passenger's side mirror and realize that my eyes are red and bloodshot. My cheeks are splotched with pink. My eyelashes are squashed together and shiny. Ana hands me her large, dark sunglasses. I put them on and step out of the car. As I catch a glimpse of myself in her mirror one last time, dressed for a meeting with large glasses on my face, I feel like Jackie Kennedy. Maybe there's a part of every woman that wants to be Jackie Kennedy, but they mean First Lady Jackie Kennedy or Jackie Kennedy Onassis. No one wants to relate to her like this.

Ana runs to the meter and goes to put quarters in but finds

herself empty. "Shit! I'm out of quarters. You head in and I'll take care of this," she says, heading back into the car.

"No," I say, reaching into my own wallet. "I have some." I put the change in the meter. "Besides, I don't think I can do this without you." Then I start crying again, blubbering, the tears falling down my face, only visible once they've made their way past the huge lenses.

JANUARY

When we got in Ben's car, he asked if I was up for an adventure and I told him that I was.

"No, I mean, a true adventure."

"I'm ready!"

"What if this adventure takes us on a road trip to a restaurant over an hour away?"

"As long as you're driving, it's fine by me," I said. "Although, I'm confused about what could possibly require us to drive an hour out of the way."

"Oh, you just leave that to me," he said, and he started the car.

"You're being very cryptic," I said. He ignored me. He reached over and turned on his radio. "You're in charge of music and possibly navigation if it comes to that."

"Fine by me," I said, as I immediately turned the station to NPR. As the low, monotonous voices started to fill the air, Ben shook his head. "You're one of those?" he said, smiling.

"I'm one of those," I said, owning it and not apologizing.

"I should have known. Pretty girl like you had to have some sort of flaw."

"You don't like talk radio?"

"I like it, I guess. I mean, I like it the way I like doctors' appointments. They serve a purpose but they aren't much fun."

I laughed, and he looked at me. He looked for just a little too long to be safe.

"Hey! Eyes on the road, Casanova!" I said. Casanova? Who was I? My dad?

Ben immediately turned back and focused on what was in front of us. "Sorry!" he said. "Safety first."

By the time we hit the freeway, he had turned off the radio. "That's enough traffic updates for me," he said. "We will just have to entertain ourselves the old-fashioned way."

"Old-fashioned way?"

"Conversation."

"Ah, right. Conversation."

"Let's start with the basics: How long have you lived in L.A.?"

"Five years. I moved right after college. You?"

"Nine years. I moved here to go to college. Looks like we graduated the same year. Where did you go to school?"

"Oh," I said. "Ithaca. My parents both went to Cornell and made me take a tour, but when I got there, Ithaca seemed a better fit. I was originally premed, but that lasted about two months before I realized I had absolutely no desire to be a doctor."

"Why did you think you wanted to be a doctor?" We were speeding up the freeway at this point. The driving was taking up less of his attention.

"Both of my parents are doctors. My mother is the chief of staff at the hospital in my hometown, and my dad is a neurosurgeon there."

"A neurosurgeon? That's intimidating," Ben added.

"He's an intimidating guy. My mom's not easy either. They were not happy when I changed my major."

"Oh, that kind of family? The pressuring kind? Overachievers?"

"They are definitely overachievers. The thing is, I'm just not like that. I'm a work-to-live not a live-to-work type of person. I like to put in my forty hours and then go have my life."

"But that doesn't sit well with them?"

I shrugged. "They believe that life is work. It's not about joy. It's not about laughter. It's not about love, really, I don't think, for them. It's about work. I don't think my dad likes saving lives as much as he likes being at the top of a field that is constantly growing and changing. I think it's about progress for them. Library science isn't exactly cutting edge. But I mean, there isn't much they can do. My parents weren't really very engaged parents, you know? So, I think when I changed my major it was, like, this moment of . . . It was a break for all of us. They no longer needed to pretend that they understood me. I no longer needed to pretend I wanted what they had."

I hadn't ever told anyone my real feelings about that before. But I didn't see any reason to tell Ben anything but the entire truth. I was somewhat embarrassed after I said it all. I realized just how vulnerable that was. I turned and looked out my window. The traffic in the opposite direction was relentless, and yet, we were flying through town.

"That's really sad," he said.

"It is and it isn't. My parents and I aren't close. But they are happy in their way and I am happy in mine. I think that's what matters."

He nodded. "You're absolutely right. Smart and right."

I laughed. "How about you? How are your parents?"

Ben blew air out of his chest but kept his eyes forward and on the road. He spoke somberly.

"My father passed away three years ago."

"Oh, my. I'm so sorry to hear that."

"Thanks." He looked at me briefly and then returned his

eyes to the road. "He died of cancer and it was a long battle so we all knew it was coming; we were prepared for it."

"I don't know if that's good or bad."

Ben let out a brief puff of air. "I don't either. Anyway, my mom is doing well. As well as you can when you've lost the person you love, you know?"

"I can't even imagine."

"No, I can't either. I've lost a father and I know how hard that can be, but I can't even imagine losing your best friend, your soul mate. I worry about her, although she insists she's okay."

"I'm sure you can't help but worry. Do you have any brothers or sisters?" I asked.

Ben shook his head. "You?"

"No, sir." I rarely met other only children. It was nice to hear that Ben was one. When I would tell people I was an only child, I felt like I was either being pitied for not having had siblings or being judged as petulant even if I hadn't proven to be.

"Awesome! Two only children! I knew I liked you." He high-fived me sloppily as he kept one hand on the wheel.

"Do I get any hints about where we are going yet?" I asked, as he merged from one freeway onto the next.

"It's Mexican" was all I could get out of him.

After two games of Twenty Questions and one game of I Spy, we finally made it to our destination. It was a shack. Quite literally. It was a shack in the middle of the road called Cactus Tacos. I was underwhelmed, but Ben's face lit up.

"We're here!" he said as he flicked off his seat belt and opened his car door. I gathered my things, and he came around to my side. He opened the door for me before I could open it for myself.

"Why, thank you!" I said over the dinging of his car, reminding us that the door needed to be closed.

"Certainly."

I crawled out and stood next to him.

"So this is the place, huh?" I said. He shut the door behind me and the dinging relented.

"I know it doesn't look like much. But you said you were up for an adventure and these are honestly the best tacos I've ever had in my life. Do you like *horchata*?"

"What is *horchata*?"

"It's rice milk with cinnamon. Just—trust me. You gotta try one." As we walked toward the taco stand, he put his hand on the small of my back, guiding me ever so gently. It felt so comforting and so natural that it made me want to turn around into his arms. It made me want to touch more of him with more of me. Instead, I stood and stared at the menu.

"If it's okay," Ben said, moving his hand up my back and now onto my shoulder, "I'll order for you. I fully respect your right to order for yourself. It's just that I've been here many, many times and I know everything on this menu."

"Be my guest," I said.

"Do you like chicken, steak, pork?"

"No pork," I said.

"No pork?" Ben said, incredulous. "I'm kidding. I don't like pork either. All right!" He rubbed his hands together eagerly.

"Perdón?" he said through the window to the man behind the counter. *"Queria cuatro tacos tinga de pollo y cuatro tacos carne asada, por favor? Queso extra en todos. Ah, y dos horchatas, por favor."*

The man showed him the size of the *horchatas* with a look that said, "Are you sure you want two of these?" and Ben nodded. *"Sí, sí, lo sé. Dos. Por favor."*

I don't know what it was exactly that made Ben seem so irresistible at that moment. I don't know if it was because he seemed so knowledgeable about something I knew nothing about (Spanish), or whether it was because any time a man spoke another language it was inherently sexy to me (because that was also true). I don't know. I just know that as I stood there, unable to understand what was being communicated around me, I thought Ben Ross was the sexiest man I'd ever seen. He was so secure in himself, so sure that this would all turn out okay. That's what it was. It was the confidence. He spoke Spanish to the man at the taco stand like it never occurred to him he might sound like a complete idiot. And that was exactly why he did not sound like a complete idiot.

"Wow," I said, as he handed me my *horchata*. "That's impressive."

"I swear that's about the extent of my knowledge," he said as he unwrapped a straw and put it in my drink. "But I'd be lying if I said I wasn't hoping to impress you."

"Well, so far, so good." I took a sip of the drink. It was sweet and cold, creamy and yet easy to drink in big gulps. "Wow, this is great too."

Ben smiled as he took a sip of his own. "I'm doing okay?" he asked.

"You're doing great," I told him. I was overwhelmed, to be honest. It had been so long since I'd had a crush on someone I'd forgotten how exciting it makes everything you do.

When our tacos were ready, Ben grabbed them from the window. They came stuffed in red and white checkered cartons. He grabbed all of them and balanced them over his forearms and in his hands.

There were no places to sit at Cactus Tacos, and so Ben suggested we sit on the hood of his car.

"These tacos look messy. I'll spill *pico de gallo* all over your car."

"It's a ten-year-old Honda. I'm not exactly precious about it."

"Fine. But I feel like you should know that I'm very clumsy and messy."

"And you forget your keys a lot."

"Well, I forget everything a lot."

"So far, it's all good by me."

We sat on his hood and we talked about our jobs and if we liked living in Los Angeles, and sure enough, I dripped taco grease onto his bumper. Ben just smiled at me. Ana called me as I was feebly attempting to clean it up and I put her through to voice mail. Ben and I talked long after the tacos were gone.

Eventually, Ben asked me if I wanted dessert.

"You have somewhere else in mind?" I asked.

"No," he said. "I thought it would be lady's choice."

"Oh," I said. I was somewhat at a loss as to what to suggest. I had no idea where we were, no idea what was around us. "Actually," I said. "Are you up for another adventure?"

"Absolutely!" he said as he hopped off the hood of the car. He put out his hand for me to grab. "Where to?"

"East L.A.?" I asked, gently. While I wasn't sure where we were, I knew we were at least an hour from my place, and East L.A. was at least thirty minutes past my apartment in the opposite direction.

"East L.A. it is, my fair maiden." He helped me off the car and opened my door for me.

"Such a gentleman," I pronounced as I positioned myself to sit down.

"Wait," he said. He grabbed me around the waist and pulled me to him. "Is this okay?"

My face was up against his. I could smell his breath. It

smelled like cilantro and onions. It smelled sweet, somehow. My heart started beating faster.

"Yeah," I said. "This is okay."

"I want to kiss you," he said. "But I want to make sure you won't be embarrassed in front of the taco stand man."

I smiled at him and looked over his shoulder. The taco stand man was staring. I was, in fact, slightly embarrassed. But it was just enough to make the situation thrilling and not enough to ruin it.

"Go for it," I said to him. He did.

As he kissed me against the car, my body pushed in toward him. My arms made their way into the crooks on either side of his neck and my hands grazed the stubble on the back of his head at the hairline. His hair felt soft and oily in my hands. I felt his chest and torso push me further against the car.

He pulled away, and I looked sheepishly at the man at the taco stand. Still staring. Ben caught my eye and looked back. The taco stand man turned away, and Ben started to laugh, conspiratorially.

"We should get out of here," I said.

"I told you you'd be embarrassed," he said as he ran around to the driver's side.

Once we'd made our way back onto the freeway, I texted Ana, letting her know that I'd call her tomorrow. She texted back asking what on earth I was doing that I couldn't talk to her. I told her the truth.

"I'm on a daylong date. It's going really well so I'll call you tomorrow."

Ana tried to call me after that and I put her through to voice mail again. I realized that me being on a date probably seemed a bit odd to her. I had just seen her yesterday morning for breakfast with no plans to date anyone, let alone date them all day.

Ben and I hit traffic. The stop and go of the freeway was made even more maddening by the sweat and exhaust from all of the cars. We had been stuck on the same stretch of road for twenty minutes when Ben asked a question I had been avoiding.

"When does this mystery place close?" he asked.

"Eh . . ." I said, embarrassed to tell him we were almost certainly not going to make it.

"It's soon, isn't it?" he asked.

"It's soon. It closes at six. We've only got about a half hour. We don't need to go. I can take you some other time."

It just slipped out, the "some other time." I didn't mean to make it clear that I wanted to see him again. I mean, in my brain I assumed we would be seeing each other again, but I also wanted to maintain some sense of mystery about the whole thing. I didn't want to show my cards that soon. I turned a little red.

Ben smiled. He knew what I'd done and decided not to press it. He just took the compliment and let it alone. "Still," he said. "I want you to get whatever it is."

"Gelato," I said.

"Gelato?" he said, somewhat disbelieving. "We're racing across town for gelato?"

I hit him in the chest with my hand. "Hey! You said you wanted to do something. It's good gelato!"

"I'm just teasing you. I love gelato. Come hell or high water I'm getting you that goddamn gelato."

As traffic started to move slightly, he veered the car onto the shoulder, flew past the rest of the cars, and got in line to get off the freeway.

"Wow," I said. "Way to take control."

"Total asshole move," he said. "But this situation is dire."

He sped through back roads and dangerously ran yellow lights. He cut a few people off and honked at them as he drove by to apologize. I directed him under unfamiliar overpasses, found unheard-of drives and lanes for him to traverse, and when we finally parked the car in front of Scoops Gelato Shop, it was 6:01 p.m. Ben ran to the door just as they were locking it.

He pounded on it politely. "Please," he said, "just . . . can you open the door?"

A young Korean girl came to the door and pointed to the Closed sign. She shook her head.

Ben put his hands together in a prayer position, and she shrugged at him.

"Elsie, do me a favor, would you?"

"Hmm?" I said. I was hanging further back on the sidewalk.

"Would you turn around?"

"Turn around?"

"I'm about to beg on my knees and I don't want you to see it. I want you to think of me as a strong, virile, confident man."

I laughed, and he continued to look at me blankly.

"Oh my God, you're serious," I said, as I laughed and resigned myself to turning around.

I looked out onto the main street in the distance. I watched cars stop at red lights and cyclists speed by them. I saw a couple walking down the street with a baby stroller. Soon, I heard the jingle of a door opening and I started to turn around.

"Wait!" I heard Ben say. "Don't move yet," and so I didn't.

Two minutes later, the door jingled again and Ben came around in front of me. In his hands were two cups of gelato, both a light brown with brightly colored spoons sticking out of them.

"How did you do that?" I asked, taking one of them from him.

Ben smiled. "I have my ways."

"Seriously," I said.

"Seriously? I bribed her."

"You bribed her?" I asked, shocked. I had never known anyone to bribe someone before.

"Well, I said, 'If you can give me two cups of whatever flavor you have left, I'll give you twenty bucks extra.' So if that's a bribe, then yes, I bribed her."

"Yeah, I'd say that's a bribe."

"Somewhat corrupt," he said to me. "I hope you can forgive me."

I stared at him for a moment. "Forgive you? Are you kidding? No one has ever bribed anyone for me before!" I said.

Ben laughed. "Now you're just making fun of me."

"No," I said. "I'm entirely serious. I think it's hugely flattering."

"Oh," he said, smiling. He laughed. "Awesome." Then he took a bite of his gelato and immediately grimaced. "It's coffee," he said, as he ran to the trash can on the sidewalk and spit it out.

"You don't like coffee?"

"Coffee is like doctors' visits and NPR to me," he said.

I took his cup from his hand and held it in the palm of mine while I ate from the other. "More for me, then," I said.

We got back in his car, and neither one of us knew quite what to do next.

"The day doesn't have to end," I said. "Does it?"

"I'm glad you said that," Ben responded. "Where to next?"

"Well, I don't know," I said. "I'm not really hungry . . ."

"What if we go back to your place?" he suggested. "I promise I won't get handsy."

I let it sit in the air for a minute. "What's wrong with handsy?" I teased him. He didn't even say anything; he just threw the car in reverse and started speeding down the street.

When we got back to my apartment, Ben took my keys out of his pocket. We walked up the stairs to my door, but halfway up the stairs, Ben realized he'd forgotten something. He quickly ran back down to his car and put money in the parking meter. Then, he flashed back up the stairs to meet me and unlocked my door. Once inside, he gingerly placed the keys on my table by the door.

"They're right here when you need them," he said. "Is that a good place to remember them?"

"That's fine. Do you want anything to drink?"

"Oh, sure. What do you have?"

"Water. I should have said, 'Do you want any water?'"

Ben laughed and sat on the couch. I grabbed two glasses and went to the refrigerator to fill them, which is when I saw the big bottle of champagne sitting there, ice cold and left over from New Year's Eve.

"I have champagne!" I said and grabbed it out of the fridge. I walked to the living room and held it up in front of Ben. "Bubbly?"

He laughed. "Yeah! Let's break open the bubbly."

We ran to the kitchen and got wineglasses. I attempted to open the bottle and failed, so Ben stepped in and popped it open. The champagne sprayed all over our faces, but neither one of us much cared. He poured our glasses, and we sat down on the couch.

It was awkward for a minute. We were stuck in silence. I

drank from my glass for a bit too long, staring at the golden bubbles. Why was it awkward now? I wondered. I wasn't sure. I stood up for a minute and felt the whoosh of the alcohol to my head.

"I'll be right back," I said. "I'm just going to go . . ." What? What was I going to go do? I wasn't sure.

Ben grabbed my hand and looked at me. He stared into my eyes. His eyes looked to be pleading with me. Just like that, I threw myself onto his lap, straddling his waist. I kissed him. My arms wandered down onto his shoulders. His hands grabbed my hips. I could feel them through my jeans. He pulled me tight as he kissed me, his arms running up my back and into my hair. It felt like he was desperate to kiss me. As we moved our heads and hands in sync, my body started to ache where it wasn't being touched.

"I like you," he said to me, breathlessly.

I laughed. "I can see that," I said.

"No," he said, pulling his face away from mine for a moment, looking at me like I was important. "I like you."

Boys had told me they liked me before. They had said it in eighth grade and in high school. They had said it drunk at parties. One had said it in a college cafeteria. Some of them looked down at the ground when they mumbled it. Some of them stuttered. Each time I had told them I liked them back. And I realized now that each time I had been lying.

No man had ever made me feel this admired before, nor had I admired someone back this much before. What had Ben done in the past few hours to make me care so much? I didn't know. All I knew was that when he said that to me, I knew that he meant it. And when I heard it come out of his mouth, it felt like I'd been waiting to hear it my entire life.

"I like you too," I said. I kissed him again and he grabbed me. He put his hands around my waist and he moved me toward him, closing what little gap there was between us. He kissed my ears and jawline, sending goose bumps up the back of my neck, for what felt like hours. I finally had to stand up. There was a cramp in my hip.

When I looked at the clock, it was after 8:00 p.m.

"Wow," I said. "This is . . . that was . . . a long time."

"Are you hungry?" he asked me.

"Yeah." I nodded, realizing that I was hungry. "Are you?"

"Yeah. What should we do? Go out? Cook here? Order in?"

"Well, pizza is out. We had that last night." We hadn't eaten it together, but I knew the way I said it implied that we had. I liked hearing myself say it. I liked that I sounded like his girlfriend at that moment—which made me feel a little insane. I was ready to get monogrammed towels for us and I barely knew him.

"Right. So my vote is order Chinese or cook here, depending on what you have." He gestured toward the kitchen. "Can I look?"

I stood up and showed him the way. "Be my guest!"

We walked into the kitchen and stood in front of the refrigerator. He stood behind me, his arms around my torso, his face in my neck. I showed him what I had, and it was sparse, although had either of us been a decent cook, I'm sure we could have come up with something.

"Well, that settles it," he said. "Where's the Chinese food menu?"

I laughed and fished it out of the drawer. He looked at the menu for only a minute. "How about we split the kung pao chicken, a bowl of wonton soup, beef chow mein, and white rice?"

"Make it brown rice and you're on," I said.

"Because this is a first date, I'm going to say okay, but all subsequent dates, absolutely not. Brown rice tastes like cardboard and I simply cannot meet you halfway on that in the future."

I nodded. "I understand. We could get two different orders of rice."

"Maybe when the romance is gone we can do that, but not tonight." He turned in to the phone. "Yes, hi. I'd like to get an order of kung pao chicken, an order of beef chow mein, and wonton soup." He paused for a moment. "No. We'd like brown rice, please." He stuck out his tongue at me, and then he gave my address, his telephone number, and hung up.

When the food came, we ate it. Ana called a few more times to try to find me. Ben made me laugh over and over; he made me cackle and hiss. He made my abdomen hurt. We kissed and we teased each other; we wrestled with the remote. When it got late enough that it was do-or-die time, I spared us both any awkward misinterpretations and said, "I want you to spend the night but I'm not going to have sex with you."

"How do you know I want to have sex with you? Maybe I just want to be friends," he said. "Ever consider that?" I didn't need to respond. "Fine. So I do want to have sex with you, but I'll keep my hands to myself."

Before meeting him in my bedroom, I thought carefully and consciously of what to wear to bed. We weren't going to have sex, so lingerie or sleeping naked was clearly out of the question. And yet, it wasn't an asexual activity. I still wanted to be sexy. I settled on a pair of very small boxer shorts and a tank top. I checked myself out in the mirror before I left the bathroom, and I had to admit, I looked accidentally sexy when it was anything but an accident.

I walked into my room to find him already under my covers. His shirt was off but the blanket was covering him. I crawled in next to him and put my head on his chest. He bent his head down to kiss me and then turned to see where the light switch was.

"Oh," I said. "Check this out." I clapped loudly twice and the lights went out. "I got it as a party favor years ago." I never used the Clapper anymore. I'd honestly almost forgotten that I'd plugged it in. Ben was floored.

"You are the coolest person in the world. Just hands down. The coolest," he said.

It was pitch dark as our eyes slowly adjusted, and then there was a buzz and small flash of light. It was my phone.

"He's STILL THERE?" Ana had texted.

I turned off my phone.

"Ana, I presume," Ben said, and I confirmed. "She must be wondering who the hell I am."

"She'll know soon enough," I said. He put his finger under my chin and lifted my head toward his. I kissed him. Then I kissed him again. I kissed him harder. Within seconds our hands, arms, and pieces of clothing went flying. His skin felt warm and soft, but his body felt sturdy.

"Oh!" I said. "The parking meter. Did you put enough money in? What if you get a ticket?"

He pulled me back to him. "I'll take the ticket," he said. "I don't want to stop touching you."

As we rolled around each other, I somehow kept to my word. I did not sleep with him that night. I wanted to. It was difficult not to. Both of our bodies pleaded with me to change my mind, but I didn't. I'm not sure how I didn't. But I didn't.

I don't remember when I fell asleep, but I do remember Ben whispering, "I'm not sure if you're still awake, but . . . thank you, Elsie. This is the first time I've been too excited to go to sleep since I was a kid."

I tried to keep my eyes shut, but my mouth couldn't help but smile wide when I heard him.

"I can see you smiling," he whispered, half laughing. I didn't open my eyes, teasing him.

"Okay," he said, pulling me closer to him. "Two can play at that game."

When he left for work the next morning, I saw him take the ticket off his windshield and laugh.

JUNE

The building is cold. The air is crisp and almost sharp. I wonder if they keep it so cold because there are dead bodies here. Then I remember that Ben's body must be here. My husband is now a dead body. I used to find dead things repulsive and now my husband is one of them.

Ana and I are called into the office of Mr. Richard Pavlik. He is a tall, thin man with a face that's generic except for the fact that it has a huge mustache across it. He looks to be about sixty.

It's stuffy in Mr. Pavlik's office. I have to imagine that people are here during the worst times of their lives, so why Mr. Pavlik can't just take the extra step and make it comfortable, I'll never know. Even these chairs are terrible. They're low to the ground and oddly sunken in. My center of gravity is basically at my knees.

I try to sit forward in the chair and listen to him drone on and on about the trivial parts of my husband's death, but my back starts to hurt and I sit back in the chair. As I do, I worry the angle is unbecoming of a lady. It looks careless and comfortable, which I am not. I am neither of those things. I sit back up, rest my hands on my knees, and grin and bear it. That is pretty much my plan for the rest of my life.

"Mr. Pavlik, with all due respect," I interrupt him. "Ben did not want to be cremated. He wanted to be buried."

"Oh," he says, looking down at the pages in front of him. "Mrs. Ross indicated a cremation."

"I'm Mrs. Ross," I say.

"I'm sorry, I meant the senior Mrs. Ross." He scrunches his face slightly. "Anyway, Elsie," he says. I can't help but feel rejected slightly. I am not Mrs. Ross to him and he does not know my maiden name, so he's jumped right to first names. "In this case, Mrs. Ross is the next of kin."

"No, Richard," I say sternly. If he can take away my last name, I can take away his. "I am the next of kin. I am Ben's wife."

"I don't mean to argue otherwise, Elsie. I simply have no record of that."

"So you're saying that because I don't have a marriage certificate yet, I am not next of kin?"

Richard Pavlik shakes his head. "In situations like this, where there is a question of who is the next of kin, I have to go by official documents. I don't have anyone else close to Ben who can confirm that you two were married, and when I looked into marital records, there was no evidence of it. I hope you understand I'm in a difficult spot."

Ana sits forward in her chair and moves her hand into a fist on Richard's desk.

"I hope you understand that Elsie just got married and lost her husband within the same ten days, and instead of being on her honeymoon on some far-off private beach she's sitting here with you implying to her grieving face that she's not married at all."

"I'm sorry, Ms. . . ." Richard is uncomfortable and doesn't remember Ana's last name.

"Romano," she says, angrily.

"Ms. Romano. I really don't mean to make this uncomfortable or unpleasant for anyone. I am so sorry for your loss. All I ask is that you have a conversation with Mrs. Ross about this, because legally, I have to take my orders from her. Again, I am truly sorry for your loss."

"Let's just move on. I'll talk to Susan about the cremation later. What else do I need to go over today?" I say.

"Well, Elsie. Everything hinges on what is to be done with the body."

Don't call it the body, you asshole. That's my husband. That's the body that held me when I cried, the body that grabbed my left hand as it drove us to the movies. That's the body that made me feel alive, made me feel crazy, made me cry and shake with joy. It's lifeless now, but that doesn't mean I've given up on it.

"Fine, Richard. I'll talk to Susan and call you this afternoon."

Richard gathers up the papers on his desk and stands to see us out. He grabs his card and hands it to me. When I don't take it, he offers it to Ana, and she takes it gracefully, tucking it into her back pocket.

"Thank you so much for your time," he says as he opens the door for us.

"Fu—" I start to say to him as I am walking out the door. I plan on slamming it when I'm done. But Ana interrupts me and squeezes my hand gently to let me know I need to cool it. She takes over.

"Thank you, Richard. We will be in touch soon. In the meantime, please get back on the phone with the marital records people and sort this out," she says.

She shuts the door behind her and smiles at me. The circumstances aren't funny, but it *is* kind of funny that I almost told that man to fuck off. For a moment, I think we might both actually laugh—something I haven't done in days. But the moment passes and I don't have it in me to push the air out and smile.

"Are we going to talk to Susan?" Ana says as we are heading to the car.

"Yeah," I say. "I guess we are." At least this makes me feel like I have a purpose, however small. I have to protect Ben's wishes. I have to protect the body that did so much to protect me.

JANUARY

At work the next day, my thoughts oscillated between focusing on tasks at hand and daydreaming. I had to promise Ana I'd drive over to her place after work to explain my absence, and I kept replaying in my head how I was going to describe him. It was always her talking to me about men and me listening. Now that I knew it would be me talking and her listening, I almost felt like I needed to practice.

I was physically present but mentally absent when Mr. Callahan cornered me. "Elsie?" he said, as he approached the counter.

Mr. Callahan was almost ninety years old. He wore polyester trousers every day in either gray or khaki. He wore a button-up shirt in some sort of plaid pattern with a cream-colored Members Only jacket to cover it.

Mr. Callahan kept tissues in his pants pockets. He kept ChapStick in his jacket pocket, and he always said "Bless you" whenever anyone within a fifty-foot radius sneezed. He came to the library almost every day, coming and going, sometimes multiple times a day. Some days, he would read magazines and newspapers in the back room until lunchtime, when he would check out a book to take home to his wife. Other days, he would come in the late afternoon to return a book and pick up a black-and-white movie on VHS or maybe some sort of opera I had never heard of on CD.

He was a man of culture, a man of great kindness and personality. He was a man devoted to his wife, a wife we at the library never met but heard everything about. He was also very old, and I sometimes feared he was on his last legs.

"Yes, Mr. Callahan?" I turned to face him and rested my elbows on the cold counter.

"What is this?" Mr. Callahan slid a bookmark in front of me. It was one of our digital library bookmarks. We had put them all over the library a week earlier to try to call attention to the digital materials we had. There was a big debate in the library about starting this initiative. We didn't have much say, to tell the truth, as we were guided by the Los Angeles Public Library system, but still, some people thought we should be doing more, some people thought we should be preserving the past. I have to say I was leaning toward preserving the past. I loved holding books in my hands. I loved smelling their pages.

"That is a bookmark about our digital library."

"What?" he said to me, asking politely but bemused.

"It's a website we have that you can go to and download materials instead of coming to the library to get them."

He nodded, recognizing what I was saying. "Oh, like if I wanted an i-book."

"An e-book, right," I said. I didn't mean to correct him.

"Wait, is it *e* or *i*?"

"E."

"Oh, for heaven's sake. This whole time I've been thinking my granddaughter, Lucia, was saying iPad."

"No," I said. "She was. You read an e-book on an iPad."

Mr. Callahan started laughing. "Listen to yourself," he said, smiling. "You sound a little ridiculous."

I laughed with him. "Nevertheless," I said. "That's what it's called."

"All right, so if I get an iPad, I can read an e-book on it that I download from the library." He emphasized *iPad, e-book,* and *download* as if they were made-up words and I was a toddler.

"Right," I said. "That's actually quite impressive how quick you got that."

"Oh, please. I'll forget tomorrow." He touched my hand and patted it as if to say good-bye. "Anyway, it sounds like I don't want anything to do with it. Too complicated for me. I much prefer the real thing."

"Me too," I said. "But I don't know how much longer the real thing will be around."

"Long enough for me," he said, and I was struck by the sadness of realizing your own mortality. He didn't seem sad, and yet, I still felt sad for him.

My boss, Lyle, came by and told Mr. Callahan we were closing.

"Okay, okay! I'll leave," he joked, putting his hands up in surrender. I watched him walk out the door, and then I tidied up and sped away to Ana's house.

"What the hell happened?! *Start* at the beginning. Who *is* this guy?" Ana said to me. I was lying on her couch.

"Ana, I don't even know how to explain it."

She sat down on the ottoman next to me. "Try."

"On Saturday night I ordered a pizza—"

"Oh my God! *He's a delivery guy*? Elsie!"

"What? No, he's not a delivery guy. He's a graphic designer. That's not . . . Just listen. I ordered a pizza but they said it would take too long to get there. So I went down to pick it up and there was this guy waiting too. That was him. That was Ben."

"Ben is the guy?"

"Ben is the guy. So I notice him, he's really cute, like too cute for me cute, you know? But he starts talking to me and it's, like, when he starts talking I just . . . Anyway, I gave him my number; he called me yesterday morning and picked me up for lunch at twelve thirty. It was the best date I've ever had. I mean, it was one of the best *days* I've ever had. He says all the right things and he's so sincere and cute and . . ."

"Sexy? Is he sexy?"

"Oh my *God* is he sexy. I can't describe it, but when I'm with him, it's like I'm with myself. I'm not worried about anything, I feel like I can say whatever I'm thinking and it won't freak him out. I'm nervous."

"Why are you nervous? This sounds *amazing*."

"It is, but this is going so fast."

"Maybe he's the one. Maybe that's why it's going so fast. Because it's right."

I was hoping she would say this. I didn't want to have to say it myself, because it seemed absurd. "No. Do you think?"

Ana shrugged. "Who knows? It could be! I want to meet this guy!"

"He's really great. I'm just . . . What if I'm getting ahead of myself? He says I'm perfect for him and he likes me and it doesn't feel like bullshit but . . . what if it's all . . ."

"An act?"

"Yeah. What if I'm being played?"

"I mean . . . being played how exactly? Did you sleep with him yet?"

I shook my head. "No, he just slept over and we slept next to each other."

"That sounds pretty sincere."

"Right, but what if he's like . . . a con man or something."

"You watch too much television."

"I know I do, but *what* if he's a con man? He's just like this really sexy, really charming, perfect man who figures out your wildest fantasies of being swept off your feet by a man who loves pizza and bribes gelato workers and is an only child and then *boom*. My money is gone."

"You don't even have very much money."

"Right, that's why I need all that I have."

"No, Elsie. I mean if he's that good of a con man, he'd target a rich person."

"Oh."

"You know what I think?" Ana moved toward me and sat so

my head was in her lap. "I think you've got a good thing going, and you're making a mountain out of a molehill. So what, it's moving fast? Just chill out and enjoy it."

"Well . . . okay . . . What if there is a limited amount of swooning in a relationship and if you use it all up too fast, then it disappears?"

Ana looked at me like I had three heads. "You're starting to stress me out. Give it a rest and stop trying to poke holes in a good thing."

I thought about this for a moment and decided she was probably right. I was freaking out about nothing at all. I did the best I could to put it out of my head.

"You good?" Ana asked me, and I nodded.

"I'm good. I'm gonna chill."

"Good," she said. "Because we need to talk about me."

I lifted my head, finally remembering the normal dynamic of this relationship and feeling much more comfortable about it. "Oh? What about?"

"Jim!" Ana could scarcely believe Jim wasn't on the forefront of my mind.

"Right! How did it go the other night?"

"I slept with him," Ana said, sounding disappointed in the act itself. "Totally not worth it. I don't know what I was thinking. I don't even like him. I think saying I wasn't going to sleep with someone made me want to sleep with someone even if I didn't really want to sleep with him. Does that make sense?"

I nodded again. Just then my phone rang. It was Ben. I showed the ringing phone to Ana, who excused herself from her own couch and I answered.

He was on his way home from work and asked if I was free.

"If you don't have plans, I could come over and see you

again tonight. I make no assumptions about sleeping over but I should be honest and tell you it's a goal of mine."

I laughed. "That sounds good. When were you thinking?"

"Have you eaten dinner yet? I could pick you up and take you out. Are you free now?"

"Oh, okay. I haven't eaten. Um . . . now? I don't know." I knew full well now was fine. I was just a little worried about looking too available, as if I had left my evening open for just this purpose. That is, in fact, exactly what I had done, but you don't ever want to admit that. "I can make that work," I said. "Want to meet me at my place in twenty minutes?"

"Yes, ma'am. I do. I'll see you then. Wear something fancy. I'm taking your ass someplace special."

"Fancy? Okay, I need thirty minutes then."

"I'll give you twenty, but I'll wait patiently in your living room for the other ten, how's that?"

I laughed. "It's a deal."

I hung up the phone and said good-bye to Ana.

"*Call me* tomorrow morning, please," she said. "And I'm saying tomorrow morning because I'm trying to be understanding, but if you get a moment to run to the bathroom and call me, I'll be waiting by the phone."

"You are my favorite person of all time," I said as I kissed her cheek.

"Not for long, I'm not," she said, and because she is a wonderful friend, there wasn't a trace of resentment. She just saw the writing on the wall.

When I got home, I ran into the bathroom. I wanted to at least get makeup on before he came in the door. I have always lived by the rule that your clothes can be a mess but if your face looks good, no one will notice. I probably believe this because I'd like to lose ten pounds but I think my face is cute. Girls that work out all day and have huge boobs but boring faces probably think the face doesn't matter if your boobs are taken care of.

Just as I had taken off my work clothes and put on a pair of black tights, the doorbell rang. I threw on a long shirt and opened the door.

"Wow," he said when he came in. He smelled great and he looked great. He was wearing dark jeans and a black button-up shirt. It was nothing special, but it somehow made him look exceptional. He leaned in to kiss me and did so gently, so as not to ruin my lipstick.

"Give me seven more minutes," I said, rushing into my room.

"You got it. I'll be on the couch here waiting patiently."

I shut my bedroom door and took off my shirt. I put on a short black sleeveless dress and black pumps, and then I added a gauzy gray cardigan to make it seem a bit less fancy. I looked in the mirror and felt that I looked a little too . . . matronly. So I pulled off the tights, put the heels back on, and walked out there.

"I think I'm under seven minutes," I said as he stood up eagerly.

"Wow."

I held out my arms in display. "Good enough for this mystery dinner?"

"You look perfect. What happened to the tights?"

"Oh." I suddenly felt whorish. "Should I put them back on?"

He shook his head. "No, not at all. Your . . . your legs look great, is all. I haven't seen you in high heels before." He came over and kissed me on the temple. It felt familiar and loving.

"Well, you've only known me since Saturday," I said as I

grabbed my purse. I took special care to make certain my keys were in there. I wasn't sure what state we would be in when we got back here, but I didn't want to create any kinks in the plan.

"Wow. You're right. It does not feel like that though. Anyway, it's not important. What is important is that you look fucking hot. Are you going to be warm enough? Fuck it. I don't care. Don't put anything else on over this."

"Wait!" I said, turning back in to the apartment as he was heading toward the door.

"Should I grab something? I hate being cold."

"If you get cold, I'll give you my jacket."

"But what if my legs are cold?"

"I'll put the jacket around your legs. Now get that beautiful ass in my car! Let's go!"

I ran right down the stairs into his front seat.

It was a warm night and we drove across town with the windows down. Once we got on the freeway, the wind from the windows made it too loud to talk so I put my head on his shoulder and closed my eyes. Before I knew it, we were parking on the Pacific Coast Highway. The dark, cool beach was to our left and high mountains to our right.

"Where are we going?" I finally asked. I could have asked earlier and he probably would have told me, but where was the fun in that?

"We are going to the Beachcomber because we can order our food sitting right over the water and I promise you won't get cold because I'll make them seat us by the fire pit."

"There's a fire pit?"

Ben smiled. "Would I lie to you?"

I shrugged. "How should I know?"

"Touché," he said. "Are you ready? The one caveat is that

we have to run across this two-lane highway with superhuman speed."

I opened my car door and took off my heels. "Okay. I'm ready." Ben grabbed my hand and we waited until the timing was right. There were a few times we almost went, and one time I thought for sure I was going to die just standing on the edge of the freeway, but eventually, with much fanfare and me screaming, we made our way across.

When we got to the restaurant, it was somewhat empty. From the look on Ben's face, I could tell this was what he was hoping for. He asked to be seated near the fire pit, and within minutes, my legs were warmed by the fire and my shoulders were cool from the sea breeze.

As I sat there, looking out onto the ocean below us and this new person in front of me, it didn't feel like my life. It felt like I was living someone else's life for a night. I didn't usually spend my Monday nights by a fire overlooking the water, being served chilled white wine and Pellegrino. I usually spent my Monday nights eating Hot Pockets while reading a book and drinking from the tap.

"This is gorgeous," I said. I put my hands toward the flames. "Thank you for bringing me here."

"Thank you for letting me," he said, as he pulled his chair closer to me.

Ben and I discussed our days and our jobs. We talked about past relationships and our families. We talked about pretty much anything other than sex, and yet, more and more, it was becoming the only thing on my mind.

His black shirt clung to his shoulders. The way he had the sleeves rolled up halfway to his elbows exposed his hands and wrists. They were thin but sturdy. Angular but delicate. As I looked at them I wanted them to touch me. I wanted them to lift me.

"You look great tonight," I said to him as I buttered my bread. I tried to sound casual. I wasn't used to complimenting a man like that and I wasn't sure how to do it without sounding creepy. "That shirt is very flattering on you."

"Why, thank you very much!" he said as his smile widened. "Thanks."

He looked down at his plate and smiled further. He looked embarrassed.

"Are you blushing?" I teased him.

Ben shook his head. "Well, ah." He looked up at me. "I'm embarrassed to say that I went to the Gap after work and bought this shirt for our date."

I started laughing. "Before you even called me?"

"Yeah. I know. It sounds very stupid. But I just . . . I wanted to look good for you. I wanted to make it a special night and . . . to be blunt, none of my shirts looked good enough for that."

"You're not real," I said.

"Pardon me?"

"You're just . . . you're not a real person. What kind of guy is that sincere about things? And that honest? No man has ever gone out to buy a new shirt just to take me somewhere."

"You don't know that!" Ben said.

The waiter came to take our order. I ordered pasta. Ben ordered steak. That's how I could tell we both knew he would insist on paying for dinner. I wasn't going to order anything extravagant on his dime, and if he'd really thought I might succeed in paying for this, he wouldn't have ordered anything extravagant on mine.

After the waiter left, I kept at it.

"Well, sure. Okay. I don't know that, but no man has ever told me he did."

"Obviously. Only an idiot would admit it. It's too obvious that I like you. I need to reel it in."

"No, no. Please don't. It feels great."

"Being liked?" he asked, as he picked up a piece of bread and ripped it in half. He popped one whole half into his mouth. I liked that he would buy a new shirt for me but he wasn't going to eat delicately in front of me. It showed that even if he wanted to put forward the best version of himself, he was still always going to be himself.

"Being liked, yeah. And liking someone so much. Being liked by the person you like so much, is maybe more accurate."

"Do you feel like things are moving too quickly?" he asked. It jarred me. Obviously, I had been thinking about that and discussing it with Ana, but if he felt like things were going too fast, well . . . I wasn't sure what I was afraid of. I just knew that even if they were going too fast, I did not want things to slow down.

"Oh. Uh. Do you? Were you thinking that?" I looked up at him from my wineglass, trying to sound carefree and blithe. I think it worked.

"No, actually," he said matter-of-factly. I was relieved to hear it. "I think you and I are just . . . Yes, we are moving quickly but we're moving at a pace that feels natural for both of us. I think?"

I nodded, so he kept going.

"Right. So, I don't see an issue. I just wanted to make sure I wasn't coming on too strong with you. Because I don't mean to overwhelm you. I keep telling myself to cut it out. But then I keep doing it. I'm typically a pretty low-key person, but I'm just . . . not low-key about you."

I felt like butter in the microwave. I had no strength left to be cool or the type of dishonest you're supposed to be this early on.

"Are we crazy here?" I asked. "I feel like you are such a different person than anyone I have ever met and I thought about you all day today. I . . . barely know you and yet I miss you. That's crazy, right? I don't know you. I guess I'm worried that we will be so into each other so quickly that we will burn out? Sort of an acute romance, as it were."

"Kind of like a supernova?"

"Hmm?"

"It's some sort of star or explosion that's so powerful it can emit the same amount of energy that the sun will emit over its entire lifetime, but it does it in, like, two months and then it dies."

I laughed. "Yep," I said. "That's pretty much exactly what I meant."

"Well, I think it's a fair concern. I don't want to rush through this so fast that we run it into the ground. I'm not sure I think it's really possible, but better to be safe than sorry." He chewed and thought. When he was done, he had a plan. "What about this? Let's give it . . . let's say, five weeks, and we can see each other as much as we want, but no one can up the ante. We can just stop ourselves from being too intense up front. Let's just hang out and enjoy each other's company and not worry about too fast or too slow or anything. And then at the end of five weeks, we can really assess if we are crazy or not. If at the end of it, we are both on the same page, then great. And if at the end of five weeks, we have burnt out or we just aren't jibing, we've only wasted five weeks."

I laughed. "Jibing?"

"I couldn't think of a better word."

I was still laughing as he looked me, slightly embarrassed. "I can think of about ten," I said and then immediately got back to the subject. "Okay. No moving forward. No freaking out about moving too fast. Just this. That sounds great. No supernova."

Ben smiled and we shook on it. "No supernova."

It was quiet for a moment, and I broke the silence.

"We are wasting our five weeks by being quiet. I need to know more about you."

Ben took another piece of bread off of the table and spread butter on it. I was glad the intensity of the moment had worn off—that things were now casual enough for him to be spreading butter. He took a bite.

"What do you want to know?"

"Favorite color?"

"That's what you're burning to ask me?"

"No."

"So ask what you really wanna know."

"Anything?"

He splayed his hands out to show himself. "Anything."

"How many women have you slept with?"

He smiled out of the side of his mouth as if I'd pinned him down. "Sixteen," he said, matter-of-factly. He wasn't bragging or apologizing. It was higher than I was expecting, and for a second, I was jealous. Jealous that there were women out there that knew him in a way I didn't yet. Women who were closer to him, in some ways, than I was.

"You? Men?" he asked.

"Five."

He nodded. "Next question."

"Do you think you've ever been in love?"

He took another bite. "I believe I have before, yes. It wasn't a great experience for me, truthfully. It wasn't . . . It wasn't fun," he said as if he was just realizing what the problem truly was after all this time.

"Fair enough."

"You?" he asked.

"I see how this is going. I can't ask any questions I don't want to answer myself."

"Isn't that at least fair?"

"That's fair. I have been in love once before, for most of college. His name was Bryson."

"Bryson?"

"Yes, but don't blame him for his name. He's a nice guy."

"Where is he now?"

"Chicago."

"Okay, good. Nice and far."

I laughed, and the waiter brought our meals. He placed them down in front of us, telling us not to touch them because the plates were hot. But I touched mine; it wasn't that hot. Ben looked at mine and then looked at his. "Can I eat some of yours if I give you some of mine?" he asked.

I angled my plate toward him. "Absolutely."

"There is one thing we need to sort out," Ben said as he reached over to eat some of my fusilli.

"Oh? What is that?"

"Well, if we aren't going to assess our relationship from this moment out until five weeks from now, we should probably sort out ahead of time when we are going to sleep together."

He caught me off guard because I had been hoping to sleep with him that night and then pretend that was never my intention. I was going to blame it on the heat of the moment. "What do you suggest?" I asked.

Ben shrugged. "Well, I guess our only real options are tonight or at the end of the five weeks, right? Otherwise, we'd be amping things up in the middle . . ." He was grinning as he said this. He knew exactly what he was doing. He knew I knew what he was doing.

"Oh. Okay. Well, in the interest of keeping things simple," I said, "why don't we just say tonight?"

Ben smiled out of the side of his mouth and pumped his fist. "Yeah!"

I felt good to be so desirable that a man would fist-pump the thought of getting to sleep with me. Especially because I would have fist-pumped the idea myself if I'd thought of it.

The rest of dinner felt a bit rushed. Or maybe it was just that I couldn't focus on eating now that it was in the air; it had been decided. He kissed me against his car before we got in. He had his hand on my upper thigh as we sped home. The closer we got to my house, the further it got. I could feel every inch of his hand on every inch of my thigh. It burned underneath his fingers.

We barely made it to the door before we were half-naked. He started kissing me in the driveway, and if I hadn't stopped it, it might have happened right there in his car.

We ran up the stairs, and when I got my key into the door he was right behind me, his hand on my ass, squeezing it, whispering in my ear to hurry up. His breath was hot on my neck. The door flew open and I ran to my bedroom, holding his hand behind me.

I fell onto the bed and kicked off my shoes. I liked hearing the double clunk they made as they hit the floor. He threw his body down on top of me, his legs between mine, and he pushed my body up and further onto the bed as we kissed with my hands around his head. He kicked his shoes off. I slid under the covers with my dress still on, and he slid in next to me. Any restraint we'd shown the night before was gone, replaced with reckless abandon. I couldn't think straight. I just moved. I operated on instinct. I wanted all of him, more of him, I couldn't get enough of him. His body made me feel so alive.

JUNE

I take a chance that Susan is still at her hotel. Ana brings me there and I call Susan from the lobby. I don't want to give her an opportunity to turn me away, which turns out to be a smart strategy because her tone makes it clear that she would have avoided me if she could have. Ana heads over to the bar as I take the elevator to Room 913.

As I approach her door, my palms start to sweat. I'm not sure how to convince Susan of this, how I plan on defending Ben's wishes to his own mother. It occurs to me that I just want her to like me. Take away everything that has happened, this is the woman that raised my husband. She created him out of nothing, and for that, a part of me loves her. But I can't take away everything that has happened; every moment of every day reeks of what has happened. What has happened is happening now.

I knock lightly on her door, and she opens it immediately.

"Hello, Elsie," she says. She is wearing fitted dark jeans with a thick belt, a gray shirt under a brown cardigan. She looks younger than her sixty years, in shape, healthy, but nonetheless, in grave distress. She has been crying, that much is clear. Her hair doesn't look brushed or blow-dried as usual. She's not wearing makeup. She looks raw.

"Hi, Susan," I say as I walk in.

"What can I do for you?" Her hotel room is more like a

hotel *apartment*. She has a large balcony and a sitting room filled with cream-colored everything. The carpet looks soft under my shoes, too delicate to walk on, and yet, I'm not at home enough in her company to suggest I take them off. I get the impression she'd like me to walk on eggshells around her, apologize for my very existence, and the carpet practically forces me to do just that.

"I . . ." I start. I'm not sure if it's appropriate to try for small talk in a situation like this or if it's better to just go right into it. How can you go right into it when the "it" is the remains of your husband? The remains of her son?

"I met with Mr. Pavlik this morning," I say. It seems close enough to the point without directly hitting the mark.

"Good," she says, leaning back against her couch. She is not sitting down. She is not inviting me to take a seat. She does not want me to be here long, and yet, I don't know how to make this a short conversation. I decide to just come out with it.

"Ben wanted to be buried. I thought that we discussed this," I say.

She shifts her body slightly, casually, as if this conversation is not a big deal to her, as if it doesn't terrify her the way it terrifies me. That's how I know she has no intention of hearing me out. She's not worried she's not going to get her way.

"Get to the point, Elsie," she says. She runs her hands through her long brown hair. It has streaks of gray near the top, barely noticeable unless you're staring at her like I am.

"Mr. Pavlik says that Ben's body is still to be cremated."

"It is." She nods, not offering any other explanation. Her candid voice, free from emotion, turmoil, and pain, is starting to piss me off. Her composure feels like spit in my face.

"It's not what he wanted, Susan. I'm telling you, that's not what he wanted. Doesn't that matter to you at all?" I say. I am trying to be respectful to the mother of the man that I love. "Don't you care what Ben would have wanted?"

Susan crosses her arms in front of her and shifts her weight. "Elsie, don't tell me about my own son, okay? I raised him. I know what he wanted."

"You don't, actually. You don't know! I had this conversation with him two months ago."

"And I've had conversations with him about this his entire life. I am his mother. I didn't just happen to meet him a few months before he died. Who the hell do you think you are to tell me about my own son?"

"I am his wife, Susan. I don't know how else to say it."

It doesn't sit well.

"I've never heard of you!" she says, as she throws her hands in the air. "Where is the marriage certificate? I don't know you, and here you are, trying to tell me what to do with my only child's remains? Give me a break, seriously. You are a small footnote in my son's life. I am his mother!"

"I get that you're his mother—"

She inches forward ever so slightly as she interrupts me, her finger pointed now toward my face. Her composure drains out of her body, the poise flees from her face. "Listen to me. I don't know you and I don't trust you. But my son's body will be cremated, Elsie. Just like his father's and like his grandparents'. And the next time you get the idea to try to tell me what to do about my own son, you might want to think twice."

"You gave this to me to do, Susan! You couldn't deal with it yourself and you pushed it onto me! First you try to stop me from even getting his wallet and keys, keys that are to my own home, by the way, and then you suddenly turn and push all of this off on me. And then, when I try to do it, you try to control it from behind the scenes. You haven't even left Los Angeles. You don't need to stay in this hotel, Susan. You can drive back to Orange County and be there by dinner. Why are you even still here?" I don't give her a chance to answer. "You want to torture yourself because Ben didn't tell you he got married? *Then do it!* I don't care! But don't keep going back and forth like this. I can't take it."

"I really don't care what you can take, Elsie," Susan says. "Believe it or not, I don't much care."

I try to remind myself that this is a woman in pain. This is a woman that has lost the last family member she had.

"Susan, you can try to deny it all you want. You can think I'm a crazy lunatic who is lying to you. You can cling to the idea that your son would never do anything without you, but that doesn't stop the fact that I did marry him and he did not want to be cremated. Don't have his body burned because you hate me."

"I don't hate you, Elsie. I simply—"

Now it's my turn to cut her off. "Yes, you do, Susan. You hate me because I'm the only one left to hate. If you thought you were doing a good job of hiding that, you're wrong."

She stares at me and I stare right back at her. I don't know what has given me the courage to be honest. I'm not a person inclined to stare anyone else down. Nevertheless, I hold her gaze, my lips pursed and tight, my brows weighted down on my face. Maybe she thinks I'm going to turn and walk away. I don't know. It takes so long for her to speak that the break in the silence is almost startling.

"Even if everything is as you say it is," she says. "Even if you two were married, and the marriage certificate is on its way, and you were the love of his life—"

"I was," I interrupt her.

She barely listens. "Even so, how long were you married to him, Elsie? Two weeks?" I work hard to breathe in and then breathe out. I can feel the lump in my throat rising. I can feel the blood in my brain beating. She continues. "I hardly think two weeks proves anything," she says.

I think about turning around and just leaving her there. That's what she wants. But I don't do it. "You wanna know something else about your son? He would be livid, to see what you're doing. Heartbroken and positively livid."

I leave her hotel room without saying good-bye. As I walk out the door, I look behind me to see a dirt stain the size of my shoe on her pristine white carpet.

Two hours later, Mr. Pavlik calls to tell me Susan has taken over burial plans.

"Burial plans?" I ask, not sure if he is mistaken.

There is a pause, and then he confirms. "Burial plans."

I wish it felt like a victory but it doesn't. "So what do I need to do?" I ask.

He clears his throat and his voice becomes tight. "Uh," he says. "I don't believe anything else is required of you, Elsie. I have Mrs. Ross here and she has decided to take care of the rest."

I don't know how I feel about this. Except tired. I feel tired.

"Okay," I say to him. "Thank you." I hang up the phone and set it down on the dining room table.

"Susan kicked me out of the funeral planning," I tell Ana. "But she's having him buried. Not cremated."

Ana looks at me, unsure of how to react. "Is that good or bad?"

"Good?" I say. "It's good." It is good. His body is safe. I did my job. Why am I so sad? I didn't want to pick out a casket. I didn't want to choose flowers. And yet, I have lost something. I have lost a part of him.

I call Mr. Pavlik right back.

"It's Elsie," I say when he answers. "I want to speak."

"Hmm?"

"I want to speak at his funeral."

"Oh, certainly. I'll speak to Mrs. Ross about it."

"No," I say sternly. "I am speaking at the funeral."

I can hear him whispering and then I hear hold music. When he comes back on he says, "Okay, Elsie. You're welcome to speak if you'd like to." He adds, "It will be Saturday morning in Orange County. I'll send you further details shortly," and then he wishes me well.

I get off the phone, and as much as I want to congratulate myself for standing up to her, I know that, if Susan had said no, I wouldn't have been able to do much about it. I'm not exactly sure how I gave her all the power, but I gave it to her. For the first time, it doesn't feel like Ben was just alive and well a second ago. It feels like he's been gone forever.

Ana heads back to her place to walk her dog. I should offer for her to bring the dog here, but I get the impression Ana needs a few hours every day to get away from me, to get away from this. It's the same thing. I am this. When she gets back, I'm in the same place I was when she left. She asks if I've eaten. She doesn't like the look on my face.

"This is absurd, Elsie. You have to eat something. I'm not messing around anymore." She opens the refrigerator. "You can have pancakes. Eggs? It looks like you have some bacon." She opens the pack of bacon and smells it. It's clearly putrid judging from the look on her face. "Never mind, no bacon. Unless . . . I can go get some bacon! Would you eat bacon?"

"No," I say. "No, please do not leave me to get bacon."

The doorbell rings, and it's so loud and jarring that I almost jump out of my skin. I turn and stare at the door. Ana finally goes to answer it herself.

It's a goddamn flower deliveryman.

"Elsie Porter?" he says through my screen door.

"You can tell him there's no one here by that name," I say to Ana. She ignores me and opens the screen to let him in.

"Thank you," she says to him. He gives her a large white bouquet and leaves. She shuts the door and places it on the table.

"These are gorgeous," she says. "Do you want to know who they're from?" She grabs the card before I answer.

"Are they for the wedding or the funeral?" I ask.

Ana is quiet as she looks at the card. "The funeral." She swallows hard. It wasn't nice of me to make her say that.

"They are from Lauren and Simon," Ana says. "Do you want to thank them or should I?"

Ben and I used to double-date with Lauren and Simon. How am I supposed to face them myself? "Will you do it?" I ask her.

"I'll do it if you'll eat something. How about pancakes?"

"Will you just run point on everyone?" I ask. "Will you tell everyone the news? I don't want to tell them myself."

"If you make me a list," she says. She pushes further. "And you eat some pancakes."

I agree to eat the damn pancakes. If you don't put maple syrup on them, they taste like nothing. I think I can choke down some nothing. As for the list, it's a silly task. She knows everyone I know. They are her friends too.

She starts to grab bowls and ingredients, pans and sprays. Everything seems so easy for her. Each movement doesn't feel like it might be her last, the way mine feel. She just picks up the pancake mix like it's nothing, like it's not the heaviest box in the world.

She sprays cooking spray on a pan and lights the burner. "So, we have two things we have to go over this morning and neither of them are pretty."

"Okay."

When she's got the first pancake under control she turns to me, the spatula wet with batter and dangling in her hand on her hip. I stare at it while she talks, wondering if it will drip onto the kitchen floor.

"The first one is work. What do you want to do? I called them on Monday, told them the situation and bought you a few days but . . . how do you want to handle it?"

Honestly, I don't even remember why I am a librarian. Books? Seriously? That's my passion?

"I don't know if I can go back," I say at first, meaning it.

"Okay," she says, turning back to the stove. The batter doesn't fall off the spatula until the last minute, until I have almost given up on it falling to the floor. It makes a small splatter at her foot, but she's oblivious.

"I know I need to, though," I add. "If only because I'm not exactly rolling in dough." I'm certainly not in a position to quit my job.

"What about Ben's . . . ?" Ana can't finish the question. I don't blame her. I can barely ask it myself in my own head.

"He had a good amount of money saved," I say. "But I don't want it."

"Well, wouldn't he want you to have it?" My pancake is done, and she delivers it to me on the table with containers of butter, maple syrup, jam, and confectioners' sugar. I push them aside. The thought of tasting something sweet right now makes my mouth sour.

"I don't know, but . . . I think it puts me in a weird position. We weren't married long. None of his family has ever heard of me. I don't want a windfall of cash right now," I say. "Not that it's a windfall, it's just more than I had saved. Ben wasn't a big spender."

Ana shrugs. "So, then maybe you should call your boss and work out when you're going back? Assuming you're going back?"

I nod. "You're absolutely right. I should." I do not want to. I wonder how long I could go before they fired me. It would be so indelicate of them to fire a widow, to fire a grieving woman, and yet, I'd leave them no choice.

"And speaking of calling people . . ." Ana flips what I hope is a pancake she's making for herself. I said I'd eat, but I'm not eating two huge pancakes. I can barely stomach this piece of shit in front of me.

"Wow, you're really going for it this morning, aren't you?" I say.

She plates the pancake, which I think is a pretty good sign she's going to eat it herself. If it was for me, she'd put it on my plate, right? "I don't mean to push you. I just think the longer you put this off, the more uncomfortable it will be. Your parents, no matter how difficult your relationship is, they need to know what has happened to you in the past few days."

"Okay," I say. She's right. Ana sits down next to me and starts on her pancake. She loads it up with butter and maple syrup. I am astonished that she can have an appetite during a time like this, that things like taste and pleasure are on her mind.

I wipe my chin and set down the napkin. "Who do you want me to call first? Let's just get this shit over with."

Ana puts down her fork. "That's my girl! You're taking life by the balls."

"I don't know if that's the case. I'm merely getting this bullshit out of the way so I can go in my room and cry for the rest of the day."

"But you're trying! You're doing the best you can."

"I guess I am," I say and grab the phone. I look to her with my eyebrows raised and the phone tilted in my hand. "So?"

"Call work first. That's an easier conversation. It's just logistics, no emotion."

"I like that you think the conversation with my parents will contain emotion."

I dial the phone and wait as it rings. A woman picks up; I can recognize that it's Nancy. I love Nancy. I think Nancy is a great woman, but as she says, "Los Angeles Library, Fairfax Branch, Reference Desk, how may I help you today?" I hang up.

JANUARY

The library was technically closed for Martin Luther King Day, but I agreed to work. We'd had a group of people, most likely high school students or fancy little rebels, come in and place the entire World Religions section out of order over the weekend. They threw books on the floor, they hid them in other sections, under tables. They rearranged the titles in no discernible order.

My boss, Lyle, was convinced that this was some sort of terrorist act, meant to make us here at the Los Angeles library really think about the role of religion in modern government. I was more of the mind that the act was harmless tomfoolery; the World Religions section was the nearest to the back wall, the furthest from view. I'd caught a number of couples making out in the library in my few years there, and they had all been in the World Religions section.

No one else was working that day, but Lyle told me that if I chose to come in and re-sort the World Religions section, he'd give me a day off some other time. This seemed like great currency to me, and since Ben was going to have to work that day anyway, I came in. I tend to like alphabetizing, which I realize makes absolutely no sense, but it's true nonetheless. I like things that have a right and a wrong answer, things that can be done perfectly. They don't often come up in the humanities. They are normally relegated to the sciences. So I've always liked the alphabet and the Dewey decimal system for being objective standards in a subjective world.

Cell phone reception is terrible at the library, and since it was empty, I had a spookily quiet day, a day spent almost entirely in my own mind.

Around three, as I found myself pretty much done piecing together the World Religions section like some three-dimensional puzzle, I heard the phone ring. I had been ignoring the phone the few times it rang that day, but for some reason, I forgot all that and ran to answer it.

I don't typically answer the phone at work, I'm often with people or filing or working on larger projects for the library, so when I answered this time, I realized it completely slipped my mind what I was supposed to say.

"Hello?" I said. "Uh. Los Angeles Fairfax Library. Oh, ah. Los Angeles Public Library, Reference Branch. Fairfax Branch, Reference Desk."

By the end of it, I'd remembered there was no need for me to answer the phone in the first place, making this that much more of a needless embarrassment.

That's when I heard laughing on the other end of the phone.

"Ben?"

"Uh, uh, Fairfax. Reference. Uh," he said, still laughing at me. "You are the cutest person that ever lived."

I started to laugh too, relieved that I had embarrassed myself only in front of Ben, but also embarrassed to have embarrassed myself in front of Ben. "What are you doing? I thought you were working today."

"I was. Working today. But Greg decided to let us all go home a half hour ago."

"Oh! That's great. You should come meet me here. I should

be done in about twenty minutes or so. Oh!" I said, and I was overcome with a great idea. "We can go to a happy hour!" I never got out of work in time to go to a happy hour, but the idea had always intrigued me.

Ben laughed. "That sounds great. That's kind of why I'm calling. I'm outside."

"What?"

"Well, not outside exactly. I'm down the street. I had to walk until I could get service."

"Oh!" I was thrilled to know that I'd be seeing Ben any minute and drinking two-dollar drafts within the half hour. "Come down to the side door. I'll open it."

"Great!" he said. "I'll be there in five."

I took my time heading to the side door, passing the circulation desk and front door on my way back there. I'm glad that I did because as I passed the front door, I heard a tapping on the door and looked up to see Mr. Callahan standing sad and confused, with his hands cupped around his eyes and fixed against the glass.

I walked up to the door and pushed it open. It was an automatic door turned off for the holiday, so it gave great resistance, but I got it open just enough to let Mr. Callahan in. He grabbed my arm with his shaking, tissue paper–like hands and thanked me.

"No problem, Mr. Callahan," I said. "I'm going to take off in about ten minutes and the library is closed, but is there something you wanted?"

"It's closed?" he asked, confused. "What on earth for?"

"Martin Luther King Day!" I answered.

"And you still let me in? I am a lucky man, Elsie."

I smiled. "Can I help you get anything?"

"I won't be but just a minute, now that I know you're in a hurry. Can I have a few minutes in the Young Adult section?"

"The Young Adult section?" It wasn't my business why, but this was out of character for Mr. Callahan. The fiction section, sure, new releases, definitely. World Wars, Natural Disasters, Sociology. All of these were places where you could find Mr. Callahan, but Young Adult was never his style.

"My grandson and his daughter are coming this week and I want to have something to read with her. She's getting too old to find me particularly entertaining, but I thought if I got a really good yarn to her liking, I could convince her to spend a few minutes with me."

"Great-granddaughter? Wow."

"I'm old, Elsie. I'm an old man."

I laughed instead of agreeing with him. "Well, be my guest. It's over to the left, behind the periodicals."

"I'll only be a minute!" he said as he headed back there, slow like a turtle but also just as steady.

I headed to the side door to find Ben wondering what the hell I'd been doing.

"I've been here for two minutes and twenty-seven seconds, Elsie!" he joked as he stepped in.

"Sorry, Mr. Callahan came to the front door and I had to let him in."

"Mr. Callahan is here?" Ben's face lit up. He had never met Mr. Callahan but had heard me talk about him, about how I found his devotion to his wife to be one of the more romantic real-life sentiments I had ever witnessed. Ben always said when he was ninety, he'd treat me the same way. I had only known Ben for about three weeks, so while it was a sweet thing to say, it was also foolhardy and arrogant. It was naïve and intoxicating. "Can I meet him?"

"Sure," I said. "Come help me put a few last books in order

and we can go find him." Ben came with me to finish up, contributing in no way to my reordering of the books. He hung back and read the spines as I told him all about finding *Buddhism: Plain and Simple* stuck up in a nook of the ceiling.

"How did you get it down?" he said, only half listening to me. His attention seemed focused on the stacks.

"I didn't," I told him. "It's right there." I pointed above us to the thin, white book stuck precariously between the metal grid and the popcorn panel. He walked toward me, standing right over me. Our bodies were so close that his shirt was touching mine. The skin on his arm just barely touched mine. I could smell his deodorant and his shampoo, smells that had become sensual to me because of how often I smelled them in sensual situations. His neck was craned upward, checking out the book in the ceiling.

"Those tricky bastards," Ben marveled, then he turned back to face me. He could now appreciate how close we were. He looked at me and then looked around us.

"Where's Mr. Callahan?" he asked. He asked it in a way that clearly let me know he was asking something else entirely.

I blushed. "He's a few walls over," I said.

"Seems pretty private back here," he said. He didn't move toward me to grab me. He didn't need to.

I giggled, girlishly. "It is," I said. "But it would be—"

"Right," he said. "That would be . . ."

Was it getting hotter? I honestly thought maybe it was getting hotter. I thought it was getting hotter and quieter, as if the air itself was becoming more intense around us.

"It would be crazy," I said, matter-of-factly, doing my best to stop this before it started. He wouldn't. I knew he wouldn't. Right there in the library? I was certain that I was the only one actually considering it. And so I put my foot down. I stepped away slightly, put the book in my hand into its place on the shelf, and announced that we needed to go check on Mr. Callahan.

"Okay," Ben said, putting his hands up in surrender. He then put one arm out as if to invite me to lead us there. I walked in front of him, and when we were almost out of the World Religions stacks, he teased me.

"I would have done it," he said.

I smiled and shook my head. I had never felt so desirable, had never realized how feeling that desirable made me feel like I could do anything in the world.

We found Mr. Callahan right where he'd said he'd be.

"What is all of this?" Mr. Callahan said to me as he saw us coming up to meet him. "I thought there would be a few books back here. This section is bigger than the new releases!"

I laughed. "There are a lot of young adult books lately, Mr. Callahan. Kids love reading now."

He shook his head. "Who knew?" Mr. Callahan already had a book in his hand.

"Mr. Callahan, I'd like you to meet Ben." I gestured to Ben, and Mr. Callahan grabbed Ben's outstretched hand.

"Hello, son," he said and took his hand back. "Strong grip on you, good to see."

"Thanks," Ben said. "I've heard a lot about you and I wanted to meet the man behind the legend."

Mr. Callahan laughed. "No legend here. Just an old man who forgets things and can't walk as fast as he used to."

"Is that for you?" Ben asked, gesturing to the book.

"Oh, no. My great-granddaughter. I'm afraid I'm a bit lost in this section. This book takes up a whole shelf, though, so I figured it's pretty popular." Mr. Callahan held up a copy of a supernatural franchise. The kind of book that gets the kids reading in the first place, even if it is insipid, so I couldn't knock it. He had the third book in his hand, and I had a hunch he couldn't tell that the whole shelf was actually four different installments with similar covers and motifs. His fine vision probably was not what it used to be, and they probably all looked the same.

"That's actually the third one," I said. "Did you want me to find the first one?"

"Please," he said.

Ben gingerly grabbed the book out of his hand. "If I may, Mr. Callahan." He put the book back in place and stopped me from picking up the first of the series.

"I'm categorically against all books about vampires in love with young women. Those books always make it seem like being bitten to the point of death is a form of love."

I looked at Ben, surprised. He sheepishly looked back at me. "What?"

"No, nothing," I said.

"Anyway," he continued, focused on Mr. Callahan. "I'm not sure it's the best influence for your great-granddaughter. I can only assume you want her to grow up believing that she can do anything, not just sit around lusting for the undead."

"You're exactly right about that," Mr. Callahan said. When Mr. Callahan was a child, he was probably raised to believe that women were made to follow men, to stay home and darn their socks. Now, he was an old man who had changed with the times, who wanted to reinforce for his great-granddaughter that she should not stay home and darn socks unless she wanted to. It occurred to me that you could see a lot in a lifetime if you stuck around as long as Mr. Callahan. He had lived through times I'd only read about.

Ben grabbed a bright blue book from the display. "Here you go. Just as popular, ten times more awesome. It's got love in it, but the love is secondary to actual character development, and you really love these characters. The girl is a hero. I don't want to spoil anything, but bring tissues."

Mr. Callahan smiled and nodded. "Thank you," he said. "You just saved me a tongue-lashing from her mother."

"It's a really good book," Ben said. "I read it in two days."

"Can I check it out, Elsie? Or . . . how does that work if you're closed?"

"Just bring it back in three weeks, Mr. Callahan. It will be our secret."

Mr. Callahan smiled at me and tucked the book into his coat, as if he were a criminal. He shook Ben's hand and walked away. After he cleared the front door I turned to Ben.

"You read young adult novels?"

"Look, we all have our idiosyncrasies. Don't think I don't know that you drink Diet Coke for breakfast."

"What? How did you even know that?"

"I pay attention." He tapped his temple with his pointer finger. "Now that you know my deepest, most embarrassing secret, that I read young adult novels written mostly for thirteen-year-old girls, do you still like me? Can we still go out, or have you just about had enough?"

"No, I think I'll stick with you," I said, grabbing his hand. The phone rang again, and Ben ran and picked it up.

"Los Angeles Public Library, Fairfax Branch, Reference Desk, how may I help you?" he said arrogantly. "No, I'm sorry. We're closed today. Thanks. Bye."

"Ben!" I said after he hung up. "That was unprofessional!"

"Well, you can understand why I didn't trust you to do it."

JUNE

What was that all about?" Ana says as she finishes her pancake.

"I . . . I got a little overwhelmed there. I just wasn't ready for it." I pick up the phone and dial again.

"Los Angeles Public Library, Fairfax Branch, Reference Desk, how may I help you?" It is still Nancy. Nancy is round and older. She's not a professional librarian. She just works the desk. I shouldn't say "just." She does a lot of work and is kind to everyone. I can't imagine Nancy saying an unkind thing about a single person. She's one of those people that can be sincere and neighborly. I've always found the two to be at odds, personally.

"Hey, Nancy, it's Elsie."

She lets out a blow of air and her voice deepens. "Elsie, I'm so sorry."

"Thank you."

"I can't even imagine—"

"Thank you." I cut her off. I know that if she keeps talking, I will hang up again. I will roll into a ball and heave tears the size of marbles. "Is Lyle around? I need to talk to him about coming back in."

"Absolutely. Absolutely," she says to me. "One second, sweetheart."

It's a few minutes before Lyle answers, and when he does, he steamrolls the conversation. I can only assume it's because he's more loath to have this conversation than I am. No one wants to be the person telling me of my responsibilities right now.

"Elsie, listen. We get it. You take as much time as you need. You have plenty of vacation days, sick days, personal time saved up," he says, trying to be helpful.

"How much my-husband-died time do I have?" I ask, trying to lighten the mood, trying to make this okay for everyone. But it's not okay for everyone, and the joke lands like a belly flop. You could fit a city bus in the length of the awkward pause between us. "Anyway, thank you, Lyle. I think it's best that I get back into my routine. Life has to go on, right?" I am all talk right now. Life can't go on. That's just a thing people say to other people because they heard it on daytime TV. It doesn't exist for me. It never will. There will be no moving on. But people not living in the valley of a tragedy don't like to hear this. They like to hear you "buck up." They want to say to your friends, to your co-workers, to the people you used to ride elevators with, that you're "handling it well." That you're a "trooper." The more crass of them want to say you're a "tough bitch" or a "hard as nails motherfucker." I'm not, but let them think it. It's easier on all of us.

"Well, great. You just let me know the day."

"The funeral is tomorrow morning and I'll take the rest of the weekend to rest. How about Tuesday?" I say.

"Tuesday sounds fine," he says. "And Elsie?"

"Yeah?" I say, wanting to get off the phone.

"May he rest in peace. We can never know God's plan for us."

"Uh-huh," I say and hang up the phone. This is the first time someone has mentioned God to me, and I want to wring Lyle's fat neck. To be honest, it seems rude to even mention it to me. It's like your friend talking about how much fun she had at the party you weren't invited to. God has forsaken me. Stop rubbing it in how great God's been to you.

I put the phone down on the kitchen table. "One down," I say. "Can I take a shower before the next one?" Ana nods.

I head into the shower and turn on the faucet, wondering how I'm going to start this conversation, wondering how it can possibly go. Are my parents going to offer to fly out here? That would be terrible. Are they not going to offer to come out here at all? That would be even worse. Ana knocks on the door, and I turn off the water. I'm sure she thinks that I'll never get out of here on my own, and I don't want to give her any more to worry about than I already have. I can get myself out of the damn shower. For now.

I put on a robe and grab the phone. If I don't do it this second, I won't do it, so let's do it.

I dial their home phone. My father answers.

"It's Elsie," I say.

"Oh, hi, Eleanor," my father replies. I feel like he's spitting in my face by saying my full name, reminding me that I am not who they intended. On my first day of school in kindergarten, I told everyone to call me Elsie. I told my teacher it was short for Eleanor, but in reality, I had liked the name ever since I saw Elsie the Cow on ice cream cartons. It was a couple of months before my mother figured out what exactly was going on, but by that time, try as she might, she could not get my friends to call me Eleanor. It was my first true rebellion.

"Do you and Mom have a minute to talk?" I ask.

"Oh, I'm sorry. We're on our way out. I'll call you some other time. Is that okay?" he says.

"No, actually, I'm sorry. I need to speak with you now. It's rather important."

My father tells me to hold on.

"What is it, Eleanor?" My mother is now on the phone.

"Is Dad on the line too?"

"I'm here. What did you want to say?"

"Well, I believe I told you about a man I was seeing. Ben."

"Uh-huh," my mother says. She sounds like she's distracted. Like she's putting on lipstick or watching the maid fold the laundry.

"Well," I start. I don't want to do this. What good comes of this? What good comes of me saying it out loud? Of hearing it through their ears? "Ben was hit by a car and passed away."

My mother gasps. "Oh my God, Eleanor. I'm sorry to hear that," she says.

"Jesus," my dad says.

"I don't know what to say," my mother adds. But she can't stand not saying something so she pulls something out of her ass. "I trust you've informed his family." My parents see death every day, and I think it has made them numb to it in a lot of ways. I think it's made them numb to life too, but I'm sure they'd just say I'm too sensitive.

"Yeah, yeah. That's all taken care of. I just wanted you to know."

"Well," my mother says, still pulling words out of thin air. "I imagine this is a hard time for you, but I hope you know that we feel for you. I just . . . My word. Have you had time to process? Are you doing okay?"

"I'm not okay, exactly. The other thing I wanted to tell you is that Ben and I were married in a private ceremony two weeks ago. He died as my husband."

It's out of my mouth. I have done my job. Now all I have to do is get off the phone.

"Why did you marry someone you barely knew?" my father asks, and there it is, off and running.

"Your father's right, Eleanor. I don't even know . . ." My mother is livid. I can hear it in her voice.

"I'm sorry I didn't tell you," I say.

"Forget telling us!" she says. "What were you thinking? How long had you known this man?"

"Long enough to know that he was the love of my life," I say, defensively.

They are silent. I can tell my mom wants to say something.

"Just go ahead," I say.

"I knew your father for four years before I agreed to even go on a date with him, Eleanor. We dated for another five before we got married. You can't possibly know enough about a person after a few months."

"It was six months. I met him six months ago," I say. God, even I know this sounds paltry and embarrassing. It makes me feel so stupid.

"Precisely!" my dad pipes in. "Eleanor, this is terrible. Just terrible. We are so sorry you have been hurt like this, but you will move on. I promise."

"No, but, Charles," my mom interjects. "It's also important that she understands that she needs to take more time with her decisions. This is exactly—"

"Guys, I don't want to talk about this right now. I just thought you should know I'm a widow."

"A widow?" my mother says. "No, I don't think you should consider yourself a widow. Don't label yourself like that. That's only going to make it more difficult to rebound from this. How long were you two married?" I can hear the judgment in her voice.

"A week and a half," I say. I'm rounding up. How sad is that? I'm fucking rounding up.

"Eleanor, you are going to be okay," my father tells me.

"Yes," my mother says. "You will be fine. You will get back up on your feet. I hope you haven't taken too much time off work at the library. You know with state budget cuts, it really isn't the time to be compromising your job. Although, I was talking to one of my friends on the board of the hospital, and she mentioned that her daughter is a law librarian. She works directly with some very high-powered attorneys on some really impressive cases. I could call her, or give you her number if you'd like. They are a bicoastal firm."

I've always known that my mother will take any opportunity to remind me that I can be better than I am now. I can be more impressive than I am now. I have the potential to do more with my life than I am doing now. And I didn't necessarily think she'd waste this opportunity out of fear of being insensitive and gauche, but I don't think I realized how seamlessly she'd be able to do it. I can hear, as she speaks, how far I have strayed from their plan for me. This is what happens when you are your parents' only child, when they wanted more but couldn't have any, when they procreated for the purpose of building mini-versions of themselves. This is what happens when they realize you aren't going to be like them and they aren't sure what to do about it.

It always bothered me until I moved out here, away from them, out of sight of their disapproving stares, their condescending voices. It didn't bother me again until right now. I have to assume it's because I didn't need them again until right now. And as much as I may say that nothing will make this better, I'm inclined to think that feeling supported by my parents would have made this just a little bit easier to bear.

"No, thanks, Mom," I say and hope that the conversation will end there. That she will give up and just resolve to sell harder next time.

"Well," my dad says. "Is there anything you need from us?"

"Nothing, Dad. I just wanted you guys to know. I hope you have a good rest of your night," I say.

"Okay, I'm sorry for your loss, Eleanor." My mother hangs up her end of the line.

"We really wish you the best, Elsie," my dad says. It catches me off guard, hearing the name out of his mouth. He is trying. It means that he is trying. "We just . . . we don't know how to . . ." He breathes audibly and restarts. "You know how your mother is," he says, and he leaves it at that.

"I know."

"We love you," he says, and I say, "I love you too," out of social convention rather than feeling.

I hang up the phone.

"It's done now," Ana says to me. She grabs my hand. She holds it to her heart. "I'm so proud of you for that one. You handled yourself really, really well." She hugs me, and I throw my face into her body. Ana's shoulder is a soft place to cry, but I've heard urban legends about the safety of a mother's arms and that sounds pretty good right now.

"Okay," I say. "I think I'm going to go lie down."

"Okay," she says. She cleans the plates from the table. Hers is an empty plate covered in maple syrup. Mine is clean but full of pancake. "If you're hungry, let me know."

"Okay," I say, but I am already in my room, already lying down, and I already know I won't be hungry. I look up at the ceiling and I don't know how much time passes. I remember that his cell phone still exists somewhere. That the number didn't die when he did. And I call it. I listen to him over and over, hanging up and dialing again.

JANUARY

It was a rainy and cold Saturday night. Well, cold for Los Angeles. It was fifty degrees and windy. The wind had started to sway the trees and make the rain fall sideways. It was only five o'clock but the sun had already set. Ben and I decided to go to a wine bar not too far from my house. Neither one of us cared that much about wine, but it had covered valet parking, so it seemed the most dry of the nearby options.

We made our way to the table, taking off our wet coats and mussing with our hair. It had been so cold outside that the inside felt warm and cozy, as if we were sitting at a campfire.

I ordered a caprese salad and a Diet Coke. When Ben ordered a pasta dish and a glass of Pinot Noir, I remembered that the whole point of this place was the wine bar.

"Oh," I said. "Cancel the Diet Coke. I'll have the same." The waiter grabbed our menus and walked away.

"You don't have to order wine if you don't want wine," Ben said.

"Well," I said to him. "When in Rome!"

Our glasses came shortly after, filled halfway with dark red. We swirled the glasses under our noses, smiling at each other, neither of us having any idea what we were doing.

"Ah," Ben said. "A faint smell of blackberry and . . ." He sipped his drink in a reserved, taste-tester sort of way. "It has a woodsy quality to it, don't you think?"

"Mmmm," I said, sipping mine and pretending to contemplate. "Very woodsy. Very full-bodied."

We both laughed. "Yes!" Ben said. "I forgot *full-bodied*. Wine people love saying things are *full-bodied*."

He started to chug his down. "Honestly," he said, "it all tastes the same to me."

"Me too," I said, as I sipped mine again. Although, I had to admit that while I couldn't speak to the tannins or the base notes or whatever else people that know wine know, it tasted wonderful. After a few more sips, it started to feel wonderful.

Our food had just been served when Ben's phone rang. He put it through to voice mail as I took a bite of my salad. He started to eat his pasta and his phone rang again. Again, he ignored the call. I finally caved and asked.

"Who is that?" I said.

"Oh," he said, clearly wishing I hadn't asked. "It's just a girl that I dated a while ago. She drunk-dials sometimes."

"It's not even seven thirty."

"She's a bit . . . What is the correct way to say this? She is . . . a party girl? Is that the polite way to say that?"

"I guess it depends on what you're trying to say."

"She's an alcoholic," he said. "That's why I stopped dating her."

He said it so matter-of-factly that it caught me off guard. It almost seemed silly because it was so serious.

"She calls from time to time. I think she's trying to booty-call me."

I wanted to laugh again at him using the expression *booty-call,* but deep down, I was starting to get jealous and I could feel the jealousy moving its way closer and closer to the surface.

"Ah" was all I said.

"I've told her I'm with someone. Trust me. It's annoying more than anything else."

The jealousy was now hot on my skin. "Okay."

"Are you upset?"

"No," I said, breezily, as if I truly wasn't upset. Why did I do this? Why not just say "Yes"?

"Yes, you are."

"No."

"You're doing that thing."

"No, I'm not."

"Yep, your chest is getting red and you're speaking in clipped tones. That means you're mad."

"How would you even know that?"

"Because I pay attention."

"Okay," I said finally. "I just . . . I don't like it. This woman you used to date—which by the way, let's just acknowledge means you used to sleep with—I don't know if I like that she's calling you to do it again."

"I know. I agree with you. I told her to stop," he said to me. He didn't seem angry but he did seem defensive.

"I know. I know. I believe you, I just . . . Look, we said we would be exclusive for these five weeks, but if you don't want to . . ."

"What?" Ben had long ago stopped eating his pasta.

"Never mind."

"Never mind?"

"When was the last time you saw her?" Why I asked this question, what I thought it proved, I do not know. You don't ask questions you don't want the answers to. I never learned this.

"What does that matter?"

"I'm just asking," I said.

"It was a bit before I met you," he said, looking down into his wineglass, sipping it to hide from me.

"How much of a 'bit' are we talking about?"

Ben smiled, embarrassed. "I saw her the night before I met you," he said.

I wanted to reach across the table and wring his neck. My face flushed with jealousy. My chest felt like my lungs were a bonfire. I didn't have a good reason. I couldn't rationalize it. I wanted to yell at him and tell him what he had done wrong, but he hadn't done anything wrong. Nothing at all. It didn't even make sense for me to be this jealous. I just . . . I wanted to believe that Ben was mine. I wanted to believe that no one had made him smile until I did, no woman had made him yearn to touch her until I had. Suddenly, the woman calling took on a personality of her own in my head. I saw her in a red dress with long black hair. She probably wore black lace bra and panty sets. They probably always matched. In my head, her stomach was flat. In my head, she liked to be on top. Instead of admitting my jealousy, instead of telling the truth, I scoured the facts and tried to find a way to blame him.

"I just don't know how much I believe you're really pushing her away. I mean, a woman doesn't call over and over if she knows she's going to be rejected."

"It's my fault she's a drunk?"

"No—"

"You're telling me you don't know any women that are so confident in their attractiveness that they don't ever hear *no*?"

"So now you're saying this woman is hot?" I challenged.

"What does that have to do with this?"

"So she is," I said.

"Why are you being so insecure right now?"

What. The. Fuck.

It wasn't necessary. I could have stayed at the table. I could have finished my meal and told him to take me home and stay at his place. I could have done lots of things. I had plenty of options. But at the time it felt like I had one option and that option was to take my coat, put it on, call him an asshole under my breath, and walk out.

It wasn't until I was standing in the rain without the valet ticket that I started to realize all of the other options I had. I saw him through the restaurant's front window. I saw him look around for a waiter. I saw him flag one down and hand over a wad of cash. I saw him grab his jacket. I just stood outside in the cold rain, hugging my jacket tighter around myself, shivering a bit and wondering what I was going to say to him when he came out. I was starting to feel pretty stupid for walking out. I was starting to feel like the stupidity of my walking out had eclipsed his insensitivity.

As he headed out to the front door, I saw through the window that he checked his phone and it was lit up again. I saw him put the call through to voice mail for the third time in ten minutes, and I grew angry again. Jealousy was so ugly. It made me feel so ugly.

I felt the gust of warm air as he opened the door and came out. When it shut, I went back to being freezing cold again.

"Elsie—" he started to say. I couldn't read this tone. I didn't know if he was going to be contrite, defensive, or irritated, so I interrupted him.

"Look," I said, closing my jacket tighter, raising my voice to be heard above the sounds of car wheels speeding through shallow puddles. "I may not be conducting myself all that well right now, but that's a hell of a thing to say to me!"

"You can't just walk out on me in the middle of a goddamn restaurant!" he yelled. I hadn't seen him yell like that before.

"I can do whatever I—"

"No!" he said. "You can't. You can't punish me for something that happened before I met you and you can't punish me for what Amber—"

"Don't say her name!"

"This is not a big deal!" he said to me. "If you knew the way I think about you and the way I think about her, this would not be a big deal." He was choking over his words as the rain snuck into his mouth.

"What does that even mean?" I said. "Don't you think that if the situation were reversed—"

"I would be jealous, yeah. To think about another guy touching you, or you . . . touching him. Yeah. I'd be jealous."

"See?"

"But I wouldn't leave you there in the middle of a restaurant looking like an idiot. I wouldn't worry you like that."

"Oh, c'mon. You weren't worried."

"Yes, Elsie, yes, I was."

"What did you think was going to happen?"

"I don't know!" he said, raising his voice again. I was so cold. The rain was so loud. "I thought maybe that this was . . ."

"Over?"

"I don't know!"

"It's not over," I said. "Just because I got upset doesn't mean that I don't want . . ." Suddenly, I wanted to hold him and make sure he knew I wasn't going anywhere. His vulnerability was so tender and touching, I almost couldn't stand it. I put my hand out and smiled at him. "Besides," I said. "We can't break up for another few weeks."

He wasn't smiling. "It's not funny," he said, his shoulders hunched, combating the rain. "I don't want to lose you."

I looked him straight in the eye and I told him what I couldn't believe he didn't already know. "Ben Ross, I'm not leaving you." Before I could even get out the last syllable, he had thrown his body against mine, his lips against my mouth. It was sloppy and imperfect. Our teeth hit, making the side of my lip sting. But it was the moment I knew Ben loved me. I could feel it. I could feel that he loved me in a raw and real way, when it's not all rainbows and butterflies, when sometimes it's fear. I could feel his fear in that kiss and I could feel the desperation in his relief. It was intoxicating and it made me feel just a little less alone. The way we felt about each other, it made him do stupid things too.

He pulled away from me, finally, and yet all too soon. I had almost forgotten that we were in public, that we were in the rain. "I'm sorry," he said, putting his thumb to the blood on his lip.

"No," I said, taking a tissue out of my jacket and dabbing his lip myself. "I'm sorry." He put his hand on my wrist and moved my hand away from his lips. He kissed me again, gently.

"You're very sexy," he said to me, as he fished his phone out of his jacket pocket. He pressed a few numbers and said finally, "Hi, you've reached the voice mail of Ben Ross. Please leave a message and I'll call you back. If this is about what I'm doing later tonight, I am busy. Don't bother asking because the answer is that I am busy. From now on, I will always be busy." He hung up the phone and looked at me.

"You didn't have to do that," I said. Ben smiled at me.

"No," he said, taking the valet ticket out of his pocket. "I really do hope she stops calling. It's not going to happen. I have a huge crush on someone else."

I laughed at him as he handed the ticket to the valet.

"It's you, by the way," he said plainly, as he pulled his jacket up over my head to protect me from the rain.

"I figured," I said.

"So are you still starving?" he asked. "Because I am and we certainly can't go back in there."

JUNE

Hi, you've reached the voice mail of Ben Ross. Please leave a message and I'll call you back. If this is about what I'm doing later tonight, I am busy. Don't bother asking because the answer is that I am busy. From now on, I will always be busy."

"Hi, you've reached the voice mail of Ben Ross. Please leave a message and I'll call you back. If this is about what I'm doing later tonight, I am busy. Don't bother asking because the answer is that I am busy. From now on, I will always be busy."

"Hi, you've reached the voice mail of Ben Ross. Please leave a message and I'll call you back. If this is about what I'm doing later tonight, I am busy. Don't bother asking because the answer is that I am busy. From now on, I will always be busy."

I listen over and over again until I know the inflections and pauses by heart, until I can hear it even when it's not playing. And then I dial again.

This time I don't get to the message. Susan picks up.

"Elsie! Jesus! Just stop it, okay? Leave me alone. I can't take it anymore! He's going to be buried! Just like you wanted. Now stop."

"Uh . . ." I say, too dumbfounded to even know how to respond.

"Good-bye, Elsie!"

She hangs up the phone.

I sit there stunned, simply staring straight ahead, eyes unfocused, but resting on one spot on the ceiling. She could have turned off the ringer, I think. She could have turned off the phone. But she didn't. She wanted to scream at me instead.

I dial Ben's number again and she picks up. "Damn it!" she says.

"You want to sit there and pretend you knew everything about your son, you go ahead. Live the lie if you want to. But don't try to bring me down with you. I am his wife. He had been scared to tell you about me for six months. Six months of him going to your house with the intention of telling you that he had fallen in love and six months of him not doing it because he thought you were too distraught to handle it. So yes, he hid it from you. And I let him because I loved him. You want to be pissed at him. *Go ahead*. You want to be in denial about what happened. *Go right ahead*. I really don't care anymore, Susan. But I lost my husband and I will call his fucking phone over and over and over if I want to because I miss his voice. So turn it off if you have to, but that's your only option."

She's quiet for a minute, and I want to hang up but I also want to hear what she has to say for herself.

"It's funny to me that you think six months is a long period of time," she says. And then she hangs up.

My fury sends me up out of my bedroom. It throws shoes on my feet. When Ana asks what I'm doing, my fury tells her I'll be back later. It pushes me out the front door, into the June heat, and then it leaves me there.

I stand outside, unsure of how I feel or what to do. I stand there for a long time, and then I turn around and walk right back inside. There's no walking away from this problem. There's no cooling off from this.

I have to pick out an outfit for tomorrow," I say when I come back in.

"No, you don't," Ana says. "I pulled out what you're wearing. You shouldn't have to think about that."

"What am I wearing?" I look at her, grateful and confused.

"I tried to find the perfect balance of sex appeal and decorum, so you're wearing that long sleeveless black shift dress I found with black pumps. And I bought you this." Ana pulls something out from under the couch. It occurs to me this couch has been her bed for days now, when I'm not using it to avoid my own.

She returns and hands me a box. I set it down in front of me and pull off the top. Inside the box is a small black hat with a thin, short black veil. It's a morbid gift, a gift you can't really say "thank you" for or say you always wanted. But somehow, this small gift fills a small chunk of the huge hole in my heart.

I slowly move toward it, delicately removing it from the box. The tissue paper crinkles around it. I move the box from my knees onto the floor and I put the hat on. I look to Ana to help me set it straight, to make it right. Then I walk into the bathroom and look at myself in the mirror.

For the first time since Ben died, I look like a widow. For the first time since I lost him, I feel like I recognize the person in the mirror. There I am, grief-stricken and un-whole. Widowed.

It's such a relief to see myself this way. I have felt so insecure in my widowness that seeing myself look like a widow comforts me. I want to run to Susan and say, "Look at me. Don't I look like a woman that lost her husband?" If I look the part, everyone will believe me.

Ana is behind me in the bathroom. Her shoulders are hunched; her hands are clasped together, fingers intertwined. She is clearly unsure if she's made a huge mistake in giving me the type of gift one hopes never to receive. I turn to her and take off the hat. She helps me set it down.

"Thank you," I say, holding her shoulder. For some reason, I don't need to rest my head on it right now. "It's beautiful."

Ana shrugs, her head sinking slightly as her shoulders sag in. "Are you sure? It's not too much? It's not too . . . macabre?"

I don't actually know what *macabre* means, so I just shake my head. Whatever bad thing she thinks this gift might be, she is wrong. Given the circumstances, I love it.

"You are a friend that I could never . . ." I choke on the words, unable to look her in the eye. "No one deserves a friend as wonderful as you," I say. "Except maybe you."

Ana smiles and seizes my temporarily not-miserable mood to slap the back of my thighs. "What can I say, kid? I love ya. Always have."

"Should I try on the whole thing?" I ask, suddenly somewhat eager for an old-fashioned game of dress-up. Ana and I used to play dress-up in college, each of us going into the bathroom to try to come up with the most ridiculous outfits for the other one to wear. This is different; this is much, much sadder, but . . . this type of dress-up is where life has taken us and Ana is on board.

"Do it. I'll wait out here."

I run into my bedroom to see that she's set aside my dress and shoes. I put them on quickly, adding a pair of black panty hose to complete the ensemble and mitigate the inherent sexiness of the veil and bare legs.

"Is it appropriate to be a sexy widow?" I call out to her while I put on my second shoe.

Ana laughs. "I've never actually seen one in person," she replies.

I step out of the door and into the hallway. When I do, I slip on the heel of my shoe and my ankle gives in. I fall flat on my ass. There is a moment when Ana stares at me not knowing what to do. She doesn't know if I'm going to laugh or cry. I think she's petrified that I will cry because this is certainly something to cry about, but I don't want to cry right now. As I look back at her, I can feel the laugh starting in my belly. I can feel it ripple through my body and then, here it is. It overtakes me.

"Oh God," I say through tears and sharp breaths. "Oh!"

Ana starts laughing loudly now too. "BAHHAHAHHHAHAHA!" she cackles. She throws herself on the floor next to me. "I don't know why," she says and breathes in sharply. "I don't know why that was so funny."

"Oh, but it was," I say as I laugh with her. I think if she wasn't here, I would have been able to stop laughing sooner, but hearing her laugh makes me laugh. My laugh grows wild and unpredictable. It grows loud and free. She is wiping her eyes and gaining her composure, but as she looks me in the eye she loses it again. When I finally get ahold of myself, I'm light-headed.

"Oooh," I say, trying to cool down. It feels so good. I can feel it in my abdomen and my back. Then I get a glimpse of myself in the mirror again and I remember why I'm here. Why I'm in the middle of the floor on a Friday afternoon dressed in black. Ben is gone. And I hate myself for laughing. I hate myself for forgetting, even for ten seconds, the man I have lost.

Ana can tell the mood has shifted; the vacation from our misery has ended and I, once again, need to be maintained. She gets up off the floor first, dusting her ass off, and gives me a hand. I rise awkwardly, flashing my underwear at her while trying to stand up like a lady. No, like a lady isn't enough. Like a widow. Widows require even more poise. Widows don't accidentally flash their underwear at anyone.

It doesn't get much shittier than this.

It's hot in the morning when Ana and I leave Los Angeles. It feels even hotter in Orange County. It feels stickier, sweatier, more terrible in every way. Southern California is always warmer than the rest of the country, and it's supposed to be less humid. But on this June morning, it's hot as hell and I'm dressed in all black.

We weren't late arriving here, but we weren't early. We weren't the type of early that you imagine the wife of the deceased to be. Susan stares at me as I make my way graveside. She was probably a full forty-five minutes early. What I want to tell her is that we aren't early because I almost didn't come, because I refused to get into the car. Because I threw myself on my own front lawn and told Ana that I honestly believed that if I went to his funeral, Ben would never come back. I told her, black mascara running down my face, that I wanted to stay there and wait. "I can't give up on him," I said to her, as if attending his funeral would be a betrayal and not a commemoration.

The only reason we were on time is that Ana picked me up off the ground, looked me in the eyes, and said to me, "He's never coming back. Whether you go or you don't go. So get in the car, because this is the last thing you can do with him."

Ana now stands next to me, wearing a black pantsuit. I

would hazard to guess she did this to allow me to shine today, as if this were my wedding. Susan is wearing a black sweater and black skirt. She is surrounded by young men in black suits and a few older women in black or navy dresses. We are standing outside in the grass. The heels of my high heels are digging into the grass, making me sink into the ground as if on quicksand. Moving my legs means pulling the heels up out of the ground as if they were mini-shovels. I'm aerating the graveyard grounds.

I can hear the pastor speaking; rather, I can hear that he is speaking, but I cannot make out the words. I believe he is the pastor that tended to Ben's father's service a few years ago. I do not know his denomination. I do not know how religious Susan really is. I just know he's speaking about an afterlife I'm not sure I believe in, about a God I don't trust. I am standing with my head down, glancing furtively at the people around me I don't know. I don't think I ever imagined attending my husband's funeral, whether it was specifically Ben's or the fictional idea of a husband I held on to until I met Ben. But if I did, I would have expected to know the people at the funeral.

I look over and see people I can only assume are aunts and uncles, cousins or neighbors. I stop trying to guess who they are because guessing makes me feel like I didn't know Ben. But I did know Ben, I just hadn't met this part of him yet.

My side of the funeral looks like a frat at a school dance. It's Ben's friends and former roommate. It's men who have one nice suit, who eat pizza every night, and play video games until they go to bed. That's who Ben was when he was here, it's who Ben surrounded himself with. It's good that they are here now, however nameless and faceless they feel in this crowd. Ana stands next to me, one of the only women our age in attendance. Ben wasn't friends with a lot of women, and ex-girlfriends would be out of place. Some of my friends offered to come, the ones that had met him a few times or gone out with us. I had told Ana to tell them, "Thanks, but no thanks." I wasn't sure how to react to them in this context. I wasn't sure how to be their host at a place where I felt like a guest.

As the pastor's voice dies down, I can sense that my turn to speak is coming. I am relieved when his hand gestures first to Susan.

Susan moves toward the top of the grave and opens a manila folder. Should I have brought a manila folder? I barely prepared anything. Thinking of what to say was so awful, so ulcer-inducing, that I simply didn't do it. I couldn't do it. I decided I was going to wing it. Because nothing could be worse than lying in bed thinking of what to say over your husband's dead body, right? At least that's what I thought until I saw Susan's perfectly preserved manila folder. She hadn't cried on it or ripped it up. She hadn't folded the corners over and over out of fear. It is straight as a board. I bet the paper inside isn't even scribbled on. I bet it's typed.

"I want to start by saying thank you to everyone in attendance today. I know this is not the way anyone wants to spend a Saturday morning." She half chuckles to herself, and the rest of us make a noise resembling a snort so that she can move on. "Some of you were with me a few years ago when Ben and I commemorated Steven, and I know I said then that Steven would have wanted us to enjoy this day. He would have wanted us to smile. I happened to have known that for a fact because Steven and I talked about it before he passed. We lay in the hospital together, when we knew it wasn't going to get any better, when we knew the end was near, and he told me, as I told you then, 'Make it fun, Susie. My life was fun, make this fun too.' I wasn't able to spend Ben's last moments with him." Her face starts to scrunch and she looks down. She regains her composure. "But in many ways he took after his father, and I can tell you, Ben would have wanted the same thing. He had fun in life, and we should do our best to find the fun in his death. It's senseless and painful, but it can be happy and I promise to try to make today a day of celebration of who he was. I thank God for every day I had with him, with both of them. We can lament that Ben is gone, but I'm trying to, I'm choosing to, I'm . . ." She laughs a rueful laugh. "I'm doing my best to instead think of Ben's time in my life as a gift from God. One that was shorter than I'd like, but miraculous nonetheless." She makes eye contact with me for a short period of time, long enough for both of us to notice, and then her eyes are back to the page. "No matter how many days we had with him, they were a gift. So in the spirit of celebration, I wanted to tell you all a story about one of my favorite, favorite Ben moments.

"He was eighteen and leaving for college. As many of you know he went to college close by, only an hour or two away, but it was much farther than he had ever been from me and I was terrified. My only son was moving away! All summer long I was crying on and off, trying to hide it from him, trying not to make him feel guilty. The day came to take him to school. Well, actually, wait." She stops, no longer reading from the paper. "The other part of this you need to know is that we have a guest bathroom in the house that we never use. No one ever uses it. It was this big family joke that no one had set foot in the guest bathroom for years. We have a bathroom downstairs that guests always use and an extra bathroom upstairs that I had deemed the guest bathroom and insisted it had to be redone and gorgeous because guests would use it, but no guest ever used it. I've never even had to clean it. Anyway . . ." she continues.

"As Steven and I are moving Ben in, we bring in the last of his stuff and I just start bawling my eyes out, right in front of his new roommate and his parents. It had to be mortifying for him, but he didn't show it. He walked me out to the car and he hugged Steven and I, and he said, 'Mom, don't worry. I'll come back next month and stay a weekend, all right?' And I nodded. I knew that if I didn't leave that minute, I'd never be able to. So I got in the car and Steven and I had started to drive away when Ben gave me one last kiss and said, 'When you get sad, check the guest bathroom.' I asked him to explain what he meant, but he smiled and repeated himself, so I let it go, and when I got home, I ran in there." She laughs. "I couldn't wait another minute, and as I turned on the light, I saw that he had written 'I love you' across the mirror in soap. At the very bottom it said, 'And you can keep this forever because no one will ever see it.' And I did, it's still there now. I don't think a single other person has ever seen it."

I look down at the ground just in time to see the tears fall off my face and onto my shoes.

JANUARY

It was the day before our five-week deal was up. For the past four weeks and six days, Ben and I had been spending all of our time together, but neither one of us was allowed to mention words like *boyfriend, girlfriend,* or more specifically, *I love you*. I was very much looking forward to tomorrow. We had spent the day in bed, reading magazines (me) and newspapers (him), and he had been trying to convince me that it was a good idea to get a dog. This all started because of the pictures of dogs for adoption in the classifieds.

"Just look at this one. It's blind in one eye!" Ben said as he shoved the newspaper in my face. His fingertips were covered in gray ink. All I could think was that he was getting the ink all over my white sheets.

"I see him!" I said back, putting down my magazine and turning toward Ben. "He's very, very cute. How old is he?"

"He's two! Just two years old and he needs a home, Elsie! We can be that home!"

I grabbed the newspaper from him. "*We* can't be anything. *We* aren't talking about anything that would progress our relationship in any way, shape, or form. Which a dog most certainly does."

Ben grabbed the paper back. "Yes, but that ends tomorrow and this dog might get adopted today!"

"Well, if he gets adopted today then he's okay, right? We

don't need to step in and help him," I said, smiling at him, teasing him.

"Elsie." Ben shook his head. His voice turned purposefully childish. "Before, when I said that I was worried that the dog wouldn't find a good home, I wasn't being entirely honest about how I felt about this dog."

"You weren't?" I said, falsely shocked.

"No, Elsie. I wasn't. And I think you knew that."

I shook my head. "I knew no such thing."

"I want this dog, dammit! I don't want anyone else to have it! We have to get it today!"

We had been joking up until then, but I was starting to feel that if I said I'd go get it that day, he'd put his clothes on and be in the car within minutes.

"We can't get a dog!" I said, laughing. "Whose house would it even live at?"

"Here. It would live here and I would take care of it."

"Here? At my house?"

"Well, I can't keep him at my house! It's a shithole!"

"So, really, you want *me* to get a dog and you want to play with it."

"No, I will take care of the dog with you and it will be *our* dog."

"You are cheating. This is . . . this is progressing the relationship. This is a huge . . . just a huge . . . I mean . . ."

Ben started laughing. He could see that he was making me nervous. The conversation had started to teeter on moving-in territory, and I was way too eager to discuss the idea. So eager that it embarrassed me and I did everything I could to hide it.

"Fine," he said, putting one arm around me and the other behind him on the pillow. "I won't talk about this at all today. But if Buster is still around tomorrow, can we discuss it?"

"Buster? You want to name the dog Buster?"

"I didn't name the dog! It says in the ad that his name is Buster. If it were up to me, we'd name the dog Sonic. Because that is an awesome name."

"I'm not getting a dog and naming it Sonic."

"Fine, how about Bandit?"

"Bandit?"

"Evel Knievel?"

"You would end up calling it Evel for short. That's terrible."

Ben was laughing at himself. "Please don't tell me you'd want to name a dog Fluffy or Cookie."

"If I was going to have a dog, I'd name it something based on what it looked like. You know? Really take into account the personality of the dog."

"Has anyone else told you you're the most boring woman on the planet?" Ben asked me, smiling.

"They have now," I said. "What time is it? We have to meet Ana soon, I think."

"It's five forty-seven p.m.," he said.

"Ah!" I jumped up off the bed and into a pair of jeans. "We're already going to be late!"

"We're meeting her at six?" Ben asked, not moving. "She's always late."

"Yes! Yes! But *we* still have to be on time!" I was reaching around the side of the bed searching for my bra. I didn't like the way my breasts looked in certain positions, and I found myself running around the room with one arm covering them.

Ben got up. "Okay. Can we just check to see if she'll be there on time?"

I stopped looking a moment to stare at him. "What? No. We have to leave now!"

Ben laughed. "Okay, I will get us there at six oh five," he said as he put his pants on and threw a shirt on over them. He was suddenly ready to go, and I was nowhere near it.

"Okay! Okay!" I ran into the bathroom to see if I'd left my bra there. Ben followed me in, helping me. He found it before I did and threw it at me. "Don't cover your boobs on my account. I know you think they look bad when you are bent over, but you're wrong. So next time just let 'em hang free, baby."

I looked at him in stunned silence. "You are so fucking weird," I said.

He picked me up like I weighed three pounds. My body was straight against his, my legs tight together, my arms on his shoulders. He looked at me and kissed my collarbone. "I'm weird for loving you?"

I think he was just as shocked he'd said it as I was. "To love parts of you, I meant." He put me down. "I meant, to love parts of you." He blushed slightly as I found a shirt and put it on. I smiled at him like he was a child who had very adorably hidden my car keys.

"You weren't supposed to say that," I teased him as I put on mascara and got my shoes.

"Ignore it please!" He was now waiting by the door for me.

"I don't think I can ignore it!" I said as we exited my front door.

We got in the car and he started the engine. "I really am sorry about that. It just came out."

"You broke the rules!" I said again.

"I know! I know. I'm already embarrassed. It's . . ." He trailed off as we headed down the street. He was pretending to be focused on driving, but I could tell all of him was focused on this sentence.

"It's what?"

Ben sighed, suddenly serious. "I made up the whole five-week thing because I was afraid I'd tell you I loved you too soon and you wouldn't say it back and I'd be embarrassed, and now here I am, I waited all these days to tell you and I . . . I still told you too soon and you didn't say it back and I'm embarrassed." He played the end off like a joke, but it wasn't a joke.

"Hey," I said, grabbing his arm. He was stopped at a red light. I turned his head and looked him in the eye. "I love you too," I said. "Probably before you did. I've been waiting to say it all month, practically."

His eyes looked glassy, and I couldn't tell if he was tearing up or he was perfectly fine. Either way, he kissed me and held my gaze until the cars behind us honked. Ben immediately started paying attention to the road again.

"I had this whole plan!" He laughed. "I was going to wake up early tomorrow and go into the bathroom and write 'I love you' on the mirror with a bar of soap."

I laughed. "Well, you can still do that tomorrow," I said, rubbing his hand. "It will mean just as much to me then."

Ben laughed. "Okay then, maybe I will." And he did. I left it there for days.

JUNE

I can't help but feel for Susan after her eulogy. She has made me love my husband even more than I did when he was alive.

Susan walks to her place along the grave, and the pastor asks for me to make my way to the front. I can feel myself sweating out of nervousness on top of the sweat already there from the heat.

I pull my heels out of the ground and stand at the top of Ben's grave. For a minute, I just stare at the box, knowing what is inside, knowing just days earlier that body had put a ring on my finger. Knowing even more recently, that body had gotten on a bike and headed up the street to get me cereal. That body loved me. They say that public speaking and death are the top two most stressful events in a person's life. So I forgive myself for being so scared I almost faint.

"I," I start. "I . . ." I stop. Where do I even begin? My eye catches the casket in front of me again, and I stop myself from looking at it directly. I will fall to pieces if I keep thinking about what I'm doing. "Thank you for coming. For those of you who don't know me, I want to introduce myself. My name is Elsie and I was Ben's wife."

I gotta breathe. I just gotta breathe.

"I know that you've probably all heard by now that Ben and I eloped just a few days before he passed away and I . . . know that puts us all in a difficult position. We are strangers to each other, but we share a very real loss. I had only been dating Ben a short while before we got married. I didn't know him for very long. I admit that. But the short amount of time that I was his wife," I say, "was the defining part of my life.

"He was a good man with a big heart, and he loved all of you. I've heard so many stories about you. I've heard, Aunt Marilyn, about the time you caught him peeing in your backyard. Or Mike, he told me about when you two were little and you used to play cops and robbers, but you both were robbers so there weren't any cops. These stories were part of why I grew to love him in such a short span of time, and they're part of what makes me feel so close to all of you."

I want to look these people in the eye when I say their names, but to tell the truth, I'm not entirely sure which of the older ladies is Marilyn and which of the young men is Mike. My eyes scan the people looking at me and then they move briefly to Susan. She has her head down, tucked in her chest.

"I guess I just want you all to know that at the end of his life, he had someone who loved him deeply and purely. He had someone who believed in him. I took good care of him, I promise you I did. And I can tell you, as the last person to see him alive, I can tell you, he was happy. He had found a happy life for himself. He was happy."

Susan catches my eye as I step back into place. This time she nods and puts her head back down. The pastor steps back up to lead, and my brain drifts to somewhere else, anywhere else but here.

As I stand next to Ana, she puts her arm around me and gives me a squeeze. The pastor offers Susan and me small shovels to spread dirt on the casket. We both step forward and take them, but Susan grabs the dirt with her hand instead and gently throws it on Ben's casket, so I do the same thing. We stand there, together but separate, side by side, dusting the dirt off our hands. I find myself jealous of the dirt that will get to spend so many years close to Ben's body. As I dust off the last of the dirt and Susan starts to move back toward her place in the crowd, our hands graze each other, pinkies touching. Out of reflex, I freeze, and when I do, she grabs my hand, if only for a split second, and squeezes it, never looking at me. For one second, we are together in this, and then she goes back to her spot and I retreat to mine. I want to run up to her. I want to hug her and say, "Look at what we could be to each other." But I don't.

I head back to the car and try to ready myself for the next phase of this day. I break it down into baby steps in my head. I just need to sit here in the front seat as Ana drives us to Susan's house. I just have to put one foot out of the door after she parks. Then the other foot. I just have to not cry as I head into her home. I just have to give a consternated smile to the other mourners as we walk in together. That's as far as I get before we are parked outside of Susan's house, one in a long line of cars against the sidewalk. Do the neighbors know? Are they looking at this invasion on their street and thinking, Poor Susan Ross. She lost her son now too?

I get out of the car and straighten my dress. I take off my hat with the veil and leave it on the front seat of Ana's car. She sees me do this and nods.

"Too dramatic for interiors," she says.

If I open my mouth I will cry and spill my feelings all over this sidewalk. I simply nod and tighten my lips, willing the knot in my throat to recede, to let me do this. I tell myself I can cry all night. I can cry for the rest of my life, if I can just get through this.

When I find myself in front of Susan's house, I am shocked at the sheer size of it. It's too big for one person; that much is obvious from the street. My guess is she knows that already, feels it every day. It's a Spanish-style house in a brilliant shade of white. At night, it must serve as a moon for the whole block. The roof is a deep brown with terra cotta shingles. The windows are huge. Bright, tropical-looking flowers are all over her front lawn. This house isn't just expensive; it takes a lot of upkeep.

"Jesus, what did she do? Write Harry Potter?" Ana says as we stare at it.

"Ben didn't grow up crazy rich. This all must be recent," I say, and then we walk up the brick steps to Susan's open front door. The minute I cross the threshold, I'm thrown into the middle of it.

It's a bustling house now full of people. Caterers in black pants and white shirts are offering people things like salmon mousse and shrimp ceviche on blue tortilla chips. I see a woman walk by me with a fried macaroni and cheese ball, and I think, If I ate food, that's what I'd eat. Not this seafood crap. Who serves seafood at a funeral reception? I mean, probably everyone. But I hate seafood, and I hate this funeral reception.

Ana grabs my hand and pulls me through the crowd. I don't know what I was expecting from this reception, so I don't know whether I'm disappointed or not.

Finally, we make our way to Susan. She is in her kitchen, her beautiful, ridiculously stocked kitchen, and she is speaking to the caterers about the timing of various dishes and where things are located. She's so kind and understanding. She says things like "Don't worry about it. It's just some salsa on the carpet. I'm sure it will come out." And "Make yourself at home. The downstairs bathroom is around the corner to the right."

The guest bathroom. I want to see the guest bathroom. How do I run upstairs and find it without her knowing? Without being terribly rude and thoughtless? I just want to see his handwriting. I just want to see new evidence that he was alive.

Ana squeezes my hand and asks me if I want a drink. I decline, and so she makes her way over to the bar area without me. Suddenly, I am standing in the middle of a funeral dedicated to my husband, and yet, I am not a part of it. I do not know anyone here. Everyone is walking around me, talking next to me, looking at me. I am the enigma to them. I am not a part of the Ben they knew. Some of them stare and then smile when I catch them. Others don't even see me. Or maybe they are just better at staring. Susan comes out from the kitchen.

"Should you go talk to her?" Ana asks, and I know that I should. I know that this is her house, this is her event, and I am a guest and I should say something.

"What do I say in a situation like this?" I have started saying "situation like this" because this situation is so unique that it has no name and I don't feel like constantly saying, "My new husband died and I'm standing in a room full of strangers making me feel like my husband was a stranger."

"Maybe just 'How are you?'" Ana suggests. I think it's stupid that the most appropriate question to ask the mother of my dead husband on the day of his funeral is the same question I ask bank tellers, waiters, and any other strangers I meet. Nevertheless, Ana is right. That is what I should do. I breathe in hard and hold it, and then I let it out and I start walking over to her.

Susan is speaking with a few women her own age. They are dressed in black or navy suits with pearls. I walk up and wait patiently next to her. It's clear that I want to cut in. The women leave pauses in the conversation, but none feel big enough for me to jump in. I know that she can see me. I'm in her sight line. She's just making me wait because she can. Or maybe she's not. Maybe she's trying to be polite and this isn't about me.

Honestly, I've lost perspective on what's about me and what isn't so . . .

"Hi, Elsie," she says to me as she finally turns around. She turns her back away from her friends, and her torso now faces mine. "How are you?" she asks me.

"I was just about to ask you that," I say.

She nods. "This is the most fucked-up day of my life," she says. The minute the word *fuck* comes out of her mouth, she becomes a real person to me, with cracks and holes, huge vulnerable spots and flaws. I see Ben in her, and I start to cry. I hold back the tears as best I can. Now isn't the time to lose it. I have to keep it together.

"Yeah, it's a hard day," I say, my voice starting to betray me. "Your speech was . . ." I begin, and she puts her hand out to stop me.

"Yours too. Keep your chin up. I know how to get through these things, and it's by keeping your chin up."

This is about all I get from Susan, and I'm not sure if it's a metaphor or not. She is pulled away by new arrivals that want to prove what good people they are by "being there for her." I walk back over to Ana, who is now near the kitchen. The waiters are running back and forth with full and empty trays, and as they do, Ana keeps pulling bacon-wrapped dates off the full ones. "I did it," I say.

She high-fives me. "When was the last time you ate?" she says, devouring the dates as she asks.

I think back to the pancake and know that if I tell the truth, she's going to force-feed me hors d'oeuvres.

"Oh, pretty recently," I say.

"Bullshit," she says as another waiter comes through with shrimp. She stops him, and I cringe.

"No," I say, perhaps too boldly. "No shrimp."

"Dates?" she says, handing her napkin over to me. It still has two left. The dates are big, and the bacon looks thick around them. They are gooey from the sugar. I don't know if I can do it. But then I think about all the seafood here and I know this is my best bet. So I take them and eat them.

They. Are. Decadent.

And suddenly my body wants more. More sugar. More salt. More life. And I tell myself, That's sick, Elsie. Ben's dead. This is no time for hedonism.

I excuse myself and head upstairs, away from the food and toward the guest bathroom mirror. I know where I'm going as I walk up the stairs, but I'm not consciously moving there. I feel pulled there. As I get further up the stairs, I can hear a number of voices chattering and people chewing. There are quite a few people hanging out in the guest room. Everyone has come up to see the bathroom mirror. I don't turn the corner and go into the room. I stand at the top of the stairs, not sure what to do. I want to be alone with the mirror. I can't bear to see his handwriting with an audience. Do I turn back around? Come back later?

"That eulogy was convincing," I hear a man's voice say.

"No, I know. I'm not saying it wasn't convincing," says another voice, this one higher, womanly, and more committed to the conversation.

"What are we talking about?" comes a third voice. It's gossipy, and I can tell just by the tone, the speaker's got a drink in her hand.

"Ben's widow," says the woman.

"Ohh, right. Scandal," the third voice says. "They weren't even married two weeks, right?"

"Right," says the man. "But I think Susan believes her."

"No, I know Susan believes her," the woman says. "I believe her too. I get it. They were married. I'm just saying, you know Ben, you know the way he loved his mom. Don't you think he would have told her if this was the real deal?"

I slowly step away, not wanting to be heard and not wanting to hear whatever comes next. As I walk down the steps to find Ana, I catch a glimpse of myself in one of Susan's mirrors. For the first time, I don't see myself. I see the woman they all see, the woman Susan sees: the fool who thought she was going to spend her life with Ben Ross.

FEBRUARY

It was a Tuesday night and Ben and I were tired. I had had a long day at the library, pulling together a display of artifacts of the Reagan administration. Ben had gotten into an argumentative discussion with his boss over a company logo that Ben was lead on. Neither one of us wanted to cook dinner, neither one of us wanted to do much of anything except eat food and go to bed.

We went out for dinner at the café on the corner. I ordered spaghetti with pesto. Ben got a chicken sandwich. We sat at one of the wobbly tables out front, with two wobbly chairs, and we ate alfresco, counting the minutes until it was appropriate to go to sleep.

"My mom called me today," Ben said, pulling red onions out of his sandwich and placing them on the wax paper underneath.

"Oh?"

"I just . . . I think that is part of why I am stressed out. I haven't told her about you."

"Well, don't worry about it on my account. I haven't told my parents about you either."

"But this is different," he said. "I am close with my mom. I talk to her all the time, I just, for some reason, I don't want to tell her about you."

I was confident enough by this point that I had Ben's heart, that the issue here was not me.

"Well, what do you think is stopping you?" I asked, finishing my pasta. It had been watery and unsatisfying.

Ben put his sandwich down and wiped the excess flour off his hands. Why on earth do fancy artisan sandwiches have flour on them?

"I'm not sure. I think part of it is that I know that she will be happy for me but concerned . . . er . . ."

"Concerned?" Now I was starting to think maybe I *was* the issue here.

"Not concerned. When my dad died, I spent a lot of time with my mom."

"Naturally," I said.

"Right, but also, I was worried about her. I wanted to make sure she always had someone around. I didn't want her to be alone."

"Sure."

"And then as time went on, I wanted to give her a chance to move on herself. To meet someone else, to find her new life. To really . . . leave the nest, kind of."

I chuckled slightly, subtly, to myself. What kind of son wants to help his own mother leave the nest?

"But she just didn't."

"Right. Well, everyone is different," I said.

"I know, but it's been three years and she's still in that same house, alone. My mom had the exterior of the house redone after my dad died. I think to keep busy maybe? I don't know. She got money from the life insurance policy. When that was done, she added an extension. When that was done, she had the front yard redone. It's like she can't stop moving or she'll implode. But she hasn't changed much about the place inside, really. It's mostly as my father left it. Pictures of him everywhere. She still wears her wedding ring. She isn't moving on."

"Mmm-hmm," I said, listening.

"I'm worried that my meeting you, meeting this fantastic girl who is perfect for me . . ." he said, "I'm worried it will be too much. I'm worried she'll feel left behind. Or . . . that I'm moving on too quickly or something. There's nothing left in the house to change. And I feel like she's about to"—he didn't say it lightly—"crash."

"You feel like you need to stagnate because she is stagnating? Or that you need to keep her at bay for now until she settles?"

"Kind of. For some reason, I just think, when I tell my mom I'm in a really great relationship, some part of her isn't going to be ready for that."

"I guess I don't understand why it's so dramatic. I mean, you've dated other girls before."

"Not girls like you, Elsie. This is . . . you are different."

I didn't say anything back. I just smiled and looked him in the eyes.

"Anyway." He went back to his sandwich, finishing it up. "When I tell my mom about you, it's going to be serious because I'm serious about you and I don't know . . . I'm worried she'll take it as a rejection. Like I'm no longer there for her."

"So I'm a secret?" I asked, starting to feel bothered and hoping I was misunderstanding.

"For now," he said. "I'm being such a baby, scared of my mom. But if you don't have a problem with it, I just want to be delicate with her."

"Oh, sure," I said, but then felt myself speaking up. "But not forever, right? I mean, you'll tell her eventually." I didn't say the last part as a question and yet, that's exactly what it was.

Ben nodded as he finished chewing. "Absolutely!" he said. "When the time is right, I know she'll be thrilled." He rolled up the wax paper from his sandwich. He pitched it toward the trash can and missed. He laughed at himself, walked over, picked up the ball of paper, and put it in the trash can. By the time he grabbed my hand and started to lead us back to my place, I had come around to his way of seeing it.

"Thank you, Elsie. For understanding and not thinking I am a gigantic douchey mama's boy."

"You're not scared your mom will be mad at you," I said. "That would make you a gigantic douchey mama's boy. You're just scared to hurt her feelings. That makes you sensitive. And it's one of the reasons I love you."

"And the fact that you understand that about me and it's a reason you love me, makes you the coolest girl in the world," he said, as he put his arm around me and kissed my temple. We walked awkwardly down the block, too close together to walk gracefully.

When we got to my apartment, we brushed our teeth and I washed my face, both of us using the sink in our own perfectly timed intervals. We took off our jeans. He took off his shirt and handed it to me silently, casually, as if it were now an impulse. I took it and put it on, as he turned on the one bedside lamp and picked up a book with a wizard on the cover. I got in beside him and put my head on his shoulder.

"You're going to read?" I asked.

"Just until my brain stops," he said, and then he put the book down and looked at me. "Want me to read to you?" he offered.

"Go for it," I said, thinking that it sounded like a nice way to fall asleep. My eyes were closed by the time he got to the end of the page, and the next thing I knew it was morning.

JUNE

I tell Ana I want to go, and within seconds, we are headed for the door.

"What's the matter?" Ana asks.

"No, nothing. I'm just ready to leave," I say. Ana's keys are in her hand, and my hand is on the doorknob.

"You're leaving?" Susan asks. I turn to see her a few feet behind me.

"Oh," I say. "Yes, we're going to make the drive back to Los Angeles." What is she thinking right now? I can't tell. She's so stone-faced. Is she happy I'm leaving? Is this all the evidence she needs that I don't belong in their lives?

"Okay," she says. "Well." She grabs my hand and squeezes it. "I wish you the best of luck, Elsie."

"You too, Susan," I say. I turn around and catch Ana's eye, and we walk out the door. It isn't until my feet have hit the cement in her driveway that I realize why I am so bothered by what she just said, aside from how disingenuous it was.

She thinks she'll never see me again. It's not like I live in Michigan. She could easily see me if she wanted to. She just doesn't want to.

When we get home, I run to the bathroom and shut the door. I stand against it, holding the knob still in my hand. It's over. Ben is over. This is done. Tomorrow people will expect me to start moving on. There is no more Ben left in my life. I left him in Orange County.

I lock the door behind me, calmly walk over to the toilet, and puke bacon-wrapped dates. I wish I had eaten more in the past few days so I'd have something to give. I want to expel everything from my body, purge all of this pain that fills me into the toilet and flush it down.

I open the bathroom door and walk out. Ana is standing there, waiting.

"What do you want to do?" she asks.

"I think, really, I'm just going to go to sleep. Is that okay? Do you think that's bad? To go to sleep at"—I look at the clock on my cell phone; it is even earlier than I thought—"to go to bed at seven oh three p.m.?"

"I think you have had a very hard day and if you need to go to sleep, that's okay. I'm going to go home and let my dog out and I'll be back," she says.

"No." I shake my head. "You don't need to, you can sleep in your own bed."

"Are you sure? I don't want you to be alone if you—"

"No, I'm sure." I don't know how she's been sleeping here for all of these days, living out of a backpack, going back and forth.

"Okay." She kisses me on the cheek. "I'll come by in the morning," she adds. She grabs her things and heads out the door, and when it closes, the apartment becomes dead and silent.

This is it. This is my new life. Alone. Quiet. Still. This isn't how it was supposed to go. Ben and I had mapped out our lives together. We had a plan. This wasn't the plan. I've got no plan.

FEBRUARY

Ben called me from the car to tell me he would be late. Traffic was backed up.

"I'm stuck on the 405. Nobody's moving and I'm bored," he said to me. I had been at lunch with Ana and had just left and made my way home.

"Oh no!" I said, opening up my front door and placing my things on the front table. "How far away are you?"

"With this traffic I can't even tell, which sucks because I want to see you," he said.

I sat down on the couch and kicked my shoes off. "I want to see you too! I missed you all morning." Ben had spent the night with me and left early to make the visit down to Orange County. He had planned on telling his mother about us and wanted to do it in person.

"Well, how did it go?" I asked.

"We went out to breakfast. She asked a lot about me. I kept asking about her, but she kept turning the conversation back to me and there just . . . there wasn't an opening to say it. To tell her. I didn't tell her."

He didn't say the phrase "I'm sorry," but I could hear it in his voice. I was disappointed in him for the first time, and I wondered if he could hear it in mine.

"Okay, well . . . you know . . . it is what it is," I said. "Is traffic moving? When do you think you'll be home? Er . . . here. When do you think you'll be here?" I had started to make this mistake more and more often, calling my home his home. He spent so much time here, you'd think he lived here. But paying rent in one place and spending your time in another was just the way things were done when you were twenty-six and in love. Living together was something entirely different, and I was showing my hand early by continuing to make that mistake.

"You keep doing that!" he teased me.

"Okay, okay, it was a mistake. Let's move on."

"The freeway is clearing up so I should be there in about a half hour, I think. Then I think I'll move in, in about four months. We will get engaged a year after that and married within a year after that. I think we should have time alone together before we have kids, don't you? So maybe first kid at thirty. Second at thirty-three or thirty-four. I'm fine to have three if we have the money to do it comfortably. So, with your biological clock, let's try for the third before thirty-eight or so. Kids will be out of the house and in college around fifty-five. We can be empty-nested and retired by sixty-five. Travel around the world a few times. I mean, sixty is the new forty, you know? We'll still be spry and lively. Back from world travel by seventy, which gives us about ten to twenty years to spend time with our grandkids. You can garden, and I'll start sculpting or something. Dead by ninety. Sound good?"

I laughed. "You didn't account for your midlife crisis at forty-five, where you leave me and the kids and start dating a young preschool teacher with big boobs and a small ass."

"Nah," he said. "That won't happen."

"Oh no?" I dared him.

"Nope. I found the one. Those guys that do that, they didn't find the one."

He was cocksure and arrogant, thinking he knew better, thinking he could see the future. But I loved the future he saw and I loved the way he loved me.

"Come home," I said. "Er, here. Come here."

Ben laughed. "You have to stop doing that. According to the plan, I don't move in for another four months."

JUNE

I lie in bed all morning until Ana shows up, and she tells me to get dressed because we are going to the bookstore.

When we walk into the behemoth of a store, I follow Ana along as she picks up books and puts them down. She seems to have a purpose, but I don't much care what it is. I leave her side and walk toward the Young Adult section. There I find a trio of teenage girls, laughing and teasing each other about boys and hairstyles.

I run my fingers over the books, looking for titles that I now own on my own bookshelf, their pages torn and softened by Ben's fingers. I look for names I recognize because I got them from work and brought them home to him. I never guessed correctly, the books he'd want to read. I don't think I ever got one right. I didn't have enough time to learn what he liked. I would have learned though. I would have studied it and learned it and figured out who he was as a book reader if I'd just been given enough time.

Ana finds me eventually. By the time she has, I'm sitting on the floor next to the E-F-G section. I stand up and look at the book in her hand. "What'd ya get?"

"It's for you. And I already paid for it," she says. She hands it to me.

The Year of Magical Thinking by Joan Didion.

"Are you fucking kidding me?" I say, too loudly for a bookstore, even though I realize that's not the same as a library.

"No," she says. She's taken aback by my reaction. Hell, so am I. "I just thought, you know, it's a really popular book. There are people out there going through what you are going through."

"You mean there are millions of misguided friends buying books for their sad friends."

She ignores me.

"There are other people that have gotten through this, and I wanted you to know that if all those stupid people can do it, you, Elsie Porter, can do it. You are so strong and so smart, Elsie. I just wanted you to have something in your hand you could hold and know that you can do this."

"Elsie Ross," I say, correcting her. "My name is Elsie Ross."

"I know," she says, defensively.

"You called me Elsie Porter."

"It was an accident."

I stare at her and then get back to the issue at hand.

"There is no getting through this, Ana. But you won't ever understand that because you've never loved someone like I love him."

"I know that," she says.

"No one could. Certainly not a goddamn book."

My job is books, information. I based my career on the idea that words on pages bound and packaged help people. That they make people grow, they show people lives they've never seen. They teach people about themselves, and here I am, at my lowest point, rejecting help from the one place I always believed it would be.

I walk out of the bookstore.

I walk down streets with cracked pavement. I walk down neighborhood roads. I walk through large intersections. I wait at stoplights. I press the walk signals over and over. I avoid eye contact with everyone in front of me. I get hot. I take my sweatshirt off. I get cold and I put it back on. I cross through traffic jams by weaving in between cars, and somehow, I find myself in front of my house, looking up at my door. I don't know how long I've been walking. I don't know how long I've been crying.

I see something at my door, and from a distance I think maybe it's the marriage certificate. I run up to it and am disappointed to see it's just the *Los Angeles Times*. I pick it up, aware of the fact that I have been so unaware of current events since the current event. The first thing I notice is the date. It's the twenty-eighth. That can't be right. But it has to be. I highly doubt that the *L.A. Times* printed the date wrong and I'm the only genius that figured it out. All of the days have been blurring together, bleeding from one into the next. I didn't realize it was so late in the month. I should have gotten my period days ago.

MARCH

"You're a goddess," he said to me, as he lay down on his back, sweaty in all the right places, his hair a tangled mess, his breathing still staccato.

"Stop it," I said. I was light-headed and my body felt hollow. I could feel sweat on my hairline and upper lip. I tried to wipe it away, but it kept coming back. I turned toward him, my body naked next to his. My nerves were overly sensitive. I could feel every place his body was touching mine, no matter how subtle or irrelevant.

It was quiet for a moment, and he grabbed my hand. He pulled our clasped hands onto his bare stomach and we rested them there. I closed my eyes and drifted off. I was awakened by his snoring and realized that we should not be napping in the middle of the day. We had movies to see and plans to get dinner. I got up and cracked a window. A chill quickly took over what was a muggy room.

"Ugh, why did you do that?" Ben groaned. I stood next to him and told him we had been sleeping long enough. He pulled me back down to the bed. He put his head on my chest as he tried to wake up.

"I have to say, I am really glad you went on that NuvaRing thing," he said, once he was alert. "I don't have to worry about anything. I can just fall asleep after."

I laughed. So much of Ben's happiness was based on his love for sleep. "It's not in the way or anything?" I asked.

He shook his head. "No, not at all. It's like it's not there, honestly."

"Right," I said. "But it is there."

"Right."

"You saying that just made me paranoid."

"About what?"

"You can't feel it at all? What if it fell out or something?"

Ben moved his body upright. "How would it fall out? That's absurd."

He was right. That was absurd. But I wanted to check just in case.

"Hold on."

I walked to the bathroom and shut the door. I sat down and braced myself but . . . it wasn't there.

My heart started beating rapidly and my face began to turn hot. The whole room felt hot. My hands were shaking. I didn't say anything. I couldn't. And soon enough, Ben knocked on the bathroom door.

"You okay?"

"Uh . . ."

"Can I come in?"

I opened the door, and he saw my face. He knew.

He nodded. "It's gone, right? It's not there?"

I shook my head. "I don't know how! I don't understand how." I felt like I had ruined both of our lives. I started crying.

"I'm so sorry, Ben! I'm so sorry! I don't understand how this could have happened! It's not . . . I did exactly what I was supposed to! I don't know how it would have just *fallen* out! I don't! I don't!"

Ben grabbed me. By this time he had put his underwear back on. I was still naked as he clutched me.

"It's going to be okay," he said. "We have plenty of options."

To me, when a man tells you that you have options, he means you can get an abortion.

"No, Ben," I said. "I can't do that."

Ben started laughing. Which was weird because there was nothing funny about it.

"That's not what I meant. At all. And I agree. We won't do that."

"Oh," I said. "Then what are you talking about?"

"Well, we don't know how long it's been gone, right?"

I shook my head, embarrassed. This was completely my fault. How could I be so incredibly careless?

"So, we can get the morning after pill for this one. But we might not be out of the woods for anything days ago."

"Right. Right."

"So, if it ends up that next month, your period is late and you are pregnant, then I'm going to grab your hand and take you with me to the courthouse right across the street from my office. We're getting a marriage license and I will marry you right then and there in front of the judge. That doesn't scare me. Diapers scare me. But spending my life with you doesn't scare me. Not one bit. And trust me, I do not want a baby right now. We can't afford it. We don't have a lot of time. We don't have the resources. But you bet your fucking ass that if you're pregnant, we will figure out a way to make it work and we'll look back on it and say that you losing that NuvaRing was the smartest thing we ever did. So don't cry. Don't stress. Whatever happens happens. I'm here. I'm not going anywhere. We are in this together and we will be fine."

No one had ever said that to me before. I didn't know what to say.

"Does that work for you? I want to make sure you feel the same way," he said.

I nodded.

"Okay. Just for the record, I hope you're not pregnant because—" He started laughing. "I am not ready to be a dad."

"Me neither," I said and then corrected myself. "To be a mom, I mean." It was quiet for a while. "When is your lease up?" I asked.

"It's month to month." He smiled.

"I think you should move in."

"I thought you'd never ask."

And then, for some masochistic and stupid reason, we had sex again.

JUNE

I am sitting in the bathroom, not sure what to do. My period is nowhere to be found. And for the first time since Ben died, I find myself excited about something. Scared, for sure. Nervous, most definitely. I am anxious in every conceivable interpretation of the word.

What if I'm pregnant? Maybe my life with Ben isn't over. Maybe Ben is here. Ben could be living inside me. Maybe our relationship isn't a ghost. What if my relationship with Ben is a tangible piece of the world? What if Ben is soon to be living and breathing again?

I run to the pharmacy down the street, the very same one that Ben biked to when he was getting my cereal. Normally, I avoid this street, I avoid this store, but I have to know. I have to know as soon as possible whether this is real. I know that having a baby won't solve anything, but it could make this better. It could make this easier. It will mean that Ben will never truly leave my life. I yearn for that feeling so badly that I can't take my usual detour. I take the most direct route.

I run past the intersection where I lost him, the intersection that fractured my life from one long joyride to a series of days, hours, and minutes that are insufferable. As I fly through the crosswalk, I hear a small crunch under my feet and I am too scared to look down. If I see a Fruity Pebble, I might just drop to the middle of the road, willing cars to run me over, and I can't do that now. I might have a baby inside me.

I get into the pharmacy and I run right past the food section. I know that it was the last place Ben did anything. I know he stood in that aisle and he picked a box of cereal. I can't look at it. I head to the family planning aisle and I buy four boxes of pregnancy tests. I rush to the cashier and tap my foot impatiently as the line moves slowly and inconsistently.

When it is finally my turn, I pay for them, and I know the cashier thinks he knows what's going on, a woman my age buying boxes of pregnancy tests. He probably thinks he gets me. He doesn't. No one could ever understand this.

I run home and race into the bathroom. I'm nervous and I don't have to pee, so it takes me quite a while to finally pee on a stick. I do two just to be sure. I figure I have the other two left over if I need them.

I set them down on the counter and look at the time. I have two minutes. Two minutes until I know what the rest of my life is going to look like.

Then I start to realize, I have to be pregnant. What are the chances I'm not? I must be. I messed up my birth control, I had unprotected sex multiple times, and it's just a coincidence that my period, which is never late, is now late? That doesn't make any sense. My period is days late. That can only mean one thing.

It means I'm not alone in this. It means Ben is here with me. It means my life, that felt empty and miserable, now feels difficult but manageable. I can be a single mother. I can raise this child by myself. I can tell this child all about his father. About how his father was a gentle man, a kind man, a funny man, a good man. If it's a girl, I can tell her to find a man like her father. If it's a boy, I can tell him to be a man like his father. I can tell him his father would have been so proud of him. If he's gay, I can tell him to be like his father *and* find a man like his father—

which would be the best of all worlds. If she grows up to be a lesbian, she won't need to be or find anyone like her father, but she'll still love him. She'll know that she came from a man that would have loved her. She'll know she came from two people that loved each other fiercely. She'll know not to settle for anything less than a love that changes her life.

I can tell her about the time we met. She'll want to know. She'll ask over and over as a child. She'll want to keep pictures of him framed around the house. She'll have his nose or his eyes, and just when I least suspect it, she'll say something that sounds like him. She'll move her hands in a way that he did. He'll live on in her and I won't be alone. I won't be without him. He's here. He didn't leave me. This isn't over. My life isn't over. Ben and I are not over. We have this. We have this child. I will dedicate my life to raising this child, to letting Ben's body and soul live on through this child.

I grab the sticks, already knowing what they say, and then I drop to my knees.

I am wrong.

There is no child.

No matter how many sticks I use, they keep saying the same thing. They keep telling me Ben is gone forever and that I am alone.

I don't move from the bathroom floor for hours. I don't move until I feel it. I am bleeding.

I know it's a sign that my body is fully functioning, that I am physically fine. But it feels like a betrayal.

I call Ana. I say I need her and I'm sorry. I tell her she is all I have left.

PART TWO

AUGUST

Are things easier with time? Maybe. Maybe not.

The days are easier to get through because I have a pattern to follow. I'm back at work. I have projects to occupy my mind. I can almost sleep through the night now. In my dreams, Ben and I are together. We are free. We are wild. We are what we were. In the mornings, I ache for my dreams to be real, but it's a familiar ache, and while it feels like it might kill me, I know from having felt it the day before that it won't. And maybe that's how some of my strength comes back.

I rarely cry in public anymore. I've become a person about which people probably say, "She's really bounced back quite nicely." I am lying to them. I have not bounced back nicely. I've just learned to impersonate the living. I have lost almost ten pounds. It's that dreaded last ten that magazines say every woman wants to lose. I suppose I have the body I've always wanted. It doesn't do me much good.

I go places with Ana, to flea markets and malls, restaurants and cafés. I've even started to let her invite other people. People I haven't seen for ages. People who only met Ben a few times. They grab my hand and say they're sorry over brunch. They say they wish they could have known him better. I tell them, "Me too." But they never know what I mean.

But when I'm alone, I sit on the floor of the closet and smell his clothes. I still don't sleep in the middle of the bed. His side of the room is untouched. If you didn't know any better, you'd think two people lived in my apartment.

I haven't moved his PlayStation. There is food in the refrigerator that he bought, food I will never eat, food that is rotting. But I can't throw it out. If I look in that refrigerator and there are no hot dogs, it will just reinforce that I am alone, that he is gone, that the world I knew is over. I'm not ready for that. I'd rather see rotting hot dogs than no hot dogs, so they stay.

Ana is very understanding. She's the only person that can really get a glimpse of this new life I lead. She stays at her place now, with an open invitation for me to come over anytime I can't sleep. I don't go over. I don't want her to know how often I can't sleep.

If I can't have Ben, I can have being Ben's widow, and I have found a modicum of peace in this new identity. I wear my wedding ring, even though I no longer insist people call me by my married name. I am Elsie Porter. Elsie Ross only existed for a couple weeks, at most. She was barely on this earth longer than a miniseries.

I still have not received the marriage certificate, and I haven't told anyone. Every day I rush home from work, expecting it to be waiting for me in the mailbox, and every day, I am disappointed to find a series of credit card offers and coupons. No one alerted the national banks that Ben is dead. If I didn't have other things to be miserable about, I'm pretty sure this would set me off. Imagine being the kind of woman that gets over her dead husband only to find his name in her mailbox every day. Luckily, Ben never leaves the forefront of my mind, so I can't be provoked into remembering him. I am always remembering him.

I read somewhere to watch out for "triggers," things that will remind you of your loss right out of the blue. For instance, if

Ben loved root beer and had this whole thing about root beer, then I should stay away from soda aisles. But what if I went into a candy store and saw, unexpectedly, that they had root beer and I started crying right there in the store? That would be a trigger. The reason why this is completely irrelevant to me is that root beer doesn't remind me of Ben. Everything reminds me of Ben. Floors, walls, ceilings, white, black, brown, blue, elephants, cartwheels, grass, marbles, Yahtzee. Everything. My life is trigger after trigger. I have reached a critical mass of grief. So, no, I don't need to avoid any triggers.

The point, though, is that I am functional. I can get through each day without feeling like I'm not sure I'll make it to midnight. I know when I wake up that today will be just like the day before, devoid of honest laughter and a genuine smile, but manageable.

Which is why when I hear my own doorbell at 11:00 a.m. on a Saturday and I look through my peephole, I think, God *dammit*. Why can't everyone just leave *well enough* alone?

She's standing outside my door in black leggings, a black shirt, and a gray, oversize, knit vesty-sweater thing. She's over sixty fucking years old. Why does she always look so much better than I do?

I open the door.

"Hi, Susan," I say, trying hard to sound like I'm not pissed she's here.

"Hi." Although, just from the way she greets me, I feel like this is a different woman than the one I met almost two months ago. "May I come in?"

I open the door fully and invite her in with my arm. I stand by the door. I don't know how long she plans on staying, but I don't want to imply she should stay longer than she wanted.

"Could we talk for a minute?" she asks.

I lead us into the living room.

As she sits, I realize I should offer her something to drink. Is this a custom in all countries? Or just here? Because it's stupid. "Can I get you anything to drink?"

"Actually, I wanted to ask if you'd like to go to lunch," she says. Lunch? "But first, I wanted to bring you something."

She pulls her purse from over her shoulder onto her lap and sorts through it, pulling out a wallet. It's not *a* wallet. I know that wallet; its leather worn down in places by my husband's fingers and molded around his butt. She hands it over to me, losing her balance slightly as she leans so far forward. I take it from her softly. It might as well be a Van Gogh, that's how delicately I am approaching it.

"I owe you an apology, Elsie. I hope you can forgive me. I offer no excuses for my behavior. The way I spoke to you, there is no excuse for being so cold and, truthfully, cruel. I treated you so poorly that I . . . I'm embarrassed about my actions." I look at her and she keeps talking. "I am incredibly disappointed in myself. If someone treated my child the way I treated you, I would have killed them. I had no right. I just . . . I hope you can understand that I was grieving. The pain in front of me felt so insurmountable, and to learn that my only child didn't feel comfortable telling me about you . . . I couldn't face that too. Not at that time. I told myself you were crazy, or lying, or . . . I blamed you. You were right when you said I hated you because you were the only one around to hate. You were right. And I knew it then, that's why I tried so hard to . . . I wanted to make it better, but I just couldn't. I didn't have it in me to be a kind person." She stops for a minute and then corrects herself. "Even a decent person."

She looks at me with tears in her eyes, a look of somber and grave regret across her face. This sucks. Now I can't even hate her.

"It's awful to say, but I just . . . I wanted you as far away from me and as far away from Ben as possible. I think I thought if you'd just go away, then I could deal with the loss of my son and I wouldn't have to face the fact that I lost a part of him a long time before he died."

She looks down at her own knees and shakes her head. "That's not . . . that's not what I came here to talk about. Never mind. Anyway, I wanted you to have his wallet and this."

She pulls his wedding ring out of her purse.

I was wrong.

I do have triggers.

I start crying. I put that wedding ring on him myself, my hand shaking while his was steady as a rock. I remember seeing it on him the next day thinking that I never knew how sexy a wedding ring was on a man until it was my ring, until I put it there.

She comes over to me on the couch and holds me. She takes my left hand and she puts the ring into it, balling my fingers up into a fist as she holds me.

"Shh," she says. "It's okay." She puts her head on top of mine. My head is buried in her chest. She smells like a sweet, flowery, expensive perfume. She smells like she's worn the same perfume for forty years, like it's molded to her. Like it's hers. She is warm and soft, her sweater absorbing my tears, whisking them away from my face and onto her. I can't stop crying and I don't know if I ever will. I feel the ring in my hand, my palm sweating around it. My fist is so tight that my fingers start to ache. I let my muscles go, falling into her. I can hear myself blubbering. I am wailing loudly; the noises coming out of me feel like blisters. Once I have calmed, once my eyes have gotten control of themselves again, I stay there. She doesn't let go.

"He loved you, Elsie. I know that now. My son wasn't a very romantic person, but I doubt you ever knew that. Because he was clearly very romantic with you."

"I loved him, Susan," I say, still stationary, inert. "I loved him so much."

"I know you did," she says. "He kept a copy of his proposal in his wallet. Did you know that?"

I perk up. She hands the paper to me, and I read it.

"Elsie, let's spend our lives together. Let's have children together and buy a house together. I want you there when I get the promotion I've been shooting for, when I get turned down for something I've always hoped for, when I fall and when I stand back up. I want to see every day of your life unfold. I want to be yours and to have you as my own. Will you marry me? Marry me."

"Will you marry me?" is crossed out and replaced with the more forward statement. "Marry me."

This isn't how he proposed. I don't even know what this is. But it feels good to know he struggled with how to ask me. This was one of his attempts. His handwriting was so very bad.

"I found it in his wallet when I went through it. That's when I got it. You know? Like it or not, you are the truth about Ben. He loved you fiercely. And just because he didn't tell me, doesn't mean he didn't love you. I just have to keep telling myself that. It's a hard one to make sense of, but anyway, you should have these things. He would want that." She smiles at me, grabbing my chin like I am a child. "I am so proud of my son for loving you this way, Elsie. I didn't know he had it in him."

It feels nice to think that maybe Susan could like me. I am

actually overwhelmed by how nice that thought feels. But this is not the Susan I know. And it makes me feel uneasy. If I'm being honest, part of me is worried she's going to wait until my defenses are down and then sock me in the stomach.

"Anyway, I would love to get to know you," she says. "If that is okay with you. I should have called before I came up here, but I thought"—she laughs—"I thought if I was you, I'd tell me to fuck off, so I didn't want to give you the chance."

I laugh with her, unsure of what exactly is going on and how to respond to it.

"Can I take you to lunch?" she asks.

I laugh again. "I don't know," I say, knowing my eyes are swollen and I haven't showered.

"I wouldn't blame you for asking me to leave," she says. "I was awful, when I think about it from your point of view. And you don't know me at all, but I can tell you that once I realize I'm wrong, I do everything to make it right. I've thought about this for weeks and I wouldn't be here if I wasn't ready to do better. I really do want to get to know you and I'd love to just . . . start over." She says "start over" like it's a refreshing thought, like it's something people can actually do. And because of that, I start to feel like maybe it is possible. Maybe it's easier than it feels. We will just start over. Let's try again.

"Yeah," I say. "We can try again."

Susan nods. "I'm so sorry, Elsie."

"Me too," I say, and it isn't until I say it that I realize I mean it. We sit there for a minute, considering each other. Can we do this? Can we be good to each other? Susan seems convinced that we can, and she's determined to take the lead.

"All right," she says. "Let's get composed and head out."

"You are much better at composure than I am."

"It's a learned trait," she says. "And it's entirely superficial. Hop in the shower, I'll wait here. I won't poke through anything, I promise." She puts her hands up in the air to signify swearing.

"Okay," I say, getting up. "Thank you, Susan."

She closes her eyes for just half a second and nods her head.

I head into the bathroom, and before I shut the door, I tell her she's welcome to poke through anything she likes.

"Okay! You may regret this," she says. I smile and get in the shower. While I'm washing my hair, I think of all the things I have been meaning to say to her for weeks. I think of how I've wanted to tell her the pain she caused me. I've wanted to tell her how wrong she was. How little she really knew her own son. How unkind she has been. But now that she's here, and she's different, it doesn't seem worth it.

I get dressed and come out into the living room, and she's sitting on the sofa, waiting. Somehow, she's put me in a better mood.

Susan drives us to a random restaurant she found on Yelp. "They said it was private and had great desserts. Is that okay?"

"Sure," I say. "I'm always up for someplace new."

Our conversation, when not about Ben, doesn't flow as freely. It is awkward at times, but I think both of us know that is to be expected.

I tell her that I am a librarian. She says that she loves reading. I tell her that I am not close with my parents; she says she is sorry to hear that. She tells me she's been working on occupying her time with various projects but can't seem to stick to something longer than a few months. "I realized I was too fixated on the house so I stopped renovating, but truthfully, renovating is the only thing that keeps me occupied!" Eventually, the conversation works its way back to the things we have in common: Ben, dead husbands, and loss.

Susan tells me stories about Ben as a child, about embarrassing things he did, tricks he tried to play. She tells me how he would always ask to wear her jewelry.

The visual of Ben in women's jewelry immediately cracks me up.

She drinks her tea and smiles. "You have no idea! He used to always want to dress up as a witch for Halloween. I would explain to him that he could be a wizard, but he wanted to be a witch. I think he just wanted to paint his face green."

We talk about Steven and how hard it was for her to lose him, how much of Steven she used to see in Ben, how she feels like maybe she suffocated Ben, trying too hard to hold on to him because Steven was gone.

"I don't think so," I say. "At least, from my point of view, Ben really loved you. He worried about you. He cared about you. We talked about you a lot. He . . ." I don't know how much I should tell her about Ben's intentions and worries, about why he never told her about me. But it feels so good to talk to someone that knew him as well as I did, that knew him better than I did. It feels good to have someone say, "I know how much it hurts," and believe them. It all just rolls off my tongue and into the air faster than I can catch it.

"He was scared that if you knew that he was with someone, in a serious relationship, that you would feel left out, maybe. Not left out, but . . . like he was moving on and there wasn't a place for you. Which wasn't true. He would always have a place for you. But he thought that if you heard about me, that you'd feel that way and he didn't want that. He kept putting it off. Waiting for the right time. And then the right time never came and things with us progressed to the point where it was weird he hadn't told you already, which made him feel bad. And then it just became this big thing that he wasn't sure how to handle. He loved you, Susan. He really, really did. And he didn't tell you about me because he was thinking of you, however misguided. I'm not going to say I totally understood it. Or that I liked it. But he didn't keep it from you because you didn't matter. Or because I didn't matter. He just, he was a guy, you know? He didn't know how to handle the situation gracefully so he didn't handle it at all."

She thinks about it for a minute, looking down at her plate. "Thank you," she says. "Thank you for telling me that. That's not what I thought happened . . . It's not necessarily good news, but it's not entirely bad, right?" She is unsure of herself, and it's clear that she is grappling with this. She's trying very hard to be the Susan I'm seeing, but my guess is, she's not quite there yet. "Are we at a place where I can make a gentle suggestion?" she says. "From one widow to another?"

"Oh. Uh . . . sure."

"I poked," she says. "In my defense, you did say it was okay, but really, I'm just nosy. I've always been nosy. I can't stop myself. I tried to work on it for years, and then I just gave up around fifty. I just resigned myself to it: I am nosy. Anyway, I poked. Everything of Ben's is still in its place. You haven't moved a thing. I looked in the kitchen. You have food rotting in the fridge."

I know where this is going and I wish I'd told her she could not make a gentle suggestion.

"I'd like to help you clear some things out. Make the place yours again."

I shake my head. "I don't want to make it mine, it's ours. It was ours. He . . ."

She puts her hand up. "Okay. I'm dropping it. It's your place to do with what you want. I just know, for me, I waited too long to move Steven's things into storage and I regret that. I was living in this . . . shrine to him. I didn't want to move his little box of floss because I thought it meant I was giving up on him—which I realize sounds crazy."

"No, that doesn't sound crazy."

She looks me in the eye, knowing that I am doing the same thing, knowing that I am just as lost as she was. I want to convey to her that I like where I am in this. I don't want to move forward.

"It is crazy, Elsie," she says. It is pointed but kind. "Steven is alive in my heart and nowhere else. And when I moved his things out of my eyesight, I could live my life for me again. But you do what you want. You're on no one's timetable but your own."

"Thank you," I say.

"Just remember that if you wade too long in the misery of it, you'll wake up one day and find that your entire life is built around a ghost. That's it. I'm off my soapbox. I'm in no place to tell you your business. I just feel like I know you. Although, I realize I don't."

"No." I stop her. "I think you do."

After lunch, Susan drops me off at my apartment and kisses me on the cheek. Before I jump out of her car and make my way up my own steps, she says to me, "If you ever need anything at all, please don't hesitate." She laughs in a sad way, as if it's funny how pathetic what she is about to say truly is. "You're the only person I have left to be there for," she says.

I unlock my door and settle in, staring at Ben's wedding ring on the counter. I think about what Susan said. We were or are, technically, family. What happens to the relationship you never had with your mother-in-law when your husband dies?

I sit down, holding Ben's wallet in my hands, rubbing the worn edges. I take off my wedding ring, put his around my ring finger, and slide mine back on to hold it in place. His doesn't fit. It's a thick band many sizes too large, but it feels good on my finger.

I look around the house, now seeing it through Susan's eyes. So many of Ben's things are strewn about. I see myself twenty years from now, sitting in this very place, his things stuck, frozen in time. I see myself how I'm afraid others will see me. I am a Miss Havisham in the making. And for the first time, I don't want to be that way. For a fleeting minute, I think that I should move Ben's things. And then I reject the idea. Ben's things are all I have left. Though it does occur to me that maybe Susan knows what she's talking about. Susan seems at peace but hasn't lost that sadness about her. As long as I have that sadness, I still have Ben. So if Susan can do it, maybe I can too.

I go to the refrigerator and pick up the hot dogs. The package is soft and full of liquid. Simply moving it from its place on the shelf has elicited some foul, rancid reaction. The entire kitchen starts to reek. I run to the garbage cans outside, the liquid from the bag dripping on my floor on the way out. As I put the lid on the garbage can and walk back in to clean up and wash my hands, I laugh at how ridiculous it is that I thought Ben lived on through rancid hot dogs. The hot dogs are gone and I don't feel like I've lost him, yet. Score one for Susan.

When Monday comes, I feel the familiar relief of distraction. I go to work, eager to start research on the new display case for this month. Most months, Lyle tells me what to feature, but lately he's been letting me choose. I think he's still scared of me. Everyone here treats me with kid gloves. At certain times I find it charming or at least convenient; at other times I find it irritating and naïve.

I choose Cleopatra for this month, and start pulling together facts and figures that I can show easily with photos and replicas. I am hovering over a book containing images of what the currency looked like in her time, trying to decide how relevant that is, when I am stopped by Mr. Callahan.

"Hi, Mr. Callahan," I say, turning toward him.

"Hello, young lady," Mr. Callahan says.

"What can I help you with?"

"Oh, nothing. I find myself a bit bored today is all," he says slowly and deliberately. I get the impression his mind moves faster than his body can at this point.

"Oh! Nothing striking your fancy?"

"Oh, it's not that. I've just been stuck in the damn house for so long, walking back and forth to the library. I don't have anywhere else to go! Nothing else to do. The days are all starting to fade away."

"Oh," I say. "I'm sorry to hear that."

"Would you have lunch with me?" he asks. "I'm afraid if I don't spend time with someone or do something interesting my brain is going to . . . decay. Atrophy. You know . . . just . . . wither away." I pause before answering, and he fills the void. "There's only so many goddamn sudoku puzzles a man can do, you know? Excuse my language."

I laugh and put the book down. I look at my watch and see that his timing is almost perfect. It's 12:49 p.m. "I would love to, Mr. Callahan," I say.

"Great!" He clasps his hands together in a rather feminine way, as if I've given him a pair of pearl earrings. "If we are going to have lunch together, though, Elsie, you should call me George."

"All right, George. Sounds like a plan."

Mr. Callahan and I walk to a sandwich shop nearby, and he insists on buying my lunch. To tell the truth, I have left-over pizza waiting for me in the office refrigerator, but it didn't seem appropriate to mention that. As Mr. Callahan and I sit down at the small café table, we open our sandwiches.

"So, let's hear it, miss. Tell me something interesting! Anything at all."

I put down my sandwich and wipe the mayonnaise from my lips. "What do you want to know?" I ask.

"Oh, anything. Anything interesting that's happened to you. I don't care if it's sad or funny, scary or stupid. Just something. Anything I can go home and recount to my wife. We're starting to bore each other to tears."

I laugh like I think Mr. Callahan is expecting, but to tell the truth, I want to cry. Ben never bored me. God, how I wish I'd had time to find him positively mind-numbing. When you love someone so much that you've stuck around through all the interesting things that have happened to them and you have nothing left to say, when you know the course of their day before they even tell you, when you lie next to them and hold their hand even though they haven't said one interesting thing in days, that's a love I want. It's the love I was on target for.

"You look sad," he says, interrupting my one-person pity party. "What's the matter?"

"Oh, I'm fine," I say. "I just . . . got a funny bit of mustard I think."

"No." He shakes his head. "You've looked sad for some time. You think I don't see things because I'm an old fart, but I do." He brings his finger to his temple and taps it. "What is it?"

What's the point in lying? Who benefits from it anyway? Propriety says not to discuss such intense matters in public, but whom does that serve? This man is bored and I am broken. Maybe I'll be a little less broken in telling him about it. Maybe he'll be a little less bored.

"My husband died," I say. I say it matter-of-factly, trying to work against the intensity of the conversation.

"Oh," he says, quite surprised. "That's heartbreaking to hear. It is interesting, like I asked, but just terrible. I didn't realize you were married."

"You met him," I say. "A few months ago."

"No, I remember. I just didn't realize you were married."

"Oh, well, we had only just married when he died."

"Terrible," he says, and he grabs my hand. It's too intimate to feel comfortable, and yet, it doesn't feel inappropriate. "I'm sorry, Elsie. You must be in such pain."

I shrug and then wish I could take it back. I shouldn't shrug about Ben. "Yes," I admit. "I am."

"Is that why you were gone for a while before?" he says,

and my face must change. It must convey some sort of surprise because he adds, "You're my favorite person here and I'm here every day. You think I don't notice when my favorite person isn't around?"

I smile and bite into my sandwich.

"I don't know you very well, Elsie," he says. "But I do know this: You are a fighter. You've got chutzpah. Moxie. Whatever it is."

"Thank you, Mr. Callahan." He gives me a disapproving glance. "George," I correct myself. "Thank you, George."

"No thanks needed. It's what I see. And you will be okay, you know that? I know you probably don't think it now, but I'm telling you, one day you'll look back on this time and think, Thank God it's over, but I got through it. I'm telling you."

I look doubtful. I know I do because I can feel the doubt on my face. I can feel the way it turns down the corners of my mouth.

"You don't believe me, do you?" he asks, picking up his sandwich for the first time.

I smile. "No, I'm not sure I do, George. I'm not even sure I want that."

"You're so young, Elsie! I'm eighty-six years old. I was born before the Depression. Can you even imagine that? Because I'll tell you, during the Depression nobody could imagine me still living now. But look at me! I'm still kicking! I'm sitting here with a gorgeous young lady, having a sandwich. Things happen in your life that you can't possibly imagine. But time goes on and time changes you and the times change and the next thing you know, you're smack in the middle of a life you never saw coming."

"Well, maybe."

"No, not maybe." His voice gets stern. He's not angry, just firm. "I'm going to tell you something no one who is still alive knows. Well, except my wife, but she knows everything."

"Okay," I say. I am done with my sandwich and he has barely started his. I am usually the one done last, but I now realize that's because I am rarely the one listening.

"I fought in World War Two. Suited up right in the beginning of 1945. Toughest time of my life. Honest to God. It just wreaked havoc with my faith in God, my faith in humanity. Everything. I'm not a man fit for war. It doesn't sit well with me. And the only thing that got me through was Esther Morris. I loved her the minute I saw her. We were eighteen years old, I saw her sitting with her friends on the sidewalk across the street, and I just knew. I knew she would be the mother of my children. I walked across the street, I introduced myself, I asked her out, and six months later we were engaged. By the time I found myself in Europe, I thought for sure I wasn't going to stay long. And I was right, because I was only there for about eight months before I was shot."

"Wow," I say.

"I was shot three times. Twice in the shoulder. One grazed my side. I remember being in that medical tent, the nurse hovering over me, the doctor rushing to my side. I was the happiest man on earth. Because I knew they'd have to send me home and I'd see Esther. I couldn't believe my luck that I could go home to her. So I recovered as fast as I could and I came back. But when I got home, Esther was gone. No sign of her."

He sighs, but it seems more a sigh of old age than one of heartbreak.

"I still don't know where she went. She just up and left me. Never told me why. I heard rumors from time to time that she'd taken up with a salesman, but I don't know if that's true. I never saw her again."

"Oh God," I say, now grabbing George's hand. "That's awful. I'm so sorry."

"Don't be," he said. "I waited around for years for her to come back. I wouldn't leave the town we lived in, just in case she came lookin' for me. I was devastated."

"Well, sure," I say.

"But you know what?"

"Hmm?"

"I took each day as it came, and it led me to Lorraine. And Lorraine is the love of my life. Esther is a story I tell young women in libraries, but Lorraine makes me feel like I could conquer the world. Like the universe was made for me to live in it. The minute I met her, she just set my world on fire. I forgot about Esther just as fast as she forgot about me, once I met Lorraine."

"I don't want Ben to be a story I tell young women in libraries though. He was more than that. That's what I'm afraid of! I'm afraid that's what he'll end up," I say.

George nods. "I know. I know. You don't have to do it exactly like I did. I'm just trying to tell you that your life will be very long with zigzags you can't imagine. You won't realize just how young you are until you aren't that young anymore. But I'm here to tell you, Elsie. Your life has just begun. When I lost Esther, I thought my life was over. I was twenty. I had no idea what was in store for me. Neither do you."

George is done talking, and so he finishes his sandwich and we sit in silence. I contemplate his words, remaining convinced that living any part of the years I have before me would be a betrayal to the years behind me.

"Thank you," I say, and I mean it. Even if I can't recover from loss like he did, it's nice to know that someone did.

"I should thank you!" he says. "I am certainly not bored."

That afternoon, I further compile research on Cleopatra. It occurs to me that Cleopatra had two great loves and look how they vilified her. At least she had a son and a dynasty to commemorate Caesar. At least she could put him on coins and cups. She could erect statues in his honor. She could deify him. She had a way to make his memory live on. All I have are Ben's dirty socks.

When I leave work on Friday afternoon and head home for the empty weekend in front of me, it occurs to me that I could call Susan. I could see how she is. I think better of it.

I walk in my front door and put my things down. I go into the bathroom and start running the shower. As I'm disrobing, I hear the cell phone in the back pocket of my pants vibrating against the floor. I fumble to get it, and as I answer, I see that it is my mother.

"Hi," she says.

"Oh. Hello," I answer.

"Your father and I just wanted to see how you were doing. See how you were . . . uh . . . dealing with things?" she says. Her euphemism irritates me.

"Things?" I challenge.

"You know, just . . . we know you are having a hard time and we were sitting here thinking of you . . . I just mean . . . how are you?"

"I'm fine, thank you." I am hoping this conversation will be over shortly, so I don't bother turning off the shower.

"Oh good! Good!" Her voice brightens. "We weren't sure. Well, we are just glad to hear you are feeling better. It must have been a strange feeling to be caught up in the grief of his family, to be in the middle of all of that."

I turn the shower off and lose my energy. "Right," I say. What's the point of explaining that I was his family? That this is my grief? That when I said I was fine I just said that because it's something people say?

"Good," she says. I can hear my father in the background. I can't make out any of what he is saying, but my mother starts to get off the phone. "Well, if you need anything at all," she says. She always says this. I don't even know what she means by it.

"Thanks." I shut off the phone, turn the faucet back on, and get under the water. I need to see Ben. I need just a minute with him. I need him to show up in this bathroom and hug me. I just need him for a minute. One minute. I step out of the shower, grab my towel and my phone.

I call Susan. I ask her if she'd like to have lunch tomorrow and she says she's free. We agree on a place halfway between us, and then I put on a robe, get in bed, smell Ben's side, and fall asleep. The smell is fading. I have to inhale deeper and deeper to get to it.

Susan has suggested a place in Redondo Beach for lunch. Apparently, she and Ben came here often over the years. Sometimes, before Steven died, they would all meet up here for dinner. She warns me not to expect much. "I hope you're okay with chain Mexican restaurants," she says.

The restaurant is decorated with bulls, hacienda-style tiles, and bright colors. It's aggressively cheesy, wearing tacky like a badge of honor. Before I even reach Susan's table, pictures of margaritas have accosted me about nine times.

She's sitting in front of a glass of water when I find the table. She gets up immediately and hugs me. She smells the same and looks the same as always: composed and together. She doesn't make grief look glamorous, but she does make it look bearable.

"This place is awful, right?" She laughs.

"No!" I say. "I like any place that offers a three-course meal for nine ninety-nine."

The waiter comes to drop off a bucket of tortilla chips and salsa, and I nervously reach for them. Susan ignores them for the moment. We order fajitas.

"And, you know what?" Susan says to the waiter. "Two margaritas too. Is that okay?" I'm already face-deep in tortilla chips, so I just nod.

"What flavor?" he asks us. "Original? Mango? Watermelon? Cranberry? Pomegranate? Cantalo—"

"Original is fine," she says, and I wish that she'd asked me about this one too because watermelon sounded kind of good.

He gathers our sticky red menus and leaves the table.

"Shit. I meant to ask him for guacamole," she says after he leaves, and she starts to dig into the chips with me. "Sir!" she calls out. He comes running back. I can never get waiters' attention once they've left the table. "Can we get guacamole too?" He nods and leaves, and she looks back at me. "My diet is a joke." Who can count calories at a time like this? I feel good that Susan can't either.

"So," she says. "You mentioned it on the phone but I don't understand. Your mom said she thought you'd be over it by now?"

"Well," I say, wiping my hand on my napkin. "Not necessarily. She just . . . she called and asked how I was handling 'things.' Or 'the thing'—you know how people use that terminology like they can't just say 'Ben died'?"

Susan nods. "The euphemisms," she says. "As if you won't remember that Ben is dead if they don't say it."

"Right! Like I'm not thinking about it every moment of the day. Anyway, she just asked and I said I was fine, like . . . I'm not really fine, but it's just a thing you say. Anyone that asked me that would know that when I said 'Fine' I meant 'Fine, considering the circumstances.'"

"Right." The basket is now empty, and when the waiter comes to drop off the margaritas, Susan asks him to fill it up.

"But my mom honestly thought I was fine, I think," I say. "I think she was hoping I'd say I was fine and that if I did say that, it would mean that she didn't need to do anything and I was back to my old self. Like nothing ever happened."

"Well, to her, nothing did happen." Susan takes a sip of her margarita and winces. "I'm not much of a drinker, I'm afraid. I just thought it would be festive of us. But this . . . is a bit strong, no?"

I take a sip of mine. "It's strong," I say.

"Okay! I thought I was being a baby. Anyway—you were saying?"

"Actually, I think you were saying."

"Oh. Right. Nothing happened to her. You two rarely talk, right?"

"Right."

"It seems like she's just one of those people that can't empathize or even sympathize. So, she doesn't know how to talk to you because she doesn't understand you."

I don't talk about my family often, and when I do, I speak in short sentences and dismissive comments. But Susan is the first person to see what's going on and give it a name. Or . . . at least a description. "You're right," I tell her.

"Don't worry about your parents. They are going to do what they would want someone to do for them, and it's going to be entirely different than what you need. And I say, give up trying to make the two fit. Not that I'm some expert. I just noticed that when Steven died there was a large difference between what I wanted from people and what they wanted to give me. I think people are so terrified of being in our position that they lose all ability to even speak to us. I say let it go."

By the time she's done talking, my margarita is gone. I'm not sure how that happened. Our fajitas come, sizzling and ostentatious, if fajitas can be ostentatious. They are just so big and require so many plates and people to bring them. There is the plate for the side dishes, the pans of chicken and vegetables, the case for tortillas, both corn and flour, and the condiments of guacamole, cheese, salsa, and lettuce. Our table looks like a feast fit for a king, and the chicken is frying so loudly on the skillets that I feel like the whole restaurant is looking.

"It's a bit much, isn't it?" Susan asks demurely. "I think it's great though, the way they bring it to you like it's a presentation. There's absolutely no need for them to have the chicken still grilling on the table. None at all."

The waiter comes back to check on us. Susan orders us each another margarita. "Watermelon for me," I interject. Susan agrees. "That sounds good; watermelon for me too."

We talk over our steaming lunches about politics and families; we talk about traffic and movies, news and funny stories. I want to be able to talk to Susan about things other than life and death, other than Ben and Steven. It seems possible. It seems like I could know her regardless of the tragedy between us. But Ben is what we have in common, and so the conversation will always come back to Ben. I wonder if it's unhealthy to fixate out loud. If being obsessed with Ben's death is something I'm only supposed to do in my own head. I also wonder how much I can truly rely on her.

"Do you have a plan for when you're going to stop his mail?" she asks me casually, while she is picking at what's left off the hot plate in front of her with her fork.

I shake my head. "No," I say. "I don't even know really how to do that." That's not all of the truth. The other fact is that I'm scared that would cause the post office to hold the marriage certificate too since it will have his name on it. I don't want to have his mail stopped until I have it.

"Oh, it's easy. We can do it today if you want," she says.

"Oh," I say, trying to think of a way to stop her and realizing I have no real excuse but the truth. "Well, I'm still waiting for the marriage certificate," I say. "I don't want to stop the mail in case they try to hold that too."

"What do you mean?" she says, peeling an onion off the plate and putting it in her mouth with her hands.

"It hasn't come yet and since both of our names will be on it, I'm worried they might keep it with his old bills and stuff instead of sending it through to me."

"It hasn't come yet?" Her voice indicates that there must be some misunderstanding. For so long, I've been worried to tell anyone that it hadn't come yet. I've thought they'd think I was lying about our marriage. I was afraid they would use it to convince themselves of the one thing I'm scared to be: not relevant. But Susan's voice doesn't convey a moment of doubt. She sounds only concerned about a clerical error or logistical mistake. It doesn't even occur to her to question whether I've been completely full of shit. I have to admit that she's come so far since I met her. She must move so quickly through emotional turmoil.

"No, I don't have it yet. I've been checking the mail every day, opening up even the most innocuous of envelopes. It's nowhere."

"Well, we need to start calling people, figuring out where it is. Have you called the county to check and see if it's at least in their records?"

"No," I say and shake my head. Honestly, I hadn't thought it was that big of a deal until I said it out loud. I hadn't wanted to face the logistical nightmare of figuring this out.

"Well, that's got to be the first step. You need to find out if the original license made it to the county."

"Okay," I say. Her concern is making me concerned.

"It's okay," she says and grabs my hand. "We'll figure it out."

The way she says "we," that she doesn't say "You will figure it out," makes me feel like I'm not alone. It makes me feel like if I can't get myself out of this, she will get me out of this. It makes me feel like I'm high on a tightrope, losing my balance, but seeing the net underneath me. "We" will figure this out. Ana has made similar sentiments to me, but all those times I knew that she couldn't help me. She could hold my hand, but she couldn't hold me up. For the first time, I feel like it's not up to only me. Nothing is up to only me.

"So you'll call on Monday?" she says. "Call the county and find out?"

I nod. It's clear she's assuming we got married in Los Angeles County and I don't have it in me to correct her. Part of me wants to. Part of me wants to revel in the truth with her. Tell her everything. But I know it's not that simple. I know that our newfound connection is still too tenuous for the whole truth.

"Should I ask for the check?" she asks me.

I laugh. "I think I need to wait out that last margarita," I say, and she smiles.

"Dessert then!"

She orders us fried ice cream and "dessert" nachos. We sit there, spoons in the ice cream, licking the chocolate around the bowls. It's what I imagined sisters did with their mothers when their fathers were away on business. When I get in the car, I think of a few things I forgot to say and I find myself looking forward to seeing Susan again to tell her.

Ana has been patient with my recovery, expecting nothing, supporting everything, but I can tell that I am starting to wear on her. Being my friend means she is pulled into this even though it has nothing to do with her. I can only assume that, after a while, even the most understanding and empathetic of people would start to wonder just how long it will be before we can have honest to God fun again. Fun that doesn't end in a sorrowful look from me, fun that isn't laced with what I have lost. She knew me before Ben, she knew me during Ben, and now she knows me after Ben. She's never said it, but I would imagine the me she knew before Ben was probably her favorite.

Ana said she'd be at my place at eight to pick me up, but she calls at seven asking if I mind if she brings this guy she has been seeing.

"Who have you been seeing?" I say. I didn't know she was seeing anyone.

"Just this guy, Kevin." She laughs, and I suspect he's right there next to her.

"I'm just some guy?" I hear in the background, confirming my suspicion. I can hear her shush him.

"Anyway, is that okay? I want him to meet you," she says.

"Uh, sure," I say, taken aback. You can't say no in a situation like this. It's rude and weird, but I wonder, if the rules of propriety allowed it, what I would have said.

"Cool," she says. "Be there at eight to pick you up. You still want to go to that ramen house?"

"Sure!" I overcompensate for my apprehension by being outwardly perky and excited. It feels obvious to me, but she doesn't seem to notice. Maybe I've been getting really good at hiding my emotions, or maybe she's not paying attention.

APRIL

Ben and I were waiting in the front of the movie theater for Ana. She was twenty minutes late and the tickets were on her credit card. The movie was starting in seven minutes. Ben was one of the only people I knew that looked forward to the previews more than the actual movie.

"Can you call her again?" he asked me.

"I just called her! And texted. She's probably just parking."

"Ten bucks she hasn't left the house yet."

I slapped him lightly across the chest. "She's left the house! C'mon. We won't be late for the movie."

"We're already late for the movie."

He said this would happen. I said it wouldn't happen, but here we were, just like he said we would be. He was right.

"You're right."

"There she is!" Ben pointed toward a woman running through the food court to the movie theater. There was a man behind her.

"Who is that?" I asked.

"How would I know?"

Ana slowed herself as she reached us. "I'm sorry! I'm sorry!"

"I'm sure you had a good reason," Ben said to her. You could hear in his voice that he had no expectation of a good reason. Ana jokingly glared at him.

"Marshall, this is Elsie and Ben." The man behind her extended his hand to us, and we each shook it. "Marshall is going to join us."

"All right, well, let's get to it, shall we? We're already missing previews!" Ben said.

"Well, I still need to print the tickets. Will you guys go get us some popcorn?"

Ben looked at me incredulously and rolled his eyes. I laughed at him. "I want a Diet Coke," I said.

Ben and Marshall ran ahead to the concession as Ana and I picked up the tickets from the kiosk.

"Who is this guy?" I said to her. She shrugged. "I don't know. He keeps asking me out and I finally just relented and invited him here to get it over with."

"So it's true love, I guess," I said. She picked up the tickets and started walking toward Ben and Marshall.

"True love, schmoo love," she said. "I'm just trying to find someone that doesn't bore me to tears for a little while."

"You depress me," I said, but I wasn't paying attention to her when I said it. I was looking at Ben, who was asking the cashier for more butter on his already buttered popcorn. I was smiling. I was grinning. I was in love with the weirdo.

"No, you depress me," she said.

I turned to her and laughed. "You don't think that one day you'll meet 'the One'?"

"Love has made you sappy and gross," she said to me. We had almost met up with Ben and Marshall when I decided to tell her the news.

"Ben's moving in," I said. She stopped dead in her tracks and dropped her purse.

"What?"

Ben saw her face and caught my eye. He knew what was

going on, and he smiled at me mischievously as he put a handful of popcorn into his mouth. I smiled back at him. I picked up Ana's purse. She pulled me aside by my shoulders as Ben watched, standing next to a very confused Marshall.

"You are crazy! You're basically sending yourself to a prison. You wake up, he's there. You go to sleep, he's there. He's going to always be there! He's a great guy, Elsie. I like him a lot. I'm happy that you two found each other, but c'mon! This is a death sentence."

I just looked at her and smiled. For the first time, I felt like I had something over her. Sure, she was stunning and gorgeous and lively and bright. Men wanted her so badly they'd hound her for dates. But this man wanted me, and unlike Ana, I had felt what it was like to be wanted by someone you wanted just as badly. I wanted that for her, but there was a small part of me that felt victorious in that I had it and she didn't even know enough to want it.

SEPTEMBER

Ana and Kevin are only three minutes late. She opens my door with her own key. Ana looks hot. Really hot, spared-no-expense, pull-all-the-punches hot. I am dressed like I'm going to the grocery store. Kevin is right behind her, and while I am expecting some overly tailored douche bag with hair better than mine, I find a much different person.

Kevin is short, at least shorter than Ana. He's about my height. He's wearing jeans and a T-shirt; looks like he got the grocery store memo too. His face is nondescript. His skin is mostly clear but somewhat muddled; his hair is a shade of brown best described as "meh," and he looks like he neither works out nor is a slovenly couch potato.

He leans toward me, around Ana. "Kevin," he says, shaking my hand. It's not a bold handshake, but it's not a dead fish. It's polite and nice. He smiles and I smile back. I see him take in his surroundings, and I start to look around my house as well, as an impulse. I see my living room through his eyes. He no doubt knows about me, knows that my husband is dead, knows that Ana is my best friend; maybe he knows that I feel like he is trying to take her away from me. As he looks, I feel self-conscious about all of Ben's things around us. I want to say, "I'm not some crazy woman. It's just too hard to put these away yet." But I don't, because saying you're not crazy makes you seem crazy.

"Shall we?" Ana says. Kevin and I nod. Within a few seconds we are out the door. We cram into Kevin's Honda. I offer to take the backseat, and I squeeze myself into it by ducking and crunching behind the passenger-side door. Why do two-door cars exist? It is the most cumbersome of all tasks to try to wedge yourself into the backseat of one.

On the way to the restaurant, Ana is clearly trying to give Kevin and me a common thread upon which to build a relationship. It feels so strange. I get the distinct impression that Ana is trying to make sure Kevin and I get along. She's trying to make sure I like Kevin. She's never done that before. She's never cared. Most of the time, meeting me is their death knell. She uses me to let them know that she doesn't need alone time with them, that we are all friends. This isn't that. She's not kicking him out the door. She's inviting him inside.

"How did you guys meet?" I ask from the backseat.

"Oh, at yoga," he says, paying attention to the road.

"Yeah, Kevin was always in my Tuesday night class and he was just so bad"—she laughs—"that I had to personally help him."

"I've tried to explain to her that instructors are supposed to help their students, but she seems to think she was doing me a favor," he jokes, and I laugh politely as if this is hilarious. I'm missing whatever it is this guy has going for him. "Worked out in my favor though, since it got her to ask me out."

"Can you believe that, Elsie?" Ana says, half turning her face toward me in the backseat. "I asked him out."

I thought he'd been joking.

"Wait," I say, leaning forward. "Kevin, Ana asked you out?"

Kevin nods as he enters the parking garage and starts to look for a parking space.

"Ana has never asked anyone out the entire time I've known her," I tell him.

"I've never asked anyone out in my entire life," she clarifies.

"So why Kevin?" I ask and immediately realize that I have not phrased it in a polite way. "I just mean—what made you change your mind? About asking people out, I mean."

Kevin finds a spot and parks the car. Ana grabs his hand. "I don't know." She looks at him. "Kevin's different."

I want to vomit. I go so far as to make a vomit noise as a joke to them, but neither of them finds it funny. They aren't even paying much attention to me. I realize, as I try to climb out of the backseat of this shitty little car without injuring myself, that Kevin has hijacked my dinner plans with Ana and they are just letting me come along as a courtesy. I am a third wheel.

You try being a widow and a third wheel. You will never feel more alone.

We get to the restaurant, and it seems pretty cool, actually. Kevin and Ana are having a good time regardless of whether I am.

"How long have you two been dating?" I ask. I'm not sure what to expect, or rather, I don't expect anything.

"Uh"—Kevin starts to think—"just about a month?" he says.

Ana looks somewhat uncomfortable. "More or less," she says, and then she changes the subject. How could my best friend have been dating someone for the past month and never mentioned him to me? I refuse to believe that she talked about him and I wasn't listening. That's not who I am, even now. I try to listen to other people. How could Ana go from a person who would never settle down, never care about a man, to a woman who asks a man out and invites him to crash dinner with her best friend? And she did this all on her own time, never mentioning it to me, as if it were a side project of self-development that she didn't want to reveal until it was complete.

After dinner, they drive me back to my house and say good

night. Kevin kisses me on the cheek sweetly and looks me in the eye when he says it was nice to meet me. He says he hopes to see me again soon, and I believe him. I wonder if maybe the thing that Kevin has going for him is that he is very sincere. Maybe Ana is attracted to how genuine he is. If that's the case, I can understand.

I call her a few hours later, and my call goes through to voice mail. I'm sure they are together. I try again in the morning, and she puts me through to voice mail again but texts me and says she'll call later. She's still with Kevin. Kevin is different. I can feel it. I can see it. It makes me nervous. I've already lost Ben. I can't lose Ana. She can't change her personality and priorities now. I'm just barely hanging on.

She calls me Sunday afternoon and offers to come over. When she gets here, the first words out of her mouth are "What did you think of him? Adorable, right?"

"Yeah," I say. "He was really sweet, I liked him a lot." This isn't entirely untrue. Even if I don't see exactly what about him is exceptional, he still seemed perfectly nice and likable.

"Oh, Elsie! I'm so glad to hear you say that. I've been nervous for you two to meet and he was over yesterday afternoon and asked if he could join our dinner and I wasn't sure how to—" She cuts herself off. "I'm just really glad you liked him."

"He was cool. He seems a bit"—how do I say this?—"out of character for you though, am I right?"

She shrugs. "Something just clicked in me," she says. "And I realized that I want to love someone, you know? I mean, everyone wants to love someone, right? I think I just mean, I finally feel ready to be with one person. And of all the people I've dated in the past, I think the problem was that I wasn't into *them*. I was just into how much they were into me. But Kevin is different. Kevin wasn't even into me. We would stay after and I would be helping him with his poses and touching him in these ways, you know how yoga is. And most men perk up when you get that close, they make it sexual when it isn't sexual, but not Kevin. He was just really genuinely trying to get the pose right. So I started kind of . . . trying to make it sexual . . . just to see if I could get his attention, but he was just really focused."

So I was kind of right. It's the sincerity that has made her smitten.

"And I think I just . . . I want to be with someone that approaches things like that. That doesn't think of me as a thing to possess or obtain. So I asked him out and he said yes and it made me so nervous, but I was proud of myself that I did it, and then from our first date, I just felt this . . . connection . . ."

I start to get mad because a strong connection on first dates is for Ben and me. It's not common, it doesn't just happen to everyone. And she's watering it down. She's making it seem like it's not mine anymore.

"I don't understand why you didn't mention it sooner," I say.

"Well." Ana starts to grow uncomfortable. "I just . . . you are dealing with your own stuff and I didn't think you wanted to hear about this," she says, and that's when it hits me. Ana pities me. Ana is now the one in love; Ana is the happy one; I am the sad one; the lonely one, the one to whom she doesn't want to rub it in.

"What made this 'click' just happen?" I ask. My words are sharp; my voice is bitter.

"What?" she asks.

"It's interesting that you just 'changed' like that. You go from being this . . . kind of . . . from someone who . . ." I give up on trying to name it. "Well to turn around now and be the poster child for love. What made you change your mind?"

"You," she says. She says it as if it will pacify me, as if I should be happy. "I just realized that life is about love. Or at least, it's about loving someone."

"Do you hear yourself? You sound like a Valentine's Day card."

"Whoa, okay," she says as a reaction to the anger in my voice. "I'm sorry. I thought you'd be happy for me."

"Happy for you? My husband died and I'm sitting here miserable and alone, but you've learned from this whole experience how to love. *Congratulations, Ana! We're all really happy for you.*"

She is stunned, and unfortunately, because it is a silent stunned, I am able to continue.

"Let's all celebrate for Ana! She's found true love! Her life wasn't perfect enough with her perfect apartment and her perfect body and all of these men chasing her, but now, she's evolved enough to see in my husband's death a life lesson about the importance of love and romance."

Ana is now almost in tears, and I don't want her to cry but I can't stop myself.

"Was it love at first sight? This romance of yours? Are you going to get married next week?"

By now, all I have as evidence of how much Ben loved me is how quickly he knew he wanted to marry me. I honestly think that if Ana says Kevin has already started talking about marriage I will lose the only piece of life I have left in me.

"No." She shakes her head. "That's not it."

"Then what is it, Ana? Why are you doing this to me?"

"What am I doing to you?" she finally explodes. "I haven't done anything *to you*. All I did was meet someone I like and try to share it with you. Just like you did months ago to me and I was happy for you!"

"Yeah, well, you weren't widowed at the time."

"You know what, Elsie? You don't have to be a widow every second of every day of your life."

"Yes, Ana, I do."

"No, you don't. And you think you can just tell me to fuck off because you think I don't know anything, but I know you better than anyone. I know you sit here at home alone and think about what you've lost. I know it consumes you. I know that you keep his things around like they are a fucking medal for how tortured you are."

"You know what—" I start, but she interrupts me.

"No, Elsie. I'll tell you what. Everyone may tiptoe around you, myself included, but at some point someone needs to remind you that you lost something you only had for six months. Six months. And I'm not saying this isn't hard, but it's not like you're ninety and you lost your life partner here. You need to start living your life and letting other people live theirs. I have the right to be happy. I didn't lose that right just because your husband died."

It's quiet for a moment, as I look at her with my mouth wide open in shock.

"And neither did you," she adds, and she walks out the door.

I stand there for a few minutes after she leaves, frozen. Then I reanimate. I walk into the back closet and find the pillow I stuffed in a trash bag right after he died, the pillow that smells like him. I just stand there, smelling it through the open hole at the top of the bag, until I can't smell anything anymore.

Ana calls me over and over again during the week, leaving messages that she's sorry. That she should never have said those things. She leaves text messages saying much the same. I don't answer them, I don't answer her. I don't know what to say to her because I'm not mad at her. I'm embarrassed. I'm lost.

I did only know Ben for six months. I didn't even celebrate a birthday with him. I only spent January to June with him. How well can you really love someone if you haven't seen him through an August or an autumn? This is what I was afraid of. I was afraid that because I hadn't known Ben *long,* I hadn't known him *well.* I think I needed someone to say it to me before I could really think about it. And after thinking about it, over the course of the week I avoid Ana, I decide that that theory is wrong. It doesn't matter how long I knew him. I loved him. I still love him.

Then I think that maybe it is time to start putting his things away, because if I did love him, if our love was real, and it did matter, then what is the harm in putting some of his things in boxes? Right? I'll be okay, right?

I don't call Ana to help me. I'm not sure I could look her in the eye. Instead, I call Susan. When she answers the phone, she immediately asks about the marriage certificate, and I have to admit that I have not called the county yet. I tell her that I didn't have enough time, but that is a lie. I did have the time.

I just know that if they tell me they do not have a record of our marriage, I will not be able to move his things into storage. I know it will make me hold on tighter to his old clothes and toothbrush. I need to believe the government knows we were married. Otherwise, I'll have to prove it to myself in arbitrary and pathetic ways. I am trying to move forward. I am trying to make arbitrary and pathetic things of the past.

MAY

Ben was sweaty. It was a hot spring day. I had all of the windows open in the apartment; the door had been open for the past few hours as we hauled things up the front stairs. There was no point in turning on the air conditioner. All the cold air would have just flown right out the front door. I threw Ben a bottle of water as he headed down the stairs for another round of boxes.

"Thanks," he said to me as he hit the sidewalk.

"Almost done!" I said.

"Yeah, but then I have to unpack everything!"

"Well, sure, but we can do that slowly, you know? Over the course of a few days if you want."

Ben made his way to the moving truck and started pushing boxes toward the back edge. I played with a few of them to see which one was lightest, and then I took that one. I knew that the proper way to face a challenge was head-on, and in that spirit, I should have taken the heavy ones first, but my arms had started to quiver and my legs were feeling unreliable. It had been a full day of unpacking and unloading, after a full night of packing and loading. I was starting to phone it in, and I was all right with that.

With the lightest box, a box that was still rather heavy, in my hands, I made my way up the stairs. As I got to the door, Ben called to me. "What did you do?" he asked. "Take the lightest box you could find?"

"It's not all that light, you know! You should pack better next time!"

"I'm hoping there won't be a next time," he yelled up at me. I was inside, setting the lightest heavy box down on the floor. I was trying to bend from the knees or whatever, but I finally just plopped it down on top of the others using what muscles I had left in my back.

"I just mean if we move someplace together." I was waiting at the door, holding the screen open for him. He walked up the stairs, straight past me, and put down his box. We started to walk out together. We were both out of breath, albeit me more so than him.

"This hasn't taught you anything about the perils of moving?" he asked, as he rushed ahead.

"No, you're right," I said. "We should stay here forever. I don't ever want to move another thing."

The sun started to set as we brought in the last of it. This was the beginning of something. We could both feel it. It was us against the world.

"Do you think you'll be able to handle my dirty dishes?" he asked with his arm around me, kissing my head.

"I think so," I replied. "Do you think you can handle the fact that I always want it to be ninety degrees in the house?"

"No," he said. "But I will learn."

I kissed his neck because it was as far as I could reach. My calves didn't have the power to get me any higher. Ben moaned. It made me feel powerful to elicit that type of reaction without even meaning to. It made me feel like one of those women that oozes sex appeal in even the simplest of tasks. I felt like the Cleopatra of my apartment.

I rubbed my nose further into his neck. "Stop it," he said

falsely, as if I was doing something tawdry. "I have to return the truck by seven."

"I wasn't trying anything!" I said.

"Yes, you were! I'm too tired!"

"I wasn't trying anything, really. I'm tired too."

"Okay! Fine!" he said, grabbing me and pulling me toward my bedroom. Our bedroom. It was now filled with his stuff on the floor and resting against the walls.

"No, really. I'm so tired."

And just like that the tides shifted. "Fine! I'll do all the work," he said. He laid me on the bed and lowered himself on top of me. "I love you," he said, kissing my cheeks and my neck. "I love you so much. I feel like the luckiest guy in the world."

"I love you too," I said back to him, but I don't know if he heard me. He had started to focus on other things.

Thirty minutes later, I was naked and leaning over him, resting his head on a pillow and asking if he wanted me to take him to the hospital.

"No! No," he said. "I think I just threw out my back."

"Isn't that what old men do?" I teased him.

"Look at how much crap I lifted today!" He winced in pain. "Can you get me my underwear?"

I got up and gave it to him. Then I put on my own. I wrapped my bra around me and threw on a T-shirt.

"What should we do?" I asked. "Do you want medicine? Should you see a doctor?" He was still trying to get his underwear on himself. He could barely move. Not wanting to see him struggle, I grabbed the waistband of his underwear. I shimmied the back up under his butt as subtly as I could. Then I pulled the front up to his waist. I pulled the blanket from the foot of the bed and I laid it on top of him.

"Do we have any ibuprofen?" he asked me.

There it was. "We." The best kind of "we." Do "we" have ibuprofen?

"I don't myself, I don't think," I said. "Any in the boxes?"

"Yeah, in a box marked 'Bathroom.' I think I saw it in the living room on the floor."

"Okay," I said. "I'll be right back." I kissed his forehead and went into the living room.

I scanned the boxes across the room and finally saw one labeled "Bathroom." It was under plenty of other heavy boxes. I was sure it was one of the first ones we'd unloaded. I moved box after box until I got to it, and then I opened it to find another labyrinth inside. After way too long, I found some ibuprofen and brought it to him with a glass of water.

He lifted his head slightly, eyes scrunched from the pain. He thanked me.

"You're welcome," I said.

"Elsie?" he moaned.

"Yeah?"

"You're gonna have to return the moving truck."

"Totally fine," I said, even though having to drive that huge truck through Los Angeles traffic was not my idea of a good time.

"You actually, uh . . ." he started. "You have to leave now. It's due back in twenty minutes. I'm sorry! I didn't think about how long it would take you to find the ibuprofen."

I jumped up and threw on a pair of pants.

"Where are the keys?" I asked.

"On the front seat."

"Where am I going?"

"Lankershim and Riverside."

"It's in the *valley*?"

"That was the cheapest one I could find! I picked it up on my way home from work."

"Okay, okay. I'm out of here." I kissed his cheek. "Are you going to be okay here alone?"

"I'll be fine. Can you bring me my cell phone just in case?"

I put his phone by the bed and started to take off. "Hey," he called. "Will you pick up dinner too?"

"Of course I will," I called out. "You pain in the ass."

SEPTEMBER

Susan shows up at my door bright and early on Saturday morning. She has in her hands a bag of bagels and cream cheese, and a carton of orange juice. Under her arm is a package of flattened boxes.

"I thought we could use refreshments," she says as she steps in.

"Awesome," I say and put them in the kitchen. "Do you want one now?" I call out to her.

"Sure." She appears in my kitchen. Her voice is next to me and quiet, instead of far away and shouting like I expected.

I put two bagels into the toaster oven, and Susan and I step into the living room. She scans the space. I can tell she is assessing what is Ben's. My guess is she is doing this both because these objects indicate the job in store for us and because they belong to her dead son.

The toaster dings. I pull the bagels out, and when I do, they burn the pads of my fingers. I put the bagels on plates and shake my hands wildly, hoping to mitigate the pain. I've never been sure what the logic is in this gesture, but it's an instinct, so maybe it works. Susan looks at me and asks if I'm all right, and for a moment I think that this is my shot to get out of this. I can say they really hurt. I can say I'm in no position to be using my hands. They do still hurt. Maybe I should see a doctor. But then I realize when I get home from the doctor, Ben's stuff will still be right here in front of me.

"Nothing I can't handle," I say. We pour large glasses of orange juice and sit down at the table. Susan asks where we are going to begin, and I say, "The living room. I need to work my way up to the bedroom." She tries to make small talk as we eat, asking about my job and my friends, but all either of us can think about is the task ahead. It's almost a relief when our bagels are gone. Now, we have to start.

Susan plops herself down in the living room and starts folding boxes. I still have all of the boxes from when he moved in. It wasn't even five months ago. I grab what I have and meet her in there. I take a deep breath, put a box in front of me, and unplug his PlayStation, putting it in the box.

"Annnd done!" I joke, but Susan insists on taking it as a cry for help. She stops folding and speaks to me in a gentle voice.

"Take your time. We are on no one's timetable but yours, you know." I know, I know. She keeps telling me.

"Have you thought about whether you're going to keep all this stuff or try to sell some of it? Give any of it away?"

It hadn't occurred to me to do anything other than store it, honestly. I just figured I'd put it in boxes and shove it in the closet. The thought of giving the things away, of not owning them anymore, it's too much for me.

"Oh," I say. Maybe I should aim toward that. I should hope that one day I can give it away or sell it. One day I will. "Maybe we should divide things into categories as we pack," I say. "Some boxes for keeping, some for giving away, and maybe another for trash. Not trash, I mean. Just like . . . things that are of no use to anyone. It's not trash. If it was Ben's it's not trash."

"Hey," Susan says. "Don't be so hard on yourself. Ben can't hear you call his stuff trash, and even if he could, it wouldn't matter."

I don't know why it is so jarring to hear, because I don't believe that Ben can hear me. I just thought Susan believed Ben is here; Ben is with us.

"You don't believe that Ben is . . ."

"All around us?" she says in a half-mocking way. She shakes her head. "No, I don't. I wish I did. It would make things a lot easier for me. But no, either he's gone-gone, his soul having disappeared into the ether, or if he's been transported somewhere else, if his heart and mind are reincarnated or just somewhere else, I don't think he'd still be here on earth as himself. I don't see . . . it just seems like something people tell victims' families, you know? 'Hey, it's okay. Ben is always with you.'"

"You don't think Ben is with you?"

"He's with me because I love him and I loved him and he lives in my memories. His memory is with me. But no, I don't see how Ben is here. After Steven died, I thought maybe he was lying in bed next to me at night, watching me. Or maybe he was some omnipotent force looking over Ben and I, but it did no good. Because I just didn't believe it. You know? Do you believe it? Or maybe what I should say is *Can* you believe it? I wish I could."

I shake my head. "No, I don't think he can hear me. I don't think he's watching me. It's a nice idea. When my brain wanders, I sometimes think about what if he's hearing everything I'm saying, what if he's seeing everything I'm doing. But, it doesn't really make me feel any better. Whenever I start to think about where he is now, I ultimately just focus on what his last moments were. Did he know they were his last moments? What if he'd never left the house? What if I'd never asked him to . . ."

"To what?"

"He was doing me a favor when he died," I tell her. "He was

buying me Fruity Pebbles." It feels like I've finally put down a barbell. Susan is quiet.

"Was that a confession?" she says.

"Hmm?"

"That doesn't matter. You know that, right?"

No, I don't know that. But I'm not sure how to say that, so I don't say anything.

"You will do yourself a world of good the minute you realize that does not matter. You can play the scenario out a million times, whether he goes to get the cereal or he doesn't," she says. "I'm telling you, he'd still end up dying. It's just the way the world works."

I look at her, trying to figure out if she truly believes that. She can see my skepticism.

"I don't know if that's true," she says. "But that is one thing we *have* to believe. Do you hear me? Learn how to believe that one." She doesn't let me speak. "Get the box," she says. "We're gonna start in the bathroom."

We pack away his toothbrush and his hair gel. We pack his deodorant and his shampoo. It's a small box of things that were only his. We shared so many of the things in here. Susan smells the shampoo and deodorant and then throws them in with the other things.

"When you are ready, this is a throwaway box, right?" Susan asks. "I mean, this is trash."

I laugh. "Yeah, that will be trash."

We move on to the kitchen and desk area, where most of Ben's stuff is also trash. We fill boxes and boxes of crap. I wonder if some of these things are being put right back into the boxes they came here in. We make our way back into the living room, and Susan starts packing his books. She sees a collector's set on one of the shelves.

"May I have this?" she says. "It took me months to convince him to read these books," she said. "He wouldn't believe me that young adult books can be great."

I want them, but I want her to have them more. "Sure," I say. "You should take anything you want. He'd want you to have his things," I say. "He loved those books, by the way. He recommended them to anyone that would listen to him."

She smiles and puts them by the door as she finishes packing the rest of his young adult collection into boxes. "Is this a sell or a keep box, by the way?"

"I'm not sure yet," I answer. She nods. She continues putting books into boxes until she is too exasperated. "Jesus Christ, how many young adult books can one person read?" she says.

I laugh. "He read them a lot. I mean, like one a week sometimes. And he refused to get them from the library. Which was annoying because I work at the library, but he insisted upon going to the bookstore and buying them. I'd bring them home and he'd just let them sit and collect dust until I returned them."

She laughs. "That's my fault," she says. "When he was a kid, my one luxury was buying books. I never wanted to go to the library."

"What?" Sacrilege!

She laughs again, embarrassed. "You're gonna be mad."

"I am?"

"I hate the way they smell, library books."

"You are killing me, Susan. *Killing me.*" I grab my chest and feign a heart attack. The way library books smell is the best smell in the world, other than the smell of the pillow I have trapped in a plastic bag.

"I know! I know! When Ben was a kid, he'd want to go to

the library because they had board games and those chairs with the . . . what are they called? The chairs where they are like this big, soft ball . . . Oh, damn it, what is the word?"

"Beanbag chairs?"

"Yes! He used to love sitting in beanbag chairs, and I would make him go to the bookstore with me instead so I could buy books that didn't smell musty. Totally my fault. I'm sorry."

"You are forgiven," I say, although I'm still hung up on the fact that she doesn't like the smell of library books.

MAY

I got home and Ben was still in bed. He'd been staring at the ceiling for the past hour and a half. It took me forever to get to the rental place in that huge truck, and then I picked up his car that he left there and headed home, only to remember he wanted dinner. I picked up McDonald's and made my way home.

"You okay?" I called out to him as I got into the apartment.

"Yeah, but I still can't move that well," he said.

"Well, you'll be happy to know I almost crashed about four times in the damn truck going up Laurel Canyon. Why do they let normal people drive those things?"

"I wouldn't exactly say you're normal," he said. "But I understand your point."

I put the bag of McDonald's on the bed and helped him to get to a sitting position.

"I really think I should call the doctor," I said.

"I will be fine," he told me and started to eat. I followed suit, and when I was done, my fingers covered in salt, my mouth coated in grease, I took a big sip of my large soda. I lay back, finally resting after the long day. Ben turned on the television and said he wanted to watch something. Then it all got fuzzy and I fell asleep.

I woke up the next morning to an empty bed.

"Ben?" I called out. He answered from the living room. I

walked out there and found that a whole section of boxes had been unloaded.

"How are you feeling? Are you okay?"

"I'm fine," he said. "As long as I stay upright and don't twist, I feel fine."

"I really think you should see a doctor. That doesn't sound good."

"Quit nagging me, wife," he said and smiled. "Can I remove some of your dumb books? I want a place to put all of these," he said. He gestured awkwardly to stacks and stacks of paperback books.

"Maybe we should just buy a new bookshelf," I said.

"Or maybe you should donate some of these lame classics to the library. Do we really need two copies of *Anna Karenina*?"

"Hey! It's two different translations!" I said. "You can't just come in here and throw my stuff out because you need room, you jerk!"

"I'm not saying we should throw it out," he said. "Just . . . donate it." He opened the book up and smelled it and then thrust his head away. *"Owow!"* he exclaimed and rubbed his back. "These books smell all old and gross, Elsie. Let's at least get you some new books."

I grab *Anna Karenina* out of his hand and put it back on my shelf. "I doubt your books smell all that great," I said. "Any book you have for a long time starts to smell of must. That's how it works."

"Yeah, but I don't buy my books at used bookstores and flea markets," he said. "I get 'em hot off the presses so they stay fresh."

"Oh for heaven's sake! Books aren't bagels. They don't go stale," I said as I pulled one from the stack. It had a teenage girl standing in front of what appeared to be an oversize falcon. "Seriously?" I said.

"Let's do a little experiment," Ben said. "What's *Anna Karenina* about?"

"It's about a married aristocratic woman who falls in love with a count but she can't—"

"I am falling asleep just listening to you. Do you know what this book is about?" he asked me, grabbing the falcon-cover book from my hand. "This book is about a group of kids who are part human, part bird." He said it plainly, as if the facts spoke for themselves. "This is a better book."

"You haven't even tried to read *Anna Karenina*. It's an incredibly moving story."

"I'm sure it is," he said. "But I like my books to take place 'in a world where . . .' "

"In a world where what?"

"Just in a world where . . . anything. In a world where love is classified as a disease. In a world where the government chooses your family for you. In a world where society has eliminated all pain and suffering. I love that kind of stuff."

"That last one was *The Giver,*" I said. "Right? You're talking about *The Giver*?"

"If you tell me you don't like *The Giver,* this relationship is over," he said to me. "I have a zero tolerance policy on not appreciating *The Giver*."

I smiled and grabbed his copy of *The Giver.* I opened it up and smelled the pages. "I don't know . . ." I teased. "Smells a little musty."

"Hey!" he yelled, trying to pull the book away from me. But the pain was too excruciating. He was wincing and crying out. I took my keys off the table.

"Stand up," I said. "We're going to the goddamn doctor."

"Not until you admit you loved *The Giver*," he muttered.

I knelt down to help him up, and I told him softly, "I loved *The Giver*."

He smiled and groaned as he got up. "I knew it," he said, unfazed. "You want to know a secret though?"

I nodded.

"I would have adjusted the policy for you." Then he kissed me on the cheek and let me help him out to the car.

SEPTEMBER

We have packed up most of his things by the afternoon, saving the bedroom and closet for last. We grab the rest of the boxes and head in there.

I throw the boxes onto the bed and look at the room. I can do this. I can do this. If I can't, Susan will. So at least it will get done.

"Come on!" she says. "Let's go." She opens a dresser and starts throwing clothes into boxes. I watch as striped shirts and dirty jeans are pulled out of their rightful home. I start taking clothes out of the closet with their hangers. You don't realize how dead clothes look on their hangers until the person who owned them is . . . Anyway, I don't even bother to take them off the hangers. I simply throw them in the box with the rest of his clothes. I have made my way through the closet and through his nightstand before Susan is done with the dresser. She has a look on her face like she's fine, but I spot her smelling a shirt before she puts it in the box. She sees me catch her.

"I've just been trying to see if anything still smells like him, you know? It's hard to remember anymore, what he smelled like."

"Oh," I say. "Sorry, I think I smelled all the smell off that stuff."

"Oh." She laughs. "That explains it then."

I think about whether I have it in me to share what I have left of Ben. I know that I do. "Hold on," I say.

I grab his pillow in the trash bag. I untie the top of the bag and hand it to her.

"Smell it," I say, and she looks at me somewhat hesitantly, but then she lowers her face into it, her nose grazing the pillow itself. "That's it," she says. "Oh God. That's him." Her eyes close, and I can see the tears falling down her cheeks. For the first time since the hospital, I see what happens when she lets herself lose it.

MAY

We spent the day at the doctor's office, sitting in cramped chairs with a room full of people with contagious diseases. Ben reminded me multiple times that we did not need to be there. But once we saw the doctor, he seemed very concerned that Ben take it easy. We left with a prescription for Vicodin.

We got home and Ben called to order Chinese. He ordered us the usual, and I overheard him tell the man on the phone that he wanted both white rice and brown rice. I remembered how he told me on our first date that ordering both would be a sign that the romance was gone, but I couldn't help but feel warmed by his doing it now. Ben and I were a team. We knew each other's wants. We knew each other's needs. We knew when to split up and compromise. We weren't each putting our best foot forward. We weren't waiting to see if this was right for us. We dove headfirst into this and here we were, one of those couples that doesn't put up with the other person's stupid shit. I liked brown, he liked white. We ordered both. Nothing fancy anymore. The novelty was gone for us and what we were left with was . . . awesome.

We got into bed that night, and even though we had not unpacked the bedroom, Ben was dead set on finding one thing. Concerned that he not bend or twist, I insisted upon looking for it myself. He directed me through boxes, and eventually, I made my way to a box so light that it felt like it was packed with air. I brought it to him, and he opened the box with joy. It was a dirty pillow.

"What is that?" I asked, horrified that that thing was entering my bed. It was covered in drool spots and orange puddles of . . . something.

"It's my favorite pillow!" he said, putting it down on top of one of my pillows, pillows that I thought were now "ours," but in comparison to his ugly, dirty pillow felt decidedly "mine."

"Please get that thing off my bed," I said.

"Our bed, baby," he said to me. "This is our bed. And our bed should have our pillows. And this is our pillow now."

"No," I said with a laugh. "I don't want that to be our pillow. I want that to be a pillow you used to have when you lived on your own."

"Well, it can't be that. I can't sleep without this pillow."

"You've been sleeping here for months without that pillow!"

"Yeah, but this is my own house now! I pay rent here! I need this pillow in a place where I pay rent."

"Ugh," I relented. "Just put a damn pillowcase on it, would you?"

"Sure." He walked to the linen closet and came back proud as a peacock. He then rolled himself delicately into bed.

"Did you take the Vicodin? It will take the edge off," I said.

"What do I look like? A man that can't handle a little pain?" he asked as he moved toward me slowly and put his head on his pillow. "You wanna try it out? It's *really* comfortable."

I shook my head. "No, thank you."

"Oh, come on. You can lie on it for five seconds. It's a part of us now," he said, teasing me.

"Fine! Fine!" I moved my head to lie on it. "Oh my God, that thing smells awful."

"What? No, it doesn't!"

"I can't believe you thought my books smelled bad. That pillow is terrible!" I laughed.

"No! It smells fine." He smelled it to make sure. "You just have to get used to it, is all."

"Yeah, okay," I said. I turned out the light. He fell asleep within minutes, and I lay there feeling like the luckiest girl in the world that this weirdo next to me was mine; that he lived here; that he had the right to demand his stinky pillow stay in my bed. I smelled it once more as I fell asleep, and I couldn't imagine ever getting used to it, but before long, that was exactly what I had done.

SEPTEMBER

The boxes are mostly packed. Ben's things are almost entirely out of sight. I can see only brown cardboard for miles. I kept his USC sweatshirt and a few of his T-shirts. I left his favorite cup in the cupboard. Susan put some books and photos in her car to take with her. She added a random notebook he'd written in and a few other things that are meaningless to anyone else but mean everything to a mom.

Now that it's all in boxes, there isn't much reason for Susan to stay here.

"Well," she says with a sigh. "I guess that's the last of it."

"I guess so," I say. I feel surprisingly stable.

"All right," she says, nodding. It's the kind of nod that says she doesn't know what to say next; she doesn't know what she's thinking. She gasps for air.

"I guess I'll . . . head home," she says. "It's, uh, this is hard. I don't want to leave but I . . . I mean, it's not like I'm leaving him, you know? I think it's more just . . . I had this to look forward to, if that makes any sense? I'm not making any sense. I'm going to go."

I hug her. "It makes all the sense in the world to me."

"Okay," she says. She breathes out. She breathes with focus. She gathers herself. "Okay, I'll give you a call next weekend."

"Sounds great."

She opens the door and walks out. I turn to see my apartment.

His things are in boxes, but I do not feel that I have lost him. It's a subtle feeling, but it's real. I am now just a little bit ready to realize the beauty of progress, of moving on. I decide to seize the moment. I grab three boxes of clothes and load them in the car. When I'm done with those, I grab two more. I don't go back in for more because I'm afraid I'll lose my nerve. I tell myself this is for the best. This is good!

I pull up in front of Goodwill and park my car. I take the boxes out and walk inside. A large man comes to greet me.

"What do we have here?"

"Some men's clothes," I say. I can't look at him. I'm staring at the boxes. "All good condition."

"Wonderful!" he says, as he takes the boxes from me. "Would you like a receipt?"

"No," I say. "No, thank you."

He opens the boxes and dumps their contents into a bigger pile of clothes, and even though I know that it's time for me to walk away, I can't help but stare. They are no longer Ben's clothes. They are just clothes in a pile of clothes mixed with other clothes.

What have I done?

Like that, they are gone. The man has taken the large pile and shoved it into the back room. I want those clothes back. Why did I give someone else Ben's clothes? What will he wear? I want to jump over the counter and sort through what they have back there. I need to get his clothes back. Instead, I am frozen and in shock over what I have done. How did I do that? Why did I do that? Can Ben see, from where he is, what I have done?

"Ma'am?" the man calls out to me. "Are you okay?"

"Yes," I say. "I'm sorry."

I turn around and get in my car. I can't turn the key in the ignition. I can't shift the car in drive. I just bang my head against the steering wheel. I let the tears fall down on the beige interior. My cheek is blaring the horn and I don't care.

I leave the keys on the front seat of my car and I get out. I just run. I run and run even though it's cold outside, even though my body is starting to heat up faster than it should. Even though I feel like I'm giving myself a fever. And then I stop, instantly and abruptly, because I realize that I cannot outrun myself. I go across the street and walk along the sidewalk until I see a bar. I don't have my wallet, I don't have my keys, but I walk in anyway. It's early enough in the day that they let me right in and then I sit at the bar and I drink beers. I drink beer after beer until I can't feel my nose. When I'm done, I pretend I'm going to the bathroom and then I sneak out the back, not paying, not tipping, not even saying thank you. By the time I get home, knowing full well I've locked myself out, I'm just plain sick.

I puke on my own front lawn. It's barely 8:00 p.m. Neighbors see me and I ignore them. I sit down on the grass when I'm done and I pass out. I wake up around 11:00, and I'm too discombobulated and inebriated to remember where my keys are. I do the only thing that I can do to get back into my house. I call Ana.

"At least you called me," she says as she walks up to the sidewalk to meet me. "That's all I care about."

I don't say anything. She walks up my steps and unlocks my front door. She holds it open for me.

"Are you drunk?" she says, rather shocked. If it were any other time in my life, she'd probably think this was funny, but I can tell she doesn't, even though I kind of do. "That's not like you."

"It's been a rough couple of days," I say and plop myself down on my own sofa.

"Do you want to talk about it?"

"Well, my husband died, so that was hard." I don't want to talk to her about any of this. I don't want to talk to anyone.

"I know," she says, taking my sarcastic remark as something genuine. She can't possibly think that was really my answer. Instead, she is treating me sincerely so that I have no choice but to be sincere. It's crafty, I'll give her that.

"I moved his stuff out," I say, resigning myself to the therapy session that is going to come my way. I don't want to talk to her about our last conversation, about our fight, although I'm sure she's going to force that on me as well. She moves toward me on the sofa and puts her arm around me. "I gave away some of his stuff to Goodwill," I tell her.

Goodwill! That's where my keys are.

"I'm sorry, Elsie," she says. "But I'm proud of you. I'm really, really proud of you for doing it." She rubs my arm. "I don't know if I'd be able to do it if I were you."

"What?" I say. "You were insisting that I needed to start moving on! You said I should do it!"

She nods. "Yeah, because you should. But that doesn't mean I didn't know it was hard."

"Then why did you say it like it was easy?"

"Because you needed to do it and I knew that you could. No one wants to do it."

"Yeah, well, no one else has to."

I want her to leave and I think she knows that.

"I'm sorry about the other night. I was out of line. I'm truly sorry," she says.

"It's fine," I say, and I mean it. It is fine. I should be apologizing too, but I just don't want to talk to anyone right now.

"All right, well, I'm going to go," she says. She gathers herself and leaves.

"I love you," she says.

"Me too," I say back, hoping it passes for an "I love you too." I do love her, but I don't want to say it. I don't want to feel anything. I see her drive away out of my front window, and I think that she is probably going to meet up with Kevin somewhere and she'll tell him all about this little episode of mine and he'll grab her hand and he'll say, "You poor baby, that sounds difficult," as if the world has conspired against her, as if she doesn't deserve this. I hate them both for being able to sigh, make a couple of serious faces about how hard this must be on me, and then go to the movies and laugh at dick jokes.

I walk to the Goodwill the next morning and get my car. My keys are sitting on the front seat where I left them, and yet, no one has stolen anything. It pisses me off, to be honest. It pisses me off that of all times, the world conspires to help me *now*.

At work on Monday, I am scowling at strangers. When they ask me to help them, I do it with a frown on my face, and when I'm done, I curse them under my breath.

When Mr. Callahan makes his way toward me, I have little energy left.

"Hello, my dear," he says as he moves to touch my arm. I instinctively pull away. He doesn't seem to take it personally. "Bad day?" he asks.

"You could say that." I grab the handle on a cart of books to reshelve. It's not technically my job to put them back, but it seems like a good way to graciously end the conversation. Mr. Callahan doesn't get the hint. He walks with me.

"I had a bad day once," he says, grinning. It's a classic cheer-up routine, and it's wasted on me. I don't want to cheer up. I'm honestly not sure I even remember how to smile naturally. What do you do? You pull the corners of your mouth up?

"Bad joke," he says, waving his hand in an attempt to both dismiss the joke and let me off the hook for not laughing at it. "Anything I can do for you?"

"Oh," I say, my eyes focused on the bookshelves above me. I don't even remember what I'm looking for. I have to look at the book in my hand again. The details aren't registering. The call number falls out of my head before my eyes make it back up to the shelf. "No, thanks," I say.

"I've got two ears, you know!" he says.

My face contorts into impatient confusion. "I'm sorry?"

"For listening, I mean. I'm good at listening."

"Oh."

"Anyway," he continues. "You'd rather be alone. I get it. Just know the offer stands. I'm always here to listen." He looks at me a minute, perhaps trying to break through my empty stare. "And I wouldn't say that to just anybody," he says, smiling as he pats my hand gently, and he leaves me to the cart.

I wish I had it in me to tell him he's a good man. I wish I had it in me to say thank you. I just don't. I can't smile at him. I don't even say good-bye. I let him walk away and I turn to the bookshelves as if he was never there. I forget, once more, the number of the book I have in my hand, and instead of checking again, I drop it right there on the cart and I walk away.

I step outside and take a breath. I tell myself to get it together. I tell myself that this situation I'm in is no one's fault. I am by the bike rack, pacing, when I see a young couple with a baby. The man has the baby strapped to his chest, the woman is carrying a diaper bag. She is cooing to the child, the man is looking down. She kisses the man on the lips and laughs as she maneuvers awkwardly around the baby. They play with the baby's hands and feet.

Why me and not them? Why couldn't that guy have died? Why am I not here right now with Ben looking at a sad woman pacing on the street, on the edge of a nervous breakdown? What right do they have to be happy? Why does everyone in the world have to be happy in front of me?

I go back inside and tell Nancy I'll be in the Native American section. I tell her I'm researching the Aztecs for next month's display. I stand in the aisle, running my fingers over the spines, feeling the cellophane crackle as I touch it. I watch as the Dewey decimal numbers escalate higher and higher. I try to focus only on the numbers, only on the spines. It works for a moment, for a moment I don't feel like I want to get a gun. But in that moment, I crash face-first into someone else.

"Oh! I'm so sorry," he says to me, picking up the book he's dropped. He's my age, maybe a bit older. He has black hair and what is probably a permanent five o'clock shadow. He is tall with a firm body and broad shoulders. He is dressed in a faded T-shirt and jeans. I notice his brightly colored Chuck Taylors as he picks up his book. I move to get out of his way, but he seems to want to stop and talk.

"Brett," he says and puts out his hand. I shake it, trying to move on.

"Elsie," I say.

"Sorry to bump into you like that," he says. "I'm not that familiar with this library, and the librarians here aren't very helpful."

"I'm a librarian here," I say. I don't care if he feels awkward.

"Oh." He laughs shyly. "That is embarrassing. I'm so sorry. Again. Wow. This isn't going well for me, huh?"

"No, I guess not," I say.

"Listen, would you let me buy you a coffee, as an apology?" he asks.

"No, that's okay. It's not a big deal."

"No, really. I'd like to. It would be my pleasure," he says, and now he's smiling like he thinks he's cute or something.

"Oh," I say. "No, I really should be getting back to work."

"Some other time then," he says. Maybe he thinks I'm being demure or shy. I don't know.

"I'm married," I say, trying to end it. I don't know if I'm saying that because I think it's true or just to get him off my back, the way I used to say "I don't think my boyfriend would like that" when I was single and hit on by homeless men outside convenience stores.

"Oh," he says. "I'm sorry, I didn't . . . I wasn't expecting that."

"Yeah, well," I say as I lift up my hand and show him.

"Well," he says, laughing. "If it doesn't work out with you and your husband . . ."

That's when I punch him in the face.

I'm surprised at how satisfying it is to make contact: the crack of fist to face, the sight of just the smallest trickle of blood out of a nose.

You are not supposed to punch people in the face. You're especially not supposed to punch people in the face while you are at work. When you work for the city. And when the person you punch in the face is kind of a baby about it and insists that the library call the cops.

When the cops get here, I can't do much to defend myself. He didn't hit me. He didn't threaten me. He didn't use incendiary language. He did nothing to provoke me. I just assaulted him. So, as embarrassing and over the top as it is, I am being arrested. They don't handcuff me. One cop even seems to think this is funny. But apparently, when the cops are called because you punched someone and they show up and you say, "Yes, Officer, I hit that person," they have to at least bring you down to the "precinct." One of the police officers escorts me to the backseat of the squad car, reminding me to duck as I get in. As he shuts the door and heads to the front seat, Mr. Callahan comes outside and catches my eye. I should be ashamed, I'm sure. But I just don't care. I look at him through the backseat window, and I see him crack a smile at me. His smile slowly turns to laughter, a laughter that seems to be equal parts shock and newfound respect, perhaps even pride. The car starts to pull away, and Mr. Callahan gives me a sly thumbs-up. I find myself smiling, finally. I guess I do remember how to do it. You just turn the corners of your mouth up.

When we get to the police station, the cops take my things and book me. They put me in a cell. They tell me to call one person. I call Ana.

"You what?" she says.

"I'm at the police station. I need you to come bail me out."

"You're kidding, right?"

"I'm entirely serious."

"What did you do?"

"I punched someone in the library stacks, somewhere between 972.01 and 973.6."

"Okay, I'm coming," she says.

"Wait. Don't you want to know why I punched him?" I ask.

"Does it matter?" she asks, impatient.

It feels like hours until she's here, but I think she actually gets here pretty quickly. I see her standing in front of my cell and . . . ha-ha-ha, how the fuck did I get here in a jail cell? She's with the officer that arrested me. I am free to go, he says. We'll wait to see if Brett presses charges.

Ana and I exit the building and we are standing outside. Ana hands me my bag of things. I now think this is really funny. But Ana doesn't agree with me.

"In my defense, Mr. Callahan also thought it was funny," I say.

Ana turns to me. "The old guy?"

He's not just an old guy. "Forget it," I say.

"I called Susan," she says. It's almost a confession.

"What?"

"I called Susan."

"Why?"

"Because I think I'm out of my league here. I don't know what to do."

"So you told on me to my mom? Is that it?"

"She's not your mom," Ana says, sternly.

"I know that," I say. "I just mean that's kind of what you've done, right? You don't want to deal with me so you're trying to get me in trouble?"

"I think you've gotten yourself in trouble."

"He was being an asshole, Ana." She just looks at me. "He *was*! How did you even get her number anyway?"

"It's in your phone," she says, like I am stupid.

"Fine. Forget it. I'm sorry I called you."

"Susan will be at your place in about an hour."

"She's coming *over*? I have to work until five," I say.

"Something tells me they won't want you back at work today," Ana says.

We get in her car and she drives me to mine. I get out and thank her again for bailing me out. I tell her I'm sorry to be difficult and that I will pay her back.

"I'm just worried about you, Elsie."

"I know," I say. "Thanks."

I drive myself home and wait for the knock at the door.

Susan knocks, and I open the door. She doesn't say anything. She just looks at me.

"I'm sorry," I say. I don't know why I'm apologizing to her. I don't owe it to her not to get arrested. I don't owe it to anyone.

"You don't need to apologize to me," she says. "I just wanted to make sure you were okay."

"I'm fine."

She comes in and kicks off her shoes. She lies down on my couch. "What happened?" she asks.

I blow out a hard sigh and sit down.

"This guy asked me out," I say. "And I said no, but he kept at it and I told him I was married—"

"Why did you tell him you were married?" Susan asks.

"Huh?"

"I tell people I'm still married all the time, and I do it for the wrong reason. I do it so I can feel married. So I don't have to say out loud that I am not married. Is that what you're doing?"

"No. Well." I stop and think. "I am married," I say. "I didn't divorce him. We didn't end it."

"But it ended."

"Well, but, not . . . we didn't end it."

"It ended," she says.

Why must everything be a life lesson? Why can't I just act like I'm married and everyone leave me the hell alone?

"Well, if I . . ." I trail off. I'm not sure of my defense.

"Go on," she says. It seems like she knows what I'm going to say, but I don't even know what I am going to say.

"If we stopped being married when he died . . ."

She waits for me to finish my thought.

"Then we were barely married."

Susan nods. "That's what I thought you were going to say."

My lips turn down.

"Who cares?" she says.

"What?"

"Who cares if you were barely married? It doesn't mean you love him any less."

"Well, but . . ."

"Yes?"

"We were only together for six months before we got married."

"So?"

"So, I mean, being married is what separates him from just some guy. It's what proves he's . . . he's the love of my life."

"No, it doesn't," she says. I just stare at her. "That doesn't matter at all. It's a piece of paper. A piece of paper you don't even have, by the way. It means nothing."

"It means everything!" I say.

"Listen to me; it means nothing. You think that some ten minutes you spent with Ben in a room defines what you meant to each other? It doesn't. You define that. What you feel defines that. You loved him. He loved you. You believed in each other. That is what you lost. It doesn't matter whether it's labeled a husband or a boyfriend. You lost the person you love. You lost the future you thought you had."

"Right," I say.

"I was with Steven for thirty-five years before I lost him. Do you think I have more of a right to pain than you do?"

The answer is yes. I do think that. I've been terrified of that. I've been walking about feeling like an amateur, like an impostor, because of it.

"I don't know," I say.

"Well, I don't. Love is love is love. When you lose it, it feels like the shittiest disaster in the world. Just like dog shit."

"Right."

"When I lost Steven, I lost love, but I also lost someone I was attached to."

"Right."

"You didn't have as much time as I did to be attached to the man you loved. But attachment and love are two different things. My heart was broken *and* I didn't remember how to do things without him. I didn't remember who I was. But you, you lived without Ben just last year. You can do it again. You can do it sooner than me. But the love, that's the sharp pain that won't stop. That's the constant ache in your chest. That won't go away easily."

"I just feel like I had him for so little time," I say. It's difficult to talk about. It's difficult because I work so hard to keep the self-pity at bay, and talking like this, talking about all of this, it's like opening the door to my self-pity closet and asking its contents to spill all over the floor. "I didn't have enough time with him," I say, my voice starting to break, my lips starting to quiver. "It wasn't enough time. Six months! That's all I had." I lose my breath. "I only got to be his wife for nine days." I now begin to sob. "Nine days isn't enough. It's not enough."

Susan comes closer to me, and she grabs my hand. She pushes my hair back off my forehead. She catches my eye.

"Sweetheart, I'm telling you, you love someone like that, you love them the right way, and no time would be enough. Doesn't matter if you had thirty years," she tells me. "It wouldn't be enough."

She's right, of course. If I'd had ten more years with Ben, would I be sitting here saying, "It's okay, I had him long enough?" No. It would never have been enough.

"I'm scared," I tell her. "I'm scared that I'll have to move on and meet someone and spend my life with them and it will seem like"—my voice cracks again—"it will seem like Ben was . . . I don't want him to be 'my first husband.'"

Susan nods. "You know, you're in a much different position than I am, and I forget that sometimes. No one begrudges me giving up on my love life. They understand. They know I won't date again. They know I've had my one love and I'm done. But you, you have to meet someone else in this life. I can't imagine how much of a betrayal that would feel to me if I had to do it."

"It *is* a betrayal. All of it feels like betrayal. I had this amazing man—I can't just find another one and forget about him."

"I understand that, Elsie. But you have to find a way to remember him and forget him. You have to find a way to keep him in your heart and in your memories but *do* something *else* with your *life*. Your life cannot be about my son. It can't."

I shake my head. "If my life isn't about him, I don't know what it's about."

"It's about you. Your life has always been about you. That's what makes it your life," she says and smiles at me. "I know nine days is short. I know six months is short. But, trust me when I tell you, if you go on and you marry someone else, and you have kids with them and you love your family and you feel like you would die without them, you won't have lost Ben. Those nine days, those six months, they are a part of your life now, a part of you. They may not have been enough *for* you but they were enough to change you. I lost my son after loving him for twenty-seven years. It's brutal, unending, gutting pain. Do you think I don't deserve to grieve as much as someone who lost their son after forty years? Twenty-seven years is a short time to have a son. Just because it was short, it doesn't mean it didn't happen. It was just short. That's all. Forgive yourself for that, Elsie. It's not your fault your marriage lasted nine days. And it doesn't say a goddamn thing about how much you loved him."

I don't have anything to say back. I want so badly to take all of her words and fit them like the pieces of a puzzle into the hole in my heart. I want to write those words down on little pieces of paper and swallow them, consume them, make them a part of me. Maybe then I could believe them.

I'm quiet for too long; the mood shifts somehow in the silence. I relax and the tears start to dry. Susan moves on, gently. "Did they fire you?"

"No," I say. "But I think they are going to ask me to take some time off."

She looks happy to hear this news, as if it all falls into her master plan.

"Stay with me in Newport then," she says.

"What?"

"Let's get you out of this apartment. Out of Los Angeles. You need a change of scenery for a few weeks."

"Uh . . ."

"I've been thinking about this for a few days, and this is a sign that I'm right. You need time to sit and feel sorry for yourself and get it all out so you can start over. I can help you. Let me help you."

I try to think of a good reason to say no, but . . . I simply don't have one.

MAY

I don't like going home as much as I used to," Ben said to me. We were walking along the streets of Venice Beach. I had wanted to go for a walk in the sand, and Ben always liked to people-watch in Venice. I preferred the quiet, romantic beaches of Malibu, but Ben loved to watch the weirdos along the boardwalk.

"Why?" I asked him. "I thought you said your mom's house was really nice now."

"It is," he said. "But it's too big. It's too empty. It's too . . ."

"What?"

"I don't know. I always feel like I'm going to break something. When my dad was alive, it was not an impressive house. He never cared about that stuff and he hated spending money on, like, crystal vases."

"Your mom has a lot of crystal vases?"

"She could never have them when he was around, so I think she's trying to make the most of the situation."

"Right. She's doing everything she wanted to do when he was around but couldn't."

"Yeah," he said. "But, not really. It's more like she's buying everything she wanted but she's not *doing* anything."

"Well, maybe buying is doing. Maybe for her, that's what's working. Also"—I hesitated to say it and then decided to push it out of my mouth—"maybe it comes from the same place as what you're going through, you know? About how you aren't telling her about us?"

Ben looked at me. "Well, that's because . . ." he started and couldn't seem to find the words to finish. "Maybe," he said, resigned. "I'm just going to tell her soon. Because it's never going to be the right time, and now, I'm just outright lying. Before it was a gray area, but I live with you now. We live together." His mood took a dive, and I could see the moment when it crashed. He let out a heavy sigh. "I've been lying to her."

Maybe I should have made him call her right then. Maybe I should have told him he was right, he was lying. But I couldn't let him be sad. I couldn't watch as he became disappointed in himself.

"You're not lying," I said. "You're doing this your way and now you can see that you really do need to tell her, and you're gonna do it," I said, as if it was the simplest thing in the world.

"Yeah, no, you're absolutely right." He nodded with purpose. "I let this go a bit too far obviously, but it's actually not a big deal. She'll be happy for me. She'll love you." He looked at me with genuine affection. He truly could not understand a world in which people might not like me, or more realistically, a world where people might feel indifferent toward me.

Ben quickly averted his gaze to avoid eye contact with the very thing he wanted to stare at. "Are you seeing this?" he asked me through his teeth. "Are you seeing what I'm seeing?"

"The old guy in the yellow thong skateboarding with a dog?" I asked quietly.

"I promise you, no one is doing that in Malibu," he said, as he put his arm around my shoulders.

I laughed and let him lead me further down the street. He watched the passersby as I disappeared into my own head. I was suddenly nervous about finally meeting his mom. I started to imagine how it would go.

We'd all meet at a formal dinner. I would have to wear a nice outfit and go to a nice restaurant. I'd probably bring a sweater but forget it in the car. I'd be cold the whole time but never say anything. I'd want to go to the bathroom, but I'd be too nervous to even excuse myself. I'd smile so fake and huge that I'd start to feel a little dizzy from all the oxygen. Ben would sit in between the two of us at a round table. We'd face each other head-on. And then I figured out what was really nagging at me. What if the whole time I was sitting across from her, maintaining perfect posture, worrying if there was something in my teeth, she would be thinking, What does he see in her?

OCTOBER

Before I go to Susan's, I discuss taking a leave of absence from my job. Lyle says that he's not comfortable with me coming back right away, and I tell him I understand. But he says when I'm ready my job is here for me. I think Nancy had a lot to do with that, but I just say thank you.

I meet Ana for breakfast and tell her I'm going to stay with Susan.

"What?" she asks. "I just wanted her to talk some sense into you, not take you away." She is clearly unnerved by this. She's throwing food into her mouth quickly. She's barely tasting it before getting more.

"I know," I say. "And thank you for calling her. I think I need to get out of here for a while. I need to find a way to move on. I don't think I can do that here. At least, I can't start it here."

"How long are you leaving for?" She looks like she might cry.

"Not long. A few weeks, tops. I'll be back soon, and you can drive down all the time."

"You really think this is going to help?" she asks me.

"I know that I want it to help," I say. "And I think that's the point."

"Okay," she says. "Do you want me to get your mail and check on the house?"

"Sure," I say.

"Okay." She doesn't say it, but I get the feeling there is a small part of her that is happy to see me go. I have drained her. If I ever stop feeling sorry for myself, it will be time to start feeling sorry for what I've been putting Ana through. I'm not there yet, but I know it's coming. "I like Kevin," I say.

"Okay," she says, not believing me.

"No, really. I was just thrown for a loop is all. I really like him."

"Well, thank you," she says diplomatically. Eventually, I leave and get in my car full of clean clothes and toiletries. I put the address into my phone, pull out of my parking space, and head south.

I ring the doorbell with my bag on my shoulder. I feel like I'm here for a sleepover. Somehow, the house looks so much more inviting this time. It looks less like it will eat me alive when I step into it.

Susan comes to the door with her arms open wide for a hug. She looks genuinely thrilled to see me, which is nice, because I feel like for the past few weeks I simply have not been someone people would be thrilled to see.

"Hi!" she says.

"Hi," I say, a bit more timidly.

"I have a whole evening planned for us," she says before I've even crossed the threshold. "Chinese food, in-home massages, *Steel Magnolias*."

I look at her when I hear *"Steel Magnolias."*

She smiles sheepishly. "I never had a girl to watch it with!"

I laugh and put my things down. "That actually sounds great."

"I'll show you to your room," she says.

"Geez, I feel like I'm at a hotel," I say.

"I decorate when I can't face the day. Which seems to be most days now." The heaviness of her admission startles me. It's always been about me when we talk. I almost don't know what to say to a woman that has lost both her husband and her son.

"Well, I'm here now," I say, brightly. "I can . . ." What? What can I possibly do?

She smiles at me but I can tell her smile can become a frown at any minute. Somehow, it doesn't. She U-turns back to happier thoughts. "Let me show you the guest room!"

"The guest room?" I ask.

She turns to me. "You didn't think I was going to let you sleep in Ben's room, did you?"

"Kind of, I did."

"I've spent far too much time in there, these past couple of weeks, and let me tell you: It only makes it sadder." She doesn't let the emotion deter the moment again. She's dead set on moving through this. She leads me to a gorgeous white room with a white bedspread and white pillows. There are white calla lilies on the desk and Godiva chocolates on the nightstand. I'm not sure if the candles are new, but they haven't been used before. It smells like cotton and soap in here. It smells so good. The whole thing is stunning, really.

"Too much white? I'm sorry. I might be overeager to use the guest room finally."

I laugh. "This is gorgeous, thank you." There is a robe on the bed. She sees me notice it.

"For you, if you want it. I want you to feel pampered here. Comfortable."

"It's great," I say. She's thought of everything. I look behind her to the bathroom and can see Ben's soap message to her.

She sees me looking at that as well. "I couldn't bring myself to wash it away when he was here, I know I won't ever wash it away now."

There it is, finally. I remember trying to find it the last time I was here. I remember why I gave up. And yet, it's right in front of me now. It's like it finally found a way to get me here. His handwriting is so imperfect. He had no idea what he was doing when he did that. He had no idea what it would mean to us.

Susan breaks the silence. "Okay, get settled in, do whatever you wanna do. Masseuse comes in about two hours. I figure we can order Chinese food shortly after that. I'm going to go watch trashy crap television," she says. "And my only rule is that you forget about the real world while you are here and just cry anytime you want to. Get it out, you know? That's my only rule."

"Sounds good," I say, and she takes off. I find myself slightly uncomfortable here, which takes me by surprise because I have been so comfortable around her recently. She has brought me such comfort. But I am now in her house, in her world. I am also in the house that Ben grew up in, and it feels fitting to cry. Yet, I'm not on the verge of tears. In fact, I feel okay. I can't help but think that maybe because it's okay to cry, I can't.

MAY

"Marry me," he said.

"Marry you?" I was in the driver's seat of his car. I had just picked him up from the doctor's office again. He had bent down to pet a dog that morning and his back had re-spasmed. Apparently, this can happen when you don't take the pain medication the doctor prescribes. Ben got a lecture on how he needed to take the pain medication so he would move normally again and work out the muscles. I had told him that earlier in the week, but he didn't listen to me. So there I was, driving him home from the doctor once again. Only this time, I was being proposed to while he was drugged out on painkillers in the passenger seat.

"Yes! Just marry me. You are perfect," he said. "It's hot in here."

"Okay, okay. I'm taking you home."

"But you will marry me?" he asked, smiling over at me, watching me drive.

"I think that's the painkillers talking," I said.

"Drunk words are sober thoughts," he said, and then he fell asleep.

OCTOBER

I sit out by Susan's pool, reading magazines and getting a tan. Susan and I play gin rummy and drink a lot of iced tea. The days come and go, and I have nothing to show for them. I walk through her herb garden, and sometimes I pick lemons from her fruit trees and then put them in my drinks. I'm finally gaining weight. I haven't stepped on a scale, but I can see the roundness back in my cheeks.

When the days start to cool down and the Santa Ana winds take over the nights, I sometimes sit by the outdoor chimney. I think I'm the first one to light it. But after the first couple of times, it starts to smell like a warm, toasty campfire, and if I close my eyes long enough, I can convince myself I'm on a traditional vacation.

Otherwise, Susan is usually with me, guiding me through her own little version of Widow Rehab. She starts to cry sometimes but always seems to stop herself. I'm pretty sure at night in bed alone is the only time she can really let herself go. Every once in a while when I am trying to fall asleep myself, I can hear her sob from the other side of the house. I never go to her room. I never mention it the next day. She likes to be alone with her pain. She doesn't like to share it. During the day, she wants to be there for me, show me how this is done, and I'm happy to oblige. However imperfect, her system is working for her. She's functional and composed when she needs to be, and she is in tune with her feelings in her own way. I guess I am learning from the best because I do feel a little bit better.

When Susan isn't around, sometimes I sneak into Ben's old bedroom. I imagined it would be here waiting for him, frozen in time from when he left it. I thought maybe I'd find old high school trophies and pictures of prom, maybe one of those felt flags I've seen people pin on their walls. I want to learn more about my husband. I want to consume more information about him. Spend more time with him. But instead, I find a small room that had been cleared out long before Ben died. There's a bed with a blue striped comforter, and in one corner, a half-torn sticker from some skateboard company. Sometimes, I sit on the bed and hear how quiet this house is with just one person in it. It must be so quiet for Susan when I am not here.

I think of a world where I am a mother of three, married to a handsome man. We own an oversize SUV, and he coaches girls' soccer. He is faceless, nameless. To tell the truth, in the scenario, he doesn't matter. I keep trying to think of a way to work Ben into this new life I could have. I could name my son Ben, but that feels too obvious and, quite frankly, too small a gesture. I am beginning to understand why people start funds and charities in other people's names. It would feel good to work at the Benjamin S. Ross Foundation for Not Eating Fruity Pebbles. But I know there isn't actually anything to rally against for him.

To tell the truth, I lack passion for much of anything. Sometimes I wish I had passion for something—which, if you think about it, is a kind of passion in itself. Albeit, somewhat weak.

Susan always plans things for me to do to keep me busy, even if it is just a structured day of lounging and watching television. Sometimes the "camp counselor" shtick she has going on can be a bit grating, but it's not my place to tell her to back off. She wants to help me and she is helping. I'm just that little bit more functional each day.

"My friend Rebecca is in town tonight," she says to me one afternoon. "I was thinking we could all go out to this new Mediterranean place I found."

This is the first time that Susan is inviting me out with any of her friends. It seems odd, somehow, to participate in something together that involves other people. I'm not sure why, though. It feels like this alliance is a private one, one not to be shared. As if she's my mistress mother. But I think I'm really just scared of what to call her. How will she introduce me? "This is my son's widow?" I don't want that.

"Oh, I don't know," I say. I'm fiddling with the pages of a magazine I read days ago. The pages are transparent and curled at the edges from when I left it by the edge of the pool and attempted a cannonball.

"Please?" she says.

"I mean—" I start. She abruptly sits down and puts her hands out, as if she's about to make a great proposition.

"Look, Rebecca isn't the best. She's kind of . . . snobby. Well, she's really snobby. And I could just never stand her snobby little attitude about our kids. When her oldest got into Stanford, it was Stanford this and Stanford that and whoopity-do, isn't Patrick the smartest kid in the world? She always acted like Ben was such a disappointment."

"Wow, okay, now I really don't want to go. And I don't understand why you want to go," I say.

"Well, get this!" Susan says excitedly. "She always, always wanted a daughter. Always. She's got two boys. Neither married yet." Susan catches herself and blushes. "I'm a terrible person, right? I am. I'm trying to use my daughter-in-law to make my friend jealous."

I don't know whether it's that I already hate Rebecca or that I like the idea of indulging Susan, but I agree. "Should we wear matching dresses?" I say. "Maybe tell her we just got back from pottery making together?"

Susan laughs heartily. "Thank you for understanding that I am sometimes a total bitch."

We take naps and then get ready for dinner. I can hear Susan changing her clothes over and over. It's odd to see her so insecure. When we get to the restaurant, we are told that Rebecca has already been seated. We walk through the dining area, Susan just the littlest bit in front of me, and I see her make eye contact. Rebecca stands up to greet us. "Only two minutes late!" Rebecca says, and I see Susan start to roll her eyes. Rebecca turns to me. "So this is the daughter-in-law you won't stop talking about."

And I realize that, more than anything, what made me want to come to dinner was that for the first time, I feel like I am Susan's daughter-in-law, plain and simple. The bizarre circumstances don't matter. I am someone's new, shiny daughter-in-law.

NOVEMBER

Ana is coming down to visit tonight. Susan invited her to stay for the weekend and she accepted. She should be here any minute, and I am excited to show her how nice it can be to just sit by a pool and feel the sun beating down on you. I went to the store this afternoon to get us snacks and wine coolers. I got the wine coolers because I thought they were funny, but then I drank one this afternoon, and you know what? They are actually pretty tasty.

Ana shows up around six, and Susan has a whole dinner planned. I get the impression Susan is deathly bored. I think my being here makes it easier to fill her days, but before Ben died, before she and I became close, she was supremely, soul-suckingly bored. She's in a lot of book clubs, but as far as I can tell, that's about it. So when Ana comes for dinner, it gives Susan an excuse for a seven-course meal.

I walk into the kitchen and find an extra apron. I put it on and splay my hands out. "What can I do?" I ask.

Susan is chopping vegetables so fast I'm sure she's about to lose a digit, but she doesn't. Her cutting board is full of various chopped stuff that she slides easily into a big bowl.

"Can you hand me that jar?" she asks. I do. She sprinkles whatever the hell is in it, possibly Parmesan cheese, onto the salad and puts the salad on the table.

"Salad's ready. The roast beef is cooking. Mashed potatoes

are mashed. Yorkshire pudding is in the oven. I think I'm pretty much done," she tells me. "I hope Ana isn't on a diet. I cooked all the food in Orange County."

The doorbell rings, and I answer. Ana is wearing a white dress and a black cardigan; she's holding a bottle of wine in one hand and her purse with the other. I've spoken to Ana on the phone many times since I got here, but it swells my heart to see her face. She is the life I want back.

She hugs me, and I can smell her perfume. It reminds me of our early twenties, when we went to bars and I stood in the corner nursing a fruity drink while she was in the center of the room. It reminds me of Sunday morning brunches and hangovers. A single life. A single life I loved before I knew anything better.

It's been so long since I've smelled Ben that I have forgotten the scent. I could recognize it in an instant, but I can't describe it, I can't feel it. I knew this would happen. I feared this would happen. Now that it has, it's not so bad. It is. But it isn't.

"You look great!" she says. It brightens my mood immediately.

"Thank you! So do you!" I don't like that our conversation has a somewhat formal quality to it. We are best friends, and best friends don't talk like this.

We walk into the kitchen, and Ana hugs Susan. "What can I do?" Ana asks, and Susan waves her off.

"You girls are so polite," she says. "I'm almost done. Have a seat. Do you want a drink?"

"At least let me get those," Ana says and starts looking for glasses.

"Top cupboard above the dishwasher," Susan says without looking. Ana grabs three glasses and pours us some wine.

It's about five minutes before we sound like ourselves again, and I think how odd it is that I've only been away from Ana for a few weeks, and yet, I already feel estranged. Then it occurs to me that I haven't been away from Ana for a few weeks. I've been away from her since Ben died. I let myself die when he did. I wonder if it was longer than that. I wonder if when I met Ben, part of me lost Ana. If so, I want her back. I want what we had back.

MAY

Ben's back had gotten so bad he couldn't move. He had called in sick to work for three days. I tried to go to work on Monday but left halfway through the day because he was stuck and didn't think he could get out of bed by himself. By Wednesday, I had given up trying to go to work and just stayed with him.

He was pathetic about the pain and acted like a huge baby. He would groan and complain as if he had flesh-eating bacteria every time I asked him how he was doing. But to me, he was adorably ill. I liked being needed by him. I liked making his food for him, running his baths for him, massaging his muscles. I liked caring for him, taking care of him. It made me feel like I had a real purpose. It felt so good to make him feel even the littlest bit better.

It had been a few days since he'd asked me to marry him, but I was having a hard time ignoring it. He was just drugged up. But what if he did mean it? Why was I so affected by it? It was just a silly thing he said when he was on Vicodin. But how much does Vicodin really mess with you? It doesn't make you say things you don't mean.

I think I was just overly excitable about it because I loved him in a way I'd never thought possible. I knew that if I lost him, if I had to live without him, it would crush me. I needed him and I didn't just need him now, I needed him in the future. I needed him always. I wanted him always. I wanted him to be the father of my children. It's such a silly statement now; people say it all the time, they throw it around like it's nothing. And some people treat it like it is nothing, but it wasn't nothing to me. I wanted to have children with him someday. I wanted to be a parent with him. I wanted to have a child that was half him and half me. I wanted to commit to him and sacrifice for him. I wanted to lose part of myself in order to gain some of him. I wanted to marry him. So I wanted him to have meant it. I wanted it to be real.

As he got better and better, he asked me to take one more day off work to spend with him. He said that I had been so great to him, he wanted one day to return the favor. It wasn't difficult to oblige him.

I woke to him standing over me with a tray of breakfast foods.

"Voilà!" he said, grinning as he watched me. I sat up in bed and let him set the tray in front of me. The tray was full of things I would normally consider mutually exclusive: a bagel *and* a croissant; French toast and waffles; cream cheese and butter. He'd even toasted a Pop-Tart.

"I think I went a bit overboard," he said. "But it was all really easy. You can get all of this at your local grocer's freezer."

"Thank you," I said. I smiled and kissed his lips as he bent down toward me. He didn't moan or wail in pain.

"Are you taking the pain medication finally?"

"Nope!" he said proudly. "I just feel better."

"You just feel better?"

"Yes! This is what I mean. You people and your Western medicine," he said with a smile. "I really feel fine. I swear."

He walked around the side of the bed and sat down next to me. He stared at my food as I began to attack it.

"Did you want some?" I offered.

"Took you long enough. Jesus," he said as he grabbed the Pop-Tart. "Were you going to eat this all yourself?"

I kissed his cheek and took the Pop-Tart out of his mouth. I offered him a waffle instead. "I was really looking forward to this. Brown sugar and cinnamon is my favorite flavor." I bit a huge chunk out of it before he could try to wrestle it back from me. He resigned himself to the waffle.

"I think we should get married," he said. "What do you think of that?"

I laughed, completely unsure of how serious he was. "Why do you keep joking like that?" I said. I sounded more exasperated than I wanted to.

"I'm not joking," he said.

"Yes, you are." I finished the Pop-Tart and wiped my hands. "Stop joking about it or you'll end up married," I said.

"Oh, is that so?"

"Yes, that's so."

"So, if I said, 'Let's go get married today,' you'd go get married today?"

"What are you doing? Daring me?"

"I'm just asking a question, is all," he said, but the tone of his voice wasn't one of a hypothetical question. I suddenly became embarrassed and anxious.

"Well, I just . . ." I said. "*You* wouldn't."

"Would *you*? That is my question."

"You can't do that! You can't ask me if I would if you wouldn't!"

He grabbed my hand. "*You* said I wouldn't. I didn't say that."

"Are you asking me to marry you for real?" I asked, finally unsure of how else to figure out what conversation we were actually having.

"I want to be with you for the rest of my life and I know that it is soon, but I would like to marry you. I don't want to ask you to marry me if it freaks you out or you think it's crazy."

"For real?" I was too excited by this idea to trust my own ears.

"Elsie! Jesus! Yes!"

"I don't think it's crazy!" I said. I grabbed him as tears started building in my eyes. I looked at him.

"You don't?" I could see his eyes start to water as well. They were growing red. His face was no longer carefree. It was sincere and moved.

"No!" I could no longer control my voice. I could barely control my limbs.

"You'll marry me?" He grabbed my head on both sides and focused my face on his. I could feel my hair crinkling between his hands and my ears. I knew we both looked silly on our knees in the middle of our crumpled bed, but I could focus on nothing but him.

"Yes," I said softly and stunned, and then it grew louder and louder. "Yes! Yes! Yes!" I said, kissing him. He was holding on to me tightly. I have no doubt that some of our neighbors thought they were overhearing something they shouldn't have.

We fell back onto the bed and proved them right. "I love you," he said to me over and over. He whispered it and he moaned it. He spoke it and he sang it. He loved me. He loved me. He loved me.

And just like that, I was going to be part of a family again.

NOVEMBER

By the time Sunday afternoon rolls around, Ana has been well indoctrinated into this new, luxurious lifestyle.

She, Susan, and I are lying out by the pool. The weather has started to cool during the nights, but the days are still hot enough to lie outside. Given that it's early November, it makes me especially glad to live in Southern California. Winter is upon us, and yet, I can barely feel a chill.

Ana read an entire book this weekend. Susan cooked every meal as if she was a gourmet chef. I mostly lazed around like I have been doing, getting to the point where I am so bored that I yearn for some sort of life again. A couple of times yesterday I pondered whether to pick up a hobby. No final decision has been made.

We are all in a little bit of a food coma from the soufflé Susan made for our "lunch dessert," as she called it. We are all quiet at the moment, but I decide to break the silence.

"So what are you and Kevin doing this week?" I ask.

"Oh, not sure," Ana said. "Although, did I tell you? He asked me to meet his parents."

"He did?" I ask.

"How long have you two been together?" Susan asks.

"Oh, just a few months now. But I really like him. He's . . ."

"He's really sweet," I say to Susan. I mean it, so it comes across like I mean it and I think it touches Ana. I still maintain that he's a bit blah all around, but you don't need spice in the boyfriend of your best friend. You need him to be reliable, kindhearted, and sincere. You need to know he won't hurt her, if he can help it. You need to know he has good intentions. By all of those accounts, I like Kevin. (But he's boring.)

"Are his parents from around here?" I ask.

"He's from San Jose. So it's a few hours' drive, but he said he really wanted them to meet me."

This touches a nerve with Susan. I can see it. Ana probably can't, but I've done nothing but sit around with this woman for five weeks now. I know her like the back of my hand. I also knew her son and I'm learning that they aren't altogether terribly different people.

Susan lightly excuses herself as Ana and I continue to talk. I remember when I was happy like she is, when Ben felt invincible to me like I'm sure Kevin feels to her now. I remember how I felt like nothing in the world could take that feeling away from me. There was nothing I could not do. But instead of hating her for being happy, I can see now that I am feeling melancholy, nostalgic, and a little jealous. It's not perfect, but it's certainly a lot healthier than last month.

Ana gets her things ready, and I walk her out to her car. She's meeting Kevin for dinner tonight in L.A., and I don't begrudge her leaving early for it. I'm also exhausted from the company. I've been alone so many hours lately that talking to two people at once has been a struggle for my attention span.

"Oh!" she says, turning toward her car and digging through it. "I forgot that I brought your mail." She finds it and hands me a big chunk of envelopes. I already know that some of them will have Ben's name on them. Truth be told, I was happy to let the piles accumulate in my mailbox hours away. If my marriage certificate isn't in here, I'm gonna wig out.

"Awesome," I say and give her a hug. "Thank you. For this, and for coming here. It really means a lot to me."

"I miss you, girl," Ana says, as she gets in her car. "But you seem happier. Just a little."

I don't want to seem happier, even if I do feel it a little bit. It feels wrong to be labeled "happier," even if it is incremental. The woman that loved Ben as fiercely as I did would never feel any degree of happy after losing him.

"Drive safe," I say. "Tell Kevin I said hi."

"You got it."

When she's gone, I rifle through the envelopes looking for one from the County Recorder's Office. I come up short. My stomach sinks, and I know that I have to call them tomorrow. I cannot ignore this problem. I cannot pretend it doesn't exist. I need to know what is going on with the legality of my marriage. I have to face it.

At the bottom of the stack is a hand-addressed envelope. The writing is shaky and uneven. I don't have to look at the return address to know who it is from.

Mr. George Callahan.

I put the other envelopes on the sidewalk and sit down on the curb. I tear open the envelope.

Dear Elsie,

I hope you don't mind that I asked the library for your mailing address. They were hesitant to give it to me, but an old man has his ways. First of all, I wanted to tell you that I don't know why you punched that guy but that I hope you won't mind me telling Lorraine about it. It was the most interesting thing to happen in months!

The real reason I am writing is because Lorraine is not well. The doctors have taken her from our home and she is now staying in the hospital. Unfortunately, old age is really starting to catch up to her. I am staying with her here at Cedars-Sinai. Sometimes I take a cab back to our home and get some of her things, but most of the time, I stay right here next to her. She is sleeping most of the time, but that's all right by me. Just being next to her, hearing her breathe, feels like a miracle sometimes.

I wanted to say that I am sorry for telling you to move on. I am now looking at the prospect of living without the love of my life, and I find it daunting and miserable. I do not know how I will live a day after I lose her. I feel like I am standing on the edge of a huge, black hole, waiting to fall.

Maybe there is one person for everyone. If so, Lorraine was mine. Maybe the reason I was able to get over Esther was because she wasn't the right one. Maybe the reason you can't get over Ben is because he was.

I just wanted you to know that even at almost ninety, I'm still learning new things every day, and I think I am learning now that when you lose the thing you love most in the world, things can't be okay again.

I'd like to say I miss you at the library, but truthfully, I don't get down there very much.

As I've reread this now, I realize it's a little bit of a mopey letter, so I hope you'll excuse my rambling.

Thanks for listening.

Best,

George Callahan

I walk inside and ask Susan where her stationery is. She gives me some, and I sit down at her kitchen table. I write until my hand feels like it's going to fall off. My palm feels cramped, my fingers ache. I have been holding the pen too tightly. I have been pressing the pen down too hard. I read over what I have written and see that it makes absolutely no sense. It is barely legible. So I throw it away and I write what my heart is screaming at him.

Dear George,

I was wrong. You are wrong.

We can live again. I'm not sure if we can love again, but we can live again.

I believe in you.

Love,
Elsie

MAY

We had filled the day with discussions about how to get married and where to get married and when to get married. I realized I didn't know the first thing about marriage. Logistically, I mean. How does one get married? What does one need to do?

I found out pretty quickly that Ben was thinking of a real wedding. He was thinking of a wedding with bridesmaids and white dresses, flowers in the centers of round tables. Champagne flutes. A dance floor. I wasn't opposed to that; it just hadn't occurred to me. His proposal felt unorthodox; our relationship felt electric and exciting. It seemed strange to seal it with something so conventional. It felt more appropriate to put on some clothes and drive down to city hall. Large weddings with long guest lists and speeches felt like things that people did when they had been together for years. They felt rational and practiced, well thought out and logical—like a business decision. I wanted to do something crazy. Something you'd only do if you were in as much love as we were.

"Okay, so you're thinking a small wedding?" he asked me.

"I mean, it can be as big as you want it to be," I said. "If it were up to me, there wouldn't be anyone there. Just me, you, and the officiant."

"Oh wow, okay, so you're talking about straight-up eloping," he said.

"Aren't you?"

"Well, I was thinking we could do it with our families and really plan something, you know? But now that you say it, eloping does sound much easier. Certainly more exciting," he said as he smiled at me and grabbed my hand.

"Really?" I said.

"Yeah. How does one go about eloping?" he said, and when he did, his eyes were so bright, his face almost maniacally excited, I knew he was on board.

"I have no idea." I laughed. Everything felt funny to me. Everything felt invigorating. I felt light and giddy, like the wind could knock me over.

"Ah!" he said, excited. "Okay! Let's do it! Let's get married now. Can we do it today? Can we, like, go somewhere right now and do it?"

"Now?" I said. We hadn't even showered yet.

"No better time than the present," he said, grabbing me into his arms and holding me. I could tell he was smelling my hair. I just lay against his chest and let him.

"Great," I said. "Let's do it today."

"Okay." He ran out of the room and grabbed a suitcase.

"What are you doing?" I asked him.

"Well, we're going to Vegas, right? Isn't that how people elope?"

"Oh!" Honestly, that thought hadn't even occurred to me. But he was exactly right. Vegas was where people went to do those things. "Okay! Let's go."

Ben was throwing clothes into the bag and checking his watch. "If we leave in the next twenty minutes or so, we can be there by 10:00 p.m. I'm sure there are chapels open at ten."

That's when it hit me. This was really happening. I was about to get married.

NOVEMBER

"You okay?" Susan asks me from the kitchen. I am addressing the envelope to Mr. Callahan.

"Actually, I am really good. You okay?"

"Mmm-hmm," she said. "I wanted to talk to you about something actually."

"Oh?"

"Well." She sits down next to me at the breakfast nook table. "I closed Ben's bank account."

"Oh," I say. I didn't know she was going to do that. I don't really know if it's her place to do that.

"It really is none of my business," she said. "But I did it because I knew that if you did it, or if I tried to get you to do it, you would not take the money."

"Oh," I say. "I don't feel comfortable—"

"Listen." She grabs my hand. "You were his wife. He would want you to have it. What am I going to do with it? Add it to the pile of money I was left from Steven? It means more in your hands, and Ben would want it that way. It's not some extravagant amount. Ben was a smart guy, but he wasn't brilliant with money. Neither was his father. Actually, if I hadn't taken out the life insurance policy on Steven when we were in our twenties, I'd be in a much different place right now, but that's beside the point. Take the money, okay?"

"Uh . . ."

"Elsie," she says to me. "Take the damn money. I didn't spend forty-five minutes on the phone with the bank convincing them I had the authority to do it for my health. I did it behind your back so I could deceive you enough to get the check in your name." She smiled at me, and I laughed.

"Okay," I say. It doesn't even occur to me to ask how much it is. It seems irrelevant and somehow perverse, like knowing what color underwear your dermatologist is wearing.

"By the way, while we are talking about uncomfortable and depressing things, what did the county say about your marriage certificate? Did you call?"

I am ashamed. I feel like I stayed out past curfew when I knew we had church tomorrow morning. "No."

"What is the matter with you?" she asks me, and her voice is clearly exasperated.

"I know. I need to get it."

"Not just for you, Elsie. For me too. I want to see it. He never told me about it. He never confided in me why he was doing it. I just . . . I want to see the fucking thing, you know? Look it in the face and know it's real."

"Oh," I say.

"Not that your marriage wasn't real. I know you well enough to know that's true. But I just . . . you have a kid and you daydream about him getting married. Getting married was the last big thing he did and I wasn't there. Jesus, was I so terrible that he couldn't tell me what he was doing? That I couldn't have been there?"

I was surprised that this was coming up now because she seemed like it was all behind her, but now I understood that it had never been behind her. It had been right there on the surface the whole time, so large and imposing that it colored everything she saw.

"He wasn't . . ." I say. "You weren't terrible. It wasn't that. It had nothing to do with that."

"Well, what then?" she asks me. "I'm sorry that I sound upset. I'm trying not to sound . . . I just . . . I thought I knew him."

"You did know him!" I say, and this time I am grabbing her hand. "You did know him. And he knew you and cared about you. And maybe the way he did it was misguided, but he loved you. He thought if he told you . . . he thought you couldn't handle it. He worried that you wouldn't feel like you two were a family anymore."

"But he should have told me before you two got married. He should have at least called," she says to me.

And she's right. He should have. He knew that. But I didn't.

MAY

We were two hours outside of Las Vegas when the cold feet set in. Ben was driving. I was in the front seat calling wedding chapels. I also called hotels to see where we could stay the night. My body was thrilled and anxious. The car could barely contain me, but I could see that Ben was starting to tense.

He pulled over into a Burger King and said he wanted a burger. I wasn't hungry, I couldn't possibly eat, but I got one too and let it sit in front of me.

"I'm thinking we should go to the Best Little Chapel," I told him. "They take care of everything there. And then we can stay at either Caesars Palace, which has a pretty good deal on a suite, or interestingly enough, the Hooters hotel has really cheap rooms right now."

Ben was looking at his burger, and when I stopped talking he put it down abruptly. I mean, he basically dropped it.

"I need to tell my mom," he said. "I can't do this without telling my mom."

"Oh," I said. Honestly, I hadn't even thought about his mom, or my own parents. I had briefly thought about inviting Ana to come and be a witness, but I quickly decided I didn't want that either. I just wanted Ben and me, together. And whoever the officiant was.

"Don't you want to invite Ana or something?" he asked. I

did not like the turn the conversation had taken. The turn in the conversation was about to create a turn in the trip, which had the very real consequence of a turn in this marriage.

"Well, no," I said. "I thought we just wanted it to be the two of us."

"I did," he said. "Well, no, you did." He wasn't being combative, but I was still feeling defensive. "I just think that I was being overzealous before. I think I should tell my mom. I think if she found out afterward that she would be heartbroken."

"Why?" I asked.

"Because she wasn't there. That her only child got married and she wasn't there, I don't know."

This was what I had been afraid of. Suddenly, I felt my whole life slipping away from me. I'd only been engaged for four hours, but in those four hours I saw a life for myself that I wanted. Just in the time we had been in the car, I'd thought so much about what our night would be like, what our tomorrow would be like, that I was already attached to it. I had replayed it so many times in my mind that I felt like I'd already lived it. I didn't want to lose what I thought I already had. If Ben called his mother, we weren't going to get back in the car and drive straight to Nevada. We were going to get back in the car and drive straight to Orange County.

"I don't know if that's . . ." I started, but I wasn't sure how to finish. "This is about you and me. Are you saying you don't want to do this?"

"No!" he said. "I'm just . . . maybe we shouldn't be doing this right now."

"I cannot believe you." I thought I was going to leave it at that, but the words kept coming out of my mouth. "I didn't make you propose to me. I wasn't the one who suggested we get married in the first place. This was all your doing! I have been telling you for months to tell your mother! So how the fuck do I end up two hours outside of Las Vegas jilted in a Burger King, huh? Explain that to me."

"You don't understand!" He was starting to get animated and upset.

"Why don't I understand? What part of this don't I understand? You asked me to marry you. I said yes. I suggested we elope. You said yes. We got in the car. We're halfway to Nevada and you're calling it off while you're eating a fucking Whopper."

Ben shook his head. "I can't expect you to understand, Elsie." Our voices were starting to attract attention, so Ben got up from the table and I followed him outside.

"What does that mean?" I yelled at him, pushing the door out of my way like it was the one doing this to me.

"It means you don't have a family!" He turned to face me. "You don't even try to get along with your parents. You don't understand how I feel about my mom."

"You're kidding me, right?" I couldn't believe he'd said that. I wished I could have time-traveled back to five seconds before so I could have stopped him from saying that and we could have continued on with our lives without him ever having said that to me.

"No! I'm not kidding. You don't get it."

"Oh, I get it, Ben. I get it. I get that you're a coward who hasn't had the balls to tell his mom he's even dating someone and now, and now I'm getting screwed for it. That's what I get."

"It's not like that," he said, but his voice was resigned. It wasn't passionate.

"What is it then?"

"Can we just get in the car?"

"I'm not getting in the car with you," I said as I crossed my arms. It was colder outside than I would have liked and my jacket was lying on the front seat, but I didn't want to go near that car, even if I had to suffer for it.

"Please? Don't make a scene out here. I'm not saying we shouldn't get married. I want to marry you. I just . . . want to tell my mom first. There's no need for us to rush this."

"You've had six months to tell your mom! And you always come up with a reason why not. How many times have I heard 'Now I'm really going to tell my mom'? But you know what? She's not a part of this relationship. This is about you and me. It's about what you want and what I want. And what I want is to be with the kind of man that wants to marry me so bad, nothing will stop him. I want to be loved by someone who loves me so much he can't think straight. I want you to love me in a way that makes you stupid and impractical. I *want* to rush into this. Rushing into it is romantic. It makes me feel alive. It makes me feel like I am jumping off a cliff and I know I'll be *fine* because that is how much *I trust you*. And I deserve you jumping off a cliff for me because I am prepared to do it for you. You think I don't know anything about family because I don't get along with my parents? Ana is my family. I love her more than I could possibly love another person, other than you. And I thought about her and I thought, No, I don't need her here for this. I just need Ben. So fuck you, I don't know family. That's not what's happening here at all. What's happening here is that I am ready to risk everything for you. And you are not ready to do it for me."

Ben was quiet for a long time. He had started to cry. I thought that it was a manly cry and couldn't help wanting to hold him despite my furor.

"How do things get fucked up so quickly?" he said. His voice was quiet. It wasn't a whisper. It was just sad. It lacked the confidence I was used to hearing in him.

"What?" I said. My tone was curt and pissed.

"I just don't understand how things can go from great to shitty so quickly. I don't know how I got us here. I love you so much, and I should have told my mom earlier, and I didn't and . . . All of those things you just talked about, I want those. I want that with you. I want to give that to you. I love you the way you want to be loved. I'm telling you that. I am the man to do that for you. I just don't know how I derailed so quickly from showing you that."

He turned to me, his eyes drying up but still pleading. "I want to marry you," he said.

"No, Ben," I said and I started to turn away from him, but he grabbed my arm. He grabbed it hard. "I don't want you to—"

"You are right," he said. "You are right. I want that. I want you. I want what you said. I want to risk everything for you. I want to be stupid with you and reckless with you. I will figure out a way to tell my mom. We'll tell her together and she'll love you. And . . . I want you."

"No, it's not . . . it shouldn't be . . ." I said, trying to find the words that meant "I don't want to do this now because it's all ruined." I settled on "You don't have to do this. I'll calm down and we can wait until we tell your mom." The minute I said it, I believed it. It softened me to see that I needed to be there for him as much as I needed him to be there for me.

Ben listened to me, but he was unmoved. "No! I was wrong! I got scared. But I want you. Please." He got down on one knee. "Marry me."

I was silent and unsure. Was this good for him? Was it what

he wanted? He seemed so genuine now. His eyes were pleading with me to listen to him, to marry him. But I didn't want to have forced his hand. I didn't want this to be something he did because I made him do it. And yet, Ben looked so in love with me, truthfully. He looked like all he wanted in the world was me. It looked so real. It was real. Ben yelled from the base of his throat. *"Marry me, Elsie Porter! Marry me!"*

I pulled him up from the pavement and held him. "I don't want you to do anything that— " I stopped myself and asked what I felt. "Are you sure?"

"I'm sure. I'm so sorry. I'm sure."

A smile crept onto my face faster than I could stop it. "Okay!" I exclaimed.

"Really?" he asked as he spun me around. I nodded. "Oh my God," he said. He buried his head in my shoulder. "I love you so much. I love you so much."

"I love you too. I'm sorry," I said. "I shouldn't have said those things. I just . . . I didn't realize how much I wanted to marry you until . . . It doesn't matter," I said. "I'm sorry. We can take all the time you need."

"No," he said. "I don't need any time at all. Get in the car. We're going to Vegas."

He opened my car door and then got into his side. Before he started the engine, he grabbed my face and kissed me, hard.

"Okay," he said, breathing in deeply. "Nevada, here we come."

NOVEMBER

It was my fault," I say to her. "He wanted to tell you before we got married. He was ready to call it off, actually, until he had time to tell you. But I convinced him not to."

"Oh," Susan says. She is quiet and thoughtful. "When was this?"

"We were on our way to Las Vegas. He wanted to turn around and drive home. He wanted to wait until you knew. Give you the chance to be there."

"Oh," she says. "I didn't realize you were married in Las Vegas." The tone in her voice isn't judgmental necessarily, but it certainly brings out any insecurity I might have over having been married in the tackiest place on earth.

"But I didn't want to. He said I didn't understand family, and at the time I told him that was a terrible thing to say to me, but I think he might have had a point."

"Hmm," she says.

"Anyway, I'm sorry. He wanted to tell you. He didn't feel comfortable doing something so big without you. He loved you. He cared about you a lot and I didn't understand. I was being selfish and I just . . . I really, really wanted to marry him. I think on some level Ben made me feel like I wasn't alone anymore and I thought . . ." I start to cry. "I think I was afraid that you'd tell him how ridiculous we were being and he would listen to you. I knew that if he talked to you, he would listen to you. I was afraid I'd lose him."

"But why would you break up because of that? You wouldn't. At the very most, he'd just decide to wait longer to get married."

"You're right." I shake my head, disappointed in myself. "You're absolutely right. But it didn't feel that way at the time. It felt so scary. We were standing at a rest stop and it was the difference between turning right out of the lot and turning left. It felt so *real*. It felt so . . . I wanted to belong to something, belong to someone, you know?"

"Mmm," she says. I don't even know what I'm about to say next until it comes out of my mouth.

"I think I wanted to meet you after we were married, because I thought . . ." Ugggggh, the lump in my throat is so huge, the tears waiting to drop are so heavy. "My own parents don't seem to think very much of me, and I thought, if you met me before . . . I thought you wouldn't like me. You'd want someone better for your son. I was afraid to give you that chance."

"Wow," she says. "Okay." She pats my hand and gets up from the table. "I just need a little while to gather my thoughts. There is a lot of stuff going through my mind right now and I know that not all of it is rational."

"Okay," I say. "I just wanted you to—"

"Stop talking," she snaps at me. She breathes in deeply and breathes out sharply. "God dammit, Elsie."

I stare at her, she stares back, trying to bite her tongue.

"You don't make it easy," she says. "I try so hard! I try so hard."

"I know you do, I just—"

She shakes her head. "It's not your fault. It's not your fault." She isn't speaking to me, I don't think. "It just . . . *ah*. You couldn't have waited? You couldn't have given me a chance? You didn't even give me a chance."

"I know, Susan, I just . . . I was scared!"

"With everything that I've gone through? You couldn't have just said all of this from the beginning?"

"I didn't know how to say it . . ." I tell her. If I'm being honest with myself, I have to admit I'm not sure I knew it was relevant until I put the pieces together, until I really thought about it.

"I have been thinking for months that my son never even wanted me at his wedding, and now you're telling me he did and you stopped him."

I am quiet. What can I say?

"Elsie!" she yells. She is shrill and teary. I don't want the old Susan back. I want her to stay new Susan.

"I'm sorry!" I say. My eyes start to blur, my lips quivering. "I just . . . Susan, I want you and me to be okay. Are we okay?"

"I'm going to go. I'm going to leave this room. I . . ." She turns and puts her head in her hands and then she breathes in.

She leaves the room, and it suddenly feels so big and hollow.

It is the next morning before Susan feels composed enough to talk to me. I can only imagine what thoughts ran through her mind all night. I have a feeling she spent a great deal of the previous evening hating me and calling me names in her head.

"Thank you for telling me that last night," she says, as she sits down next to me in the living room. I had been fast-forwarding through the contents of her TiVo and eating one of her Danishes from the kitchen. I'll tell you, it feels weird to be a guest in someone's house when they are rip-shit pissed at you.

I nod to her.

"I can't imagine that was easy to tell me, but truthfully, it is good news to me. It makes me feel better to know that Ben had the inclination to tell me. Even if he didn't actually do it."

I nod again. It's her time to talk. I'm just keeping quiet.

"Anyway, it's in the past. I didn't know you then, you didn't know me then. It does neither of us any good to hold grudges. Ben made his own decisions, regardless of how we may have tried to influence them. He is responsible for what he did. You are not. I am not. He loved you enough to marry you the way he did. What mother doesn't want that for her son? You know, you have a boy and you raise him right and you hope that you've raised the kind of son that knows how to love and does it well. Especially as a mother, you hope that your son is sensitive and passionate; you hope that he knows how to treat women well. I did my job. He was all of those things. And he loved. He spent his short time on this earth loving. He loved you."

"Thank you," I say. "I'm still sorry I didn't tell you that earlier."

"Put it out of your head." She waves her hand at me. "The other thing that I want to tell you is . . . I would have liked you," she says. "I don't pretend to understand your relationship with your parents. That is between you and them. But I would have liked you. I would have wanted you to marry my son."

Hearing her say that, I get the feeling that I have done all of these things out of order. I should have met her, then married him; if I did, maybe this wouldn't have happened. Maybe Ben would be here next to me, eating peanuts and throwing the shells in an ashtray.

"Thank you," I say to her.

"I've thought a lot about you and I recently. I think I haven't truly begun to cope with Ben's death. I think that I am still mourning for my husband, and the loss of my son is . . . it's too huge to bear. It's too large to even begin to deal with. I think having you as a part of my life, helping you to deal with this, I think it's helping me to avoid dealing with it. I think I thought that if I could help you to get to a place where you could live again, that I would be able to live again. But I don't think that's the case.

"When Ben was little, he used to get in bed with Steven and I and watch *Jeopardy!* every night. He didn't understand any of the questions, but I think he liked hearing the blooping noises. Anyway, I remember one night I was lying there, Ben between us, and I thought, This is my family. This is my life. And I was so happy in that moment. I had my two guys. And they loved me and I belonged to them. And now, I lie in that same bed and they are both gone. I don't think I have even begun to scratch the surface of what that has done to me."

She doesn't break down. She's calm but sincere. She's lost. I don't think I could see it before because I was so lost. I'm still lost. But I can see that Susan needs . . . something. She needs something to hold on to. For me, she was that something. She was the rock in the middle of the storm. I'm still in the middle of the storm but . . . I need to be a rock too. I realize it's time I was supportive as well as supported. I think the time for "This Is All About Me" actually ended quite some time ago.

"What do you need?" I ask. Susan seems to always know what I need, or at least thinks she does with enough confidence that she convinces me too.

"I don't know," she says, wistfully, as if there is an answer out there somewhere and she just doesn't know where to start looking. "I don't know. I think I need to come to terms with a lot of things. I need to look them in the eye." She is quiet for a minute. "I don't believe in heaven, Elsie." This is where she cracks. Her eyes tighten into little stars, her mouth turns down, and her breathing becomes desperate. "I want to believe so bad," she says. Her face is now wet. Her nose is running. I know what it feels like to cry like that. I know that she's probably feeling light-headed, that soon her eyes will feel dry as if they have nothing left to give. "I want to think of him happy, in a better place. People say to me that he's in a better place, but . . . I don't believe in a better place." She heaves again and rests her head in her hands. I rub her back. "I feel like such a terrible mother that I don't believe in a better place for him."

"Neither do I," I say to her. "But sometimes I pretend I do," I say. "To make it hurt just a little less. I think it's okay to pretend you do." She rests her weight on me and I can feel that I am holding her up. It's empowering to be the one holding someone else up. It makes you feel strong, maybe even stronger than you are. "We could talk to him if you want," I say. "What does it hurt, right? It doesn't hurt anything to try, and who knows? Maybe it will feel good. Maybe it will . . . maybe he will hear us."

Susan nods and tries to gain her composure again. She sighs and breathes deep. She wipes her face and opens her eyes. "Okay," she says. "Yeah."

MAY

"We're in Nevada!" Ben screamed as we drove over the state line. He was emphatic and exhilarated.

"Wooo!" I yelled after him. I put both fists up into the air. I rolled down my window and I could feel the desert air rushing in. The air was warm but the wind had a chill. It was nighttime, and I could see the city lights in the distance. They were cheesy and ugly, overwrought and overdone. I knew I was looking at a city of casinos, a city where people were losing money and getting drunk; but none of that mattered. The city lights looked like they were made just for us.

"Which exit did you say?" Ben asked me, a rare moment of logistics in an otherwise very emotional car ride.

"Thirty-eight," I said and grabbed his hand.

It felt like the whole world belonged to us. It felt like everything was just beginning.

NOVEMBER

It's evening by the time we muster the strength to try to talk to him. It's a warm November night even by Southern California standards. We have the sliding glass doors open around the house. I try to direct my voice to the wind. Speaking into the wind seems just metaphorical enough that it might work.

"Ben?" I call out. I had planned to follow it up with some sort of statement, but my mind is a blank. I haven't spoken to Ben since he said he'd be right back. The first thing I say should be important. It should be beautiful.

"If you can hear us, Ben, we just want you to know that we miss you," Susan says, directing her voice toward the ceiling. She points her head upward as if that's where he is, which tells me there has to be some small part of her that believes in heaven after all. "I miss you so much, baby. I don't know what to do without you. I don't know how to . . . I know how to live my life thinking that you're there in L.A., but I don't know how to live my life knowing that you aren't on this earth," she says, and then turns to me abruptly. "I feel stupid."

"Me too," I say. I am now thinking it matters significantly whether you actually believe the dead can hear you. You can't just talk to the wall and convince yourself you aren't talking to a wall unless you believe.

"I want to go to his grave," she says. "Maybe it will be easier there."

"Okay." I nod. "It's too late to go today but we can go up first thing tomorrow morning."

"Okay," she says. "That will give me time to think about what I want to say."

"Okay, good."

Susan pats me on the hand and gets up. "I'm going to go to bed early then. My mind needs a rest from this." Maybe she really does need a rest, but I know she's going in there to cry in peace.

"Okay," I say. When she's gone, I look around the room and walk aimlessly around the house. I go into Ben's bedroom and I throw myself on his bed. I breathe in the air. I stare at the walls until I can no longer see them. I know that I am done here. I may not be ready for my life back, but it is time to stop avoiding it. I lie in Ben's room for as long as I can stand it and then I get up and rush out.

I walk over to my room to start to gather my clothes. I want to do it quickly, before I lose my nerve. There is a part of me that wants to stay in this purgatory for as long as I can, that wants to lie out by the pool all day and watch TV all night and never live my days. But if Ben could hear me, if Ben could see me, that isn't what Ben would want. Also, I don't think I'd want that for myself.

I get up in the morning and collect the rest of my things. I walk out into the kitchen and Susan is there, dressed and ready to go, drinking a cup of coffee, sitting at the kitchen counter. She sees that my things are packed behind me and she puts down her coffee. She doesn't say anything. She just smiles knowingly. It's a sad smile, but a proud smile. A bittersweet and melancholy smile. I feel like I'm going away to college.

"We should take two cars," she says. She says it as a realization to herself but also, I think, to spare me from having to say it. From having to spell out that after this, I'm going home.

Susan gets there a bit before I do, and as I drive up, I see her standing at the entrance to the cemetery. I thought perhaps that she would have started without me. That she might want time alone with him, but it looks like she needs a partner in this. I don't blame her. I certainly wouldn't be doing this alone. I park the car and catch up to her.

"Ready?" I say.

"Ready," she says. We start the long walk to his gravestone. When we get there, the headstone looks so brand-new it's almost tragic, like when you see grave markers so close together you know it was a child. Susan kneels on the ground in front of Ben's grave and faces his headstone. I sit down next to her.

She breathes in deeply and seriously. It is not a casual breath. She pulls a piece of paper out of her back pocket and looks at me, shyly. I nod my head at her, urging her, and she starts to read. Her voice is without much emotion at first; she truly is reading the words on the page rather than speaking.

"I just want to know you're okay. I want to know that you didn't suffer. I want to believe that you are in a better place, that you are happy and have all the things in life that you loved, with you. I want to believe that you and your father are together. Maybe at a barbecue in heaven, eating hot dogs. I know that's not the case. I know that you are gone. But I don't know how to live with that knowledge. A mother is not supposed to outlive her son. It's just not supposed to happen."

Now she starts to lose her public speaking voice, and her

eyes drift from the page onto the grass beneath her. "I know that you believed it was your job to protect me and take care of me. If I had one last thing to say to you, Ben, I think I would want to tell you this: I will be okay. You don't need to worry. I will find a way to be okay. I always do. Don't worry about me. Thank you for being such a wonderful son. For being the son that you were. I couldn't have asked for anything more from you other than just more time. I want more time. Thank you for loving Elsie. Through her, I can see that you grew into exactly the type of man I hoped you would. And the two of us . . . will be okay. We will make it through. So go and have fun where you are and forget about us. We will be okay."

That is what true love is. True love is saying to someone "Forget about us. We will be okay," when it might not even be true, when the last thing you want is to be forgotten.

When Susan is done, she folds the piece of paper back up and wipes her eyes, and then she looks at me. It's my turn and I have no idea what I'm even doing here, but I close my eyes to breathe in deeply, and for a second, I can see his face as clear as if he were right in front of me. I open my eyes and . . . here goes.

"There's a huge hole in my heart where you used to be. When you were alive, I used to sometimes lie awake at night and listen to you snore and I couldn't believe how lucky I was to have found you. I haven't wanted to be whole again without you. I thought that if I were okay, it meant that I had truly lost you but . . . I think if you heard that logic you'd think I was an idiot. I really do think you'd want me to be happy again someday. You'd probably even be a little mad at me for all the wallowing I've done. Maybe not mad. Frustrated. You'd be frustrated. Anyway, I'm going to do better. I could never forget you,

Ben. Whether we were married right before I lost you or not, in the short time I knew you, you worked your way right into the soul of me. I am who I am because of you. If I ever feel one tenth as alive as I felt with you . . ." I wipe a tear from my eye and try to gain control of my wavering voice. "You made my life worth living. I promise you I am going to do something with it."

Susan puts her arm around me and rubs my shoulder. We both sit there for a moment and stare at the grave, at the gravestone. As I let my eyes lose their focus on what's right in front of me, I realize that I am in a sea of gravestones. I am surrounded by other people's loss. It has never been so clear to me that I am not alone in this. People die every day and other people move on. If everyone that loved all of these people has picked themselves up and moved on, I can do it too. I will one day wake up and see the sun shining and think, What a nice day.

"Ready?" Susan asks, and I nod my head. We pull ourselves up off the ground. The grass has made our knees wet. We walk in silence.

"Have you ever heard of supernovas?" Susan asks me as we head toward the front gate.

"What?" I almost stop in my tracks.

"Ben was really into space as a kid and he had all of these space books. I used to read them to him when he couldn't sleep, and I always loved the little chapter in this one book he had on supernovas. They shine brighter than anything else in the sky and then fade out really quickly. A supernova is a short burst of extraordinary energy."

"Yeah," I say.

"I like to think that you and Ben were like that," she says to me. "That you ended abruptly, but in that short time, you had more passion than some people have in a lifetime."

I don't say anything. I just take it in.

"Anyway," she says. "You headed home?"

I nod. "I think I'm ready for it."

"All right," she says. "Well . . . I guess this—"

"Do you want to get dinner on Friday?" I ask her. "At the Mexican place?"

She looks surprised but pleased. "I would love that."

"I know you're not my mother. I know that. But I really enjoy your company. Even if the circumstances are a bit strange, I like you."

Susan puts her arm around me and kisses me on the head. "You're one hell of a woman," she says to me. "I'm lucky to know you."

I laugh shyly. I think I am blushing. "Me too," I say, nodding, hoping it's clear just how much I mean it.

She shakes her head to avoid crying. "All right!" she says, slapping me lightly on the back. "Get in the car! Go home. If you need me, call me. But you can do this. You got this."

"Thanks," I say. Our hands lightly touch. I squeeze hers and then I walk away. I'm only a few steps from her when I turn around. "Hey, Susan?" I say. She turns around to see me. "Same goes for me. If you need me, just call."

She smiles and nods. "You got it."

I take the coastal highway instead of the interstate. I look out the window more often than I should. I try to appreciate each moment that I have. At one point, a song comes on the radio that I haven't heard in years, and for four minutes, I let myself forget who I am and what I'm doing. I'm just me, dancing in a car heading north on Pacific Coast Highway and it's not so bad. It's not so bad at all.

When I pull into my driveway, my apartment looks bigger and higher up than I remember. I get the mail and search through it for the marriage certificate. It's not there. However, in the mail is a check from Citibank addressed to me. I go up the steps and I let myself in the house.

It smells familiar. It's a scent I didn't even know I missed until I smell it. Everything is where I left it. It was frozen in time while I was in Orange County. I breathe in deeply and I don't smell Ben here. I just smell myself.

I sit down on my couch and organize the rest of the mail. I clean up some old dishes. I make my bed. I clean out the refrigerator and then take out the trash. As I come back in, I stop and look at the envelope from Citibank. It feels petty to be thinking about how much money I've just inherited, but I have to open the envelope at some point. So here we go.

Fourteen thousand, two hundred sixteen dollars and forty-eight cents, paid to the order of Elsie Porter. Huh. I don't know when I stopped considering myself Elsie Porter Ross, but it seems to have been some time ago.

Here I am, six months after I got married: husbandless and fourteen thousand dollars richer.

MAY

"The gazebo ceremony takes place outside in the . . . well, gazebo," she said to me from behind the counter. She was about fifty and appeared to be putting on a fake southern accent. That or she was just from the deep, deep South. Ben was in the bathroom and had left the planning up to me.

"Oh, it's a bit cold, right?" I said. "I think just the simplest thing you have is fine."

"You only get married once, honey. Don't you want to make it special?" How did she not understand that this was special? Pomp and circumstance meant nothing to me as long as I got to be with this man. She must not have understood how lucky I was to have him. She must have thought I was marrying just anybody and I needed a gazebo to make it spectacular.

"I think we are good," I said. "What's this one? The simplicity package? We'll take that one."

"Okay," she said. "How about rings? Do you have an engagement ring that we should match it to?"

"Nope!" I said proudly. "No engagement ring." Honestly, the thought hadn't even occurred to me.

"We'll be getting her one though," Ben said, and he came toward us.

"Oh, stop it," I said.

"Well, do you two want silver or gold?" she asked.

"Gold," I said, but Ben said, "silver," at the same time.

We both quickly swapped our answers to match and missed again.

"Baby, I just want what you want," he said to me.

"But I want what you want!" I said.

"Let's do what you want for this because I want to eat at Hooters after this and I need compromise points."

"You want to eat at Hooters for our first meal as a married couple?"

"If it makes you feel any better, it's because of the wings, not the boobs."

The woman ignored us. "Okay so . . . gold?"

"Gold." She pulled out a tray of gold bands, and Ben and I tried some on until we found ones we liked and ones that fit. Ben paid the bill, and I told him I'd pay for half of it.

"Are you joking? We're not going Dutch on our wedding," he said to me.

"All right, lovebirds. Do you want to order any copies of the certificate?"

Ben turned toward me, his face asking me to answer.

"Yes," I said. "One copy should be fine, I would think."

"Okay, I'll add that to the final charge," the woman said as she put her hand out expectantly. "Do you have the license?"

"Oh, not yet," Ben said. "We need to fill that out, I guess."

The woman put her hands down on the counter, as if to halt everything. "You need to walk down to the Marriage License Bureau. It's about three blocks down. I can't do anything else until you get that filled out."

"How long will it take?" I asked.

"Half hour if there's no line," she said. "But there's often a line."

There was no line. We were seated and filling out paperwork within minutes of walking in the door.

"Oh, I didn't bring my social security card," he said when he got to the question about his social security number.

"Oh, I don't think you need it," I said. "It just asks for the number."

"Well," he said, "I never remember the number."

"Oh." What a remarkably mundane hurdle to find ourselves up against. My excitement started to deflate as I realized this might not happen after all. Maybe we couldn't get this done. He might need to call his mom for it, and then where would we be? "You know what? We can wait until you have it," I said.

"What?" he said, appalled at the idea of waiting. "No, I'm almost positive I know what it is. Here," he said as he wrote it down. "I know it's either 518 or 581, but I'm pretty sure it's 518." He finished writing it and put the pen down triumphantly. He walked right up to the window, handed in the paperwork, and said, "One marriage license, please!" Then he turned toward me. "We're getting married, baby! Are you ready?"

NOVEMBER

I put the check in a drawer where I won't forget it and I look around my apartment. It feels like mine again. It feels like I can live a life here of my own. I know that I envisioned a life for Ben and me here. I imagined we'd move out one day when we had kids. I even imagined that one day, Ben would be moving boxes out of the house by himself while I looked on, eight months pregnant. That life is not going to happen for me. But now I realize that there is a world of possibilities. I don't know what it's going to look like when I move out of this apartment. I don't know when it will be. And that, in its own way, is kind of thrilling. Anything could happen.

My cell phone rings, and it's a number I don't recognize. For some reason, I decide to answer it anyway.

"Hello?"

"Hello, is this Elsie Porter?" a woman asks.

"It is."

"Hi, Ms. Porter. This is Patricia DeVette from the Clark County Recorder's Office in Nevada," she says. I swear my heart stops beating for a moment. "I have a . . . We don't usually call people directly, Ms. Porter, but I have been filing some paperwork here and I wanted to speak with you about your county record."

"Okay . . ." I say. Oh God. I avoided this moment so long that it decided to take matters into its own hands and crash into me.

"It's taken me a while to figure out what exactly went on here, but it appears that Ben Ross put the wrong social security number on your marriage license. I've left a number of messages for Mr. Ross and have not heard back."

"Oh."

"I'm getting in touch with you, Ms. Porter, to let you know that the marriage has not yet been filed with the county."

And here it is. What I have feared all along. Ben and I are not legally married. During Ben's lifetime, we were never recognized as a legal union. My worst nightmare has come true, and as I stand here on the phone, silent, I am surprised to learn that I don't collapse. I don't break down.

"Thanks, Patricia. Thank you for calling," I say. I'm not sure what to say next. It's such an odd predicament to be faced with. All I've wanted since Ben died was proof that we meant something to each other. Now, I realize that no piece of paper can prove any of that.

"Well," I hear myself say. "Ben passed away."

"I'm sorry?"

"Ben died. He's dead. So I'm not sure if you can still file it."

"I'm so sorry, Ms. Porter. I'm so sorry to hear that."

"Thank you."

I get the distinct impression that Ms. DeVette doesn't know what to say. She's quiet for a few breaths before she speaks again. "Well, I can still file it," she says. "Since it's overdue paperwork representing a legal union that did take place. But it's entirely up to you. We don't have to."

"File it," I hear myself say. "It happened. It should be a part of the county record."

"All right, Ms. Ross, will do. Can I get his real social security number?"

"Oh," I say. "What number did he put on the document?"

"518-38-9087."

"Just change the 518 to 581."

"Great, thank you, Ms. Ross," Patricia says to me.

"Thank you for calling," I say.

"And Ms. Ross?" she says as she is getting off the phone.

"Hmm?"

"Congratulations on your marriage. I'm sorry about your husband."

"Thank you for saying that," I say to her. When I put the phone down, I feel a short, sound sense of peace. I was Ben Ross's wife. No one can take that away from me.

MAY

Elsie Porter?" the officiant said to me.

"Yes?"

"Ben Ross?"

"Yes."

"Are you two ready?"

"Yes, sir," Ben said. The officiant laughed and shook our hands. "My name's Dave," he said. "Let's get this show going."

"Okay!" I said, my arms pumped.

"Would you turn to face each other?" he asked, and we did.

"Ben and Elsie, we are gathered here today for you to celebrate one of life's greatest moments and give recognition to the worth and beauty of love, as you join together in vows of marriage."

I couldn't see the officiant; I just kept staring at Ben. He was staring back at me. His face was lit up. I couldn't believe how animated his smile was; I'd never seen anything like it. Dave continued to talk, but I couldn't hear him. I couldn't make out the words. It felt like the world had stopped, like it was paused and muted, like I was frozen in time and space.

"Did you two prepare vows?" Dave asked, as he brought me back to reality.

"Oh," I said, looking at Ben. "No, but we can. Wanna wing it?" I said to Ben.

"Sure." He smiled. "Let's wing it."

"Ben? Would you like to go first?" Dave asked.

"Oh, okay. Sure." Ben was quiet for a minute. "Are vows, like, supposed to be promises you make or just . . . like anything you want to say?" he whispered to Dave.

"Anything you want to say is fine," he said.

"Oh, okay." Ben breathed in sharply. "I love you. I feel like I loved you from the moment I saw you in that pizza place, but I know that doesn't make sense. I can't live my life without you anymore. You are everything I have ever wanted in another person. You are my best friend, my lover, my partner. And I promise that I will spend the rest of my life taking care of you, the way you deserve to be taken care of. My whole life I was never looking for something bigger than myself, and then I met you and I want to dedicate every day of my life to you. You are it for me. You are why I am here. Without you, I am nothing. So thank you, Elsie, for being who you are, and for spending your life with me."

Tears were forming in my eyes, my throat felt like I'd swallowed a brick.

"Elsie?" Dave prompted me.

"I love you," I said and broke down. I couldn't make out words in between my blubbering. As I looked at Ben, I saw he was crying too. "I just love you so much," I said. "I never knew what it was like to love someone so much and to be loved so well," I said. "For the rest of time, I will be by your side, Ben. I will dedicate my life to you."

Ben grabbed me and kissed me. He pulled us together so tight, there was no room to breathe. I kissed him back until I felt an arm between us.

"Not yet, son," Dave said, pulling us apart and laughing. "We still have a small formality to take care of."

"Oh," Ben said, smiling at me. "Right."

Dave smiled and turned to him. "Ben, do you take this woman to be your lawfully wedded wife?"

"I do," he said, looking directly at me.

"And do you, Elsie, take this man to be your lawfully wedded husband?"

"I do," I said and nodded, smiling widely.

"Then by the power vested in me by the State of Nevada, I now pronounce you husband and wife."

It was dead quiet for a minute as we were both frozen. Ben looked at Dave expectantly.

"Now, son!" Dave said. "Now's your chance. Kiss the bride. Give her everything you've got."

Ben grabbed me and spun me. He kissed me hard on the lips. It felt so good, a kiss like that. It just felt so good.

Dave chuckled to himself and started to walk away. "I'll let you kids calm down," he said and, before he made it through the door, "You know, I marry a lot of people, but I have a feeling about you two."

Ben and I looked at each other and smiled. "Do you think he says that to everyone?" Ben asked.

"Probably," I said, and I threw myself onto his body. "Are you ready to go to eat wings?"

"In a minute," he said, running his hands through my hair and then pulling me closer. "I want to spend a few seconds looking at my wife."

NOVEMBER

I pick up the check and I get in the car. I go to Citibank and cash it. I have a purpose and an energy I've lacked for some time, but I know what I want to do and I know I can do it.

The bank teller cashes the check somewhat hesitantly. She has no reason not to cash it, but I imagine she doesn't often have a twenty-six-year-old woman come in and cash a fourteen-thousand-dollar check. I ask for it in hundreds.

It won't fit in my wallet, so I have to take it in a few money envelopes. I get in my car and I drive to the biggest bookstore I can find. I walk into the store feeling like my purse is on fire, and my mind is reeling. I am wandering in circles before an employee asks if she can help. I ask her how to find the young adult section, and the young woman leads me to it. She splays her hand out to show me the shelves—stacks and stacks of books, brightly colored with titles in large display print.

"I'll take it," I say.

"What?" she says back to me.

"Can you help me get it to the register?"

"The whole section?" she asks me, shocked.

It's too many books to fit in my car, too many books to take anywhere by myself, so the store agrees to have them delivered. I take three stacks myself and put them in my car, and then I drive myself to the Fairfax Library.

I see Lyle the minute I walk in, and he comes over to me.

"Hey, Elsie. Are you okay?"

"I'm good," I say. "Can you help me get some stuff out of my car?"

"Sure."

Lyle asks me how I've been and if I feel like coming back to work. He seems eager not to talk about my "episode," and I am thankful for that. I tell him I will be back at work soon and then we make our way to my car.

I open the trunk.

"What's this?" he says.

"This is the beginning of the Ben Ross Young Adult Section," I say.

"What?"

"I'm having another truckload delivered tomorrow and donated to the library in Ben's name."

"Wow," he says. "That's very generous of you."

"There's only one stipulation," I say.

"Okay?"

"When the books start to smell musty, we gotta get rid of them. Donate them to another library."

Lyle laughs. "What?"

I grab a book from the trunk and fan its pages in front of Lyle's face. I smell them myself. "Smell how clean and new that smells?" I say.

"Sure," Lyle says.

"Once they start smelling like library books, we're gonna donate them to another library and replace them with this." I hand Lyle the rest of the cash. It's wrapped in an envelope, and I'm sure it looks like we're dealing drugs.

"What the . . ." Lyle says to me. "Put that away!"

I laugh, finally seeing this from his perspective. "I should probably just write a check . . ."

Lyle laughs. "Probably. But you don't have to do this."

"I want to," I say. "Can we have a plaque made?" I ask.

"Sure," he says. "Absolutely."

"Awesome." I put some books in his arms and grab some myself, and we head into the library.

"You're sure you're okay, Elsie?" he asks me as we head into the building.

"Positive."

Ana comes over for dinner. We eat, just the two of us, on my couch and we drink wine until it's time to stop. I laugh with her and I smile. And when she goes home that night, I still have Ben in my heart and in my mind. I don't lose him just by having a good time without him. I don't lose him by being myself with her.

DECEMBER

I give myself time to adjust, and then one morning when I feel up to it, I go back to work. The air in Los Angeles has officially cooled down and hovers around forty-five degrees. I put on a jacket I haven't worn since last winter and I get in my car. While a part of me feels shaky about this next part, the part where I start my job again for real and I put the past behind me, I walk through the doors. I walk up to the admin offices and I sit down at my desk. There aren't a lot of people in the office yet this morning, but the few that are clap for me as I walk in. I see there's a major donor pin on my desk. They aren't clapping for me because I'm a widow back at work. They are clapping for me because I did something good for the library. I am something to them other than a woman who lost her husband. There is more to me than that.

The day goes by as days at work do. I find myself enjoying the camaraderie of my job for the first time in months. I like being needed here. I like talking to people about books. I like it when kids ask where to find something and I can squeeze in a mini-lesson on the Dewey decimal system.

Around noon, the boxes of books are delivered and brought to my desk. I don't have the shelf set up yet, so they sit on the floor, burying my desk. I recognize some of the titles. Ben used to have some of them before I gave them to Susan. Others look new to me. Some look pretty interesting; others look mind-numbingly stupid. As I take stock, I laugh about the fact that my husband used to love to read children's books. Life never turns out like you think. You don't think you'd end up with a man that likes to read literature aimed at twelve-year-olds; you also don't think you'll lose that man so soon. But if that's the case, I have many more surprises left in my life, and they can't all be bad.

I call Susan and tell her about the books. I can't tell if she's laughing or crying.

"You actually said to them that the books can't get musty?"

"Yep," I say from my desk. "They have to donate them someplace else."

She laughs, even if she's crying. "I might finally take out a library book then," she tells me. I laugh. "Actually," she says, "I want to do it too. I'll add to the fund. I don't want them to ever run out of fresh-smelling books."

"Really?" I ask, excited. "Oh, man! We can make it the Ben and Susan Ross Young Adult Section."

"No, your name should be there too. Oh! And Steven's! It should say The Ross Family Young Adult Section. For the four of us. Cool?"

I try not to acknowledge the tenderness of the moment, but I can't help but be overwhelmed.

"Okay," I say, my voice small and quiet.

"E-mail me later and tell me where to send the check, okay? I'll call you this weekend."

I hang up the phone and try to go back to work, but my mind is fluttering from one thing to another.

Mr. Callahan doesn't come through the doors all day. I ask Nancy when she saw him last.

"Oh, geez," she says. "It's been at least two months."

When five o'clock rolls around, I excuse myself and head to Cedars-Sinai hospital.

I ask the nurse at the front desk where I can find Mrs. Lorraine Callahan. The nurse looks her up in the computer and says there is no Lorraine Callahan currently admitted. I get back in the car and drive down the street from the library. I find the house I think is Mr. Callahan's.

I walk up to the front door and ring the doorbell. It doesn't seem like it's ringing so I knock on the door. It takes a few tries before he comes. When he does, he opens the door and looks at me through the screen.

"Elsie?" he says, disbelieving.

"Hey, George, can I come in?"

He opens the screen and makes room for me at the door. The house looks disheveled and sad. I know that Lorraine is not here.

"How are you, George?"

"I'm fine," he says, not really listening to my question.

"How are you?" I say, this time more sincere, more pointed.

His voice turns to a quiver. "I can't even get out of bed most days," he says. "It's not worth it."

"It is," I say. "It is worth it."

He shakes his head. "You don't know," he says. "No one does."

"No, you're right about that," I say. "You two were together for so long. I can't begin to imagine how lost you must feel. The thing is though, George, you may be old, but you have a lot of fight in you. Lorraine wouldn't want you to go down this easy." I grab his shoulder and focus his eyes on mine. "C'mon," I say. "Let's go get a beer."

And just like that, I am there for someone. I am not the one in pain. I am not suffering. I am helping. My life without

Ben felt like it was nothing, but here I am, doing something with it.

Mr. Callahan nods his head reluctantly and puts on his shoes.

"Think they'll card me?" he says. We both laugh, even though it wasn't that funny. We have to find little ways to smile. No matter how strong you are, no matter how smart you are or tough you can be, the world will find a way to break you. And when it does, the only thing you can do is hold on.

When Mr. Callahan and I get to the bar, he goes straight for the bartender. I hang back for a minute before I meet him. I breathe in and out. I look at what's around me. A guy comes up to me and asks what a gorgeous girl like me is doing here during a happy hour. He asks if he can buy me a drink.

I don't say yes, but I also don't punch him in the face. Mr. Callahan agrees with me that I'm making progress. Plus, New Year's Eve is just around the corner, and who knows what the year will bring.

JUNE

We woke up in the hotel room in Las Vegas. The bed was wide; the sheets were luxurious. There was a Jacuzzi bathtub within four steps of the bed. The bright shining sun was already finding its way through the curtains, peeking around the edges and through the middle. My life had never felt so exciting, so full of possibilities.

Ben was still asleep when I woke up. I just watched him sleep. I put my head on his chest and listened to his heartbeat. I read the news on my cell phone. Even the most ordinary things felt like Christmas morning to me. Everything had this tint of peace to it. I turned on the TV and watched it at a low volume while Ben slept next to me. I waited for him to wake up.

When it got to be 11:00 a.m., I turned to him and lightly shook him awake.

"Wake up, baby," I said. "We have to get up soon."

Ben barely woke from his stupor. He put his arm around me and buried his face in his pillow.

"Come on, Husband," I said to him. "You gotta get up."

He opened his eyes and smiled at me. He lifted his mouth off the pillow and said, "What's the rush, honey? We have all the time in the world."

ACKNOWLEDGMENTS

I owe a great deal of thanks to my agent, Carly Watters, and my editor, Greer Hendricks. You both saw what I was trying to do, you believed in this story, and you made it better, brighter, and more heartbreaking. Thank you. And thank you to Sarah Cantin at Atria for your faith in this book. You are the gatekeeper and it's you who let me through.

I also want to thank the friends who cheered me on along the way: Erin Cox, Julia Furlan, Jesse Hill, Andy Bauch, Jess Reynoso, Colin and Ashley Rodger, Emily Giorgio, Bea Arthur, Caitlin Doyle, Tim Pavlik, Kate Sullivan, Phillip Jordan, Tamara Hunter, and Sara Arrington. Your collective faith in me made me stupid enough to think I could do this.

It's crucial that I acknowledge the bosses and teachers who believed in me: Frank Calore, Andrew Crick, Edith Hill, Sarah Finn, and Randi Hiller. I am so grateful to have had you all as mentors in my life.

Thank you to the Beverly Hills Public Library for giving me a quiet place to write that sells delicious fudge and strong iced tea, and to the community at Polytechnic School for being so supportive.

I cannot let this opportunity go by without mentioning the man who lost the love of his life and posted about it on Craigslist. You, sir, are a far more beautiful writer than I and the tenderness with which you speak brings me to tears every time I read your post. And I've read it a lot.

To the Reid and Hanes families, thank you for embracing me with the warmth you have.

To Martha Steeves, you will always be in my heart.

I have endless gratitude for the Jenkins and Morris families. To my mother, Mindy, my brother, Jake, and my grandmother, Linda: Your belief that I can do anything I set my mind to is why I believe it. I can't think of a greater gift to give a person.

And lastly, to Alex Reid, the man who taught me how a perfectly sane woman can fall madly in love and get married in a matter of months: Thank you for being the inspiration for every love story I find myself writing.

FOREVER, INTERRUPTED

Taylor Jenkins Reid

QUESTIONS AND TOPICS FOR DISCUSSION

1. The plot of *Forever, Interrupted* isn't strictly linear and, instead, alternates between Ben and Elsie's courtship and Elsie's mourning. How did this affect your reading experience? Why do you think the author made this narrative choice?

2. At various points throughout the novel, Elsie and Ben voice the concern that perhaps their relationship is progressing too quickly. Before reading this, would you have thought that two people could be ready to marry after six months of dating? Did *Forever, Interrupted* affect your opinion one way or another?

3. Romantic love may seem like the driving force behind *Forever, Interrupted*, but in what ways does friendship also shape the novel? In particular, how does seeing Elsie in the role of a friend—and not just as Ben's girlfriend and wife—add to our understanding of her? What do her interactions

with Ana, as well as with Mr. Callahan, reveal about her as a character?

4. Elsie is furious with Ana when she tries to give her a copy of *The Year of Magical Thinking,* Joan Didion's memoir about losing her husband, and laments, *"My job is books, information. I based my career on the idea that words on pages bound and packaged help people. That they make people grow, they show people lives they've never seen. They teach people about themselves, and here I am, at my lowest point, rejecting help from the one place I always believed it would be"* (p. 164). Do you share Elsie's perspective about the power of books? Why might this belief system be so painful for her to embrace immediately after Ben's death?

5. Do you understand why Ben never told his mother about his relationship with Elsie? Why do you think Elsie didn't push him harder on this?

6. Why is it important to Elsie that she and Ben were legally married? What do you think about Susan's point of view, that, *"It means nothing. You think that some ten minutes you spent with Ben in a room defines what you meant to each other? It doesn't. You define that. What you feel defines that. You loved him. He loved you . . . It doesn't matter whether it's labeled a husband or a boyfriend. You lost the person you love. You lost the future you thought you had"* (p. 249)?

7. Turn to the scene where Ben and Elsie are driving to Las Vegas and, as a group, read aloud the argument that they get into. Could you see each point of view, or did you side more with Elsie or Ben? Should one of them have handled the conversation differently?

8. When Elsie first arrives at Susan's house, she realizes: "*I can't help but think that maybe because it's okay to cry, I can't*" (p. 260). Can you find some other concrete examples of the grieving process that are illustrated in the book? Were there particular moments of Elsie's (or Susan's) mourning that especially resonated with you?

9. Ana and Mr. Callahan each try to offer Elsie words of comfort and wisdom after Ben dies. At the time, she mostly rejects what they have to say. How has Elsie's point of view changed by the end of the novel—and have Ana's and Mr. Callahan's perspectives shifted as well?

10. Elsie has a very distant relationship with her parents. How do you think their absence from her life affects first her courtship with Ben—and then later, her experience of mourning? Do Elsie's views on family change over the course of the narrative? Do you think the novel distinguishes between what constitutes friendship and what constitutes family?

11. Ben and Elsie's relationship is twice likened to a "supernova." Discuss the two different contexts that this comparison appears in. Ultimately, do you think it is an applicable analogy for their love?

ENHANCE YOUR BOOK CLUB

1. Pretend you are casting the film version of *Forever, Interrupted*. Who would play Elsie and Ben? Susan and Ana? What about Mr. Callahan?

2. Revisit Susan's quote in question #6. Do you think this argument could be applied to the institution of marriage more generally? That is to say, if it doesn't matter whether Elsie and Ben were married for nine days or zero, does marriage matter at all?

3. In *The Year of Magical Thinking* (the book Ana buys for Elsie), Joan Didion writes: *"Marriage is memory, marriage is time. Marriage is not only time: it is also, paradoxically, the denial of time."* What do you think she means by this?

4. The evening of their first date, Ben and Elsie prepare to order Chinese food and quickly discover that they do not agree on their rice preferences. When Elsie suggests that they get two different orders of rice, Ben responds, *"Maybe when the romance is gone we can do that, but not tonight"* (p. 68). Can you think of something that has in the past (or would in the future) signify to you that you're past the early stage of a relationship? How does a concept like "romance" in a relationship change or manifest differently over time?

5. If Ben hadn't gone out for Fruity Pebbles that night—if he had lived—what do you think would have been in store for Elsie and Ben's marriage? And do you think Elsie would be as close to Susan?

Read on for a look at Taylor Jenkins Reid's
compelling new novel

The Seven Husbands of Evelyn Hugo

Available from Washington Square Press

NEW YORK TRIBUNE

Evelyn Hugo to Auction Off Gowns

BY PRIYA AMRIT MARCH 2, 2017

Film legend and '60s It Girl Evelyn Hugo has just announced that she will auction off 12 of her most memorable gowns through Christie's to raise money for breast cancer research.

At the age of 79, Hugo has long been an icon of glamour and elegance. She is known for a personal style both sensual and restrained, and many of Hugo's most famous looks are considered touchstones of the fashion and Hollywood archives.

Those looking to own a piece of Hugo history will be intrigued not only by the gowns themselves but also by the context in which they were worn. Included in the sale will be the emerald-green Miranda La Conda that Hugo wore to the 1959 Academy Awards, the violet soufflé and organdy scoop-neck she donned at the premiere of *Anna Karenina* in 1962, and the navy-blue silk Michael Maddax that she was wearing in 1982 when she won her Oscar for *All for Us*.

Hugo has weathered her share of Hollywood scandals, not the least of which being her seven marriages, including her decades-long relationship with film producer Harry Cameron. The two Hollywood insiders shared a daughter, Connor Cameron, who is no doubt the influence for the auction. Ms. Cameron passed away last year from breast cancer soon after turning 41.

Born Evelyn Elena Herrera in 1938, the daughter of Cuban immigrants, Hugo grew up in the Hell's Kitchen neighborhood of New York City. By 1955, she had made her way to Hollywood, gone blond, and been re-christened Evelyn Hugo. Almost overnight, Hugo became a member of the Hollywood elite. She remained in the spotlight for more than three decades before retiring in the late '80s and marrying financier Robert Jamison, older brother of three-time Oscar-winning actress Celia St. James. Now widowed from her seventh husband, Hugo resides in Manhattan.

Preternaturally beautiful and a paragon of glamour and daring sexuality, Hugo has long been a source of fascination for moviegoers the world over. This auction is expected to raise upward of $2 million.

1

CAN YOU COME INTO MY office?"

I look around at the desks beside me and then back at Frankie, trying to confirm to whom, exactly, she's talking. I point to myself. "Do you mean me?"

Frankie has very little patience. "Yes, Monique, you. That's why I said, 'Monique, can you come into my office?'"

"Sorry, I just heard the last part."

Frankie turns. I grab my notepad and follow her.

There is something very striking about Frankie. I'm not sure that you'd say she was conventionally attractive—her features are severe, her eyes very wide apart—but she is nevertheless someone you can't help but look at and admire. With her thin, six-foot-tall frame, her short-cropped Afro, and her affinity for bright colors and big jewelry, when Frankie walks into a room, everyone takes notice.

She was part of the reason I took this job. I have looked up to her since I was in journalism school, reading her pieces in the very pages of the magazine she now runs and I now work for. And if I'm being honest, there is something very inspiring about having a black woman running things. As a biracial woman myself—light brown skin and dark brown eyes courtesy of my black father, an abundance of face freckles courtesy of my white mother—Frankie makes me feel more sure that I can one day run things, too.

"Take a seat," Frankie says as she sits down and gestures toward an orange chair on the opposite side of her Lucite desk.

I calmly sit and cross my legs. I let Frankie talk first.

"So, puzzling turn of events," she says, looking at her computer. "Evelyn Hugo's people are inquiring about a feature. An exclusive interview."

My gut instinct is to say *Holy shit* but also *Why are you telling me this?* "About what in particular?" I ask.

"My guess is it's related to the gown auction she's doing," Frankie says. "My understanding is that it's very important to her to raise as much money for the American Breast Cancer Foundation as possible."

"But they won't confirm that?"

Frankie shakes her head. "All they will confirm is that Evelyn has something to say."

Evelyn Hugo is one of the biggest movie stars of all time. She doesn't even have to *have* something to say for people to listen.

"This could be a big cover for us, right? I mean, she's a living legend. Wasn't she married eight times or something?"

"Seven," Frankie says. "And yes. This has huge potential. Which is why I hope you'll bear with me through the next part of this."

"What do you mean?"

Frankie takes a big breath and gets a look on her face that makes me think I'm about to get fired. But then she says, "Evelyn specifically requested you."

"Me?" This is the second time in the span of five minutes that I have been shocked that someone was interested in speaking with me. I need to work on my confidence. Suffice it to say, it's taken a beating recently. Although why pretend it was ever really soaring?

"To be honest, that was my reaction, too," Frankie says.

Now *I'll* be honest, I'm a little offended. Although, obviously, I can see where she's coming from. I've been at *Vivant* for less than a year, mostly doing puff pieces. Before that, I was blogging for the *Discourse*, a current events and culture site that calls itself a newsmagazine but is, effectively, a blog with punchy headlines. I wrote mainly for the Modern Life section, covering trending topics and opinion pieces.

After years of freelancing, the *Discourse* gig was a lifesaver. But when *Vivant* offered me a job, I couldn't help myself. I jumped at the chance to join an institution, to work among legends.

On my first day of work, I walked past walls decorated with iconic, culture-shifting covers—the one of women's activist Debbie Palmer, naked and carefully posed, standing on top of a skyscraper overlooking Manhattan in 1984; the one of artist Robert Turner in the act of painting a canvas while the text declared that he had AIDS, back in 1991. It felt surreal to be a part of the *Vivant* world. I have always wanted to see my name on its glossy pages.

But unfortunately, for the past twelve issues, I've done nothing but ask old-guard questions of people with old money, while my colleagues back at the *Discourse* are attempting to change the world while going viral. So, simply put, I'm not exactly impressed with myself.

"Look, it's not that we don't love you, we do," Frankie says. "We think you're destined for big things at *Vivant*, but I was hoping to put one of our more experienced, top hitters on this. And so I want to be up front with you when I say that we did not submit you as an idea to Evelyn's team. We sent five big names, and they came back with this."

Frankie turns her computer screen toward me and shows me an e-mail from someone named Thomas Welch, who I can only assume is Evelyn Hugo's publicist.

From: Thomas Welch
To: Troupe, Frankie
Cc: Stamey, Jason; Powers, Ryan

It's Monique Grant or Evelyn's out.

I look back up at Frankie, stunned. And to be honest, a little bit starstruck that Evelyn Hugo wants anything to do with me.

"Do you *know* Evelyn Hugo? Is that what's going on here?"

Frankie asks me as she turns the computer back toward her side of the desk.

"No," I say, surprised even to be asked the question. "I've seen a few of her movies, but she's a little before my time."

"You have no personal connection to her?"

I shake my head. "Definitely not."

"Aren't you from Los Angeles?"

"Yeah, but the only way I'd have any connection to Evelyn Hugo, I suppose, is if my dad worked on one of her films back in the day. He was a still photographer for movie sets. I can ask my mom."

"Great. Thank you." Frankie looks at me expectantly.

"Did you want me to ask now?"

"Could you?"

I pull my phone out of my pocket and text my mother: *Did Dad ever work on any Evelyn Hugo movies?*

I see three dots start to appear, and I look up, only to find that Frankie is trying to get a glimpse of my phone. She seems to recognize the invasion and leans back.

My phone dings.

My mother texts: *Maybe? There were so many it's hard to keep track. Why?*

Long story, I reply, *but I'm trying to figure out if I have any connection to Evelyn Hugo. Think Dad would have known her?*

Mom answers: *Ha! No. Your father never hung out with anybody famous on set. No matter how hard I tried to get him to make us some celebrity friends.*

I laugh. "It looks like no. No connection to Evelyn Hugo."

Frankie nods. "OK, well, then, the other theory is that her people chose someone with less clout so that they could try to control you and, thus, the narrative."

I feel my phone vibrate again. *That reminds me that I wanted to send you a box of your dad's old work. Some gorgeous stuff. I love having it here, but I think you'd love it more. I'll send it this week.*

"You think they're preying on the weak," I say to Frankie.

Frankie smiles softly. "Sort of."

"So Evelyn's people look up the masthead, find my name as a lower-level writer, and think they can bully me around. That's the idea?"

"That's what I fear."

"And you're telling me this because . . ."

Frankie considers her words. "Because I don't think you can be bullied around. I think they are underestimating you. And I want this cover. I want it to make headlines."

"What are you saying?" I ask, shifting slightly in my chair.

Frankie claps her hands in front of her and rests them on the desk, leaning toward me. "I'm asking you if you have the guts to go toe-to-toe with Evelyn Hugo."

Of all the things I thought someone was going to ask me today, this would probably be somewhere around number nine million. Do I have the guts to go toe-to-toe with Evelyn Hugo? I have no idea.

"Yes," I say finally.

"That's all? Just yes?"

I want this opportunity. I want to write this story. I'm sick of being the lowest one on the totem pole. And I need a win, goddammit. "Fuck yes?"

Frankie nods, considering. "Better, but I'm still not convinced."

I'm thirty-five years old. I've been a writer for more than a decade. I want a book deal one day. I want to pick my stories. I want to eventually be the name people scramble to get when someone like Evelyn Hugo calls. And I'm being underused here at *Vivant*. If I'm going to get where I want to go, something has to let up. Someone has to get out of my way. And it needs to happen quickly, because this goddamn career is all I have anymore. If I want things to change, I have to change how I do things. And probably drastically.

"Evelyn wants me," I say. "You want Evelyn. It doesn't sound like I need to convince you, Frankie. It sounds like you need to convince *me*."

Frankie is dead quiet, staring right at me over her steepled fingers. I was aiming for formidable. I might have overshot.

I feel the same way I did when I tried weight training and started with the forty-pound weights. Too much too soon makes it obvious you don't know what you're doing.

It takes everything I have not to take it back, not to apologize profusely. My mother raised me to be polite, to be demure. I have long operated under the idea that civility is subservience. But it hasn't gotten me very far, that type of kindness. The world respects people who think they should be running it. I've never understood that, but I'm done fighting it. I'm here to be Frankie one day, maybe bigger than Frankie. To do big, important work that I am proud of. To leave a mark. And I'm nowhere near doing that yet.

The silence is so long that I think I might crack, the tension building with every second that goes by. But Frankie cracks first.

"OK," she says, and puts out her hand as she stands up.

Shock and searing pride run through me as I extend my own. I make sure my handshake is strong; Frankie's is a vise.

"Ace this, Monique. For us and for yourself, please."

"I will."

We break away from each other as I walk toward her door. "She might have read your physician-assisted suicide piece for the *Discourse,*" Frankie says just before I leave the room.

"What?"

"It was stunning. Maybe that's why she wants you. It's how we found you. It's a great story. Not just because of the hits it got but because of you, because it's beautiful work."

It was one of the first truly meaningful stories I wrote of my own volition. I pitched it after I was assigned a piece on the rise in popularity of microgreens, especially on the Brooklyn restaurant scene. I had gone to the Park Slope market to interview a local farmer, but when I confessed that I didn't get the appeal of mustard greens, he told me that I sounded like his sister. She had been highly carnivorous until the past year, when she switched to a vegan, all-organic diet as she battled brain cancer.

As we spoke more, he told me about a physician-assisted suicide support group he and his sister had joined, for those at the end of their lives and their loved ones. So many in the group were fighting for the right to die with dignity. Healthy eating wasn't going to save his sister's life, and neither of them wanted her to suffer any longer than she had to.

I knew then that I wanted, very deeply, to give a voice to the people of that support group.

I went back to the *Discourse* office and pitched the story. I thought I'd be turned down, given my recent slate of articles about hipster trends and celebrity think pieces. But to my surprise, I was greeted with a green light.

I worked tirelessly on it, attending meetings in church basements, interviewing the members, writing and rewriting, until I felt confident that the piece represented the full complexity—both the mercy and the moral code—of helping to end the lives of suffering people.

It is the story I am proudest of. I have, more than once, gone home from a day's work here and read that piece again, reminding myself of what I'm capable of, reminding myself of the satisfaction I take in sharing the truth, no matter how difficult it may be to swallow.

"Thank you," I tell Frankie now.

"I'm just saying that you're talented. It might be that."

"It's probably not, though."

"No," she says. "It's probably not. But write this story well, whatever it is, and then next time it will be."